Books by Carol Louise Wilde

Books of the Nagaro Chronicle

Gift of Chance (1)

Covenant of the Sword (2)

Return to Lankura (3)

Thief of Slaves (4)

Future titles in this series: Heir of Darion (5), Brothers of the Blood (6), & Legacy of Loros (7)

Praise for Carol Louise Wilde's *Gift of Chance*

"Our young hero awakens, stripped of his memories, in a strange and dangerous land. Something has pushed him to his limits, and maybe it's better not to remember. As dreams help him piece his past together he discovers he's innately a man of honor. He is also a man of anger. *Gift of Chance* will appeal to lovers of world-building fantasy. Wilde's commitment to her characters lights every page with their passion, and hers."

  -- Petrea Burchard, author of *Act As If: Stumbling Through Hollywood with Headshot in Hand* and the novel *Camelot & Vine,* and instructor at the Story Kitchen.

"*A Gift of Chance*, by Carol Louise Wilde is the first of a fantasy series that centers around a young man who has mysteriously lost his memory. He's taken in by a kindly fisherman's family and because he can't remember his true name, he decides to call himself Nagaro, which means 'no one'. As the story unfolds, Nagaro is repeatedly plagued by terrifying dreams that show him glimpses of his past. He struggles to remember, but at the same time, he's afraid of what he might learn. The emotional heart of this book revolves around Nagaro's harrowing journey to the truth of who he is. He and his friend Taru, the fisherman's son, are tested in a most horrific way, and in the process, they both discover the breadth of their strength and courage. *A Gift of Chance* is a fine debut from a promising new talent in the epic fantasy genre. I, for one am eagerly awaiting the next installments in the series."

  -- Leslie Ann Moore—Author of the award-winning *Griffin's Daughter Trilogy* and the *Nuetierra Chronicles*.

"[...]Wilde has created a main character who immediately comes alive in her story *Gift of Chance: Book 1 in the Nagaro Chronicle*. Nagaro is sure to capture the hearts of fans, and he will stay with them long after the last page is read."

  -- *Writer's Digest* Self-Published Book Awards reviewer's comments.

The  Chronicle 1

Gift of Chance

Carol Louise Wilde

Dedication

For my husband, Gerry, without whose support, encouragement, and patience, this book (and indeed the entire series) would never have been possible. You will always be the hero of my chronicle.

Acknowledgements

The foundation of learning to write fiction is reading it, and so I am forever grateful to my mother who firmly believed in reading to her children. I must also acknowledge my test readers and critics because the mirror lies, and we are all a little blind. First, I doubt this work would have been written without Kristie McCue, my dear friend who read it almost chapter by chapter as I wrote it. Her thumbs-up on the first installment gave me the first clue that perhaps I was not deluding myself, and she continued to bolster my confidence by closing almost every phone conversation with the words, "Send more chapters."

Others read the manuscript of this first volume in more completed form. Marie Lim, Aubry Lyons, Suzanne Coulter, J. Goldberg, Kari Kopach, my husband, my mother, my brother Paul, and my son Arthur read the earliest version. Later drafts were read by Sherry Hintz and Douglas Hufnagel (both through www.critters.org) and by Anne Bannon and Cornelia Klarner. I also received both support and helpful criticism from members of ScHoFan, a science fiction/ horror/fantasy critique group under the auspices of GLAWS (Greater Los Angeles Writers Society). Those members include, in alphabetical order: Jason Ahl, Carol Ann Alves, Sarah Beach, Lee Bohannon, Hillary Smith Cantor, Wayne Castro, Neil Citrin, John Henry Davis, Gabriel De Anda, John Gwinner, Ace Antonio Hall, Ken Hughes, Stephanie Kahl, Scott Kilburn, Katy Mann, Leslie Ann Moore, Carl and Toni Nelson, Robin Reed, Judith Swanson, Taguhi Tavitian, Sharan Volin, Lynn Ward, and Garrett Weinstein.

Finally I must mention those who helped me through the publication process with reprise mentions of Kristie McCue, who edited and formatted and did so much more, and Anne Bannon, my book pub buddy who fearlessly forged a path across the treacherous terrain of book publishing and internet promotion and held my hand when terror threatened.

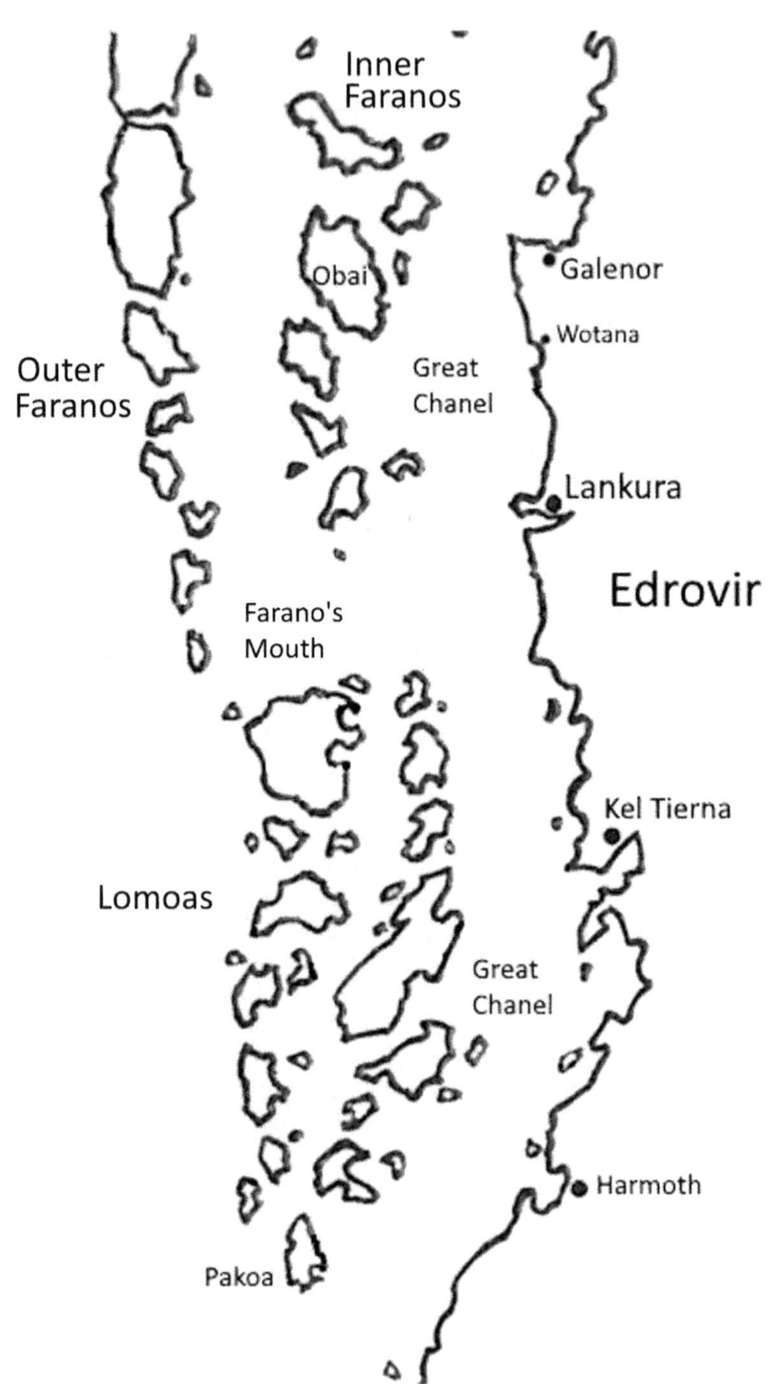

Inner Faranos
Outer Faranos
Obai
Great Chanel
Galenor
Wotana
Lankura
Edrovir
Farano's Mouth
Kel Tierna
Lomoas
Great Chanel
Harmoth
Pakoa

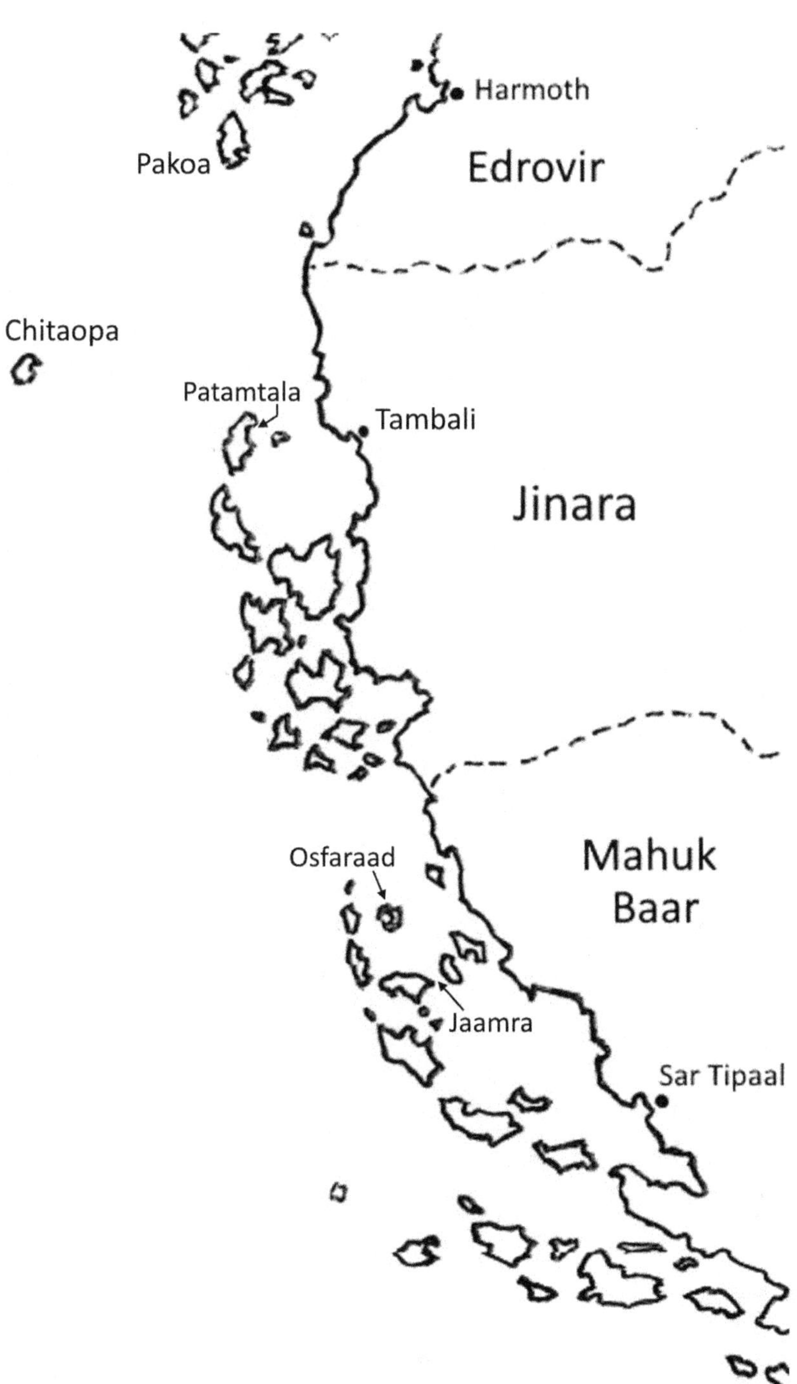

Harmoth
Edrovir
Pakoa
Chitaopa
Patamtala
Tambali
Jinara
Osfaraad
Mahuk
Baar
Jaamra
Sar Tipaal

CONTENTS

Chapter 1: The Memory Thief

He was running through the dark forest, all around him the black and silver harlequin patterns of tree-shadow and moonlight. Branches whipped at him as he ran. Brambles caught at his clothing. He laughed aloud—a wild, exultant, manic laugh.

He was free! Finally free!

He felt as if he could run forever, reveling in the power of his pumping limbs, heedless of muscles on fire from exertion and lungs that burned with each indrawn breath. He slid down a bank, splashed through the stream that lay at the bottom, and flung himself up the slope on the other side, scrambling over rocks that rose before him in a pool of moonlight.

So far... so far already, but he must go farther still...

The change was so gradual that he was unaware of it, but more and more the tree trunks began to reel and waver as they passed. The shapes of rocks and bushes leaped weirdly out of the darkness and danced erratically around him until the world seemed to be turning like a wheel, and he felt as if he were floating. The forest was becoming indistinct, shades of darker and lighter gray instead of black and silver. He staggered, his feet stumbling—and then he was falling, falling among ferns, where he lay gasping, his head spinning, too dizzy and spent to move.

Face down... damp fern leaves... finally able to breathe... the smell of musty earth... the world turning, turning...

A wave of nausea swept over him. Sweat sprang from his already drenched body, and a chill came, racking him, rattling his teeth together in his head. He lay shivering and shuddering among the fern leaves.

Time passed and with it the chill. A delicious warmth stole over him, wrapping him in its blanket. Feebly, then, he tried to move, but his muscles were as weak as water, and his head was full of warm fog so that at first he didn't notice his memories being tugged away.

Names were among the first things to be taken. His own was gone before he knew it. When he became aware that things were slipping away, he struggled against the loss. *"No..."* he murmured, *"No... Don' do that..."* But the memory-thief paid him no heed.

Shapes floated in his vision—faces of shadowy figures, bending over him. There was a girl with honey-colored hair and an expression that was kind and sad and poignantly disappointed. There were men— four men—blond or red-haired, all nameless. And a final face—as nameless as all the others—sallow, with short-cropped black hair and a nose like a hawk's beak. This face had hard black eyes that glittered coldly, chilling him, evoking an intense desire to escape. He struggled, twisting, uttering a wordless cry... and suddenly he felt as if he were falling into darkness... as if the ground had dissolved beneath him...

Now hands were grasping him... turning him over... lifting him...

He struggled to open his eyes...

Too much light!

He closed them again—tried to speak, but all that came out was a moan. A hand was laid on his forehead, and from somewhere, a very long way off, he seemed to hear someone say, *"He's burning..."* But the words conveyed no meaning to his fevered brain.

Enveloped in darkness and warm, gentle fog, he wandered into fevered dreams. The troubling faces came and went, intermingled with running and the sensation of falling. Now and again the memory-thief came, slipping into his mind, taking away memories that troubled him, pulling them behind a curtain of forgetfulness.

Such a relief to let those things go...

But other things were being taken as well, things that he wanted to keep. Weakly he sought again to resist the intangible hands of the unseen thief. But he didn't know how, and the memories kept slipping through his helpless mental fingers, until all sense of the need for resistance slipped away, and he yielded.

Chapter 2: Awakening

There was a room now, sometimes—emerging as if from a lingering mist. It was a small room with rough walls and a low ceiling of hewn timbers. He saw mostly the timbers because he was lying on a bed, looking up at them. There were faces, too—broad, brown faces with dark eyes, framed by dark hair...

Safe faces...

When he finally made his mind focus on one of the faces, he found that it belonged to a woman. She was of middle years, with lines on her forehead and at the corners of her eyes, and her dark hair was pulled back into a single long braid. Then he saw that she was smiling and holding a cup of something for him to drink.

He sat up and took the cup in his hands. It was made of earthenware and it felt smooth and solid under his fingers.

Easy to hold...

He frowned briefly, puzzled by the thought, but then he drank from the cup and the liquid it contained was warm and tasted good. The woman took the cup then and told him to rest, and he lay back down and slept.

After that he wandered less.

*

The brown faces had become people to him. There were three of them. There was the woman, and a man of about the same age with a weathered face and a close-trimmed beard, peppered with gray. He did not come often. The third was a youth of seventeen or eighteen years with a cheerful face and quick, bright eyes. He seemed to be trying to grow a beard like the older man's.

The room had become more real to him as well. Its walls were of wood above and stone below, rough but solid. There was one door and a single window that was covered with oiled skin. It allowed light to pass but no image of what lay beyond. Besides the bed in which he lay, the only furniture was a small table, two stools, and three assorted chests.

There came a time when he awoke to find the woman there, smiling kindly at him. "Would ye like some more broth?" she asked.

He nodded, then found his voice and said, "Yes, please."

"Rest then, while I fetch ye some," she answered, and went out through the door, pulling it shut behind her.

His mind seemed fuzzy, as if his head were still full of fog, but that didn't really bother him—at least not yet. He pulled himself up into a sitting position and noticed that he was quite naked under the sheets. Vaguely he wondered who had undressed him.

He noticed also that there was an object hanging around his neck. He examined it. It was a large bronze ring with no stone, but with a design cut into its square, flat top. The design depicted a half sun disk with rays—either setting or rising—encircled by leafy sprigs bearing trumpet-shaped flowers. The ring was threaded onto a silver chain with a clasp. Both the ring and the chain felt familiar in his hands. It was right that they should be there.

He examined himself then. His skin was pale, not brown like that of the three people who seemed to inhabit this house. He found he had marks on the inner sides of both arms in lines running from his elbows down to his wrists. There were some bruises and tiny red spots that looked as if something sharp had been poked through the skin, and also faded scars of older marks. Looking at them made him feel uncomfortable. There was something wrong about them, and he didn't want to think about it, so he turned his attention to the sounds of voices coming through the rough wooden door.

"Aye, he does seem t' be truly awake this time." That was the woman.

Then the voice of the young man: "Can I go in with ye then, Mother?"

"Oh, aye, it won't do any harm I suppose."

They both came in then, and he pulled the sheet hastily up around his waist. The woman sat down on one of the stools and handed him the cup again.

"Here's your broth then, dearie. Ye drink that right up now."

He was very glad to do so. When he handed the cup back to her, he said reflexively, "Thank you, *Zirdyn*."

Immediately she shook her head at him. "What's that ye're calling me? Zirdyn? I don't need any such title."

"But it's not a title," he objected. "It's just being polite. I was taught to speak that way." Somehow he knew that.

She made a dismissive gesture. "Well, ye can just call me Olomi," she said. "That's quite good enough for me. And my husband's name is Jomo. If ye go calling him *Zirda*, he'll likely choke."

The other youth had seated himself on the second stool and was leaning forward, studying him with great interest. "I'm Taru," he interjected. "What's your name?"

"I... don't know..." He frowned, and the frown deepened. The fog in his head was getting in the way, but still it seemed that he ought to know. He felt confusion, and the first note of alarm was sounding weakly in his head. "Why can't I remember my name?"

His two visitors exchanged glances. "Ye've had a fever," the woman said gently, "a very bad one. It's been three days and nights. I've heard that sometimes a fever can affect the mind. But most likely it'll pass in a day or two," she added reassuringly.

"Father was afraid ye were going t' die," put in Taru. "He was afraid we'd catch a net-full o' trouble then, when someone came lookin' for ye. Instead of a reward—"

"Taru!" Olomi gave her son a stern glance, then turned back to her patient. "Perhaps ye should rest now."

But he didn't feel like resting. A half-formed fear was fluttering in the back of his mind. "How did I come to be here?" he asked. In fact, he realized he had no idea where "here" was.

Taru answered. "I found ye lying in the forest up there behind the house." He gestured in the direction of the wall that held the window. "Father and I carried ye down here. Ye were already in a fever, so we put ye to bed. Where do ye come from? How did ye come to be in Lord Bron's forest?"

He frowned again, trying to remember. But there was nothing. Trying to think made his head hurt, so he stopped. "I only remember this place," he said. "And you, and Olomi, and the other man." Even as fuzzy as his mind was, he found this disturbing. But he wasn't ready yet for the uncomfortable thoughts beginning to surface in his mind, so he pushed them away and said, "Thank you for being so kind to me."

Olomi was shaking her head at Taru. The youth had looked as if he wanted to say something but had changed his mind. "How old are ye?" Taru asked after a moment. "Ye look about my age."

Without stopping to think, he answered. "Seventeen. I'll be eighteen in... in..." He struggled to grasp the thought that had been there, but it fled as soon as he pursued it. "Very soon," he finished weakly.

"See! I knew it!" Taru exclaimed. "I'll be eighteen in Evrel."

"Yes, that's it. Evrel." It sounded right somehow when Taru said it.

"Taru! Are ye coming, boy? The mist's almost gone." It was the voice of the older man—Jomo—calling from somewhere outside.

Taru leaped up. "Coming, Father!" he cried. Then he turned back and said, "I have t' go. It's past time we set sail."

He looked at Taru, puzzled. "Sail? Why? Where are you going?"

Taru looked surprised. "Why, out t' sea with our nets, and then to Wotana t' sell our catch and back home again. That's what we do. We're fishermen, ye know." And with that, the young man hurried out leaving Olomi shaking her head.

"Please excuse my son," she said. "He asks too many questions. Do try to rest now. I'm sure it'll all come back t' ye."

He did as she asked then, and he did sleep for a time.

*

When he next awoke, it was about midday judging by the brightness of the square of oiled skin that covered the window. He was feeling hungry. His mind was clearer but no less empty, and he now found this truly disturbing. Still, he reminded himself of Olomi's reassurances and tried not to think about it. He called for her then, a little hesitantly. When she came he asked her, still more hesitantly, about his clothes, because he had no idea what he had been wearing.

"Oh, aye, I'll get them for ye," she said and bustled out.

She soon came back with a bundle that she laid upon the bed. He examined the things with a gathering frown. The undergarments were plain, and there was a pair of black boots made of soft, supple leather. These things pleased him well enough, but the shirt was of purple silk and the britches were white satin.

"I washed them as best I could," Olomi ventured apologetically, seeing his frown. "And I mended them where they were torn."

He shook his head. "No," he said. "This is wrong. These can't be mine."

"Well, they're what ye were wearing," she replied, frowning at him in her turn.

"But why would anyone wear such things?" he wondered aloud, holding up the white britches. "They'd be no use for anything but sitting in the parlor. They'd be spoiled in a minute if there was any work to be done. What would I do around here wearing these?"

Olomi's frown dissolved, and she laughed. "Well, as t' that, I guess ye have a point," she said. "We don't even *have* a parlor. I tell ye what I'll do. I'll go and fetch ye some spare things o' Taru's. They'll be a bit short in the leg though. I fancy ye're a bit taller."

She came back quickly with a new set of garments made of brown homespun cloth, which she left for him. There was a *tirkyl*-style tunic meant to be belted at the waist and laced at the throat, with long, loose, cuff-less sleeves that could be easily rolled up. There was also a pair of pants, looser fitting than the britches. He got up, feeling weak and shaky but determined not to be deterred. The pants were a little short, but the black boots solved the problem. They were taller than the sort worn by fishermen, coming up to the knee. He was able to tuck the pants into the tops of them. The ring on the chain around his neck he left under the tirkyl next to his skin, because that felt right.

He emerged from the bedroom into the main room of the house. This room seemed to be kitchen and living room in one. It had few furnishings—a table and three chairs, two stools by the fireplace, a pair of chests, and a low bench by the door. Some shelves on one wall held dishes and cooking utensils. There were two windows in opposite walls, to the left and right. Both were open, the wooden frames that held the stretched, oiled skin having been swung wide. Sunlight brightened the room.

Under one of the windows there was a piece of canvas laid out on the floor with some folded blankets. He realized with a sudden pang of guilt that the house had no spare beds and he had displaced someone— probably both Olomi and Jomo, judging by the size of the bed he'd been lying in. The fireplace was immediately to his left, set into the wall that separated the two rooms. Olomi was kneeling there, and he saw that she was just putting a flat, round loaf of bread to bake on a large slab of stone placed among the embers.

She greeted him and he answered politely, then sat on a stool near the fire while the wonderful, warm, yeasty smell of baking bread filled the room. As Olomi moved about tending to things, he found himself listening to something. He realized the sound had been there ever since he had awakened. He'd probably also heard it in his sleep. It was so constant that he hadn't been aware of it, but it seemed louder here in this room with the open windows.

"What is that sound?" he asked. "Like a rushing wind that rises and falls, over and over?"

Olomi frowned for a moment, then suddenly laughed. "Why 'tis the sea, o' course," she said. "I've heard it for so long that I take no notice."

"*The sea!*" He rose excitedly and went to the door, which was in the wall opposite the fireplace. He opened it and stood on the threshold and stared.

The sand began perhaps fifty yards from where he stood, at the bottom of a rock-strewn slope sown with grasses and small flowering plants. Half a dozen yards beyond that, small waves were breaking. Off to his left, there was a rocky point of land jutting out into the water, and away off in the opposite direction, a longer, lower spit of land was visible. The stretch of water in between was thus a kind of very broad bay, sheltered a little from the full force of the ocean's surge. Between the tips of those two points of land, the gray and silver immensity of the ocean stretched to the horizon, broken only by the low shapes of some distant islands and the tiny sails of fishing boats. In the air over the bay, sea birds wheeled and soared.

"Have ye never seen the sea before, then?" Olomi had come up behind him.

"No... I mean, not like this... so *close*..." He blinked then as a fleeting image flickered in his mind. "I've seen it from a window, a long way off..."

He frowned again as he tried to grasp the details of the image that had come into his mind, but it faded before he could place it. With a sigh, he abandoned the effort.

He stood for some time gazing at the scene spread out before him, feeling the sea wind on his face and smelling the salty tang of it. What brought him back at last was hunger. The bread was done and Olomi offered him some. He ate so much of the loaf that Olomi shook her head at him and declared that she would have to bake another. "Still, I suppose ye needed it," she added kindly. "Ye've not had anything solid in days."

After that he went exploring.

The inside of the house didn't take long. There were only three rooms and he'd already seen two of them. The third was another small bedroom, entered through a door on the other side of the fireplace. It was as sparsely furnished as the rest of the house. Against one wall was a low frame formed of planks and filled with dried fern leaves, covered by a blanket. He guessed this was where Taru slept.

One other thing caught his eye as he turned to leave. It was a bow and quiver of arrows hanging on a hook beside the door. Carefully he lifted the bow from the hook and held it in his hand. The bowstring was unstrung. Without stopping to think, he put his right foot through between bow and string, pinned the lower limb of the bow against the outer edge of his left boot, and flexed the bow against the outside of his right thigh. Deftly he slid the small loop at the end of the string along the upper limb of the bow and slipped it into the notches at the tip. Then he lifted the strung bow with his left hand, hooked the string with three fingers of his right, and drew it back to his ear. *Yes,* he thought. This was something he knew how to do.

Carefully he eased the tension back out of the bow, unstrung it, and returned it to its hook.

Next he went outside again. Everything he could see there was as new to him as if he had wakened to life but an hour before, rather than merely waking from a fever. Looking along the shore to his right, he noticed there was a small inlet where a stream flowed into the ocean. There was a kind of narrow pier there within the inlet's shelter. It consisted of a row of three crude tripods made of logs lashed together and connected by planks laid from one tripod to the next. He supposed this must be where the family's fishing boat would be tied up if it were not out at sea.

Standing there, he drew a long breath. This place was so peaceful. It felt *safe*, and that was good, though he had no awareness of any specific danger.

And it was all so *big*... so *open*... There were no walls or boundaries, nor any... He frowned. What had he been thinking? *Guards? Why would there be guards?* He shook his head as if to shake the thought away.

He sighed. It felt good to be free to *move*, to choose what he wished to do and simply do it. He supposed this must be because he had been confined to bed for several days.

He walked down the slope to the beach and stepped out onto the sand. There he stood for a long time watching in fascination the way the waves arched up, translucent green with the sunlight shining through them, and tumbled forward into white foam that rushed across the sand towards his feet. Wave after wave broke and dissolved itself into that tracery of foam that came to him and slipped away again to be devoured by the next cascading breaker. The beach was strewn with polished pebbles, bits of driftwood, seaweed, and small shells. He stooped to pick up an object that lay like a little dish in his hand. The inside shone a beautiful rainbow-tinged pink, while the outside was a dull black.

He carried it back to the house with him and gave it to Olomi. She smiled and told him its name and thanked him for the gift, though she surely had seen a hundred abalone shells before.

He soon ventured back outside, for he was curious about the forest where they had found him. He made his way around towards the back of the house. It was spring, and there were flowers among the dune grass. The ones growing beside the house were white, deep blue, lavender, and yellow. He admired them, though he didn't know their names. Behind the house, sheltered in its lee, there were several plots of ground that he imagined would be used for growing vegetables later in the season when it came time to plant, though he couldn't have said how he knew about vegetable gardens.

About thirty yards beyond that there was a road, and twenty yards farther still lay the edge of the forest. He only got as far as the road. The ground sloped more steeply upward as he approached it, and the exertion of the climb made him acutely aware of how weak he was. He stood in the road waiting for his legs to stop shaking.

The forest covered a range of hills that rose before him, and it went on as far as he could see along the shore in either direction. It was dense and shadowy, but it was just a forest. He knew somehow that he had seen a forest before, but this one didn't look specifically familiar.

The road was narrow and unpaved, and it ran along between the forest and the sea. He could see a few other houses scattered along it in both directions and a few folk passing along it, to his left. The nearest house was about a quarter mile in that direction, beside a small river that flowed into the bay. He could make out a bridge where the road crossed the river. A few miles farther on, at the base of the long, sandy spit, he could see a cluster of roofs that must be a town.

As he stood there, a woman stepped out of the forest almost

directly in front of him and descended towards the road. She resembled Olomi in coloring and in the way she wore her hair, drawn back into a braid. She differed in that her hair had a little less gray than Olomi's, and she wore a tiny gold earring in her left ear. She smiled at him in a knowing sort of way as she drew near, and she greeted him.

"Good morning t' ye, lad."

She was carrying a basket and when she got close enough he saw that it was full of mushrooms.

"Good morning, Zirdyn." His response was reflexive.

She cocked her head at him, though she didn't comment as Olomi had done on being so addressed. "Ye're not lost, are ye, lad?" she inquired.

"No-o." He frowned. *Did he look lost?* "I came from that house, right down there." He pointed to the small fisherman's cottage where he had awakened.

"Did ye, now?" She tilted her head a little and studied him through half-hooded eyes. "That's a very good house t' be coming from. And an even better one t' be going back to. Ye do plan on going back?"

"Yes... of course." In fact, he had nowhere else to go, but he didn't feel he needed to tell her that.

"That's good." She smiled as if bestowing a blessing. "See that ye do. Very good folk they are in that house."

"They certainly seem so." He was thinking of how Olomi and her family had taken him in and cared for him.

She smiled again, a satisfied smile this time. "Good day t' ye then, lad," she said.

Turning away, she moved off along the road in the direction of the river and the town.

For a moment he watched her go, uncertain what to make of her apparent interest in him. Soon, however, his own interest returned to the broader scene that lay in the direction she had taken.

That's north, he thought, *because I know the sea is in the west.* But he wasn't sure how he knew it. He tried to bring a map into his mind and failed. The effort made his head begin to hurt again so he gave it up. His mind still felt a little fuzzy, as if the fog hadn't entirely left him. And as little as he could recall of geography, he realized that he had no memory of history at all. And that felt simply *wrong.*

Every place must have a story, mustn't it?

He shook his head, trying to clear the fuzziness away, but the action had no noticeable effect, and he was beginning to know better than to try to force memories to come.

He took a few steps along the road and became aware again of the weakness of his legs. Realizing he wasn't ready yet for more extensive exploration, he decided to return to the house by following the stream that emptied into the inlet. It emerged from the forest a short distance north of where he stood and flowed across the road in a simple ford.

He joined it at the ford and followed its course as it gurgled and splashed over rocks on its way down the slope. Coming to a deep, quiet pool near the house, he stooped for a drink, cupping the water in his hands. When the ripples cleared, he studied his reflection in the water.

He was fair-skinned, with very regular features. He had a high forehead, a narrow straight nose, and wide gray eyes. The hair that framed his face was nearly black and fell almost to his shoulders. His chin must have been shaved some days ago, though he had no recollection of it. The beginning growth of a youthful mustache and beard shadowed his upper lip and chin, and when he put his hand to it, he felt a little fine, soft stubble. He recalled that Taru and Jomo wore their hair tied at the nape of the neck. On impulse, he tore a little strip of cloth from a ragged place in the hem of his tirkyl and tied his own hair in the same fashion. Studying his image in the water he decided he liked the effect, so he left it that way when he rose and made his way back to the house.

Olomi's reaction to the change surprised him.

"Now why have ye gone an' tied your hair like a Turo?" She frowned at him. "Ye're Kelorin, or don't ye know that?"

The look on his face answered her.

"Poor dear," she said then, gently, "Ye really don't remember anything, do ye?"

He shook his head, frowning in frustration. "I know I've seen a forest before, and that I hadn't seen the sea. But I can't say what forest this is, or what lies beyond it. I have no names for anything. No map. No history. The worst of it," he added, "Is that I don't even know how much is missing—how much I *ought* to know. Maybe you could teach me?"

She readily agreed.

So they sat at the table under the window and talked while Olomi did her sewing. He was hungry for information and asked questions whenever she paused. She could only tell him what she knew, of course. She couldn't help him much with geography, for she had never traveled beyond the town he'd seen, and she had no formal schooling. The town was called Wotana. So was the river, and the bay. The country they were dwelling in, on the other hand, was called Edrovir.

"The capital of Edrovir is Lankura," she told him. "It's south o' here, twenty miles or so, at the mouth o' the River Edro. There's other cities up an' down the coast. There's Galenor t' the north, and Kel Tierna and Harmoth t' the south—beyond Lankura. If ye go much farther 'n that, I guess ye'd come t' the land o' Jinara. Every other year it seems there's a truce with the Jinari, and the years in between we're fightin' them again."

Some of the things she told him seemed to fall into place in his mind as if he'd known them before, and that reassured him. He was relieved, for example, to learn that he was right in thinking that the sea lay to the west. The coastline of Edrovir, and also of the other lands to the south, ran roughly north-south.

"What forest is this?" he asked, hoping that he might recognize the name. In this he was disappointed however.

"It's called Sobring Wood, because it belongs t' Lord Bron Sobring," she explained. "All this land south of the Wotana River is part o' Sobring Hold, for that matter, so we're subjects o' Lord Bron since we moved here. But the town o' Wotana is in Galenor Wared. That's another lord's territory."

"A '*hold*'... and a '*wared*'...?" He frowned.

"The Leithian folk call their lands 'holds' and the Kelorin call 'em 'wareds.'"

"Oh. Yes." Once she'd said it, it sounded so right that he was embarrassed for asking, but the word "Leithian" had seemingly not been in his head a moment before. "You said I was Kelorin, not Turo. How many different kinds of folk *are* there in Edrovir?"

She laughed, not unkindly. "There's only three, so ye know them all now. The Leithians are fair-skinned and blue-eyed, with hair that's yellow like straw, or reddish-colored. The Kelorin are fair-skinned too, but they have hair that's dark brown or black and eyes that are gray like yours, mostly—or sometimes as dark as mine, but blue. And the Turo, o' course, have coloring like me, or Taru, or Jomo."

He nodded. This all seemed right, but he felt more than ever the lack of a history. "How did it come to be this way? All these different folk living in one country?"

"Oh, now *that's* a bit of a tale," she said, shaking her head. "And I'm not very good at story-telling."

"I've nothing else to do but listen," he pointed out. "And I won't complain, no matter how you tell it."

She smiled at him then. "Oh well," she said. "If ye'll be as kind t' me as that, perhaps I *will* try."

So she re-threaded her needle, got her line of stitches fairly started, and began: "The Leithians and the Kelorin came t' Edrovir in the days o' my mother's mother—when she was a girl. They came from out o' the east. It was just after the Time o' Fire and Water..."

She saw his blank look and stopped. "Now, ye see?" she said. "I don't know properly where t' begin. There was a time, ye see, when fire fell out o' the sky and the sea rose up and washed over the land, and many things were smashed, or burned, or washed away. We Turo call that the Time o' Fire and Water. The Leithian and the Kelorin folk came right after that, fleeing out o' their own land, away t' the east beyond the mountains."

"Fleeing? From what?"

She bent over her needle. "From the fire falling out o' *their* sky, I expect."

"Oh." He thought for a moment, then asked, "Where did the Turo come from?"

She sighed. "The Turo have always been here. Since the beginning. We were all fisher folk then, dwelling here on the shore o' the sea and in the islands. Most of us are fishermen still, but there's some have learned other things—farming, and such. The Leithians and the Kelorin knew how t' farm, ye see, and how t' build towns an' cities, an' make things the Turo hadn't seen before. And," she added, after a little frowning pause while she focused on her needle, "some o' them called themselves lords. They divided the land up into holds an' wareds. The lands t' the east o' these hills were empty before they came, so it wouldn't ha' mattered if they'd all just stayed *there*. But they came *here* too, and made them-selves lords over the Turo."

He frowned at that. "You mean the Turo didn't choose to have them as lords?"

"Most o' them didn't."

"That doesn't seem right," he said, because it bothered him. Was it because a Turowan family had taken him, a Kelorin, into their home and cared for him during his fever? "What did the Turo do about it?"

She shrugged. "Nothing really. Turowan folk don't like trouble. And Kelorin and Leithian common folk are decent enough. It's the Leithian and Kelorin lords that made all the trouble. They came here and settled, as I told ye, but it wasn't long afore the lords took to fighting among themselves. It seems the Leithians an' Kelorin didn't trust each other— or they wanted more land. Then it was that one o' the lords—a man named Darion—put a stop to all the fighting. Partly by bein' good with a sword, and partly by bein' good with words..."

She became intent upon a difficult part of her sewing, letting her thoughts trail.

"What happened after that?" he prodded gently.

"Oh," she frowned, "Darion made all o' the lords meet in Lankura. They called it the 'Council of Lords'. And the Council o' Lords chose him t' be the first king of Edrovir. 'Darion the Great,' they called him. He made the capital city at Lankura, and built a great palace there, an' all. He was a good man and he made a good king." She sighed a little wistfully.

"So the Turo liked him too?"

"Everyone liked him. Well, almost everyone." She was making a knot and she stopped speaking to bite the thread with her teeth.

"Was he Kelorin?" he asked, hoping the answer would be yes.

"Half," she said, pulling a new length of thread from her spool. "Darion had a Turowan mother, a chief's daughter—Princess Minowei she was t' our people. But he married a Kelorin lady, and they had a son, Tevren. After Darion died, the Council o' Lords chose Tevren to rule, but he was only king for two years, afore some o' the Leithians killed him. There was nearly a very bad war after that, but some o' the lords signed a paper—the Pact of Lankura. And they chose the king we have now."

"What's *his* name?"

"Elgurn. He's a Leithian, but he has a Kelorin queen named Semorel. They've been king and queen for sixteen years. I know that 'cause that's how old their daughter is, and she was born the very year Elgurn was crowned." Olomi sighed and the needle stopped moving as she raised her eyes to gaze dreamily across the bay. "That's Princess Nevien, their only child, and a sweet girl they say, like her mother." Olomi smiled fondly as she returned her attention to her sewing. "Everyone was wondering who Nevien would wed. And then last summer, out o' nowhere, King Elgurn brought in a young man t' be her husband. He's no more 'n a boy, really—named Leyel Virden."

"Why would the king do that?"

Olomi waved a hand in the air. "Oh, it seems the marriage had been *arranged* years ago. When they were children. Noble folk do that sort o' thing, I guess. They say he's a handsome lad, but not right in the head."

"What do you mean... not right in the head?" He hadn't liked the sound of that phrase. *He* didn't feel "right in the head," himself.

"Oh, well, it seems that years ago, when he was a boy, the poor lad was taken sick with a fever so bad that he was never right afterwards. He has fits, and he's simple-minded and sickly. They say he's not likely t' live long, and maybe that's a mercy—"

"Simple-minded?" Now he felt a powerful surge of alarm. "And he has *fits?* From a fever that was *years* ago? *He never got better?*"

Olomi looked worried at his reaction. "*No-o...* I'm afraid he didn't," she faltered. "But don't ye fret," she added quickly. "Your trouble is nothing like his. Your mind's as quick as anyone's. See how much ye've learned already? Even if ye never get back all the memories ye've lost, ye can learn almost everything over again."

What about my name and my own history, he wondered. *Who is going to teach me those things?* But he didn't say it aloud because she meant well, and he didn't want to upset her any more on his account. He tried to look reassured instead.

By this time Olomi was finished with her sewing. She put the needle and thread away in her sewing box and went to get a fishing net that needed mending. The sun was already westering, so they took the bench outside to work where the light was better. They sat, each at one end of the bench, with the net spread out between them.

"What can I do?" he asked.

She gave him an odd look, but she showed him how to hold the net stretched out for her, so it was easier for her to tie the knots, and how to cut the cord with a small hooked knife.

After he had gotten a feel for the task, he asked, "Are there any Turowan lords?"

"Ah, well, there's three," she replied. "One somewhere t' the south, an' two more way up t' the north where the winters are so cold that no one else wants t' live there. They were chiefs in Darion's time, and he named them lords. No one's had the courage t' take it away from them—though I dare say there's some would like to. But most o' the Turo live like we do, under a Leithian or a Kelorin lord. Do ye understand now," she added, "Why it doesn't do for ye to be tying your hair like that? Taking Turowan ways?"

He met her gaze earnestly. "No," he said, "I don't. What does it matter whether a custom is Turowan or Kelorin, if it is a good custom? See how the wind can't blow my hair into my face when it's tied?"

"Most Kelorin wear their hair shorter."

"If it pleases me to wear mine long and tie it, why should I not?"

Olomi stared at him. Clearly she didn't know what to make of this. "It's just not the way o' things," she said at last, shaking her head. "What if your father or mother were t' see ye lookin' like a Turowan fisherman?"

"I'd tell them what I just told you, because it seems right to me."

Olomi frowned. "What if they didn't see it that way? They'd surely be angry."

"Maybe it was my parents who taught me to think this way, and that's why it feels right to me," he said. But he stopped then because it felt strange to talk about parents when his memory held not so much as a shadow of a father or a mother.

She only shook her head again. "Ye're as stubborn as Taru," she said, but she didn't try to argue with him anymore.

They turned their attention to their task after that, and so it was that Jomo and Taru found them when they came up the slope from the beach.

Taru got there first. "Hullo," he said. "Ye've tied your hair. I like it."

Taru was grinning at him and he smiled back and glanced significantly at Olomi. She threw up her hands.

"I've a name for ye," Taru went on. "Until ye remember yours. I'm going to call ye 'Nagaro'—if ye don't mind, o' course."

"Taru! That is *not* suitable." This came from Jomo, who had come up behind his son. "It's not right t' give him a Turowan name."

"But I don't know how to give him a Kelorin one," the youth protested. "And what would ye call him? 'Dearie,' as Mother does? Or 'the boy,' as I've heard ye do? He's no more a 'boy' than I am!"

Jomo frowned darkly. "A name is a good thing, but not *that* name. Not 'Nagaro.' Ye should have more respect."

As the would-be recipient of the name, he felt he ought to have some say in the matter. "Why?" he asked. "What's wrong with 'Nagaro'?"

It was Olomi who answered. "Nagaro means 'one who has no name' in the ancient tongue o' the Turo," she said quietly.

"Well it fits then, doesn't it?" He glanced defiantly at Jomo, then looked at Taru, who was grinning. "Besides, I like the sound of it."

Jomo looked as if he were going to say something, but Olomi spoke first.

"Nay, Jomo. This one knows his mind. See how he's decided t' tie his hair and I couldn't talk him out of it? If it pleases him t' be called Nagaro, then let him be so. Perhaps 'tis only for a little time."

And so it was decided.

Chapter 3: News From Lankura

Jomo and Taru had brought some fish from their day's catch and Olomi quickly set about preparing dinner. When she said she needed some water from the stream, the newly christened Nagaro volunteered to fetch it.

It was starting to get dark, and he had to pick his way carefully in the fading light. The pale moon, Talebra, was a thin crescent in the darkening western sky. Naru, the smaller dark moon, higher in the sky, was almost a quarter full. The two moons and their names were as natural to him as the color of the sky or the rising and setting of the sun, and he didn't stop to wonder at them.

Coming back carrying the full bucket, he had to rest several times because he was so weak. The last time, he stopped and set the bucket down almost under one of the windows of the little house. The window was still open, and he could hear the voices from inside quite clearly.

He heard Olomi saying, "Ye needn't ha' worried about me, husband. He's barely out of his sickbed, and he seems a gentle lad. Very well brought up."

"Ye say so? Well, that'd go along with him being a lord's son, like I said from the start."

Crouching outside the window, Nagaro frowned and listened more closely. Given the state of his memory, these fisher-folk were in a better position to speculate about his origins than he was.

"Well, he *is* very fair-spoken." Olomi's voice was thoughtful. "That's as a lord ought to be, I suppose. But he was too polite t' me, calling me Zirdyn. Me—a fisherman's wife! And he asked t' help with mending the net."

"Well, if he *isn't* a lord's son, what could he be—dressed as he was?"

"He said the clothes weren't his." Olomi paused and Nagaro could hear the sound of dishes being laid on the table. "Maybe he was a servant o' some sort, wearin' his master's livery. Or a merchant's son, all dressed up for some reason."

"Aye, well, I suppose that's possible. He might ha' fallen off a coach or a wagon—him being sick. And it bein' the middle o' the night, they might not ha' missed him right away."

"Maybe the coach was attacked by highway robbers!" That was Taru, speaking for the first time.

"Robbers!" Jomo gave a snort. "There aren't any robbers along this stretch o' road. Although..." he added thoughtfully. "There *is* some wild country a ways south o' here, where th' road turns inland..."

Olomi's voice came again. "What about those marks on his arms? If he's a lord's son?"

"Doctoring," Jomo suggested.

"And the ring he wears around his neck?" That was Taru again.

Olomi answered. "It's just a keepsake, I'd say. It's a very plain ring— not gold or anything o' that sort."

"Aye, but the chain is silver," Jomo objected. "He may not be a lordling, but he's no farmer or fisherman, I'll warrant."

There came the sound of a chair scraping on the floor and Olomi's voice said, "I'd best close the window. The air's startin' to turn chill."

Hastily, Nagaro picked up the bucket and moved away from the window and towards the corner of the house. He was thinking hard. *Was he a lord's son?* Somehow he didn't feel like one. *A merchant's son, then?* Perhaps. But the idea sparked no recollection. The clothes Olomi had shown him had just seemed *wrong*. The old ones of Taru's that he now wore weren't familiar, but they were... *better*. Why? Because they were good, honest, sensible clothes. The way he spoke was quite natural to him, and he also was aware that it was different from the speech of these fisher folk.

He had no answers, and in any case he'd reached the front door. He made sure to make plenty of noise in opening it.

Dinner was fish stew, fresh bread, and a hot golden-colored tea made from berries of a plant called *sothiril*. The stew was spicy and the flavor unfamiliar, but it was good and he had two helpings. The sothiril he was fairly sure he'd tasted before. The meal's setting could hardly have been more simple or more plain. The table and chairs were of unfinished wood. There was no tablecloth. The dishes were of unpainted earthenware. The utensils were mixed, some wood, some rudely-crafted base metal. Still, the light from the single candle in the center of the table glowed warmly on the cheerful faces of Taru's little family, and the savory aroma of the food mingled with the traces of wood-smoke in the air. Altogether, Nagaro found it all strangely comforting.

The conversation at the table soon turned to the news that Jomo and Taru had heard that day in Wotana.

"The talk is all about the Mahuk raid on Lankura," Jomo told them. "There was rumor of it yesterday, ye remember, but now it's certain. It seems it happened four nights ago. The filthy villains overran the palace and took a lot o' captives. King Elgurn had t' pay a fat ransom to get 'em back!"

Nagaro was listening with interest. "Excuse me," he ventured when Jomo paused. "Who are the Mahuk?"

Jomo stared at him for a second with his mouth open before he sputtered, "*Who are the Mahuk?* Where have ye been, lad?"

Nagaro felt his face redden.

Olomi came to his rescue. "He doesn't remember anything, Jomo, but he just needs teaching, that's all." She turned to Nagaro. "The Mahuk are sea raiders," she explained. "They come from away to the south, along the coast—from the Mahuk Baar on the other side o' Jinara. Every year they come raiding all along our coast an' in the islands. They take gold, or anything else they can get. They're very cruel, and they only ransom captives if they can get gold for 'em. So only rich folk are saved that way. Any captives they take in *these* parts end up as slaves t' row their war galleys."

"Well, they got a heap o' gold this time by all accounts." Jomo said, resuming his narrative. "They say the raiders even took some o' the queen's ladies. They didn't get any slaves, though, unless they kept the king's precious princeling, that is, an' that one surely wouldn't last long chained to an oar."

"What do ye mean? What's happened?" Olomi immediately wanted to know.

Taru spoke before his father could answer. "The Mahuk took Leyel Virden, but he wasn't among the ones they ransomed back! Everyone's sure he's dead—either died of a fit, or the Mahuk killed him. Either way they likely threw him t' the fishes."

Olomi looked shocked. "But that's horrible! Such an innocent boy to end in such a way!"

"Aye, it's a cruel end, I suppose," agreed Jomo. "But for the best, I'd say, in spite o' that. Best for him, and best for Edrovir. I'll warrant the princess is right glad t' be rid of him."

"Now that's a horrid thing t' say!" Olomi put down her spoon. "It's not as if he could help bein' as he was. And ye don't know how the princess felt about him."

"Well, I can surely guess! Ye know what folk were callin' him—a 'pretty-faced boy with no more wit than a cabbage!' He was the laughing stock of all Lankura. Of all Edrovir!"

"I know that well enough! And I think it's a shame. King Elgurn never should ha' brought him t' Lankura. It was cruel!"

"Well, I suppose that's so," Jomo agreed. "But now it's over. The princess will have another husband in nine months' time, and this time it should be a proper man at least."

There was a pause. Olomi picked up her spoon again, but she seemed to have lost her appetite.

At length Taru pushed back his plate and said, "What about Nagaro, Father? It's been four days now. Do ye still think someone will come for him?"

Jomo heaved a sigh and looked at Nagaro, who looked down at his plate. "I don't know... I've asked every fisherman I know. And the fish-sellers, and the shopkeepers. The tavern keeper in Wotana as well. There's no news anywhere about a missing boy."

"Except Leyel Virden..."

All eyes turned to Taru, who had spoken.

"What are ye saying, Taru?" Jomo demanded.

Taru looked uncomfortable. "Well... I was just thinking..." he said slowly. "The raid was four nights ago, and it was the very next morning that we found Nagaro. No one seems t' know for certain what happened t' Leyel, and well, I was thinking... Nagaro is Kelorin. And he's about the right age. And he was dressed like a prince."

Nagaro didn't like this idea at all. *It couldn't be true, could it?* After what Olomi had told him before, and the things he'd just heard Jomo say, he was quite certain he did *not* want to be the unfortunate Leyel Virden.

Jomo was nodding thoughtfully. "Aye, that's all true. And he doesn't remember enough t' say it isn't so."

"But the only thing wrong with Nagaro is his memory," Olomi put in quickly. "And that's from the fever. I've been talkin' with him all afternoon, and his mind is as quick as yours or mine."

Nagaro cast her a grateful glance.

"But I've been thinking about the fever too." Taru was carefully not looking at Nagaro. "Is it possible... I mean, if one fever could turn a person simple, could another fever somehow... put him right again?"

Nagaro felt a cold twist in his stomach. He looked desperately at Olomi and felt a wash of relief when she shook her head.

"I don't think it's likely, Taru," she said. "I never heard of a fever doin' anyone any good. Besides, it's twenty miles t' Lankura, and that's straight as a gull flies. The road's even longer. How could he ha' come so far in one night with a fever coming on him an' all?"

"Ah, well, I guess ye're right then." Taru sounded almost as relieved as Nagaro felt. Now his eyes sought those of the other youth. "I'm sorry, Nagaro," he said. "Once the question was in my head, I had t' ask it, don't ye see?"

Nagaro only nodded. He was quite willing to forgive Taru for having had the thought since it had turned out it couldn't be true.

Jomo was studying him. "Do ye remember anything at all?" he asked. "Anything that could help us find your home or your family? Have ye tried very hard t' remember?"

Nagaro frowned. "Trying doesn't seem to work. Whenever I try to remember, I get nothing—except a headache... Sometimes, when I'm not trying, things just come to me..."

"Well *don't* try then," said Taru. "That's easy enough."

Nagaro shook his head. "Even when *not* trying, I haven't remembered anything useful." He looked at Jomo. "I'm very grateful to you for taking me into your home, and to Olomi for caring for me. I wish I knew I had a family to repay you for your trouble. All I can do now—until my memory returns, or... or someone comes—is to try to earn my keep. If you'll let me stay..."

Jomo sighed. "I never thought o' ye not bein' able to tell us where ye came from." He scratched his beard and looked at Nagaro skeptically. "O' course ye can stay—what manner o' man would I be t' turn ye out with no place to go? And any help ye can be to us in the meantime is more 'n welcome. But I'm wondering what ye can do."

Nagaro realized that, in the fisherman's eyes, he still might be some lord's son, and the Turo must think lords a rather useless lot. Instinctively, he knew he was accustomed to working. "I can fetch and carry," he said. "I can gather and chop wood. And I'll try any task you care to teach me." Then a thought occurred to him. "And I can hunt in the forest with Taru's bow and bring you fresh meat."

Jomo frowned. "Hunting in the Lord's forest is forbidden," he said sternly. "That's poaching, and ye'll do six months' labor for Lord Bron if ye're caught."

Nagaro frowned in his turn. "Anyone should be allowed to hunt for food," he said. "Why else does Taru keep a bow?"

Jomo and Olomi exchanged glances, but Taru was grinning. "I call it 'target practice'," he said gleefully, ignoring his father's reproving look.

"And if some forest creature chances to come between you and the target?" Now Nagaro was grinning also.

"It'd be a sin t' let it go to waste," Taru finished with a wink.

"Well then," Nagaro said, addressing Jomo again. "If Taru will lend me his bow, perhaps I can have some 'target practice.' And I'll gather some fern leaves to sleep on tomorrow," he added, turning to Olomi. "I can make myself a bed in Taru's room—if Taru doesn't mind—so you and Jomo can have the use of your bed again."

This time, Olomi looked as if she wanted to protest, and it was Jomo who made a sign to her, and she said nothing. Taru, for his part, seemed to think it a fine idea.

During the meal Nagaro had begun to feel very tired. By now his head was beginning to swim, and all his muscles felt like wet rags, so he excused himself and went to the bedroom where he'd spent the last several days and nights. He undressed and crawled between the sheets, then lay staring up at the dark rafters, trying to find the peace that would allow him to sleep. It was a relief, of course, that these fisher-folk would let him stay with them, but who was he? And what had happened to bring him to this place?

If only his memory would come back soon... He told himself that he probably just needed more rest. Tomorrow he would surely begin to remember things—some things, at least. Why, it was even possible that he would awaken in the morning to find his memory completely restored...

With this hope glowing in his mind, he sank into slumber.

Chapter 4: The Dream

The wind whistled around the little house, waves crashed on the shore, and rain descended as if poured from the sky in bucketfuls. Nagaro sat in front of the fire with Taru, who was showing him how to work pieces of bone with a pumice stone to make arrowheads. Since Jomo and Taru couldn't take their boat out in such weather, the little family all sat huddled inside, working at various tasks by the light of the fire or of a candle. Olomi was kneading bread. Jomo was making a new net and grumbling about the weather and the fact that there would be nothing for dinner but bread and last season's moldy potatoes and dried onions.

Nagaro held up his bit of shaven bone. "How's this?" he asked. "Am I making it too thin?"

Taru considered the sharp sliver. "Well, if ye took any more off, it might be," he said critically. "But not if ye stop now. I'll show ye how t' finish the neck." He reached for the pumice stone. "It's so much better having ye here, Nagaro," he added. "I've hated foul weather days ever since my friend Gudo got too old for games and started fishing. It's good to have someone my age t' talk to again."

Nagaro nodded, though he also frowned. He liked talking to Taru too, though for him it felt like a new experience... *and of course he didn't know whether it was...* He'd been working as best he could for Olomi for days now. He'd eaten well, and his strength had returned fairly quickly so that by the end of a week, he'd judged himself more or less recovered in body. The marks on his arms had faded until all that remained on each forearm was a straggling row of little pinpoint scars that were scarcely noticeable. He was glad about all of that, and about the fact that the fuzziness seemed to be gone from his mind—or at least he thought it was. What he was *not* glad about was the state of his memory, which was no better than it had been the day he'd awakened.

And no one had come looking for him... Was he so unloved in all the world that there was no one who even wondered where he was?

"I like teaching ye things too," Taru was saying. "And it's better than ye having t' learn from my mother. I can't believe she set ye t' making stew. That's women's work!"

Nagaro shrugged. "I don't mind. She's shown me how to bake bread too."

Taru stared at him. "Ai, Nagaro!" he said. "This must be what comes o' not being able to remember anythings Ye've no idea what's fit or proper for a man!"

This time Nagaro frowned. "How can anything useful not be good to know—for a man or for a woman?" he asked. "And I *don't* just think so because I can't remember!" His glance slid away and he sat staring into the fire. *How did he know that?*

"I'm sorry, Nagaro." Taru was instantly contrite. "I know it's hard for ye. But it's only been a little more than a week."

Nagaro turned back to face the other youth, frowning fiercely. "It's been thirteen days! That's nearly *two* weeks—" He broke off. How was it that he knew there were eight days in a week? And thirteen months in a year, each four weeks long, except for the thirteenth month, Idrin, which had only seven days. How was it that he knew all of this, and couldn't remember his own name?

"Haven't ye remembered anything more?"

"Nothing *useful!* I remember chopping wood, but I can't remember *when* or *where*. I know I used to gather wood with a Turowan man. I can see him in my mind. He's missing a tooth that shows when he smiles, and he has a beard like your father's. But I can't remember his name!" Nagaro shook his head in frustration. "And there's nothing at all familiar about sleeping on fern leaves," he added. "I'm still getting used to that. I must have slept on proper beds, with feather mattresses..." He let the thought trail, aware of the contradictory implications of some of the things he'd just said.

Taru was studying him with a baffled expression. The silence began to feel awkward, so Nagaro shrugged. "It doesn't matter," he said, trying to sound as if it didn't. "I'm sure it will all come back eventually. Can you show me how to finish the arrowhead?"

"All right." Taru seemed grateful for the change of subject.

An hour later, the rain finally stopped. The clouds parted and the sun emerged in dazzling splendor. Taru winked at Nagaro.

"What d' ye say we try some target practice?"

Nagaro eagerly agreed. It would be his first chance to try shooting with the bow, and he was eager to see if the activity brought any memories.

The two young men struck off for the forest through the suddenly bright, windswept afternoon. As they approached the road, they met a Turowan woman who seemed to have just come out of the forest. Taru scarcely gave her a glance, seemingly unconcerned that she could see they were making for the lord's forest with a bow and quiver.

Nagaro recognized the woman, by the gold earring she wore, as the same one he'd met on the day of his awakening. He greeted her accordingly.

"Good afternoon, Zirdyn."

"Good afternoon t' ye, too, lad." Her greeting came accompanied by a cryptic little half smile. Her eyes strayed to the bow in Taru's hand, but she offered no comment, turning instead and walking away along the road.

She hadn't even looked at Taru's face.

As soon as her back was turned, Taru rolled his eyes.

"Ye don't have t' be callin' her Zirdyn, Nagaro," he said when the woman was out of earshot. "Folk 'll think ye're strange."

Nagaro frowned. It didn't feel right to be less formal. "I talked to her once before," he said. "Who is she anyway?"

Taru shrugged as he started across the road. "Just some woman."

"You mean you don't know her?" Nagaro was puzzled, recalling how the woman had talked about Taru's family. "Your parents must, at least."

"Not really." Taru began pushing through the undergrowth that grew thickly at the edge of the trees. "Mother talked t' her once. Seems she lives with an old man in a wagon they keep by the side o' the road, down there a ways." He gestured south, in the direction the woman had gone.

"They live in a *wagon?* Haven't they anywhere else?"

"I guess not." Taru obviously wasn't interested. "They've not been here long. I expect they'll soon move on."

Nagaro might have said more, but Taru was leading the way into the woods and his thoughts leaped back to the prospect of archery practice.

Under the broad trees, everything was still wet and dripping. Their clothes were soon dampened, but not their spirits. Taru led the way to a place where the trees grew right up against an earth embankment. There the tree trunks would be the targets, and the arrows that missed would bury their points harmlessly in the soft earth of the bank so they wouldn't be damaged and would be easily retrieved.

Taru handed the bow to Nagaro. "Can ye string it?" he asked. When Nagaro demonstrated that he could, Taru nodded his approval. "Aye," he said. "I believe ye do know how t' do this." He then chose a knotted place on a tree trunk for his target and put his first arrow into it from twenty paces. Clearly pleased with himself, he then handed the bow to Nagaro, saying, "Now it's your turn. See how close ye can come t' my arrow."

Nagaro nocked an arrow to the string and drew, feeling familiar muscles knot in his back and shoulders. He stood for several seconds, sighting the target and trying to judge the bow's draw weight. His first arrow struck a foot low. He frowned a little, but took another arrow. This one landed four inches high. His third arrow struck so close to Taru's that the feathers brushed.

"That's not bad." Taru was plainly impressed.

Nagaro's gaze was still focused on the tree. "It seems that I've been accustomed to a bow with a stronger pull," he observed. "That's why my first shot was so low. Shall we try a little more distance? It'll help me to get the feel of your bow."

Taru raised an eyebrow. "If ye like," he said.

They retrieved the spent arrows and Nagaro chose a new position a dozen paces farther back. Taru shot first. His first arrow went a little wide, grazing the tree trunk and landing in the earth beyond. His second arrow struck the trunk a foot above the mark. His third missed the trunk, though barely. Shaking his head, he handed the bow to Nagaro. "This is the limit of my skill," he said.

Nagaro set an arrow to the string, drew, and stood still for a long moment before he let it fly. The arrow struck the tree trunk an inch below Taru's. His second arrow struck the mark dead center, and his third about an inch to the right of the second.

Taru whistled. "*Hakura!* Ye're good at this, Nagaro! If I'd known ye could shoot like that, I'd never have imagined ye might be Leyel Virden."

Nagaro was frowning. "I've done a great deal of this..."

Taru glanced at him sharply. "Ye remember?"

"No." There was an edge of bitterness to his voice. "I can tell by the way it feels, that's all."

"Ye don't know who taught ye to shoot?"

And Nagaro did get a fleeting image in his mind then, and the now familiar frown creased his brow as he strove to grasp it. "It was a long time ago..." he murmured. "I was quite small. The man who taught me had to kneel down to show me how to draw..."

"Who was he?" Taro asked. "Your father?"

Nagaro shook his head. "It's no good, Taru. It's gone. But I don't think he could have been my father. He was too old. His hair was almost white."

"A grandfather, then?"

"Taru, I don't know!" Frustration made Nagaro sound angry.

"I'm sorry, Nagaro. I know ye've said remembering doesn't work when ye try too hard."

They retrieved the arrows once again. Nagaro still carried the bow. He nocked and arrow. "Come on," he said. "I've had enough of shooting at trees. Let's look for a tastier target." Without waiting for an answer, he struck off through the trees, keeping low, using the cover of the under-growth, and moving with the stealthy tread of an experienced stalker. Taru stared after him a moment in surprise, then hastily followed.

Ten minutes later, Nagaro spied a fat grouse among the ferns. He sent his arrow winging and the bird fell without a flutter, transfixed.

Taru's admiration showed clearly in his face. "Ye're good at this too," he said. "How did ye learn t' go so quietly through the brush?"

Nagaro stood still for a moment. There was more memory here. *A man was creeping ahead of him through tall ferns... turning back with a finger to his lips... beckoning...* He focused on the man. "The man who taught me to hunt was a Turo—" he began, then frowned again, and put a hand to his forehead. The memory was gone and the effort was, as usual, giving him a headache. He shook his head. "I'm afraid that's all."

"Well," Taru remarked lightly. "If he was a Turo, he surely wasn't your father. But it would be a Turo that'd teach ye to hunt like a man who wants his dinner."

Nagaro was puzzled. "Why else would a man hunt, except for his dinner?"

"Lord Bron and his folk hunt for sport. They'll chase a deer 'til it's falling down with weariness, and then they shoot it."

Nagaro shook his head. "That doesn't seem right. Here," he added, handing the bow to Taru and picking up the grouse. "Let's see if we can find one for you to shoot."

Half an hour later, they had a pair of grouse, Taru having indeed shot the second one, and they were making their way back to the house, feeling very pleased with themselves. They were almost at the edge of the forest when a thought occurred to Nagaro and he stopped and turned to Taru.

"Can you show me where you found me?"

"Aye. I think so. It was just a little way south o' here."

Taru led the way through the trees to a small clearing. Sunlight poured through a gap in the canopy of trees to illuminate a little space carpeted with ferns and bright with flowers. Larkspur grew there, as well as foxglove, queen's lace, buttercup, and scarlet flame flower.

"It was right here in this fernbrake." Taru pointed to a place where something had disturbed the vegetation. "See how some o' the ferns are still broken, and the leaves have turned brown?"

Nagaro surveyed the spot, studying the ferns and the shapes of the surrounding trees. There was nothing familiar about any of it. He scowled. "It might as well be on the dark side of Talebra for all it means to me," he murmured. "Did you look for tracks?" *Why hadn't he thought to come here sooner? Had it been the fog in his head?*

"Aye. I looked. There were only the marks o' your boots, coming from that direction." Taru pointed south. "I couldn't follow them far. The ground turns rocky there under the trees."

"How was I lying?"

"Face down. With your head t' the north."

"So I came alone... on foot... from the south..." He spoke aloud, more to himself than to Taru.

"Aye, that's what it looked like."

"Can you show me where the tracks ran?"

Taru led him across the clearing and under the trees on the far side. Almost immediately they had rock under foot and Taru stopped.

Moving out of the bright sunlight, the sudden shadow of the forest seemed very dark. In the brief moment before his eyes adjusted to the light, Nagaro thought he caught a fleeting vision of dark tree trunks rushing past. The image was gone in an instant, however. He blinked and rubbed his forehead. *Had it been a memory, or just his imagination playing tricks on him in the gloom?* "What did that fever do to me?" he wondered aloud. "Why can't I remember anything?" He felt a surge of bitter frustration. "Even if I can't remember anything else, surely I should know my own name!"

"Ye remember how t' shoot like no one I ever saw," Taru put in. "That's something."

Nagaro cast him a grateful glance, but shook his head. "My hands remember everything they've ever learned, I think, but my mind is giving me only snatches." He stared southward into the shadowed forest. "What's out there? What would I find if I went that way?"

Taru shrugged. "Not much. There's no more towns, all the way t' Lankura. Ye might find a farm or two, for all I know. A few fishermen's houses along the beach. But the coast gets rocky as ye go that way, an' there's not many safe places t' put a boat ashore."

Nagaro looked around one more time, then angrily shook his head. He was free to go anywhere he wished, but the freedom did him no good! It would be folly to strike off into the world with no clear destination.

"Let's go," he said. "We're wasting our time here."

Nagaro moved up several notches in Jomo's estimation when Taru glowingly described his performance with the bow. The birds were soon plucked, spitted, and roasted over the fire, and the family had a very satisfactory dinner indeed. When Taru suggested that Nagaro might try his hand at "target practice" on a regular basis, Jomo offered no objection whatsoever.

*

The days of Evrel slipped by. Taru celebrated his eighteenth birthday near the end of the month, and Nagaro decided to mark his as well for lack of any better information. It was a bad time for him. Taru returned from Wotana that day with a bright new knife in a leather sheath, and Jomo had also bought dried fruit and currant buns to make the occasion more festive. Taru was very proud of the knife, and generally in high good humor. Olomi was aglow with pride in her son, and Jomo, so often critical of Taru, had only good words for him that evening. Nagaro, of course, had neither a handsome gift nor loving parents to share the day. He tried to join in the buoyant mood for Taru's sake, but his heart wasn't in it. Then he became angry with himself for his selfishness, which only made him feel worse.

He was very glad when at last the family retired to their beds. He was in no mood to talk that night, as he and Taru often did, and was relieved when Taru was content simply to go to sleep. The difficulty, of course, was that he couldn't find sleep himself, but lay awake on his none-too-comfortable bed.

His frustration had been growing as the days passed. He still had no name. He had remembered nothing that could help him discover who he was or where he came from. The fact that even little scraps of memory came to him convinced him that the rest must be there inside his head. Why couldn't he get those memories to come? And why, of all things, was his own name lost to him? Here he was, entering into manhood, and the book of his life was closed to him. He didn't even know the date of his own birth—couldn't be truly sure that he had reached his eighteenth year.

As he lay in the dark, his hands sought the chain around his neck and drew out the ring that he wore. It was the one thing he had that he felt truly belonged to him. He ran his fingers over it, hoping to awaken some memory. Nothing came. He rose, distractedly, and paced the floor of the little room, treading the narrow aisle between his bed and Taru's, clutching the ring in his fist and trying hard to remember why he carried it. Still there was nothing—except that his head began to hurt.

He stopped pacing then and tried standing still, shutting his eyes tight and seeking to summon recollection by sheer force of will. This time his head began to throb violently, but still not the slightest shred of new memory came. He clenched his fingers tighter around the ring, and the pain in his head escalated. Only when it threatened to become unbearable did he finally give up the effort. He opened his eyes and let go of the ring.

Feeling angry and defeated, he sat down on his bed, massaging his aching forehead. Once he stopped trying to remember, the pain rapidly began to ebb. He shook his head. Obviously trying was the wrong thing to do. *It was as if something were resisting him... as if something wouldn't let him remember...* But that made no sense. How could a fever do a thing like that? And if not the fever, then what? Did it have something to do with the fog that had clouded his head in those first few days?

He had nothing but questions and no way to find the answers, and he knew he ought to try to sleep. Lying down again among the ferns, under his blanket, he tried to make himself very still... tried to draw his breaths in slow measure... tried to still his mind. He could hear Taru's regular breathing, telling him the other youth was sleeping peacefully, but for a long time his own mind could find no peace.

Sometime before dawn, he must finally have drifted into slumber from sheer weariness. When he did, there came a dream.

He was lying on a bed in a room that he sensed was his own room, though the dream showed it to him only dimly. All he could remember afterward were plain white plaster walls and ceiling, and white curtains drawn across the window.

There was a lady there beside the bed, bending over him. She was tall and slender, and she wore a gray gown trimmed with black lace. She was neither young nor yet old, and she had still something that could be called beauty. Her pale features might have been carved from ivory. Her raven hair, lightly mingled with strands of silver, was braided and wound about her head like a crown. Yet it was her eyes that caught and held him. They were of that rare color known as Kelorin blue, deep and dark like the evening sky fading into night. There was wisdom and serenity in those eyes, and an abiding sadness. She moved away from him, beckoning.

He rose from the bed and followed her. The shapes around him shifted as he moved. Now he walked along a hallway. On either wall were hung paintings of places that seemed familiar, like a series of windows into the world of memory that he had lost. He glimpsed them fleetingly: a garden, a river, a forest, a farmer's cottage. But always the lady in gray glided on before him, and he felt compelled to follow.

The hallway became a passage with dim gray walls. Still the lady led him forward. Now he could see beyond her to where the passage ended in a pair of wooden doors. Though the doors appeared heavy and solid, they swung wide with only a touch of the lady's hand. Beyond the doors lay nothing—only empty darkness. She turned to him again and beckoned to him once more, and he advanced to the very threshold of the void. There he stopped beside her. He was not afraid, although he knew somehow that to pass that threshold would mean that he would never return unchanged into the world he had known.

The lady gazed at him for a long moment with her eyes that were wise and serene and sad. Somehow he found his voice and asked the question that was in his mind. "Lady, are you my mother?"

Silently she shook her head. She reached out then and touched his cheek with her fingers, so lightly that it might have been only a breath of air that he felt against his skin. Then she turned and crossed the threshold, moving into the darkness as if carried on a cloud. This time, she didn't beckon for him to follow, and he remained standing in the doorway while her form receded, faded, and was lost in that infinite and formless night that contained not even stars.

Then it was that a voice spoke to him as if out of the void. It was a voice of power, and of gentleness, neither male nor female, and it said, *I wish you peace, friend, but I see that you are troubled.*

"Yes, I am." Somehow it felt perfectly natural to converse with the disembodied voice.

There was something almost like a sigh, and then: *Tell me what troubles you.*

A wave of anger rose in him, and bitterness rang in his voice. "I don't know who I am! I can't remember my past. I can't even remember my name!"

Another sigh. *Some things are better not remembered*, the voice answered him. *At least for a time. There is wisdom in the Spirit of the White Flower. Trust it and be patient, Spirit that calls itself Nagaro. Rest now, and be healed.*

The words faded, and suddenly he was standing in the room he shared with Taru. He was awake, and it was morning.

Taru was sitting up in his fern leaf bed, staring at him. "Are ye all right, Nagaro?" he asked. "I woke up, and ye were standing there. I tried to talk t' ye, but ye didn't answer."

Shakily, uncertainly, Nagaro sat down cross-legged on his own pile of fern leaves and pulled his blanket around his shoulders. It wasn't cold in the room, yet he was shivering. "I think I must have gotten out of bed in my sleep, Taru. I... I had the strangest dream..." He began to describe the dream to his friend, then, in as much detail as he could remember.

Taru's eyes grew wide as he listened. "*Hamanei mata noa!*" he exclaimed. "Surely that must be a spirit dream!"

"A spirit dream? What's that?"

"It's a dream sent by a spirit, o' course—to give ye a message. Spirit dreams are sent by the spirits of our ancestors, or by the great Guiding Spirit, Hakura Kili." Taru paused and frowned. "At least, that's who sends spirit dreams t' the Turo. Ye're Kelorin. I don't know who would send ye a spirit dream... Vothra, maybe?"

"*Vothra!*" The name leaped in his mind like a flame, and a wealth of remembered knowledge associated with that name suddenly emerged from the shadows of his mind as if a curtain that had been concealing it had been pulled away. "Yes!" he said excitedly, "That's it! I remember now... The voice must have been Vothra!"

"I don't know..." Taru said doubtfully. "Vothra *does* seem t' be like a kind o' Kelorin guiding spirit, but I've heard a lot of folk say that Vothra is dead—even Kelorin folk say it," he added hastily.

Nagaro immediately shook his head, his eyes alight with understanding. "Vothra is spirit, and spirit cannot die." He was speaking from his newly remembered trove of knowledge. "But Vothra was formed from many human spirits joined together, and during the time of the Rithral Lords—before the Time of Fire and Water—so many folk turned away from Vothra that all those spirits parted and went their separate ways. So Vothra ceased to exist, for a time. Now Vothra is gathering again. At least, that's what she believed, and now I know it must be true!"

"What *she* believed? Who is *she*?" Taru sounded as if he wasn't entirely sure he wanted to know. He was eyeing Nagaro in a strange way.

"The lady in my dream... The lady in gray."

"But who *is* she?"

And suddenly Nagaro was frowning again, struggling for memory and finding none. "I... don't know..." He shook his head. "She was someone important to me, I think, but she said she wasn't my mother. I think she's dead, too." His face clouded. Why did he think that? He felt an uncomfortable twisting in his stomach as he thought of the words from his dream. *Some things are better not remembered...*

Taru was looking worried. "Maybe ye should go talk to the dream reader in Wotana."

Nagaro was running through in his mind all the words he had heard in his dream. Suddenly he felt sure—though he didn't know why. "No," he said. "I don't need to do that. Because I know what the dream means."

"What, then?" Taru still looked worried.

Nagaro took a deep breath. "Something bad happened to me," he said. "And... and remembering it would hurt me. So I'm being kept from remembering—for a while..."

"But how can ye be *kept* from remembering?" Now Taru looked confused. "Who's doing the keeping? Vothra?"

Nagaro shook his head. "No, I don't think so. The voice was Vothra. And it said there was wisdom in something called the Spirit of the White Flower."

"Is that... spirit magic, d'ye mean?" Taru's eyes widened.

"I suppose so..." Nagaro didn't know much about spirit magic. In fact, he realized he'd known nothing about it at all until the mention of Vothra's name had opened a whole book of memories. It seemed that he'd read things about it, bits here and there. Spirit magic was very old and not often encountered. No one knew very much about it.

But he remembered something else. "I don't think I need to understand that right now," he said. "Vothra doesn't purposefully speak in riddles to confuse people. If there's anything I don't understand, I'm probably not meant to. At least not now. I think I should just try to let things be for a while..." He made himself a promise, then, to put aside his frustration and trust the voice of Vothra that had spoken to him in his dream. It wouldn't be easy, but for a while at least he'd try to have patience and let things unfold as they would.

"Well... all right..." Taru licked his lips nervously. "Ah, in that case, let's go get some breakfast. I hear Mother setting things on the table." He was clearly relieved to change the subject. It was one thing to talk about spirit dreams and quite another to have a friend who talked to spirits in his sleep.

*

By the end of that day's afternoon, Nagaro had formed a plan. That evening at dinner he was very quiet, until at length he turned to Jomo and asked, "Do you think you could teach me to be a fisherman?"

Jomo nearly dropped his spoon. "Be a fisherman? By the Spirits! Why would ye want t' do that?"

Nagaro met Jomo's eyes with an earnest gaze. "I've been thinking," he said. "No one has come looking for me. Either they don't know where to look, or... or maybe there's no one who cares enough to seek for me. Even when my memory returns, I might find that I have no place to go. And in that case, I'll need to make my way in the world somehow. Fishing seems as good a trade as any, and if it turns out I don't need it after all, there's no harm done."

Jomo considered him doubtfully. "I don't know," he said, scratching his chin. I've got fishing in my blood, and so's Taru, but ye've the look of a landsman. I don't expect ye've ever been in a boat in your life, have ye?"

The familiar frown clouded Nagaro's face as he tried to remember. "I don't think so," he admitted.

"But what difference does that make?" Taru demanded. "For everything there's a first time. Surely he can learn."

"I think ye should let him try, Jomo," Olomi said. "Nagaro is quick, he's good with his hands, and he doesn't give up. Besides that, he heeds my teaching—not like Taru, who always thinks he knows better than I how to do things he's never done before."

Taru feigned outrage. "Now see what ye've done," he said to Nagaro. "Ye've gone and spoiled her altogether."

"Well," Jomo observed. "I suppose it does no harm t' try. The next market day we'll take him to Wotana and see how he does in the boat. There's just one thing though," he added, turning to Nagaro. "Can ye swim? I'll not have ye drowning if ye go overboard, afore I can bring her around t' come back for ye."

Nagaro answered without stopping to think. "I've been swimming in a river... At least I think so." The memory had seemed to be

 Carol Louise Wilde

there, though it was gone in an instant, leaving only the vague sense of knowing.

"Only one way to be sure," observed Jomo. "And no time like this one."

Dinner was over, so the three men went down to the little inlet where the boat was tied. The light was fading and the air was a bit chill, but it would only be colder in the morning. Nagaro followed Jomo and Taru out along the planks of the narrow pier to the boat. Standing in the boat while Jomo steadied it, and feeling its motion on the water, was unsettling. He didn't have time to think about it, however, because Taru promptly stripped and dove in, calling for him to follow.

Nagaro stripped a little self-consciously, then climbed onto a plank that ran just below the gunnel, and jumped. The water of the inlet was deep, and mostly salt seawater since the tide was in. As it closed over Nagaro's head, the coldness of it gave him such a shock that he gasped and got some of it in his mouth. The bitter, briny taste gagged him, and he came up choking, spitting, and treading water.

"Don't swallow it," Taru exclaimed, laughing. "It'll make ye sick."

It turned out that he could indeed swim, though not nearly as well as Taru, who swam and dove around him like a young porpoise. Nevertheless, Jomo declared it sufficient and Nagaro felt a surge of pride at having passed this first test.

Chapter 5: Market Day

The market day dawned gray and damp, but Nagaro, eager to take the next step towards achieving his plan, was undaunted by the weather. He and Taru and Jomo went down to the boat after breakfast, carrying a basket in which Olomi had packed their lunch. Besides that, Jomo had his purse, and Nagaro proudly carried a bundle of rabbit skins that they planned to sell. Most of the skins were the product of his own efforts with the bow, and the money from the sale of those was to be his.

There was a soft wind off of the sea, and it had blown in a great bank of cloud that hung low over their heads and obscured the horizon all around. They couldn't actually see the town of Wotana, but they could see the line of the shore, and had only to sail parallel to it to be sure of reaching their destination. Jomo cast off and took the tiller while Taru set the sails.

The boat wasn't large, perhaps twenty feet in length. It had only a little bit of deck at the prow and a bit more at the very stern. Otherwise, there were only foot-wide planks running six inches below the gunnel along both sides, and also across the width of the boat in three places— fore, aft, and amidships at the level of the single mast. These planks served both as seats and as catwalks for getting about, a particularly useful feature when the whole open area amidships was full of slippery fish. The mast carried a boom with a triangular sail and also could be rigged with a triangular jib.

Nagaro sat on the aft cross-plank and watched with admiration as Taru moved nimbly along the catwalks, making adjustments to the lines. The wind wasn't strong, but there was a heavy swell, and he found himself increasingly aware of the heaving motion of the boat. Before long, he began very much to wish that he wasn't so aware of that motion, for it was having a most unpleasant effect on his stomach.

Taru, balancing along the side catwalk, saw the expression on his face. "Nagaro," he said. "Are ye seasick?"

Miserably, Nagaro nodded. A little later, to his great chagrin, he had to put his head over the side of the boat while his stomach emptied itself in a series of painful heaves. Jomo shook his head at him and muttered something about "landsman" under his breath. Taru brought him the water flask so that he could rinse the sour taste out of his mouth. "Don't worry, Nagaro," he said. "Lots of folk are sick at first. Ye just need a bit more time t' get used to it."

"Were you ever seasick?"

"Well, no," Taru admitted. "But it doesn't mean ye won't make a sailor. It doesn't mean anything really."

Nagaro wasn't so sure. He still felt wretchedly ill and thoroughly ashamed. His wonderful plan was now in jeopardy, and he was in the process of mentally chastising himself for having imagined he could do anything he chose to do just by setting himself to it, when they hove up to one of the sturdy wooden piers that jutted out from Wotana's broad stone quay.

He was very glad to get out of the boat. The steadiness of the pier at first felt as strange as the boat's motion, but the strangeness quickly faded. His nausea, however, took much longer to dissipate. Jomo strode along the waterfront, exchanging greetings as he passed various fish-sellers and fellow fishermen. Nagaro trailed miserably behind, only half listening to the banter. Taru hung back as well for sympathy's sake.

The fishermen were a mixed lot. There were all ages, from youths to graybeards. Perhaps two thirds of them were Turowan while the rest were Kelorin, though most of these were, oddly, as brown-skinned as the Turo—something Nagaro might have wondered about if he hadn't been so preoccupied with his stomach. The two groups seemed to rub shoulders with easy camaraderie despite their differences in styles of hair and clothing.

"Hoy Palu!" Jomo hailed a gray-haired Turowan fish-seller with a face like leather. "Any news for my wife today? News from Lankura?"

The fish-seller grinned. "News for my sweet Olomi, eh? Well, ye can tell my favorite lass that they held a funeral for Leyel Virden—a week ago, I guess it was."

"Buried him, did they? They found him dead?"

"I didn't say they *buried* him. They never found him neither. Just had a funeral anyway."

The other fishermen who gathered about were cocking their heads to listen and some of them now joined the conversation with more questions.

"What took 'em so long, Palu?"

"Did the king get tired o' waitin' for his princeling t' come home?"

"*Well...*" Palu drawled. "The way my cousin heard it—an' *he* heard it from his sister, whose son lives in Lankura—they officially declared the lad dead—on account o' there bein' neither word nor sign of him for so long—that t'gether with his health bein' so poor."

A Turowan fisherman sniggered. "I don't know about his *health.* Sounds like an excuse t' be rid of him, if ye ask me—so's the princess can wed someone else."

"Aye," a Kelorin fisherman chimed in. "Just 'cause he didn't turn up don't mean he's *dead.* That Leyel Virden hadn't enough brains in his head t' find his way home from three feet outside the palace gate!"

"Aye now, that's true." Palu nodded sagely. "My cousin's sister's boy actually *saw* him once in Lankura and says he had a stare like a stunned haddock!" The fish-seller did a fair imitation of a fish out of water, with goggling eyes and mouth agape, and the men all burst into guffaws.

Nagaro was standing back a bit and didn't join in the mirth. Feeling the way he did just then, he was even less inclined than usual to laugh at someone else's misfortunes. As Jomo started to move on along the quay, the fishermen at last took notice of him.

"Hai, Jomo! Is this your lost waif?" one of them called out. "That lad ye were askin' about what doesn't know who he is? The one ye've been feedin' all this time?"

"Aye, there," put in another, "maybe ye should feed him a bit better. He looks a mite sickly."

Taru turned on them. "Oh leave him alone, will ye! He just got a bit seasick 'cause he was never in a boat before!"

"Well, what was he doing in one then?" a tall, clean-shaven Kelorin shot back.

"He thought he'd learn t' be a fisherman." Jomo sought to explain. "I brought him t' market to see how he'd be in a boat."

The Kelorin, who was a tall, chisel-jawed man in his prime, fixed Jomo with a gray-eyed stare. "Well, I don't know if ye're the bigger fool or him, Jomo. If a landsmen has any sense, he'll keep t' the land."

"Aye, that's right, Gundor," agreed a young, round-faced Turowan. "Landsmen should leave the sea t' those as was born to it."

This brought a general murmur of approval mixed with derisive laughter.

Nagaro was standing silent with his face afire. He'd been listening with growing mortification to this discussion of his personal failure. Now the fishermen's mirth stung him as nothing else had in all the days since he'd awakened in the little house on the bay. His anger flared, scarlet and hot, and even as sick as he still felt, he couldn't keep silent. He took two steps forward to plant himself before the last two men who had spoken. "How was I to know the boat would make me sick?" he demanded. "It's not as if I could tell by *looking* at it! No more could Jomo tell by looking at *me!* And how is anyone to know if he can do a thing except by trying?"

The men, Jomo included, stood agape.

Taru burst out laughing. "Aye, Nagaro! That's telling 'em!"

"Nagaro, is it?" The tall Kelorin, Gundor, was looking him up and down appraisingly. "Well, ye may not know your name, lad, but ye've a spark o' fire in ye that I like t' see. Maybe I was a bit hard on ye. It's your stomach, after all."

One or two of the fishermen nodded, though others shook their heads and looked dubious. When it was apparent that nothing more was to be said on the matter, the talk turned to something else as the men returned to their tasks.

Palu gave Nagaro a look of sympathy, then turned to Jomo. "Well, maybe a boat's not just the thing for the lad," he said confidentially. "But he was game for tryin', and ye're a good man for takin' him in. The Spirits 'll bless ye for that. And it seems that he's impressed Gundor, which is worth more'n a bucket o' fish heads."

Jomo received Palu's praise with a nod and a shrug, then bade the fish-seller good day and led the way on into the market square. Nagaro forced himself to follow with his shoulders straight and his head up, though his awareness of his nausea had returned as soon as his anger had ebbed.

Taru elbowed him in the ribs. "That was a smart thing ye did," he hissed. "The only way they'll respect ye is if ye speak up for yourself."

Nagaro winced. "Is it going to matter? If boats make me sick?"

"Ai, Nagaro! That doesn't mean anything. Didn't I tell ye? Ye'll get over it. I'm almost sure ye will."

Nagaro tried to smile, but what echoed in his mind was the word *almost*. His wonderful plan didn't look so wonderful right now. What would he do if he couldn't be a fisherman? What other trade could he choose, and how would he find someone to teach him?

The town of Wotana was a sprawling maze of narrow streets lined with houses and shops built from a rustic hodgepodge of fieldstone and what looked like ships' planking. It surrounded three sides of the market square, with the fourth side occupied by the water-front with its docks and open-air fish market. This being market day, the market square was crowded with temporarily erected stalls and jostling throngs of towns-people.

Being both queasy and distracted, Nagaro took little interest in the morning's marketing. The potent mix of market smells—fish and meat, spices, wool and freshly tanned leather—did nothing for his stomach. The sale of his rabbit skins brought a respectable handful of copper rins, but even this didn't rouse his enthusiasm. Nor was there anything about the town, the marketplace, or the crowds of people that seemed to jog his memory.

At noon, they stowed their purchases in the boat, retrieved the lunch basket, and went to visit Jomo's mother. The old woman who greeted them at the door of her tiny cottage was small and stooped, with a lined face and hair that was quite gray, but her dark eyes were lively and bright. She embraced her son and grandson warmly before pausing to look Nagaro up and down. She'd heard all about him, of course, from Jomo's and Taru's previous visits to Wotana.

"So this is Nagaro," she said, "come t' visit me at last. And Olomi must be very pleased. She always wanted another son and now the wind has blown her one. But ye're so tall," she added. "What has Olomi been feedin' ye?" She laughed merrily, enjoying her own joke. Nagaro was not unusually tall for a Kelorin, but the Turo were a shorter, stockier folk, and he stood taller than either Jomo or Taru by a good two inches. Taru's grandmother was so small and bent that she had to tilt her head back to look up at him.

They ate their lunch at the table in the tiny kitchen. The old woman insisted upon treating Nagaro as if he were one of the family. This made him feel good in a way, although it embarrassed him as well. Taru called her "Gama", which was Turowan for "grandmother", and she seemed to expect Nagaro to do the same, for she gave him no other name to use. She had an apple tree that grew beside the house, and she brought out some of last season's wrinkled apples to add to the repast. Nagaro didn't have much appetite, but he ate an apple for the sake of politeness, and some bread at Taru's insistence. No one commented on the fact that he didn't want any of the dried fish, and no mention was made of his sea-sickness, for which he was very grateful.

The last thing Jomo did before leaving was to pull out his purse and count out a stack of coins for Gama. "There, Mother," he said. "That'll keep ye at least 'til next market day."

Gama kissed her son's cheek. "Ye're a good son," she said. "I know I've nought t' worry about as long as ye're in the world."

As they were going out the door, Nagaro found he couldn't escape without having to bend down so Gama could give him a parting embrace.

*

Nagaro felt better after lunch. Perhaps it was the food, or perhaps just the time that had passed. The clouds had by now burned away, the sun shone brightly, and his spirits lifted. At least for the time, he set aside his worries about his future plans. The marketplace seemed more crowded than it had been in the morning, and more interesting. There were men, women, and children of all ages present. More than half were Turowan, while the rest were mostly Kelorin with a few yellow-haired Leithians mixed in as well. Nagaro supposed he must have seen people of all three races in his life, since none of them looked strange to him.

Jomo had finished all his business in the morning, so they now strolled among the stalls, looking rather than buying. Nagaro soon real-ized he was drawing some stares, a stranger with his fisherman's pants stuffed into black boots and his hair tied back Turo-fashion. At length he also noticed that Taru was an object of interest among many of the Turowan girls they passed, and it was an interest that Taru obviously returned. As they rounded a corner from one lane of stalls into another, they nearly bumped into a Turowan girl of about Taru's age carrying a basket. Her plain brown face lit up when she saw them, though it was Taru who mostly drew her eyes.

"Good morning to ye, Tor Jomo," she said. "And Taru... and...?" Her questioning gaze indicated the unfamiliar member of the party.

Jomo returned the girl a polite nod and a "good morning, Hamani," as he passed, but Taru seemed oddly uncomfortable. "Good morning," he mumbled, then added, "Ah... this is Nagaro," in answer to her implied question.

She looked surprised at the name, but she gave Nagaro a warm smile none-the-less, and said, "Good morning, Nagaro."

"Good morning... Hamani." He smiled politely.

There happened at that moment to be a lull in the clamor of the marketplace, and a peal of female laughter came to their ears. Glancing around, Nagaro followed the sound and saw that it came from a pair of Turowan girls who were standing near a stall on the other side of the lane, a little way ahead of them. The girls were looking in their direction, and one of them was pointing at Hamani. Hamani plainly saw the looks and the pointing finger. She dropped her eyes and seemed to shrink into herself.

"Ah... we have to go." Taru gestured after his father, then tugged Nagaro after him as he hurried away, following his own gesture.

Nagaro twisted his neck to look over his shoulder. Hamani was standing still, staring after them. The expression on her face was dis-tinctly disappointed, and he thought that Taru had been rather rude. "Who was that girl?" he asked.

Taru shrugged. "Just Hamani. She lives across the road from Gama. She and I... ah... used to play together when we were... younger. A *lot* younger. She always wants t' talk to me—as if we were still children."

"Oh." Looking ahead, Nagaro saw that Jomo was still some distance ahead of them.

Taru, however, slowed down instead of quickening his pace as they came abreast of the two Turowan girls. Taru was looking alternately at the girls, who were still casting glances at him, and at his father's retreating back. "Wait a minute," he said to Nagaro under his breath, and he darted across the lane to where the girls were standing.

Nagaro watched as Taru exchanged banter with the two girls. The youth's behavior towards them was quite different from the way he had treated Hamani. The girls' behavior was different from Hamani's as well. They wore their bodices very tight and stood in poses that emphasized their hips and bosoms. They also did a lot of fluttering of their eyelashes.

Nagaro frowned and started to go after Taru, then stopped halfway across the lane, feeling awkward about intruding on the conversation. He looked back to where Hamani was still standing, just in time to surprise a look of pain on the girl's face before she hung her head and turned away. He was still trying to decide what to do when Jomo suddenly strode past him with a scowl on his face. The fisherman grabbed his son by the arm and forcibly dragged him away from the giggling girls.

Nagaro hurriedly followed and was close enough to hear Jomo mutter, "I've told ye, Taru, not those two!"

Taru gave the two girls a parting wink over his shoulder, and a wave. Then, since his father had released him, he fell in beside Nagaro. "Father doesn't like me t' talk to Panila or Lanei," he confided. "They're a bit wanton. He says I shouldn't take up with such, but Gama says he had his way with half the girls in Wotana before he settled down and married my mother and they moved to the house where we live now."

Nagaro was a little disturbed to hear such things about Jomo. "Your father seems to be very happy with your mother," he ventured. "Don't you want to find a woman you love—a woman who loves you—and marry her?"

Taru looked as if he didn't believe what he was hearing. When it became apparent that Nagaro was completely serious, he shrugged and said, "Well o' course I expect I'll marry *some* day. When I'm older. But I don't see why I shouldn't have a bit o' fun first."

This didn't sound quite right to Nagaro, but he wasn't sure how to say so, and he decided to keep his peace.

Some time later they stopped at a blacksmith's stall, which featured a display of knives of various sizes. Since these items were of interest to all three of them, they lingered for quite some time, examining the merchant's wares.

Nagaro stood, feeling the edge of a long hunting knife with his thumb and reflecting that it would be very fine to be able to make such a thing. He was just wondering whether he might study to be a blacksmith if he couldn't be a fisherman, when he heard a sweet, female voice quite close to him say, "I like your boots."

Startled, he looked up—directly into the eyes of a very pretty Kelorin girl.

She looked about sixteen, and she must have come from the back of the stall because he hadn't seen her when they first arrived. She dropped her gaze demurely when he looked at her, momentarily veiling clear gray eyes with dark lashes. When she looked up again, she smiled at him and said, "I haven't seen ye here before. What's your name?"

He had to swallow hastily before he could get his voice to come out. "Nagaro," he managed, his heart suddenly beating faster.

"That sounds like a Turowan name," she said. "Why do ye tie your hair like that?"

"Because I like it that way," he said, avoiding the subject of his odd name. He found himself feeling rather warm. "What's your name?"

"Aramei."

"That's a pretty name..."

He was trying desperately to think of something else to say, when he felt a hand grip his arm and pull him away from the stall. He turned his head, expecting to see Jomo's frowning face, but it was Taru who held his arm. "What's the matter," he asked. "Don't tell me she's wanton too."

"Not likely," Taru hissed. "She wouldn't have the chance. No one can get near her 'cause of her father, Tor Boronin. Did ye see the knife he wears? The only time I ever said a word t' Aramei, he swore he'd slit my throat if he ever saw me hanging 'round her again."

Nagaro looked back at the blacksmith, a big, burly man who stood at the other end of the stall talking to Jomo. There was a foot-long sheath hanging at the man's belt.

"It's lucky he didn't notice ye," Taru continued. "Ye'd best pick some other girl t' flirt with."

"I was just talking to her," Nagaro protested. "I wasn't flirting."

Taru gave him a searching look. "Well, maybe ye weren't," he said, "But *she* was. Girls are always flirting when they talk to boys. If she didn't want t' lie with ye she wouldn't ha' bothered."

Nagaro suspected this wasn't all that went on in the heads of young women, but he hadn't a single shred of specific memory to support his impression. Other than the kind-hearted and sensible Olomi, and Gama whom he'd just met, the Lady in Gray was the sole example of the fair sex of whom he had any recollection. He couldn't imagine any of them as flirtatious sixteen-year-olds, but then he hadn't known any of them when they were sixteen either.

He glanced back at the stall and saw that the girl was still watching him. It might have been his imagination, but he thought she looked disappointed in rather the same way Hamani had as she'd watched Taru walk away. "It must be very hard for her," he said. "Having a father like that. I don't suppose she gets to talk much to anyone. She probably just wanted to see if she liked me."

Taru gave him a pitying look. "What she wanted was t' get her hook into ye, and I'm thinking maybe she did, too. I tell ye, Nagaro, it's best ye just forget about that one."

*

Before leaving the village, they stopped at a tavern because Jomo and Taru fancied having a mug of ale. Nagaro, however, hung back as they approached the door, troubled by a thought that had come into his mind. "I don't think I should drink ale," he said. "Or wine. Vothra counsels against it."

Jomo considered him. "Well, he said. "It's no great surprise that ye're Vothrin. Most Kelorin are, but not all o' them keep their ban. But I'm sure we can get ye a cup o' sothiril. That'll likely set better on your stomach anyway."

Nagaro felt his heart sink at this reminder of the morning's failure and of the fact that going home meant traveling in the boat again. He sat at one of the tavern tables, gloomily sipping his sothiril and contemplating the bleakness of his future, while Jomo and Taru savored their ale.

When they stood up to leave, Taru suddenly turned to him. "I've been thinking, Nagaro," he said. "About ye and the boat. I think I know what ye did wrong."

"What then?" Nagaro asked, though he hadn't much hope.

"Ye shouldn't ha' sat still in the stern like that, just lettin' the boat bob ye up and down like a bucket o' fish. Ye've got to be up and moving. Set your mind on where ye're goin' and what ye're doin'. Let the boat move under ye. Balance with her."

"It sounds rather like riding a horse," Nagaro said, imagining sitting astride a horse's smooth, broad back and balancing to the motion of its strides.

"Ye can ride a *horse?*" Taru stared at him.

"Yes, of course. I mean, I think so." Nagaro was never sure of anything if he thought about it too hard. Might it not, after all, have been something he'd dreamed?

"I wish I could ride a horse," Taru said wistfully. "When Goran the trader comes, we'll have t' see if he'll let ye try one o' his. He has two horses, one for him and one for his wares."

Nagaro hunched his shoulders. "Well, I wish I could ride a boat the way you do, Taru. Right now, though, I'd settle for getting back to the house without getting sick again."

*

In fact, he did not get sick the second time. He began by standing on one of the planks, steadying himself by the mast while Taru cast off. Then he followed Taru's instructions and helped unfurl the mainsail and secure the lines. Once they were well underway, Taru brought up some more planks from the bottom of the boat and laid another catwalk down the middle, running fore-and-aft and secured by pegs that fitted into holes in the cross-planks.

"Try walking that and see if ye can get your balance," Taru suggested.

It wasn't easy. The wind was blowing more forcefully, there were whitecaps on the waves, and the boat was surging along with a bucking motion. Repeatedly, Nagaro lost his balance and ended in the bottom of the boat. He landed on his feet like a cat however. It was only a two- or three-foot drop, and as often as he fell, he got right back up onto the planks and tried again. By the time they reached their destination, he was showing marked improvement and feeling tremendously elated at the prospect that he might have a future as a fisherman after all.

Jomo was also eyeing him with more respect. "By the Spirits," he said, "ye do learn fast. We may make a sailor of ye yet. It seems I should ha' bought ye some *kuma* after all. If ye're going t' be spending the whole day on the water, ye'll be needin' it with that fair skin o' yours."

Nagaro stepped triumphantly out of the boat onto the narrow pier. "What's kuma?" he asked.

Taru answered him. "Did ye see how brown the Kelorin fishermen were? That's 'cause they use kuma stain. It's made from the shells o' kuma nuts and it'll keep your skin from burning. Ye rub it on at night, and in the morning ye're as brown as a Turo."

"Does it ever come off?" Nagaro asked. It wasn't that he minded the idea of being as brown as a Turo, but he wasn't sure he would always want to be that way.

"It wears off in a few weeks. Then ye just have t' put on some more."

"Trader Goran'll have some," Jomo put in. "He'll be coming by here any day now."

*

Nagaro lay awake that night for some time with the memories of the day's events running circles in his head. The success of his second attempt at sailing, after his initial disappointment, meant that his plan had a real chance of working. And he thought he had perhaps made a favorable impression on at least one member of Wotana's fishing community. There was also the market, selling his rabbit skins, the kindness of Taru's grandmother, and the prospect of having a chance to try riding a horse—not to mention turning his skin brown with kuma stain.

And, finally, there was Aramei. It was the image of the girl's dark lashes and soft gray eyes that was floating in his mind when he at last slid into slumber.

Chapter 6: Fisherman's Apprentice

It might have been merely coincidence that Jomo chose the first week of Nagaro's apprenticeship to careen the boat, but Nagaro suspected it was another test of his resolve.

Taru quietly agreed. "Well, it had t' be done sooner or later," he confided. "But it could ha' waited a few weeks. And if ye'll stand this, ye"ll stand *anything*."

Scraping off barnacles was both extremely tedious and very hard work. This part of the task alone took several days and Nagaro's hands soon sported blisters and cuts as proof of his diligence. He was determined, however, not to complain—at least not any more than Taru.

It was on one of these days, on a bright, cloudless morning, that Goran the Trader came to Wotana Bay. Nagaro and Taru were working close together, squatting on their haunches near the bow of the boat.

"Ow! Cut myself again!" Taru dropped his sharpened scraper and sucked a wounded thumb.

Nagaro tried to scratch an itch on his cheek with the back of his hand, not liking to use fingers fouled with the remains of scraped barnacles, and worse. "I know," he said. "Yesterday I tried to scratch my chin and got blood in my beard."

Taru made a face at him. "Is that what ye call that dirty bit o' fuzz on your chin?"

Jomo, at the other end of the boat, must have heard them. "I've told Nagaro I can take him t' town to have his chin shaved," he offered, for the third time. "He's got those rins from the marketing t' pay for it."

Nagaro frowned. "No, thank you." He and Taru were in a competition to see who could sport the better beard, and he wasn't sure whether to be annoyed or amused by Jomo's efforts to make him behave like a proper Kelorin. "Besides, I'd rather save my money for other things."

"*Jomo!*" Olomi's voice came to them from the direction of the house. "Goran's coming, and I need t' buy a needle and pins!" She was standing in front of the house, pointing with an outstretched arm to where the trader could be seen approaching along the road from the south astride a big bay, leading a laden pack horse.

Taru stood up. "What were ye just saying, Nagaro, about saving your money? Goran'll have kuma stain."

"Kuma stain!" Nagaro stood up eagerly, then looked questioningly at Jomo.

The fisherman threw up his hands. "Aye, go on. Off with ye both, then. Just see that ye come straight back when ye're finished."

Gratefully, they laid down their tools and ran to intercept the trader.

Goran turned out to be a tall, lanky Kelorin in his fourth or fifth decade, dressed in leather traveling clothes. He listened attentively to Olomi's request and laid out what he had to offer on a cloth that he spread on the ground near the front door of the little house.

While Olomi was looking over the offered wares, Nagaro boldly asked the trader about kuma stain and purchased a small clay pot containing several month's supply of the ointment for a few rins. He balked, however, when Taru jabbed him in the ribs and jerked his thumb in the direction of the horses. "Just forget it, Taru," he muttered. "I don't like talking about my memory."

Taru gave him an exasperated look, and then, stepping up to Goran, launched into a description of Nagaro's woes before Nagaro could stop him.

The trader listened while Nagaro's face burned. "Go ahead then, lad," he told Nagaro at the end of it. "I'll gladly let ye try a ride on my beast if ye think it might jog your memory."

Nagaro swallowed his embarrassment. Murmuring his thanks, he approached the trader's mount, noting the brightness of the horse's eye and the long, clean lines of its legs. He was sure, now, that he could ride, and his pulse began to quicken at the thought of it.

He put out a hand to rub the horse's muzzle, then spoke a few soft words into its ear before seizing the pommel. Putting his foot in the stirrup, he swung easily up into the saddle. As he settled himself into that familiar seat, his lingering discomfiture slipped away and he felt a sense of elation. *This was a place where he belonged!*

"I'll go no farther than those rocks," he said, pointing to an outcropping that thrust itself out into the breaking waves about a quarter of a mile south along the shore. "And I promise I'll come straight back."

The trader was eyeing him, noting how easily he sat in the saddle. "Aye, go on, lad," he said, grinning.

Nagaro took the reins in one hand, made a clicking sound with his tongue, and dug his heels firmly into the horse's flanks. The bay sprang forward, breaking into a gallop as they reached the firm surface of the road. Goran hadn't ridden far or hard that morning. The horse was young, fresh, and more than willing to stretch its legs. Impulsively, Nagaro loosed the reins and stood in the stirrups. Stretching both arms to the sky, he let out a whoop of pure joy. Then, gathering up the reins again, he rode crouching low over the horse's neck. Feeling the cord that tied his hair loosening, he pulled it off, tucked it into his belt, and let his hair whip in the wind.

It had been far too long since he had done this. *How long? A few months? A year?* He was uncertain, but it was something he'd once been accustomed to doing almost daily. The feel of the horse's powerful body surging between his knees and the rush of wind in his face brought visions of memory wheeling through his mind in rapid succession.

They were places where he'd ridden: A road beside a river through a woods... a country road running past farm houses... He remembered a man—the same man, he realized, who had taught him to shoot a bow. The man was a lean, gray-haired Kelorin, and he seemed to be a stableman by trade. As the memories came flooding, Nagaro realized that this man had shown him how to tighten a saddle girth, buckle a bridle, clean a horse's hoof, and brush its coat. This man had lifted him up, up, onto the high, broad back of a chestnut mare when Nagaro was so small that his legs, stretched as wide as he could stretch them, barely began to follow the downward curve of the animal's sides...

He was so much in the thrall of these memories, and so focused on the distant outcrop, that he didn't see the wagon come out of the forest on his left. All he knew was that it was suddenly there, moving onto the road in the path of his speeding mount.

The driver, an elderly Turowan man, with a woman seated beside him, chose that moment to tug on the reins, stopping the wagon broadside across the roadway, completely blocking Nagaro's way.

"*Vothra!*" Nagaro frantically pulled on the reins of his own mount, and the wheel of memory spun away as he brought the bay to a plunging, snorting halt just feet from the weathered planks of the wagon.

"Good day t' ye, lad, and where would ye be going?" said a female voice.

The speaker was the wagon's passenger, and he saw now that she was the woman with the gold earring. She was sitting on the far side of the driver where he hadn't been able to see her clearly before. The driver gave Nagaro an apologetic shrug.

Nagaro stared at them both as he tried to catch his breath and ease his wildly thudding heart. Taru had said the woman lived in a wagon with an old man. This must be the wagon. And the man. The wagon's canvas top, stretched over wooden hoops, was all there was to keep off the rain. The stolid, flea-bitten gray between the traces seemed completely indifferent to having so narrowly escaped a collision.

Nagaro's brows knit in frustration. The outcrop was still a hundred yards away. He was on the road to Lankura, and behind him was the tiny house that suddenly seemed like a prison. He felt a wild desire to ride on down that road—to ride until he found the places in his memory. But he didn't know where the places were, and he'd given the trader his word.

Besides, there was a wagon in his way... He realized that the Turowan woman was still staring at him, waiting for an answer. "Nowhere," he said, bitterly. "Obviously."

Without waiting for any response, he turned the horse about and rode back the way he'd come at a reluctant canter. Pulling to a halt on the grass beside the little house, he swung to the ground and handed the reins to Goran. "Thank you, Zirda," he said quietly.

The trader was looking at him ironically. "Aye," he said. "I think ye can ride, lad. Just a little."

Olomi was clutching her new needle and pins and staring at him as if she were wondering who and what he truly was.

Taru's eyes held frank admiration. "*Hakura!*" he exclaimed. "I wish I could do that!"

Nagaro shook his head. "Fishermen ride boats, not horses," he said, and his eyes were clouded.

"Did it bring ye any memories?" Goran asked.

"A few, yes. Thank you."

Olomi paid Goran the price of her purchases, and the trader packed up his wares and bade them good day. Nagaro's gaze lingered long on the departing figures of the man and the two horses.

"Come on, Nagaro. Father's waiting." Taru's voice pulled him from his thoughts.

"I almost wish I hadn't done that."

"Why? Did ye remember something bad?"

"No." Nagaro shook his head. "But I think I used to ride almost every day, just for the pure joy of it. I know now that I've always loved to ride, Taru, but I never missed it in all the days that I've been here—until now."

After a moment, he found the piece of cord in his belt and re-tied his hair. "All right then," he said. "It's time to go back to scraping barnacles."

*

After scraping barnacles came caulking. This was not quite such unpleasant work, although Nagaro went to bed with pine pitch on his hands every day they worked at it—and for a week after they'd finished.

The work kept him busy—too busy to have time to think about the state of his memory or how much he missed having a horse to ride, though his nights began to feature dreams of riding a tall, black horse— galloping, wild and swift, with the wind in his hair.

At last the boat was clean and tight and they had only to wait for high tide to float her. The night before they were to do that, he brought out his kuma ointment and, with Taru's help, covered every inch of his skin from his hairline to his waist with the stain. It was a kind of dirty yellow color when rubbed on, and he and Taru both had a good laugh about how funny he looked.

Taru didn't laugh in the morning, though, after the stain had turned brown. "Ye don't make such a bad Turo, Nagaro," he said. "I wish ye could see yourself."

That day they fished, and Nagaro learned how to cast a net and draw it in. He kept busy moving about the boat, and he wasn't sick that day, or any other, although it was many days before he felt confident enough to try a more sedentary task like handling the tiller.

*

Besides casting and drawing in the net, Nagaro learned how to sort the catch at the pier in Wotana. He learned the names of all the different kinds of fish, and which brought the best prices. He learned how to set and trim the sail, how to handle the tiller, how to tack into the wind, and how to bail when the waves washed over the gunnel. He began to understand how to read the wind and follow the rhythm of the tides. He also learned how to row the boat when the wind died, pulling in tandem with either Taru or Jomo, matching stroke for stroke with one of the two long oars that were stored under the catwalk planks along either side. He became in time almost as adept as Taru at walking the catwalk planks in all kinds of weather, balancing to the motion of the boat.

Spring slid gradually into summer. The days were so full that they ran together, and the nights found Nagaro so exhausted that he slept soundly until sunup. The state of his memory remained unchanged, but at least he was making progress in pursuit of the plan he had set for himself. Most of the fishermen were at first inclined to be amused by Jomo's strange, fair-spoken apprentice. But Gundor was a leader among them, and Nagaro had won a measure of that man's respect on his first visit to Wotana. Besides that, Nagaro was obviously so earnest in his desire to learn the fishermen's craft that the men's mirth eventually gave way to acceptance.

One other thing Nagaro learned was that no amount of skill or craft could ensure that the net would be full, or even that there would be any fish to catch at all. The Turowan fishermen talked of the waywardness of the Spirits of Wind and Wave. The Kelorin spoke of Lokundas, whose hand turned the world, sending fortune—good or ill—to man and beast alike. The hand of Lokundas touched everyone it was said, but no plea, however piteous, could touch Lokundas' heart. If there had been any Leithian fishermen in those waters, they would doubtless have complained of the fickle whims of the gods by whom they swore.

Taru taught him the names of the many different sea birds that they saw. There were gray terns and petrels and sleek black cormorants. There were four kinds of gulls, each with different markings. There were the great ungainly pelicans that flapped along low over the waves, and suddenly folded awkwardly and fell with a great splash, only to emerge from the water with fish in their beaks.

Then there was the great sea eagle that circled high in the sky and came down swift and sure as an arrow to its mark.

"The Turo call that one *taru*," his friend informed him.

Nagaro looked at him. "Are you named for the sea eagle then?"

Taru grinned. "That's right."

"Taru, the Sea Eagle. I like that." Nagaro shielded his eyes with his hand, watching the great bird circle overhead. "I wonder what my name means," he added. "My real one, I mean. The one I can't remember."

Jomo's little boat could never move as fast as a galloping horse, but Nagaro found that riding her as she surged over the swells, at the best angle to a good wind and with both sails set, gave him a sense of freedom and power that was very much akin to what he'd been accustomed to feel on the back of his big black horse. Even when they weren't moving fast, there was the sea wind in his face, the salt tang in the air, and the awesome sweep of sea and sky. The ocean had a myriad of moods that moved across its great face in shifting patterns of sunlight and cloud shadow. Its surface could be anything from smooth and glassy, to tossed and broken and flecked with foam—all according to the fickle graces of the wind.

They routinely sailed beyond the confines of Wotana Bay, out into the strait between the mainland and the Farano Islands. The nearer island chain comprised the Inner Faranos. Beyond them lay a second chain, the Outer Faranos. It was a longer chain that ran farther south, and south of that was yet another group, the Lomoas. Jomo knew all of this, though he'd never sailed so far himself. In fact, the farthest they sailed while fishing that summer was to within a stone's cast of Obai, the nearest of the Inner Faranos.

Merchant ships plied these waters, sailing between the cities along the mainland coast as well as back and forth between the islands and the mainland. These craft had two, or even three, masts. They dwarfed Jomo's little fishing boat, and the first time Nagaro saw one, he stared in undisguised amazement. Just as he had known on his first day of awakening that he'd never seen the sea close up before, so he knew that these great ships were something new to his experience. They fascinated him, and it was many weeks before he could see one, even quite far off, without stopping whatever he was doing to watch it pass. Jomo shook his head at him, and Taru laughed, but the day that a merchant ship passed within twenty yards of their little craft, even Jomo and Taru let the net lie in the water while their eyes drank in the sight. Long and tall, the great hull clove the waves. She was a two-masted craft, fore-and-aft rigged. Her sails bellied to the wind as she rode the swells, and the flag of Edrovir, white hawk upon a field of blue, floated from her main mast. They could see the figures of men on her deck.

Nagaro wondered what it would be like to stand among them.

*

There was another day, though, when Nagaro spied a ship of a different kind. They were fishing far out in the strait that day, close to the southern end of the isle of Obai. They had just finished hauling in the net and emptying the fish into the bottom of the boat. Glancing up from his work, Nagaro noticed that a two-masted craft had emerged from behind the island, bound east-southeast, about a half mile distant. The prow of it had a strange shape, and there was a rhythmic ripple of motion along the length of the hull that he didn't understand. He couldn't make out the device on the flag she flew, but he could tell that the flag was red, not blue. The course the ship was on would carry it right past their boat.

"What kind of ship is that?" he asked, pointing.

Jomo took one look at it, and swore under his breath as he put the tiller hard over to starboard to bring their bow around to a northeast heading. "Raise the jib!" he barked. "Taru, shorten those lines. We need all speed!"

Both young men leaped into action. Nagaro hauled up the jib and made the line fast. Taru pulled in the slack mainsail until it snapped taut in the wind. The little boat surged ahead, lunging over the swells, heeling hard, with both sails trimmed to the wind. Only when Nagaro saw that they were making good speed and were moving farther from the course of the unknown vessel did he ask his question again.

"What *is* that ship?"

"*Mahuk!*" Jomo spat the word.

Nagaro studied the distant ship then with even greater interest. Sitting with Taru on the high side of the boat to help keep her keel in the water, he steadied himself by a mast stay with one hand while he shaded his eyes with the other. So *that* was a Mahuk war galley. It must be the movement of the oars that he saw, rippling along the side. He'd often heard the fishermen talk of the dreaded Mahuk sea raiders. The oddly shaped prow was made for ramming other craft, and the oars were worked by galley slaves—many of them doubtless captured Turowan fishermen. He noted the tension in Jomo's face and saw that the older man''s knuckles were white where he grasped the tiller. "Do they take men at sea then?" he asked.

"At sea, or on the shore—as they can, or as they choose." Anger smoldered in Jomo's eyes. "By Hakura, I'd rather die than be a slave! I'd drown myself in the sea afore I'd let 'em take me."

"They're holding their course," Nagaro observed. "They're not coming after us."

"Look there! Ye can see why." Taru pointed towards the southern tip of the island. Emerging from behind Obai's rocky headland was another warship. It was very much like the first, save that it was flying the blue banner of Edrovir. As they watched, a second and then a third blue-bannered ship came into view.

"They also have oars!" Nagaro exclaimed.

"Aye," Jomo answered him. "But it'll not be slaves that are pulling on 'em. It'll be seamen—Lord Kuran's sea warriors—that are rowing *those* ships. The Lord of the Fleet won't be there himself, o' course. He'll be off somewhere t' the south with the main part o' the Royal Fleet. Those three are just here t' guard the islands."

"Well, it's a good thing that someone is protecting the fishermen," Nagaro remarked.

"Protecting the *fishermen?*" Jomo snorted. "And fish have feathers, I suppose! It's the *gold* men dig out o' those islands that they're protecting. Elgurn doesn't care about the fishermen. Kuran might care, bein' half Turo, himself, but he's got his orders."

Nagaro frowned. "Well Elgurn *ought* to care about the fishermen," he said with conviction. "They're his people. Turowan or Kelorin or Leithian, we're all his people."

He sounded so serious that Taru laughed at him, and Jomo gave him a hard look. "Aye lad," he said dryly, "and if ye're ever in Lankura, ye'll tell him that for me, won't ye?"

Nagaro didn't answer. His attention was all on the tall ships, now dwindling behind them. "Will there be a battle?" he asked.

"If they can catch those Mahuk devils," Jomo replied. "I think it's safe t' head more easterly now," he added, putting the tiller over. "See t' the lines, both o' ye."

"Couldn't we slacken sail a little bit, Father?" Taru's interest was suddenly as keen as Nagaro's. "I've never seen a sea battle."

"Nor have I, and I don't wish to." Jomo answered his son tartly. "I don't reckon it's healthy t' be anywhere near one." He shook his head at their disappointed faces.

*

News from the lands beyond Wotana passed from fisherman to fisherman out on the sea whenever two boats came within hailing distance, and between the fishermen and the fish-sellers when they met at the pier to buy and sell the day's catch. Nagaro listened to the news with interest, since his knowledge of the world was still sketchy and he wished to improve it. He rarely asked questions of the fishermen, however, being embarrassed to reveal his ignorance. He usually asked Taru or Olomi later, knowing neither of them would laugh at him.

The movements of the feared Mahuk sea raiders were of interest to everyone.

"They raided Galenor two days ago," old Palu informed them one day, shaking his head. "Those devils just get bolder an' bolder."

"Aye," a gray-bearded fishermen put in. "It's the first time I've heard o' them comin' ashore on the mainland anywhere this side o' Lankura. Afore this, they've only raided the islands when they've come this far north."

Gundor looked very sober. "If they can raid Galenor that's just t' the north of us, and get away with it, what's to stop 'em from raiding Wotana? Though there's nothing here they'd want—except slaves…"

There were some uncomfortable glances exchanged at that, and Palu changed the subject. "I hear the border war with Jinara's flared up again."

"Aye." Jomo sighed. "We heard that too. I don't know why they can't just settle it like decent folk."

Judging by the number of nods, this was the prevailing opinion.

Palu shrugged resignedly. "That's lords for ye. That lot just loves t' fight."

"It's not so much lords as *Leithians*," the Kelorin, Gundor, objected. "*They're* the ones what likes fightin'. It's mostly Leithians that settled along the southern border an' they've been fighting with Jinara—and with Hran too—ever since."

Nagaro, who was listening while he and Taru sorted fish, turned to his friend and asked in a low voice, "Where's Hran? I know Jinara is on the coast between Edrovir and the Mahuk Baar, but…"

Taru looked up from the fish in his hands. "Hran runs along our southern border too," he explained. "But it lies t' the east o' Jinara—so it's inland. Hran's got no seacoast at all."

One of the men must have heard Taru, for he turned about and addressed the youth. "Aye, that's right, boy. An' they say the folk in Hran have tool for hair, and skin the color o' tar."

"They're right good fighters, though." One of the other fishermen chimed in. "My uncle Olo had t' go fight the Hranji when he was no more 'n a lad. The king called for the lord o' Galenor to send men t' the border war, an' the lord called up all the Wotana lads and marched 'em off to fight. Some of 'em didn't come back, neither."

Nagaro spoke without thinking. "Doesn't the king have an army to defend Edrovir by land the way the Royal Fleet does by sea?"

"No lad." It was Gundor who answered, speaking with an exaggerated kindness that made Nagaro wince. "All Elgurn has for soldiers is the Royal Guard that protects the palace—and the City Guard, that protects the city o' Lankura. If he wants t' make war on Jinara—or Hran—he has to ask the lords t' send soldiers. Lucky for us, he's lately gotten enough soldiers to do his fightin' by calling on the lords o' the southern Holds an' Wareds."

*

For Olomi's sake, Jomo always asked Palu for news of the doings of the "great folk" in Lankura, especially about her favorite, the Princess Nevien. As the summer waxed, however, he scarcely needed to ask. The burning question was who would wed the widowed princess. It was assumed that whoever did so had a good chance of becoming the next king of Edrovir, though this was by no means automatic.

"Her three months o' mourning was only up the middle o' Dunrel, and already there are suitors everywhere," Palu complained one day. "Though she'll not be wed for another six months!"

Taru did the arithmetic. "Nine months? Why do they wait so long?"

"Ye don't know, lad?" One of the fisherman leered at him. "It's so they'll know who the *father* is."

"What father? Nobody's ever said she was with child!"

"O' course she ain't!" The man laughed derisively. "Ye don't suppose Leyel Virden was man enough t' get her that way, do ye?"

"I don't suppose he even knew how!" One of the fish-sellers put in.

There was general raucous laughter. Nagaro didn't join in. He disliked this kind of talk. Nor was it the last time he heard this particular joke. When Jomo repeated it at home, however, Olomi gave him a stern look.

"Now how do ye suppose ye know that?" she asked. "And even if 'tis so, ye should let the poor girl have her time. Why be rushin' her into another marriage when she's still so young?"

*

There was yet one more thing to distract Nagaro from his troubles: the Kelorin girl, Aramei. Since no one else seemed to describe Tor Boronin in the extreme terms Taru had used, Nagaro soon decided to ignore his friend's admonition, though he kept the decision to himself. Getting a chance to talk to the girl wasn't easy, however. It was midsummer, early in the month of Duleyin and two weeks after they had learned of the raid on Galenor, before he got his chance, excusing himself to do his own "marketing" while Jomo and Taru haggled over the price of new boots.

Aramei greeted him as soon as he stepped up to the stall.

"Hello Nagaro."

He blushed with pleasure that she remembered his name, and hoped that the kuma stain concealed it. "Hello Aramei," he said. "I didn't see you here last week."

"I was with my aunt. Father doesn't like bringing me to market, so as often as he can he leaves me with her."

"What about your mother?"

"My mother is dead."

"Oh. I'm sorry!"

"It's all right," she hastened to reassure him. "She died when I was very young. I really don't remember her." She reached out to touch his hand where it rested on the counter. "That's kuma stain, isn't it? I almost wouldn't have known ye—when I saw ye across the way—if it hadn't been for your boots."

He felt a thrill at her touch, and he was about to answer when a strident voice interrupted them.

"Aramei! By the Eyes, lass, what are ye doing?"

Instantly Aramei jerked her hand away and dropped her eyes, seeming to shrink in upon herself.

Intent as they had been on each other, neither of them had noticed the approach of her father. Now he loomed over them. And like most members of his trade, he was a man of imposing dimensions.

"We were just talking, Tor Boronin," Nagaro put in quickly.

"Just talking, were ye?" The man regarded him narrowly. "And who gave ye leave, boy, to make so free?"

Nagaro stood his ground and met the man's eyes with a direct gaze. "I didn't know I needed anyone's leave just to talk," he said. "But if that's the way of it, Zirda, then I'll ask your leave right now, if I may."

This mixture of boldness and courtesy appeared to take the blacksmith by surprise. He stared at Nagaro for several seconds before saying, "I see by your features that ye're Kelorin, but I don't know ye. Who are ye then, and from whence do ye hail?"

Nagaro held the other man's gaze. "I'm called Nagaro. I live in the house of Jomo the fisherman, a few miles south along the bay."

"Ye're a fisherman then?"

"I'm learning to be one, Zirda."

"It's a dangerous trade. This town is full o' fishermen's widows." The blacksmith frowned at him, but then turned thoughtful. "Still 'tis an honest trade," he added. "And I like a man who'll look me in the eye. Very well, lad, ye have leave to talk t' my daughter. Supposin' only that she wishes to talk to *you*. Ye can sit at the back o' the stall." The blacksmith indicated a pair of stools with a wave of his hand.

Nagaro returned his attention to Aramei. She wasn't looking at the ground any more. In fact, she was looking at him with shining eyes.

So they sat together, side by side, in the shade at the back of the blacksmith's stall while Tor Boronin manned the counters at the front of

 Carol Louise Wilde

it, talking to customers and looking over his shoulder from time to time to make sure that talking was all that was going on behind him.

Nagaro thought it an odd arrangement but supposed they might manage a private conversation if they kept their voices low.

Aramei sat twisting her hands in her lap. She looked down at them, then up at him. "Father's never let me do this before."

"Really? Why not?" Nagaro had placed his own hands on his knees, finding nothing else to do with them.

"I suppose he thinks he's protecting me. It was very brave of ye to stand up to him like that."

She was giving him that shining-eyed look again. He'd liked it the first time, but now it seemed a bit too much. "It wasn't brave," he protested. "I just had to say something, because he wasn't being fair— taking me to task for breaking a rule when I'd no way of knowing there was a rule to be broken."

She giggled. "Ye don't know my father very well."

"Of course not. I just met him. But he treated me decently enough once I explained the misunderstanding."

She giggled again and shook her head at him, making her glossy brown hair dance. "There wasn't any rule, silly! Father just didn't like us talking."

Nagaro felt his face grow hot. "Oh... I..."

But Aramei had stopped laughing. She dropped her eyes. "And I shouldn't have touched your hand."

"My hand? What's wrong with touching my hand?" And then he remembered the hot little thrill that had gone through him at her touch, and he reddened again. In fact, sitting so close to Aramei was making him feel a little warm all over.

"Aunt Minda would say it was very forward."

"Oh..." He wasn't at all sure he understood.

She was studying him, frowning in puzzlement. "Haven't ye ever done anything like this before *either?*"

"No—" he began, and stopped. It *felt* true, but he really had no idea whether it *was* true.

Fortunately Aramei didn't pursue the issue. Instead she asked, "Are ye *really* living with Taru's family?"

"Yes."

She wrinkled her pretty nose. "I don't like Taru. My friend Hamani is terribly stuck on him, and he treats her like a piece of old rag."

"I'm... sorry... about that." Nagaro had seen enough to know that the latter part was true, but he felt he should defend his friend, so he added, "Taru's all right, really. He probably just doesn't know how she feels about him."

"Well if he doesn't, he must be blind. *I* think it's because she's so plain. But she can't help that, can she? She's terribly nice, and very well brought up. Not like Lanei or Panila that he's always talking to. *They're* not well brought up at all! They're terrible flirts, *and...*" Aramei lowered her voice and leaned towards him. "I've *heard* things. About what Lanei's been doing with boys behind her father's woodshed!"

She sat up again, prim and straight, but not before he had caught a whiff of lavender that he found unaccountably distracting. *Did she wash her hair with lavender? And where had that idea come from?*

She was waiting, looking at him expectantly. Her gray eyes held a challenge and he knew he needed to say something. "All I know is that Taru and his family have been very good to me," he ventured. "They took me in when I had nowhere else to go."

"Oh." Her expression softened. "I suppose that *would* turn your thinking a little." She wrinkled her nose again. "Let's talk about something *else* then. Shall we?"

"All right."

There was a pause that grew uncomfortably long. Nagaro couldn't for the life of him think of anything to say. It didn't help that the sensation of warmness kept creeping over him. He knew what it was, and he was annoyed at himself for feeling it just because he was sitting with a pretty girl.

It was Aramei who eventually broke the silence. "Ye're not from anywhere around here, are ye?" she asked. "Your speech is... different..."

This was treacherous territory. He swallowed. "I... I came from the south..."

Aramei looked as if she were thinking of asking for clarification, but just at that moment, her father interrupted their conversation by telling her it was time to help pack up the wares.

Nagaro breathed a sigh of relief even as he looked about. The sunlight was slanting steeply across the market and he knew he'd better find Jomo and Taru. He rose to excuse himself.

"Will ye come talk to me again?" Aramei asked, looking at him from under her lashes. "Next market day?"

He hesitated. "Yes... If I can get away from the others..."

As he hurriedly threaded his way through the closing market, he was mentally kicking himself for having been so tongue-tied. He should have asked her about where she lived, or what she liked to do... what she thought of her Aunt Minda... *anything...*

*

Nagaro told Taru about his progress with Aramei that evening as they lay on their fern leaf beds.

Taru was incredulous. "Tor Boronin let ye talk to his daughter?

How'd ye manage that?"

Nagaro shrugged. "I just asked."

There was a rustle of fern leaves as Taru rolled over. "Ye're either very brave, or quite daft. Either way ye won't get leave t' do more than talk, I'll wager."

"Talking is enough for now, though I expect I might get leave to marry her by asking, one day, if I chose."

Taru sat up. "What are ye saying, Nagaro? One minute ye're just talking, and the next ye want to *marry* her?"

Nagaro remained on his back, turning his head to meet his friend's eyes. "I didn't say I wanted to marry her *now*," he objected. "I said I might get leave to by asking *some day*. But I don't know her well enough yet to know if I'd want to do that. I'm trying to find out. *That's* why I wanted to talk to her."

Taru flopped back down on his fern leaves. "What will ye do if ye want t' kiss her?"

Nagaro frowned up at the rough-hewn ceiling beams. "Well I don't think I'd ask leave for *that*," he said seriously. "Kisses are always stolen, aren't they? In stories, I mean."

"What then? Haven't ye ever kissed a girl?"

"I don't think so. It didn't feel as if I'd ever even just *talked* to one..."

"Ai!" Taru exclaimed. "Where have ye been living? On the dark side o' Talebra?"

It was a question Nagaro couldn't answer. And that was the trouble, of course. It always came back to the unsettling fact that he simply didn't know...

Chapter 7: The Green-Eyed Girl

"Ye still haven't kissed her?"

Nagaro frowned as he tossed a silver sardine into the appropriate bucket in the row standing on the edge of the pier. The boat bobbed gently under him and bumped against the wooden pilings. The sun beat on his shoulders and the mingled odors of fish, tar, and brine assaulted his nostrils. He stooped to pick up another fish. "No," he said, "her father is always there. And besides, I've only talked to her a few times."

He wished Taru wouldn't push him. It was late summer, near the end of Oteyin, the eighth month, and he still wasn't sure what he thought of Aramei. She'd talked about how strict her father and her aunt were, how she spent her days learning how to cook and sew, how she liked to pick berries with her friends in the fields at the edge of town. He had talked about what it was like to be a fisherman, how glorious it felt to be out on the sea in a boat, and all the things he was learning about the fisherman's trade. She was pretty, she stirred his blood, and she seemed nice enough—except for not liking Taru. Nagaro was pretty sure that Taru really didn't know about Hamani's feelings for him... but he and Aramei had agreed not to talk about that...

Taru was shaking his head at him. "Well, that's just what ye get for setting your sights on Tor Boronin's daughter," he said. "O' course, Father keeps me away from the ones I'm after too. But I've got an idea that's sure t' help us both." He squatted down beside Nagaro among the remaining fish and the puddled seawater in the bottom of the boat. Glancing behind him to make sure Jomo was busy in the bow, he leaned closer and continued in a conspiratorial whisper.

"I'll ask Father to let us spend the winter in town with Gama. We'll say we're going t' help her with things. That way we won't be stuck in the house all winter, miles from anything *interesting*, if ye know what I mean."

Nagaro frowned. He knew exactly what Taru meant, and it worried him to think of what Taru might get up to while spending a winter in town. Still, it would mean more chances to talk to Aramei, and Wotana would be a change... "I suppose we could help keep her house in repair," he ventured as he tossed the last three mackerel into the mackerel bucket.

"That's the idea!" Taru grinned slyly. "We'd live in Gama's house, and during the day we'd do chores for her. Then at night, we'd—"

"Ye'd *what?*" Jomo suddenly loomed over them. "Your Gama has Hamani t' look in on her. And if she needs anything done afore I can get to it, there's Hamani's father to help her. Ye're not thinkin' half so much o' your Gama as ye are o' that Lanei creature. And that girl will lie with anything male on two legs! One o' these days, some young buck's going t' get her with child, and when her father comes knockin' on doors, I don't want him to come knockin' on mine."

Taru stuck out his chin. "How would he ever know the right door? There'd be too many t' choose from. That's the beauty of it."

Jomo gave his son a hard look. "It's not who did it. It's who she *says* did it. Lanei 'll pick whoever she fancies the most, and I can tell she fancies ye, Taru—Hakura knows why."

"What's the chance it'd happen? I'd be careful—"

"Ye'll be careful, all right. Ye'll spend the winter at home where I can keep an eye on ye!"

Taru scowled. "When are ye going t' stop treating me like a child?"

"When ye start showing some sense!" Jomo frowned darkly at his son. Then his face cleared and he sighed. "Or when ye get t' be too much a man for me t' stop ye from doin' what ye please—and that's going to be soon enough. I know I can't keep ye from makin' mistakes forever, but this winter I want ye at home, and that's the end of it."

Taru grumbled something. He picked up a fish, angrily flung it at a bucket and missed, which meant that he had to climb onto the pier to retrieve it. He went, muttering all the way.

Nagaro had kept silent during the exchange. He thought Jomo made good sense but he knew better than to say so to Taru. While the other youth was busy locating the errant fish among the array of buckets and tackle on the pier, he picked up each of the few fish that remained and sorted them into their proper places.

Jomo nodded approvingly. "There's a job well done, Nagaro. Ye go on and do your bit o' marketing. Taru and I 'll start the bargaining with the fish-sellers."

"Hey!" Taru stood on the pier looking down at them. "*I* just might have some marketing o' my own!"

Jomo shot his son a look. "I know all about your marketing—"

"But *he's* just going to see Aramei! Ye know that!"

"Aye. And when ye get interested in a nice girl like that, ye'll have the same privileges. Now pick up some o' those buckets and let's get on with this." With that, Jomo grasped a pair of bucket handles in each fist and stamped off in the direction of the fish market.

"I'm sorry, Taru." Nagaro stepped up onto the boat's gunnel and leaped nimbly onto the pier beside his friend. "I won"t go either, if he's going to play you a trick like that."

Taru had been looking after his father with a face like thunder, but he dropped his scowl when he heard Nagaro's words. "Don't be daft," he said. "Just see that ye kiss her this time so it won't be wasted. And at least it won't be as dull at the house as last winter, not with both of us there together." He gathered up the remaining buckets and started after Jomo.

Nagaro watched him go, then heaved a sigh and hastily went to scrub his hands with sand and rinse them in a bucket of seawater. Aramei didn't like it if he smelled too much of fish...

*

The afternoon had been hot, and the wind from the sea was very welcome as it wafted through the marketplace, carrying a medley of scents to where Nagaro and Aramei sat in the blacksmith's stall. The too-sweet smell of over-ripe fruit mingled with the tang of peppers and the pungent odors of spiced meat and wood smoke. The breeze stirred Aramei's dark hair where it lay against her slender neck or flowed over the shoulders of her butter-yellow blouse. Her eyes looked almost lavender in the shadow at the back of the stall. As always, Nagaro enjoyed looking at her. But she was being too quiet today. Ordinarily he could count on her to do more than her share of the talking, but not this time... He finally asked, "What's wrong?"

She looked down at her hands, and chewed her pretty lip, and at last she said, "Hamani told me that 'Nagaro' means 'man who has no name.'" She looked back up at him. "However did ye ever get a name like that?"

It was Nagaro's turn to avoid her eyes. Since the first day that he'd sat with her, he had steered their conversations away from the state of his memory. He wasn't ready to talk about it. *Maybe after his memory came back, but not now...* He stared at the packed earth floor in the far corner of the stall. He might have tried to make up a tale, but he couldn't think of one, and he really didn't like to lie. So he took a deep breath, raised his eyes, and told her the story.

Her gray eyes went wide as she listened.

"Ye don't know who ye are then?"

"No. Not really..."

"But... that must be very hard," she said, looking at him with pity in her eyes—pity that somehow stung.

"I'd... rather not talk about it." He didn't want to tell her just exactly how hard it was.

She frowned. "What if ye don't ever remember?"

"Then I'll be Nagaro... and be a fisherman."

"And if ye do remember?"

"Then perhaps I'll be a fisherman with a different name." It was, after all, a possibility.

Aramei was not so easily answered however. "What if ye remember, and ye have to go away?" she asked, her eyes troubled. "I always knew ye were different." She searched his face. "What if there's someone waiting for ye, somewhere... a girl maybe?"

And for that, he really had no answer. "I don't think there is..." he began, but he didn't want to explain why he thought so. His fragments of memory had never shown him any woman but the Lady in Gray, but that didn't necessarily mean anything, and he didn't want to tell Aramei about the flashes of memory that had shown him a life so different from anything she had known.

He was trying to find words, when a breathless voice from the front of the stall cut across his thoughts.

"Have ye heard, Tor Boronin? Reith Hurn is dead!"

"Reith Hurn dead?" Boronin stepped over immediately to address the white-haired Turo who was leaning across his counter. "How'd that happen?"

"He got killed in the border war! Almost a week ago, and the news only just came t' us. Came in with the fishermen, and it's spreadin' like the plague. This 'll mean trouble for sure!"

The news-bearer hurried on to tell others folk, and Boronin turned around, shaking his head. "I don't know about trouble, but there'll not be much more buying and selling done this day if I know Wotana folk. The men'll be gathering at the tavern t' talk about it. Ye just run on home, Aramei, and tell your Aunt Minda we'll have an early dinner tonight." With that, the blacksmith started to pack up his wares.

Nagaro looked at Aramei, who had stood up and was worriedly chewing her lip. "Who is Reith Hurn?" he asked, keeping his voice low.

"Don't ye know?" She stared at him. "He's one o' the Pact Signers."

"Oh. Right." This was serious. It explained the part about "trouble." "Ah, I guess I'll be going now, since you have to go home anyway," he said quickly.

He was relieved to have the excuse, though he felt like a coward for using it. All the way back to the fish market, he kept seeing in his mind the look she'd been giving him just before the news had come... The shadow in her eyes...

*

The fish market, when he reached it, was in an uproar. All work had ceased and everyone was standing about talking and gesticulating. He found Jomo in deep conversation with old Palu.

Taru was standing behind his father, fairly vibrating with excitement. "Lord Reith is dead, Nagaro! I can't believe it! A great warrior like him, and he's gone and got himself killed. One o' the Pact Signers!"

Nagaro had heard all about the six lords who'd signed the Pact of Lankura that had put an end to Edrovir's civil war. They were the six most powerful lords—three Leithian, and three Kelorin—and they had replaced the full Council of Lords established by Darion. The change had struck Nagaro as a bad idea as soon as he'd heard about it. "So now there are only five Pact Signers," he said. "Which is sure to cause trouble because they make up the King's Council, don't they?"

"Aye, lad, ye're right." Jomo shifted his position to include the two youths in his conversation with Palu. "Now there's three Kelorin Pact Signers, and only two Leithians." He shook his head. "And they're not *just* the King's Council. They *choose* the king. It's in the Pact. None o' them are allowed t' take the crown, but they choose the one that does. And with Reith dead, the numbers don't match."

"Is there no plan for what to do if one of them dies?" Nagaro asked.

"Not that I've ever heard of." Jomo turned to Palu. "Do ye know anything I don't?"

The fish-seller shook his hoary head. "No, I've never heard tell of any plan. And these old ears have heard an ocean o' news in their time."

"Well that's not a very good design then, is it?" To Nagaro it seemed a shocking oversight. "Not having made any provision for deaths, I mean. They'll all die eventually. What will happen then?"

Jomo rolled his eyes at this, and Palu whistled between his teeth. They were both past commenting on Nagaro's vocabulary, but the old fish-seller said, "Ye're the wise one, aren't ye? Ye'd ha' planned for it from the beginning, I suppose?"

"I dare say I would! If it had been up to me..." Nagaro saw how they were looking at him and felt his face redden. "Of course, that would have been hard," he added, "since I was no more than a babe at the time."

At that, everyone laughed, and the awkwardness passed. After a few more words, Jomo bade old Palu good day. He'd already sold all of their catch and had heard enough news. So the three of them collected their buckets and headed back to the boat.

"What do folk think is going to happen?" Nagaro asked as they cast off and he and Taru prepared to raise the sail.

Jomo had taken the tiller. He shrugged. "Some are sayin' they'll choose another lord t' take Reith's place—a Leithian, o' course."

"A new Pact Signer?"

"Aye," Taru put in. "But he wouldn't *be* a Signer, seeing as how he didn't *sign*. That's what the rest are saying."

"How would they choose him? Who would do the choosing?"

"It might be King Elgurn," Jomo answered. "Or what's left o' the Council. More likely, both together. 'Course, the *other* thing they're saying is that there might be a new Pact—or else there *won't* be, and there'll be a war. We all have t' hope those bloody fool lords don't want that. It sounds like everyone in Lankura is running 'round like hens without their heads. And we don't need *that* spreadin' to the rest o' the country. They'd better find a way to fix this."

Their conversation continued all the way back to the little house where Olomi was waiting for them. She had her own ideas, and she expressed them over dinner.

"I'm not sorry t' be rid o' Reith Hurn," she declared. "After all, it was him that murdered King Tevren."

"Lord Reith murdered King Tevren?" Nagaro paused with his fork in mid-air. This was a detail he hadn't heard before. "Why wasn't he executed?"

Olomi set down her cup of sothiril and sniffed primly. "Oh, it was *supposed* to ha' been something according to the *law.*" She waved a hand in the air. "A *challenge*, is what the Leithians called it. The Kelorin called it murder. And the sad thing is, he killed Queen Lindra too—an *accident*, they said that was. And o' course no one knows for sure what happened t' their baby boy—whether he took sick and died afore his parents were killed, as it was claimed, or whether the Leithians killed him, too. Or whether he was hidden away somewhere and is still alive."

"Aye," Jomo put in. "And o' course, all the fuss over the deaths of Tevern and Lindra started a war. I don't know that it ever would have ended, either, if it weren't for the Pact o' Lankura. Part of what the Pact did was t' make it official that Reith wasn't guilty o' murder."

"Oh." Nagaro had finished eating and now pushed back his plate. "I didn't know there was a baby," he said. "Would the Leithians really have killed a helpless little child?"

"Leithians would do anything." Taru was busy mopping up the last crumbs of fish on his plate with a piece of bread and now offered his two-rin's worth.

Jomo shrugged. "They say they didn't."

Taru rolled his eyes. "Would ye expect them to admit it?"

"Well, no, probably not. And it's a fair wager that they wouldn't ha' wanted that baby to grow up t' be a man."

"Why not?" Nagaro asked.

"They were afraid he'd be chosen king after Tevren. Most o' the Leithians didn't want Tevren for their king, ye see. When the Council o' Lords chose him after Darion died, they were split pretty near down the middle—the Kelorin for it, and most o' the Leithians against."

"Just because Tevren was Kelorin?"

"Aye." Jomo heaved a sigh. "They were afraid of having a whole line o' kings all of Darion's get. They didn't trust that a Kelorin king would treat Leithians right."

Olomi stood up and started to gather up the dishes. "The Leithians tried to get Tevren t' marry a Leithian lady," she said. "But he followed his heart and married Lindra."

Nagaro handed her his empty cup. "Well he should have married the woman he loved," he said. To him that seemed obvious.

To his surprise, Jomo and Taru nearly choked trying to keep from laughing.

"Hush now, ye two!" Olomi gave them reproving glances. "And the Spirits bless ye, Nagaro," she added with feeling. "I expect that's what *he* thought too."

Jomo stood up. "Marrying for love is all very well for ordinary folk," he said severely. "But kings have got no business doing it. When that Kelorin queen o' his bore Tevren a son, it was the end o' them both... Probably of all three."

*

It was only when Nagaro lay down to sleep that night that he realized that Taru had forgotten to ask him about kissing Aramei. Considering how his talk with her had gone, he was glad to have been spared the question. Once Aramei was in his mind, however, he couldn't seem to get her out of it, nor could he manage to sleep. He was tossing and turning well after Taru began to snore.

Weariness eventually overcame him, and when he did sleep, he had a dream.

There was a girl bending over him, her face quite close to his, as if she meant to kiss him. Her skin was fair, her features finely molded. Her hair was a rich light brown, touched with gold, like the color of honey, and her eyes were as green as clear sea-water with the sun shining through it. The green eyes were fixed upon his face, studying him as if searching for something. Whatever those eyes were seeking, however, they didn't find it, for they grew clouded. She drew away from him, then rose and turned, moving to stand just out of reach. He saw that she was wearing a long white shift of some material so thin and fine that the light from a candle on the table behind her shown through it, outlining the form of her body beneath—a form as lovely as her face.

He wanted to do something—to say something—but he found he could neither move nor speak. He couldn't even turn his head. A wave of panic swept over him as he struggled vainly to sit up and to loose his tongue. The more he struggled, the more he seemed to be bound by immobility. It began to seem as if the canopy of the bed were bearing down on him, that it might crush him. It came to fill his vision so that all he could see were the carved wooden panels that decorated its underside. He struggled harder, desperately trying to cry out—

Abruptly, the paralysis broke and a wordless cry sprang from his throat as he jerked to a sitting position. At the same time he flung up his arms, to thrust off the paneled canopy, but his hands touched only air. And in that instant, the vision snapped and he found that he was sitting on fern leaves in the dark—drenched in sweat, his heart pounding.

Taru stirred in the darkness and his voice said sleepily, "What is it, Nagaro?"

"I... I had a dream... about a girl..."

"Who? Aramei?" Taru was immediately wide awake. "I have lots of dreams about girls—Lanei or Panila or Samiya. Mostly about Lanei. I dream that I'm holding her, and—"

"It wasn't that kind of dream! It wasn't pleasant at all! I couldn't move, I couldn't speak, and the girl just turned away. It wasn't Aramei either. It was a different girl. She had gold-brown hair and green eyes, and—Oh, *no!* By the Eyes of Vothra's Mind, Taru! She was wearing a nightdress!"

"*What?*" Taru sounded shocked. Nagaro didn't often swear.

"She was wearing a nightdress. That means I must have been in her bedchamber! Taru, I have to stop what I'm doing with Aramei."

"But ye're not doing *anything* with Aramei!" Taru protested. "Ye're just *talking* to her. Are ye saying ye have t' stop not doing anything with one girl because ye had a dream about not doing anything with another? That's daft even for you! Besides," he added, "ye don't even know if the girl in your dream is real. Maybe your mind made her up. Or maybe ye just wanted to be in her bedroom, so ye dreamed that ye were. I've never done anything with Lanei, but I dream about it all the time."

Nagaro shook his head, forgetting that his friend couldn't see him in the dark. "That's not the point, Taru. Don't you see? It doesn't matter if she's real or not, because she *could* be. I don't remember enough to know she isn't! I could be promised. I could even be married!"

"But if ye don't remember, surely ye can't be blamed." Taru yawned audibly.

"I'm not worried about being *blamed*. I'm worried about doing the wrong thing—about hurting someone."

There was silence as Taru digested this. "Well, I guess it wouldn't be good t' have two girls fighting over ye," he said after a moment. "I've heard that women can be pretty vicious about that sort o' thing." There was the sound of another yawn. "Why don't ye just go back to sleep, Nagaro? I'm sure it'll look better in the morning."

Nagaro gave up trying to make Taru understand. He lay back down and closed his eyes, but he kept seeing the image of the green-eyed girl in his mind, and remembering the feeling of not being able to move.

*

He meant to explain his decision to Aramei, though he wasn't sure what he was going to say. As it turned out, she wasn't at the blacksmith's stall on the next market day. Or the next, or the next... Each time he didn't find her, he slunk quietly away. How could he tell Tor Boronin that he was going to stop seeing his daughter when he couldn't explain why? After failing to find her the third time, he stopped trying, thinking Aramei must have decided to stop seeing him.

It was two weeks later that he and Taru and Jomo arrived at the pier in Wotana to find the fishermen once again in an uproar. Questions were flying furiously amongst a group gathered on the quay.

"*Another* Pact Signer dead?"

"How'd it happen?"

"Which one is it this time?"

Gundor and his crew-mate were at the center of the group. They both looked shaken. "It's Berinar Sundorin." Gundor had to raise his voice to be heard. "We got the same news from two different boats. It happened four days ago."

"Berinar? A Kelorin this time? That's a relief."

"It's *suspicious*, I'd say. It evens things up. *Four* Pact Signers. Two an' two."

"But, how did it *happen?*"

"If ye'll give me a chance, I'll tell ye!" Gundor flung up his hands for silence. "The tale goes like this. He was ridin' home from Lankura when he stopped at an inn for his dinner and decided t' stay the night. He was taken sick about midnight, an' died afore morning."

"Ha! Poison!"

"It had t' be Dreigen then!"

"Aye! The king's lore master must ha' done it! He poisoned Darion, didn't he?"

"That's what they all say—"

But Gundor was shaking his head. "Dreigen was in Lankura the whole time. And Berinar looked well when he left. If it was Dreigen, he used some kind o' magic, and they'll never prove it."

"They never proved that he poisoned Darion either, but everyone says—"

"That was twenty years ago!"

"What if it was?"

The talk went on, but Jomo pulled the two youths away. There was a boat-full of fish waiting to be sold.

"Well," he said as they started setting up to sort their day's catch, "it looks like they fixed it."

Taru was squatting by the gunnel, dipping up seawater in a bucket to keep the fish fresh. "*Was* it Dreigen, d' ye think?" he asked.

Jomo, down among the fish in the bottom of the boat, cast him a look. "I'm not saying it was Dreigen, and I'm not saying it wasn't. I don't need t' know the *how* of it. A Leithian Pact Signer got killed, and now a Kelorin one is dead. The numbers didn't match, an' now they do. Somebody fixed it."

Nagaro took the bucket of water from Taru and began pouring a little into each of the sorting buckets on the pier. "Could the Leithians have been behind it? Maybe someone followed Berinar to the inn."

Jomo shrugged. "I'll not argue against that, but it doesn't matter. What matters is, there won't be any war. This'll be the end of it."

"You don't think there'll be a Leithian killed in reprisal?"

"No. There's more t' be lost than gained by that, and everybody knows it."

There didn't seem to be any more to say, so they turned their full attention to the fish. It took nearly an hour to sort their catch, and by that time some of the excitement had died down. Apparently, a death that evened-up the Pact Signers' numbers wasn't as alarming as one that put them askew.

They moved on to the fish-sellers, and Jomo fortunately found one who wasn't too preoccupied with the news to deal with them. The two men were just starting negotiations, with Nagaro only half listening, when a female voice spoke behind him.

"Hello, Nagaro."

"Aramei?" He spun about as his stomach tried to tie itself into a knot.

She was standing a few feet away, in front of another fish-seller's stall. The light of the westward-tending sun was behind her, making a nimbus of her hair.

"Father says ye haven't been coming to the stall."

He couldn't read her eyes with the light behind her, but she sounded hurt.

"I *did* come. I looked three times, but you weren't there."

Aramei made an annoyed gesture. "Aunt Minda's been ill and I've had to tend her. I'm only out with her today because she insisted on doing her own marketing." She cast a glance at a woman with graying hair being waited on by the fish-seller's wife.

"Oh." He felt like a fool. "I... didn't know..."

This time, she very plainly frowned. "Ye could have asked Father."

Nagaro couldn't meet her eyes. "I... didn't want to talk to him," he said, floundering. "I... listen... Aramei, I'm sorry. After I talked to you the last time, I had a dream. About a girl." He forced himself to look at her. "I don't think we should go on..."

Something had frozen in her face. "I understand," she said. But from the way she said it, he could tell that what she understood wasn't what he'd meant.

"I don't know who she is," he began, "but until I can find out—"

"It's all right." She stepped back. "She'll be waiting for you."

"Aramei—"

But she turned away from him to follow her aunt who was moving on along the line of stalls. He watched her go until other jostling shoppers eclipsed his view of her slender figure.

"Let her go, Nagaro." Taru's voice spoke from behind his shoulder. "Ye'll find a better one."

Nagaro went through the rest of the afternoon under a storm-cloud of guilt. He didn't try to explain to Taru that finding a "better one" wasn't the issue—that until he had his memory back, he couldn't even try. Nor was *that* the issue. His handling of Aramei had been all wrong. With a memory that reached back only a few months, he'd had no right to start talking to her in the first place. *Why hadn't he seen that?*

That night he dreamed, but not of the green-eyed girl. This time he was running—running through a dark forest, dodging among pools of shadow and patches of moonlight, driven by an intense and unexplained desire to escape.

He awoke in a cold sweat, immensely glad to be done with the dream, only to find in the days that followed that the dream wasn't done with him.

Chapter 8: Shaking Things Loose

Nagaro woke with a cry and sat up, again, with his heart pounding. *Why did this keep happening and how long was it going to go on?* He looked around the bare little bedroom. At least this time it was morning.

Taru rolled over on his fern-leaf mattress and gave him a look that was equal parts sympathy and exasperation. "*Another* nightmare?"

Nagaro nodded. He shivered as he pulled his blanket up around his shoulders. "I was running through the forest again. In the dark. It's *always* dark in the forest. And I know I'm running away from something, but I've no idea what! It's been the same, five times this week, and twice I dreamed about that green-eyed girl..."

Taru sighed. "All right, I give up," he said, conceding a long-standing argument. "They're not just ordinary dreams. But what do ye think they mean?"

Nagaro was staring unseeing at the wall beyond Taru's head. "I think they're memories," he said. "But for some reason, they're stuck on that forest... and on that girl... Those two things have to be connected somehow. And there have got to be more memories wherever those are coming from." He sighed, bringing his focus back to Taru's face. "If only I could find a way to shake something else loose—like I did when I rode that horse months ago." He let go of the blanket to massage his temples. "I'm getting really tired of that forest!"

He also didn't like the way the dreams about the girl made him feel. In the last one, she'd been showing him a tree she used to climb, and when she asked him a question, he'd said, "You are very beautiful." The words had seemed all wrong—stilted and wooden. He'd felt over-whelmed by awkwardness, an intense desire be somewhere else. But instead of going, he'd just stood there, enduring the look of disappoint-ment in those beautiful green eyes. And when at last he had tried to say something else, he'd found he was struggling again—struggling against some resistance. As before, the struggle had awakened him to leave him lying in the dark, still burning with embarrassment, tangled in the dream's net of frustration...

"What if ye tried going into the forest after dark? D'ye think that would do it?"

Nagaro blinked. "It might..." He frowned, considering the idea. He'd promised himself five months ago that he would be patient, because the Spirit had said that some things were better not remembered—*for a time...* Well he had been patient, hadn't he?

"All right," he said. "Let's try it. And I want to do it soon. There's always moonlight in the forest dreams, and Talebra is nearly full right now."

Taru sat up in bed and reached for his clothes. "Maybe we can try it tonight. If it doesn't rain."

It was late in Sedrin, the ninth month, and the season for fishing was over. Darkness would come early, but the weather had been stormy for days and this particular day was no exception. The morning passed, overcast, with intermittent gusty winds and rain. In the afternoon, Jomo braved the weather to walk to Wotana for some needed supplies. He returned wet and dripping.

As evening approached, however, the rain stopped, though the sky was still partly obscured by a bank of clouds blowing in off the ocean. Nevertheless, Nagaro and Taru decided to go out as soon as it was fully dark and hope for the best.

The wind had died, and the clouds were thinning a little when they set out. Talebra betrayed her presence as a bright patch in the clouds just above the crest of the hills. The shrouded moon gave little light, however, and they had no lantern. They had to pick their way up the slope to the edge of the woods with great care.

A few steps under the eaves of the forest, the darkness seemed complete.

Nagaro stopped under the trees. "This isn't going to work," he said. "How can it bring me any new memories if I can't see anything?"

"Let's just try a little farther." Taru's voice answered him, close by on his left. "Since we're here."

"All right." Although he had agreed, Nagaro remained doubtful. The memories that had come to him so far had all involved images. Here he was so blind. He put his hand out to touch a rough tree trunk and groped his way forward a few steps, testing the ground with his feet as he went. He found another tree, the bark of this one smooth under his fingers.

He was about to speak again, to say that this was useless, when there came into his mind, suddenly and very clearly, a memory of the physical sensation of feeling a smooth plastered wall with his fingertips, of taking cautious steps on flagstones. He was suddenly filled with apprehension, and...

...hands were seizing him, gripping his arms and forcing him down onto the flagstone floor, pinning him there—spread-eagled on his back.

He struggled desperately against the hands, but they held his arms securely, and there was the weight of what felt like a knee on his chest. A sudden flare of light dazzled his eyes. There were forms against the light... shapes of people, but he couldn't make out their faces... Fingers began prodding his left forearm and a sharp pain stabbed him there. He struggled more violently, but still to no avail. Then a strange, unpleasant sensation washed over him, and it was as if the ground were dissolving underneath him and he was falling... falling helplessly into darkness...

Nagaro gasped and staggered where he stood, so that his hand broke contact with the tree trunk. The memory was instantly gone, but his heart was beating so hard that the force of it shook his entire body.

"*By the Eyes!*" he muttered.

"What is it?" Taru's voice, coming out of the dark, sounded alarmed.

"I don't know! A different memory... and it's gone now." Nagaro drew a breath and let it out, long and slow, trying to steady himself. "It wasn't what I expected. I was being... attacked in the dark—"

"Attacked! Hamanei mata noa! By who?"

"I don't know! But I don't like this. Let's go back to the house."

"All right." Taru sounded more than willing.

The young Turo was very quiet at first as they walked, but curiosity soon go the better of him. "Where d' ye think it happened? What kind of place was it?"

Nagaro shivered. "It was inside a building. A hallway, maybe, with a flagstone floor. The wall felt like plaster. I couldn't see anything at first, as if it were a pitch-black night—just like back there under the trees. And then there was too *much* light, and I couldn't see because it was in my eyes. And at the end of it, I felt like I was falling... It felt like it was going to be the end of *everything!*"

"Well obviously it wasn't," Taru said, too quickly.

Nagaro could see the whites of his friend's wide eyes in the feeble moonlight that leaked through the veil of clouds. "I don't want to try that again," he said.

"I can't blame ye for that. And let's not tell my parents. It'd only frighten my mother."

They finished the walk in silence.

*

Nagaro was tense all through dinner. There was little conversation while the family ate their fried fish and potatoes. Finally, with the dishes cleared away, Olomi asked her husband for the news from Wotana and Jomo immediately launched into an account of the latest developments in the tale of the princess's suitors.

The topic had been bandied about for months, and Nagaro had taken an interest for the sake of increasing his knowledge of the larger world, though the suitor's names initially meant nothing to him. By the end of the summer, the field of contenders had narrowed to a short list, and it now appeared that two men had risen to the top of that list. They were Gillard Marchent, a Leithian lord fifteen years older than the princess, and young Fargil of Galenor. The folk of Wotana had a particular interest in Fargil since he was the son of their own Wared lord.

"It's got t' be Fargil," Taru declared. "I saw him ride by on the road once, and he looked so fine up there on his horse, proud and strong. And everyone says he's a good man."

"Oh, he's a decent lad, all right—as lords go." Jomo seemed to feel the need to display a more tempered enthusiasm. "And it would surely do Wotana no harm t' have our lord's son wearing the crown one day. But he's too young. He's green as sea-grass."

"He's three years older than me!"

"Just as I said. Green as sea-grass."

"He wouldn't be wearing the crown 'til he was older," Olomi looked up from putting the dishes on the shelf. "Elgurn's not likely t' die soon."

"That's true," Jomo conceded. "There'd be time for him to learn a little wisdom, I suppose."

"Besides," Olomi added, "anything would be better than Gillard."

"No argument there."

Nagaro smiled to himself. He had yet to hear anyone in Wotana speak well of Gillard Marchent, though folk were never inclined to say why. He suspected they would have thought ill of anyone who was in competition with Fargil. "When will they choose?" he asked.

Jomo got up from the table and stretched. "In about a month—around the end o' Todrin." He yawned widely. "And the marriage would be in the middle o' Finorel, well before the end o' the year. If not then, it'll be after the turning of the year, t' steer clear o' the dark days of Idrin."

Nagaro nodded knowingly as he pushed his chair back and stood up. The majority of folk in Wotana considered the seven days of Idrin, arround the winter solstace, an inauspicious time, although Vothrin teaching said this was only superstition.

"Well, that's all good." Taru stood up as well. "And it'll be none too soon. We'll finally be able t' talk about something else!"

*

As Nagaro lay down to sleep that night, the memory of what had happened in the woods crept back into his mind. He couldn't help wondering what had happened to him. Who had attacked him—and why?

When eventually his mind drifted, and sleep took him, he dreamed.

At first he was running again through the moonlit forest, between walls of tree trunks, under a ceiling of overarching branches. Then the image swam and flowed, and the forest became a dark corridor, more sensed than seen. He was moving along it, feeling his way—trying to be quick and quiet, his heart in his throat. *If he could go just a few more steps...* But the dream shifted again and he was lying on his back while faces loomed over him in the darkness, belonging to shadowy figures.

The green-eyed girl was there. Her expression was kind, and sad, and a little disappointed—but nothing worse. He tried to move, but couldn't. He tried to speak to her, but that also proved impossible. And after her, there came a parade of other faces... Four Leithian men—the first with a close-trimmed, red-blond beard, and shrewd blue eyes that looked at him with pity and apparent distaste. The second—big, blond, and ruddy-faced—leered at him and laughed derisively. The third was tall and thin, with disheveled red curls and a look in his grey-green eyes that said he wished he were somewhere else. The fourth, and last, was younger than the others, blond and handsome, but with a long scar on his cheek and cold blue eyes that belied the honey in his smile.

After the Leithians there came one more face, sallow, with short-cropped black hair and a high-bridged nose, hooked like a hawk's beak. This man's hard black eyes glittered with fierce excitement. For some reason, those eyes chilled Nagaro to the core. Under their gaze, he felt a desperate desire to escape. The face bent closer... The eyes burned... The lips parted in a hungry smile... He fought desperately against the immobility of the dream, and this time the effort finally jerked him awake, forcing a cry from his lips.

"*No!*" He sat bolt upright, shuddering, his heart hammering against his ribs. He stared at Taru who was staring back at him, wide-eyed in the dim light of morning.

"Did ye dream something different?" Taru asked. "Like ye hoped?"

"Ye-es..." Nagaro deliberately unclenched his hands. He felt chilled from within as much as from without. "Some of it was like the memory in the forest—but there was more." Haltingly, he described the faces. "I don't know why that last man scared me so," he finished. "He didn't *do* anything except look at me. That's all any of them did. But feeling that I couldn't move made everything worse! I'm sure they're real, though, just like the Lady in Gray. The green-eyed girl, the Leithian men, and that hawk-faced man... they all must be people I knew."

Taru sat up straighter. "Do ye think those men are the ones that attacked ye? Was that why ye were running?"

"It's possible." The thought had already occurred to Nagaro. "But if I was running away from... wherever they were... it would have to be somewhere around here."

"Well, there isn't anything I know of around here like the place ye talked about before," Taru said. "Not for miles. There's just Wotana. And Sobring Hall—Lord Bron's big house. It's away t' the east, on the other side o' the hills."

Nagaro frowned. "It wouldn't be a lord's house if it had plain plaster walls. It would have to be something smaller than that..."

Taru began to gather his clothes while his thoughts ran. "Smaller than a lord's house..." He broke off. "There *is* a smaller house! Down in the bottom of the valley that's just on the other side o' the ridge behind our place."

"What's it like?"

"It had two floors... an' lots of windows, but that's all I remember. I came within bow-shot o' the place by accident when I was hunting. I'd no mind t' be taken for poaching, so I lit out o' there right away. That was two years ago—maybe three."

Nagaro rubbed his chin. "I think I'd like to see it... Do you think you could find it again?"

Taru stopped moving, his tirka in his hands. "I thought ye didn't want t' try anything like the forest again."

Nagaro swallowed, remembering how very shaken he had been. He reached for his own pants. "The forest was dark, like my dreams," he said. "We'd do this in broad daylight."

"Oh. All right." Taru sounded much more reassured than Nagaro felt. "I'm sure I could find it. Especially in this season with the trees going bare." He pulled his tirkyl over his head. "O' course, that means there'd be hardly any cover if there was anyone there t' see us." He frowned, then brightened. "We could pick up sticks... pretend we just came for firewood. No one would pay us any mind."

But now Nagaro was worried. "I don't want to be seen, Taru—if it's the place I escaped from. I don't want to risk being recognized."

Taru laughed outright. "Nagaro, no one's going t' recognize ye—unless maybe they get a *really* close look. With the kuma stain, and your hair an' beard and all, ye look like a Turowan fisherman!"

Nagaro raised one hand to his face and rubbed the youthful beard that clothed his cheeks. He had to laugh too. Taru was right. The changes he'd made in his appearance during the past year made a pretty fair disguise.

*

Nagaro insisted that they not set out to investigate the mysterious house unless they had several hours of daylight. It was therefore two days before they got their chance—an entire afternoon with nothing to do but find something to shoot for dinner. Nagaro expressed concern about taking the bow, but Taru shrugged it off. "We'll look at the house first and hunt afterwards," he said. "If we bundle our sticks around the bow, no one'll notice it."

So they set out up the slope behind the house, towards the crest of the ridge, making for a low point that formed a sort of notch. Autumn was fading into winter and the deciduous trees were nearly bare. The leaves still clinging to them were pale and faded, and those trodden under foot had lost most of their color as well. The only real cover was provided by juniper bushes, and on the higher slopes, by pines.

Once through the notch, they started down the other side. They clambered out onto an outcropping of rock to get a view of the valley spread out below them and saw their destination. The cluster of roofs and bit of clearing in the trees was almost directly below them, in the very bottom of the valley.

"Do you mean to say you went all that way by *accident?*" Nagaro asked suspiciously.

"Well, not *exactly* by accident," Taru admitted. "I saw it from here, and I was curious, so I decided t' do a bit of exploring. I didn't mean t' get so close though. That part was an accident."

They began to pick up fallen sticks as they made their way down into the valley. They were careful not to encumber themselves too much, however, collecting only enough to lend credence to their story that they were gathering firewood.

Nagaro felt his stomach tighten when they caught their first glimpse of the house close up through the leafless branches of the trees. From a distance it had looked deserted, but as they drew closer they saw a wisp of smoke issuing from one of several chimneys. The windows on the ground floor weren't shuttered, but there didn't seem to be any people about. They circled cautiously around to one side, staying about twenty yards distant.

In addition to the two-story house, there turned out to be a stable, a few other outbuildings, and a strip of fenced land along the stream that would be pasture when the spring brought forth new grass.

"I'll wager Lord Bron doesn't use it in the winter," Taru observed as they stood looking up at the empty windows at one end of the main building. "It's probably for hunting, and the smoke just means there's someone here t' look after the place."

Nagaro nodded. The buildings and their surroundings all seemed utterly unfamiliar, and he was both disappointed and a bit relieved. He would learn nothing from this expedition, but neither would he have to confront anything unpleasant. "I don't think I've ever been here before," he said. "We've wasted our time."

Taru shrugged. "There was no other way t' find out."

"The place that I escaped from must have been somewhere else," Nagaro murmured, "but the size and layout of this place do remind me a little of Averwin—"

He stopped dead. *Averwin...* "Taru!" he cried, "That's the name of the place where I grew up! Averwin!"

Taru met his excited gaze with a blank look and a shake of the head. "I've never heard that name before."

At that moment, the sound of a distant hunting horn suddenly pierced the stillness of the winter valley. It was followed by shouts and the baying of hounds, and the latter sounds were drawing nearer.

"Ai!" Taru cried in alarm. "Hunters! And they're coming this way!"

The horn sounded again, distinctly closer, and they could now hear the sound of large bodies crashing through the undergrowth a short distance up the valley. It sounded as though the hunting party was coming straight down the stream that threaded the valley's bottom. Nagaro and Taru were standing directly in the hunters' path.

The two young men exchanged fearful looks and dashed back in the direction from which they'd come. It was one thing to say they were innocently gathering wood and quite another to risk being ridden down by galloping horses or being set upon by hunting dogs. As they hurriedly picked their way across the stream, a wild-eyed doe came bounding along the edge of the watercourse, dodging among the tree trunks. She saw them and made a frantic leap that carried her across the stream, then plunged up the farther bank and disappeared into a leafless willow thicket.

A third time the horn rang out, blaring in their ears, and in the next instant the hounds and the horsemen came into view. By this time, Taru and Nagaro had put the stream behind them and were climbing the slope they'd descended earlier, moving among clumps of evergreen juniper that offered some cover.

"Wait, Nagaro!" Taru panted. "Stop! We're out o' their way. They make a fine show, and I want to watch!"

Nagaro turned and stood beside his friend, breathing hard. The pack of hounds was crossing the stream, following the doe's scent. The hunters came crashing after them. There were half a dozen of them, blond men with bows and quivers, mounted on snorting, steaming horses. As the leader came abreast of where the young men stood, he reined in a little before wheeling his mount to cross the stream, and Nagaro got a good look at him. He was a big, broad-shouldered man who gripped the reins in one beefy hand and his bow in the other. His straw-colored hair was slick with sweat, his square, red face contorted in fierce excitement.

Nagaro stared at the man in horror. His world seemed to freeze as terror nailed him where he stood. Then he dropped his sticks and flung himself face down behind a juniper bush.

Taru swore and ducked down beside him. "What are ye doing, Nagaro? They'll pay us no heed as long as we stay out o' their way!"

Nagaro had his eyes squeezed shut. "Is he gone?"

"Who?"

"The one with the red face!"

Taru stuck his head up. "They're all gone."

"Did he see me?"

"If he did, he didn't care. By the Spirits, Nagaro, what ails ye?"

Nagaro opened his eyes, first relieved, then embarrassed. He got unsteadily to his feet. "I'm sorry," he mumbled. "He looked like one of the men in my dream..."

Taru was trying to pick up all the sticks, his and Nagaro's, but he stopped to stare wide-eyed at his friend. "The big man with the red face? The one in front?"

"Yes."

"Ah, Nagaro... I think that was Lord Bron. Ye're not sayin' ye were running away from *him* when ye came to us, are ye?"

"I... don't know..." Nagaro reached shakily for his share of the sticks. He blinked and found that he couldn't picture the man he'd just seen clearly enough to know whether it was the same man or not. "I'm not sure..." *Yet it had seemed so clear a moment before.* "I've been hearing Lord Bron's name since the day I woke up," he said. "If I'd ever known him, wouldn't I have recognized his name?" It seemed to make sense... but... *Had the Spirit of the White Flower just done something?* He turned to look back at the hunting lodge. "I still don't remember this place. Nothing else here fits any of my dreams." He shook his head in bafflement. "Come on. Let's go home."

Taru gave him a look, but no argument.

They started back up the slope. When they reached the top of the ridge, Nagaro took all of the sticks so Taru had his hands free for the bow. There was no sense in wasting good firewood, he reasoned, and his nerves were still so frayed after what had happened at the hunting lodge that he didn't think he could aim properly.

Near the edge of the forest, they had the good luck to spot a rabbit and Taru brought it down with a clean shot. At least they could return to the house with both fuel and meat.

*

"Does Lord Bron have... a daughter?" Nagaro asked that night as he and Taru were preparing for bed.

Taru stopped and looked hard at him. "Aye, he does. But I've never seen her, so I couldn't tell ye what she looks like."

Nagaro looked away. Taru had obviously guessed what he was thinking. "I don't *know* that I was running away from Lord Bron," he said. "But if I *was*... and if he had a *daughter*..."

"She could be the girl ye seen in your dreams." Taru finished the thought for him.

Nagaro raised his eyes. "Yes, but there's more. How far away is Sobring Hall?"

Taru cocked his head. "Ten or twelve miles, at least. Maybe fifteen. But it's east, Nagaro. Not south."

"I was in a fever, Taru. I might have been wandering around for some time. But I'm thinking, what if Lord Bron comes *here?* Could I be putting your family in danger?"

Taru actually laughed. "In all my life, he's never set foot on this side o' the hills. He hunts in his forest, with his son and a pack o' Leithian men—like ye saw today. But Leithian women don't go hunting, so *she'll* not be with them. And there was no sign that he knew ye. So he's got no cause t' come here, so long as we don't go pokin' around that place any more—or go to Sobring Hall looking for your green-eyed girl."

Nagaro shivered. "No, I wasn't planning to do that. I need my memories, Taru, but I guess I'll have to find some other way of shaking them loose."

The question was: how?

Chapter 9: Waking Visions

The days passed without an obvious answer, but the dreams kept coming. And night after night of dreams—about the green-eyed girl, about running or being attacked, about faces that made him squirm like a worm on a hook or want to flee in terror—began to wear on Nagaro.

"If only I'd dream about something *pleasant*," he complained one afternoon.

Taru shot him a sympathetic look. The two young men were sitting on the floor in front of the fire, straightening green sticks for arrow shafts by drawing them through a groove in a hot rock. Jomo and Olomi were sitting at the table by the window, working together on a new fishing net. Outside, rain dripped steadily from the eaves.

Taru levered the rock back into the fire to let it get hot again. "The ones about the girl must be pleasant at least," he said.

"Not really..." Nagaro hesitated. It was always hard to explain things about the girl to Taru. "The things I do in those dreams don't feel right."

"What d' ye mean?"

"Well, in the last one, I was sitting with her beside a pool of water, watching fish swimming in it. And when one of them swam up close under the bank, she said, 'You can almost touch it.' And when she said 'touch it,' I... I put my *whole arm* into the water. Without even rolling up my sleeve! It was a stupid thing to do, and I don't know why I did it! I got soaking wet, of course, and the worst of it is... she laughed..."

It hadn't been an unkind laugh, but the memory still stung.

"Oh." Taru was plainly baffled. "Maybe ye just didn't know anything about fish back then?"

"Maybe. But I surely knew about water—and about shirts!"

*

In the afternoon, during a lull between storms, the two youths went hunting. The whole world was gleaming-wet and rain-washed. The air under the trees was rich with the smell of damp earth. It was a good smell that brought Nagaro a sense of peace, though he couldn't say why. The leaves had fallen later here and lay everywhere on the ground, a carpet of scarlet and gold. The autumn woods were very quiet, almost silent, except for the occasional snap of a twig under their feet and the tinkling sound of water when they drew near the stream.

They were following the stream's course, picking their way along the bank, when Nagaro chanced to glance across the stream through the bare branches of a young alder tree. Suddenly, without any warning, he seemed to be looking through a different curtain of branches at a different scene. Image followed image then, all so clear and compelling that he came to a halt on the spot and stood mesmerized, oblivious to his surroundings.

Taru, who had the bow and had therefore been in the lead, eventually realized he was alone. Retracing his steps, he found Nagaro standing rigid beside the barren alder, apparently staring at nothing.

"Nagaro?" Taru touched his friend on the arm. "What's happening? Do ye see something?"

Nagaro started and blinked, roused from his trance-like state. He shook himself and met Taru's questioning gaze with eyes full of excitement. "I just remembered the house where I grew up! This morning I wished I would dream something pleasant, and I think the spirit just answered me. The memory was so clear—as if a curtain opened in my mind. But it closed when you touched me. I wish you hadn't."

"I'm sorry, Nagaro!" Taru's eyes reflected his regret. "But I had no way o' knowing. Can ye tell me about it as we walk?"

They started forward again. "What was the house like? Taru asked.

Nagaro focused on the memory. The house he'd seen felt entirely right to him. "It had two floors, with half a dozen rooms below, and another half dozen above," he explained. "My room was at the top of the stairs. I used to play on the stairs when I was little—and on the terrace too. The terrace was at the back of the house. It was covered with a roof so it was dry in the winter and cool in the summer. And it had climbing vines on trellises spaced all around it, so you could look out between them and see the garden and the pasture and the river. In the winter, when the leaves were off the vines, you could look out through their branches..." He paused. "That's how the vision began," he added. "Looking through branches."

Taru gave a low whistle. "It sounds very grand."

Nagaro shook his head. "It was just a country house. A merchant or a lord might keep a house like that, to enjoy a few days in the country from time to time." Somehow he knew this.

"But ye said ye grew up there. Did ye live there all the time?"

"Ye-es... I think so..."

"Why would ye be living in a place like that?"

This time Nagaro frowned and could only give his all-too-frequent response. "I don't know. But I was right when I said I remembered the name of the place. It *was* called Averwin."

Taru just shook his head. "I told ye I've never heard of it."

Nagaro's excitement was undiminished. "But it's a new memory, Taru. A gift from the Spirit of the White Flower. If I wish for it, maybe there'll be more."

He set himself to fervently wishing, then, as they continued along the stream course. He had no luck with the bow that afternoon, perhaps being too distracted, and had no more visions either. Fortunately, Taru shot a fat grouse.

That evening, after dinner, Nagaro and Taru sat in front of the fire, passing a little time before going to bed.

Nagaro was staring into the flames, watching them waver and dance. A trace of wood smoke in the air made his eyes water and he blinked. Taru was saying something but he wasn't really listening. He was tired from not having slept well the night before—or the night before that. The flames began to blur in his vision...

He blinked again... and suddenly the curtain reopened in his mind. He was in another place, another time. He was a child, sitting at a long table in a room lit by a fire that was burning in a large fireplace. Before him were paper, pen, and ink, and he was carefully tracing the letters of the *reivinkor*, the Kelorin alphabet. The Lady in Gray was there, standing beside his chair. She spoke words of encouragement, reached out to guide his hand...

The scene shifted. He was sitting at the same table and the lady was sitting beside him this time. Before him lay an open book, a primer with pictures and words written large. He was running his finger along under the words and struggling to put together the sounds of the letters. Occasionally the lady corrected him...

Another shift, and he was sitting cross-legged on the floor in front of the fire. In his lap he had a slate and he was writing numbers on it with a piece of chalk... There was more... Absently he picked up a piece of charcoal and began making marks with it on the hearthstone.

"What are ye doing?"

The voice was Taru's, but it seemed to come from far away. Nagaro answered from the place where his mind was wandering. "Writing my name."

"Which name?"

This time the question jerked him back to the present, and in that instant the curtain closed. He blinked and stared in momentary bewilderment at Taru's questioning face. Then the significance of his friend's words sank in.

Which name? *Which indeed?* Eagerly he looked down at the hearthstone, but he was disappointed by what he saw there.

"I've written 'Nagaro,'" he said bitterly. "I just had another vision, about learning my lessons this time, in the house that the spirit showed me while we were out hunting. The Lady in Gray taught me—reading, writing, sums, history. All of that just came to me—*but not my name!*"

And he realized something else. "The Spirit of the White Flower must have purposely kept the names out of that vision! The Lady in Gray was there—over and over again—talking to me. But she never once said my name!" *Nor had he said hers. And where, where were his parents?*

Taru was staring at him, open-mouthed. "That's... amazing," he said, but his eyes were drawn back to the hearthstone. He examined the letters written there with great interest.

Watching him, Nagaro suddenly realized what else his friend's first question had revealed. "Can't you read, Taru?"

Taru shook his head without answering.

Nagaro became aware that Olomi was standing over them, looking down at the hearth stone. Glancing up, he discovered that Jomo had come over as well. They both looked a little awestruck, and he realized he'd been speaking loudly enough that they must have overheard everything he'd said.

Jomo shook his head, bemused. "There aren't more 'n a few dozen people in Wotana that know their letters," he said. He looked at Olomi. "Now didn't I say from the start that Nagaro seemed like he had some schooling?"

"Can ye write *my* name?" Taru asked.

"Of course." Nagaro was glad to shift the conversation away from the subject of spirit magic. He picked up his piece of charcoal and wrote the four letters.

Taru admired them.

Nagaro began to write again. "This is 'Olomi,'" he said, "and this is 'Jomo.'" He looked up at the older fisherman. "Do you have a family name?"

Jomo shrugged. "We use Nareyo," he said. "Because we have to have a name when we pay the tax. It just means 'sea-man'. 'Narei' is 'sea' and the 'o' sound on the end makes it a man, like the 'o' in 'Nagaro'.

"I see." Nagaro wrote "Nareyo" after "Jomo."

Taru was closely watching Nagaro's hand as he formed the letters. "Nagaro," he said suddenly, "could ye teach me to do that?"

Nagaro shrugged. "I don't see why not."

Jomo snorted. "Why waste your time with something that's of no use t' ye?"

"Because I want to!" Taru's eyes blazed. "If Nagaro is willing to teach me, why shouldn't I learn?"

"Ye're a fisherman. Fishermen don't need t' know their letters."

Olomi intervened. "Let him try, Jomo, if he wants to so much. He'd be the first in the family on either side t' know his letters—and, who knows? He might just want to be something other than a fisherman someday." She looked down at the hearthstone and turned to Nagaro. "But ye'll have t' find something else besides my hearthstone for your lessons," she added sternly. "Just see what a mess ye've made of it."

*

Nagaro lay down that night with his mind full of anticipation. He had wished for pleasant memories, and some had come—*twice*. He'd always known that he had an education. The subject had just never come up in this place where there was no need for it. It was a surprise, however, to find it was the Lady in Gray who had taught him. Had she been his tutor? And would there be more such memories? Would they come in his dreams? Jomo and Olomi had asked him a few questions about the Spirit of the White Flower, and he'd done his best to answer, explaining that he thought his memories were at last coming back and downplaying how disturbing his dreams had become. If only the dreams would be different now... *If only he could get some sleep...*

He must have drifted off eventually, for he was jolted awake out of a succession of dreams containing only the same dark images that had plagued him for weeks. The last one ended in the all-too-familiar sensation of falling into oblivion, which was what woke him.

Groaning, he rolled over and resettled himself, then lay in the dark listening to Taru snore softly as he tried to calm himself and get over his disappointment. He'd hoped the benign influence of the Spirit of the White Flower might assert itself over his dreams, but it seemed that nothing had changed.

Since Vothra made no pretense of being able to answer prayers, and he was far from certain of the capabilities of the Spirit of the White Flower, he offered a prayer addressed to no one in particular. *Please*, he thought, *I'm so tired. When I close my eyes this time, just let me sleep 'til morning.* Then he drew a breath, let it out, and closed his eyes.

It might have been his imagination, but it seemed he heard a single word, whispered through his mind...

Sleep...

When he awoke, he found the light of morning dimly suffusing the little bedroom, and he felt more rested than he had in days.

*

For two days he waited in vain for more visions. Those two days were nothing but rain. And the nights brought only the familiar nightmares.

On the third day, the rain stopped, and Nagaro and Taru went out to gather driftwood for the fire. The storms had left mounds of debris on the beach, some natural, some shaped by human hands. It was a dreary day. There was no wind, and a thick gray blanket of clouds hung low over land and sea. The waves slapped half-heartedly against the sand and slipped away with a muffled shushing sound. It was cold, and the smell of the sea was heavy in the air.

Walking on the firm, wet sand just beyond the reach of the waves, Nagaro stopped to pick through a tangle of seaweed, and something white caught his eye. It turned out to be a piece of smooth plank with white paint still on it. "Look, Taru!" He called to the other youth, who was a dozen paces ahead of him. "Wouldn't this be perfect for writing on with charcoal?"

He tugged the plank loose from the entangling seaweed, straightened, and then stood stock still with the object in his hands, his mind suddenly awash in vivid memories.

Taru had heard him and turned back, but seeing Nagaro's abstraction he waited for his friend to return to the present before saying, "Ye had another vision, didn't ye?"

Nagaro let his breath out. "Yes." He looked at the piece of plank in his hands. "I think this had something to do with it. The Lady in Gray painted pictures on smooth pieces of wood like this, and that's what I just remembered. She painted lots of pictures—of places around where we lived. She hung them in the upstairs hall, mostly. And I had one in my room, of horses. She painted a picture of me, too, around my seventeenth birthday. I remember having to sit still for hours while she worked on it."

"Well, I can't say I see much use in that," Taru said. "But at least it wasn't anything bad."

Eagerly, Nagaro nodded. "I think the Spirit of the White Flower has decided to give me back the good parts of my memories. The parts it won't do me any harm to know."

"But why now?"

Nagaro's eyes clouded. "Maybe because it's losing its hold on the bad parts—the dreams I've been having... what came to me in the dark woods... and Lord Bron... If I'm going to remember all those bad things anyway, it might as well give me the good parts to balance them."

"Oh." Taru looked hopeful. "Does that mean everything's going t' come back?"

Nagaro looked back down at the piece of plank. "I hope so," he said. "The spirit must still have some control though. The dreams don't really *tell* me anything. They just hint. And all the names that could help me find my way home are missing from the both the dreams and the visions—my name, the name of the Lady in Gray, and of all those men. I don't think that's a coincidence." He wiped some sand off of the painted surface with the sleeve of his tirka. "Come on. Let's take what we have back to the house."

That evening they began Taru's education, working with the piece of painted board. They marked on it with charcoal and wiped it clean with a bit of rag, over and over. "These are the letters of the reivinkor," Nagaro explained. "Each one has its own sound. All you have to do to write is put the letters together in the right order, and reading is just saying back the sounds of the written letters."

Taru squirmed. "Twenty-eight letters, Nagaro! Why are there so many?"

"Because that's how many sounds you need to write what we call the Common Speech, which is New Kelorin with some Leithian words mixed in."

"Why is it called the reivinkor?"

"It's named for Reivin, the woman who designed the letters. She lived hundreds of years ago, in Kelor, far over the western sea."

"How do ye know all this?"

"From my lessons—and from reading books, Taru. But you'll never be able to read anything if you don't pay attention to this."

*

The waking visions continued to come. Almost every day, at least once, the curtain in Nagaro's mind would open without warning and close again just as capriciously. The memories seemed to be triggered by things, often little things, and they were so absorbing that they completely displaced whatever he was doing. The nights were still ruled by darker images, punctuated at intervals by dreams involving the girl with the sea-green eyes and honey-colored hair.

It was the middle of Todrin, the tenth month, before Nagaro's memory yielded up a name. It came while he was helping dig up the last of the potatoes they had planted. It must have been the smell of the damp earth and the feel of it on his hands that was the trigger, for Nagaro suddenly got a clear image of his hands cupped around the roots of a plant while an old Turowan man showed him how to nestle it into a hole and fill the earth in around it. There was affection in the man's brown eyes, and approval in his gap-toothed smile.

Taru's voice broke into the vision. "What is it this time?"

Nagaro felt a surge of fierce excitement. "Chula!" he said. "The gardener's name was Chula! He taught me how to plant and harvest. And how to lash sticks together and tie knots and carve little wooden boats to sail in the river."

Other names came in the days that followed. There was Hinda the cook, and Thorlan the stableman, who had shown him how to handle a horse and shoot at a target. And there was Bodano the farmer, who had taught him how to stalk game and read animal tracks. But their names drew only blank looks from Taru, Jomo, and Olomi. And still the Lady in Gray continued to be nameless, and his nights were haunted by the green-eyed girl, the four Leithian men, and the hawk-faced man, also still as nameless as before.

*

By the beginning of the eleventh month, Nondorin, Nagaro could remember how he'd learned to ride and shoot and hunt. He remembered climbing trees and swimming in the river in the summer, picking berries in the forest in the autumn, and making snow forts in the winter.

"Did ye have any friends? Taru asked. "Lads your age, t' play with?"

Nagaro shook his head. "No." As far as he could tell, there had no playmates of his own age, and of his mother or father there was still no sign.

"Weren't ye lonely then?"

They were making arrowheads again, sitting on the floor by the open door while Olomi baked bread on the hearth. The fresh bread aroma mingled with the salty sea air. It was a rare clear day, and the late autumn sunlight streamed in. The rush of the waves sounded a familiar rhythm.

Nagaro frowned at the arrowhead he was holding. "I don't think I knew that I should have been."

There was a pause while the pumice stones scraped.

Eventually Taru put his stone down. He studied his arrowhead. "Will ye be going back there?" he asked. "When ye remember how t' find the place, I mean." He didn't meet Nagaro's eyes.

"I suppose so..." Nagaro caught the look of regret that crossed Taru's face before the other youth suppressed it. "I mean," he added quickly, "I'll have to see what it makes sense to do. After I know what happened."

"O' course ye will." Taru flashed him an awkward smile, and they both went back to work.

Nagaro heaved an inward sigh. The place he remembered was the place where he belonged—or had belonged... Sometimes, though, he wondered... *Even if his memory returned completely, would he be able to go back?*

*

A week later, winter struck with a vengeance. Overnight the temperature plummeted and the rain turned to snow. Keeping the shed stocked with firewood became a high priority, and it wasn't long before Jomo was showing concern about the supply of money he had saved to buy food.

"Will there be enough t' see us through 'til spring?" Olomi asked anxiously one day as Jomo was counting the coins he kept stored in a little wooden box.

Jomo gave her a sharp glance. "I hope so. But winter's come early, it seems, and last season's fishing wasn't as good as I would ha' liked. And we've one more mouth t' feed..."

Nagaro was sitting just a dozen feet away and couldn't help overhearing The house was often too small for easy privacy. He felt a twist of guilt. "I'm sorry, Jomo," he began. "You can have the rins I've saved if it will—"

Jomo stopped him with a raised hand. "Don't ye fret, Nagaro," he said, with a reassuring smile. "Ye've brought us a good spot o' meat with your hunting. Just see ye keep doin' that, and I'm sure we'll manage."

Nagaro could only nod and say, "I'll do my best." He didn't like to mention how tired he often was from lack of sleep, or the way the visions came without warning. The truth was that hunting was becoming more difficult for him every day.

Chapter 10: The Turning Of The Year

He was lying on his back, staring up at the carved panels on the underside of the wooden bed canopy. The stylized vines and flowers and ornate scroll-work were presented to his eyes in minute detail. He knew them excruciatingly well, and they were of no interest to him whatsoever. The green-eyed girl was lying beside him, their bodies close but not touching. He couldn't see her face, but he knew she was crying. Silent sobs were shaking her body and he could feel them through the mattress. She was crying, and he was saying nothing... doing nothing...

In the end, it was the girl who spoke. "I'm sorry..." she said in a voice that quavered. "Leave me now... please..."

Without a word, he rose. Stepping onto the floor beside the bed, he walked around the foot of it, treading first on elegant Jinari carpet, then polished wood. He crossed to the door without pausing to look back, opened it by turning the sculpted brass doorhandle, stepped through, and closed it behind him.

In the chamber beyond, he stopped as if held by some imperative, and stood still in the darkness, barefoot and bare-legged in his nightshirt. The oak floor was cold under his feet, and he shivered. This room was also a bedchamber, but the canopied bed was empty and unused, its brocade coverlet neatly arranged.

He stood there... and stood there... as if waiting for something... until the dream faded.

Nagaro opened his eyes and stared at the rough-hewn ceiling beams of Taru's room. He wondered, as he had before, why the girl so often wept. He'd dreamed about it repeatedly, in dreams that were different enough to represent different nights. His response, on the other hand, was always the same: rigid inaction and stony silence. *Why had he never done anything to comfort her?* It was no wonder she had asked him to leave.

And why was there a second bedroom? One that wasn't used? Both rooms were richly appointed, suggesting far more wealth than he had known during his childhood...

He blinked blearily and pushed the thoughts away. He knew so much more now about his past life, but these dreams still didn't connect to what he knew, and he was never going to simply guess the answers. Besides, it was morning. The oiled skin on the window glowed with a wan light. He was still tired, as he always was these days, but there was no point in trying to sleep any more right now. There would only be more dreams.

The room was cold. And empty, he realized. Taru must have decided to let him sleep. There was a trace of wood-smoke in the air—which meant someone had already kindled the fire in the outer room—but the house was too quiet. There should be the sounds associated with breakfast. Then he noticed that Taru's blanket was gone. The dried fern leaves were exposed in all their dusty splendor. In the next instant, he remembered guiltily that there were other things to worry about besides his own life's secrets. Olomi was ill, and it was the third day of Idrin.

She had been ailing for several days, cooking the meals but scarcely touching her own food. Doing little but sit by the fire... Then yesterday, she had made their breakfast and gone back to bed. There would have been neither lunch nor dinner if Nagaro hadn't used the last of the flour to bake two loaves of bread. Taru and Jomo had both rolled their eyes at the idea of him doing women's work, but it hadn't kept them from eating their share of the bread.

Shivering, he fished under the covers for his clothes. He kept them under the blanket all night so they wouldn't feel like ice in the morning. Finding them, he dressed as quickly as possible. He was pretty sure he could guess where Taru's blanket had gone, and he took his own with him when he left the little bedroom.

He found Taru and Jomo sitting silently at the table, just finishing a breakfast of yesterday's cold bread and warmed-over sothiril. The way they sat hunched over their cups and the expressions on their faces told a tale before either of them uttered a word.

"I can't get her out o' the bed." Jomo said grimly as he accepted the offered blanket. "She's not put anything in her stomach since the day afore yesterday. I mean t' go to town this morning to see the medicine woman, and t' buy beans and flour. I was just waiting for ye to show your face, Nagaro, so there'd be someone t' watch her while I'm gone."

"That's so I can hunt and gather firewood," Taru explained.

"I could do those things," Nagaro protested. "You should stay with your mother."

But Taru shook his head. "Ye can't go out alone, Nagaro. Not the way your head has been. Ye'd fall asleep on your feet, or your mind would go wandering, and ye'd freeze t' death."

Nagaro caught himself in a yawn and looked sheepish, knowing Taru's points were well taken. He went hunting as often as he could, but always with Taru now because his lapses into waking dreams presented a real danger. Taru's task was to shake him out of his trances, though it was still Nagaro who usually carried the bow. They both knew his skill was greater, and the family needed meat. "All right," he said. "I'll make some soup. The broth may do her good."

There was no rolling of eyes at the suggestion this time.

It was snowing outside and Taru was afraid his father might lose his way. Jomo was determined to go on foot, however, and confident he could follow the road. So the older man dressed in knitted woolen leggings under his pants. He then donned one of the family's two sealskin coats and a pair of knitted gloves, shouldered an empty pack, and set off. Even before he rounded the corner of the house, his figure was nearly lost in the gray-white swirl of falling flakes.

Nagaro set to work to make the soup with Taru helping to locate ingredients. There was nothing to put into the pot but onions, potatoes, and a few scraps of dried fish. Nagaro sat at the table, struggling to focus his sleep-starved mind on cutting up the vegetables.

Taru paced and fretted. "Why'd this have to happen in Idrin?" he wondered aloud. "In the dark days? It could ha' been any time, and the whole of Idrin's only seven days long! What've we done that the Spirits are sending us such bad luck?"

"You haven't done anything." Nagaro stood up, blinking eyes that were smarting from the onions. He covered another yawn, then began to transfer hand-fulls of chopped onions and potatoes to the pot of water that he'd hung on a hook over the fire. "The Vothrin Writings say there's nothing to fear about the dark days of Idrin. They were just the last few days that were left at the end of the year when they made the calendar. And the fourth of Idrin is Mid-Winter's Day, the shortest day of the year. That's why it's so dark." *He was trying not to think about the possibility that Olomi might die...* Belatedly he remembered the dried fish and added it to the pot.

"Your Kelorin folk celebrate the turning of the year on the fourth o' Genorel, just like everyone else," Taru observed pointedly. "So there's three days that are clear, outside of Idrin, to make ready for the New Year's feast."

Nagaro sighed. "It's a very old custom and I suppose they saw no reason to change it. I *am* worried about your mother, though. It's so cold and—"

"And we've put every blanket in the house over her!" Taru actually wrung his hands. "And Father said she was *still* shivering!" He dropped onto the stool Nagaro had just vacated and sat there worriedly gnawing a thumb nail.

Nagaro squatted on the hearth and stirred the contents of the big iron pot. "Soup will warm her from the inside," he said, trying to sound reassuring. He put the spoon down and poked the fire with a blackened stick. "We need more wood. Could you fetch some from the shed?"

"There isn't any." Taru stood up and squared his shoulders. "I said I'd have t' gather some. Remember?"

"Oh. Right. Is it still snowing? I don't want *you* to get lost."

"I won't." Taru sounded as confident as his father. "After all, if I get turned about, all I have to do is go downhill 'til I strike the road, and north 'til I strike the stream. Don't worry. Just tend t' that soup and sit with Mother."

So Taru dressed as Jomo had done and ventured forth.

Nagaro sat alone for a time, stirring the pot, trying not to worry and not to doze. He tasted the soup and added another onion and a pinch of salt. When there was nothing left to do but let it simmer, he went to sit beside Olomi's bed.

He found her sleeping. She looked very fragile. The bones of her cheeks stood out and her eyes were sunken. Looking at her, he wondered what it would have been like to have a mother like her.

It seemed that the Lady in Gray had, in large measure, raised him. But who was she? Had she been a tutor? A governess? A maiden aunt perhaps, set to the task of instructing him? She was there throughout all the memories of his childhood. Besides his lessons and the ways of Vothra, she had taught him the formal courtesies used between folk of noble rank, and to show respect to all people regardless of their station. She had taught him to work with his hands and with his mind to make himself useful in the world. She had taught him to give freely to others who were in need. And she had taught him to shun the ways of power. Yet she continued to have no name.

Olomi stirred and let out her breath in a little sigh, startling him out of his thoughts. He reached out and took her hand. She opened her eyes then, and saw him. She squeezed his hand. "Nagaro," she said weakly. "My second son."

He was touched by her words. So he kissed her hand because he didn't know what to say—and because it was something he had been taught to do, to show that he felt honored.

She shook her head at him. "That's your high-born up-bringing again," she said. "And too fine for the likes o' me." There were tears in her eyes. "Somewhere," she added, "there must be a woman who is very proud o' ye."

He frowned. "I think the Lady in Gray was proud of me... sometimes," he said. "But she didn't often say so."

Olomi sighed softly. "'Tis that way with mothers... and fathers... We fear t' give too much praise, lest we spoil the child."

He nodded. "I know you're proud of Taru. I see it in your face some-times. And I've seen the way Jomo watches him when we're out on the sea. Taru has mastered his sea-craft well, and his father is proud of that, though he never says so."

Feeling awkward speaking of such things, he rose and excused himself to go out and stir the soup again and to taste it. "I can bring you some broth in a little while," he told her when he returned. "But it isn't ready yet."

She smiled again and closed her eyes.

He settled down once more to wait and watch, but he was so tired that he soon began to drift. It must have been the talk of mothers that triggered the vision.

The curtain opened in his mind, and he was in another place and time. Fleetingly, he glimpsed the Lady in Gray lying on a bed, but the image was gone in an eye-blink, replaced by an image of her sitting at a writing desk under a window whose indirect light haloed her seated form. He approached her, for he had questions. She gave him answers. The scene shifted again as his memory jumped years ahead. Still other visions followed... Then, as suddenly as it had opened, the curtain closed again.

Nagaro let out his pent-up breath in a long sigh. He found that he was holding his ring in his hands, and he noticed with relief that Taru was there, sitting on the other stool at the foot of the bed, watching him. Olomi was awake and watching him as well.

The discontinuity of Taru's presence didn't disturb him because such things happened so often now. Instead, he noted that Taru couldn't have been there long because his hair was still sprinkled with tiny drop-lets that must be melted snowflakes.

"Ye've been wandering." Olomi's voice was husky.

He nodded.

"What did ye see this time?" Taru was always eager to know. "Were there any new names?"

"No." Nagaro heaved a sigh. "I think I would like some soup first," he added. "If it's ready. Then I'll tell you about it."

The soup was indeed ready. He and Taru each brought back a bowl, as well as a cup of broth for Olomi. They sat her up and helped her drink it, then laid her down again and sat on their stools to give their attention to their own bowls and spoons. Nagaro ate in silence, but he was aware of their expectant eyes.

"Ye don't have t' talk if ye don't want to," Olomi said.

"No, it's all right." He drank the last of the soup from his bowl, and set both bowl and spoon on the floor. He pushed his stool back a little so he could lean against the wall. The ring still hung outside his shirt, and he fingered it as he spoke.

"I never knew my parents," he began. "I was a foundling, left at the Lady in Gray's doorstep with nothing but the blanket I was wrapped in and this ring. I think she wanted a child, because she had no husband and no children of her own, so she kept me instead of giving me to one of the farmers' wives." He paused to draw a breath and let it out, not meeting their eyes. After a moment, he continued. "There was a tale among the farm folk 'round about that I was the lady's bastard child, fathered by her murdered lover. I was nine or ten when I heard that story and asked her about it. She told me it wasn't true."

"Were ye adopted then?" It was Taru's question.

Nagaro sighed. "She treated me like an adopted son, giving me her name. But I never called her mother, and her family never accepted me. I never met any of them. She'd had a falling out with her parents because she refused to marry according to their choosing. She wanted to marry the man she loved, but her parents disapproved, and there was some sort of battle of honor between the man and her brother in which her brother killed the man. After that, she declared she would never marry, so her parents sent her away to the little country house where I grew up. She lived there in a kind of exile, and she always wore gray because it's the color of mourning."

He paused again. The room was very quiet. "It's no wonder no one has ever come looking for me," he finished finally. "My Lady Guardian— the Lady in Gray—is dead. And her family would be glad to be rid of me. I have no one in the world... and no place to return to..."

Olomi spoke softly in the silence that followed. "I'm sorry, Nagaro."

"It's all right," he said. "I'm not really surprised. It all makes sense now."

"Ye have us."

"Yes," put in Taru. "O' course ye have us."

Nagaro looked at the floor. "Thank you."

"And it does explain a lot o' things," Taru offered after a moment. "Ye're not a lord's son, but ye were raised like one."

"Something like one, yes."

"And ye could be a fisherman, now, if ye wanted..."

"Yes. I could." Nagaro didn't meet Taru's eyes.

"Ye don't *know* that your parents are dead..." Olomi put in.

Nagaro sighed. "No, but in seventeen years no one ever came to claim me. Someone cared for me enough to try to give me a better life. Perhaps my father was a farmer with too many mouths to feed already, or perhaps my mother was a farmer's daughter finding herself with a child and without a husband. However it was, I am grateful, because I did have a very good life... for seventeen full years—until something happened to ruin it."

He sat staring at the ring in his hands, then abruptly slipped it back inside his shirt. "I used to look into people's faces when I went riding," he said. "Looking for some sign—someone who looked at me too long, or who turned away too quickly. I gave it up a long time ago. It was clear there was no one who knew anything among the folk who lived close by, and I didn't ride far because my Lady Guardian didn't want me to— and I was obedient." He laughed a little sadly. "At least I was once I got old enough to understand her story. She'd had enough pain, and I didn't want her to suffer on my account. So I didn't cross her—at least not when it came to anything important."

"Ye must have loved her very much," Olomi said softly.

He swallowed hard. "Yes."

He had thought her the wisest person in the world—so calm and sad. Hers had been such a strong and graceful spirit. She had made peace with the fate that Lokundas had sent her. Once she had told him that the hardest thing had been to forgive her brother. Yet even that she had managed to do, for she had spoken of what he'd done without any anger at all. Thinking about her, Nagaro's throat felt tight.

"I hope she is with Vothra now," he said. "It was what she always wanted."

*

Jomo returned in mid-afternoon, bringing flour and dried beans, as well as honey, some healing herbs, and a bag of apples from Gama's tree. The medicine woman had given him instructions to make up a sauce of the apples, together with the honey and the herbs, and to feed this to Olomi.

It seemed to Nagaro that Olomi was already a little better, but the three of them set to work to make up the concoction anyway and administer it to their patient. Nagaro was glad of the activity since it gave him something to think about besides the implications of his most recent vision. Eventually, with Olomi resting comfortably, Taru actually pitched in to help Nagaro prepare a pot of seasoned beans for their dinner. By nightfall Olomi was clearly on the mend, for she was able to get out of bed and sit by the fire. Jomo was sure his medicine was responsible and no one wanted to argue with him.

With his wife safely settled on a stool by the hearth, Jomo finally remembered the news—rather distressing news at that. The whole town was in mourning for Fargil. He'd been set upon and slain on the road between Galenor and Lankura in the middle of Finorel.

"They made it look like a robbery," Jomo explained. "His purse and horse and sword were gone."

"How do we know it wasn't then?" Nagaro asked.

"Well for one thing, it isn't common for highway thieves t' kill those they rob. And they're saying that it was done with a narrow blade, an assassin's knife. So o' course everyone in town is sure he was murdered t' keep him from marrying the princess."

Taru had been sitting silent, stunned. Now his face darkened. "It must ha' been Gillard," he growled. "He's the one that stands t' gain from it, the filthy rotter!"

Jomo shrugged resignedly. "It could ha' been anyone who favored Gillard over Fargil, or anyone that favors one o' the other suitors. What *is* sure is that Gillard is most likely now t' win the princess's hand."

Olomi looked up from her seat by the fire. "Poor Nevien," she said. "If that happens, I'm afraid it'll go hard with her."

Jomo nodded grimly, though he made no answer.

*

That night, Nagaro dreamed about the hawk-faced man. He'd often dreamt of the man bending over him as he lay immobile on a narrow bed, but this time the sinister figure sat in a small drab room, hunched over a table like a carrion crow, his pen scratching endlessly. Occasionally he raised glittering black-onyx eyes and spoke. Nagaro felt a deep stirring of anger, mingled with the usual paralyzing fear—emotions so powerful they seemed to drown out the meaning of the hawk-faced man's words. When he awoke, trembling and drenched in sweat, he could remember nothing of what the man had said.

Lying there, feeling the lingering reverberation of his anger, he thought that he might have tried to hurt the man with his bare hands if he'd dared—or if he'd been able. He had never in his life felt such anger towards anyone else, as far as he knew, and it disturbed him deeply.

*

It was a harsh winter as well as an early one. Genorel was colder than usual, with heavy snow. Gathering enough wood and finding game to hunt became a constant challenge. With worries about the family's survival on his mind, and with the distraction of his dreams and visions, Nagaro had little time to think about the solution of his life's mystery or what direction his future might take.

Whenever he and Taru weren't hunting, they were gathering wood. They scoured the forest for it and collected every scrap that washed ashore. The wood was often wet and they had to carefully lean it up against the walls inside the woodshed so it would dry. One day, as they were stowing a pile of freshly-gathered driftwood in the shed, Nagaro picked up a clean, straight stick about three feet long. He stopped, standing outside the woodshed door, holding one end of the stick and staring at it, his breath steaming in the cold. Memories seemed to flow from the thing, and he began to move with the memories...

Taru, working inside the shed, missed the other youth and went to the doorway. He saw Nagaro raise the stick in a kind of salute, as if it were a sword. Grinning, he picked up a similar stick of his own, imagining that Nagaro was remembering some childhood game, for what boy hasn't played that sticks were swords? Wasting no time on salutes, he lunged at his friend. Nagaro deftly beat the attack aside. Then, with a movement too quick to follow, he twisted Taru's stick from his hand and sent it spinning off across the icy ground.

"Hey!" Taru rubbed his stinging fingers, and cast Nagaro a look of reproach.

Nagaro was keenly examining the stick in his hand. "It just needs a guard," he said. "So many of the best defenses use the guard. We could lash a crosspiece here... make one for each of us..." He looked up and met Taru's gaze, and there was an eager gleam in his gray eyes. "I can teach you some good moves, Taru."

Taru's shoulders sagged. "Ye've had schooling in swordsmanship," he said resignedly.

Nagaro nodded. "Three years with Swordmaster Fendar. Come on. Let's find some pieces of wood for guards and take our sticks inside so they can dry better."

Taru considered him. "Well, all right," he said. "As soon as we're finished here... But the first thing ye're going t' teach me is how to knock the stick out of *your* hand."

Nagaro looked at his friend, and then at the other stick lying on the trampled snow. "Oh," he said, rubbing his forehead. "I'm sorry, Taru. In a formal practice bout, it takes three hits to win, but disarming your opponent always wins the bout even if you're behind on hits. I saw an opportunity to disarm you, so I did it without thinking."

Taru gave Nagaro an odd look, but the idea of learning some real swordsmanship plainly appealed to him. So they finished their work and took their chosen sticks and cross-pieces inside and laid them close to the hearth, explaining to Jomo and Olomi what they were for so that no one would put them on the fire. Olomi smiled indulgently, but Jomo shook his head. "Mind ye don't neglect your tasks," was all he said.

The two youths sat down in front of the fire and got out the writing board to fill the time before dinner. Taru wrote words for practice, saying them aloud. Nagaro sat, trying to listen and watch for mistakes, but his mind wandered. The fire was warm and bright. He was tired, as always, and the newly reclaimed memories of sword practice were running in circles in his head. The memories stirred others, and he drifted...

Taru presently became aware of his friend's silence and glanced at him. When he saw that Nagaro was staring into the fire, unseeing, he heaved a sigh and waited.

The trance lasted some time, and when at length Nagaro came out of it and shook himself, there was a look of resolution in his eyes that hadn't been there before.

"What did ye see?" Taru asked.

Nagaro glanced at Jomo and Olomi, where they sat working at the table by the window. "Ask me tonight."

Taru raised an eyebrow, but then he shrugged. "Will ye look at my letters then?"

Nagaro tried to, but found it hard to concentrate. He put his head down on his folded arms where they rested on his up-raised knees, and a moment later jerked awake with a start when his arms slipped.

He kept yawning during dinner.

"Perhaps ye should go to bed," Olomi suggested.

"No," he answered quickly, thinking of his dark dreams. "Not yet." But half an hour later, he went anyway. Taru made a show of yawning and stretching, and went after him.

Nagaro sat on the fern leaves in the dark bedroom with his back against the wall and his blanket wrapped around his shoulders. He heard Taru stretch out on his own bed with a rustle of fern leaves.

"All right," came Taru's voice. "What did ye learn that ye didn't want my parents to hear?"

Nagaro drew a breath. "I know why I did all that training in swordsmanship," he said. "I was going to try to join the Royal Fleet or the City Guard. Even without having the support of her family, my Lady Guardian thought her name might get me a commission."

"The Fleet! Or the City Guard!" Taru's voice conveyed awe. Then he asked, "What's a commission?"

"It means you start at the most junior officer rank, instead of as a common soldier or seaman. Most of the commissions go to the sons of noble houses—or to the wealthy merchant class, who are able to buy them."

"Oh." There was a pause, then, "Do ye still want t' do that?"

"I don't know..." Nagaro said cautiously. "There'd be no hope of a commission now, with my Lady Guardian gone. But it seems a shame to waste all that training, especially after what it cost her."

"What d' ye mean?"

Nagaro picked up a piece of fern leaf and began twisting it around his finger. "We never had much extra money. And Fendar's fee was high. He took me on at half his usual price, because he said I showed promise and he could tell that My Lady really couldn't pay the full amount. She still had to sell one of the horses and some of her books, and I think some of her jewelry as well. I felt bad about that... but not bad enough to tell her not to do it. I wanted that training so much..."

The silence grew between them. Nagaro wished there was enough light to see his friend's face. He'd lost the piece of fern leaf, and he felt about for another one.

Finally Taru said, "Ye don't want t' be a fisherman, do ye, Nagaro?"

"No." He was relieved that Taru understood.

"Which would it be, the Fleet, or the Guard?"

Nagaro didn't hesitate. "The Fleet. I always thought I'd like it better, but I'd never been in a boat until I came here. Now that I have, I'm sure."

He sat in the dark then, waiting for what he expected would come next.

"Nagaro?"

"Yes?"

"D' ye think I could try t' join the Fleet too—even though I haven't any training with a sword?"

It was exactly what he'd expected from Taru, and it was another reason why Nagaro had wanted to talk to him alone. "Anyone can try," he answered. "I'm sure most of the common recruits wouldn't have the kind of sword training that I have. That would be an advantage for me. But you're ahead of me in sea-craft, and that would be an advantage for you." He paused, then said, "What do you think your father would say?"

"I don't care," was Taru's immediate response. "Didn't he say that I'm getting too old for him t' tell me what to do? Anyway, I can always come back here and be a fisherman if it doesn't work. When d' ye plan to leave?"

Nagaro let out the breath he'd been holding. "The big recruitment comes around Midsummers Day at the end of Dunrel, but I can't plan anything yet."

"Why not?"

This was the hard part. He still held the piece of fern in his hands, and he now began to tear off little pieces of it. "I still don't have all of my memories. I think I know how my whole life went up until the last year before I came here, but most of the last year is missing... except for the ugly bits I'm getting from my dreams..."

"Ye think the dreams are all from the last year?"

"Yes. And there's something very *wrong* about them. When I finally remember everything, it could change the plans I can make. There might be... other things I have to do."

"What sort o' things?" Taru wasn't making it easy for him.

"Well... I mean... I think I must have been married to the green-eyed girl." There, he'd said it. He heard the rustle of fern leaves as Taru sat up in the dark.

"Married! What makes ye think so?"

Nagaro took a deep breath. "Well, I've... ah... dreamed about being in bed with her."

Taru gave a low whistle, obviously impressed. "And ye're *sure* it's a memory?"

"Yes..." He broke off, recalling how unpleasant those dreams were and knowing that Taru was imagining something quite different.

The young Turowan was speaking again. "I still don't see why it means ye were married."

Nagaro felt suddenly very tired. "I was wearing my nightshirt. I don't see how it could mean anything else—not the way I was brought up."

"Well, ye *were* raised by a woman—a lady too. I suppose that would make a difference."

Nagaro didn't feel it was his place to offer Taru moral instruction, but this was too much. "I was raised Vothrin, Taru, that's all. And the Writings are very clear about this. I've read them myself. Doesn't your Guiding Spirit ever tell you that some things are just *wrong?*"

There were a few seconds of silence.

"Well... not exactly..." Taru faltered. "I mean... Hakura Kili doesn't make any rules, and neither do the World Spirits. If ye make them angry, they'll punish ye by sending ye bad luck. But there's no telling what they'll take it into their heads t' be angry about. Does Vothra make rules, then, and punish ye for breaking them?"

Nagaro leaned his head wearily against the wall. "No. The Path isn't rules. It's just..." He searched for the right word. "*Advice.* But it's advice based on the wisdom of hundreds of lives. So straying from the Path can bring its own punishment because you're more likely to come to grief that way."

"And Vothra's advice is t' marry a girl before ye lie with her? I can't see why. What's the harm if she's willing?"

Nagaro sighed. "What if you get her with child? Do you just walk away and leave her to raise the child alone, or manipulate some other man into marrying her? Then the child grows up without a father, or with someone who isn't really his father—and everybody knows it. And if you're forced to marry the woman, when you don't really want to, you're hurting yourself too."

"I hadn't thought about all o' that."

Nagaro felt that he really, really needed to sleep. He was so tired. "It just makes sense," he said, yawning, "not to risk fathering a child with a woman you don't care about enough to want to marry..." He stopped speaking. He was thinking about the green-eyed girl, lying beside him, quietly weeping.

The silence stretched for several long seconds until Taru said, "Did ye care that way about the green-eyed girl?"

Nagaro felt sick. "That's part of what feels wrong. I don't seem to have cared for her at all! In the dreams, I never kiss her or hold her. I scarcely even talk to her. I can't understand why I treated her so badly."

"Was she not very pretty? Or was she stuck-up maybe? Or bad-tempered?"

"Actually she's very pretty. She seems perfectly nice too. All I can think of is that I must have been forced into a marriage I didn't want. It must have been after my Lady Guardian died, because she would never have done that to me—not after the way her life was ruined."

"Maybe ye're just mistaken somehow."

"Maybe." Nagaro was really tremendously tired. "I can't think any more, Taru. I have to sleep. It's just this: If I *am* married, or if there could be a child, I can't just turn my back and walk away. Maybe the marriage could be dissolved... Maybe it already has been..." He stifled another yawn. "I just can't plan anything until I know, that's all."

"All right," Taru said. "Then we have to wait t' make our plans. I just hope it isn't long."

"I hope so too. Now good night, Taru."

Unable to keep his eyes open any longer, Nagaro stretched himself out on the ferns and pulled his blanket close around him. He fell asleep almost immediately. Of course he dreamed.

Chapter 11: The Harness Shed

It was night. He was moving through the dark garden, trying to hurry... trying to find a good place... The girl with the sea-green eyes was clutching at his arm, trying to stop him, begging him to come back. He shook himself free of her and ran, but it was hard to run because his legs were beginning to shake. He knew he only had a little time before he'd have to lie down, but he didn't want to lie down here. The garden was dark, cold, and wet with recent rain. The sky was overcast. There was neither moon nor stars to comfort him. It seemed a bleak place in which to die.

Ahead of him there was a light that looked like an open doorway. He headed for it, struggling against the shaking of his limbs that was growing worse with every step. And then the pain began, a burning sensation in his extremities that grew and spread until it ran throughout his body, making every movement an agony.

The girl caught up with him again as he reached the doorway. She was saying something about medicine, but he didn't want medicine. By this time, he was staggering because he was shaking so violently and the pain was searing through him. His vision was beginning to cloud, but he could see that the room he'd entered was a shed, full of saddles, bridles, and carriage harness. Someone had left a lantern burning on a hook, so there was light. It seemed a little warmer, and there was the comfortingly familiar smell of leather. Very soon, none of it would matter, but still it was better than the darkness outside. Gratefully, he let himself sink to his knees in the warm pool of lantern light.

The pain was running along his every nerve now like knives of fire, and the shaking of his body was uncontrollable. He toppled forward onto the rough-worn floorboards, his muscles jerking spasmodically. His breath came in ragged gasps. He was fighting for consciousness, trying to recite in his mind the words of the Writings... All pain ends... all pain ends... and death is the path to a new beginning...

The girl was pulling at his shirt. She was saying something... Something about going to fetch someone... But he mustn't let her do that...

"No!" He forced the word out. "Don't go!" He wanted to say, "Let me die," but it was too late. Every inch of his body was on fire and he had to clamp his teeth shut to keep from screaming. He was no longer aware of the girl, or the light, or the hard floor under him. His mind was overwhelmed, his body consumed by white-hot flame, and then he was screaming, though he scarcely knew it.

Out of the maelstrom of blinding agony, emerged a long gray passageway. He was moving along it, towards the great double doors that opened at its end—opened into outer darkness. Vothra would be there, and the Lady was with Vothra. He was not afraid. Pain was an abstraction now. What mattered was to reach those doors, to cross that threshold. He was almost there... But something was holding him back... Someone had hold of his arm...

Now someone was shaking him, and he was aware that there was a person bending over him in the dim light, saying his name. The passage and the doors were gone. "Why didn't you let me die?" he asked.

"*Nagaro!* What are ye *saying?*" The anguish in Taru's voice was unmistakable.

With a shock, Nagaro realized he was awake. There was no pain, but he felt utterly drained. He groaned and sat up in the darkness. "I'm sorry, Taru. I wasn't talking to you. My mind was still in my dream."

"Ye don't want to die?"

"Of course not. Why would I want to die...?" He broke off then, for he realized that, in his dream, he had wanted exactly that.

Light suddenly suffused the room as Jomo's figure loomed in the doorway. He was clutching a lighted candle, and there was a worried look on his face. Olomi appeared behind her husband. Her eyes were wide with alarm and she hugged a blanket about her shoulders.

"What's the matter?" Nagaro asked, alarmed in his turn by the looks on their faces.

Taru answered him. "Nagaro, ye were screaming."

"Oh." He was embarrassed. "I'm sorry. I'm all right—really. It was a dream, that's all—just a bad dream. Please go back to bed."

It took some effort to convince them. He didn't mention any details of the dream. He didn't want to talk about it, especially not in front of Olomi.

At last they went. After they had gone, Taru insisted on fetching another candle, which he lit from the embers of the fire and placed on the floor between their beds. So the two young men sat for a time, wrapped shivering in their blankets, staring at each other across the candle flame. Taru was watching Nagaro with a haunted look. At length, when the silence in the little house had stretched long enough, the young Turo spoke, keeping his voice low.

"Hakura Kili and all the Spirits, Nagaro! Ye really scared me. First it sounded like ye *were* dying, and then, when ye said *that...*"

"I'm sorry." Nagaro leaned his back against the wall. "In the dream, I was trying to die, and something wouldn't let me, and just then, you woke me. That's all."

"That's *all*? Nagaro, why would ye be trying t' die?"

"I don't know," Nagaro said wearily. "There was pain in the dream, but even before the pain started, I was looking for a good place to die. It seemed I knew what was coming. I very nearly did die, too. The doors were right in front of me. The void was right there."

Taru's eyes were round with horror. "What would ha' happened if I hadn't wakened ye?"

"I suppose I would have wakened on my own when the dream ended."

"Ye *suppose?*"

"Well, of course." Nagaro studied his friend's anxious face. "It was a *dream*, Taru," he said patiently. "A memory dream about something that happened in the *past*. I almost died *then*, not *now*." He rubbed his forehead, trying to think. "The green-eyed girl was there. She was trying to hold me back. I think she wanted to get someone to 'help.' Maybe she did—even though I told her not to—" He saw the look on his friend's face. "Honestly, Taru, dreams don't kill people."

"I don't know..." Taru was shaking his head, his eyes still haunted. "Ye didn't hear yourself, Nagaro. Ye kept screaming, and screaming—like someone was tearin' ye apart or something. I've never heard anyone scream like that before in my life!"

Kept screaming and screaming... Nagaro stiffened. "I have," he said, suddenly appalled. He could hear it in his mind... a voice... a woman's voice... screaming and screaming... over and over. "*No!*" he cried, because suddenly he knew. He clamped his hands over his ears, trying futilely to shut out the memory of the sound. "Oh no! Vothra, *no!* It was *her*—the Lady in Gray! *She died like that!*"

"How? What happened?"

"I don't know!" As suddenly as it had come, the memory was gone. But he knew what the image was that went with those screams. That beautiful, quiet, graceful woman—the strongest and wisest person he had ever known—had died, screaming and writhing in agony.

The terrible wrongness of that death made him feel sick. He leaned his head against the cold stone of the wall and shut his eyes to hide his tears. After a moment, he felt Taru's hand on his shoulder as the other youth tried awkwardly to comfort him.

A little later he found the strength to speak again. "That's *how* she died, but I don't know *why*. And it seems as if the same thing happened to me—in the dream I just had. It was almost the same, except that for some reason I didn't die..."

"What could it possibly have been?" Taru wondered.

"I don't know!"

Taru clearly didn't know what else to say, and Nagaro needed to sleep. So he curled up on the fern leaves under his blanket. Taru insisted on leaving the candle burning, and tried to sit up and watch, but Nagaro closed his eyes.

Weary though he was, sleep didn't immediately come. He dreaded what he might dream, but it wasn't the ordeal in the harness shed that he feared. It was instead the thought of reliving the final agony of his Lady Guardian. Finally, too weary to think about what Vothra could or couldn't do, he silently prayed: *Please, Vothra, I don't want to see that... or hear that in my dreams... Please just let me sleep...* Then he at last relaxed and let the tide of oblivion take him.

*

The shining image of Vothra's sign, that had been called the "circle-within-a-circle-joined," was floating in the darkness before his eyes.

The sign faded... and out of the darkness came the Lady in Gray, with a face still and pale and eyes that seemed to look right into his soul. She spoke to him, and afterwards when he awoke, he remembered every word with perfect clarity.

"Do not grieve long for me," she said, her voice like gentle music. "Vothra gathers, and soon I will join that gathering, for which I have so long prepared. It is with Vothra's aid that I send you this, my Death Dream. I cannot give you strength to face your own end. That you must find for yourself. I can only offer you this council for your spirit's peace: Do not allow anger to rule you in the moment when you have power. You must remain true to yourself, although you have just cause for anger. Remember what is written in the Book of Vothra concerning pain. It will help you in your ordeal which surely is to come. 'All pain ends, if only in death, and death is not an end, but the path to a new beginning.' Remember, and farewell."

The dream didn't wake him so much as it simply faded, leaving the sign of Vothra floating again before his eyes. That image faded too, and he found that he was awake, lying on his fern leaf bed with the first faint light of dawn tinting the oiled skin on the window.

He lay there quietly, staring up at the beams that supported the roof. *He knew he had dreamed that dream before.* And he found that he felt better, for his Lady Guardian had surely gotten her wish to be one with Vothra. It helped to know that...

And she had warned him about anger...

Taru was sleeping soundly, curled in his own bed. The candle had guttered in a frozen puddle of wax on the floor between them.

*

"I don't like it, Nagaro. It gives me shivers."

That was Taru's reaction. They were getting dressed and Nagaro had just described the second dream and the sense that he had dreamed it before.

"What *is* a Death Dream, anyway?"

Nagaro knew the answer. Perhaps it had come with the dream. "It used to be, long ago—before the time of the Rithral Lords—that Vothra would help each person who died to send one message, in the form of a dream, to someone left among the living. Those were called Death Dreams." He paused, and his eyes clouded. "The Lady in Gray must have died some time ago, and that's when the dream first came to me. This was just a memory of it."

"Where'd the memory come from then? Who sent it this time?"

"Vothra maybe... Just before I fell asleep, I prayed to Vothra."

Taru started pulling on his pants. "What did that mean about anger and pain... and *death?*"

Nagaro's fingers paused in the midst of lacing his tirkyl. "It must have been something about the bad thing that happened to me—that's being kept from me. That passage from the Writings, 'all pain ends...' is meant to help a person face pain, or death, with courage."

"Right. That's why I don't like it. Why did your Lady in Gray think ye'd be facing things like that?"

"She knew what was coming. She believed I was going to die—and soon. And I was repeating those very words from the Writings in the dream about the harness shed. So that must have happened *after* she sent me her Death Dream."

"Well anyway," Taru cut in, "If it's an old dream, whatever it was must be over already—and ye're still alive. So it's all right, isn't it?"

"I suppose so..." Nagaro had finished dressing, and he now rose to follow Taru to breakfast. But he wasn't sure of his answer. He *had* almost died in that harness shed. And it didn't feel finished.

*

By unspoken agreement, they didn't talk about the harness-shed dream in the days that followed. At first Nagaro was aware of Taru watching him surreptitiously as if fearful he might slip into a waking dream and act out some death wish. But nothing happened. No visions came, and the nights were free of disturbing dreams.

After a week of this, Taru finally said, "I don't understand, Nagaro. Is it all over?"

Nagaro shook his head. "I still don't know what happened. Maybe the Spirit of the White Flower is just letting me rest."

The absence of both dreams and visions did indeed allow Nagaro to rest, and to do other things. Winter was waning, and their lives were easing with the warming weather. Nagaro and Taru had finally finished making the wooden practice swords, and the lessons in swordsmanship began.

Whenever it was daylight and they had no other duties, the sound of their sticks cracking against each other could be heard. They went at it outside when the weather permitted, and if it didn't, they moved inside when Olomi permitted. Taru's reading and writing lessons were relegated to the evenings. Nagaro used what he remembered from his own instruction. He worked at building up Taru's skills in a systematic way and drilled him hard.

Taru quickly mastered several methods of disarming an opponent, but disarming Nagaro if the other youth didn't choose to allow it was another matter. Still, it was a matter of pride with Taru, and he persisted in trying to take Nagaro by surprise. Such tactics usually evoked reflexive responses from Nagaro so that Taru got the worst of it. One day he threw down his weapon in disgust after another failed attempt.

"I'll never be able t' do it!"

Nagaro stooped to pick up the wooden sword and handed it back to his friend. "I've had three years of training, Taru, and you've had a few weeks. You're doing very well. I know a few more tricks, that's all."

"About a hundred, I'd say! And ye're so *fast!* Either ye're terribly good at this, Nagaro, or I'm just terribly bad."

Nagaro considered his friend soberly. "I think maybe I *am* good," he admitted. "My Lady Guardian said Fendar was a skilled swordmaster— one of the best—and he seemed pleased with me. Near the end of the third year, I overheard him telling her there wasn't much more he could teach me. Towards the end, I think I really beat him several times too. The trouble is, he could have been playing with me, and I've never fought anyone else, so I don't know for certain."

"Well, if everyone else is as good as ye are, there's no hope for *me!* That's sure."

Nagaro laughed. "I felt completely useless at the beginning too, Taru. So it's surely too soon to say. Now stand on guard, and let's try that last defense again."

Olomi watched them practicing sometimes. She wasn't smiling anymore, for this was clearly not some boyish game. Both young men were taking it far too seriously, and Nagaro's skill was obvious, even to her untrained eye. She looked at him more and more as if she were seeing something she'd never seen before.

So, too, did Jomo. The Turowan fisherman might have no use for swordsmanship, but there was a part of him that couldn't help admiring such obvious prowess in any manly art.

"Do ye know what I think?" he said privately to Olomi one day, after they had been watching the two young men. "I think Nagaro would be very dangerous with a real sword. And I don't think he was ever meant t' be a fisherman."

Olomi nodded silently. This was not a harmless, useful skill, like hunting with a bow or riding a horse. Swordsmanship was a deadly art that had no proper purpose save to kill.

*

"Do ye think ye could kill a man?"

It was Taru who asked the question. He and Nagaro stood beside the woodshed, breathing hard after a particularly vigorous bout. Despite the chill morning air, they were both sweating.

Nagaro frowned. "I don't know," he said. "I suppose if someone is trying to kill you, you do what you must. If you're going to be any kind of a warrior, on sea or land, you have to be prepared to kill your enemy."

"I don't think it'd be hard t' kill a Mahuk." Taru spoke with conviction. "The way they make slaves o' poor honest folk."

"Well, it's Mahuk that we'll be fighting if we join the Fleet." Nagaro paused, then added, "Your parents have been watching us, Taru. They must surely guess something of what we mean to do. I feel badly that we haven't told them anything."

Taru wasn't concerned. "We'll tell 'em in good time," he said easily. "Ye were right about what ye said before. Ye have to wait." He paused and glanced sidelong at Nagaro. "Ye still haven't had any more dreams?"

Nagaro shook his head. "No—except ordinary ones about hunting and fishing and doing sword practice. I wish *something* more would come. Vedorel is half gone and Madrel is coming. It was in Madrel that I came here, so it's been nearly a full year that I've been 'Nagaro'."

"I thought ye liked the name."

"I do. It feels very... *comfortable* after all this time. I wonder if my own name will feel strange when I finally remember it." Nagaro frowned, then shrugged. "Come on. We'd best put the practice swords away. We promised we'd shoot something for dinner."

*

The approach of spring meant they could at least consider taking the boat out again, but spring was also a time for mists along that part of the coast. There were morning mists that sometimes persisted into afternoon, and the mist returned in the evenings with the cooling of the air. Often there wasn't enough time in between to do much fishing, and if the mist took too long to clear there was no point in taking the boat out at all. Jomo chafed at the inactivity on mist-locked days. Taru and Nagaro just shrugged and went hunting.

They ranged far up the wooded hillside one afternoon in search of game, which was still scarce after the hard winter. Though the morning mist still hung over the water, it had retreated from the land. The snow was long gone, and the damp earth wore a haze of new green where the first blades of grass were springing. Bare gray branches were beginning to bud. Even the evergreen pines and firs on the upper slopes were putting out new growth of a lighter, brighter shade of green.

"I don't understand why ye did so much hunting," Taru said as they skirted a greening thicket.

Nagaro shrugged. At least he knew the answer now. "It was part of my work to help keep meat on the table."

Taru stopped to stare at him in surprise. "I didn't think lords and ladies worked at all, and I always thought they had plenty of everything—because o' the tax."

"There were only three farms that paid tax to my Lady Guardian, and part of it went to the crown. We had our own goats and chickens and a vegetable garden. But aside from that, there was only one tenth part of the harvest from three farms that had to support a household of five—because we had three hired people. From the time I was old enough to do anything useful, I always worked. I helped with anything I could around the house and grounds, and I did service to the tributary farmers."

"Service *to* the farmers?"

"Yes." Nagaro's gaze grew distant. "It's an old idea, but my Lady Guardian took it very seriously. It comes from the Second Corner of Kelorin Law—the one that says lords should be chosen by the people that they lead. The people support the lord, so the lord should serve the people in return."

Taru was eyeing him askance. "Where d' ye get all this, Nagaro?"

"From a book of Kelorin law. My Lady Guardian had a great many books."

"Did she make ye read them?"

"Of course not. I just did."

"Why?"

"I liked to. And there wasn't much else to do on winter evenings."

They hit a particularly steep part of the hillside and were silent, saving their breath, until they paused at last to rest in a spot that offered a wide view of the forest and the bay. The fog lay like a blanket drawn up to the shore. White fading to gray, it covered Wotana Bay and stretched away to the western horizon, interrupted only by the blue-green crests of some of the islands that rose high enough to thrust themselves clear of it. The road was visible as a mud-colored ribbon winding along the forest's margin, and the bare slope beyond it led down to the pale sand of the beach. Away to the right they could see a gray jumble of slate roofs that was the of the town of Wotana. Jomo's little house lay directly below them, a thin trickle of smoke rising from its chimney to lose itself in the clear air.

Standing there, Nagaro realized that this was the widest view he'd ever had of the place that had become his world, and he found himself turning to the south, the direction from which he believed he had come. The barren forest stretched away in that direction to the limit of vision.

But there was something moving on the dirt road, moving slowly northward. It was an old gray horse pulling a canvas-covered wagon. Both were familiar. *So*, he thought, *the woman with the gold earring and the old man who travels with her must have decided to come back.* He realized that he hadn't seen them for months. He'd assumed they had moved on with the coming of winter. Seeing the woman reminded him of the day of his waking. He raised his eyes from the wagon to stare again into the south.

"If I was running away from something, what was it?" He spoke his thought aloud. "And *where* could I have been running from, if it wasn't Lord Bron's hunting lodge? There's nothing out there."

Beside him Taru nodded. "I know," he said. "Is it time t' do some more shaking?"

"Maybe. But, *how*?"

Taru had no answer, and they returned their attention to hunting. They startled a grouse, and Nagaro shot it on the wing. Some time later, he spotted a rabbit and came to a halt, handing the bow to Taru and whispering, "Your turn." It was a clear shot, and well within Taru's skill. Soon they were heading back down the slope with their prizes.

"Did your Lady in Gray *make* ye work for the farmers?" Taru asked as they were nearing the bottom.

Nagaro frowned. "She told me to do it, if that's what you mean. But I never really minded. She did service too. She used to make clothes for Bodano's two little children. She made warm clothes from the furs of animals I killed as well, and gave them to whoever needed them. And she tended the sick. She bought herbs and medicines from Luka—an old Turowan medicine woman who came every autumn and set up her tent in our pasture."

"Service from a lord." Taru shook his head, bemused. "I'd like t' see that. But we don't get much in the way o' service from Lord Bron."

"I've noticed you don't," Nagaro answered, dryly. "And he has a law against poaching, too. My lady let the householders hunt in our bit of woods as much as they needed. If the winter was hard and the game was scarce, we all suffered alike."

As they stepped out onto the road, they nearly walked into the woman with the gold earring. She was moving northward along the road with her basket on her arm.

Nagaro managed to say, "Good day, Zirdyn."

She returned his greeting with a trace of her enigmatic smile. A thought occurred to him, and he asked, "Have you heard any news from the south?"

She looked keenly at him. "That I have," she said. "And I expect ye'll not have heard it here, since it comes from Lankura. The princess was wed in Genorel, t' Gillard Marchent."

Nagaro seemed to feel a little shadow cross his heart.

"Well, it's not as if that's unexpected," Taru put in jauntily.

The woman gave Taru a rather cool glance. "No," she said. "Not unexpected. Good day t' ye both." Then she turned and continued on her way.

Taru looked after her and shook his head. "Strange woman," he said. "And I didn't think it was the season for mushrooms."

Nagaro frowned. "I'm not sure mushrooms have a season." He'd noted that the wagon was nowhere in sight. "I wonder where she makes her camp."

Taru shrugged and started on down the last slope to the house. "I could scarcely care less," he flung over his shoulder. "It's not as if she's anything to us, or we to her."

Nagaro sighed. "You're right of course." He hurried after his friend.

*

It was Taru who told his parents the news at dinner. "We heard it from the traveling-wagon woman," he said.

"Ye mean Boka?" Olomi asked. "The one with the little ring in her ear?"

"Aye, that's the one."

"Genorel." Jomo shook his head. "They scarcely waited a month out o' respect for Fargil."

Olomi's face tightened. "And to wed her to Gillard! I *had* hoped the king would have more care for his daughter."

Nagaro hastily swallowed the mouthful he'd been chewing. "I know everyone here liked Fargil better, but no one's ever told me what they have against Gillard."

Olomi didn't answer, but she pressed her lips together disapprovingly.

Jomo cleared his throat. "Gillard's got a hungry way about him when it comes to young women," he explained. "He's been in trouble more 'n once for having his way with this one or that one. He's had t' fight some challenges over it. And so far, he's always come out on top, so there's been nothing t' make him change his ways. They say he's got a scar on his face from one o' those challenges, but he nearly killed the other man. He'll use that poor girl hard, I'm thinking—and be looking around for other seas t' fish at the same time." Jomo sighed and shook his head. "It's a bad turn o' luck for the princess—her first husband wasn't any kind o' man, and the second one's the wrong kind."

That was the end of the conversation on the subject, but Nagaro's thoughts kept circling around it all the rest of the evening and even after he lay down to sleep that night. The idea of the young princess being mistreated bothered him a great deal.

When he finally slipped into slumber—after weeks of having dreamt of nothing more sinister than hunting and fishing—he dreamed of the green-eyed girl.

Chapter 12: A Turn For The Worse

She was teaching him a dance she called "Road to Seralind." They were in the bedchamber that he thought was hers—the one with the big bed with the wooden canopy. This time it was day. The room was brightened by sunlight streaming through a pair of windows in the wall opposite the bed. As they moved through the dance's figures, they wove in and out of the two bright patches of sunlight on the polished floor.

The dance was done as a couple, moving sometimes around the outline of a circle, and sometimes into the circle and back out again. They had no music, so the girl was humming the tune, breaking off at intervals to explain the steps. She gave good instructions and he learned the dance quite easily. It seemed to him that one part of his mind was following the girl's words while another part—the real part—was paying little attention to the steps and far more to the graceful movement of her body next to his. The dance required them to move side by side, each with one arm about the other's waist and the other hand resting on their partner's. He was aware of her slender body, warm and supple against his encircling arm, and the touch of his hand on hers. For once he wasn't wishing he were somewhere else.

They finished the dance and she drew away, turning to smile at him. He felt himself smile automatically in return.

"That was really quite good," she said. "I believe I could teach you anything." Her eyes clouded for a moment as her brows knit in a frown, but whatever the thought was, she seemed to put it aside, for she smiled again. "I'll teach you some more dances. Would you like that?"

"Yes." The word sounded stiffly polite, an automatic answer, yet it wasn't false for all that.

"Which one would you like to learn next?" she asked. "The Balandir? Or maybe Tavinskala, or 'The Ivy Vine'?"

"You are very beautiful."

He was aware that the phrase sounded stilted—aware of having said it too many times—but just at that moment, the words really did seem to fit. She was wearing an ivory-colored gown with blue and gold embroidery, and the sunlight from the window was finding golden highlights in her hair. Her eyes sparkled like liquid emeralds. She was undeniably beautiful, yet for some reason, all pleasant feelings were swept away by a wave of bitter anger the moment he uttered the words.

The dream dissolved, but the emotion still hung there, making his stomach knot.

He lay in the darkness, trying to make sense of what he was feeling. Had he been angry at the girl? No, he knew she was innocent, though he couldn't say how he knew it. Some of his anger had surely been directed outward... but some of it was directed inward as well. He frowned. *He had been angry with himself... Why?*

Then he knew. It was the way his thoughts had been straying. He hadn't *wanted* to find the girl attractive—hadn't wanted to let himself want her. *But why not?* That he didn't know—had no way of knowing...

Eventually he slept again, but when he awoke in the morning the dream about the girl immediately leaped back into his mind and the knot returned to his stomach.

*

Taru's reaction to news of a new dream was quick and to the point. "Does this mean ye'll finally get all the answers?"

"I don't know." Nagaro let his breath out in a weary sigh. They were just about to begin sword practice on the level ground beside the woodshed, and Nagaro was stretching his muscles, his wooden sword in his hand. "But the anniversary of the day I came here must be very close. It was near the end of Madrel."

"What? Do ye think the spirit is aiming t' make it a year?"

That very idea had occurred to Nagaro during breakfast, and once it was in his head, it was impossible to get it out again, even though there was no real reason to assume any such thing. The hope—and the dread—in his heart were immune to rational persuasion. "There's been more than enough time for the spirit to show me anything it wanted," he said. "Why did it *not* start right away—and then stop and start again— except to make it take a full year?"

Taru nodded sagely. "Aye, that's the sort o' thing spirits do. They like round numbers. What did ye find out this time? In your dream?"

"Not much, really..." Nagaro made an experimental lunge to stretch his leg. "She was teaching me a dance."

"A *dance?*" Taru stared at him. "Ye mean like what we do at festival? Hold hands in a circle, and take three steps t' th' right, and stamp, and three steps t' th' left?"

Nagaro shook his head. "Not that kind... a court dance... the kind high-born folk do."

"Oh. So... were ye going to have t' dance *at the court?*"

"Not necessarily. I mean... I don't know. She was teaching it to me, and I was learning it, and, at the end... something made me angry..." Nagaro found he really didn't want to describe the dream any further. He suspected that Taru would understand some of it *too* well, and the rest of it not well enough. He covered his discomfort by making another lunge, ostensibly to stretch the other leg.

Taru was doing his own stretches. "Well, *I'd* surely be angry if I had to learn some fancy court dance," he said as he lunged. "But I'd think your spirit would have better things t' show ye than *that.*"

"I'm... ah... sure it will." Nagaro straightened out of his second lunge and raised his sword in a salute. "On your guard, Taru!"

They circled. When Taru attacked him, Nagaro parried. Inwardly, he relaxed, focusing on the straightforward demands of sword practice. He wanted to recover his lost memories, but there were things about the dream he would rather not talk about.

He'd been married to a girl he didn't want to love...

*

That night, he dreamed he was standing, looking out of a window. It was daylight outside, bright and clear, and the window was open, letting in air tinged with the scent of brine. It was a high window, on a second or third floor, and he could see a long way. There was a large garden laid out below, in which he could make out the deep pink of roses and the white of *farusia* blossoms. The garden sloped upwards as the land rose towards the crest of a ridge, topped by a wall. There was a sort of saddle in the ridge with the lowest point directly in front of him, and through that low point, he could see a distant patch of blue-gray that he knew must be the sea.

He knew it was all he'd ever seen of the sea, and all he would ever see of it. A poignant sorrow welled up in him. It was hard, so very hard, to be fated to die so young. Vothra would guide his passing, and his spirit would go on to another life, but he didn't feel finished with this one, not by far. There was so much that he'd never done, or seen, or known... so much he would never have a chance to do, or see, or know. It was terribly unfair. Anger came then, white and hot, burning the sorrow away and searing a knife-like gash across his soul.

The intensity of the anger woke him. He lay in the darkness for a long moment, tense and trembling, before his rage was swept away by a wave of gratitude as he realized that he was awake and it had only been a dream.

But it was also a memory. For he had been there—staring out that window. He had felt those feelings and thought those thoughts. It made him doubly grateful that the fate he had foreseen had not come to pass. After another moment, he realized that he had glimpsed this memory on the day of his awakening, when Olomi had asked him if he'd never seen the sea. Even then, the sight of it had stirred him. Now he thought he knew why, and he offered up silent thanks to Lokundas for the gift of standing on the shore and watching the waves roll in, and of sailing on the sea.

Still, the dream left a lingering unease. It appeared he had cheated death... or had somehow kept death from cheating him...

*

Taru's reaction was predictable. "More about dying," he said, with a shake of his head. Then he added, "But obviously ye didn't. So ye needn't worry about it."

The two young men were hunting again, and Nagaro now paused with the bow in his hand, turning to meet his friend's eyes. "I can't just ignore it, Taru. It fits in with all my dreams about running away from something. It suggests I was a prisoner." He felt a chill and glanced about him at the greening woods.

The setting could hardly have been more incongruous for speaking about death. The air around them was still laden with moisture, but the sun was setting the mist aglow, and the warmth of its light was unmistakable. Flowers were beginning to open, and the wood would soon be hopping with rabbits and aflutter with grouse.

Nagaro shook off his dread. "I was supposed to have died, Taru. The Lady in Gray expected it. I expected it. But for some reason it didn't happen."

"What was supposed t' kill ye?" Taru was curious in spite of himself.

"I suppose it was whatever came on me in the harness shed. Some kind of illness..."

Taru shivered visibly. "Well ye must ha' got better," he said hastily. "Now can we talk about something else?"

Nagaro frowned. He'd been chased through the woods and attacked in a dark hallway. He'd been a prisoner waiting to die... and married to a girl he didn't love. The pieces didn't fit together. He would have liked his friend's help with this puzzle, but Taru was too squeamish about any mention of death. He sighed. "Right," he said, looking around at the newly-green woods. "Let's go that way." He pointed ahead through the trees to a spot where the light was brighter. "It looks like a good place for rabbits."

*

Nagaro's dreams continued in the days that followed. The four Leithian men made their reappearance. No longer only faces bending over him, they now appeared as full figures in diverse settings. It was as if the Spirit of the White Flower were presenting him with a cast of players, though they still remained nameless and never addressed him by name.

"What are they doing?" Taru asked.

"Walking together. Talking. Sitting at dinner..."

It was the end of a dreary mist-wrapped day in early Madrel. The two youths had just finished restocking the woodshed with timber that the sea had cast up on the fog-shrouded beach. They were sitting side by side in the shed's open doorway, talking and watching the drifting mist. The world might as well have ended twenty feet from where they sat. The once-bare earth of their practice field now sported a carpet of star flower, sand verbena, and heal-all, a carpet that began at their feet and faded away into the pale gray fog. The plants were already in bloom, though the colors of the flowers were muted by the fog-filtered light. The air was almost still, and redolent of the sea. There was no other sound in the world but their voices and the soft, ever-present rush and hiss of invisible waves breaking on the unseen shore.

"Sitting at *dinner?*" Taru gave him a disbelieving look.

"Yes. At a long table, with a linen cloth on it. With silver knives and forks, and china dishes, and glass goblets..."

Taru's eyes grew round. "They must be great lords!"

"I don't know about that..." Nagaro frowned. "I mean, they must have had money, surely. They're also always very well-dressed. But merchants have money. And sometimes I see them alone, sitting at a little table beside the door in a plain, bare room..."

"What d' they talk about?"

"I don't know." Nagaro's frown deepened. He bent and plucked a stalk of heal-all. The action shook loose a shower of tiny droplets that had condensed out of the fog. "They're never talking to *me*, and I can't really hear what they're saying. But I can read their expressions... and I'm learning things..."

"What sort o' things?"

"That the bearded man is the leader. The others treat him with respect—or at least they make a show of it. The man with curly red hair is the only one I'd trust. His smile looks honest. He disagrees with the bearded man the way friends disagree, without getting angry. The big, blond man with the red face—"

"The one that looks like Lord Bron?"

"Yes. He *argues.* And when he does, his face gets redder. He always backs down and smiles, but the smile goes away as soon as the bearded man isn't looking. And the youngest man—the one with the scar on his face—never disagrees *or* argues. By the look in his eyes, he'd like to, but instead he just bows and smiles. There's calculation behind his eyes, but the bearded man doesn't see it. He only sees the smiles and the bows, the trappings of respect."

"Oh." Taru's eyes had begun to glaze. It was too much for him, and he didn't know what to make of any of it.

They sat in silence for a long moment. Finally Taru asked, "What are *you* doing in these dreams—while the men are walking and talking and eating their dinners?"

Nagaro was toying with the sprig of heal-all. He held it to his nose. The pungent smell of the crushed stem was strong enough to overpower the pervasive sea-scent that wafted through the mist. "Nothing really," he said. "Just standing... and looking... or sitting... or eating my own dinner..." *And feeling angry...* But he didn't want to say that.

"Well, it all sounds quite boring t' *me*." Taru got to his feet, brushing off the seat of his pants. "I can't think why your Spirit is showing ye such dull things."

"I suppose the men played parts in what happened during that last year of my life." Nagaro stood up as well. He started to discard the stalk of heal-all, then decided to give it to Olomi instead. She brewed a tea from the leaves that she believed could ward off illness. "At least these aren't really *bad* dreams—not like the ones about the hawk-faced man."

Taru cast him a sympathetic glance as he set off through the mist, following the wall of the house to keep his bearings. "It's almost time for *our* dinner," he said.

Nagaro shivered and went after him.

The Leithian men did nothing worse than make him angry, but the hawk-faced man was another matter. That sallow countenance, with its hooked beak of a nose and fierce black eyes, always struck him with terror. The man's absence from the most recent dreams was odd considering how often he'd appeared in the past, sitting at the table in that bare little room. Nagaro drew a worried breath. It was too much to hope that he was done with that ominous apparition. No, the hawk-faced man would return. When he did, would it signal a turn for the worse?

Nagaro paused at the door of the little house and took his turn to stamp the water from his boots on the flat stone that served as a door step. He glanced over his shoulder into the drifting mist. Anything might be out there, anything at all. His past was out there somewhere... His future might be waiting. But for now, he had to go in and eat his dinner and pass an hour or so until it was time to seek his bed. His heart filled up with dread like a cup of dark water at the thought that the hawk-faced man might visit him that night. Hurriedly he stepped inside and closed the door.

*

The evening passed as he'd imagined it would, and when he went to bed, he did dream. But the dream was one he'd never dreamed before—and nothing he could possibly have expected.

He lay immobile on a narrow bed in the small, bare room where the hawk-faced man had so often sat at his table, writing. This time, however, the bearded Leithian was there. The man had drawn up a chair and was seated beside the bed, talking to him.

The tone of the man's voice suggested earnestness, but the pale blue eyes revealed too little of his soul. "I never meant you harm," the man was saying. "I swear it by all the Gods. I've never wished your death, but I'm afraid that... circumstances... now make it inevitable."

The man was watching him closely, as if looking for some sign of a response. But he seemingly lay frozen, incapable of speech or movement in spite of the anger rising in him.

"I would save your life if I could," the man continued. "But it is beyond my power. Only give me an heir, and I swear I will make the end easy. I'll find some merciful way... There's no reason you should suffer... *as she did...*" The pale glance slid away from him.

Inwardly, he raged. He would have struck the man if he could have moved, and his mind was screaming the words he couldn't say: *I will give you nothing, you murderer! Do you think I'm so afraid of pain?*

The man's pale gaze came back to him, and when next the Leithian spoke, he seemed to be trying his best to be persuasive. But Nagaro felt only cold fury at the words. Mutely he struggled to move... to sit up... to lash out...

"I have given you my daughter," the man was saying, "the most precious thing I possess. Is it such a hard thing I ask of you? After all, the girl is gentle and kind... and very fair to look upon. Only give me an heir—it will be your heir as well. Why die and leave nothing behind?"

Whatever else the bearded man might have said, Nagaro didn't hear it. He'd been struggling ever more desperately against the paralysis of the dream, and at that moment he at last jerked free of it and sat up among the tattered fern leaves of his bed, his heart hammering against his ribs and his fists clenched in rage.

It was morning, and Taru was staring at him. "What's the matter, Nagaro? Ye look like ye want to punch someone."

"I had another dream..." He stopped and took a deep breath, deliberately unclenching his fists.

"About the hawk-faced man?"

"No!" Nagaro shook his head. "The bearded one!" In spite of his efforts to calm himself, he felt his jaw muscles tighten, and his words had come out harsh and angry-sounding. He took another deep breath. "I can't talk about it yet. Maybe after breakfast."

Taru gave him a searching look. "All right," he said after a moment, and he got up to open the small window. "Just as I thought," he remarked as he peered out. "It's thick as Mother's fish stew out there. We won't be sailing for an hour or two at least. The ferns are growing tall along the stream now, and it's time we had fresh fern leaves for our beds. We'll cut some after breakfast. We can talk then."

*

"I don't understand." Taru paused with a wet fern leaf in his hands. "Ye're saying that the bearded man is the green-eyed girl's *father?* And he was going t' kill ye if ye *didn't* get her with child?"

They had found a particularly lush bed of ferns where the stream exited the forest's edge. The mist was thinner under the trees, but still everything was dripping.

"*No!* I was going to die no matter what!" Nagaro slashed hard at the fern stems. The knife he carried was an old one of Taru's. Its blade was notched, and it never held an edge for long, but it was sharp enough for this work and the fern leaves jerked suddenly free in his hand, showering him with water. "The man was saying that he'd give me a merciful death if I gave him what he wanted—an heir—"

"And ye weren't going t' do that?"

"Of course not! However I was going to die, I'm sure he had a hand in it! I'm sure he was responsible for the death of my Lady Guardian too. I wasn't going to give him *anything!*"

Nagaro flung the fern leaves on the ground. He'd managed to stifle his emotions during breakfast, but as he spoke of the dream now, his anger welled up like hot blood. It was more than mere anger. It was pure hatred—hatred that started with the bearded Leithian and extended to all of the others. He wanted to stop them from forcing him to do things... from hurting him... He wanted to stop them from hurting anyone ever again...

Glancing at the knife in his hand, he suddenly saw a vivid image of that hand plunging the knife into someone's belly. The action was accompanied by a surge of fierce exultation, borne on the tide of his rage. The next instant, the exultation was replaced by horror. *Had the image been a memory of something he'd done? Or merely something he'd wanted to do?*

"Vothra!" The knife fell from his nerveless fingers, landing point downwards, standing straight up in the soft earth like an omen. "Vothra save me," he murmured. "Is that the answer? *Did I do murder?*"

The morning seemed for a moment to close in around him and he heard a roaring in his ears. What did the *Book of Vothra* say? *Vengeance does not become the noble heart. It is a poison of the spirit...*

Taru was eyeing his friend warily. He'd never seen Nagaro as angry as he'd been a moment before—nor as shaken as he now appeared. "Are ye all right, Nagaro?" he asked.

"Yes... *No.*" Nagaro drew a long shuddering breath and let it out slowly, trying to let both anger and horror run out with it. Stooping, he picked up the knife. He stared at it, holding it gingerly. No new images came into his mind. He looked at Taru. "I just imagined putting a knife into someone's belly," he said. "I don't know if it was a memory. Vothra knows I was angry enough to do it." He sat down heavily on a stone. Laying the knife on the ground, he took his head in his hands.

Taru found a seat as well. "Nagaro," he said, "ye mustn't take it so. Ye don't really know what happened."

Nagaro spoke dully. "It would make sense, though—if I killed the bearded man... or the hawk-faced one." He looked up into Taru's eyes. "I would have had to have been terribly angry to do it because it goes against Vothra's teaching." He paused. "Do you remember the first dream I had—a year ago? Vothra said, 'Rest your spirit, and be healed.' Healed of hurt, I thought it meant. But it could have meant healed of anger—they're both wounds of the spirit. I couldn't understand why my name was being hidden from me, when I've remembered so many other things. But it makes sense if I'm being sought somewhere by that name... *for murder...*"

"But we didn't hear of any murder!" Taru objected. "Not at Sobring Hall or anywhere else."

"It could have been hushed up. High-born folk hate scandals."

"But ye said the bearded man murdered the Lady in Gray! So he would ha' deserved it!" Taru's eyes begged for agreement.

Nagaro frowned. "I don't *know* that he did. I suppose it *might* save me from execution if I had just cause..."

The words of the Lady's Death Dream came to him: "*Do not allow anger to rule you... though you have good cause to be angry... You must be true to yourself...*" The Lady had warned him against this pitfall of the spirit. Had he fallen into the trap in spite of her warning? Had his anger driven him to vengeance?

There were pages and pages in the *Book of Vothra* on the subject of killing. Since he'd set his heart on joining the Royal Fleet or the City Guard, Nagaro had read all those pages with great interest. He knew that Vothra would prefer it were unnecessary to kill at all. Just as clearly, Vothra recognized that some reasons for killing were more acceptable than others. Self defense or protection of the innocent were acceptable reasons. Armed combat could be acceptable when a city or country found itself unjustly under attack. Vengeance, on the other hand, was not.

Nagaro couldn't hope to explain all of this to Taru, but he felt he had to say something. "The bearded man was never armed, so far as I can remember," he said. "So killing him the way I just imagined would have been murder. And if I did murder, I'd be no better than he was. It's not good to hate a man enough to kill him."

"I hate the Mahuk enough t' kill *them*," Taru protested. "And ye said ye could do that too, didn't ye?"

"I think I could, in battle. When you're facing an enemy, sword to sword, you both know it's slay or be slain, and you're both prepared to kill and to die. Even in battle, though, it isn't good to let anger rule you."

Taru sighed. "Well, ye've an awfully fine sense o' honor considering the man was going t' kill ye!"

Rising, Nagaro picked up the knife. Very deliberately, he grasped a handful of fern leaves and cut the stems with a quick, clean stroke. "He was going to give me an easy death if I did what he wanted. But I chose the hard death—the one he said was 'inevitable.' I think that's what I was trying to do in the harness shed, Taru—trying to die *my* way, rather than his." That much made sense to him. He also understood now why he hadn't wanted to find the green-eyed girl attractive...

Taru stood up. "I still say ye're only guessing about what happened, Nagaro," he said. "Ye should wait and see. Wait until your Spirit o' the White Flower lets ye remember the rest of it. I'll wager ye'll find it's not as bad as ye think."

"I expect that you're right." Nagaro spoke as calmly as he could. He wanted to believe the words, but his heart misgave him.

Taru was looking around, as if looking for some way to change the subject. The morning had brightened considerably since they'd entered the forest. "The mist is lifting," he said. "Father may want t' sail soon. We've cut about as much as we can carry. Let's take these back t' the house and see what the weather looks like out on the bay."

Nagaro was glad to sheath his knife and pick up an armful of fern leaves. It wasn't easy, though, to put the dream out of his mind. Walking behind Taru, he tried to remember whether there had been a knife anywhere in any of his dreams. He couldn't recall seeing one, and that made him feel a little better.

They had stepped out from under the eaves of the forest, directly above the house, and were descending towards the road. Intent as he was on his own thoughts, Nagaro was taken by surprise when Taru suddenly stopped dead in front of him.

"Nagaro," Taru said, and there was a peculiar edge to his voice. "What kind o' ship is that, there in the bay?"

Nagaro stared. The mist was evaporating under the warmth of the morning sun. Out over the bay, it had lifted clear of the water, but fragments of it still drifted on the stirring breeze. Riding in the middle of the bay, the long, low shape of a ship was unmistakable. The details were indistinct, however, for the air between was still heavy with vapor so that lines were softened and colors muted by the distance.

"A war galley!" Nagaro murmured.

"Whose?" Taru had dropped his armload of fern leaves.

Nagaro let his fall as well. "I can't tell. I can't make out the color of her banner."

At that moment, a violent commotion erupted from the house below them. There were shouts—of many voices—Olomi's rising shrill over the rest. A number of figures burst into view from around the corner of the house. They wore uniforms of black and crimson. Swords swung at their sides.

"Mahuk!" Nagaro's stomach twisted.

And then he saw that they were dragging Jomo. The fisherman was fighting like a wildcat. He had his knife out and was wielding it so savagely that he was making it impossible for them to completely subdue him. None of them seemed as yet to have noticed the two youths at the top of the slope above the house.

Taru's reaction was immediate. He gave an anguished cry. "*Father! I'm coming!*" And the next instant, he was plunging down the slope, his knife flashing in his hand.

At the cry, Jomo looked up and saw his son. "No, Taru!" he cried. "*Run for the forest!*" Heedless, Taru pelted on.

It seemed cowardly to think of running away, but Nagaro understood. There were seven or eight Mahuk warriors there, most of them big, burly men. "Come back, Taru!" he cried. "They'll only take you too!" But he might as well have been addressing the western gale. Taru was drawn by a power stronger than sense or reason—the tie of common blood that binds brother to brother and father to son.

Nagaro drew the old notched fishing knife from its sheath. He started after Taru, then stopped again. He couldn't possibly catch up with his friend in time to stop him, and the Mahuk were too many for the three of them to fight. Frantically he looked around for some source of aid, but the nearest house was a quarter mile away to the north along the curve of the bay. The Mahuk longboat was drawn up on the sand near the inlet where Jomo's boat was moored. The raiding party would be gone with their victims long before he could summon help.

He heard a voice call, then, from the forest behind him. He spun and saw a woman standing by the edge of the road. It was the woman with the gold earring, Boka. She was beckoning to him frantically— urging him to save himself. But how could he abandon his friend?

Desperately he swung back to the scene below, just in time to see Taru fling himself at the nearest warrior. He watched in anguish what happened next. Taru didn't manage to land a single blow. The warriors were aware of his coming. His intended victim dodged, grabbing at Taru and throwing him to the ground. Two of the others closed on the young Turo before he could get up. In an instant, they disarmed him and pinned his arms behind him.

Jomo, having helplessly witnessed the capture of his son, sagged in defeat. The two warriors who held him quickly wrested the knife from his hand.

Nagaro stood for one instant more—torn between loyalty to his Turowan family and the knowledge that it would do no good for him to share their fate. In that instant, Olomi joined the fray, emerging from the little house with a wailing cry, bearing a burning branch from the hearth fire.

She could not possibly prevail. This desperate act of courage was only likely to earn her death. Yet she came. Her unbraided hair streamed behind her as she wielded her firebrand with a fury known only to the heart of a woman who sees her chosen man and her only son simultaneously in peril. Her unorthodox assault caught the Mahuk off guard. Some moved to dodge the burning brand. Others circled to outflank her. Taru struggled wildly in the hands of the man who held him. Jomo stood as if transfixed. His eyes were on the figure of his wife, and in those eyes were mingled admiration and despair.

The sight of Olomi in danger was too much for Nagaro. The balance of his indecision tipped.

"*Olomi! No!*" He sprang forward and went charging down the slope at a dead run to hurl himself upon the first Mahuk who moved into his path.

The warriors would probably have made as short work of him as of Taru had they not been distracted by Olomi. As it was, none of them saw him coming. Even so, he fared only a little better than his friend. He managed to knock the sea warrior off balance and to sink his knife into the man's shoulder. The warrior recovered quickly, however, and rounded on him with an oath, striking Nagaro's forearm a savage blow.

Pain stabbed through Nagaro's arm, and his fingers involuntarily loosed their grip on the knife. It flew from his grasp. He dove to retrieve it but was brought up short by an arm suddenly flung around his throat from behind. He struggled, but the arm squeezed, harder and harder, choking him.

His vision began to go gray and he dropped to his knees, scarcely aware of his arms being twisted behind his back. Then, suddenly, the grip on his throat relaxed and he sagged, gasping, in the hands of his captors.

He stumbled to his feet with his arms pinned, his vision clearing just in time to witness Olomi's end. He was aware of Jomo shouting for Olomi to run away, but by the time he looked, she had nowhere left to run. She was trapped between the wall of her own house and a semi-circle of armed warriors. One of the other Mahuk had drawn his sword. The decorations on the man's uniform proclaimed him an officer, the leader of the group. Like the rest of them, he was black-haired, tawny-skinned, and narrow-eyed, and he advanced upon Olomi with a mocking smile.

Olomi held her ground, the smoldering brand raised before her protectively. Her eyes still held defiance. She was only a few paces from Nagaro, but try as he would, he couldn't free himself—couldn't reach her.

The Mahuk captain was flicking his sword at her, toying with her. The other warriors were all shouting things in their tongue, whether taunting Olomi or urging their captain on, Nagaro couldn't tell.

The Mahuk captain could have prolonged the sport, but he saw no profit in it. This fisherman's wife was only a woman, of an inferior race—not worth the trouble. Still, she had angered him by interfering. So, when at length she made a little lunge at him, the warrior captain deftly beat the branch aside and leveled the point of his sword at her breast. Continuing his thrust, he pierced her through with no more ado than had she been a target made of straw.

She fell without a cry, crumpling to the ground and lying still.

"*Olomi!*" The word was wrenched from Nagaro like a sob. The last image his mind held of her was as she lay there on the spring earth, her eyes staring blindly upward at the brilliant blue sky above Wotana Bay, her black-and-silver hair falling among the early star flower and yellow heal-all.

Taru's cry was the inarticulate howl of a wounded animal.

Jomo exploded into motion. Exactly what the fisherman did to free himself Nagaro never knew, but suddenly the warrior who'd been holding him was on the ground, and Jomo had got a knife in his hand. He charged at the Mahuk captain, slashing wildly at him. Caught off guard, the warrior dodged, avoiding a cut to the body but getting raked across the face instead. The Mahuk let out a bellow of rage and pain. He clutched his left eye with one hand, blood streaming between his fingers, as he struck at Jomo's knife arm with his sword.

The stroke laid the flesh open to the bone, but Jomo seemed not to feel it. He stood with his head up, his arms spread wide as if in invitation. With an oath, the Mahuk ran him through. The fisherman fell, toppling like a tree under the woodsman's axe, but even as he fell it seemed there was a look of triumph on his face.

The Mahuk warriors around the circle had all fallen silent, their faces hard to read. The captain strode to the fallen Turo. He kicked the dead man viciously and spat on him, venting his wrath. Then he turned towards Taru who was hanging, white-faced, in the hands of the man who held him.

For a moment it seemed the furious Mahuk would slay the young

Turo as well, but he mastered himself. This little raid had cost him too much already. He had likely lost an eye by the hand of a mere fisherman and allowed himself to be provoked into a display of anger in front of his men. He had also killed one of the three new slaves the raid would have earned them. Too late he realized that the suffering of a galley slave would have been a far better payment for his eye than the quick, clean death he had given the fisherman.

The Mahuk captain barked an order. When none of his men moved quickly enough to obey, he stepped forward himself and struck Taru a solid blow to the side of the head with the butt of his sword.

Nagaro had been standing almost still throughout this whole performance. In his mind, he was repeating part of a battlefield prayer: *Vothra guide these spirits in crossing the abyss, and welcome them to your embrace. For these were true hearts who have given all they knew how to give.* He knew that Olomi and Jomo hadn't been Vothrin, but the prayer was all he could think of, and he felt the need to somehow honor their passing.

He watched as Taru was struck down, falling limp in his captor's hands. He had no time to wonder about his own fate, for in the next instant, something struck him hard on the back of the head, and the world went out like a snuffed candle.

Chaper 13: Behind The Curtain

He was creeping down the hallway, feeling his way along the wall in the dark, trying not to make a sound. If he could get out the back door and onto the terrace, he thought he'd be safely away. After that, he had only to run to the nearest farm. Bodano would surely help him save the Lady Maramine.

He had to get her away from these men. They had done something to her—something to her mind. He didn't believe their story that she'd been taken ill with a fever. For days he hadn't been allowed to see her, while that horrid hawk-faced man they called a healer had tended her. She was very ill, they told him—too ill to see anyone, and in the meantime he'd found himself essentially a prisoner in his own house. Every time he'd tried to go out, one or more of the three Leithians had stopped him, speaking blandly but blocking his way. He shouldn't leave the house now, they said, with the Lady Maramine so ill. She might call for him at any time. Yet they hadn't let him see her—until today...

When at last he'd been allowed to see the lady, he had found her changed—so terribly changed that he had immediately been alarmed. Lying in her bed, propped up on pillows, she had shown no animation. Her face had been pale and still as a mask, her beautiful dark eyes, normally so full of intelligence, had been strangely empty. Her voice, when she'd spoken to him, had carried none of its usual nuances. More than that, her words had been all wrong. He should accept this offered marriage, she'd told him. It was a fine opportunity for him, far better than the Fleet or the Royal Guard. He must consider his future, for she hadn't long to live, and in this way he'd be well provided for. It was a complete turnabout from anything she'd ever said before.

In the context of her supposed sudden illness, those words *could* have sounded sensible. He might have accepted them if he had thought they came from her heart. But her words had sounded like a speech learned by rote. He didn't want to believe she was dying—couldn't believe that her "illness" was natural. But standing there in her chamber, in the presence of the Leithians and the hawk-faced healer, he hadn't been able to question her—hadn't dared to offer any argument. Instead he had spoken words of agreement and given her his promise when she asked for it. He'd done his best to sound sincere, and tried to appear to have been persuaded. Afterwards though, he had returned to his room to wait for nightfall, a plan forming in his mind—the plan he was now trying to execute.

He had to go to the householders for help. There was no one else. Old Thorlan had left his post as stableman a year ago and gone to live with his daughter a dozen miles away. Chula was away visiting his ailing mother. Even Hinda the cook was gone—sent away, he assumed. In her place was a different woman, docile and silent.

He had waited for darkness to come, then waited two hours more until the house was silent. He'd gotten out of his room and down the stairs without being detected. Now, as he groped his way past the kitchen doorway, he felt a rising sense of elation as he anticipated success. It was only a few steps more to the door at the end of the hall...

But he celebrated too soon. A sudden sound of movement from the dark recesses of the kitchen made his heart jump into his throat, and before he could react, he was seized from behind by strong hands that twisted his arms behind his back and forced him to the floor.

"Where do you think you're going, *whelp?*" It was the snarling voice of the big Leithian—Bron, they called him.

"Let me up!" He twisted futilely under the big man's weight.

"So you can finish running away? Is this how you keep your promise to the Lady? Ungrateful, lying, little pup!"

He clamped his mouth shut on the words he would have liked to say—that he'd meant to come back with help for Maramine. Nor did he cry out when the big man's knee ground painfully into his back. Bron didn't seem to like him, though he had no idea why, and the reason didn't matter. He wouldn't give the man the satisfaction of knowing that he'd hurt him.

There was light suddenly. Someone had lit a candle or uncovered a lantern. Pinned as he was, face down on the floor, he still could see little.

"Shall I fetch our 'healer,' then?" That was the voice of the scarred man. As usual, it had an unpleasantly insinuating quality, and the word "healer" was uttered as if it were a joke.

"Aye, do that, Gill. Tell him the little bird was trying to fly away, just as I said he would."

He heard the sound of footsteps ascending the stairs.

"Just wait until that serpent gets his fang into you." The big man spoke gloatingly. "You'll be more cooperative then, I think."

He had no idea what that meant, but he didn't like the sound of it.

A third voice spoke then—that of the tall, thin Leithian—sounding uncomfortable and hesitant. "I still don't think we should do this, Bron.

Elgurn may not like it."

"By the Mark, Kale!" The big man responded angrily. "He told us to secure the boy's cooperation, and this is the only way to do it! He left me in command, and I want to have something to show for the time we've spent."

"But I don't think this is what he meant. And he'll be here tomorrow. We could wait, and see if he wants to change the plan."

"We tried his plan, and you see how well it worked! *Kroneg's Blood*, man! This boy is nothing but a stubborn, self-willed, little cur. There's only one way we'll ever get 'cooperation' from him!"

Again the knee dug into his back.

At this point, footsteps sounded on the stair, and the big man made a hissing sound through his teeth. "They're coming! Say no more of this, Kale. We don't want to argue in front of *him*."

The footsteps proceeded towards them along the hallway, and at length there came the voice of the hawk-faced man, coldly precise and emotionless. "Turn him over, Zirda, if you would, and hold his arms."

The pressure on his back was removed, but only long enough for the big man to roll him over. Immediately he was pinned again, with a knee on his chest and his arms each held flat against the floor by one of Bron's beefy hands. He struggled desperately, but the big man outweighed him by a hundred pounds. He knew that calling for help was useless. There was no one under that roof who could give him aid.

"Would you be so good as to sit on his legs, Zirda? I can't have him kicking me while I work." This request from the hawk-faced man was aimed at the tall, thin Leithian. The man, Kale, obeyed, though he seemed reluctant.

The hawk-faced man was kneeling at his left side now, though his view was blocked by Bron's massive chest. He could see that Gil was holding a candle to give the healer light. Now his left wrist was being pinned as well. He felt his sleeve being pulled up. Fingers probed along his forearm, and there was a sudden sharp jab of pain. "What are you doing?" he cried, trying vainly to pull his arm free.

"You'll find out soon enough." The big man's face loomed close over him, leering.

His alarm escalated sharply as the pain in his arm continued. Then abruptly the pain ceased, and he felt a wash of relief, only to have panic grip him again a few heartbeats later when his vision began to swim and then to dim, so that the candle flame became a wavering smudge of light beyond the twisting dark shadow that was Bron's head and torso. Then, just as his terror was reaching a crescendo, he had a sickening sensation of falling... falling... downward into darkness, as if the floor had dissolved away beneath him...

*

He was drifting... slowly... upwards... to a nebulous place where he floated, wrapped in a vague, formless night that numbed his mind and muffled his senses. After some indefinite time, he became aware that he was lying on a surface. Perhaps it was a mattress. Small sounds began to penetrate the dense cloud that enveloped him. Gradually the sounds came to have meaning: the creaking of a chair... the sigh of an indrawn breath... a scratching, as of a pen on paper...

He came slowly to an awareness that he was lying on his back on a bed in a dark place—and that he was not alone. Someone was sitting nearby, writing...

Writing in the dark? Were his eyes shut? He tried to open them, but the darkness remained and he couldn't tell whether he'd succeeded or not. Was it truly dark? Or was he blind?

Alarmed, he tried to put his hand to his face, but his hand wouldn't move. In a wave of panic, he tried to roll onto his side... To sit up... To cry out... But his body remained immobile, and no sound issued from his lips. Cold terror twisted his stomach. Desperately he fought to calm himself. *This had to be a dream.* But somehow he knew it wasn't.

Abruptly, there was the scrape of a chair on a wooden floor, and the sound of footsteps approaching the place where he lay. "Open your eyes." There was no malice in the voice, only a chilling coldness.

His eyes opened at the words as if of their own accord, and he saw that he was in his own room, lying on his own bed. The room was dimly lit by candlelight, indicating that it was still night. The man who had spoken was standing over him. It was the hawk-faced healer.

"You are awake, then. Excellent." The man's black eyes glittered avidly in the pools of shadow under his dark brows. His voice cut the air, cold and sharp as the blade of a knife.

"You will have discovered that you cannot move," the man was saying. "That is the effect of the *heskial*—a liquor distilled from the flowers of the *heskia* vine—which I have put into your blood. Do you see this?" The man held up a small glass vial containing a quantity of pale brown liquid. "It is a truly marvelous tincture. Only a fraction of a dram was required to put you into your present state."

Frantically he strove again to move his body, not wishing to believe what he was hearing. His redoubled efforts proved fruitless, however, and his panic began to rise again.

The man meanwhile continued speaking as coolly as if he were discussing the prospect of rain, or the price of grain at market. "The marvelous power of heskial is that it completely subverts the conscious will while sparing thought and understanding. Thus you have no power to move or to speak, while I, or anyone, can command you with a word.

Moreover, any instruction I give you now you will carry out at the appointed time, though it may be hours or even days hence. And though you have no control over your voice or body, you are yet aware of all that transpires. Remarkable, is it not?"

Horror gripped him at these words. Surely this explained what had been done to the Lady Maramine—and now it was being done to him!

The hawk-faced man had moved away from the bed, perhaps to return the vial to its place. He couldn't be sure because he couldn't turn his head to follow the healer's movements.

The man returned, carrying an hourglass that had just been turned over. He set the hourglass down just out of sight. There was the sound of it contacting a hard surface, presumably the top of the small bedside table. The man then drew up a chair beside the bed, seated himself, and calmly continued his discourse.

"You are wondering, perhaps, how I was able to put the heskial into your blood. It was by use of this device." The man produced a small object from somewhere about his person, and held it up in front of his helpless victim's eyes. It seemed to consist of a thin, needle-like thorn about an inch long, with a sack-like pod attached to its base.

"It's called a bladder-thorn," the healer continued. "Another marvelous invention of the Jinari. It's a pity that we are so often at war with them, for it makes it difficult at times to get certain materials. I have an ample supply of bladder-thorns, however. See how cunningly the thing is made? The thorn comes from the *scapala* tree and it is naturally hollow almost to the tip. All that is needed is to drill a tiny hole, there, just behind the point, and to attach the pliable pod from a marshbladder plant to the other end. So, by compressing and releasing the bladder, liquid may be drawn in through the hole. Then, when the tip of the thorn is driven through the skin into the interior of a vein, a simple squeeze of the bladder ejects the liquid directly into the blood. It's an exquisitely simple design—most ingenious, don't you agree?"

At this point, the man paused in his speech and turned towards the bedside table, apparently to check the level of sand in the hourglass. He was plainly talking to pass the time while waiting for something, but he also seemed to take pleasure in the one-sided conversation. It was a pleasure related more to his fascination with his topic, however, than to any desire to inform his victim.

After a moment the hawk-faced man turned back to the inert figure on the bed, and resumed speaking, this time on the subject of the drug he had used. "Our knowledge of heskial comes from the work of the Jinari lore master, Obiari, who recorded his observations on its properties. I have a copy of the scroll. It's an excellent piece of work— very finely reasoned, very detailed... Yet it leaves a number of unanswered questions. Ever since I secured a quantity of this remarkable liquor several years ago, I have been most eager to conduct a study of my own, to extend Master Obiari's excellent work. I lacked a suitable subject, however... *until now.*"

Mentally, that "suitable subject" was screaming in protest. There was nothing he could do, however, except listen with mounting horror to the healer's words.

"Circumstances could scarcely have aligned themselves better," the man went on. "Bron was quick to agree to the idea of this alternative plan, should you prove stubborn. And so your little escape attempt was most fortuitous. Now my master will have this marriage that he desires, and I the opportunity that I have sought for so long. And you? You will have the privilege of contributing to a work of lasting significance in the annals of herb lore. With luck, I may obtain enough material to prepare a treatise on the subject."

This was an abomination! In his rage at the idea of being so used, he willed his body to lash out and strike the man, but his arm remained where it lay, as if nailed to the bed. He struggled to move it again, and again... with no more success. A terrible sense of helplessness rose in him, threatening to overwhelm him, until he realized that direct confrontation with his paralysis was fueling his panic, and he tried instead to make his mind as still as his body was compelled to be. This helped, and after a while he found he could think again. He was half convinced the hawk-faced man was mad. The man was most surely not a healer, for he lacked any feeling or compassion.

In the meantime, the hawk-faced man seemed to be studying him, and the man's tone became reflective as he continued speaking. "I must say that you were foolish not to accept what was offered to you—being what you are. A fatherless bastard shouldn't expect too much. He should learn to accept what is given to him by his betters." *(Had there been a hint of bitterness?)* "You should be glad you have a pretty face, high-born manners, and a mother who is of noble birth. I had no such advantages. Yet even a fatherless bastard may go far if he is clever and mindful of opportunity. I am an example." *(Definitely a note of pride, there.)* "My mother sold me into service to an apothecary when I was ten. I worked hard and kept my eyes cast down. The man found me apt and made me his apprentice. I took that opportunity to learn all that I could of herb lore, until I surpassed my master. So, in time, I came to the attention of Lord Harl Sobring and thus was able to become the official lore master to a noble house."

The man paused. "There have been... other opportunities... since then. I've taken them as they've come. You should have taken what was offered, as I said. It was a mistake to think that you have any choice in the matter." There wasn't even contempt in these last words. They were simply a statement of fact.

Lying there, helpless, he was trying to think, and it seemed to him that the hawk-faced man had revealed his identity. The man was plainly a master of herb lore, masquerading as a healer. If the hawk-faced man served Elgurn, then who could he be but the king's dreaded Lore Master, Dreigen!

The hawk-faced man glanced again in the direction of the bedside table. "I think we might begin," he observed mildly. Rising, he picked up the hourglass, its sand still flowing. "Get up," he commanded. "Go to the table, and sit in that chair."

Now he felt his body move to comply, even as his mind was crying *No!* His body sat up. His legs swung over the edge of the bed. He stood, and his legs carried him across the floor to the table on which the candle burned. His body bent and seated itself on the chair that awaited him.

Abomination and horror! This was, if anything, even worse than the paralysis—this feeling his body move of its own accord in response to the words of this dreadful man! And try as he might, he was helpless to stop it. No effort of will, no rebellion of mind, no defiance of spirit, were to any avail. His muscles simply did not obey him. His body had become a wooden puppet, and the hawk-faced man held the strings! He could only sit as he'd been commanded, awash in outrage and mounting dread, waiting to see what would happen next.

The hawk-faced man had followed him, bringing the hourglass, and seated himself on the other side of the table. A large, bound notebook lay open in front of him, as well as pen and ink. The man took up the pen, dipped it, and made a note in the notebook. Then he raised his eyes.

Seen clearly in the candlelight, the man's face was gaunt, angular, and tawny-skinned. His eyes were as hard and black as bits of polished jet, and as cold as a moonless midnight in Idrin. He spoke again.

"Place your hand close to the candle flame—so. No, the left hand. We don't want to risk damaging the other."

His left arm extended itself, holding his hand less than a finger's breadth from the candle flame as instructed, nearly touching it. Almost immediately the heat of the flame began to burn his fingers.

The hawk-faced man waited several excruciating seconds while the pain intensified.

He would have cried out, but he had no voice. Nor could he draw back his hand! His spirit writhed in helpless agony.

After perhaps ten seconds that seemed like an eternity, the man spoke again. "Withdraw your hand now, and let me see it."

Even when removed from proximity to the flame, his hand still stung and throbbed violently, and there was an area covering parts of two fingers and a portion of the palm where the skin glowed an angry red.

The hawk-faced man examined the hand with keen interest. "Yes," he murmured. "It is as I thought. The skin is burned. There is no reflexive action for self-protection at this stage. We must try again in a quarter of an hour." Picking up the pen and re-dipping it, the man glanced again at the hourglass and made another entry in the big notebook.

Inwardly he shuddered, utterly appalled. *The man was a monster!* What might he do next? Bid him put his hand right into the flame? Leave it there until the flesh charred?

But, no. The hawk-faced man finished writing, turned, and bent to rummage about in something that lay on the floor beside his chair. Presently the man produced a small pot and applied some salve to the burned hand. This immediately reduced the pain to a dull ache, though he doubted it was done for his comfort—more likely to avoid damaging the man's precious experimental subject.

The hawk-faced man picked up the pen again, and held it poised over the page. "What is your age?" he asked. When no answer came, a frown flickered across his face. "Ah," he observed after a moment, "I am forgetting what I learned from working with the woman. You cannot answer questions unless previously instructed how to do so. We shall try again. *Tell* me your age."

This time he felt his lips and tongue move. "Seventeen." The word came out flat-sounding to his ear.

The hawk-faced man's pen scratched briefly across the paper. After a moment, he laid it down. "Henceforth, when asked your age, you will speak your age. When you are asked your name, you will speak your name. If you are asked how you are feeling, you will answer that you are well..."

There followed a list of instructions in a similar vein, directing him to make appropriate responses to a host of mundane questions. Following delivery of these instructions, the man tested each of them. Having thus satisfied himself that all were carried out as he intended, the man brought out a piece of paper with writing on it.

"I believe we shall deal with the letter now. It wouldn't do to neglect my master's wishes." This statement was accompanied by a smile that revealed strong, yellow teeth, but not a trace of warmth. "I've taken the trouble to write this out in advance, and I will now read it to you. When in the future I tell you it is time to write the letter, you will go to the nearest writing desk, take pen and paper, and write out exactly what I am about to read to you. You will then sign your name to it." The hawk-faced man proceeded to read aloud what was written on the paper.

Listening to this dictation, he felt a growing outrage at the words that were being, in effect, put into his mouth. The document was a letter addressed to his presumptive bride-to-be. In it, the writer—which was to be him—expressed his eager anticipation of this union, stating that he'd been told of her great beauty, and that he could scarcely wait to meet her. It included a promise to send in advance a portrait of himself so that she might see what he looked like. This, of course, could only refer to the painting of him that the Lady Maramine had finished but two weeks before.

For some reason, it angered him beyond all reason to think of the lady's painting being used in this way. He began to repeat over and over in his mind "I will not listen. I will not do it," seeking to drown out the meaning of the words being read to him. The result was that, by the time the reading was finished, he wasn't sure what the closing of the letter had been. In any case, he knew he couldn't possibly recall the exact wording of the entire text. It seemed to him that the hawk-faced man would be thwarted in his intent, and the thought gave him some satisfaction.

The reading of the letter being complete, the man consulted the hourglass and determined that a quarter of an hour had passed. There followed another command to place his hand near the candle flame. The man didn't wait so long this time to tell him to remove it, however, for it was apparent that he was again going to be burned. The man recorded this in his notebook and turned over the hourglass to begin again.

By this time, a warm glow of morning suffused the curtains at the window. The silent woman who served as cook came and brought them breakfast on a tray. The man told him to eat, and so of course his hands took up the cutlery and put food into his mouth, and he chewed and swallowed. Had it been up to him, he would have eaten little, for he was far too distressed to have any appetite. In the meantime, the hawk-faced man consumed his own breakfast absently, while writing intermittently in his notebook.

This process consumed another quarter of an hour according to the glass, and so the candle-flame test was repeated again. This time, his hand jerked away involuntarily at the first sensation of heat and pain.

"Ah, very good," was the hawk-faced man's comment, as his pen scratched again across the notebook page. "The protective response has returned. It's safe to try a little more activity now. Before, had you stumbled or tripped, you would have made no move to catch yourself and could have easily been injured. We should now have approximately four hours before the effects of the drug begin to wear off."

How his heart leaped at those words! The drug would wear off, and he would be free! If he could then just find some way to escape, he might still be able to get help and return to rescue Maramine. He had only to endure four more hours. With these hopeful thoughts in mind, he resolved to face whatever those four hours might bring with as much equanimity as he could muster.

Presently the hawk-faced man rose and made for the door, commanding him to follow, which his body did against all his will and desire. The man led him out of the room and down the hallway to the library, which also served the Lady Maramine as a study.

The room contained a writing desk, and also a number of bookcases, some comfortable chairs, and a low table under the window. The only occupant of the room was the tall, thin Leithian named Kale, sitting with his head bent over a book. Kale was a man of middle years, long-limbed and gangling, with curly red hair that was starting to gray. When the healer and his charge appeared in the doorway, Kale put down his book and rose.

As he entered the room on the heels of the hawk-faced man, he saw Kale's expression change. The red-haired Leithian had an open, honest face, and the look of shock that it registered when their gazes met spoke volumes. He realized he must have worn just such a look when he'd seen the shocking change in the Lady Maramine.

The hawk-faced man simply ignored Kale's expression. He asked the Leithian, with cool politeness, if he would find and bring the other two men. Kale murmured a word of agreement and slid past them gingerly to exit the room.

As soon as Kale had gone, the hawk-faced man turned to him. "Go and stand there by that chair. Then turn around and face the door." His body responded as instructed. "You are to approach and greet courteously the first man who enters the room."

They had not long to wait, and the first one to come through the door was Bron. Gill and Kale followed close behind.

He seethed with fury as he recalled the role that Bron had played in his current enslavement, but he couldn't prevent his body from stepping forward and approaching the big Leithian. His right hand extended, and from his mouth came words, courteous but wooden. "Zirda, I give you greeting."

Bron was of about the same age as Kale, with close-cropped white-blond hair and a ruddy complexion. He didn't take the extended hand, but a mocking smile flickered across his florid face. "Well, well, now," he observed. "Isn't he a docile pup this morning." Then, turning to the hawk-faced man, he added, frowning. "But it would be better, Dreigen, if he showed me more respect."

So he'd been correct about the identity of the hawk-faced man. The confirmation brought no comfort.

"If it please you, My Lord Bron," came the Lore Master's well-oiled response, "he speaks as he has been taught—and not by me. If you wish him to speak differently, you have but to instruct him."

"I see. Put that hand down, boy."

He had stood rigidly with his hand still extended while Bron was speaking. Now the hand returned to his side. Inwardly he burned with indignation.

"I want you to greet me again, boy. But this time bow and address me as 'My Lord.'"

The Lady Maramine had taught him all the courtly graces, and so his body now executed a very creditable bow and he uttered the words, "I give you greeting, My Lord," with courteous tone, if flat inflection. Had he been in control of his voice, he would have choked on the words.

"That's better." The big man smiled broadly.

He thought he read triumph in the piercing blue eyes.

The man named Gill approached him, then, and looked him up and down with his usual smirking smile. Gill was about thirty years old, significantly younger than Kale or Bron. The scar on his right cheek was a pale, narrow line running from the corner of his eye to his jaw. He was handsome despite the disfiguring mark, or would have been had there been any trace of human kindness in his ice-blue eyes. He spoke almost casually. "Now bow to *me*, boy."

His body again complied.

"He does that rather well, I think, but will he truly do anything he's bidden?"

"Within the limits of his ability, and if you make your instruction clear, Zirda," was the smooth response.

The Leithian bestowed his smirking smile upon the hawk-faced man. "I wonder..." he mused indolently. "If I were to place this sword in his hand,"—he touched the hilt of the blade that swung at his hip—"and bade him to cut off your swarthy head, Dreigen, would he do *that?*"

The darker man's nostrils flared ever so slightly and his black eyes glittered. His voice was smooth as satin, however, as he answered. "He would try, Zirda, but I very much doubt he would succeed, since I could halt him with a word."

"Ah. Quite so. He would make a poor assassin then, it seems. But, no matter. He is meant for... other uses."

The scarred man turned back towards him. "Can you dance, boy?" he inquired, then frowned when there was no response.

"He will not answer a question if not instructed, Zirda. You must command him. If he can do it, he will. If he does not, he cannot. Either way, you are answered."

Gill raised an eyebrow. "So? Very well then. Show me, boy, how you dance The Ivy Vine."

Nothing.

"Is that too difficult?" Gill's smirk widened. "Well, it *is* a Leithian Dance. Show me the Balandir then. That one is Kelorin."

Still nothing.

He had never had any interest in learning to dance, and so the Lady Maramine hadn't taught him. It was a deficiency for which he was, at that moment, profoundly grateful.

Gill went on to try the names of several other dances, also to no effect. Now he smiled contemptuously. "It seems he is entirely ignorant," he observed dryly. "Let's try something else. Stand on your left foot, boy."

His body immediately complied.

After several seconds, Gill remarked, "Well, at least it seems he has good balance, so there's some hope. Put your foot down, boy." Then another thought seemed to occur to the man. His ever-present smile grew wider, but not more pleasant. "Now sing for us 'The Maid Went Over the Meadow.'"

It was a popular and rather bawdy ballad. He'd never sung it aloud. Indeed, he never sang anything. The Lady Maramine had told him gently, years ago, that he had best leave singing to others because he had no ear. He knew the song, however. Thorlan had sung it frequently and loudly while mucking out the horses' stalls. With consternation, he felt himself draw breath and felt his mouth open to begin the first verse.

"*Stop!*" Kale had been hovering in the background, looking unhappy, throughout this exchange. It was he who had spoken, and he added, with surprising vehemence, "You've no call to make sport of him!"

With tremendous relief, he felt his mouth close again. Although Kale's command had apparently been directed at Gill, it seemed to have worked on him as well.

"I don't see the harm." The scarred Leithian negligently flicked a wrist. "He surely has no idea what he's doing."

"Oh, but he does," Dreigen interjected. "According to the work of Master Obiari, a man under the sway of heskial is fully conscious."

"Is he *really?* How interesting! But then, how can you *tell?*" Gill was quite unperturbed by the hawk-faced man's revelation. Kale looked horrified.

At this point, Bron interrupted. "If you please, gentlemen," he said, "we're wasting time with this. The hour is approaching when we must show what we've accomplished." He turned to Dreigen. "Have you gotten the letter from him, as I requested?"

The Lore Master smiled unctuously. "He will write it whenever I bid him, My Lord. He could do it now. Or—if I might make a humble suggestion—perhaps it would be a good demonstration if my master were to see him do it?"

Bron considered, frowning. "Can you be sure he'll do it properly?"

"Oh, yes. Quite sure." The hawk-faced man exuded confidence.

"Very well, then," Bron agreed. "See that he's ready, Dreigen." He beckoned for the other two Leithians to follow him downstairs, where they would await their lord's arrival.

Dreigen used the time to further instruct his charge. The Lore Master seemed to be trying to anticipate things his master might ask. He was both ingenious and thorough. "Enough, I think," he said at last. "Go sit in the chair by the window. Take up that book and read until he comes."

The book was the one Kale had been reading, a book of Vothrin poetry. Though his eyes followed the lines, and his hands turned the pages, he scarcely noticed what those pages contained. He was wondering how much time had passed and how much still remained for him to endure. *Perhaps three hours more*, he told himself. He anticipated that the writing of the letter would go badly for Dreigen, and he wondered what the consequence would be. Eventually, he heard voices and footsteps in the hall, and he steeled himself to face the indignities he knew must follow.

Bron, Kale, and Gill entered the room. With them came the bearded Leithian, Elgurn, the King of Edrovir. He was an imposing man of fifty years. Almost as tall as Kale, he seemed taller, for he carried himself as straight as a pikestaff. He moved with an unstudied confidence that made it clear he was accustomed to giving orders and having them obeyed. He wore his blond hair cut short. His beard, copper mixed with silver, was impeccably trimmed. He seemed uncharacteristically tense as his pale blue eyes swept the room.

"You must be quick about this," he was saying to Bron. "I can't stay long. There's an urgent matter that requires my attention. Where is the boy?"

The hawk-faced man stepped forward. "He is there, My Lord King, reading by the window."

This was his cue, according to his recent instructions. His hands put down the book. He stood, and walked across the room, stopping to bow deeply before the bearded man. As his body straightened, his mouth produced the words, "I give you greeting, My Lord King." Having completed this performance, he stood frozen, burning with resentment and humiliation.

The bearded man's expression was pleased at first, but it quickly changed to a frown. He spun upon the hawk-faced man. "What have you done to him?" he demanded.

The Lore Master's face was a mask of surprised aggrievement. "It is only heskial, My Lord. The same as I used with the lady."

The bearded man's frown deepened. "I didn't give you leave to do this."

Dreigen cast down his eyes in an artful simulation of humility. "I beg your pardon, My Lord King," was his smooth response. "My Lord Bron gave permission."

Now the bearded man turned his frown upon the big, red-faced Leithian. Bron, feeling the king's disapproval, made haste to offer an explanation. "My Lord, your orders were to secure his cooperation and we have done so."

The bearded man put a weary hand to his brow. "I would have preferred his *willing* cooperation, Bron."

"But it's clear you'll never get that, My Lord. The boy is willful and stubborn, and lacking in all filial obedience." Bron's tone was reasonable and persuasive, the open contempt he displayed for his charge at other times was not in evidence.

Kale suddenly stepped forward. "Say rather that he was not taken in, My Lord. The change in Maramine was too great, her behavior too unnatural."

The king's eyes narrowed shrewdly. He glanced from Kale to Bron. "I see," was all he said.

Bron was clearly nettled. "My Lord, he tried to run away! We had to do something!"

The king drew in his breath sharply. "Yes, of course you did," he said, frowning. "Still, I don't like to see him like this."

"If I may speak, My Lord," The Lore Master's voice was buttered silk. "The boy will do anything required of him—with a little careful instruction. Speak to him, My Lord. Ask him a few questions."

At this, the bearded Leithian raised a blond eyebrow and turned towards him, where he still stood statue-like. Frowning slightly, the king addressed him, not unkindly. "How do you feel this morning?"

His lips moved. "I am well."

"Have you had your breakfast?"

"Yes."

These were questions he'd been told how to answer.

The man was studying him thoughtfully. Now he asked, "What was the book you were reading?"

"A book of poetry." The hawk-faced man had cleverly instructed him to answer as accurately as he could any question concerning books he had read.

"And the last poem you read—what was it?"

He wasn't at all sure of the answer to this question, and was utterly shocked to hear his voice respond, "The Song of Karidei." It was as if some other part of his mind had known the answer.

Kale spoke then, gently, and a little sadly it seemed. "Tell us, please, the last two lines of that poem."

Now he really had no idea of the answer. He didn't know the poem, and he'd paid no attention while he'd been "reading" it. Yet again, that other part of his mind—the puppet part, he decided to call it—seemed to know, for his mouth moved and words came out of it. "Though burning gold, or iron cold, may weave my prison bars, my spirit wakes to wander still the shadows of the stars."

The king started, and he gave Kale a sharp look. The lanky Leithian only nodded, however, his expression unreadable. "Yes," he said. "That is the final couplet of The Song of Karidei. I was reading the poem earlier this morning and those lines have stayed in my memory."

His heart leaped a little at Kale's words. Had Kale meant those lines to be a message for him? That his spirit was still free, even though he seemed a prisoner within his own body?

"It's quite remarkable," the bearded man was saying. "He has the countenance of one who is walking in his sleep... and yet to have such detailed recall..."

"That is the great power of the drug, My Lord," Dreigen interjected quickly. "A mind under heskial remembers everything in minute detail. Therefore he is exquisitely instructable. With your permission," the man added silkily, "I have prepared a demonstration." So saying, the Lore Master turned to him and said, "It is time now to write the letter."

Upon hearing this cue, his body turned to face the writing desk, walked to it, and seated itself—all without his volition. His hands found paper, a pen, and ink, and proceeded to begin to write. He could only watch in frustrated humiliation as the words flowed effortlessly from the tip of the pen, formed in his familiar firm, even hand. He couldn't remember all of the exact words of the dictated letter, but he recognized them. The puppet part of his mind seemed to have gotten them perfectly, and his hand continued without the slightest hesitation right into and through the part he'd tried to drown out with other thoughts. The hawk-faced man's confidence had not been misplaced after all.

So it appeared there was nothing he could do to prevent the puppet part of him from obeying the puppet-master. This discovery was a blow, to be sure. Still, he told himself, it didn't really matter. When the drug wore off, he would make his escape...

His hand had finished the body of the letter, and it proceeded to add his signature, as instructed.

"Excellent," came the voice of the Lore Master, who must have seen his hand put down the pen. "Now bring the letter to me."

His body complied. The hawk-faced man took the letter from him, scanned it quickly, then handed it to his master.

The king read the letter through carefully, with a look of approval growing on his face as he read. "This is very good," he observed. "Yes, this is perfect. One couldn't ask for better. The bit about the portrait is a good idea too. I saw the thing hanging in the hall, and it's a good likeness." He sighed. "If only this letter spoke his true feelings."

"Ask him, My Lord," was Dreigen's instant response.

The king again crooked an eyebrow, but he turned nevertheless to address the writer of the letter. "So," he asked archly, "are you now willing to marry my daughter?"

"Yes, My Lord," the puppet part of him answered. This subject had been covered by the Lore Master's recent instructions.

"And the prospect pleases you?" The pale blue eyes bored into him.

"Yes, My Lord." His mouth spoke the words blandly while inside he writhed as his mind screamed silently, *No, no, no!*

The bearded Leithian looked surprised. He chewed his lip. "This could yet work," he murmured. Then he frowned, turning to Dreigen. "Does he know what he's saying?"

"Oh yes, My Lord, he knows."

The king looked troubled. He shook his head, still frowning. "Yet it must be only the heskial that makes him so compliant. Take away the drug, and I don't doubt that we'd find him as unwilling as before."

"If I may speak, My Lord." Gill broke in with well-feigned sincerity. "The boy has yet to meet your daughter. The young lady's charms are, shall we say... considerable? Once he sees the maid he is to wed, or once he finds himself wedded to her..."

The king's expression softened at the mention of his daughter. He smiled. "Now surely you are right, Gillard," he said. "If we present him with the deed accomplished, he may find his lot pleasant enough after all. Feminine grace may well succeed where all our efforts have failed." He nodded decisively. "Yes, we will try this way."

Having made his decision, the king wasted no time. He turned first to Dreigen. "I wish to have the wedding in a month's time. Can you have him ready?"

"Consider it done, My Lord," was the smooth reply. The bearded man seemed not to mark how the hawk-faced man's eyes gleamed with satisfaction.

Next the king turned to Bron. "I trust you to see that the boy comes to no harm in the meantime."

"Of course, My Lord." Bron's tone was mild and acquiescent. Only his eyes revealed his true feelings, a sign the king again seemed not to see.

"Good," the king continued. "I will ride now, for I must be in Glenarl before sunset. Send the portrait on as soon as you can." (That was to

Bron.) "The letter I will deliver myself."

So saying, the king turned to the supposed author of the letter. Approaching him, the bearded Leithian smiled broadly as he folded the piece of paper and thrust it into his tirka. "I will see you, then, in a month's time, my boy," he declared heartily. "And I look forward to welcoming you into the family." With that, the man clapped him on the back so forcefully that his feet had to take a small step to keep from losing his balance. He saw Bron smile at this, and Gill was smirking behind his lord's back. The king saw none of it however. "See to it," he said curtly over his shoulder to Bron. Then he turned on his heel and strode from the room.

Inwardly, he was fuming at the king's presumption, not to mention Gill's insinuation that any girl's charms, however great, would cause him to forget what was being done to him. He was more determined than ever to make his escape. *How much longer now? Perhaps two hours... Or two and a half...*

He was conducted back to his room by Kale, the gangling Leithian having volunteered for the task when Dreigen indicated that he had to go and "see to the lady." Once in the bed chamber, Kale politely bade him to sit in one of the chairs at the table. The Leithian sat in the other and studied his face searchingly. There was pain in the man's gray-green eyes.

"I am sorry for this..." the man began after a moment, then broke off and looked away, running his fingers through his graying curls.

He could sense the Leithian's sympathy, but he could do nothing to acknowledge it. And the man seemed uncomfortable about having spoken, since he made no further effort to communicate.

After staring across the room for a minute, Kale glanced down and noticed the Lore Master's journal on the table. Idly the Leithian opened it and silently read a little. The man frowned, turned the page, and read a little more. An expression of distaste appeared on his face, and he closed the book and pushed it away. After another minute of staring distractedly at the walls, the Leithian got up to prowl nervously about the room. He offered no comment on what he'd read.

When their lunch was brought, Kale took the tray from the silent woman and set it on the table. "Here," he said gently. "Please eat some of this good food." After watching him woodenly move several bites of food into his mouth, the man poured two cups of sothiril, and set one at each place. "Please take some drink to wash it down," he said.

By thus phrasing his directives in the form of polite suggestions, Kale created the illusion that his charge's responses were voluntary, although the Leithian surely knew that they were not. Kale ate his own lunch with little apparent enthusiasm.

Immediately after lunch, the hawk-faced man appeared in the doorway, and Kale promptly excused himself. His backward glance said quite plainly that he was torn between conflicting impulses—reluctant to leave his charge in the hands of the Lore Master, but glad to be done with his uncomfortable duty and to make his own escape.

Dreigen had entered carrying a cup, which he set upon the table. "Take that and drink it all," he directed.

His hand picked up the cup as he was commanded, and he drank. The liquid in the cup appeared to be water, though it had a slightly bitter taste that he didn't like. He had no choice, however, but to drink all of it. As his hand set the cup down, he saw the Lore Master turn over the hourglass to start the sand running. The man then opened his notebook and proceeded to make some notation. At length he put down the pen and raised his hard, black eyes.

"Henceforth, you will answer this question, whenever I ask it, as accurately as you are able. Do you feel any faintness?"

"No." The word came out flat, without inflection, though inwardly he was greatly alarmed. What was the man about this time? And what had he just been made to drink?

Dreigen spoke as if in answer to his thought. "I have given you your second dose of heskial. It is somewhat slower to take effect when taken by mouth, but no less potent."

More heskial? And it had come before the previous dose had even begun to wear off! Wildly he strove for even the slightest hint of voluntary movement, but there was nothing. What a fool he'd been to imagine that this monstrous man would allow him any chance to escape!

Through his rising panic, he became aware that the Lore Master was still speaking. The man's voice was as cool and matter-of-fact as if he were explaining how to brew sothiril. "Although the method is slower, it is much easier, as I'm sure you will agree. Furthermore, it spares the skin of your arm—and also my supply of bladder thorns." Here the man glanced at the hourglass. "Do you feel any faintness now?"

"No." Again his lips produced the word.

Dreigen nodded and made note of the response in his book. "We have perhaps a few minutes before you will begin to feel it," he observed blandly. "Still, it is better not to risk waiting too long. Go to the bed and lie down."

His body complied with the instruction, and presently he was lying on his back, as immobile as he'd found himself hours earlier at the start of this waking nightmare. Inside, his spirit beat frantically against the confines of his inert flesh, as a caged bird might beat its wings against the bars of its prison. As the seconds slipped by, he strove to calm himself, for he knew the panic did no good. But it was more than he could do to keep his thoughts from slipping in the direction of despair. *What could he possibly do now... and what was going to become of him?*

He could not turn his head, and his eyes were fixed on the beams of the ceiling. After some agonizing period of time, the beams began to waver and twist as his vision blurred. Abruptly, then, the hawk-faced man was standing over him. The man's face also seemed to twist and bend, becoming a hideous mask.

"Do you feel any faintness now?" The words seemed to reach him from a distance.

"Yes." His own voice seemed to come out slowly, as if with an effort.

The man was speaking again, and the words fell into his mind and stuck there like daggers thrown one after the other, even as his vision began to fade into grayness.

"There is another fascinating property of heskial," the Lore Master was saying. "If this drug is given repeatedly, without allowing the subject to recover fully between doses, it acquires such a grip upon the flesh that the body becomes unable to live without it. If the drug is then withheld, the subject experiences shaking of the limbs and increasing pain. Unless the drug is given again, the flesh is overwhelmed within a matter of thirty minutes, or an hour, and death ensues. Master Obiari lost his second subject in this way—quite accidentally it appears. In the lady's case, six doses were required to reach this point. Your case I expect will be similar..."

And now he was floating in a sickly gray sea in which he couldn't make out the form of anything identifiable, yet his mind still clung to a slender thread of awareness. The thoughts that flickered through that mind made his spirit quail, for the full horror of the situation was now apparent. There would be no rescue of the Lady Maramine. For her it was already too late, and death was her only escape. Soon it would be too late for him as well. But how long would the Lore Master keep him alive... and what would he be forced to endure before the end?

A voice came to him dimly, saying, "Are you feeling faintness..." His mouth moved, but he never heard the answer, if indeed there was one, for he was falling... falling into darkness...

*

He struggled against darkness, and a throbbing pain in his head, fighting his way upward, seeking light and consciousness. As it turned out, there was no light, and consciousness brought only pain and confusion. Groaning, he put a hand to his aching head. The fact that he could move voluntarily and produce sound told him that he was awake and free of the heskial. *Had he been dreaming?*

Relief flooded through him... and ebbed in turn. *It had happened exactly that way... All that, and more... There had been nearly a year of bondage under heskial...* He knew he had just been reliving the beginning of that ordeal, but what had happened to end it? How could he be alive and yet be free?

Confused images of life on the shores of Wotana Bay then pushed into his mind, and his thoughts spun vertiginously as two sets of memories collided. He struggled to understand where he was.

Lying still in the blind darkness, he reviewed the evidence of his other senses. He was lying curled on his side on damp planks... He heard the creak of timbers... felt the undulating motion of sea swells... There was a strong odor of mingled tar and stale sea water. When he tried to move his legs, he found that he was chained to something by his left ankle. Reaching and twisting, he followed the chain with his hands until it met a vertical wall of planks.

He was on a ship. Chained to a bulkhead!

With sudden clarity, he understood. The memory of the time he'd spent with Taru's family came sharply into focus, and he remembered the brutal way that time had ended. The Mahuk sea-warriors must have knocked him senseless. They must have taken him to their ship. He was a prisoner in the stinking black bilge of a Mahuk war galley.

Even as this realization sank in, there came another. The mental curtain that had shielded him in Wotana from the worst parts of his past was gone as completely as if it had never been. His mind was laid bare to the full memory of a nearly year-long nightmare. Born of that nightmare came an overwhelming tide of emotion—a roiling mix of pain and rage and humiliation. Hot tears stung his eyes, and a sob escaped him.

"Nagaro? Are ye awake?"

Taru's voice came from only a few feet away in the dark, sounding taut and raw as if the young man had been weeping. "I woke up about an hour ago, I think. I must ha' dozed again. It seems t' be night now." The voice paused. "Nagaro? Can ye hear me?"

"*Ye-es...*" It was all the answer that he could manage, and it came out sounding half-strangled.

"Are... are ye all right? Did they hurt ye too much?" This time Taru sounded worried.

Of course his friend must mean the Mahuk raiders... *Not those other men.* With an effort, Nagaro mastered himself enough to say, "Only my head... but that's not my trouble."

"What then?" Taru asked, but he got no answer. After a moment he ventured, "If ye're weeping for my parents, it's very good of ye, Nagaro. I've shed my tears already." The words were brave, but the ache in the young man's voice suggested the rawness of his wound.

"I'm sorry, Taru... I... I can't think of that now." Nagaro was aware he was being selfish, but he couldn't help it. His own pain was too great.

"What *is* it then, Nagaro? *What's the matter?*" Now Taru sounded alarmed.

He knew he needed to say something, but it was hard. He groaned. "It's all come back, Taru. I remember everything..."

There was a moment's hesitation. "Have ye killed someone? Is that it?"

"*No...*" He hadn't killed anyone, but he had wanted to... He'd even planned how he would do it. *He'd been so angry... more angry than it was good for anyone to be.*

"But... ye must remember who ye are. That's good, isn't it?"

A wave of revulsion washed over him. "*No! No, it isn't!*"

"But... why not?"

"Because..." He shuddered. "...*because... I'm... Leyel Virden!*"

There was a stunned silence, then Taru said, "But... ye *can't* be!" After another silence, he added, "I mean, if *ye're* Leyel Virden, who was that in Lankura?"

Nagaro squeezed his eyes shut against new tears that started to flow and swallowed hard. "It was me... *It was all just me!*"

"But *how?*" Taru was plainly struggling. "Was I right after all? Did the second fever somehow put the first one right?"

"*No!* The first fever never happened!" It helped to focus on specific questions. "That was a lie they told...to... *to cover up what they did to me!*"

He heard a chain rattle as Taru moved in the dark. Then he felt his friend's hand fumbling to grasp his arm. "*What* did they do? Who are *they?*"

"The men from my dreams. They were my *keepers...*" He spoke with bitter derision. "The red-faced man *was* Bron Sobring. The other two were Kale Fendred... and Gillard Marchent..."

"But they're all lords!" Taru sounded shocked. "I can't believe this! Lord Bron and—"

"—and the bearded man was Elgurn... and the hawk-faced one was *Dreigen.*" He nearly choked on the last name.

"The *king?* And his *lore master?*"

"It was Dreigen, mostly... But Elgurn should have stopped it! He said he didn't like it... but he just let it go on... *and on...*" Nagaro stopped. He wasn't making sense.

"Nagaro, what did they do? Tell me!"

He drew a long painful breath and began haltingly to explain as best he could. Taru led him on with questions, drawing the truth out of him. It got a little easier once he got started. It helped that Taru already knew some parts of the story.

"*Hamanei mata noa!*" Taru murmured when at last he understood. "There's bad spirit magic in this *heskial!*"

"Yes... very bad! It was like... like... being a wooden puppet with strings. The kind you see in the market..."

For eleven months, from Medrin to the end of the following Madrel, he had been Dreigen's helpless puppet...

"I couldn't do *anything*—except whatever I was told! I couldn't *stop* myself from doing it either—*no matter what it was!*" The memory of a hundred excruciatingly embarrassing scenes paraded through his mind, mocking him all over again. "And things kept happening that weren't in my instructions, and then I just *stood* there... stupidly... So everyone thought I was an *idiot!* What else could they think? And they said the cruelest things—right there in front of me—because they didn't think I understood!" A sob caught in his throat and he swallowed hard. "I was the laughing stock of all Lankura. Of all Edrovir! You heard what they were calling me in Wotana. '*The pretty-faced boy with no more wit than a cabbage*'—"

"Nagaro, don't! Please! My father didn't know it was you! Anyone who knows ye, knows ye're not like that—"

"*But nobody knows me, Taru!*" His voice caught on a sob, and he had a struggle to master himself. This was the very heart of his pain. He had to make Taru understand. After a moment he continued, more steadily. "Everyone in Edrovir *thinks* they know who Leyel Virden was, Taru. But I can count the number of people who really do on the fingers of my two hands!"

Taru could find no immediate response, and Nagaro lay in the dark with the agony of his thoughts echoing in his brain. The worst of it was, those who knew the truth were either servants and farmers—people of no account—or else they were the powerful people who had hurt him. *What was he to do now if he ever got off of this ship? He had no home to return to. He couldn't show his face in Lankura—couldn't speak his name anywhere in Edrovir.* He felt a fresh surge of bitter rage every time he thought of how completely his name, his reputation—his entire life— had been destroyed.

When he spoke again it was with barely suppressed fury. "Everyone believes Leyel Virden is dead. They think he met his end in the belly of a Mahuk war galley. Well, let it be so! I'll bury him here, and I swear I'll never use that name again! From this day on, I will be only Nagaro!"

Taru could do no more than murmur awkward words of sympathy.

Chapter 14: Words In The Dark

The two young men lay for a time in the foul, damp darkness, nursing their aching heads while the Mahuk ship carried them south into the gathering night, far from lands and waters they had known. Nagaro grew calmer as the first wave of his pain and anger ebbed. The emotions were still there, under the surface, but having spent a year with Taru's family helped to put some distance between him and what he'd suffered in Lankura.

"They left us some food and water," Taru said at last. "I already ate and drank. Ye should have the rest." Feeling blindly in the dark, the young Turo put things into Nagaro's hands—a strip of dried meat, a chunk of hard biscuit, and a stoppered gourd of water.

Nagaro devoured all of the food. He'd had nothing since breakfast and was so hungry that the rancid meat and stale biscuit almost tasted good. He drank sparingly of the water, though, pointing out that they might want it later. "How do you know it's night?" he asked.

"There was a bit o' light showing around the edges of what looks like a trapdoor up there above us, but it's gone now."

"Oh."

They lay quietly, feeling the ship's motion and listening to the creak of timbers. After a little while, Taru began to talk about the deaths of his parents and of how bad he felt that he hadn't been able to help them.

"I didn't even get my knife into one o' those brutes," he said bitterly. "I wasn't any use at all."

"I didn't do a lot better," Nagaro pointed out. "Rushing in without thinking... I should have gone for the man's sword instead of trying to use my knife. If I could have gotten my hand on a sword—"

"They would ha' just killed ye too. There were eight o' them!"

"I suppose you're right."

"We should ha' run back t' the forest—just as Father said. Why did I never *listen* to him, Nagaro? Why did I always argue? Now he's gone an' I'll never have another chance to learn what he was trying t' teach me!"

Nagaro struggled for an answer. "You still remember all the things he ever told you. You have that."

"I guess so..." Taru sighed. "I told my father I was sorry," he went on miserably, "before ye came running in t' join us. And d'ye know what he said? He said, 'It's all right.' That's the last thing he ever said to me! How could it be all right, Nagaro?"

This time Nagaro answered without hesitation. "If he said it was all right, then it *was* all right, Taru. He wouldn't have said anything he didn't mean. Not at a time like that."

"But *how* could he have meant it?"

"By not running away, you showed courage, Taru. And loyalty." He paused. "Your father was proud of you."

"Do ye really think so?"

"I know he was." Nagaro swallowed hard. "He was proud of your mother too. If she'd stayed hidden in the house, she'd still be alive. But she could no more have done that than you could have run away and hidden in the forest. She would have saved you both if she could."

"I know." Taru's voice turned bitter. "She shouldn't ha' died like that, Nagaro! If I can get out o' here—if I ever get my hand on a sword—I swear I'll make those rotters pay!" He sighed. "But she would ha' pined for Father. So if he had t' go, maybe it's best she went with him. And my father always said he'd rather die than be a slave, so I guess it's better for him too."

Nagaro nodded in the dark. "Your father chose his death, Taru. It took a lot of courage to stand there and take a sword thrust that way. Both of your parents were very brave." Nagaro didn't say all that was in his mind, that it was Olomi's death that had made Jomo resolve to seek his own.

"Well, they're gone," Taru said, his voice catching a little. "But I'll see them in Hanuroa."

Nagaro said nothing. He knew Hanuroa was the Turowan spirit world—the realm of the dead—but he didn't believe in such a place. The Writings of Vothra told him that the spirits of Jomo and Olomi would live again. Perhaps they'd already been reborn as tiny babes somewhere. That thought eased the anguish he felt over the violent manner of their deaths, but he never expected to see either one of them again, and that gave him sorrow.

They were long silent, and after a time, they both slept.

*

When Nagaro next woke, his head felt a little better. He lay listening to Taru's breathing and concluded that his friend was still asleep. At length, he sat up cautiously and found that it made his head throb some, but nothing worse. He investigated the chain that held him, feeling with his hands. It was about two feet long and composed of heavy iron links. The cuff that encircled his bare ankle was leather rather than iron, but very thick and strong. It was fastened to the chain by a massive rivet. He rubbed his ankle where the leather had already begun to chafe. "They've taken my boots," he muttered. "Those were good boots."

He remembered being fitted for an entire new wardrobe after he'd been brought to the palace, because his own clothes had been deemed "unsuitable." In fact, he now knew that the tall black boots had been the only thing remaining to him that were truly his...

No, not quite the only thing! Hastily he felt inside his tirkyl and was hugely relieved to find his ring still there on its chain. The Mahuk must not have searched him, doubtless not expecting a fisher-lad to have anything of value. But they would surely find it when they stripped him to the waist to bare his back for the lash.

Working by feel in the dark, he tore a strip of cloth from the hem of his tirkyl. He then unclasped the chain from his neck and slid the ring off of it. The chain he discarded by flinging it into the darkness. He tore a bit from one end of the strip of cloth to wrap around the ring, then threaded the remaining strip of cloth through the cloth-wrapped ring and tied the strip around his waist, pushing it down out of sight inside the waistband of his pants.

Just as he was finishing, he heard Taru move in the dark.

"What are ye doing, Nagaro?"

"Hiding my ring. I haven't been carrying it since I was twelve just to have some Mahuk make off with it." Briefly he explained what he'd done.

"That's a good idea," Taru said approvingly. "But I'm surprised the Leithians let ye keep it."

"It's only bronze. It can't be very valuable. High-born folk aren't going to steal a thing like that."

"Oh. No, I suppose not." There was a pause, filled with rhythmic creaking, the slosh of bilge water, and the muffled susurration of the sea against the outside of the ship's hull. At last Taru said, "Nagaro, how are we going t' get out o' this?"

Nagaro shivered in the dark. "I don't know."

"When they take us on deck, maybe we could jump overboard and swim for shore."

Taru sounded so hopeful that Nagaro hated to point out the flaw in this plan. "I can't swim with this chain, Taru. It would take me straight to the bottom."

"But they'll have t' take the chain off, to take us up on deck, won't they?"

"It's not meant to come off, Taru. The cuff is riveted. The lock is at the other end of the chain, where it's fastened to a ring in the bulkhead. The chain is going wherever I go."

There was silence while this sank in, then the sound of Taru's chain rattling. "*Hamanei!*" he muttered after a moment. "I don't think I could swim with that either." There was another silence. Then Taru spoke again, more thoughtfully. "The cuff's only leather. A sharp blade would cut through it."

Nagaro had already thought about that too. "A very sharp blade, maybe—like a Mahuk sword. It would take a lot of sawing with something like my old knife."

"So, if we can get our hands on a sword... or a good knife..." Taru sounded hopeful again.

"If I can get my hands on a sword, I'll be cutting something besides this leather! But the Mahuk must know what a slave could do with a sharp blade. It's not going to be easy, Taru."

"What's to be done then?"

Nagaro let out a long breath. "We'll have to wait for an opportunity—endure whatever happens for as long as we have to, and be ready to act whenever we get the chance." He paused, then added grimly, "I didn't live through the hell of heskial just to die like this. If I can survive *that*, I can survive anything!"

For a little while longer they talked about escape, but eventually they fell silent. Nagaro nearly dozed. He started when Taru spoke again.

"Was it the heskial that ye thought was going t' kill ye in the harness shed?"

Nagaro drew an uneven breath. He didn't like thinking about any of it, much less talking about it, but Taru deserved an answer. "Yes... except that what would have killed me was it wearing off. As long as Dreigen kept giving me more, I'd live, but—"

"But ye didn't like the way ye were living," Taru supplied.

It was a serious understatement, but accurate. "Whenever it started to wear off, there were a few minutes when I could move... Before the shaking would start... and the pain—" He had to stop for a gulp of air because his chest felt tight. "I'd try to get away whenever I could move. I was trying to die—"

Taru's sharp intake of breath was plainly audible in the dark pit of the ship's bilge. "*Ai, Nagaro!*"

"It was the only way out! Or I thought it was..." He shuddered, and swallowed. "I never got far. The shaking came on fast... and then they'd catch me. They told everyone that I had fits—that I needed 'medicine.' But it wasn't medicine. It was heskial."

"So that's what saved ye in the harness shed?"

Nagaro swallowed. "Yes. Nevien fetched Dreigen. He came... just in time... *I was so close.*"

Taru's chain rattled in the dark. "Why didn't ye tell someone what was going on?"

"*Because I couldn't speak!* Even when it wore off enough so that I could *move*, I couldn't *speak* right away. By the time I might have, there was too much pain. Dreigen told Elgurn he needn't worry that I'd ever tell anyone. By the time I could speak, I'd be screaming..."

Dreigen hadn't been quite right. He'd managed to say "No, don't go" to the princess in the harness shed. Those had been the only words of his own that he had spoken in all the time he'd been under the sway of the heskial.

"What about your Lady in Gray? What happened t' her?"

This was even more treacherous ground. Nagaro needed to master his emotion before he could speak. "She was Maramine Virden... *They murdered her—*" He choked.

"By the Spirits! *Why*, Nagaro?"

"Do you really want to know?" Nagaro's voice was tight with rage. "*Shall I tell you?*" He didn't wait for an answer. "Dreigen used Maramine to figure out how to use the heskial. But once he had *me*, he didn't need *her*! So he persuaded Bron to let her die—by stopping the drug." He shuddered at the memory. "*And they made me watch!* So I'd see what would happen if I tried to escape!"

"*Ai! Nagaro!*" A world of horror rang in Taru's words.

The scene was so vivid in Nagaro's mind: *Maramine lying on her bed, writhing in agony... screaming... and screaming...* "I couldn't *help* her, Taru! I couldn't *speak*... I couldn't *move*... *I couldn't even weep!*"

Emotion threatened to overwhelm him, to strangle his voice. With an effort, he swallowed past the painful constriction in his throat and steadied himself. When he could speak again, he said, "Bron plainly wished he'd never agreed to it. Kale ran out of the room. Dreigen was so... so *cold*... To him it was just another *experiment!* But Gill... Gill was the worst! I swear he *enjoyed it—*" Nagaro choked and drew a shuddering breath. "And *then*—right in the middle of it—Elgurn came... a day before they expected him. He walked right into it."

"Hamanei mata noa! What did he do?"

Nagaro tried to laugh. It came out as a harsh, strangled sound. "He had no more stomach for it than Bron! He was shouting... swearing... demanding that Dreigen stop it somehow. But Dreigen said there was nothing to be done. It was too late to save her with another dose of heskial. When Elgurn heard *that*, he swore by all the gods he owned! He picked up one of the bed pillows, and he pressed it over my Lady's face! And he held it there until she stopped moving..."

Nagaro was shaking. He couldn't say any more. He had watched in agonized, immobile silence while Dreigen probed the lady's throat with his long fingers, then raised his hard, dark eyes and said those three horrible words: "She is dead."

After a long moment he found his voice again. "That's how my Lady died. Elgurn smothered her—because he couldn't bear to listen to her screams."

"The king? I can't believe it..." Taru stumbled on.

But Nagaro wasn't listening. The memory of what had happened next was still playing in his mind. Elgurn had flung the pillow away, then turned and seen him sitting at the opposite end of the room. "What is he doing here?" the king had demanded. No one had answered, so the king had turned on Dreigen and said, "I want you to release the boy!" Dreigen had calmly explained why he couldn't. Nagaro remembered the king's words. "There is no cure? No counter-drug? You're quite sure?" And Dreigen's flat response had been, "There is none, My Lord." Elgurn's face had been ashen as he demanded, "Do you mean to tell me that you've killed them both?"

Dreigen's reply had been utterly infuriating in its coolness. "Oh no, My Lord. The lady died by your hand, and the boy still lives. He will live as long as you wish him to, and do whatever you ask." For a moment it had seemed that Elgurn might strike the Lore Master, but the moment had passed. And when next the king had spoken it had been with icy calm. "Why did you never tell me that the heskial would kill?" Dreigen's answer had been smoothly matter-of-fact. "You never asked, My Lord. But, what of it? The lady's death is not inconvenient. Her family has disowned her and will make no inquiry. And the boy is of no account. Once he's fulfilled his purpose, he is surely of no further use."

Elgurn had stood stonily for perhaps half a minute after that, the expression on his face unreadable. Then he'd turned on Bron and Gill. Bron had started to protest, "My Lord... I never imagined it would be like this! He didn't tell me!" Elgurn had cut him off with, "Enough!" Then he'd strode to the door and called for Kale.

Kale had come, entering the room with an expression like that of a man who's been watching demons dance upon his own grave. Elgurn had addressed them all then, saying, "The Lady Maramine died of a fever of the brain. Remember that! It is at least half true." Then he turned to Kale and said, "Take the boy to his chamber and bid him sleep." Kale had done as instructed with his usual gentleness, but Nagaro knew he would never have been able to sleep if the heskial hadn't made the instruction an imperative. It had been during that sleep that Maramine's death dream had first come to him—the dream in which she had warned him not to be ruled by anger...

"Nagaro?"

He shook himself. "What is it, Taru?"

"I asked ye a question. Why did the king choose ye for this?"

"Why me?" Nagaro remembered what Dreigen had said. He spat

the words. *"Because I'm a fatherless bastard with nice manners and a pretty face!"*

"But surely he should ha' chosen some high-born lad..."

Nagaro frowned. He'd had a theory about that. He saw no reason to doubt it now. "Elgurn must have believed the tale that Maramine was my mother," he said. "Dreigen certainly did. That would have given me noble blood on one side. And I was schooled well enough to pass for nobility if appearance was all that mattered. We had no family to protect us since Maramine's family had disowned her. Elgurn could do whatever he had to with us to get what he wanted."

"And he wanted... what? An *heir?* Like in your last dream?"

"Not *just* an heir, I'm sure—one he could control, one that no other noble house had any interest in. Of course, he didn't tell me any of this when he offered me the hand of the princess, but—"

"The *king* made that offer? *Himself?*"

Nagaro shifted his position. The hard planks under his shoulder were making it ache almost as much as his head. He turned on his side and tried to use his arm for a pillow. "Yes, but I didn't know he was the king. He didn't tell me. Neither did Maramine. And he wasn't wearing his crown when he came to Averwin. He just rode up one day and talked to Maramine for about an hour in her study. Then she came out and told me that this man had come to make a proposal. She said I should listen and think carefully about what he said, but that the choice was mine. Then she sent me in to see him. He introduced himself as 'Lord of Harlind.' I knew Harlind was the name of the Royal House, but I thought he was some *other* lord of Harlind."

"And he asked ye to go to Lankura and marry the princess?" Taru's tone said plainly that he was having trouble believing what he was hearing.

"Well, yes..."

"And ye just said *no?*"

"I didn't *just* say no. I was polite about it. I thanked him for the offer, and told him I was honored, but I didn't want to do it."

"But why, Nagaro? Why'd ye turn it down?"

Nagaro bridled. He had never thought the offer might sound good to Taru. "Because I had no wish to marry a girl I'd never met!" he said vehemently. "Or to live in a palace and wear satin pants! I didn't want to spend my time smiling and bowing and attending ceremonies. I wanted to join the Fleet or the Royal Guard!"

"Oh. Right." Taru didn't sound entirely convinced, but he didn't press the matter. Instead, he asked, "What did Elgurn say when ye told him?"

"He just said 'very well,' and told me I could go. He talked to my

Lady some more, and then he left. Since she didn't seem upset about what I'd done, I supposed that the man would just find somebody else. But a week later, the three Leithians came—with Dreigen. And... it all started..." Nagaro's voice trailed off.

"It seems t' me the king went to an awful lot o' trouble..." Taru said cautiously.

Nagaro frowned. His head was beginning to throb again, but he tried to explain. "Elgurn didn't set out to go to so much trouble," he said. "Using the... heskial... on my Lady Guardian to try to convince me was Dreigen's plan that Elgurn just agreed to. And after *that* didn't work, it was Bron who let Dreigen use it on *me*. Elgurn only agreed to *that* after it was already done. He thought it would be temporary. Dreigen didn't tell him the drug would kill me until after he'd killed Maramine..."

Nagaro's voice died but his thoughts ran careening on. *He'd thought that would be the end of it, that Elgurn would tell them to kill him and have done. But the king had kept trying... and trying... for eleven long, horrible months...*

With an effort he forced himself to think about something else—to focus on the dark and the damp and the stink of the bilge. He tried to find a more comfortable position on the planking. Eventually he said, "I wonder where the ship is now."

"By the length o' the swells, I'd say that we're in deep water." Taru's voice came confidently out of the darkness.

"That makes sense. I'd expect them to have made for the open sea. Beyond the islands."

"And I think the wind's dropped. We're not making as good way as we were the first time I woke up. I can tell by the sound she makes as she cuts the water."

Nagaro stirred again. "You don't think they're rowing?"

"I'm pretty sure that'd feel different. And sound different."

"I suppose you're right. We'd hear the oars splashing... or something..." Nagaro fell silent. They would soon be learning more about the rowing than they wished to know.

"Nagaro?"

"Yes?"

"If ye'd just agreed t' marry the princess, what would ha' happened after the king got his heir?"

Nagaro laughed a short, bitter laugh. "*If* I'd lived that long, I doubt I would have lived much longer. I'd have been in somebody's way. And without a powerful house behind me to threaten reprisal, I'd have been murdered like Fargil. He was the son of the Lord of Galenor, and all he did was court the princess. But somebody didn't want him to win her, so he met with some convenient highway thieves."

"Hamanei! Getting mixed up in court doings sounds dangerous!"

Nagaro nodded in the dark. "That's another reason I didn't accept Elgurn's offer. If I'm going to risk my life, I'd rather it was in a clean fight with a sword in my hand than have someone poison me or stick a knife in my back!"

This was an argument Taru could appreciate. "By all the Spirits!" he exclaimed. "It's a good thing ye got away! And ye'd best not be going back, either!"

"I don't intend to." Nagaro muttered the words, then fell silent. He was thinking again of all he had lost. "If there's anything else you want to know, Taru, you'd best ask me now," he said. "Once they put us in with the other slaves, there won't be any chance to talk about it."

"Ye're right about that." Taru paused. "Let me think... At least now I understand about the harness shed."

Nagaro's chain clinked as he shifted in the darkness, waiting with some trepidation to see what else his friend might ask. If Taru thought he understood the incident in the harness shed, Nagaro was content to let him think so. *It had been near the end of the whole ordeal—only days before the Mahuk raid—*and it had happened as a result of Elgurn's way of dealing with his daughter's squeamishness...

The king had ordered Dreigen to reduce the dose of heskial and to time it so that it would wear off when he and Nevien were together in the evening, in her chamber. That had given him a few minutes of control before the shaking started. Elgurn had tried to persuade him to use that time to *cooperate*... But he had used the opportunity to run away instead—to try to find a place to die...

But that wasn't all he'd thought about doing that night. There had been a ceremonial sword and a pair of daggers on the wall in the sitting room, just across the hall, and Elgurn had been in his chamber just a few doors away. But killing Elgurn would have been of little use. Elgurn was the master, but Dreigen was the instrument. And in the end, he'd decided not to try to kill Dreigen either. Why? Because of the words of Maramine's death dream, urging against vengeance? He wished it had been so. But the truth was that he'd been afraid—afraid that he would fail... afraid to think what form the Lore Master's vengeance might take. *Oh, there were surely fates much worse than death...* So on that night, he'd run away, all the way out into the garden, to the harness shed. It was the farthest he'd ever gotten... the closest he'd ever come to dying...

"Nagaro? Are ye still married t' the princess?"

Oh, Vothra! It was a question Nagaro was unprepared for, and a host of mortifying memories instantly flooded his mind. *That marriage...*

He remembered the wedding all too well... It had been performed in the garden with a minimum number of guests, and it might have gone quite smoothly if Nevien hadn't twice strayed from the script so that the puppet part of him had missed its cue. Both times, Elgurn had stepped in to whisper an instruction into his ear, but not before he'd stood silent for far too long. It must have looked as if he'd forgotten his lines and lacked the wit to improvise—or even to ask for help. And then, at the end of it, there had been that clumsy excuse for a kiss...

With an effort, he jerked his thoughts clear and tried to answer Taru's question. "How can I be bound by that marriage?" he demanded. "The words I spoke were put into my mouth. And besides that, it was never consummated."

"What does that mean? *Con-soo-may-ted?*"

Turning crimson in the dark, Nagaro explained.

"What? Not even *once*?" Taru was incredulous. "I know ye didn't want t' give the king what he wanted, but I thought ye couldn't help doing what they told ye t' do. How could ye be married all those months and *never...?*" His voice trailed off as it dawned on him what he was asking.

There was silence, in which the sounds of the ship's bilge seemed suddenly to fill the darkness. At last Nagaro said, "She didn't want me."

"But, Nagaro, why wouldn't she?"

Nagaro tasted bitter bile. "How *could* she, Taru?" he asked wretchedly. "The way I was... The way I *seemed* to be... She didn't know what was going on. Her father kept everything from her. But I had to *obey* her! She only had to shake her head, or say one word... to... to override any other instructions..."

"*I'm sorry, Nagaro!*" Taru's tone was agonized. "*I never should have asked!*"

"It's all right," Nagaro answered, too quickly. "I wanted it that way."

Which was true, as far as it went. He had been glad, then, of anything that thwarted Elgurn's plans. Now, however, as he looked back, the memory of Nevien's rejection hurt his youthful pride—though he couldn't blame her for it. It would have been funny, if it hadn't been so horrible. Dreigen had bent him to his will in so many ways, yet the Lore Master had failed to achieve Elgurn's cherished goal because he'd had no idea how to win the heart of a maid! In retrospect, the thought gave Nagaro some small measure of satisfaction.

Dreigen had surely never been with a woman in his life, and the man's instructions in the art of romance had been ludicrously inadequate. At first, Dreigen had instructed him to tell the princess she was beautiful every time she asked a question he hadn't been told how to answer. It might have seemed a clever cover-all—if she hadn't asked so *many* questions! How many times had he said, "you are very beautiful," the very first day? Of course Nevien had quickly realized the words were empty. Dreigen had kept refining the instructions, but the damage had been done. If Nagaro hadn't been so angry, he never could have borne it.

And the king had known something was wrong. When Nevien had failed, month after month, to conceive, Elgurn had confronted Dreigen. But the Lore Master had blamed everything on the princess. It was *her* reluctance that was ruining Elgurn's plans. His proposed solution? To instruct the idiot prince to *ignore the girl's protests*. Nagaro remembered vividly—painfully—the king's response. *"I will not have my daughter raped by this* thing *you have created!"*

He writhed at the thought. The puppet part of him could have forced itself upon her, even hurt her. He could never have lived with that. Fortunately, they had tried it Elgurn's way instead—reducing the dose of heskial...

He realized Taru was speaking.

"Well, if ye don't think it was a proper marriage, at least ye're not going t' think ye have to go back to Lankura on account of it," his friend was saying. "That's something. But what I'd really like t' know is why ye didn't die—and how ye escaped."

Nagaro shook off the memories that had held him in thrall. This was safer ground, except that Taru wasn't going to like the answer.

"I don't know."

"What? Ye *still* don't?"

Nagaro blew air through his teeth. "There's still a gap in my memory—a much smaller one. I thought everything would be clear when the Spirit of the White Flower released its hold on me, but I still don't know what the Spirit of the White Flower *is*, or how it came to help me. I don't even remember the attack on the palace—"

"Not at *all?*"

Nagaro drew a long breath. "I remember being with Nevien in her chamber. I had drunk some wine, and I felt very strange—like my head was on fire. I stood up... and then everything just fades out. Nothing else is clear until after I woke up in your house on Wotana Bay."

There was a little silence, until Taru said, "Do ye remember running through the forest?"

"I don't know, Taru. I've dreamed about it so much, I suppose it must have happened. But it's always seemed unreal... And your house is twenty miles from Lankura. Could I really have run that far in a single night?"

Taru had no immediate answer. After a moment, he said, "Do ye think there was something in the wine?"

Nagaro heaved a sigh. "Maybe. Or it could just have been the wine itself. Or maybe it was just the fever..."

Neither of them spoke for a time, until Taru said, "Are ye sure ye would ha' died without the heskial? Maybe Dreigen lied about that."

Nagaro had thought about that too. "Dreigen lied to Elgurn about a number of things," he said. "But I don't think he was lying about that. I came so close to dying in the harness shed. Another minute, and I think it would have been too late. In the end, *something* saved me from the heskial, though he said there wasn't anything that could. Either he was lying about *that*, or there was something even he didn't know about."

There was another pause. Then Taru said, "I think' ye must have had the help o' the Spirits that night." The young Turo spoke reverently. "I never heard of your Spirit o' the White Flower before, but there's all kinds o' spirits, and some of them take it into their heads t' look after people. Your Spirit o' the White Flower must be one of those."

"Maybe..." The Vothrin writings made no mention of the Turowan World Spirits, but Nagaro believed it was Vothra's voice that had told him about the Spirit of the White Flower, so he said no more.

They passed the gourd between them and each took a swallow of water. Then they lay in the dark, feeling the motion of the ship and letting their thoughts run.

"Do ye know what I think, Nagaro?" Taru suddenly asked. "I think the king wanted your seed."

"*What?*" Nagaro was so astonished that he sat up in the darkness in spite of his aching head.

"I think he wanted your seed because of how ye can ride, and shoot, and handle a sword. He was hoping your son'd be good at those things too."

"What am I, a prize stud horse?" Nagaro didn't like the idea at all. But Taru's mind was sharp, and it ran along paths more devious than his own. It made sense to give his friend's idea serious consideration. All he could think of, however, was how Maramine had sometimes brought in extra money by selling the services of the tall black stallion he'd so loved to ride—until she had been forced to sell the horse to help pay Fendar's fee...

Fendar's fee... Fendar the swordmaster... He groaned aloud. "You might just be right, Taru," he said. "Not about the riding and shooting, I think, but swordsmanship is a useful talent for a king—because of the Right of Challenge." It was a Leithian custom, but one even Darion had been forced to observe. The Right of Challenge allowed any lord who thought himself more suited to the crown to challenge the king in single combat.

"Well, ye *are* good..." Taru ventured.

Nagaro was silent for a long moment. Then he said, "I think I have a gift for swordsmanship." He sighed. "Do you remember what I told you about Master Fendar?"

"Your swordmaster? Aye."

"When I was in Lankura—that summer—there was a sword tourney at the palace, and I had to sit in the audience. The best swordsmen from all over Edrovir were there. Fendar took second place."

Taru whistled. "And ye said ye beat him once or twice?"

"I won half of the last six bouts we fought. That was when Fendar told Maramine there wasn't anything more he could teach me. I thought he might have been holding back with me, but, watching that tourney, I... well... I think I could have made it some way up the ranking."

"*Hakura!* Nagaro, we've got t' get ye a sword somehow so ye can teach these devils a lesson!"

Nagaro was suddenly very aware of the dark and the damp and the pain in his head. He lay back down on the planks. "I'm not saying I wouldn't like to try, Taru," he said. "But it's been two years since I held a sword, and that was only a dull-edged one meant for practice. I've never fought for blood—much less killed anyone—"

"Aye, but there's a first time for all things!" Taru brushed the objections aside. "Ye've been practicing, too, even if our swords *were* made o' wood!"

Nagaro didn't answer. He doubted he could say anything to dampen Taru's enthusiasm, and his friend's theory did seem to fit. It really did look as if his past troubles might have begun because he'd possessed a desirable talent—one he might be expected to pass on to his descendants. Eventually he asked, "What hour do you suppose it is?"

"I don't know, Nagaro. Surely past mid-night."

"Then we should try to sleep. Tomorrow is going to be hard."

They both fell silent. Nagaro curled up on his side, pillowing his head in the crook of his arm. He let his breath come, slow and easy, trying to empty his mind. Gradually he began to drift and the first jumbled images of a dream began to coalesce.

The princess Nevien was there, walking away from him on the arm of a blond-haired man. She turned back, looking over her shoulder, a furtive gesture... There was fear in her eyes. And the man turned then, too, as if following her glance. His handsome face was marred by a long scar. He smiled, a chillingly empty smile that showed his teeth. There was a hunger in his eyes...

Nagaro jerked awake. The dream images fled, but the thought that had wakened him still held him in its grip. "*No!*" he cried. "By the eyes of Vothra's mind! I can't let them do it!"

"What...?" Taru's voice came sleepily.

"They've married the princess to Gillard Marchent! He was *horrible!*" Nagaro was sitting up again, feeling for the chain that held him. "Kale didn't do much to help me, but at least he felt sorry for me. Bron hated me for no reason at all. But Gill was the worst! He didn't care two rins about me. He just enjoyed being cruel! I can't *bear* to think they've married Nevien to that man!"

"Well, I don't know what ye're going t' do about it," Taru observed. "They're lords, and ye're not. And besides, ye're chained to a bulkhead."

Nagaro gave his chain a futile yank. "But... she was kind to me—as kind as could be expected anyway..." In fact, she had treated him rather as a mother treats a small child whose inappropriate behavior stems from innocence and ignorance. It had been humiliating, but he couldn't blame her for it. "If I hadn't run away—"

"If ye hadn't run away, ye'd be dead by now," Taru said matter-of-factly. "Be sensible. Even if ye were free, ye couldn't go back there. They'd surely kill ye! Ye'll just have to trust the king t' look after his daughter."

Nagaro let the chain drop from his fingers. Taru was right. Resignedly, he lay down again on the cold planks. He didn't doubt that Elgurn cared for his daughter, but he also knew what the king was capable of putting the girl through to achieve his ends. *How many nights had she lain beside him and wept?* He tried to put the thought out of his mind, willing himself to lie still, trying to clear his mind again so he could find slumber.

The slow seconds ticked past. "Nagaro?" Apparently Taru wasn't sleeping either.

"Mmm."

"What does your name, *Leyel*, mean anyway?"

Nagaro resisted the impulse to say that it wasn't his name anymore. Taru meant no harm. "It's a kind of gift," he said. "A gift of chance, or a gift unlooked-for. I suppose that's what I was to Maramine, in the beginning." He paused, feeling the raw edge of a new pain. After a moment he said huskily, "In the end, I was the death of her. She died because I said no to the king."

"It wasn't your fault, Nagaro. Ye didn't know."

"No. I didn't." He sighed. She had told him the choice was his. She'd even seemed pleased by his choice. But he doubted she had known what would come of it.

"Try not t' think about it, Nagaro. Try to sleep."

It wasn't easy. Nagaro lay awake for a long time, thinking. No, he wasn't to blame for Maramine's death, any more than Taru was to blame for Jomo's or Olomi's. Those deaths had been cruel and unnecessary, the result of men acting badly. In a world where all men sought to do good, such things would not be. Was it possible, he wondered, that there could ever be such a world? Vothra bade every spirit to strive for it. Nagaro frowned in the darkness. Vothra also said that everyone should use whatever gifts they were given to do good in the world. Nagaro wasn't sure how he could use his gift for swordsmanship to do good when he couldn't go back to Lankura to join the Royal Fleet, but he determined that he would try to find a way if only he could get free. Lying there in the dark, listening to the groaning of the ship's timbers and the wash of waves against the hull, that thought brought him enough peace that he was at last able to sleep.

Chapter 15: The Oar Deck

They awakened to the sounds of feet tramping to and fro on the planks above their heads. This evidence that it was morning was corroborated by the appearance of a narrow line of light around the edges of a square in the planking above where they lay. A third sign seemed more ominous—a rhythmic, muffled thudding that accompanied a noticeable change in the motion of the ship, each thud coinciding with a distinct forward surge.

"They're beating a drum to mark the time for the rowers," Taru explained. "I heard it sometimes when one of our own war galleys came close t' Father's boat."

The sea warriors came for them about two hours later. They had just drunk the last of the water, and Nagaro was trying with little success to make out the shapes of their surroundings by the tiny glimmer of light, when there suddenly came a scraping of wood from the direction of the square of planking they'd concluded was a trapdoor. An instant later, the trapdoor opened and light flooded in as a ladder was lowered. Momentarily dazzled, Nagaro instinctively rolled into a crouching position, uncertain what to expect. As his eyes adjusted, he saw that Taru was crouching as well. Fleetingly, he made out the dimensions of the long, low cavern that was the ship's hold, cluttered with spare timbers, planks, coils of rope, and barrels of tar. Then the light was partially occluded as a warrior descended the ladder. Two more followed.

The men approached Taru first since he was closer to the ladder. Two of them lunged at the young Turo, grabbing him and pinning his arms. The third used an iron key that he carried on a loop of cord to unlock Taru's chain from the ring embedded in the bulkhead. As the men dragged Taru towards the foot of the ladder, Nagaro moved forward, still crouching, until his chain brought him up short. He couldn't get close to them, and in any case, none of the three carried a sword or blade of any kind.

Taru cast him a worried look but went up the ladder when the warriors released his arms and made it clear they wanted him to ascend. When his head reached the level of the trapdoor, other hands reached down from above to haul him upward.

The warriors waited only until Taru was securely held above before returning for their second captive. Nagaro made no effort to resist, but went up the ladder, dragging his chain behind him.

The trapdoor led to a triangular room in the bow of the ship. It was lit by a pair of portholes on each side and contained various chests and barrels as well as another ladder, leading upwards. There were a number of sea warriors there already. Nagaro recognized some of them from the raiding party that had come ashore at Wotana Bay. One of these, a broad-shouldered man with grizzled hair and an ugly scar over his right cheekbone, held Taru. The young Turo stood sullenly with his right arm twisted painfully behind his back. Nagaro soon found himself secured in the same way by one of the other men.

As the last Mahuk sea warrior emerged from the trapdoor, one of the others re-fastened it with a wooden batten. As this one straightened, Nagaro recognized him as another member of the raiding party. Nagaro realized with a shock that this man was no more than a youth, smooth-faced, and no older than he or Taru.

The man who had used the key was burly and barrel-chested, with a crooked nose and markings on his uniform that indicated he was an officer. He crossed to a door in the aft wall, and flung it open, holding it so while he exchanged words with someone on the other side. It was through that open door that Nagaro got his first glimpse of the oar deck. He had an impression of a large space lit only by a few lanterns and the light that entered through the oar ports. Two double rows of ragged, half-naked men bent and strained rhythmically at the huge oars to the throbbing drumbeat. He expected that he and Taru would be dragged through the doorway, but the crooked-nosed officer closed the door again when he had finished speaking, and the two friends were pressed instead to climb the second ladder, guards ahead of them and behind.

The second ladder took them up into the ship's forward cabin where it was clear that most of the ship's warrior crewmen made their beds. The walls bore double or triple tiers of bunks all around, and the space between was fitted for the slinging of hammocks. Nagaro and Taru were forcibly marched through this room and out by another door onto the deck of the ship, where they found themselves blinking in the full light of a sun-washed morning.

The brilliance of the sunlight made Nagaro's head begin to ache once more. Still, the feel of the fresh, salt wind on his face was wonderful after a night spent in the close, foul air of the ship's hold. They had no time to savor it, however, being immediately marched across the deck, dragging their chains, to the foot of the great foremast. At the base of the mast was a heavy iron ring set in the wood, and to this ring their chains were made fast. Only then were their arms released.

Most of the sea warriors now stepped away from them, moving off across the deck. Two remained, standing at a little distance with impassive faces and crossed arms, apparently on guard. Nagaro ignored them even as he ignored his aching head. He'd often wondered what it would be like to stand on the deck of one of these big ships. Under other circumstances he would have admired the great mast, the size of a tree trunk, or studied the rigging of the huge foresail. Now, however, his eyes swept the horizon, searching for land.

His heart sank. The only land he could see was a series of islands on the port side of the ship. They were a very long way off, no more than dark silhouettes with the morning sun behind them. Even if he could have freed himself and his friend from their chains, they could never have swum so far. Since the islands lay to port, he knew they must be sailing south along the seaward side of the Outer Faranos. The ship was making good headway under the combined power of oar and sail. From where he stood, Nagaro couldn't see the oars, but he could feel the forward surge each stroke produced.

Abruptly his thoughts were interrupted by the voice of his friend. "Ai, Nagaro! They're going to brand us!" Taru pointed past the mast to where a group of men had gathered amidships.

Nagaro followed his friend's gesture. As he looked, two of the clustered men moved aside and he saw that they were gathered around a brazier of glowing coals, set in a large tub of sand. Several iron rods protruded from the brazier, and one of the men now lifted one of these. The end of it was shaped into some sort of design. It glowed bright red.

Taru uttered a low groan. "I've heard o' this, but I hoped it wasn't true. I don't want t' be branded, Nagaro!"

Nagaro didn't like the idea either. He noted that some of the men in the group at the brazier wore swords, as did a number of other warriors idling about the deck. He didn't see what he could do, though, even if he could manage to get his hand on a blade. There were too many Mahuk and nowhere to go, with or without the chain on his leg.

Three men left the group around the brazier and approached the captives. They bore no weapons. One of them, the barrel-chested man with the crooked nose, planted himself in front of the two young men. He pointed at Taru's tirkyl. "Take off shirt!" he commanded in accented Common Speech. "Now!"

Taru folded his arms across his chest and looked defiant. The man barked an order to the other two crewmen in their own tongue, and several of them immediately grabbed Taru and began pulling off his tirkyl. Taru resisted vigorously, twisting and struggling in the grip of his captors. The only result was that the men pulled more roughly. There was a sound of tearing cloth, and the rent garment was flung unceremoniously on the deck. Released, Taru stood glowering, bare chested, with his fists clenched.

The big man with the crooked nose nodded his satisfaction and then turned his attention to Nagaro. "Take off shirt!" he commanded as before, pointing at Nagaro's tirkyl. Nagaro returned the man's stare coldly. Then, very deliberately, he removed his tirkyl. With exaggerated care, he began to fold the garment.

"*Bishka!*" It was one of the other men, the one with the scar on his face and streaks of gray in his hair, who suddenly swore and tore the tirkyl from Nagaro's hands, flinging it away across the deck. The man with the crooked nose merely laughed, and issued another order to his two subordinates.

They took Taru first. The two crewmen seized and held the young Turo, while the crooked-nosed officer unfastened the end of his chain from the mast. Then they dragged him away across the deck in the direction of the brazier. Nagaro could only watch helplessly, shivering without a shirt in the chill sea air.

Taru fought every inch of the way, alternately bracing with his bare feet against the deck planking and kicking furiously at his captors' legs. Despite his efforts, he was forced down onto the deck beside the brazier. Two of the sea warriors attempted to hold the young Turo still for the branding, but he redoubled his efforts, twisting wildly, kicking, and even trying to bite his tormentors.

Taru couldn't have kept up this fight for long, but the scar-faced officer didn't wait for him to tire. The man aimed a vicious kick at the youth's belly, catching him just below the ribs. Taru doubled up on his right side, clutching his stomach in pain. The other warriors took immediate advantage. It required but an instant to press the hot iron against the naked skin of the young Turo's left shoulder. Still crippled from the kick, and unprepared for the suddenness of the iron, Taru screamed. It was a piercing sound that cut across nerves like a knife. A moment later, the warriors dragged Taru's sagging body back to the foot of the foremast. There they dropped him, locking his chain once again to the iron ring.

Taru lay moaning on the deck, his right hand clutching his wounded shoulder, his left arm wrapped protectively across his bruised belly. Where his hand gripped his side, the knuckles showed white. Before he was dragged away, Nagaro caught one glimpse of his friend's face. Taru looked pale about the lips, and his eyes were wide with pain and shock.

Nagaro put up only token resistance, enough to show that he didn't willingly submit to this cruel indignity. He'd seen the ineffectiveness of Taru's efforts. There was nothing to be done but bear it as best he could.

After all, he felt that pain was something of which he had some experience.

All too quickly, he found himself pushed roughly down onto the deck beside the brazier. A dozen strong hands held him on his side with his left shoulder facing up. He saw the bright red iron raised. He looked away, his eyes seeking a distant point where the ship's rail met the bright blue morning sky. Just above the spot, there was a single tiny wisp of cloud like a gull's feather of purest white. He willed himself to keep his eyes on that bit of cloud. In his mind he repeated like a litany the words from the Book of Vothra: *All pain ends, if only in death, and death is not an end but the path to a new beginning...* Even so, he had to clamp his teeth together with all his strength to keep from crying out when the iron struck. The searing pain was ten-fold more intense than that of Dreigen's candle flame, and it struck suddenly at full intensity—nothing like the slowly-building pain of heskial withdrawal.

All pain ends, if only in death... and death is not an end...

He kept his eyes on the wisp of cloud, but someone moved to block his view. His focus broken, Nagaro looked up at the figure standing over him. With his mind full of pain, it took him a moment to notice that the man's right arm was in a sling. A bulge under the warrior's shirt further revealed where the man's shoulder had been bandaged. Dimly Nagaro realized that this must be the man he'd stabbed with his fishing knife.

As if in response to the dawning comprehension in Nagaro's eyes, the man lashed out at him, kicking him savagely in the ribs with the toe of his boot. The sudden new jolt of pain, on top of the agony of his burn, was too much. A moan escaped from between Nagaro's clenched teeth. *"Shaku raal!"* The words were spoken with satisfaction and fine contempt. With that, the warrior turned on his heel and stalked off across the deck.

Nagaro shut his eyes. *All pain ends... All pain ends...* He felt himself being dragged across the smooth, hard deck planks. The motion ceased. Chain rattled. He didn't need to open his eyes to guess that his chain had once again been locked to the foremast. Close beside him, he could hear Taru's ragged breathing. His own burned shoulder screamed agony, and his ribs hurt with every indrawn breath.

All pain ends... All pain ends...

A shadow fell across his face, and almost involuntarily he opened his eyes, fearing some new cruelty. The figure of a man loomed over him, grim-faced and hard-eyed, speaking words in the Mahuk tongue. Nagaro's mind registered gold insignia on the man's scarlet tunic, and a new leather patch covering the man's left eye. It was the ship's captain—and the man who'd led the raiding party. The man bore the grim reminder of Jomo's handiwork. Nagaro couldn't find the strength to care. He closed his eyes again and kept them so, even when a booted foot prodded him painfully in the side. There followed another stream of gloating words, among which "shaku" was several times repeated, and more painful prodding.

Nagaro groaned loudly, hoping the man would be satisfied by this expression of his misery. Apparently it worked, for the captain laughed harshly, and Nagaro felt the morning sun on his face again and heard the sound of boots moving off across the deck.

Some indefinite time later, Nagaro felt a hand touch his arm. Reluctantly he opened his eyes, imagining that it must be Taru. Instead he found the Mahuk youth he'd noticed earlier, kneeling beside him with a pot of salve in his hand. His face impassive, the young man indicated by gestures his intent to apply some of the pot's contents to the wound on Nagaro's shoulder. "This make it better," he said.

Surprised at being shown such consideration, Nagaro only nodded mutely. The touch of the youth's fingers was surprisingly gentle. Nevertheless, it at first caused the pain to escalate almost unbearably. Nagaro gritted his teeth hard, but after a moment he found himself able to relax a little as the blinding pain receded to a dull throbbing that was a considerable improvement over what it had been before the ointment was applied.

In the meantime, the young man had moved on to attend to Taru, who lay curled about himself with his eyes tight shut. The Mahuk youth reached out and attempted to pull Taru's hand away from his burned shoulder. Taru's eyes flickered open briefly. "*Devil's get!*" he growled through clenched teeth. He clutched his shoulder more tightly, winced, and gasped at the pain caused by his own touch.

The young man frowned slightly and shook his head. "It not heal without *chutapaak*," he said, and tried again to move Taru's hand. This time Taru let go, but then he blindly struck the youth's hand away.

Nagaro sat up gingerly. He was feeling somewhat better since the salve had begun to work. "It's all right, Taru," he said. "Let him do it. It makes the pain better."

Taru's eyes snapped fully open at the sound of his friend's voice. He stared at Nagaro as if trying to focus. "It's all right," Nagaro repeated. "Let him put the salve on the burn. It will hurt worse at first, when he touches it, but then it will get better."

The young man glanced from Taru to Nagaro and back again. Then he scooped some of the salve from the little pot and gingerly reached out to apply it to Taru's wound. This time Taru allowed it. As the youth applied the salve, the young Turo winced violently and began to mutter, "*hamanei mata noa... hamanei mata noa...*" Taru had found his own litany.

When the young Mahuk had finished his task, he replaced the cover on the pot of salve and moved to go. On an impulse, Nagaro reached out and gripped the young man's arm. The youth froze, staring at him with something like alarm in his eyes. Nagaro held the other's gaze until the alarm faded. "Thank you," he said then, and released his hold. The young warrior rose hastily and moved away, his face once again an impassive mask.

Nagaro lay painfully back down on the deck. He was not, however, allowed to rest for long. The crooked-nosed officer with the key returned with four other warriors, and the two captives were dragged to their feet. They were then marched, staggering, back across the deck to the forward cabin, and down the ladder to the triangular room adjoining the oar deck. There they were flung down, chained to the aft wall bulkhead, and left to themselves.

Both young men were feeling a little better by this time, though their burns still smarted and they were bruised and sore. They managed to sit up, supporting themselves against the planks of the bulkhead. After a time, Nagaro examined the brand on his shoulder, trying to make out the shape of the mark. It was a thing rather like a figure eight with an "S" lying on its side across the middle of it. "I wonder what it means," he said aloud.

Taru gave a bitter laugh. "It's the mark o' whichever bloody Mahuk warlord thinks he owns us." He frowned angrily. "Branded like cattle!" he muttered. "I'll carry this mark 'til the day I die. Ai, Nagaro, I'm glad my father didn't live t' see this!"

Nagaro sighed. "I don't like it either," he said. "But it's only a mark on my skin. They can't put their mark on my spirit, unless I put it there myself."

"Huh! What good are *words?* They won't wash this mark away! And what did ye go and thank that young devil for anyway? He was just following orders."

Nagaro studied Taru's face. "I'm sure he was—about putting on the salve," he said. "But he could have been much less gentle about it."

"So ye thanked him for *not* kicking ye? Is that it?"

"No." Nagaro frowned, trying to put into words the feeling that he'd had. "He's very young, Taru. Perhaps he hasn't yet learned to be cruel."

"Nagaro, *he's a Mahuk!*"

"Yes. And I'm a Kelorin, and you're a Turo."

"The Mahuk are *different!*" Taru gestured in the air. "They're not like us. They're born cruel!"

"I don't see how they could be. There are good and bad among all folk. That's what I think."

"What *ye* think! Nagaro, ye don't know what ye're talking about!"

Nagaro sighed and let the matter drop.

They sat in silence until the grizzled, scar-faced man emerged from the oar deck and tossed them some lumps of food and a water gourd. "Eat shaku!" he growled, and disappeared through the door again. It was exactly the same fare they'd been given below in the hold. Having had no breakfast, they consumed it hungrily.

Half an hour later, the door leading to the oar deck swung open again. This time the crooked-nosed man came out followed by the scar-faced man, the beardless youth, and another young man. The crooked-nosed officer stopped in front of Nagaro. "Up!" he commanded with a jerk of his thumb. Nagaro considered the man for several seconds, then deliberately and painfully got to his feet. Resistance, he reasoned, would likely only earn him more bruises. Taru also stood up when commanded, scowling darkly. The scar-faced man quickly stepped around and got Taru's arm twisted behind his back in the now familiar hold. The youth moved to do the same to Nagaro. He wasn't so quick about it, and Nagaro suspected he could have foiled the young man's effort, though he didn't see any point in trying. There was still nowhere he could go.

So he and Taru were at last marched to the door, and through it into the cavernous oar deck. Nagaro, in the lead this time, nearly gagged as he stepped across the threshold. The atmosphere of the place was thick with the mingled odors of excrement and unwashed human bodies. The great oars were shipped for the time being, and the drum was silent. The slaves were at rest, slumped at their benches.

They appeared a wretched lot—unkempt, filthy, and clad only in the ragged remains of whatever pants each man had been wearing at the time of his capture. They sat facing aft as oarsmen must. Some didn't even turn their heads to look as the two new slaves were pushed along the strip of open deck between the two rows of benches. Others stared, sullen or dull-eyed. Only a few showed real interest in the new arrivals.

Nagaro couldn't make out their faces clearly at first, other than the shine of their eyes, in the dim light coming from the oar ports and from the three dirty lanterns hung at intervals along the central ceiling beam. As his eyes adjusted to the gloom, he discovered that about a third of them were men of the Mahuk Baar. Most of the rest were Turowan, as he'd expected, with a scattering of pale-skinned Kelorin. A single blond head on the starboard side marked a Leithian.

As they neared the stern, they passed a man whose appearance made Nagaro start. For an instant, he felt his heart thud in his chest and sweat prickle along his sides. This slave had black hair and eyes, and hawk-like features that closely resembled those of Dreigen, the king's Lore Master, though his skin was a shade darker. He couldn't have been there long, as his hair was still quite short and his chin bore only a little growth of stubble. Lean to the point of emaciation, the hawk-faced slave didn't turn or meet Nagaro's eyes, but stared fixedly before him.

The two new slaves were marched almost all the way to the stern of the oar deck, near the high platform where the big drum stood. They were jerked to a halt there at the end of the rows of benches. Most of the benches held pairs of slaves, but the last one on each side of the center aisle was empty and the two just forward of that on the starboard side each held a single man, in both cases seated on the side of the bench that was closer to the ship's hull. Taru and Nagaro were roughly pushed down, each beside one of these un-paired men. Nagaro was placed on the more forward bench and Taru the aft. Their chains were locked fast to iron rings set in the deck planking.

There followed an exchange of words among the four crewmen. Then all four left by way of one of two doors in the aft bulkhead, flanking the drum platform.

Nagaro's benchmate was a massive young Mahuk of about his age, judging by the scantiness of the beard on his chin. The young man's black hair hung lank about his ears, framing a flat, square face. He stared stonily at Nagaro through narrow black eyes. Nagaro gave the young man a tentative smile, and extended his hand in greeting. The other youth, however, made no move to take the offered hand. He continued to stare at Nagaro, his eyes narrowed to mere slits.

Before he could think of what to do next, Nagaro's attention was claimed by Taru's benchmate. This man was vocal and animated, unlike most of the unfortunate occupants of that pit of misery. A Turowan in his early twenties, with an overgrown beard and hair tied with a scrap of dirty rag, he had an ugly scar where his upper lip had been split and had healed badly. "Welcome aboard, mate," he said, addressing Taru with mock joviality. His ironic smile revealed a missing tooth behind the scar on his lip. "My name's Moraga. What's yours? I hope ye're not another lumberin' landsman. The last one didn't live one season."

Taru grasped the man's extended hand. "My name is Taru. I'm a fisherman."

"A fisherman, eh? Good!" Moraga slapped his own chest. "Merchant seaman, that's what I be. What about that one?" he added, jerking a thumb at Nagaro. "Is he with ye? Seems to be a Kelorin tryin' to look like a Turo. Never saw any do that before."

Taru gave a short laugh. "That's Nagaro. He does what he chooses."

"*Nagaro?* That's *no name* for a man, hey?" Moraga chuckled at what he apparently considered a good joke. "How'd he come by it?"

Nagaro belatedly realized that he had given no thought to how he would explain his name. Before he could think of anything, Taru spoke again with casual ease.

"It began as a jest, and it's been so long now that we've both got used to it."

"Have ye, now?" Moraga glanced from Taru to Nagaro, then finally addressed the latter. "Be ye a fisherman too, mate?"

Nagaro promptly replied. "I was learning the trade when we were taken. But since I was learning from Taru's father, and he's dead, I'd say my apprenticeship is over."

Moraga stared. Nagaro's manner of speech was evidently outside of his experience. "A *prenta*-ship?" He repeated slowly. "What kind o' ship is that?" He turned back to Taru. "I say, mate, where'd ye find that one, anyway?"

"In a fernbrake." Taru answered with a perfectly straight face.

Moraga raised an eyebrow. "Have ye thought about puttin' 'im back then?"

Before Taru could say anything, Nagaro answered. "I'm sure he has. Only he's got enough sense not to try." He punctuated his words with the most wicked smile he could muster. It was, in fact, much more effective than he imagined. His beard was coming in fairly well, it was very black, and his teeth showed very white in contrast.

Moraga drew back a little, looking startled, until Taru burst out laughing. The sound of the young Turowan's unfettered merriment was shockingly incongruous in that dismal place.

It was at that moment that the door in the aft bulkhead in front of them opened, and the Mahuk crew members filed back onto the oar deck. The grizzled, scar-faced man came first, carrying a long, black whip coiled in his hand.

Moraga hastily gripped Taru's arm and made a shushing motion. He mouthed, "No more talk," and turned to face aft. He wasn't quick enough. The scar-faced Mahuk had heard laughter on the oar deck, coming from the near end of the starboard row of benches. With a negligent flick of his arm, the man sent the long, black lash snaking out as he passed. The forked end caught Taru across the shoulders, making him suck in his breath sharply through his teeth.

"Nobody laugh here, shaku! Nobody but Raak." The man jabbed his thumb at his own chest and let out a loud guffaw to illustrate. Then he strode on along the aisle between the benches, flicking his lash this way and that as he went, wherever he saw something that wasn't to his liking. Startled gasps and moans followed him.

In the meantime, the crooked-nosed man, who appeared to be in command of the oar deck, began barking orders. A small, gnarled man with a game leg, whom Nagaro hadn't seen before, mounted the three steps to the aft platform, seated himself at the huge drum, and took a heavy, padded stick in his hand. At a nod from the crooked-nosed man, he struck the drumhead twice with the stick in rapid succession. Two great thuds reverberated down the length of the oar deck.

"That means 'un-ship the oars'," Moraga muttered as he bent down to seize the shaft of the great oar that lay across the deck at his feet. Nagaro's benchmate was already moving to do the same. Nagaro made haste to assist the Mahuk youth. The oars had been partially shipped for a rest break. A little less than half their length was still extended through the oar ports. What now needed to be done was to slide the oar shafts out into the fully-extended position, and hold them there so that the blades remained high and clear of the water. The first part was easy, the second required strength and a certain amount of weight. Nagaro had the impression that his benchmate could have performed the task unassisted. Determined to make his presence felt, Nagaro leaned hard on the oar shaft.

There came three more rapid thuds from the drum. "Now we *start rowing!*" Moraga grated through his teeth.

As one, the slaves leaned forward, swinging the oars through the long back stroke, blades still held clear of the waves. *Thud!* The drum sounded again. The oar blades dipped and bit the water. Then came the power stroke, the slaves hauling with all their strength on the huge oar shafts, putting their arms and legs and backs into it, bracing their feet against short planks placed for the purpose. *Thud!* The drum sounded. Up came the oars for another back stroke. *Thud!* Down again for another power stroke. *Thud... Thud... Thud... Thud...* The drum rolled on relentlessly, beating out a ponderous rhythm.

Nagaro already knew how to row, but the massive oar was more than twice as long, and four times as heavy, as the ones used to propel Jomo's small fishing boat. It took a large, strong man to handle one of these oars alone. Even with two men, the work was hard. It wasn't long before his arms and legs began to ache. His sweat ran, and his breath came raggedly. The drum throbbed on and on. Forward, and back. Forward, and back. Push. *Pull.* Push. *Pull.* The time seemed endless. Nagaro's side began to hurt where he had been kicked. His head ached as well, and the burn on his shoulder began to sting viciously as salty sweat trickled into the wound...

Thud... Thud... Thud... Thud... Push. *Pull.* Push. *Pull.*

How much longer?

Nagaro's vision began to cloud, and his head throbbed in time to the drum. His mind began to drift. His sweat-slicked palms slipped on the smooth oar shaft, and the big oar faltered in its motion. The young Mahuk grunted and bore down harder to finish the back stroke as Nagaro fumbled to regain his grip. There was a sudden whistle, and a crack, as the lash of the whip cut Nagaro across his back. The new, sharp sting brought him fully awake. He grabbed for the oar shaft, held it, and threw himself anew into the next power stroke...

How long they rowed, he afterwards had no idea. Towards the end, he moved in a haze of pain, his muscles screaming agony. His burn felt as if it were again in contact with the red-hot iron. His chest was on fire with every breath. Three times more he faltered, and three times the whip brought him back. In the end, he was doing little more than riding the oar as his benchmate propelled it, aiding the effort mainly with the weight of his body flung alternately forward and back.

Then, suddenly, it was over. The drum beat out a slowing tempo, at the end of which there were three quick thumps—the signal to stop. Nagaro slumped forward, his head falling onto his knees. His mind slid into blackness.

*

When he came to himself, he found that he was lying awkwardly where he must have fallen, on the planks between his bench and Taru's. The rank smell of the filthy decking was in his nostrils. Nagaro struggled up with a groan and pulled himself stiffly onto the bench. Taru was sitting slumped against Moraga, and Nagaro saw that a number of red welts crisscrossed the young man's back.

Taru roused himself when he heard his friend stir. Turning around, he gave Nagaro a wan smile. "Are ye with us again? Good. I'd be out still, myself, if it weren't for Moraga here. He's kept shakin' me."

Nagaro massaged the aching muscles of his arms and thighs. The effect of the ointment must have completely worn off, for his shoulder stung cruelly. By comparison, the sting of the stripes on his own back seemed to be the least of his pains. "How long has it been since the drum stopped?" he asked.

Moraga answered him. "Two hours, maybe."

"Two hours!"

Moraga snorted. "Taru tells me they hit ye both on the head hard enough t' knock the sense out o' ye. It'll take some days for ye to be right again."

Nagaro felt the back of his head with his fingers. The spot was very tender. Pressing on it made little points of light swim in his vision, so he left it alone. "I'm terribly thirsty," he said. "I don't suppose there's any water."

Moraga shook his head. "Ye missed the first round o' water, I'm afraid. I got yer friend up for it, but I couldn't reach ye well enough to rouse ye, an' old stoneface, there, wouldn't lift a hand." He gestured dismissively at Nagaro's benchmate. "They'll come 'round again with water in a little while. We're no good to 'em if we die o' thirst."

Nagaro sat in silence then, trying to rub the soreness out of his arms and legs. After a while, he looked around. None of the slave handlers was present, but there was little talk on the oar deck. A muttered conversation here and there was all he could hear above the creaking of the ship's timbers. Most of the slaves had either no spirit or no strength for talk. Many appeared to be asleep—or perhaps unconscious—sprawled in the narrow spaces between one bench and the next. Nagaro noticed that the dark-skinned, hawk-faced man had toppled sideways from his bench and had fallen halfway out into the aisle between the two rows of rowing benches.

Turning to Moraga, Nagaro asked, "What manner of man is the dark one there? Of what people?"

Moraga glanced in the direction Nagaro was pointing. "Him? He's a Jinari, and he's done for by the look of 'im. We had a Jinari once before, and he went the same way. Wouldn't eat."

"Do you mean they choose to starve themselves to death?"

Moraga shrugged. "All I know is, they don't eat."

At that, one of the slaves across the aisle from Nagaro spoke. "I've heard that the Jinari don't eat meat, nor any other part of an animal," he observed. The speaker was a weathered Kelorin with grizzled hair and a beard gone quite gray.

Nagaro stared at him. "Why not?"

"I suppose their god told 'em not to," the man replied with a shrug. "Naturally, they won't eat the dried meat. And they won't touch the biscuit either, 'cause it's made with beef fat."

"Oh." Nagaro turned around again to study the still, dark form of the Jinari, trying to understand how any god could ask a man to accept death rather than violate such a ban. There couldn't be much fat in the dry, hard biscuit they were fed. His thoughts were interrupted by the opening of the port-side door in the aft bulkhead.

The murmur of voices stopped, silence sweeping like a wave from the stern to the bow end of the oar deck, even though it was only the two younger crewmen who came this time. The beardless youth, and the other young man only slightly older, each carried a water skin on his shoulder and a gourd dipper in his hand. The dippers they filled from the skins and passed among the slaves, carefully seeing that each man got only one dipper-full. The younger one took the starboard side, and the older one, the port.

When the beardless youth handed Nagaro the full dipper, he did so gingerly, as if he feared that this strange new slave might try again to grab his arm or speak to him. Nagaro made no such attempt, but merely drank his water thirstily and handed back the empty dipper. The gourd was filled again, and Nagaro reached out, took it, and passed it to his benchmate. The massive young slave's eyes flickered as he took the dipper. Nagaro studied the youth's impassive face as he drank. He recalled Moraga saying that the young man had made no effort to rouse him when the water had been brought earlier.

Before moving on to the next bench, the young sea warrior brought out the little pot of salve from the black sash that girded his scarlet tunic. He applied some more of the stuff to the burns on the new slaves' shoulders. The youth focused studiously on the task and wouldn't meet Nagaro's eyes. The salve brought immediate relief.

The two slave handlers continued systematically along the length of the oar deck, skipping those slaves that could not be roused. They made an effort to waken these only if the other slaves around them failed to do so. A single poke with the toe of a boot was all that the older one seemed willing to do. The younger one appeared willing to try two or three prods before moving on. When they reached the sprawled form of the Jinari, both young men stopped and exchanged words.

The Jinari's bench was on the port side, which was the older youth's domain. Accordingly, that one prodded the still form with his foot, once, then a second time. He muttered "*bishka*" when there was no response. More words passed back and forth. The two young men seemed to be arguing.

At length, the younger Mahuk knelt down beside the unconscious man. He dribbled a little water into his dipper. Lifting the Jinari's head, he attempted to pour the liquid into the man's mouth. The action elicited a feeble cough. The young man dribbled some more water into the gourd and tried again. This time the water must have gone down, for the youth looked up at his companion and uttered some excited words. The older youth's response was dismissive, however, and he pointed to the starboard-side benches as if telling the younger one to get back to work. With apparent reluctance, the younger slave handler left the Jinari where he lay and returned to the task of dispensing water to the remaining slaves on his side of the ship.

When they had finished, the two young crewmen left the oar deck by the way they had entered, returning almost immediately with the crooked-nosed Slave Master. All three went to inspect the Jinari. As Nagaro watched, the crooked-nosed man squatted down and made a thorough examination of the unconscious man. Then he stood up and shook his head. He issued some rapid orders, and the two younger sea warriors promptly saluted and left the oar deck. The crooked-nosed man remained, standing beside the Jinari and glancing now and again towards a spot among the ceiling beams. There Nagaro could make out what appeared to be a covered hatch, doubtless leading to the deck above.

Presently, there was a scraping of wood, and the hatch cover was slid aside. Brilliant afternoon sunlight flooded through the hole, causing the slaves to flinch and cover their eyes.

When Nagaro was able to look again, he saw that the crooked-nosed man had apparently unlocked the Jinari's chain and dragged the limp body a few feet to the spot directly below the open hatch. A rope had been lowered through the hatch from the deck above. It ended in a kind of harness, which the Slave Master was in the process of securing about the body of the Jinari. When he was finished, he gave a signal to the men above. The creak of a windlass could be heard, the rope became taut, and the unconscious man was lifted jerkily upward to disappear through the bright square of the opening. The hatch cover was then slid back into place, and the Slave Master departed again through the starboard aft door.

The Jinari's benchmate was left alone. Nagaro leaned forward to address Moraga. "There's no one paired now with that big Turo. What will happen?"

Moraga grunted. "Don't worry about him. He's a Lone Man."

"A Lone Man?"

"Aye. 'Cause he can manage the oar *alone*. The Slave Master likes t' have one or two o' them. Pairs 'em with the weakest men."

"I see." It made sense. "What will they do with the Jinari?"

Moraga gave Nagaro a quick glance, then looked away. "He's one for the fishes."

"But he's still alive!" exclaimed Taru, who had been listening.

Moraga shrugged. "Don't matter. He can't row, and he'd be dead soon anyway. This is quicker. Maybe kinder too."

A little later Nagaro heard a distant splash. If any of the others heard it, they said nothing, though several shifted on their benches.

After a time, Nagaro turned his attention once again to his benchmate. He had noticed that the young man's dark gaze flicked from one to another of his fellow slaves as each of them spoke, as if he were following their conversation. The youth's face, however, remained blank and unreadable. When the young man chanced to look at him, Nagaro made a decision. He returned the glance, looking his benchmate straight in the eyes. "You're very strong," he said. "I'm sorry I wasn't more help with the rowing. You had to do more than your share." The youth's eyes remained fixed on Nagaro, and he frowned slightly, but he made no answer.

Nagaro tried again. "I am called Nagaro," he said, tapping his chest as he pronounced his name. "What is your name?" He gestured at the other man with an open hand.

"What are ye talkin' to *him* for?" Demanded a voice from behind Nagaro. "He's one o' *them*."

Nagaro turned to look at the speaker, a ragged, middle-aged Turo who was sitting on the bench directly behind him. The man nodded at him. "Tego's my name," he added and extended a gnarled, calloused hand. Nagaro didn't take the hand. Instead he pointed at the brand on the shoulder of the young Mahuk sitting beside him. "He's got a brand on his shoulder just like you and me," he said evenly. "I'd say that makes him one of *us.*"

The man named Tego frowned. "Ye can't trust any o' them," he said matter-of-factly.

"I don't see why not."

The young Mahuk's eyes had gone from Nagaro to Tego and back again, following this exchange. Now, suddenly, he spoke. "Pavo Maat," he said, putting his hand on his chest. His voice was incongruously soft for a man of his size.

"Ahoy mates, ol' stoneface can speak!" Moraga exclaimed. "He was chained next t' me for two weeks, and never said a word the whole time."

Nagaro ignored the Turo's comment. He kept his eyes on his benchmate's face. "Is that your name?" he asked. "Pavo Maat?"

The youth's glance shifted to Moraga and back again to Nagaro. He inclined his head once. "I... name... Pavo Maat," he said, slowly.

Nagaro extended his hand. "Well met, friend Pavo Maat," he said. And this time the big youth took the hand, enveloping Nagaro's slender fingers in his big, thick ones and giving them a painful squeeze. "You *are* strong," Nagaro said, ruefully shaking his hand and flexing the fingers.

The young Mahuk smiled then. It was a hesitant, almost shy, smile that gave his face an entirely new aspect—no longer closed and wary, but open and vulnerable.

At this point, the gray-bearded Kelorin on the other side of the aisle spoke up. "I wouldn't get too friendly with any o' the Mahuk if I were ye."

"Who are you, and why do you say that?" Nagaro asked.

"My name is Mendorel," the man said. "And I'll tell ye why. The Mahuk slaves aren't innocent like us. They're criminals that are put here for punishment."

Nagaro frowned. He turned back to his benchmate, who was eyeing him warily again. "Pavo Maat, is this true?" Nagaro asked, carefully keeping his voice even. "Are you here because you broke some law of your people?"

Pavo Maat regarded him for several seconds. Then, very deliberately, he nodded.

"What did you do?"

The young man answered slowly, trying to find words in the Common Speech. "I kill... *shupat*... belong Lord Baalkir."

Nagaro frowned slightly. "What is a *shupat*?" He looked around. "Does anyone know?" He was met with blank stares.

"Maybe it's a *who*," Moraga growled darkly.

Taru had been watching the exchange with an uncertain look on his face, but now his eyes grew suddenly hard. "Aye," he put in. "Maybe he killed the lord's servant or guard or something."

Nagaro turned back to Pavo Maat. "Can you help us to understand what *shupat* is?"

Pavo Maat frowned in concentration. After a moment he put his hands up to the top of his head, one on each side, pointing upward, with the fingers cupped. Then he took his hands down and made a hopping motion with one of them.

"A *rabbit?*" It was Taru's quick mind that came out with it first. "He's saying he killed a rabbit!"

Pavo Maat made the hopping motion with his hand again. Then he held up two fingers. "Two shupat," he said. "Kill for... eat. Very hungry."

Nagaro shook his head. "Poaching. If you ask me, it shouldn't even be a crime." He turned bsck to Mendorel. "I've killed dozens of the lord's rabbits. This man is less guilty than I am!"

Mendorel was looking thoughtful. "Aye, so it would seem," he said.

"Ye mean ye're going to *believe* him?" It was the Turowan named Tego who spoke.

Nagaro turned around to face him. "What can the man gain by a lie, here in this place?"

Tego shrugged. "He can get ye t' call him *friend*."

"Well," Nagaro observed, "if he values such coin as that, how bad a man can he be?"

Tego gaped at him, working his way through Nagaro's logic. "Ye know... ye have a point," he said after a moment. "And I think I'd like it if ye called *me* friend." For the second time, he put out his hand. This time Nagaro took it, grinning. "Well met, friend Tego," he said.

Taru had been staring at Pavo Maat. "How long will your punishment be?" he asked. "How long must ye row for what ye did?"

The young man's eyes betrayed no emotion as he answered. "Until I die," he said calmly.

Taru was clearly shaken by this pronouncement. "Ye mean ye're sent here t' *die* just for killing *two rabbits?*"

Pavo Maat nodded once. "Shupat belong Lord Baalkir. Law say... be slave for kill shupat. I kill shupat. Now I belong Lord Baalkir." The young man sounded not so much contrite as simply resigned to his fate. He'd made a bad gamble, and now he was paying for it.

Taru was outraged. "These Mahuk are surely the most horrible folk—" He broke off, seeing the look on Pavo Maat's face. The young Turo frowned. "What did ye do before this?" he asked instead. "How did ye live?"

Pavo Maat frowned hard. Then he stood up and pantomimed a motion with his arms and upper body. It was unmistakably the movement of casting a net. "Take fish," he said, and sat down again on his bench.

"Ye were a *fisherman?*" The look on Taru's face now was comical. One could almost see preconceived notions about the order of the world rearranging themselves behind his eyes. He was realizing that he might have more in common with this Mahuk youth than with Nagaro.

The young man nodded. "Fisher-man," he said, trying out the word. "I fisherman. My two brother... fisherman. My father fisherman..."

"Your father is a fisherman too?"

A shadow crossed Pavo Maat's face. "My father die," he said. "Two... year. Sea take."

Taru's sympathy was immediate. "The sea took my grandfather— my father's father. I never even knew him. But my father was alive only yesterday." The freshness of his pain made Taru's voice suddenly turn hard. "He *should* be alive still—only your captain killed him!"

Pavo Maat's eyes narrowed. He shook his head. "He not my *heeruk!*" He spat for emphasis. "*Urchak tok-Faar*... bad man! No *kajadeem!*" He said quite a bit more, then, in the language of the Mahuk Baar. Another of his people, sitting behind Tego, said something in response, and a third man sitting near Mendorel on the port side added his own comment. A ripple of muttered speech ran the length of the oar deck.

"What is it?" Moraga asked. "What're they on about?" He looked pointedly at Nagaro.

"Aye," said Tego. "Ye're the one that started talkin' to him. Ye have t' ask him."

Nagaro turned to his benchmate. "Pavo Maat," he said, "my friends want to know what you and your folk are saying."

The youth ernestly met his questioning glance. "Say many thing..." he responded. "About *heeruk*—is you say 'cap-tan'—Urchak tok-Faar."

"Is that the captain's name?" Nagaro asked. "Urchak...?"

"Urchak tok-Faar." Pavo Maat nodded. "We say he bad. Hear *Mautep* talk. Mautep say... Urchak kill... uman."

Mendorel spoke up in answer to Nagaro's blank look. "He's saying the Mahuk slaves heard the crew talking. That word 'Mautep'—seems t' mean 'warrior'. I think he's saying the captain killed a woman..."

Pavo Maat nodded vigorously. "Urchak bad. No *kajadeem*... He kill uman!"

"Oh, the captain killed a woman all right," Taru growled. "*He killed my mother!*"

"That's right," Nagaro interjected. "Taru's mother tried to fight the warriors with a burning stick—and the captain killed her. Then Taru's father got hold of a knife and put out the captain's eye, so the captain killed him too."

This drew an exclamation from Pavo Maat that was followed by a rapid stream of words in his own tongue, directed at the other Mahuk slaves.

There was a general muttering that ran the length of the oar deck, then a ragged cheer from those who had the strength for it.

"What is it? Moraga asked. "What are they cheerin' for?"

Pavo Maat smiled grimly. "They say is *good!* That Taru father... he take Urchak eye for kill uman... is good! Taru father good man!"

Moraga and Tego exchanged stunned glances, and the look on Taru's face showed that he was moved by this unexpected tribute to his father. No one had any opportunity to speak of it further, however, for at that moment the starboard aft door opened and the slave handlers returned to the oar deck—all of them this time, including the lame man who beat the drum. His presence was a sure sign that the slaves would have to row again.

*

The second session of rowing went very much like the first except that Nagaro's muscles began to scream in agony even sooner. The lash fell on him repeatedly, and before the end he was moving in a gray haze that slid into blackness as soon as the drum stopped.

This time, it was Pavo Maat's strong hands that eventually pulled him out of it—dragging him up onto the rowing bench again and back to half-consciousness.

"Water..." Nagaro croaked. He was answered, not by the dipper, but by a bucket of icy sea water that sluiced across the planks where he had been lying a moment before. Groggily he stared at his drenched feet. "What...?" he wondered aloud. He looked enquiringly at Pavo Maat, but the young man held a finger to his lips.

Nagaro looked around him. The two young slave handlers were on the oar deck. The younger one was standing quite close to him and the empty bucket in the youth's hands immediately explained the source of the sea water. The older youth was unhooking a second bucket from a line that descended from the open hatch. Evidently the two young men were washing down the deck between the benches. It was, as it turned out, a daily activity rendered necessary by the fact that the slaves had no privy. The two youths had apparently started from the bow and were therefore almost finished.

Nagaro noted hazily that the square of sky showing through the open hatch was the deep blue of advancing evening. He shook his head to try to clear it, but this only made the world start to go gray around the edges, and he gripped the edge of the bench to keep himself from falling. Immediately he felt Pavo Maat's big hand grab hold of his arm, steadying him. Without thinking, Nagaro said, "Thank you." Pavo Maat instantly put his finger to his lips again. Turning around, Nagaro saw the beardless young Mahuk looking at them. The youth's eyes flicked back and forth between Nagaro and Pavo Maat and he frowned slightly. After a moment he turned away and went back to his task.

After the cleansing of the deck, the water skins and dippers were brought around. Nagaro felt much restored after he'd drunk some water. When at length the two young slave handlers disappeared through the door in the aft bulkhead, he turned to Pavo Maat and asked a question that had been troubling him.

"Why didn't you help me after the first time we rowed? I missed getting water and Moraga said you didn't wake me." The other youth returned his glance uncomfortably, but didn't speak. "Was it because I'm not Mahuk?" Nagaro asked after a moment.

Pavo Maat answered then, his voice very low and a little hesitant. "Some of it," he said. "Some Turo not good to Hashtep... You say 'Mahuk.'" He glanced meaningfully at Moraga's back. Then his eyes slid away to stare off across the shadowy oar deck. "Is more too... You not strong. Maybe you go die. If man go die here... better die quick."

"I see." Nagaro was well aware that the slenderness of his build made him appear less robust than the average Turowan, though in fact he'd found himself to be Taru's equal in most matters of strength. There was the matter of the blow to his head, however. If Moraga was right about that, he should be doing better in a few days—if he could survive that long. "I will get stronger if you help me," he said earnestly.

Pavo Maat's glance came back to rest upon him. "Yes," he said. "I help." Then he added, "Here man get strong—or he die."

"I have no intention of dying in this place," Nagaro stated flatly.

Mendorel must have heard him. "Sooner or later, we'll all die in this place," he observed with calm fatalism.

"Not us!" This was from Taru.

At that, Moraga joined the debate. "Well I'd like t' know how ye plan to avoid it, mate."

"We're going to escape, o' course!"

"*Escape?*" Moraga laughed mirthlessly. "D' ye hear that, Mendorel? They think they're going to escape!" In answer, the gray-bearded Kelorin only shook his head sadly.

"Just how d' ye plan t' do it?" Moraga inquired.

"I don't know yet," Taru admitted. "But we'll find some way. Why, if Nagaro can just get his hand on a sword, he'll cut those sea warriors t' ribbons!"

"*Taru!*" Nagaro exclaimed. "Don't tell them that!"

"What's this?" Moraga looked from Taru to Nagaro and back again. "I thought he was a fisherman. Now ye're tellin' me he's a warrior?"

"I said I was *learning* to be a fisherman—" Nagaro began.

"A warrior that's learning t' be a *fisherman?*" Now Moraga sounded frankly incredulous.

"I am *not* a warrior." Nagaro was exasperated. "I've just had some schooling in swordsmanship, that's all."

"Nagaro doesn't like to boast," Taru put in. "But he's really good with a blade."

"Taru!"

"Is he, ye say?" Moraga looked Nagaro up and down with obvious skepticism.

"It doesn't matter much how good he is," Mendorel observed. "He'll never get his hand on a sword here. The Mahuk aren't fools. They know better'n to bring any kind o' blade onto the oar deck."

At that moment, they were interrupted as the two young slave handlers re-entered the oar deck carrying baskets of dried meat and biscuit for the slaves' evening meal. All talk among the slaves ceased while the food was distributed and then hungrily devoured. Once the food had been consumed, the crooked-nosed Slave Master and his scar-faced lieutenant, Raak, appeared. The order was given to fully ship the oars and close the oar ports for the night. Raak's whip ensured that all of the slaves complied. There followed one final round of water. Then the lanterns were extinguished and the oar deck became as black as a pit.

All the slaves were weary, and most of them were unaccustomed to conversation in any case, so when the lights were put out, there was a general rustle of movement as they made themselves as comfortable as they could for the night. Nagaro had nowhere to sleep except the strip of deck between his bench and Taru's. The planks were still damp with sea water and none too sweet-smelling, but he was too tired to care. He and Pavo Maat stretched out, side by side and head to foot, as dictated by where their chains were bolted. He was so exhausted that he fell almost immediately into a deep, dreamless sleep.

Chapter 16: Slaves

In the days that followed, the ship continued on its southerly course. The grueling rhythms of the oar deck repeated themselves, day after day, with insignificant variations. The need to survive and adapt to his new situation allowed Nagaro no time to think about the life he'd left behind or its lingering questions. Physically, his condition improved. His burned shoulder and bruised ribs healed. The effects of the blow on his head faded, and he became able to finish a bout of rowing without losing consciousness. Taru improved in a similar fashion, and the lash fell on both of the friends less frequently. So they settled grudgingly into the cruel misery of a life lived at the end of two feet of chain secured to an iron ring in the floor. The stink of the place offended Nagaro at first, but his nostrils soon became so full of it that he could no longer remember what clean air smelled like.

The work was brutally hard. Those whose bodies broke under the strain were simply discarded, but that grim attrition was less troubling than the discovery that there were some men whose minds had broken, although their bodies were strong enough to bear the work. Tego's bench mate was one of these. A weathered Turowan with matted gray hair and beard, Tego called him "Lopo" meaning "old man." Lopo's body was lean and hard from moving the great oar, but when he wasn't rowing, he sat mumbling to himself or slept curled up on the floor. Tego would rouse him as needed, to drink or eat or avoid a soaking. On the second day, Nagaro tried talking to Lopo while they waited their turn for water, but the gaze the old man turned on him held no understanding.

"It ain't no use, mate," Tego said, tapping his temple with a gnarled finger. "His mind has gone, long time since."

"Gone where?" Taru asked.

"Can't say for sure. Home, maybe. Or maybe Hanuroa."

There was a Kelorin two benches back who talked endlessly about his "little bit o' house on the bay," and a Turowan across the aisle who never spoke at all—whose body went through all the motions necessary to ensure his survival while his eyes stared vacantly, seeing nothing.

Then there was Mendorel's bench partner, a simple-minded young

Turowan called Otao. Mendorel was gentle with him, faithfully waking him whenever necessary. Otao just as faithfully returned the favor, grinning in fatuous self-congratulation whenever Mendorel thanked him. It was hard for Nagaro to watch Mendorel treating a man in his twenties like a child. But Otao's mind was very like a small child's, and there was no reason to suppose that a different mind was imprisoned in his skull.

Nagaro talked to Pavo Maat whenever he could. The young Mahuk asked to be called simply Pavo, Maat being his family name. Pavo's command of the Common Speech improved steadily from his conversations with Nagaro. It seemed the young man had a gift for languages, though it helped that Nagaro was patient and enjoyed teaching him.

Pavo taught Nagaro about the ship, its crew, and the ways of the Mahuk Baar. Nagaro learned that the ship's name was *Fist of Death* in the tongue of the Mahuk Baar. The slave-taking raid that had resulted in Nagaro's and Taru's capture had been a diversion from the main purpose of the voyage—taking gold from the Faranos. Such diversions were necessary because slaves were in short supply, as the harshness of their existence took its toll. The *Fist of Death* was now speeding southward to re-join the fleet of the warlord who owned her, Baalkir jir-Akaan, to whom the ship's captain, Urchak, owed allegiance. The man Nagaro had stabbed in the shoulder was the first mate, Haotef, Urchak's second in command. Nagaro's standing among the slaves rose several notches after Taru made it known how Haotef had been wounded.

Nagaro also learned the names of the five members of the oar deck crew, whose quarters were reached through the pair of doors in the aft bulkhead. Baruk, the Slave Master, was the crooked-nosed officer who commanded the oar deck and who kept the key that could unlock their chains. The man with the whip, Raak, was the Slave-Driver, Baruk's lieutenant and the chief enforcer of his commands. The lame drummer was called simply Ul, and the two young slave-tenders were named Fataan and Roheed. Nagaro was particularly interested to learn that the latter one, the youth to whom he had spoken, was Lord Baalkir's nephew, the only son of the warlord's younger brother.

He learned that the slaves from the Mahuk Baar referred to themselves as *Hashtep*. It was their word for their own race. The language they spoke was *Hashti*. In contrast, *Mautep* referred specifically to the ruling warrior class of the Hashtep people. The word *shaku*, which Nagaro had heard so often, simply meant "slave" and was offensive and insulting even when it was accurate. Worse than shaku was *shaku raal*, which meant "slave dog." Nagaro's interest in these linguistic details rather amused the other Edroviran slaves, though even Moraga had to admit that the opening of communication with the Hashtep had advantages. The Hashtep slaves could understand the conversation of the ship's crew, after all, which gave them access to more detailed information about the ship's location, course, and other external events than the Edroviran slaves could glean by peering out the oar ports. This fact was brought home in the second week of Nagaro's and Taru's captivity.

It was just after dawn that a sudden commotion arose on the deck overhead while Fataan and Roheed were performing the morning's sea-water dousing. The Hashtep slaves listened eagerly to what they could hear through the open hatch and to the conversation of the two young sea warriors. Presently Pavo leaned close to Nagaro and spoke in a low voice. "Mautep see many Droviri ship," he explained. "All together."

Nagaro passed this information to Taru and Tego, and it was conveyed throughout the oar deck by means of cautious whispers. Next, repeated shouts of *Hatakei Raal!* were heard from above, and Fataan exchanged rapid speech with Raak, who was manning the windlass. The hatch was hurriedly closed, the buckets collected, and the two young Mautep departed the oar deck in apparent haste.

"What has happened?" Nagaro asked, as soon as the slave tenders had gone.

"Droviri ship is belong man we call Hatakei Raal," Pavo explained. "That mean 'dog that run.' He captain all Droviri ship. Now we row very hard—or Mautep fight!"

Nagaro turned excitedly to Taru. "That must be Lord Kuran Kel!" he exclaimed. "They've sighted the Royal Fleet!"

"Maybe Kuran'll capture the ship," Taru said hopefully, "and then we'll all be freed!"

"More likely drowned than freed," Moraga said grimly. "That's *if* they catch us."

"Aye," Mendorel put in. "Ye'd best hope that they don't. Kuran never misses a chance to sink a Mahuk warship."

At this point, further discussion was cut off by the return of the oar deck crew. Old lame Ul fairly sprang up the steps to the drum platform to beat out the signal to un-ship the oars. Baruk mounted the steps as well and stood tensely gripping the wooden rail that surrounded the platform. Raak strode swiftly down the center aisle, his lash flicking to left and right. The expression on his face made it clear that he was in no mood for laughter this time. "*Row, shaku!*" he thundered. "*Row for keep your life!*"

And row they did. Even being fresh from a night's rest, Nagaro was pushed so hard that he nearly lost consciousness with his hands still on the oar before they were at last allowed to stop.

They learned through the Hashtep that the ships of Edrovir had given chase, but that the *Fist of Death* had outdistanced them. Still, the slaves were put to the oars again when they were barely rested, and again driven very hard. Three more times that day they were made to row as if for good measure, even though there had been no further sightings of the Droviri fleet.

Despite Moraga's and Mendorel's warnings, Taru and Nagaro were chagrined that the *Fist* had escaped Lord Kuran's fleet so easily. Nagaro wondered aloud whether the *Fist of Death* was an unusually fast ship.

"*Fist* is come from Sar Tipaal," was Pavo's proud response. "Is my home. Lord Baalkir make many ship there. Very fast ship! We go there in storm time. Work there. Make ship. You see!"

"You mean they will make us work in a shipyard in the winter?" Nagaro asked. "A place where they build ships?"

Pavo nodded his affirmative. Taru, of course, felt bound to say that they would be gone from the oar deck long before winter came. Nagaro was far from sure of that, but he held his peace.

Four days later, events repeated themselves, except that this time the ships that were sighted belonged to another Mautep warlord—one named Angkat.

"These Mautep attack *each other?*" Taru gasped, when they were finally allowed to rest after making their escape.

"Mautep Emperor is get very old." Pavo explained. "Mautep need new Emperor. So they fight. See which one is most strong."

Nagaro was massaging his aching biceps. "Don't they have a better way than that to choose an Emperor?"

Pavo shook his shaggy head. "No. Only fight. But they not fight very hard. Is more about *kajadeem*—what you call 'honor'."

While they continued, under sail, awaiting the next order to row, Pavo managed to explain that there was little kajadeem in a fleet of ships attacking a lone vessel like the *Fist of Death* under most circumstances, but in this particular case, the goal would have been to seize the gold she carried. Had they overtaken the *Fist*, Lord Angkat's warriors would have boarded rather than rammed her. The crew of the *Fist* would have put up a brief fight to demonstrate their courage before honorably surrendering to Angkat's overwhelming numbers. The victors would then have been honor-bound to spare the lives of the *Fist*'s crew, the gold would have been transferred to Lord Angkat's ships, and all parties would have gone their ways.

These were new ideas to Nagaro and the other Edroviran slaves. The notion that the Mautep people had a well-developed sense of honor sparked considerable debate.

"If they've got so much honor, why d' they make slaves of honest men what never did 'em any harm?" Moraga demanded. "I'd just set sail out o' Harmoth on a ship bound for the Lomoas with a hold full o' wheat when they attacked us."

"And I was a seaman on a gold ship out o' the Faranos," Tego put in. "They could ha' taken the gold for all I cared—though it was thievin'— but why'd they have t' be takin' me and me mates?"

Pavo's answer to this was simple. "Mautep say only Mautep know kajadeem. Sea-man that is not warrior not know it. Droviri man—man from Edrovir—not know it. They say, why give honor to man who not know what it is?"

"You should treat every man with honor!" Nagaro's response was prompt and emphatic. "No matter who he is and regardless of whether he understands it. The man who doesn't know *that*, is the man who doesn't know honor!"

"Hoo-ee!" Moraga rolled his eyes. "Just listen t' this one!"

Mendorel stared at Nagaro from across the aisle. "Where did ye learn that?" he asked.

"It comes out of the *Book of Vothra*. The Writings say you shouldn't wait to see how a man will treat you. You should give him the best you know how to give. If I had the book here, I could show you the words in a minute."

"Ye mean t' say ye've *read* the *Book of Vothra*?" Mendorel inquired.

Nagaro was surprised in his turn. "Well, not *all* of it," he admitted. "But I've read that part. Haven't you read any of it?"

Mendorel shook his head. "My old mother used t' quote verses she remembered—telling us to follow the path an' all. But we never had a copy in the house."

Nagaro frowned. Apparently some of his experiences were unusual even among other Kelorin. He was spared any need to explain, however, by the sudden appearance on the oar deck of Baruk, Raak, and Ul.

The slaves were made to row yet again until they were exhausted before there was at last a welcome rest. Then came the food and water and the cleansing of the deck. Finally the lamps were extinguished and darkness closed around them.

Nagaro lay awake for a time. He could hear Pavo's even breathing beside him. It seemed that all the other slaves were sleeping. Though he was weary, sleep would not come. He thought he heard someone stirring across the aisle from where he lay. "Mendorel," he called softly. "Are you awake?" There was a little pause, then the answer.

"Aye."

"I haven't heard your story. How do you come to be here? Somehow you don't seem like a seaman."

"I'm not, lad," Mendorel replied. "I'm a 'lumbering landsman' as Moraga would say, though I've not let on to him," he added. "I'm a candle-maker by trade, from Kel Tierna. It'll be a year ago come Madrel that I took it into my head t' take a ship to Harmoth to visit my uncle. I'd no reason to go by ship save that I'd never been to sea, and I fancied giving it a try." He sighed. "So, what do ye suppose happened? A day out o' Kel Tierna, the sea-raiders attacked us."

Nagaro winced. "That's a hard turn of luck."

"Don't I know it!" Mendorel gave a bitter laugh. "And it gets worse. Most o' the crew took to the boats when they saw that the ship was going to be taken. I could ha' got away like that myself, but I was afraid to get off that nice big ship into one o' them tiny little boats. Lokundas is laughing at me still, I'm sure."

There was a little silence. Then Mendorel spoke again, very softly. "I have a wife and three children in Kel Tierna, and a little shop in Kettle Street. I was teaching my two boys the trade. The older one's only just now sixteen. I do wonder how they're faring without me."

"Mendorel, I'm sorry..." Nagaro couldn't think of anything else to say. There was no *good* way to become a slave, but Mendorel's tale struck him as more cruel than most. The silence stretched long, and Nagaro was at last drifting toward sleep when the older man's voice pulled him back.

"Nagaro?"

"Yes?"

"I've been meaning to tell ye something." The other man paused as if trying to find words. At length he ventured, "This place is... different... since ye and your friend came."

"Different?" Nagaro was puzzled. "How?"

"More... *alive*, I'd say. It used to be a man might talk to only one or two others—those as sat close to him. We never talked t' the Hashtep, nor they to us. We didn't know enough to call 'em Hashtep, for that matter. Now all the news goes up and down the whole deck. We're all comrades." Mendorel paused again, then said, "Before ye came, I'd been thinking o' taking the Jinari's way out."

Nagaro rolled over, and raised himself on his elbows. "You mean... starve yourself until you couldn't row and they threw you overboard?"

"Aye. There's others have done it. I don't fancy drowning, mind ye, but... well... there didn't seem much point in going on. But it's different now. Not *really* different, I mean—I still don't expect I'll ever see my wife again. I expect I'll die here... one way or another, like I said. I'm just thinking I'd rather stay alive as long as I can, that's all."

Nagaro turned onto his back again, to lie staring up at the shadowy beams above him. "I'm glad you've decided to live, Mendorel," he said. "But if you change your mind again and decide to seek death, I'll understand."

Neither man said anything more after that, and eventually they both slept.

*

The *Fist of Death* traveled south through the waters of the Mahuk Baar. Eventually she arrived in Sar Tipaal, where the stolen gold would be unloaded and sent to fill Lord Baalkir's coffers. At Sar Tipaal, the *Fist* also made rendezvous with Lord Baalkir's other ships. The warlord's entire fleet was tied up at the quay, waiting to be re-provisioned. The Mautep crew enjoyed the chance to spend time ashore, while the slaves were left chained at their benches in the stifling gloom of the oar deck.

The only benefit the slaves derived from being in port—besides not being forced to row—was the addition of some small, sour, orange fruits called *kuamka* to their numbingly monotonous diet. Nagaro found he rather liked kuamka. Taru, however, turned up his nose at them and would have refused to eat any if Moraga hadn't grimly informed him that if he didn't eat at least some he'd get sick and his teeth would fall out.

"Sometimes they give us onions," Moraga told them. "Ye have t' eat the onions too. Same reason." He made a face.

"Onions wouldn't be so bad," Taru grumbled, gingerly biting down on one of the kuamka fruits. "I like onions."

Pavo was doubled over, staring through his oar port, which faced north.

"Is the shipyard over there?" Nagaro asked. "Can you see it?"

"No." Pavo shook his head. "That on other side of ship. Not see from here."

"Will they take us there now?" Taru wondered.

"Only in storm time. Last storm time I live many day there in slave house. This time we be only few day in Sar Tipaal. We stay in ship." Pavo hadn't turned to look at the other slaves when answering their questions. He remained doubled over, staring out of the oar port.

"What are you looking at then?" Nagaro finally asked him.

"My home is there." Pavo answered, still without turning. "Six mile past city. I not can see it, but in my heart I know."

"Oh." Nagaro understood. After a moment, he ventured, "Is your mother there?"

"No." This time the young Hashtep did turn his impassive face towards Nagaro. "My mother dead. Many year. I have two brother there, name Taan and Katuk. Taan, he is big man. Two year more old than me. Katuk is five year more young. He have twelve year when they take me. Now thirteen." Pavo turned back to the oar port. After a moment, he said, "I know Taan take good care of Katuk. Teach him how to be good fisherman."

Nagaro sat silent. He knew that Pavo's father had been killed two years before. How hard it must have been for this family. Long bereft of a mother, they'd lost the father, and a year later the second son.

Taru had been listening with half an ear. "When I get close to *my* home, I'm going t' find something sharp," he said, fingering the cuff on his ankle. "I'll start workin' away at this leather. Just a little bit at a time, 'til I have it off."

Pavo shifted his big frame. "I try that."

"You did?" Taru sounded a little deflated. "Ah... what did ye use to cut it with?"

"I use this." Pavo reached down to touch the hasp of the lock that held his chain to the ring in the floor. "I move leather... on it... so." He demonstrated, bringing the cuff on his left ankle up against the hasp and rubbing up and down.

Taru examined the hasp on his own lock. "It's not very sharp," he observed. "It'd take a long time t' wear through the leather that way."

Pavo nodded. "I work many, many day. I maybe... half done. Then Fataan see. He tell Raak. And Raak do this." Pavo twisted round on his bench to show them his back, which was cris-crossed by whip scars.

Taru winced. "That must ha' hurt."

Pavo nodded emphatically. "Hurt very much! I not try that again. Take too long, and Mautep sure to see. Get more stripe on back. Same happen to you."

Taru was not easily deterred however. "What if I was t' pretend to get sick and die," he asked. "When they took me up on deck t' throw me overboard, I could swim away!"

This time Mendorel spoke up. "That'd never work," he stated flatly. "In the first place, ye'd never fool Baruk. He'd poke ye and prod ye 'til he got some sign o' life. And if ye *did* fool him, they'd see ye start swimming and go after ye with one o' the longboats."

Moraga snorted. "There'd be no need for longboats," he said. "They weights the bodies down wi' stones. I've seen it, lookin' out the oar port. Bags o' stones, tied t' the feet."

So Taru had to think some more. When Lord Baalkir's fleet sailed out of Sar Tipaal harbor, he was still thinking.

*

After Sar Tipaal, the *Fist*'s crew went about their work in earnest. For several weeks, Lord Baalkir took his six ships up and down the coast and among the islands of the Mahuk Baar, engaging the fleets of rival warlords. This posed great risk to the slaves.

First, there was the danger of the *Fist* being rammed and sunk. A rammed ship could fill with water very quickly, and when that happened her crew would waste no time saving the slaves. And boarding, the pre-ferred tactic of the Mautep sea-warriors, required controlled speed and maneuverability in close quarters—which meant the use of oars. The wind couldnt be relied on for such close work.

Moraga explained the danger. "Ye don't want t' have your hands on one o' these oars if a ship hits the other end of it," he said. "When a ship hits the outboard end, the inboard end, she *moves!* That's how I got this." He indicated his scarred lip. "I was lucky though. Me mate—what was sittin' on the other end o' me bench—got his head stove in. Killed 'im just like *that*, it did." He snapped his fingers for emphasis.

Since the oars and slaves were both valuable, the Mautep made an effort to prevent harm to either. There was a speaking-tube that communicated between the oar deck and the main deck above, and Baruk kept his ear to it during any action. There was also a double set of signals—one verbal and one drum-talk—that told the slaves what to do. They all knew the code by heart and knew their lives depended on getting the oars shipped quickly at a moment's notice.

Nagaro and Taru experienced the ramming of another warship for the first time during their first sea battle, and it was something Nagaro would never forget. The slaves were given no warning of the captain's intent until just before the *Fist*'s metal-clad bow struck home. Then, at the last moment, the order was given to lift their oar blades and brace themselves with their hands and feet. Within the space of a dozen heartbeats, the impact came, and the slaves were nearly flung from their benches. Above the hideous crashing and splintering of timbers, Nagaro heard the shouts and screams of men—masters and slaves—aboard the vessel the *Fist* had struck.

Immediately after the impact, Baruk shouted the order to back-paddle, and the drum beat out a new sequence. The slaves instantly obeyed, pushing on the oars with all their might. They knew the risk. If the *Fist*'s ram were not freed in time, their own vessel would be dragged down by its sinking victim. Frantically they leaned back, lowered the oars into the water, and pushed, as metal and wood screeched against each other. The cries from the other ship receded, reassuring the *Fist*'s slaves that they were out of danger. Yet, even as the drum ceased and Nagaro felt relief flood through him, there came a horrible rushing, gurgling roar, a rending of timbers, and rising above it the agonized screams of helpless slaves being carried to their deaths as the rammed ship went down.

Nagaro leaned on his oar, his sides heaving, murmuring prayers for the passing of those souls. His heart was sick with the knowledge that he had been part of the instrument that had claimed those lives. *If only he'd known...* But of course the Mautep never let their slaves know when their ship was on a ramming course.

They also learned first-hand the danger of flailing oars before that month was out. In earlier encounters, the ship's bow had been raked, and also her starboard side, but in both cases the signal had been given and the oars shipped in time. This time they weren't so lucky.

The battle trumpets sounded loudly from the deck above, and they knew the *Fist* had been ordered into the fray. Baruk barked orders, and the drum began to sound a quickening tempo. The slaves rowed, tense with apprehension under Raak's whip. Nagaro was counting oar strokes—in an effort to distract himself from the impending danger—when Moraga chanced to catch a glimpse of a looming hull through his oar port. There had been no signal from Baruk. Perhaps those on deck had missed giving it.

"*Get down!*" Moraga screamed, letting go of his oar, even as he threw himself down between the benches and pulled Taru down beside him.

Pavo instantly echoed the warning in Hashti and followed Moraga's example.

Nagaro, Tego, and the other slaves on the adjacent benches let go of their oars and dived for cover as well.

There followed a horrible series of thuds, and the repeated *crack* of splintering wood. The inboard ends of oars lashed wildly above the heads of the cowering slaves. Someone screamed, the gut-wrenching sound coming from close to where Nagaro lay. It was poor, mad Lopo. The old man had either not understood or not heeded the warning. All through the ensuing battle, he lay moaning where the oar had flung him.

Before the end, the *Fist* was boarded and all hands were called up on deck to ward off the attackers. When it was all over, Raak and Baruk returned to the oar deck to survey the damage. What they found revealed that Moraga's and Pavo's warning had done its work well—though the two slaves got no reward from the Mautep.

Lopo was the only casualty, but the oar had broken both his arms and several ribs. Fractured bone protruded through bleeding skin. His left leg, by which he was chained to the floor, was twisted and dislocated. Baruk declared the injuries too severe for mending. Lopo cried out piteously as Fataan and Roheed lifted him, and again when the rope harness tightened around him and the windlass hauled him up to the deck above. Presently, the hatch was closed and the slaves heard him no more. So Lopo made his journey to Hanuroa.

The fleet had to make for port following this incident, as seven oars had been broken and the *Fist* had too few spares. Three new Hashtep slaves were brought aboard as well. Tego got one of the three as his new benchmate, a silent and stoic Hashtep named Laash, big enough to be a Lone Man, who'd been sentenced to the galleys for stealing three eggs and a loaf of bread. The *Fist* also took on several barrels of onions. For days afterwards, Nagaro had to listen while Moraga complained bitterly and Taru extolled the virtues of the tear-inducing bulbs.

The weeks went by, grueling days of rowing punctuated by the sudden intense terror of battle and brief stops in ports along the coast, or among the islands of the Mahuk Baar. Spring passed into summer. Nagaro's kuma stain had faded, to be replaced by a patina of mingled sweat and grime. His beard grew full, and his hair grew lank down his back. He kept it tied as best he could with a bit of dirty rag. He was growing strong from the constant rowing. Rope-like muscles bunched and knotted under the skin of his arms, shoulders, back, and thighs as he pulled on the oar. He wasted no time worrying about the loss of the kuma stain. He knew he must look nothing like the idiot prince who had once been paraded through the streets of Lankura.

As long as the *Fist* remained in Mahuk waters, escape was out of the question, since any land they could hope to reach would be hostile. At first Taru chafed and fretted about this, but as the weeks passed, the young Turo's mood drifted increasingly towards resignation. Nagaro gritted his teeth and bent to his oar. Nothing could be done until the ship fared farther north.

Late in the summer, Lord Baalkir found some pressing business on the mainland and at last sent his fleet north, back into waters claimed by Jinara or by Edrovir. The purpose was simple: *piracy*. Constant warring with rival fleets was costly, and taking foreign merchant vessels was one way the Mautep warlords financed their campaigns. The activity also allowed them to capture foreign slaves to help replace those lost in the skirmishes.

The waters off of Jinara were scarcely any better for escape plans than those of the Mahuk Baar, as long as Jinara and Edrovir were at war. No one was sure what fate would befall an escaped Edroviran slave in Jinari hands. Matters were further complicated because the slaves couldn't easily determine the ship's position. Pavo unfailingly passed on to Nagaro anything the Hashtep learned from the conversations of the Mautep. Otherwise, they had to rely on sightings of known landmarks, glimpsed through the open oar ports. Even when they were at last sure that the *Fist* was in Edroviran waters, the friends were still frustrated by the lack of a plan or any opportunity for escape.

Entering Edroviran waters brought a trickle of news from home to the Droviri slaves. When merchant ships were overtaken by the Mautep sea raiders, the merchant seamen usually took to their boats and fled, but occasionally unfortunate Edroviran seamen were taken. It was from these that news of Edrovir came to the oar deck of the *Fist of Death*, and this was how the slaves first heard rumors of the plague that was sweeping the land.

As the summer waned, the picture sketched by these rumors came into focus. The war with the Jinari had been going badly for Edrovir, and King Elgurn had gathered a force and ridden south to succor the southern lords. The king's coming had turned the tide—until some of his warriors had begun to sicken and die. By the time Elgurn and the other lords realized there was a plague coming out of Jinara, it was too late. The disease had already been creeping northward from the border, and when the Edroviran host fled homeward in disarray, the men spread contagion across the entire kingdom.

This news caused great alarm to those slaves who had family in Edrovir. Taru shook his head in concern over his Gama and others he knew in Wotana. Nagaro worried about the Wotana folk as well—Gama, certainly, but also Aramei. He even wondered about the welfare of the Princess Nevien.

Either the Mautep captains knew less about the plague than their slaves, or else they believed that the disease couldn't cross water. In any case, Lord Baalkir's war galleys continued to seek ships to prey upon off the southern coast of Edrovir well into Oteyin. Even when the merchant ships became scarce as the plague waxed, Lord Baalkir's captains continued to ply those waters, hoping for one or two last prizes.

Instead, they were surprised late one afternoon among the Lomoa Islands by ships of the Royal Fleet under the command of Kuran Kel.

Chapter 17: Plague!

The battle was violent but brief. After each side saw one of its ships go down, both decided to pull back. The sun was by then descending into the sea as an orb of crimson fire, and it would soon be too dark to fight in any case. So the Edroviran fleet made for Pakoa Harbor while the Mautep captains put the setting sun to starboard and sailed south with all speed. The last thing Captain Urchak did before doing so was to direct his warriors to pluck several crewmen from the sunken Droviri ship out of the sea. In doing this, Urchak broke with established Mautep custom. Trained enemy fighters might find means of doing mischief, even on an oar deck. But the Mautep ships had been long out of port, and the *Fist of Death* had fared less well than Urchak would have liked. Too many of her rowing benches were empty.

The slaves were driven long and hard as the *Fist* fled south with the rest of Lord Baalkir's fleet, but at last the order was given to ship oars. The drum had no sooner ceased than Baruk began moving slaves from bench to bench to make room for Urchak's human spoils of war. The Slave Master never paired new slaves together, always placing each new man with a seasoned one who knew the signals used on the oar deck of the *Fist of Death*.

Up until this time, Nagaro and Taru had remained with their original benchmates, but this now changed. Taru was moved to the last aft bench, one that had been empty, while Moraga was moved to the empty bench on the opposite side of the center aisle. Nagaro was moved one bench aft to what had been Moraga's seat next to the hull, leaving Pavo unpaired in the seat behind him. Another space was made by moving Tego across the aisle to the vacant seat beside a Turowan lone man, leaving Laash unpaired in his seat behind Pavo.

The Hashtep had gotten wind of what was happening above decks well before Baruk began his rearrangements. Word of the taking of the Edroviran seamen had been passed around the oar deck in low whispers, arousing much curiosity. No one there had ever seen one of Lord Kuran's sea warriors. When at last the new captives were brought in, one by one, they were in rather sorry condition. They'd been stripped down to their dark blue uniform pants, still wet with seawater. Newly branded, their faces pale and drawn with pain, they staggered down the center aisle and sank into their appointed seats without resistance.

There were five of them, the first being a flaxen-haired young Leithian who was placed next to Moraga on the port side. The second was a Kelorin, a big, muscular man with an ugly gash on the side of his head, who stumbled several times as he traversed the length of the oar deck to be placed next to Taru. Nagaro glimpsed the man's face as he was shoved past, and was struck by the slack jaw and glassy eyes.

Nagaro's new benchmate was the next to be brought in, a bedraggled Kelorin youth who sank into his seat and promptly put his head down on his knees. He was followed by a small, wiry Leithian of about thirty-five years with close-cropped sandy hair and haggard eyes. This man was paired with Pavo on the bench behind Nagaro. The last man was a lean, weathered Kelorin with grizzled hair who was placed in the empty space beside Laash, behind Pavo's bench. The Mautep crewmen then departed, and it became safe for the slaves to talk. Nagaro heard muttered words exchanged behind him, though the youth beside him still kept his head down.

Taru tried speaking to his new benchmate. "Bad night for a swim, eh?" he inquired. The man turned to look blearily at the young Turo, but made no response. Taru tried again. "My name's Taru. What do they call ye, mate?" This time the big Kelorin didn't even turn his head. Taru rolled his eyes. "It seems Lord Kuran's sea warriors think they're too good for the likes of us," he announced to no one in particular.

Nagaro frowned at this judgement, and considered addressing the man himself. Further conversation was cut short, however, when Fataan and Roheed entered with a round of water.

Taru had to shake his new benchmate twice to get him to take the ladle. Roheed retrieved the ladle gingerly, studying the big Kelorin's face with worried eyes. Moving two steps farther forward, Roheed halted beside Nagaro's benchmate. Head still down, the Kelorin youth seemed oblivious. Nagaro touched the young man's shoulder, and the youth started and sat up, staring at him wide-eyed.

Nagaro discovered that the young sea warrior had fine features and wide-set eyes of deepest Kelorin blue. He stared back, transfixed by those eyes. They stirred memories of the Lady Maramine. With an effort, he pushed the memories aside and motioned past the youth to where Roheed stood waiting with the dipper.

The young Kelorin dragged his own eyes away from Nagaro's, and turned. Seeing the dipper, he immediately took it and drank thirstily. When he passed the re-filled dipper to Nagaro, the youth glanced quickly at him and just as quickly away again. As soon as Roheed moved on along the deck, the Kelorin youth put his head back down on his knees and remained so until the two slave-tenders had again left the oar deck.

Once Roheed was gone, Nagaro decided to risk talking to his new benchmate. "My name is Nagaro," he ventured. "What's yours?"

The young man raised his head then, and gave Nagaro a lingering look. "Simion," he answered, then added, "I'm sorry. I... I need to rest," and he put his head back down again.

Nagaro twisted around to address the same question to Pavo's new benchmate, behind him. The sandy-haired Leithian shook himself out of a gloomy reverie to reply simply, "Tredhold Ferth."

Before any more could be said, Baruk returned with the rest of the Mautep oar deck crew, and the slaves knew that they would have to row again, even though it was already night outside the oar ports. The Mautep must still have feared pursuit, for Raak drove the slaves long and hard. The five former sea warriors picked up the drum signals quickly: Raak's lash was scarcely needed for them, though he applied it anyway out of spite. Simion kept the pace until very near the end, when he flagged and Nagaro had to work hard to keep the big oar moving.

Taru's silent benchmate seemed to grip the oar almost automatically, moving flawlessly forward and back with the rhythm of the oar for as long as the drum kept up its beat. When the drumbeat stopped, however, the man's hands slipped from the oar shaft and he slumped forward, then slid to the floor to lie like a dead thing. Seeing this, Raak prowled over to prod the fallen man with his boot, He laughed derisively before leaving the tending of the slaves to Roheed and Fataan.

When Roheed arrived later with the waterskin and the dipper, Taru kicked his benchmate none too gently. In response, the big man groaned and dragged himself back onto his bench. He mechanically drank his share, then sat, swaying. When Roheed came around again a little later with his pot of salve, the young Mautep's ministration drew not so much as a twitch from the big Kelorin. When the food was brought, the big sea warrior showed no interest, and he sat silent and unmoving during the sluicing of the deck. Half a minute after the aft door had closed behind Fataan and Roheed, the man toppled backward, landing with his head at Simion's feet, his body draped awkwardly over his bench. His eyes were shut and he appeared unconscious.

Simion stared, frozen, at his crew mate.

Nagaro frowned and addressed Taru. "Will you help me lift him back over the bench?" he asked. "We shouldn't leave him like this."

"I don't know why I should bother with him," Taru said stiffly. "Let the Mautep move him if they don't like where he's lying."

Nagaro gave his friend a sharp look. "Simion will need to sleep in this space," he pointed out. Taru merely shrugged. "Do whatever ye like," he said sullenly.

Nagaro sighed and turned to Simion. "Will you help me move him?"

Dully, Simion nodded.

Nagaro rose and knelt at the fallen man's head, putting his hands under the big Kelorin's shoulders to try to lift him. Immediately he drew back with a cry. "He's burning with fever!"

This time Simion sprang up, his eyes wide with fear. "The plague's taken him!"

"*Plague!*" A frightened murmur ran the full length of the oar deck. Nagaro felt a twist of fear in his stomach.

"It's plague, isn't it, Tred?" Simion was speaking to the sandy-haired Leithian on the bench behind him. The wiry little man looked grave. "Aye, it's likely," he answered grimly. "I'd hoped it was the head wound, but it's not like Worin to suffer so with such a scratch. If it's plague, he'll be delirious in an hour or two and we'll see the purple patches on him by morning."

"Are you a healer then?" Nagaro asked. "Can you help this man?"

The Leithian's weary gaze shifted from Simion to Nagaro. "I was ship's doctor on the *Fairwind*, that's gone to the bottom with a dozen good men still inside of her," he answered bitterly. "Not to speak of all the ones we had to bury at sea because of the contagion. As for Worin, there's little I could do for him here even if I could reach him."

"Are we all going t' die, then?" The question came from Mendorel. The graying Kelorin sounded more resigned than fearful, though there were alarmed stirrings and muttered words from other quarters.

Tredhold shrugged. "Even at its worst, this plague will kill no more than one man in four. With good care, it's no more'n one in ten."

Nagaro studied the Leithian. "What sort of care?"

The man's brow furrowed. "Give the man plenty o' water and fresh air, keep him cool... and wait. If he's strong enough, he'll live. If not..." The healer shrugged again. "The juice of some kinds o' fruit has virtue," he added. "Sour fruits with a bitter peel, like lemons and limes."

"Do you think onions would serve?" Nagaro asked.

The Leithian looked first startled, then thoughtful. "They might, at that—" he began.

Moraga had been listening from across the aisle, and he didn't give the healer a chance to finish. "What are ye on about, Nagaro?" the Turo demanded. "Ye know the Mautep'll throw the man overboard as soon as they see he's got the plague. They'll throw us all overboard afore they let the plague get a hold on this ship!"

"Throw him overboard!" Simion sounded horrified.

Tredhold muttered "Barbarians!" under his breath.

Nagaro gave his benchmate a sympathetic look. "I'm afraid Moraga is right," he told the young man. "Unless we can persuade the Mautep that they have more to gain by some doctoring..."

"*Persuade* the Mahuk?" Tredhold was incredulous.

Nagaro turned back to the Leithian healer. "They never seem to have enough galley slaves," he observed calmly. "If they know there's a good chance a man will recover..."

Moraga let out a harsh laugh. "It's Nagaro that ye should be treatin' for fever now, healer! He must be raving!"

Nagaro ignored Moraga. He turned to address Tredhold's benchmate. "Pavo," he said. "Do you think they'll make us row again tonight? What have the Hashtep heard?"

Pavo quickly exchanged words with several of the other Hashtep slaves in Hashti, and turned back to Nagaro to answer. "I not think we row, Nagaro. Hashtep hear Mautep say they see no sail behind us."

Pavo's speech drew astonished looks from Simion and Tredhold and their crew mates, which Nagaro ignored. Turning to Simion, he said, "The Mautep will come soon to put out the lanterns. They'll likely haul your mate out of here tonight if they find him with fever, but if you help me move him back to his side of the bench, they may not notice, and he'll live at least until morning. Then we can see what the new day brings. Perhaps it's not the plague that ails him."

Simion nodded his acquiescence, and together they were able to lift Worin and move him back to his own side of the bench.

Taru grumbled about having the sick man near him.

"You have the last bench, so you have plenty of room to lie down without touching him," Nagaro pointed out. "Simion doesn't."

Nagaro and Simion had just finished their task when the two young slave tenders returned, as predicted, to extinguish the lanterns, and the oar deck was plunged into darkness.

*

Nagaro woke some time before dawn to the sound of a mumbled voice close by in the darkness. He didn't have to listen long to know he was hearing the Kelorin sea warrior, Worin, talking in his delirium. By the sound of it, the man's fevered mind was reliving some battle he had fought. Nagaro rolled over, feeling sick at heart. He tried to cover his ears with his hands, but couldn't shut out the sound of the fevered man's voice.

Morning light, when it came, clearly revealed the first dark purplish lesions on Worin's arms and neck. When the slave tenders came, Roheed took one look and made for the aft door with Fataan on his heels. They both returned with rags wrapped around their hands. Raak came with them to direct them, while Baruk manned the windlass.

When Tredhold understood what they were about to do, he stood up angrily. "Here, now!" he cried. "There's no need to take him—"

The healer's words were cut short by Raak, who struck the Leithian savagely in the face with the butt of his whip. "*No talk, shaku!*" the Slave Driver snarled.

Tredhold sat down heavily, clutching his hand to his mouth. There was blood showing between his fingers.

In due course, the sick man was raised through the hatch, and the hatch was closed. The empty seat beside Taru was filled by moving Tego from across the aisle, leaving the Turowan lone man to row alone, and the Mautep departed. It was a calm morning, and the seas were quiet, so they all heard quite distinctly the soft splash as Worin's fever-wracked body slid into the oily swells. Simion bowed his head, his lips moving in silent prayer. The weathered, gray-haired Kelorin sitting behind Tredhold spoke the words that must have been in the minds of all of his crewmates. "Now that's a sorry end for a sea warrior! Fair makes me sick, it does."

"Aye." Tredhold spoke up painfully, still nursing his bloody lip. "But he'll ride with Kroneg tonight. He wasn't Leithian, but Worin surely had the Mark o' the Warrior God upon his brow."

"Aye, that's so!" The other Leithian sea warrior, the flaxen-haired youth sitting beside Moraga, echoed the healer's sentiment.

"What are they talking about?" Nagaro wondered aloud, more to himself than to any of those around him. He was surprised when Simion answered.

The young Kelorin had been sitting still, studying his hands, but he now shot Nagaro a sidelong look. "The Leithians believe that Kroneg, their warrior god, bears a wound on his forehead from which a trickle of blood forever flows," he explained. "They say he uses that sacred blood to mark the foreheads of his chosen, the greatest warriors, whose spirits will join him to ride forever on a great battlefield in Seralind, where they believe their spirits go when they die." With that, Simion returned to the inspection of his digits.

"Oh, I see." The Leithians meant to honor their lost comrade with their words. Nagaro foresaw a very different future for Worin's spirit, another life that might well contain neither swords nor battlefields, but he raised his voice and said, "So Worin must have been a mighty fighter then."

"Aye, he was," Tredhold declared. "Worin was the best swordsman on the *Fairwind,* and one o' the best in the whole Fleet." He dabbed again at his lip with the back of his hand, and added, "Whatever did ye mean by talking about persuading the Mahuk of anything, mate? I'm lucky I didn't lose a tooth!"

"I'm sorry," Nagaro answered earnestly. "I had no chance to warn you that Raak is a brute—not the man I'd choose to try to reason with. Even Baruk would be better. But the one I'd start with is the youngest one, Roheed."

"You mean that beardless boy?" the healer exclaimed. What could he do even if he'd listen to ye—which I doubt."

"I hope he might be able to reason with Baruk," Nagaro explained. "And he might have some influence. He's the nephew of Lord Baalkir, the warlord who owns this ship."

"He's the warlord's *nephew?* What is he doing tending slaves on this stinking oar deck then?" The weathered Kelorin spoke from behind the healer.

"I don't know," Nagaro admitted, frowning.

"I tell you." Pavo spoke up. "His father send him to work on warship so he can learn how be warrior. He start most low place. So he learn like common sea-man. Nagaro is make good choice. Roheed not so much cruel."

"Well, that's as may be," Tredhold observed dryly. "But he was just here, helping to carry poor Worin away."

Pavo nodded. "Roheed follow order," he said. "Mautep think they get rid of plague. Sick man gone. No more plague."

There was a murmur among the other slaves. It was Mendorel who gave voice to their thoughts. "Do ye think they could be right, healer?" he asked the Leithian.

Tredhold sighed. "Only time will tell," he said. "Myself, I doubt it. Lord Kuran tried to keep the Fleet clean o' the plague by keeping us at sea as long as he could. But when we fell short o' rations, we had to put into port long enough to take on supplies. Three days after that, we had the first man with fever. Two days later, we had two more, and two days after that there were another five. The other ships had plague as well. We were headed for harbor on the island of Pakoa, to tend our sick, when we spied these Mahuk ships and Kuran decided we had to run 'em off." The healer drew another long sigh. "From what I've seen, the plague could sweep through this oar deck like a wind in the grass. May the Gods help us now!"

*

Three days passed and no one spoke of the plague. It seemed that no one wanted to think about it, and indeed the denizens of the oar deck had little energy for talk. It was the very end of Oteyin. Each day, the sun was like a torch burning in the cloudless sky, and the oar deck was a stifling pit. The wind scarcely stirred the glassy swells, and Lord Baalkir's fleet crept southward under slack sails. Only when the slaves were made to row did the ships make good headway. When night came, the heat dissipated slowly, and it was only in the few hours before dawn that there was any real relief.

During those three days, Nagaro found Simion a disquieting bench-mate. The youth was very reticent when it came to speaking to the other slaves, but oddly inclined to confide in Nagaro. Though he rarely met Nagaro's eyes, he seemed to wait for a moment when none of the other slaves were listening, and then try to draw Nagaro out by volunteering some detail of his personal life.

On the first day, Nagaro learned that the young man came from Lankura, having been born and raised in that city. "And what of you?" Simion asked, his eyes on his hands, clasped in his lap. "Where do you hail from?"

The question made Nagaro acutely uncomfortable, but he felt it would be rude not to answer. "I grew up in the country," he said, wishing he were still paired with Pavo who had never pressed him for his history. He was relieved when Baruk gave the order for the drum to sound again, even though it meant bending his back to the oar in the sweltering heat.

*

"My father is a wool merchant," Simion confided on the following day while he and Nagaro were leaning, exhausted, on their oar during a rest break. "My whole family trades in cloth—or something related to it," Simion went on. "Every one of them, including my two older brothers. Even my sister married a weaver. Do you have any brothers or sisters?"

"No." Nagaro answered tersely, not inclined to volunteer any additional information.

"So how does your father make his way in the world?" Simion cast him a glance, veiled by dark lashes.

"I really don't know." Nagaro winced. *That* would need some further explanation. "I was a foundling," he added hastily, before Simion could ask. "So I never knew my father." That was true, and it should be safe...

"Oh! I'm very sorry!" Simion seemed genuinely distressed. This time his deep blue eyes stayed on Nagaro's face for several heartbeats before he guiltily looked away.

"Don't worry about it," Nagaro muttered, averting his own gaze. "It doesn't matter." After a moment, he risked a glance at the youth and caught Simion's gaze on him again, then saw it hastily withdrawn.

Fortunately, the rowing break came to an end again at that point. But the next time the oars stopped moving, Simion offered something more revealing. "I had a falling out with my father," he confessed, his eyes cast down. "So I ran away from home to join the Royal Fleet."

"You did? Isn't that a bit... extreme?" It was such a shock to Nagaro that anyone with a home and a father would willfully choose to abandon them that he didn't consider the wisdom of the question.

Simion's shoulders hunched and he seemed to draw into himself.

"My father didn't understand..." His voice trailed off. Then he shook himself, rallied, and said, "I was on my first mission as a Fleet warrior when *this* happened."

"Oh." Nagaro could well appreciate the cruelty of Lokundas' hand. "That's hard," he said. "I imagine you might wish you'd stayed home."

This earned him a fleeting smile and a lingering look that turned into a curious, questioning one. "If you don't have a father, how did you live?"

"I was learning to be a fisherman."

"A *fisherman?*" Simion stared now in obvious disbelief. "You don't seem like a fisherman... or a country lad, either." His slim brows came together. "Were you ever in Lankura...?"

For an instant, Nagaro froze. Those deep blue eyes were searching his face. Then he tore his own eyes away to sweep the shadowy expanse of the oar deck, wildly searching for some inspiration. *He couldn't tell the truth... and he couldn't just lie...*

Just then Baruk shouted an order for the rowing to resume.

It had been a narrow escape. All through the rest of that afternoon, Nagaro kept catching Simion's eyes on him. He thought the youth looked troubled, and found himself dreading the thought of further questions. It happened, however, that they had no further opportunities for talk before the dousing of the lamps that evening, and the silence that followed made private talk impossible for the rest of the night.

When Nagaro lay down with his head near Simion's feet, he found that he couldn't sleep. He'd begun to worry that the young man had recognized him from the time he had spent in Lankura. He told himself he must be mistaken, that he couldn't resemble Leyel Virden in anything except the features of his face that weren't covered by his beard. In every other respect, he must seem to be a completely different person. He told himself that, at worst, Simion might be troubled by a resemblance he couldn't place—or an improbable chance resemblance between Nagaro and the idiot prince—but he couldn't entirely convince himself.

He lay awake for what felt like hours. with the oppressive heat worsening his insomnia. The Mautep had made the single concession of leaving the two overhead hatches open at night, but still insisted that the oar ports be securely covered in case there were a change in the weather. There was therefore no cross-ventilation. The air on the oar deck barely stirred.

Eventually, Nagaro must have fallen asleep, but the morning came too soon and he could scarcely rouse himself enough to eat his morning biscuit. He still felt groggy by the time the drum signaled the day's first turn at the oars, and the rowing seemed to exhaust him more than usual. After the drum stopped and the slaves had shipped the oars, he clutched the edge of the bench to steady himself against the roll of the swells and closed his eyes.

He must have dozed sitting up, but a voice speaking close to him brought him out of it. It was Simion, saying something... something about his father. Nagaro tried to focus on the other youth, but he couldn't quite follow what the young man was saying.

When Simion paused expectantly, Nagaro felt that he should say something. "I don't even know who my father was," he ventured after a moment. Simion stared at him as if he'd said something strange. Nagaro shook his head, trying to clear it, but he still felt half asleep. "Excuse me..." he murmured. "I need to rest." With that, he lowered himself to the planks between the benches and lay down, closing his eyes.

His mind drifted...

Someone was shaking him. He opened his eyes. Taru was leaning over him, looking worried. "Are ye all right, Nagaro? They've brought the food."

"Of course I'm all right." Nagaro frowned. "I just didn't sleep well last night. It was so hot..." With an effort, he pulled himself back up onto his bench. He felt a little better for having slept but his head felt muzzy and he was sure he needed more rest. He didn't really have any appetite, but he forced himself to eat a few bites of everything, especially the onion. He gave the rest to Pavo, who never seemed to get enough. He was very thirsty, though, and drank all of his water when it came.

Before long, the slaves were put to the oars again. By now the full heat of the day was upon them. For Nagaro, the rowing quickly faded into a suffocating blur that seemed to go on interminably. By the time the drum stopped, he felt as if his head were stuffed with hot wool. He didn't even try to help Simion ship the oar, but immediately let himself slide down onto the planking and again closed his eyes. *If he could just rest a little more...*

*

"Nagaro! What ails ye, man?"
He jerked his eyes open. Taru's face seemed to float in front of him. He couldn't quite focus on it, but he knew he should try to answer... "Too hot..." was all he managed to say. Then he shut his eyes again. It was too hard to keep them open.

There was a hand on his forehead. "*Hamanei mata noa!*"

"Fever?" someone asked, but Nagaro didn't hear the answer. Once again he was drifting...

*

"Nagaro, get up! Ye have t' row or they'll throw ye overboard!"
"*Wha...?*"

Hands were grabbing him, pulling him up onto the bench. Someone took hold of one of his hands and actually curled his fingers around something smooth and hard. He was looking at the thing. Some tiny part of his mind, a long way off, knew that it was called an "oar." "Row..." he murmured. "Overboard..." Mechanically he placed his other hand next to the first...

He was moving now in time to the throbbing thuds of the drum... Forward and back... Forward and back... Lean... *Pull!* Lean... *Pull!* A hot tongue of pain licked across his back. Lean... *Pull!* Lean... *Pull!* Over and over... *How long had it been? Would it ever end...?*

*

He wasn't rowing anymore.

Not rowing... Overboard... They were coming now to throw him overboard, but the ropes would not stay on him. They fell away. He was rising... rising up, up out of the oar deck. The faces of the other slaves were turned up, staring in amazement, to watch him go. Up, out of the hatch, and up, and up... High above the ship he floated, looking down. Mautep faces now turned upwards, astonished, to watch him soaring away over the sea. He was flying... free! High above foam-tipped waves, then dipping low so he could watch the fish swimming in the depths of translucent green. Then up again and turning to the north...

He would fly home... home to Averwin! They would all be there,, Thorlan and Bodano, Hinda and Chula... good old Chula! And the Lady Maramine, of course... But they'd told him the Lady was ill. He had to hurry. Fly faster... faster... But he didn't know the way...

Where was Averwin? It was in a place where there was a river, and a forest, and a road, a road that ran between farms on either side... He was riding home along the road... Turning in at the gate... Swinging down from the back of the tall black horse to stand on the grass... Autumn grass at Averwin... Under the tree, with its leaves all gone to gold, by the side of the pasture... Luka was sitting cross-legged on the grass. Ancient Luka, medicine woman, smiling up at him with bright, dark eyes in a face like creased leather, her hair gone almost white. She was holding up a sprig of dried herbs... telling him that this would surely make the Lady well again...

*

Fingers were probing along the inside of his right forearm. *"No!"* He tried to pull his arm away. "Not the thorn! Don't do that to me again! Never again!"

But still the fingers held him. He opened his eyes. Dreigen's face shouldn't be so pale. The man's hair was blond, the eyes pale blue... "I'll never give you what you want," he said to the pale blue eyes.

"What do ye think I want?" the man asked. "Who do ye think I am?"

Why was Elgurn trying to trick him? *"I'm going to kill you!"* he told the blond man, speaking with all his pent up fury. The fingers immediately let go. The face drew back...

He got up from the narrow bed in the horrid little room. He walked past Dreigen, the Lore Master, sitting at the table, writing in his big book. Writing, always writing... "I'm going to kill you too," he told Dreigen, with terrible calm. The Lore Master never looked up, never stopped writing.

He moved across the room, out through the door, along the hall, and across to the sitting room. In the sitting room there was a sword... and two daggers... hanging on the wall... A pretty sword with polished stones and gold tracery on the hilt and hand guard... The sword would be the most satisfying... It would go right through a man. Ah, but to die by a sword was a warrior's death. That was too good for them... Better make it a dagger then... He reached for one of the clean, bright daggers, matching partners to the sword. But his hand closed on air...

*

Hands were seizing hold of him, pulling him up, making him sit. He struggled to get away. "No!" he cried. "Let me go!" The edge of a cup was being forced against his lips. Dreigen's face floated before his eyes, and a voice said, "Drink this."

"No!" He pushed it away. "I won't drink your potion!"

"Drink it. All of it!" Again the cup was there. "No!" he cried again, "I'll never give you what you want!"

"Nagaro, it's water! Drink it!"

The familiar voice seemed to come from very far away... somewhere behind him...

"Taru? What are you doing here?" He tried to twist around, but someone gripped his chin and turned his head back to the front. Suddenly he was looking into deep blue eyes—like the evening sky fading into night—in a pale face, framed by dark hair.

"My Lady?" he said. "I thought you were dead..."

A voice spoke from somewhere, saying, "Please... you're very sick. You need to drink some water. It's just water. I swear it in Vothra's name."

Hands were there, holding the cup again. Such a funny cup, like a little bowl with a handle sticking straight out of it... "Yes," he murmured, and he let the hands pour water into his mouth. He swallowed it. His throat felt swollen. More water, and again more... He swallowed it all.

"Now rest," said the voice. "Lie down and close your eyes."

Gratefully, he obeyed. "Yes..." he murmured, "My Lady..." Fingers gently caressed his forehead as he drifted into an easy sleep.

Chapter: 18: Roheed Jir-Akaan

Nagaro opened his eyes to near darkness. His head felt clear, clearer than it had in... how long? The sounds he heard around him in the gloom told him he was on the oar deck. There was the creak of the ship's timbers, and the rush and gurgle of the sea swirling against the *Fist's* great sides. There was another sound as well. From more than one side, came the murmuring of half-articulate voices—the voices of delirium.

Cautiously, Nagaro sat up. The action made his head spin briefly, and his muscles felt like limp rags. His skin was still slick with sweat, and his pants clung damply to his thighs—signs of how recently his fever had broken. He looked around the shadowy cavern of the oar deck. At the far end, one of the three lanterns was burning, but it flickered, nearly guttering. Here and there an oar port was open, and dim light came through. He could make out little in the gloom but the indistinct shapes of benches and the vague recumbent forms of the men nearest to him.

The light suggested it was either dusk or dawn outside, but Nagaro had no idea which. Weakly, he crawled to his own oar port, unfastened the cover, and peered out. A light breeze fanned his face. It wasn't quite dark outside. The sky glowed a deep and luminous azure that darkened towards the distant horizon, indicating that the sun, the source of illumination, must be on the other side of the ship. There was nothing to be seen beneath that sky but the great, blue-black expanse of the sea. Knowing that he was on the starboard side of the ship, and assuming the vessel was still on a southerly course, Nagaro concluded that he was looking west into the open ocean and that it must be just before dawn rather than just past sunset.

The cool air felt wonderfully refreshing, and he would have stayed longer to enjoy it if it hadn't been so uncomfortable to crouch with his head held down there at the level of the oar port. He straightened and turned. Just at that moment, the one remaining lantern went out. With a shock, Nagaro realized that it must have been left burning all night. Something was definitely amiss aboard the *Fist of Death*. The scattering of open oar ports at such an hour was wrong as well... as was the presence of so many fevered slaves on the oar deck.

Nagaro decided to leave his own oar port open. Fresh air was better for sick men, and he didn't care if he risked punishment. There was clearly no danger from the weather. As he turned again to secure the cover of the oar port in the open position, the gathering light fell across his hand and arm, and he noticed for the first time a number of purplish lesions—the hallmark of the plague. Curiously, he examined them. They were smaller than the ones he'd seen on Worin's skin, and they were already fading. This confirmed what he had already guessed—that he had passed through the dark tunnel of the plague and emerged on the other side. How long, he wondered, had he been in a fever?

He turned his attention to the men around him—the ones who lay close enough for him to reach. He located them half by feel and half by sight. The light did seem to be growing stronger, confirming his conclusion that dawn was on its way.

Simion lay curled like a child, half under the bench. The young man moved restlessly as Nagaro studied him, murmuring jumbled words. Nagaro reached out and felt Simion's arm. He found the skin hot and dry. At his touch, the young Kelorin uncurled himself, and Nagaro made out the shine of his eyes in the glimmer of light from the oar port. The youth seemed to be looking at Nagaro, but it wasn't certain what he was seeing.

"Please, Mother," the young man murmured. "Talk to him. Tell him I'm still his son..." Nagaro frowned, recalling that Simion had told him he had run away from home to join the Fleet. For a moment, he crouched by the young man's head, waiting to see if the youth would say anything more, but Simion lay quiet and the gathering light allowed him to see that the young man's eyes were closed again. The arm that lay curved across his belly bore the beginnings of a number of dark plague lesions.

Nagaro turned then and sought Taru, remembering dimly that his friend had roused him from a fevered sleep to make sure that he rowed. It seemed that he remembered something also about water, but of that he was less certain. His brow creased in a frown. How much of what he remembered had he actually said out loud—and who had heard what he'd said?

Taru lay sprawled, as far from his bench as it was possible for him to lie with his ankle chain still fastened to the floor ring. Nagaro was only able to reach the young Turo's foot and ankle, and he couldn't be very sure of his friend's condition just by the feel of them. Nagaro was at least certain that Taru was alive, for he felt rather warm to the touch. And by the rise and fall of his chest, the young Turo seemed to be breathing easily and quietly, with no sign of delirium.

Tego was lying within easy reach. The older Turowan seemed only to be sleeping soundly, quite free of fever.

Pavo and Tredhold were another matter. Even before he touched Pavo's skin, Nagaro knew what he would find. The young Hashtep was tossing restlessly on the planking, a mumbled stream of Hashti issuing from his swollen lips. A hand laid on Pavo's forehead found the young Hashtep on fire with fever. Tredhold the healer was in a somewhat better state, though clearly ill as well. The Leithian didn't feel as hot as Pavo, and he moved when Nagaro touched him. The healer's eyes were open, but he looked past Nagaro and said, quite distinctly, "Hold 'im up now and give me the dipper. We have t' get some water into him..."

Water. They all needed water, especially the sick men. Nagaro was very worried about Pavo. It was apparent that the Mautep hadn't been throwing fevered slaves overboard, but it wasn't clear whether any doctoring was being done. Nagaro pulled himself weakly to a seat on his bench and twisted around to face the ship's bow. Raising his voice above the sounds of timber and wave and the fevered mutterings, he called out. "Hallo! Is anyone awake?"

Two benches forward, the grizzled Kelorin sea warrior promptly sat up, peered at him, and answered. "Ahoy there, matey! Nagaro, is it? Have ye come through it then?"

"I think so," Nagaro responded. "I'm weak as a babe, but my head is clear, and the spots are fading." Then he added, "I'm sorry. I'm afraid I never heard your name."

"It's Landros. Landros Torenin."

Nagaro smiled weakly. "Well met, friend Landros. Can you tell me what has been happening? The last thing I remember clearly is being made to row."

"Aye," the Kelorin answered him. "That would ha' been three days ago. That was the last time they made us row. They were working us hard, too. And then, all of a sudden, three slaves just fell over."

"Three at once?" Nagaro was startled. "All with plague?"

"Aye." The sea warrior nodded. "Ye were one o' them. Another was young Gurd, that's one of my mates..." It appeared that Landros meant the flaxen-haired Leithian paired with Moraga. "And that great Mahuk lad over there." Landros pointed to where the simple-minded Otao lay. "It happened all at once. like I said. So, seeing as how we were down three oars, the slave master—what's his name? Baruk?—he hollered for the drummer to stop. And what d' ye think? The drummer no sooner beat out the signal to halt, than three more slaves keeled over.

Three more? That was six, Nagaro thought. Tredhold was right. The plague was moving fast through the oar deck. "What did the Mautep— the Mahuk—do?" he asked.

Landros laughed shortly. "Oh, well, first they poked at a couple o' the lads that were down. Then they did a lot o' jabbering. And then they high-tailed it off o' this oar deck like the ship was afire. I reckon they're not so brave, these Mahuk, when it comes t' plague!"

"Have any of them been back since?"

"Those two young bucks came—once," Landros answered grimly. "That evening... They made us ship the oars and close the ports. And they left us two water skins and those dipper things. That's the last I've seen o' them. Those of us that were able-bodied passed the water around that night—and the next day. Every time, there were fewer of us. Then the water ran out. That was yesterday evening."

"There's no water, then, for these poor men?"

Landros shook his head. "Nary a drop."

"Do you think they'll bring more?" Nagaro asked doubtfully. He was suddenly aware that he was very thirsty. Knowing there was no water made it worse.

Landros shrugged. "Maybe." He didn't sound very hopeful. "But I'm thinking they're too much afeared o' the plague."

Nagaro sat staring across the dim oar deck. "I remember something about water," he murmured. "But it's all very confused. I must have been out of my head with fever."

"Aye, that ye were." Landros seemed to be studying him narrowly in the gloom. "They had a peck o' trouble getting water into ye yesterday. Fighting with 'em ye were, and saying ye were going to kill poor Tred. What was that all about anyway? It seemed ye thought someone was trying to do ye harm."

Nagaro frowned uncomfortably. He had a pretty good idea what it had been about. "Just the fever, I suppose," he said. Then, to change the subject, he asked, "What about the rest of the fleet? I didn't see any other ships out there."

"And ye won't," Landros replied. "They just kept their slaves rowing when our lot stopped. They've left us behind to limp along with this lame breeze."

Nagaro was surprised by this news. Were the Mautep really all so afraid of plague that they'd abandon an entire shipload of their own? "How many of the men are sick?"

"It was almost a third o' them last night, but it wouldn't surprise me if it was closer to half by now. My benchmate, here, was starting to wobble on his pins last night and this morning he's talking nonsense. 'Course there might be some more that's coming around again, the way ye've done. If ye wake up Tred, there, he'll have more to say I'm sure."

"Tred? You mean the healer?" Nagaro looked down at the Leithian where he lay, twitching and muttering on the floor boards. "I'm afraid the fever has a pretty good hold on him."

Even in the poor light, Nagaro could see the dismay on Landros' weathered features. "By the Eyes!" the grizzled seaman exclaimed. "Not Tred!" Landros leaned over the healer's bench and gave the Leithian a good shake. "Tredhold, ye great barnacle! Rise and shine there, matey!"

The healer uttered an inarticulate sound, and his eyes half opened. "No, no... it's adder's tongue for chill blains..." he murmured thickly, "an' sandwort for fever blister..."

Landros uttered a groan. "*Blood and bilge water! By the Eyes and Ears!* What's to become of us now—if Tred's gone?"

"He's not gone!" Nagaro was alarmed by Landros' reaction. "Don't you remember what he said? Most of these men will recover with just a little bit of tending. Tredhold told me everything there is to do—" He broke off, frowning. "Of course," he muttered, "we can't do any of it without water." Desperately his eyes swept the oar deck. Outside the sun must have risen above the horizon. A good deal more light was coming in through the open oar ports on the starboard side of the ship, although it still was not very bright without the lanterns.

There were at least thirty-five men on the oar deck, all chained to their places—unable to save themselves from death if the Mautep chose not to give them the means to do so. Nagaro felt a wave of anguished frustration. It was unthinkable that they should all be left to die of plague or of thirst in this place. Abruptly, he turned to face aft and cupped his hands to his mouth to make his voice carry.

"Roheed!" he shouted. "Roheed! Roheed jir-Akaan!"

Nothing happened, except that Tego sat up and blinked owlishly at him. Across the aisle, Mendorel rolled over and said, "Is that Nagaro shouting? He's out of his head, Tego. Can't ye make him lie down?"

Nagaro paid no attention. He cupped his hands and shouted again. "Roheed! Roheed jir-Akaan!"

Tego looked from Mendorel to Nagaro and back again. "I don't think it's the fever, Mendorel," he said. Then to Nagaro, "What are ye, daft, man? Ye know it's forbidden t' speak when any o' the Mautep are about. Raak 'll flay ye alive for makin' so bold as t' call one o' them by name!"

Nagaro met Tego's eyes. "Well," he observed grimly. "That would at least be quicker than dying of thirst." He raised his hands to his mouth and shouted again. "Roheed jir-Akaan!"

Abruptly, the aft port door burst open, and Roheed strode onto the oar deck. The young Mautep was dressed in shirt, pants, and boots, without the scarlet tunic or sable sash that normally completed his uniform. His hair was disheveled and his face looked drawn. He cast his gaze about the dim oar deck, frowning, undoubtedly seeking whoever had dared to call his name.

Tego, as soon as he heard the door open, immediately lay down, feigning sleep. Mendorel promptly did likewise, and a sound of rattling chain behind Nagaro suggested that Landros had decided to follow the more experienced slaves' example.

Wishing to leave no doubt as to his guilt if there was to be any punishment for his actions, Nagaro stood up, though his legs would scarcely hold him. He was lucky, in fact, that the sea was calm and the deck not moving much beneath him. He lowered his voice, not shouting any longer. "Roheed jir-Akaan," he said, inclining his head in acknowledgment of the other man.

Roheed's glance fastened on him. "You!" he exclaimed. The young Mautep glanced over his shoulder as if to be certain he had closed the door behind him. Then he turned back and took a few steps towards Nagaro, stopping again with a worried frown as he became aware that he was approaching the recumbent forms of Taru and Tego. He fixed his eyes once more on Nagaro and spoke low and urgently. "You do not call Mautep! Not say my name! They kill you for do that."

Nagaro regarded the young man steadily. "They will not kill me," he observed calmly, "if you do not tell them." He'd noticed that Roheed's words were uttered in Common Speech that was more articulate and less accented than that of the other Mautep. He had no time, however, to wonder how Roheed came by his knowledge of the Edroviran language, though he was glad of it since it made his task easier.

The young Mautep had been gaping at him, still frowning. Now his frown deepened "Why you call?" He demanded, suspiciously.

"Water," Nagaro said simply. "We need water here, or we will die." He spread his arms, gesturing to include the men lying all about him.

Roheed shook his head. "Urchak say give no more water to shaku. Shaku have plague. All go to die."

Nagaro tried to keep the desperation out of his voice. "No," he said carefully. "These men will not all die. Most of them will live—with a little doctoring. Look at me," he added, pointing to the spots on his arm. "I had plague. I was one of the first, but I am better now—because my friends gave me water. Now some of them are sick, but I have no water to give them."

Roheed looked away. "Is not me say water, or no water," he said, and it seemed to Nagaro that the young Mautep didn't like what he was having to say. "Urchak say no water for shaku."

"Then we will surely all die," Nagaro said quietly. "Of plague... or of thirst." He looked hard at Roheed, but the youth avoided his eyes. Nagaro took a deep breath and played his last gambit. "Do you think, Roheed jir-Akaan, that Lord Baalkir will be pleased to lose a whole shipfull of slaves, when it didn't have to be so?"

Roheed stiffened. The look in his eyes was something between shock and reproach. "You not speak name of Lord Baalkir—" he began. Then he stopped, as if he read something in Nagaro's face that changed his thought. "How you know I have name jir-Akaan?" he asked suddenly.

Nagaro shrugged. "My friend, Pavo Maat, told me." He indicated where the young Hashtep lay. "Now he's very sick. Please give us water."

This time Roheed didn't look away. "Is not me say no water," he repeated. And with that, the young Mautep turned on his heel and strode away, disappearing back through the aft bulkhead door and pulling it firmly closed behind him.

Nagaro stared numbly at the closed door.

Tego sat up. "So we're all t' die—captain's orders," he growled. "If that ain't just like the Mahuk!"

Nagaro sat down heavily on his bench and took his head in his hands. He felt terribly tired, and terribly thirsty, and there was a sick feeling growing in the pit of his stomach that had nothing whatever to do with hunger or the plague.

"Don't take it so hard, laddie. At least ye tried." That was Landros, speaking from behind him.

Nagaro shook his head. "Oh, Roheed, I judged you a better man," he murmured. Then he slid down onto the planks beside Simion. "Vothra, I'm tired," he said to no one in particular. "I need to rest..." He stretched himself out and closed his eyes, trying to shut out the sound of fevered murmurings and forget how thirsty he was.

*

"Hst! Nagaro!" Someone was shaking him. Blearily he opened his eyes. Tego was reaching under his own bench to shake him by the arm. "It's Roheed," the weathered old Turo informed him in a hoarse whisper. "Ye'd best have a look."

Nagaro sat up and stared. Roheed stood uncertainly, just in front of the aft door. The young Mautep carried a pair of bulging water skins, one on each shoulder. He was tensely staring across the oar deck, and his whole demeanor suggested that at any moment he might change his mind and bolt. When his gaze fell on Nagaro, however, the youth seemed to make a decision, for he suddenly stepped forward and came right down the center aisle to the level of Nagaro's bench. Turning to port, Roheed set down one of the water skins within reach of Mendorel. The grizzled Kelorin sat up unabashedly and pounced on it. Turning towards the bow, he hissed, "Hoy! Which one o' ye's got the dipper?"

Roheed frowned and made a shushing sound. Then he crossed quickly to Nagaro's side. He knelt on the deck and set down the second water skin.

Nagaro found his voice. "Thank you," he said hoarsely.

Roheed gathered his feet under him but did not stand up. Instead, he remained squatting near Simion's feet, regarding Nagaro intently. "You know plague," he said suddenly. "You know what to do?"

Nagaro frowned. "Yes..."

"You are *dakataar*? Man make sick people better?"

"A healer?" Nagaro asked, then shook his head. "No, I'm not a healer. That man—" he pointed to Tredhold "—was a ship's doctor. Before the fever took him, he told me what to do."

Roheed moved over to study Tredhold for a moment. The Leithian was moving restlessly, mumbling in fevered dreams. The young slave handler shook his head and returned quickly to Nagaro. "You tell me what to do," he said urgently.

"Tell... you?" Nagaro was puzzled.

Roheed glanced furtively at the door through which he'd entered, although it was securely closed. He looked back at Nagaro. "We have plague," he said. "Up there." He gestured toward the deck above their heads. "Our dakataar... he is dead. Die in fight with Hatakei Raal."

Nagaro hesitated only for an instant. "There isn't much to do," he said. Then he told the young Mautep what Tredhold had told him, finishing with, "The strong ones will live. That's all I know."

Roheed stood up. "Thank you," he said. Then he turned around and left the oar deck the way he had come.

"By the Eyes!" Landros exclaimed after Roheed had gone. "It looks like ye're not such a poor judge o' men after all, matey!"

"I don't know 'bout that," Tego put in quickly. "Seems t' me that boy just used the water to buy him some answers. Why'd ye go an tell him, Nagaro?"

Nagaro sighed. "Fair is fair," he said. "I asked him for water to help my mates. He asked for information to help his. And, as far as buying answers goes, he gave us the water before he asked his questions. And that water didn't come by captain's orders. Ah! Here's the other dipper." Someone had passed the implement to Landros, who now straddled the bench in front of him, leaned forward, and stretched out his hand to give it to Nagaro.

"Here, Tego," Nagaro offered. "Get yourself a drink."

Tego shook his head. "No, ye should take some first," he said. "We wouldn't have this water if it weren't for ye takin' a chance on callin' that Mautep lad."

Nagaro didn't argue. He filled the dipper and drank gratefully. The water was tepid, and as always, it tasted of leather, but it still felt wonderfully soothing to his parched throat. He would gladly have taken a second dipper-full, but he restrained himself. There was no telling how long this water would have to last them. *If the Mautep became too busy with their own sick... or if Roheed took fever without having persuaded any of the other Mautep that it was worthwhile to keep the slaves alive...*

Nagaro passed the dipper and skin to Tego, then turned his attention to Taru. Leaning out over the bench in front of him, he grabbed his friend's ankle and gave it a good shake. "Come on, Taru," he said. "Can you sit up, man?" Taru groaned. Nagaro shook him again.

"Wha' happened t' th' light?" Taru mumbled vaguely. The young Turo rolled over and sat up weakly. His face was flushed, and his eyes looked unnaturally bright. "Ohh... I don' feel good," he said and started to lie down again.

Tego moved quickly to catch his benchmate. "Here matey," he said. "Lean on the bench. Here's some water now. Can ye hold the dipper?"

"'Course I can hol' it," Taru said, and tried, but his hands were so unsteady that Tego hastily reached over to help him drink before the precious water could be spilled.

"How long has he been sick?" Nagaro asked.

"Not long," Tego answered. "He weren't quite right last night, and ye see how he is this mornin'."

Taru seemed to really focus on Nagaro for the first time. The young Turo's brow furrowed in concentration "N'garo," he said. "Ye're a very sick man... Ye should lie down..."

"I *was* sick," Nagaro replied. "But I'm better now."

"Don' ye go tellin' me ye're better!" Taru swayed drunkenly as he leaned forward to shake a finger in Nagaro's face. "Ye lie down ri' now... Or my mother'll put ye t' bed!"

Nagaro started to laugh, but he sobered quickly at the memory of Olomi. He shook his head at his friend. "If your mother were here, Taru, she'd put *you* to bed. If there were any bed, that is..."

"Oh." Taru looked around him as if only just noticing where he was. Then he said, "Ohhh... I don' feel good..." and slid back down onto the deck planking.

Satisfied that they had done all they could for Taru, Nagaro turned next to his own benchmate. It proved impossible to rouse Simion to any form of awareness.

"Please, Father... Don' say that..." the young man mumbled without opening his eyes, when Nagaro tried shaking him. "I'll do wha'ever you say..."

Nagaro still had very little strength. In the end, he managed to hold Simion up, cradling the youth's head in his lap while he filled the dipper and poured water into the young man's mouth.

Tego shook his head at him. "I'd have a care o' that one, Nagaro," the Turowan ventured. "He's a strange one."

"What do you mean?" Nagaro asked, lowering the dipper.

"I don't know. The way he was... touchin' ye when ye was sick..."

Nagaro frowned. He vaguely remembered someone stroking his forehead. In his fever, he'd imagined it was the Lady Maramine. "Was he the one who got me to take water?" he asked.

Landros answered. "Aye, that he was."

Nagaro raised the goard dipper again and carefully poured another mouthful between Simion's parted lips. "Then I'd be a pretty poor excuse for a man if I didn't do the same for him," he said quietly. He finished the task and laid Simion gently back down on the decking.

Landros got the dipper next and used it to slake his thirst. Then both he and Nagaro turned to the two men whose bench lay in between theirs. Tredhold proved difficult. Nagaro could scarcely reach the healer. Landros had better luck because he was able to get one leg over Tredhold's bench. The Leithean made feeble efforts to sit up when they shook him. Between the two of them, Nagaro and Landros managed to get him propped against the bench while Landros administered the water.

Pavo's condition appeared grave indeed. The young Hashtep lay limp and still, except for the rising and falling of his chest with each ragged breath. Leaning over his own bench, Nagaro put his hand on his friend's forehead and winced at what he felt. "Vothra," he murmured. "I pray it's not too late!" He took Pavo's head between his hands, leaning close. "Can you hear me, Pavo?" he asked, but he got no answer. Nagaro massaged the youth's temples with his fingers, continuing to speak to him, but Pavo was completely unresponsive.

"I'm afraid ye're wasting your time with that one, mate," Landros observed.

Nagaro ignored the comment. Carefully he dribbled a little water into the palm of his hand and rubbed it across Pavo's forehead. Then he leaned down and blew gently on his friend's dampened brow. Pavo's hands twitched then, and his head moved slightly from side to side. Nagaro turned to Landros. "Can you hold up his head?" he asked urgently. "So he won't choke when I try to get some water into his mouth."

Landros moved to comply, but at the same time he asked, "Why go to so much trouble for a Mahuk?"

Nagaro gave the older man a piercing glance. "Hastep, or Turo, or Kelorin doesn't matter on this oar deck!" he declared with some heat. "Besides," he added more moderately, "Pavo is my friend. He was my benchmate for five months until you and your crewmates were brought in."

"All right then, matey," Landros said hastily. "I guess I know which way the wind's a-blowing." He got his hands under Pavo's shoulders, and lifted him into a half-sitting position.

Nagaro ran a little water into the dipper. He held Pavo's jaw with one hand and carefully dribbled water into the youth's open mouth with the other. Then he massaged the young man's throat until he felt Pavo swallow. He painstakingly repeated the process until he was convinced that Pavo had consumed a full dipper's worth of the life-giving liquid. At last he gestured for Landros to lower the young man's head back onto the planking.

"Here," Nagaro said, handing the dipper to Landros. "Do what you can for Laash." Landros proceeded to minister to his fevered benchmate, venturing no comment about taking trouble over another Mahuk.

After that, Nagaro lay down to rest some more while the water skins slowly made their way from the aft to the forward end of the oar deck. He felt he had done all he could for the time being, and he trusted to the unspoken rule of comradeship that had developed among the oar deck slaves to see the process through. The plague had left him easily exhausted. He closed his eyes and slept.

He was wakened by the gentle prodding of a booted toe against his shoulder. He opened his eyes to find Roheed standing over him. Hurriedly he sat up. The young Mautep's demeanor was very different this time. The uncertainty and furtiveness were gone, and the youth had brought baskets of biscuit and dried meat. Nagaro murmured his thanks as he took the baskets. He hadn't much appetite yet himself, but he was sure some of the other slaves would be glad of the food.

Roheed shook his head at Nagaro's expression of gratitude. "Is Urchak say give shaku food," the youth informed him. Nagaro nodded his understanding, although he suspected it was Roheed's efforts that lay behind the captain's change of heart.

"We are go to Chitaopa," Roheed added, after a moment's hesitation. "Wind is good. Go to be there before night come. Take all man from ship at Chitaopa. Stay there 'til plague go away."

Nagaro nodded again, grateful to be offered so much information. "That's good," he said. "There will be fresh air and water, and everyone can rest."

It was good news indeed. The ship had stopped at Chitaopa once during the summer to take on water. Nagaro remembered the name, though he knew little else about the place, except that it was an uninhabited island where water could be found all year 'round.

After Roheed had gone again, Nagaro looked about the oar deck. A number of men were sitting up now as the food baskets moved amongst them. Nagaro had taken only half a piece of biscuit. He felt he ought to eat something, and the biscuit was all he could stomach. Many more oar ports were open now, letting in sunlight and a stirring of air. By the brightness of the light, Nagaro judged it to be about midday. The weather had clearly changed for the better. It wasn't nearly so hot, and the plunging roll of the ship's motion told him they were riding a heavy swell, confirming what Roheed had said about the wind.

He sat and nibbled his biscuit. After a little time, the water skins were passed again, this time from forward to aft. For Landros, Tego, and Nagaro, there followed a repetition of the ritual of tending to their sick comrades. Nagaro thought that Pavo seemed, perhaps, a little better, but Tredhold and Taru were clearly worse. Simion was about the same. The effort of lifting and holding the other men and pouring water between their lips exhausted him again. When they had finished the task, Nagaro lay down and slept once more.

*

"Chitaopa!"

The cry awakened him. Nagaro sat up and crawled to the oar port. Crouching down to peer out, he saw that the sun was low in the western sky. He also saw the island that was their destination. When the *Fist* had stopped there earlier in the summer, he hadn't been next to the oar port. Now, as the ship drew closer and altered course to make for the eastern shore, he was able to get a clear view of the place.

Chitaopa was a massive bastion of rock, often rising in sheer cliffs out of the foaming sea. To the east, however, on its leeward side, there was a headland that sheltered a small cove and a stretch of beach where a narrow skirt of land ran along the base of the cliff. A small stand of cedar trees grew on a low hill, and little streams cascaded down the rock face to flow through stands of bush willow and across the sand to the sea. Sea birds wheeled and circled about the cliffs on snowy wings, filling the air with their mournful cries. At the base of the cliff, near the southern end of the beach, Nagaro made out the black mouth of a cave, well above the tide line.

The crew anchored the *Fist of Death* as close to the sandy stretch of shore as they dared, and the task of disembarking her human burden— sea warriors and slaves—began immediately. There was an urgency to the work. The Mautep clearly wanted to finish while the light lasted. They took their own sick ashore first, along with those needed to tend them.

In the meantime, however, Baruk came onto the oar deck and began looking over the slaves to see which were too sick to shift themselves, which were able to stand, and which were fit enough to be put to work. The Slave Master brought Roheed with him, as well as four other Mautep whose names Nagaro didn't know. Some of these men had rags wrapped around their hands. Clearly they didn't wish to touch the plague-ridden slaves. Instead, they made the slaves do for themselves, directing them with prods, kicks, and curses. There was no sign this time of Fataan or of Raak. The slave driver's whip was quite unnecessary in any case, for the slaves were glad to forsake the foul prison of the oar deck for the more pleasant-looking environment ashore.

The slaves were taken off a few at a time. The able-bodied ones were chained together in pairs. Under the direction of the Mautep, these slaves were put to work moving their unconscious fellows one by one, and placing them in the harness so they could be hoisted to the deck above by means of the windlass. Nagaro saw Pavo, Simion, and Tredhold lifted from the oar deck in this fashion, as well as Otao, and the young Leithian named Gurd. Tego and Landros, chained together, did most of that work, and the rest was done by Mendorel and a burly Turowan called Potero.

Nagaro was deemed to be unfit for heavy labor. Instead, he found himself chained to Taru. Two of the Mautep set out to march them down the length of the oar deck, poking and prodding as they went. Walking wasn't easy because Taru was very unsteady on his feet and scarcely able to understand instructions. The free end of Nagaro's chain had been locked to one of the links of Taru's chain, close to the cuff. Accordingly, the two men had to move their left legs in step if they were to make any progress. The only way Nagaro found to manage this was to walk behind his friend, half supporting him, and calling out the steps alternately, right and left. Somehow they managed to make their way along the length of the oar deck, through the door, up the ladder, and out onto the deck above.

Descending the rope ladder to the waiting longboat was the most harrowing part. Nagaro went first. This meant that he was one step below Taru and was supposed to catch his friend in case the young Turo should fall. In fact, Nagaro very much doubted he had the strength to prevent disaster in such an event. All the way down he kept up a steady stream of instructions.

"Now move your right hand down one rung... the *right* hand. Now the right foot... down a rung. *Down*, Taru! Good. Now bring your left foot down next to your right... Good. Now the left hand..." Somehow they made it without falling and lay exhausted in the longboat, along with two other slaves, while the Mautep seamen rowed for the shore.

The island's shadow already stretched far out across the water by the time the longboat's keel ground on the sand. Standing ankle deep in a wave's foamy backwash, with his left arm firmly around Taru's chest, Nagaro stared up at the lowering cliffs of Chitaopa. *Land!* After nearly six months on the oar deck of the *Fist of Death*, he had sand under his feet and the wide open sky above him!

Taru swayed against him. The young Turo's head came up. "Are we fin'ly home?" he murmured vaguely.

Nagaro sighed. "No, Taru," he said gently. "I'm afraid we're a very long way from home indeed."

One of the Mautep prodded his back with a piece of driftwood. "Move, shaku!"

Nagaro winced. "All right, Taru," he said. "Let's go. Right foot first."

Chapter 19: Chitaopa

The island of Chitaopa offered little in the way of shelter from the elements. The cave Nagaro had seen through the oar port was the best that was available, so naturally the Mautep chose it for their own camp. The slaves were given the second-best accommodations—the little grove of cedar trees. Encircling loops of chain had been placed around the trunks of two of the stoutest trees, which stood about a dozen feet apart. The slaves were linked together in strings of three or four in the way that Nagaro was linked to Taru. The chain of the first man in each string was fastened to the loop encircling one of the trees. Placed at intervals around each trunk, these strings of pitiful humanity thus radiated out like the spokes of a wheel.

Evening had come, and Nagaro lay stretched out on a yielding bed of aromatic cedar needles. Taru lay beside him, and beyond Taru lay the next in the chain, Tredhold, with Laash closest to the tree's trunk. The sound of Taru's ragged breathing was worrying.

Roheed was moving among the slaves, distributing food and water. If the sun weren't already set, it soon would be, and the light was very poor under the cedar trees. Roheed was hurrying to finish his duty while enough light remained to see what his hands were doing. When the young Mautep reached the string of slaves next to his, Nagaro sat up. Pavo was outermost in that string and hadn't moved since he'd been laid there. Dozens of dark, purplish patches covered his arms, legs, and chest. Nagaro watched as Roheed struggled gingerly with the unresponsive Hashtep. It was clear that the young Mautep didn't much like having to touch Pavo's blotched skin. It was also clear that Roheed didn't know how to get so sick a man to take water.

Finally Nagaro could stand it no longer. "Please," he said. "Let me do that," and he stretched out his hand towards the dipper.

Roheed raised his eyes to stare narrowly at Nagaro for a moment, then silently handed over the dipper and the water skin. Nagaro's chain rattled as he moved to Pavo's side and took the young man's head onto his knees. Roheed watched intently as Nagaro worked to get water into his friend, holding up the youth's head, dribbling the liquid into his mouth, then feeling the young man's throat until he felt Pavo swallow. At length, Roheed put his hand out tentatively to feel the young Hashtep's neck.

"You can feel him swallow," Nagaro said. "Here. See?" He reached to guide the young Mautep's hand to the right place. Roheed flinched involuntarily at Nagaro's touch, but didn't pull his hand away. Nagaro dribbled some more water into Pavo's mouth and stroked his friend's throat. "There!" he said. "Did you feel it?" Roheed gave him a startled glance and nodded. Then he motioned for Nagaro to go on to the next slave in the string.

Nagaro proceeded to tend the other men he could reach. He had to make Taru sit up and move a little so he could get to Tredhold. Taru moved, but he murmured something that sounded like "Give me some more stew, Mother." Nagaro knew that Taru was getting worse, and he found the healer was very nearly as sick as Pavo. He feared for all three of them, and that fear made him bold. As he finished with Tredhold, he turned to Roheed. "I can do this work for you," he said. "I can tend all these men." He gestured to include all of the slaves under the trees. "If only you will unlock my chain so I can reach them..."

Roheed stared at him as if trying to read his face in the gloom, but the youth didn't answer.

Nagaro tried again. "Please, Roheed. I will not run away. I will not leave them—and where could I go?"

Roheed spoke then. "Only Baruk have key," he said. The silence stretched. "Maybe is way," he added, after a long pause. "I talk to Baruk." With that, the young Mautep rose and moved off to finish with the few remaining slaves—all men who could manage the dipper themselves. He then hastily passed out the rest of the dried meat and biscuit and disappeared into the gloom of fading twilight. Nagaro sat staring after him.

"Ye play a clever game, Nagaro." That was Landros' voice coming from somewhere behind him.

"Aye, but ye don't really think Baruk'll loose your chain, do ye?" Tego's voice asked from the same direction.

Nagaro sighed. "I don't know. It's Baruk's responsibility to keep as many slaves alive as he can. I showed Roheed that I could do the work—better than he—but Baruk may not believe that I won't run away."

There was a pause until Landros said, "Ye meant it then? About not running away?"

Nagaro's hands sought for Taru in the dark. His friend's head felt burning hot. "Roheed will come only two or three times a day, perhaps for an hour. I'm not sure that will be enough for some of these men," he said quietly.

*

Dawn brought a crisp, fresh breeze from the sea that stirred the branches overhead and mingled its salt tang with the fragrance of cedar. Nagaro sat at the limit of his chain, gazing out under the cedar boughs across the blue-gray expanse of the sea. Off to the southeast, very nearly at the limit of sight, he could make out the low, gray shape of a single island. No other sign of land marred the perfect sweep of the sea or interrupted the fine pencil-line of the horizon.

Nearer at hand, in the clear, blue-green waters close to shore, the *Fist of Death* lay with her sails furled, rocking easily on a gentle swell. Grudgingly, Nagaro took note of the vessel's sleek, graceful lines. Broad, slanting rectangles of red and black, like alternating swatches of blood and midnight, ran in a row along the ship's side just above the oar ports. If Nagaro hadn't known the *Fist* more intimately as a floating prison, he would easily have called her fair.

The rhythmic rush and hiss of the waves breaking on the sand came to his ears, mingled with the skirling cries of the gulls riding the morning air, scanning the sea in search of their breakfast. Beneath these sounds, there was another, far more tantalizing—the cool, liquid gurgle of water running over stones. Nagaro couldn't see the stream from where he sat, but he knew where it lay. He and Taru had crossed it on their stumbling journey from the boat to the cedar grove the previous evening. It ran a little more than a dozen yards from where he'd spent the night, amongst a stand of bush willow at the foot of the hill that bore the cedar trees.

It might as well have been a hundred miles away. The cool, life-sustaining water was exactly what Taru needed... and Pavo, and Tredhold, and at least a dozen others. It was so close, yet he couldn't reach it. As achingly beautiful as this place seemed to him after his months on the oar deck, it was nothing more than another prison—a place where the slaves might still all die of thirst if their jailors didn't bring them water from a stream that lay but a stone's throw away.

Nagaro turned from his contemplation to once again check on the condition of the sickest men who lay near him. It was the second time he'd done so that morning, and his brow creased with worry. He was smoothing Taru's damp hair when he heard voices behind him speaking in Hashti. Turning, he saw Roheed and Baruk advancing up the slope between the trees. Roheed carried a basket in one hand and a water skin on the opposite shoulder. Nagaro felt hope stir in him. He sat down with his arms about his knees to await the coming of the two Mautep.

Roheed pointed at Nagaro as he approached and said something in Hashti. Baruk grunted. Stopping in front of Nagaro, the Slave Master stared down at him for a moment, rubbing his crooked nose. Then he took the water skin and dipper from Roheed, and dropped them on the ground near Nagaro's feet.

"You, shaku! Show how give water." He pointed at Pavo's still form.

Nagaro wasted no time in complying. He poured a dipper-full and sprinkled Pavo's face and hair. The water was cold. It must have been freshly drawn from the stream. Pavo stirred, opened his mouth, and gave a little gasp. Nagaro moved quickly to lift up the young Hashtep's head and pour a little water between the parted lips. Still he had to coax a swallow at first, but after the second time, Pavo began to swallow on his own. Nagaro felt a wash of relief. Finishing with Pavo, he moved immediately to Taru's side.

Beads of sweat stood on the young Turo's forehead. Nagaro tried the same approach, with the cold, sprinkled water. Taru shook his head weakly from side to side. "...'m sorry, Father," he murmured. "...so sorry..." Nagaro shook his friend gently. He was rewarded with more mumbled words, but Taru wouldn't sit up under his own power. Frowning, Nagaro lifted Taru until the youth's head lay against his shoulder. He pressed the dipper to Taru's lips, speaking his friend's name. Taru's eyes opened, fever-bright. His hands came weakly up to grasp the dipper. With Nagaro steadying it, Taru tipped the dipper and drank.

Nagaro started to move on to Tredhold's side, but Baruk stopped him with a word and a prod of his boot. "Enough! Lie down, shaku. So!" The Slave Master gestured to show that he meant face down. Nagaro obeyed, stretching on his stomach on the cedar needles.

Baruk said something in Hashti, to which Roheed replied in a persuasive tone. Baruk's response, however, was a barked order. Presently Nagaro felt a knee pressed hard into the small of his back. He supposed it was Roheed's. His right arm was seized and twisted across his back, but the hands that held him didn't pull so hard as to cause him pain. He heard the clink of chain, and felt cold iron links being passed around his right ankle. Then he heard the click of a lock, and Roheed released him.

"Stand up!"

Nagaro rolled over in response to Baruk's order and sat up. Immediately he saw what had been done. His leg chain had been unlocked from Taru's and the free end of it fastened around his own right ankle. Though he was no longer fastened to any stationary object, he was hobbled quite effectively. Awkwardly he got his feet under him and stood. Cautiously he took two steps forward. He was limited to a stride of about twelve inches. He wouldn't be able to go any great distance with ease, or travel very fast, yet he could move about. He looked up into the faces of the two Mautep and nodded once. Baruk's eyes bored into him. Roheed's expression was hard to read.

Baruk pointed a finger at him. "You! Take care shaku!"

Again Nagaro nodded.

This time Baruk held up three fingers. "Three lash for every man die!"

Nagaro's jaw tightened, but he was carefull to keep the anger from showing in his face as he nodded a third time. In Roheed's eyes, he thought he read apology.

Baruk was apparently satisfied. With a guttural word, the Slave Master signaled it was time to depart. Turning, he strode off down the hill. Roheed made haste to follow, leaving the water skin and dipper and the basket of food behind.

Nagaro wasted no time in setting about his newly-appointed task. He worked his way among the men, tending them as they needed and taking stock of each one's condition. The plague had started at the aft end of the oar deck, and the sickest were all men who had been chained there. Laash was worse, barely able to sit up. Tredhold was too ill even to hold the dipper. Simion, Otao, Moraga and the Leithian, Gurd, were all burning hot and delirious, the skin of their arms and legs marred by purplish plague lesions.

Tego groaned when Nagaro shook him. "Aye, matey, it's got me," he acknowledged as Nagaro felt of his forehead and confirmed that judgement. "Felt it comin' on me in the night."

Landros and Mendorel still showed no sign of illness, though they were surrounded by sick men. Landros helped himself to water. He glanced significantly at the chain that hobbled Nagaro's ankles. "Is that what ye were hoping for?"

Nagaro shrugged. "It will do," he said. "Go ahead and take another dipper-full if you want it, Landros. I can get as much as we need from the stream."

Mendorel watched as Nagaro patiently tended to Gurd and Otao, who were linked to him by their chains. "Ye're a bold man, Nagaro," he observed. "I'd never have thought t' ask for such a thing." After watching as Nagaro again and again carefully poured a little water into Otao's mouth and coaxed him to swallow, Mendorel suddenly asked, "Where'd ye learn to tend sick folk like that?"

Without thinking, Nagaro answered him. "My Lady Guardian had some skill. I used to watch her, and I helped sometimes."

"Your Lady Guardian?" Landros had been listening. "Was that the lady ye were talking to in your fever? I wondered how ye came to be so fair-spoken."

Nagaro's hands froze for an instant. Then he forced himself to move again—to finish caring for Otao. On the oar deck there had been little need to explain his history—at least until Simion had begun asking questions. Now he berated himself for having spoken so carelessly. He knew he had to say something, or it would only make matters worse. As casually as he could, he said, "A lady took me in when I was a babe and raised me, but she's dead now." Having finished with Otao, he moved towards the next group of men, taking painfully short, jerky steps and not looking behind him.

The remaining men had not been chained close to Nagaro on the oar deck. He knew some names—the Turowan, Potero, a massive lone man named Nanu, a quiet Kelorin named Denoras. Others he knew only by their faces, like the mad and broken Kelorin man with the "little house on the bay." Many were Hashtep, with whom he could only communicate by gestures. A fair number were already ill, though few as gravely ill as Pavo or Simion. After he'd finished going all the way around with the water, Nagaro passed around the food. He ate a full portion himself this time. He'd found his appetite and was ravenously hungry.

It was then that the real work of tending the sick began. Nagaro went from one to another of those who were most seriously ill. He used the contents of the water skin freely to cool their fevered bodies. Tearing cloth from the legs of his own pants, he made sponges that could be soaked with the cool liquid and laid on fevered brows, or used to wipe water across burning skin. Some of the men who were still well also contributed torn portions of their clothing and helped to tend those lying close to them.

Before long, Nagaro had to make a trip to the stream to re-fill the water skin. It was to be the first of many such journeys. Awkwardly he shuffled down the slope, emerging from under the trees near the sandy place where he had crossed the stream the day before. It was late in the season, and the stream was too shallow, there where it ran over the sand, to allow him to fill the water skin. Since only the beach lay downstream, he followed the watercourse in the opposite direction. He climbed clumsily over rocks and pushed his way through bush willow until he found a place where the clear water ran sparkling over stones and collected in a little pool that had enough depth to serve his purpose.

Before leaving the stream, Nagaro took time to move some stones to dam the stream's flow a little and deepen the pool. When he stood up, he noticed some wild onions growing along the bank. He pulled up as many of them as he could carry in one hand, leaving the other hand free to steady the water skin on his shoulder. Then he trampled a path through the bush willow and made his way back to the edge of the cedar grove by a more direct route.

The sun was high by now, and the air was growing hot. Climbing the slope was hard going with his short, hobbled stride, and he was sweating freely by the time he arrived back at the cedar grove where his charges lay. He no sooner made his appearance under the trees than the voices of several men were raised, calling to him.

"Nagaro! Here! Water!"

Before that day was through, Nagaro had begun to realize the enormity of the task he'd taken upon himself. To properly care for only a few seriously ill patients would have kept him fairly busy, but he had more than a dozen such, and there were only likely to be more in the near future. His sense of right wouldn't allow him to give less attention to any man than he gave to those who meant the most to him, so he moved endlessly from one to another all that afternoon and evening. Twice more he went to the stream for water. The last time was just before nightfall to be sure they had water to see them through the night. He tried to sleep then, but was awakened repeatedly by voices calling him. Each time he went, crawling painfully on hands and knees, feeling his way among the sweating, moaning bodies with one hand while he dragged the water skin after him with the other.

Rising groggily in the dawn, Nagaro found himself granted a brief interlude of peace. He tended to his own needs, then discovered the handful of onions where he had dropped them. Casting about, he found a smooth, rounded stone and used it to crush one of the bulbs in the dipper bowl, half filled with water. Carefully, he fished out and ate the fragments. Sampling the water, he found that it had a strong tang of onion. He wasn't sure whether it would be as effective as feeding onions to a sick man, but he found that both Pavo and Taru would drink the concoction. Accordingly, he set about making more of this "onion water" and administering a dose to each of his sickest patients, offering bits of half-crushed onion directly to those who were well enough to eat it.

Before he could even finish making that first round, the slaves began to call for him. "Nagaro! Over here! Bring water!"

When Roheed came later that day and saw the onions, he asked where Nagaro had gotten them, nodding at the answer. "Where we are," he pointed in the direction of the cave, "there are kuamka. Tomorrow I maybe bring some."

Nagaro murmured his thanks.

But Roheed didn't come the next day, or the next, nor for many days thereafter. Instead, other Mautep warriors came whose names Nagaro didn't know. They silently dumped their loads of food and picked their way disdainfully among the slaves, checking leg irons and making sure the captive men weren't trying to saw through their leather cuffs.

Nagaro wondered whether Roheed's kindness had gotten him into trouble, or whether the young man had merely been stricken with the plague. In truth though, he was far too busy to give much thought to the young Mautep. All day, every day, he labored among the men, moving endlessly from one to another. Several times each day, he staggered down the slope to the stream and back up again to bring more water—

and sometimes more onions. When each night came at last, he lay down bone-weary on the cedar needles, only to have his rest disturbed by the voices of men calling his name in the darkness. Even the Hashtep, who knew no other words of the Common Speech, quickly learned to call "Nagaro! Here! Water!"

So the days soon ran together, and he lost count of how many times the sun had risen and set since they'd come to the island of Chitaopa.

*

Nagaro was glad that Pavo and Taru lay close together. At night he lay down between them to sleep. If he could spare a moment during the day, he sat beside them. Pavo improved slowly but steadily in those first days, though without returning to consciousness. Taru's illness, on the other hand, waxed and waned repeatedly. The young Turo moved in and out of delirium. When fevered, he could be heard alternately conversing with his parents or pursuing Lanei through the landscape of his dreams.

In between those fevered wanderings, Taru had lucid moments. On one of these occasions he raised his head weakly and asked a little petulantly, "How is it ye came t' be well so quick, Nagaro, when it seems I've been sick forever?"

Nagaro shrugged. "It's always been that way with me. I wasn't often sick, and when I was, it never lasted long. Old Luka, the medicine woman, used to say I was just strong that way." He frowned then, remembering how sick he'd been when Taru had found him. Surely that had been no natural fever...

On another occasion, after a particularly bad night, Taru turned hollow eyes upon his friend. "The Spirits mus' be angry wi' me, Nagaro," he murmured feebly. "This is my punishment... for not listening t' my father. Firs' I'm a slave, an' now this!"

Nagaro shook his head. "I don't believe it, Taru. If you're being punished, what did all these other men do?" Then with a grin, he added, "And what did I do to deserve to be nurse-maid to you all?"

"That's dif'rent." Taru made a weak imitation of his former jauntiness. "Ye asked for it!"

*

Few other events stood out during those days, but one that did was an experience with Simion. The Kelorin youth was wracked with fever and delirium, and Nagaro spent a good deal of time at his side trying to cool the young man's body and ease his suffering. Inevitably, Nagaro heard many of the fevered words that spilled from Simion's lips. The youth seemed tormented. First he begged his father's forgiveness, then pleaded with his mother to intercede for him. Sometimes he spoke with longing of someone named Brandle. At other times he spoke apparently to Brandle in such intimate terms that it made Nagaro blush.

Nagaro knew that there were men who loved other men. He had no direct experience with such things, but he'd read something about it in the *Book of Vothra*, and Vothra taught tolerance and compassion above all things. So whenever Simion's fevered fingers sought the comfort of another man's touch, Nagaro didn't hesitate to take the youth's hand, seeking to ease the young man's distress.

As he sat quietly holding Simion's hand early one evening, while the shadows were stealing among the twisted cedar trunks, the young man opened his eyes, those startling eyes of Kelorin blue in a face that had become thin and fragile-looking. The sick youth looked directly into Nagaro's face. "Nagaro..." he murmured softly. Then, after a moment, "You're so beautiful... Won't you say you love me?"

Nagaro stiffened, his mouth suddenly dry even as sweat prickled along his sides. After a moment he found his voice. "I'm sorry, Simion," he said, as he carefully extricated his fingers from the other young man's grasp. "I can't do that." Then he added, "You're very ill. Lie quiet and try to rest."

A little spasm passed over Simion's face and his eyes closed. Nagaro stood up hastily and backed away. Forgetting the chain that hobbled him, he tried to take too long a step and lost his balance, sitting down hard next to Landros.

"*Vothra! Lord of my choosing!*" he murmured distractedly. "I didn't mean to encourage him."

Landros cast a glance around the cedar grove. At that moment, all was quiet, and it seemed those nearest to them were sleeping. "I thought ye knew what ye were about," the old sea warrior said, speaking low, "else I would ha' said something. The boy's not to your liking then?"

"No!" Nagaro gave him a stricken look. "I only meant to give him a little comfort because he is so very ill. He was talking about a man named Brandle, and I didn't think he knew who it was that was holding his hand!"

Landros cocked an eyebrow. "Ye needn't berate yourself," he said. "I'd say Simion's had his eye on ye since the first day he stepped onto the oar deck."

"No, he couldn't have..." Nagaro began, but then he remembered the way Simion had looked at him, and the youth's efforts to talk to him, and those fingers that had stroked his forehead while he was delirious. "Why would he look at *me?*"

Landros emitted a short laugh. "Fish feathers and gull's teeth, lad! Don't ye know ye're uncommonly well-favored?"

"*What, still?*" Nagaro's tone conveyed his disgust. "Just look at me! I'm ragged. I'm filthy. I must look like a wild man!" He gestured at his unkempt beard and matted hair. "And I'm sure I must smell as bad as everything else on that wretched oar deck!"

Landros waved a dismissive hand. "After a few months at sea, a man ain't so particular about the niceties. Under the dirt, ye're still 'pretty as a picture,' as my old mother used to say."

Nagaro groaned. *Not a boy any longer, but still a "pretty face."* He put his head down on his drawn-up knees and wrapped his arms around them.

Landros was taken aback. "Hoy, now," he said. "Don't fret so much. Ye can't be more'n a passing fancy to Simion. He had something serious with Brandle Furthing from what I hear. 'Til his father and Brandle's father—Lord Madred—got wind of it."

Nagaro raised his head, curious in spite of himself. "This Brandle is a *lord's son?*"

Landros nodded. "That he is. I did some asking around after Simion signed on. It seems Simion's father caught the two o' them together and threw Brandle out into the street buck naked. Didn't know who he was... It could ha' been a public scandal, but Lord Madred managed to hush it up somehow."

Nagaro sat open-mouthed.

The older man considered him with a sympathetic eye. "My mother used to tell me that good looks was a curse," he observed. "O' course, I figured she only said that 'cause she knew I didn't have any."

Nagaro looked away. "Well, my looks haven't done me any good so far," he said bitterly.

At that point, he heard one of the men calling him. With a sigh, he got to his feet and went back to his work. In the days that followed, he continued to tend Simion as he did any other sick man, but he no longer took the young man's hand. The youth didn't speak his name again while his fever lasted.

*

For a time, the number of the sick increased, but eventually some of the men began to recover. Encouraging as this was, it didn't immediately mean a great deal less work for Nagaro. The men who had been ill for many days were reduced almost to skin and bones. Many were so weak they couldn't hold up their own heads to drink.

There came a morning when Pavo opened his eyes in a gaunt face and fixed Nagaro with a glance that held real understanding. In a feeble whisper, he asked, "What place this?" Nagaro answered him in a few words—words that didn't begin to express the relief and gratitude that filled his heart.

Gurd and Moraga returned to the waking world soon after Pavo, and soon after that, Taru came out of the last of his fevers. Simion and Tego returned to full consciousness a few days later. When Tego expressed concern about what he had said in his fever, Nagaro could honestly say that he didn't remember. "I've heard so many men either calling for their mothers or wooing their sweethearts these last few days, I can't recall which was which," he said, laughing.

Simion was stonily silent after his return to consciousness. Nagaro found that the young Kelorin wouldn't meet his eyes, and he suspected the youth had a pretty fair idea of what sort of things he'd let slip during his delirium. Perhaps he even remembered the question he had asked and Nagaro's answer.

Neither Mendorel nor Landros had ever shown any signs of contracting the plague. One afternoon, some days after Simion's recovery, Landros expressed his bafflement about it. "It's got me blowed," he remarked to Mendorel, "why we two old bilge-rotters ain't been taken sick, when all these young bucks are laid so low."

"Aye, it is a puzzle," was Mendorel's response. "I still remember the plague of 517. I was just a lad, and I nearly died of it."

Landros frowned. "Did ye? Now there's a coincidence. So did I."

Nagaro looked up from where he was about to start ministering to Tredhold. The Leithian was lying very still that morning. His condition had been improving, but he had yet to speak a coherent word. "That's your answer," Nagaro said, addressing Landros. If you've had the plague once, you won't get it again."

"But that makes no kind o' sense," Landros objected.

"But he's right, Landros," said a weak voice. "Most kinds o' sickness work that way." It took them all a moment to realize that Tredhold had just spoken.

"Tred! Ye old bilge-bucket," Landros exclaimed, "ye're alive!"

"Of course I'm alive, ye great piece o' floating drift-weed," the healer responded weakly. "Though I don't think I would be if it weren't for this man here." He turned his pale blue gaze to Nagaro. "Well done, lad."

*

Nagaro was just beginning to rejoice that some of the sickest men were out of danger when death paid its first call upon the cedar grove. Otao, the simple-minded young Turo, was the first to steal away with that unwelcome visitor. Nagaro's regret was tempered by his conviction that whatever life the young man's spirit went to next must surely be a better one. He felt much the same at the passing of the mad Kelorin whose name no one had known. No more tales of the little house on the bay would they hear.

The death of Laash, when it came, hit Nagaro much harder. Laash had been young and strong and whole of mind. Nagaro could not help feeling that he must have failed the Hashtep somehow, and he said as much to Tredhold.

The healer was only in his early thirties, but as a ship's doctor, he had seen his share of disease, injury, and death. "Ye can't possibly save them all," he told Nagaro, in a voice scarcely above a whisper. "And ye must try to remember that many o' these men owe ye their lives. I know I owe ye mine. I've been watching, and there's nothing more ye could ha' done for Laash."

Indeed, it seemed that Tredhold had been watching Nagaro much as a master might study an apprentice. "Ye'd make a good healer if ye'd a mind," he told Nagaro on one occasion. "Ye've got good hands, and the right kind o' disposition." Nagaro smiled wanly at the words, though the older man's favorable judgement pleased him.

On another occasion, however, the healer's interest was much less welcome. It was a morning, fairly early, and most of the slaves were still sleeping. Nagaro was experimenting with moistening pieces of biscuit to make them easier for the convalescent men to swallow. He sat down beside Tredhold to offer the man a piece. As he extended his hand, the Leithian reached out and grasped Nagaro's wrist, studying the skin of his forearm. "These scars on your arms," he said. "How did ye come by them?"

Nagaro's stomach turned over. Taken off-guard, he had no answer. Only someone of Tredhold's training would even have noticed the faded marks, but how could he possibly explain them? "I'd... rather not talk about it," he said, trying to make the words sound casual, and failing utterly.

Tredhold considered him, still gripping his wrist. The man's clear blue eyes held sympathy and his voice when he spoke again was gentle. "It was a bladder-thorn made those marks, I'm thinking."

This was too much. With a reflexive jerk, Nagaro wrested his arm from the Leithian's grasp. He stood up hastily and found that he was shaking. "I said I don't want to talk about it!" Casting about for a means of escape, he picked up the water skin, although it was still a quarter full. Turning, he plunged off down the slope towards the stream, moving with stiff, jerking steps, as fast as his hobble would allow.

The healer raised himself weakly onto one elbow and stared after Nagaro, a frown creasing his brow. Landros rolled over with a clinking of chain and sat up. "Now why'd ye have to go and put him out o' temper, Tred?" the grizzled Kelorin drawled. "Ye could at least ha' waited until he fetched me my breakfast."

Tredhold shook his head. "Sorry mate," he said. "I didn't know it would upset him so." His frown deepened. "But then, maybe it's not surprising, if what I'm thinking..." The healer's voice trailed off. He picked up the piece of softened biscuit from where Nagaro had heedlessly let it fall, and brushed it off.

"What is it, Tred?" Landros asked keenly. "Ye're onto something, I know. Now out with it!"

Tredhold looked around to make sure that no one else was listening, then considered his old shipmate thoughtfully. "The bladder-thorn's a very fine thing," he said at length, "for getting medicine into a man that can't swallow or can't hold anything in his stomach. But ye can also use it to get a drug into a man that's unwilling."

"*Unwilling?* But why would ye—?" Landros' eyes suddenly went wide. "Ye're thinking about how he was fighting with ye when he was in his fever."

The healer nodded. "I'd lay odds that somebody drugged that lad—more than once or twice, too. He's got dozens o' those scars."

"But why would anyone do that?"

Tredhold chewed his lip. "I don't know for certain," he said. "But if I had to guess, I'd say he was some man's catamite. I'm thinking he would have been a beautiful boy—just the kind that'd catch the eye o' some cross-tiller."

Landros gave a low whistle. "Lord o' my choosing," he murmured. "*There's* something nasty. But, wait a shake," he added. "He told me and Mendorel that a lady took him in when he was a young 'un and raised him. He said he learned some doctoring from her. He said she was dead too."

"Well, he could have started out that way," Tredhold observed, "until he caught the eye o' the crossed man—likely some kin of the lady's." Tredhold paused, thinking. "Aye," he continued after a moment. "That'd make sense, because the man would ha' needed the aid of a healer that knew how to use the bladder-thorn. Most lords have a healer at their beck and call. The lady likely wouldn't have been able to stop it—or maybe she was already dead. Nagaro fought it, though, I'm thinking. In the end, maybe he got away, or maybe the man just cast him off when he'd gotten too much grown or too hard to handle."

Landros' brow furrowed. "Well... it does seem to fit," the old sea warrior reflected. "He wouldn't want to talk about something like that. And he's none too happy about his good looks, I can tell ye that."

Tredhold merely nodded. He still held the piece of moistened biscuit. Now he absently took a bite, made a wry face, but chewed and swallowed. "It doesn't taste any better," he murmured. "But it does go down a sight easier. And that onion water o' his is good thinking. The lad's got a good head on him." The healer sighed. "If he doesn't want to talk, I suppose I'd best just let him be."

*

Nagaro was still shaking when he reached the stream. He went through the motions of filling the water skin, scarcely aware of what his hands were doing. Then he sat for a long time on the rocks of his little dam, letting his bare feet soak in the clear water of the pool. The chain had worn an open sore on his right ankle. There was a reason why the Mautep normally used leather against the skin. He'd tried repeatedly to wrap a rag in between, but it never stayed in place for long. The cold stream water felt good. It both cleansed and numbed at the same time.

Cleansed and numbed... Nagaro wished he could find such medicine for his troubled mind. He knew he'd handled the healer's questions badly, but he couldn't see what to do about it. He told himself that Tredhold seemed a decent fellow and would probably leave him alone as he had asked. Still, he would rather have given the man some sort of explanation. It seemed too late to try it now, however, even if he could think of one.

Nagaro had a natural aversion to telling outright lies. Indeed, he suspected he wasn't very good at it. He could sometimes turn an awkward query aside with an obvious jest, but partial truths were usually the only way he could convincingly manage real deception. In this case, he couldn't see how any partial truth could serve him. He would just have to leave things as they stood. Tredhold would wonder, of course, but he was unlikely to guess the truth. It was simply too improbable.

Nearly an hour had passed by the time Nagaro finally returned to the cedar grove. He was relieved to see that Tredhold appeared to be sleeping, and indeed, he'd no sooner appeared than half a dozen voices called for water.

Chapter 20: Nagaro's Choice

The days passed. Nagaro had never made any effort to mark the time, but he could feel the season advancing. The slaves were afflicted by heat less and less frequently under the cedar trees, and more and more often the nights were uncomfortably chill. In fact, the month of Sedrin was waning and the plague was at last burning itself out. There came a time when it was clear to Nagaro that he had seen the last of the deaths among the men he tended. Besides Otao, Laash, and the mad Kelorin, there were just three more—two Turowans he had scarcely known and the man named Denoras. The Kelorin was the last and in many ways the worst, for he alone asked to die.

In a clear moment between two bouts of fever Denoras looked at Nagaro and said, "don' take more trouble over me, lad. Jus' let me go."

"Are you sure?" Nagaro asked him.

"Yes, I'm sure. I'd rather die here in the clean air than rot on that oar deck. There's none left in the world t' mourn me. Just give me a little water—long as I can drink it—an' then let me go."

Nagaro respected the man's choice because Vothra allowed such choosing. It was a hard thing, though, because death didn't come quickly. The plague finished its work, leaving Denoras still alive but very weak. It took several more days for the Kelorin to die from lack of food, and in the end, water as well. Tredhold watched with something bordering on disapproval, though he said nothing. Leithians, in general, did not countenance suicide. They believed it a sin against Solbrid, the mother goddess, who was said to give life to all earth's creatures.

Three Mautep came for Denoras, as they had come for the others. At first Baruk had been one of the three, but not this time nor the time before. Nagaro supposed the slave driver must have fallen ill himself. The three men dragged the body down to the beach where they built a pyre of driftwood and burned the corpse. Later, after the ashes had cooled, one of them would return to retrieve the valuable iron leg chain. Nagaro sat long that day at the edge of the cedar grove, watching the dark smudge of smoke rise and thin and drift away, borne on the wind that blew from the sea.

*

It was not long after the passing of Denoras that the food began to run low. Nagaro first noticed that there seemed to be less in the basket when the Mautep came. Before long, the basket arrived only half full. Then they began to get a kind of starchy tuber instead of biscuit. Pavo called it *yaba* root. The roots were rather inexpertly cooked—charred on the outside and often still half raw on the inside. Even so, the slaves devoured them and always wanted more. Nagaro had to ration the food among the men more and more carefully. Some couldn't eat much yet in any case, but others had been starting to regain their strength and the shortfall of provisions now threatened their recovery.

Pavo took whatever he was given without complaint according to the stoic nature of his people. Taru, however, looked at his small charred root and shred of dried meat in dismay. "Is this all there is?" he inquired plaintively. "How's a man supposed to get his strength back on these little crumbs?"

Moraga was more strident. "What d' they mean to do now? Starve us t' death?"

Nagaro shook his head at both of them. "We've been weeks on this island," he pointed out. "And we were weeks at sea before that without putting into port for provisions. I expect the food has only lasted this long because the sick men haven't been eating."

Moraga scowled. Well don't be tellin' me th' bloody Mahuk is cuttin' themselves so short!"

Nagaro suspected that Moraga was right, although if the Mautep were reduced to eating slave rations, the situation must be dire indeed. Supposing that the situation was in fact dire, Nagaro began to venture farther afield seeking what forage Chitaopa might offer besides wild onions and kuamka fruit.

Working his way painfully along the stream bank one afternoon, he managed to find some berries ripening on twisted brambles. He also found tracks left by small animals coming down to the water to drink. Bodano, the Turowan farmer who'd taught him to hunt, had also shown him how to make a snare out of twisted grass. Nagaro had never made much use of the skill, preferring the bow, but now he set to work with a will. Before he left the stream-side that day, he'd set snares in three different places. He returned to the cedar grove with his cupped hands full of ripe blackberries.

The following morning, Nagaro found that one of the snares had caught a small, plump ground squirrel. Almost sadly, he stared at the dead creature. It was a pitifully small morsel, and he knew he had no way to cook it. Nevertheless, he extricated the animal's little body from the loop of grass, reset the snare, and carried his tiny prize back to the other men under the cedar trees.

Landros shook his head in astonishment. "Ye caught that, Nagaro? Ye're a man o' many talents."

Moraga was less impressed. "I don't suppose ye'd care t' fetch us about a dozen more," he remarked dryly. "And some taters, an' a stew pot?"

Nagaro's teeth flashed in a feral smile. "I'll do that," he said, "if you'll work on how to skin a squirrel using your teeth, or start a fire without flints. Or is anyone hungry enough to try raw squirrel meat?"

Pavo spoke up softly. "I can make fire," he said. "You find piece of tree... outside part that is flat. And stick—like this, only more long," he held up a short, straight bit of twig. "And dry leaf that take fire easy."

Nagaro gave Pavo an appreciative look. "Now that's better," he said. "Even if we can't skin it, we can roast it whole. It should be easier to get the skin off once it's cooked."

At that moment, a stick cracked behind him under a heavy tread. Nagaro turned to find one of the grim-faced Mautep staring at them. The slaves had all been so intent on what to do with the squirrel that they hadn't noticed the man's approach. Now the Mautep put out his hand and said in a commanding tone, "Give meat!"

Nagaro looked down at the dead squirrel and back up again at the scowling Mautep. He could hardly believe he'd understood.

"*Give meat!*" There was an unpleasant edge to the man's voice.

Slowly Nagaro picked up the little squirrel. He stood up, holding his catch, feeling rebellion rise within him. It was *his* squirrel... But he knew he couldn't win. Even if he and his friends fought successfully for his tiny prize, the Mautep would only come back with a greater force to punish them. Grudgingly, he extended his hand, holding the squirrel. But he stood his ground so that the other man was forced to take a step forward to seize the little carcass.

Without another word, the Mautep dumped out the paltry contents of the basket he'd been carrying onto the ground. Then he turned, taking the basket and the squirrel, and strode away.

Nagaro stood with fists clenched, staring after the retreating figure as indignant voices rose around him.

"Why'd ye give it to him?"

"That was *your* meat, Nagaro!"

"Ye shouldn't ha' let the rotter take it!"

Deliberately Nagaro uncurled his fingers. "If the Mautep are that desperate for meat—to demand a single squirrel caught by a slave—then we're all in serious trouble," he said quietly.

In the next few days, Nagaro's snares caught several more squirrels, and once a small rabbit, but he didn't bring them directly to the cedar grove. He'd found Pavo the things needed to make a fire drill, and the young Hashtep had shown him how to kindle fire with it. He then found a place among some rocks on the farther side of the hill where he could safely keep a few embers burning, and there he roasted his secret bounty over a little fire on a rack of green willow twigs. Only at sunset, when he knew they would not be disturbed, did Nagaro bring the cooked meat to share—a mouthful apiece—among the men who most needed it.

*

One morning, Nagaro awoke in the early dawn light to the touch of someone's fingers probing the sore on his right ankle. He sat up with a jerk to find himself staring into Roheed's startled face. The signs of the young man's struggle with the plague were plain to read. His cheeks were hollow and there were dark shadows around his eyes. He hadn't troubled to shave, and his upper lip bore the stubble of an incipient mustache. Staring back at Nagaro, he withdrew his hand from the other young man's ankle. "Maybe chutapak help that," he said, pointing to the sore.

Nagaro shrugged. "I do not think it will heal until the chain comes off," he said, and moved to re-wrap the rag he used for padding.

Roheed didn't move from where he knelt near Nagaro's feet. He was studying Nagaro intently. "I remember when we take you—and that one," he indicated Taru, who lay sleeping nearby. "You very far from us. Why you not run away?"

Nagaro gave him the truth. "I wanted to stop them from hurting the woman."

Roheed nodded. "But she not your mother?"

"She was his mother." Nagaro pointed at Taru. "But she was very good to me."

Roheed nodded understanding, and his eyes smoldered. "Urchak not good man!" he declared with surprising vehemence. "Is not good to kill woman!"

Nagaro smiled back at him with a flash of teeth. "I know," he said. "No kajadeem in it." This earned him a startled glance and then an unexpected question.

"What is your name?"

"Nagaro."

"Nagaro? What other name?"

"No other name... just Nagaro."

Disappointment showed in Roheed's face. "Is no one, then, to give gold to Urchak? For get you back?" he asked.

So that was it. Roheed had hoped that Nagaro might be ransomed to freedom. Nagaro shook his head. "I have no family."

Something flickered in Roheed's narrow, dark eyes. "What happen your family?" he asked keenly.

Nagaro wasn't sure what to make of the young Mautep's interest, but he didn't see why he shouldn't answer. "I don't know," he admitted. "I never had a mother or a father that I knew." He struggled to find simple words to explain. "I was a baby, found at the door..."

Roheed abruptly stiffened. His eyes widened perceptibly, but then he seemed to try to control himself. "It is not right you be here," he said. "Not right you be shaku."

Nagaro shook his head at this. "It isn't right that any of these men are here, Roheed," he answered with conviction. "None of them deserve to be shaku. It is wrong to use men this way. My people say there is no kajadeem in this."

Roheed glanced at the sleeping men all around them. His brow furrowed in a frown. "Always there be shaku," he said. "But is not right *you* be shaku." He stood up, looking down at Nagaro. "We leave Chitaopa soon," he said. "Today they make smoke inside ship—for make plague go away. Tomorrow ship sail. Food almost gone, and storm come soon. You run away to hide, they not look very much. Other ship come one day. Maybe Jinari ship. Maybe Droviri."

Nagaro stared, dumbfounded. He could scarcely believe what he was hearing. Finally he managed to say, "You *want* me to run away? But won't that make trouble for you?"

Roheed shrugged the objection aside. "Not much trouble, for one shaku. Have plenty more."

Nagaro's mind was racing. He'd never even considered the possibility of escape since he'd first told Roheed that he wouldn't run away. "But where would I hide?" he wondered aloud. He looked at his hobbled ankles. "I can't run, or climb..."

Roheed had the answer to this as well. "Up there is little cave." He pointed to the headland "I find it—no other man know. I take chain off from there," he added, gesturing at Nagaro's right ankle. "Baruk still sick, so I get key. You come to stream tonight when first star show."

Before Nagaro could say anything, the young Mautep turned and walked away from him, striking off down the hill. Though the youth moved quickly, there was a wobble to his stride that showed how weak he was. Nagaro stared after the retreating figure, his mind in turmoil.

*

The *Fist of Death* looked for all the world as if she were on fire inside. Pale wisps of smoke issued from her cabin doors, portholes, hatches, and oar ports. Nagaro sat under the edge of the sheltering cedar boughs, facing out across the cove. He'd watched as the Mautep rowed the longboats back and forth, transporting the loads of wood and aromatic herbs they meant to burn, and buckets of sand to build their fires in so they wouldn't set the ship ablaze. Now his eyes gazed upon the strange site of the smoking ship, but he scarcely saw it.

His mind was in an agony of confusion and his heart was torn. It was now about an hour past noon. Already, in this waning season, the sun had slippws behind Chitaopa's massive ramparts, and the shadow of the towering cliffs lay over the cedar grove like a weight upon the heart. There were several hours still before that unseen sun would dip below the western horizon and enough light would fade from the sky to allow the first stars to show.

Nagaro had been over everything in his mind a dozen times since the morning. The lure of possible freedom was potently appealing, yet he didn't see how he could possibly leave Taru in captivity. His first thought had been to tell Taru and the others of his dilemma, but he hadn't imme-diately done so, and the longer he thought about it, the less certain he was that he ought to say anything at all. What if Taru told him to take this chance and go? Or what if the other men suggested that he wrest the key from Roheed and set them all free? Nagaro was sure he could overpower Roheed in the youth's present weakened condition, but he was equally sure he couldn't bring himself to harm the young Mautep. He would therefore ultimately have to let Roheed go, after holding him long enough to let the slaves get well away.

He would have liked nothing better than to see all of the slaves go free, but there were two things wrong with this plan. In the first place, he'd only been able to save himself and the other slaves from dying on the oar deck because Roheed had trusted him. He had never meant to deceive the young Mautep, and he was bitterly averse to such a betrayal, even in these circumstances. He knew Roheed's career as a sea warrior might very well be ended by such an outcome, even though he was Lord Baalkir's nephew. Whatever else happened, the young man would prob-ably never risk extending his hand to a slave again.

The other difficulty was that freeing *all* of the slaves would lessen the chances of any one of them actually escaping from the larger prison of Chitaopa and winning his way to real freedom in the wider world across the sea. Whereas the Mautep might well not search very hard for a single slave, they would surely be very diligent when faced with the disappearance of the whole lot of them. Roheed's "little cave" wouldn't likely harbor them all, either, and many of the slaves were still in such poor condition that they'd be unable to get far without the help of the more able-bodied ones.

Even if the Mautep weren't in much better condition than their captives, the island offered so little cover that many of the slaves were likely to be recaptured. And those that escaped would have to survive on

Chitaopa's meager forage—already depleted by himself and the Mautep. Nagaro had no illusions that any other ship would put in at the island in the waning days of autumn. A single man might survive the winter on Chitaopa, but not a dozen or more.

Moodily Nagaro stared out over the cove, following thoughts that ran in circles. He had told the others what Roheed had said about their imminent departure, but that was all. What if he were to just quietly steal away in the night to meet Roheed? He wouldn't have to say any-thing to anyone—wouldn't give them any chance to argue or to concoct plans. He imagined himself hiding in the little cave up on the headland, watching the *Fist* sail away. Faces paraded before his eyes. Taru's came first, of course, but Pavo's was there as well, and the face of Mendorel, and those of Landros, Tredhold, and Tego—even the face of Simion, who had persuaded him to drink water when he'd been ill with the plague. He probably owed his life to Simion. If he were to leave any of these men now, how could he ever rest?

He had tried to tell himself that he would somehow find a ship and get a crew. He would search all the seas, until he found the *Fist of Death* and set her captives free... But how long might that take? He pictured living on squirrel meat, yaba root, and onions until spring came. He'd have to hide whenever he saw a sail approach until he learned what manner of ship it was. He was fairly sure Chitaopa lay somewhere near the northern border of the seas that were under Mautep control. How long might it be before an Edroviran ship would stray this far south—or would he dare to ask a Jinari captain for aid? And how could he hope to get his own ship and crew for such a dangerous undertaking as hunting for the *Fist of Death?* At best it all would take years—and galley slaves didn't have years...

Shaking himself out of his brooding, Nagaro rose and turned his back on the cove. He moved farther in under the trees, passing among the men who lay there. It was a warm afternoon, and almost all of them were asleep or dozing. Some were still weak and very much in need of the rest. Others were merely seeking relief from boredom and the growling of their empty stomachs. Nagaro gazed down at each one in turn, Pavo and Taru, Tredhold and Tego, Moraga, Landros, and Simion... As he came to where Mendorel lay, however, he found that the man was awake and watching him.

The former shopkeeper beckoned for Nagaro to sit down. A little reluctantly, Nagaro sat on the cedar needles at the man's side. Mendorel lay with one arm crooked behind his head, regarding Nagaro closely. "Are ye taking your farewells then?" he asked after a moment, keeping his voice low.

Nagaro started guiltily. "Why? What do you mean?" He also spoke low, not wishing to be overheard, even as he resisted the urge to look around to be sure that no one was listening.

Mendorel gave him a knowing wink. "I was awake this morning when your friend came to call."

"Oh." Nagaro shifted uncomfortably. "I wouldn't call Roheed my friend," he said. "We respect each other, I think, and for some reason he's taken it into his head to try to help me. But friend is too strong a word."

"Well what he is, or why he's doing what he's doing, don't matter," Mendorel observed, "as long as he keeps his word, eh?"

"I don't know..." Nagaro studied his hands. "I wish he hadn't made the offer."

Mendorel sat up. "Now, by the Eyes, lad!" he hissed. "*Why?*"

"Because I can't leave Taru!" Nagaro's response was an emphatic whisper. *Or you, or Pavo, or Tred or Landros...* "Do you think he would ever forgive me?"

"'Course he would! Ye should go, Nagaro. Nobody deserves it more than you."

"Why? Because I did some doctoring? For that I should go free while all these men go on being slaves? *It's not right!*" He fell silent, hearing Roheed's words echo in his mind: "*Always there be shaku. But you should not be shaku.*" The young Mautep wanted to set him free, but could only justify such a thing by convincing himself that Nagaro was somehow different from all the other slaves. Nagaro spoke again. "I've decided," he said, "I'm not going to the stream tonight."

"Ai now, ye can't mean that! Why, any one o' these men would jump at a chance like this!"

Nagaro shook his head. "It's not even a good chance," he said, as persuasively as he could. "You don't know that I'd ever even get off this island. I might not find enough food to make it through the winter. And when the ships come again in the spring, there'd be more Mautep ships than any other kind. I might just be caught again... No, Mendorel, I'm not going to meet Roheed."

With that, Nagaro stood up. He picked up the near-empty water skin from where it lay. "I'm going to fill this now, so I won't need to later," he said pointedly. Then he added in a lower voice, "Please, Mendorel, don't say anything to anyone."

Silently, the older man nodded, his expression unreadable.

*

It was one of the other Mautep who came with their evening food, not Roheed. Nagaro's snares had caught nothing that day, so there was nothing for him to cook and only the rations they were given to share among the men.

Nagaro stared at his own share, picturing again trying to live on squirrel meat, yaba root, and onions. The evening came. He tried not to watch the eastern sky where it showed between the branches—tried not to notice if there were stars to be seen. When the great, pale disk of Talebra rose above the eastern horizon and sent its silver beams in low under the cedar boughs, he knew the appointed hour had come and gone.

He lay down then as he always did, between Taru and Pavo. The air was cool now, and the slaves were wakeful. Snatches of low conversation could be heard from here and there under the trees. Abruptly he realized that Taru was speaking to him.

"Do ye really think we'll sail tomorrow, Nagaro?"

"That's what Roheed said."

Taru shook his head. "I still can't believe he talks to ye so free and easy. Do ye believe everything he says?" Taru seemed a little annoyed that Nagaro's instincts regarding Roheed had proven accurate.

Nagaro shrugged. "He said they were going to smoke out the ship today, and they did. The rest is probably true as well."

Taru sighed. "Well, I'm not in any hurry t' be back on that oar deck, but I'm not in any hurry t' starve either."

Pavo suddenly stirred, sitting up as if listening. Then he started. "Look!" he hissed in an urgent whisper. "See, there! He coming!"

Nagaro raised himself on both elbows and followed Pavo's pointing finger. There was a single figure coming up the hill in the moonlight and it appeared to be Roheed. Nagaro watched with mounting dread as the young Mautep approached, making straight for the place where he lay. The youth stopped a few paces outside the circle of slaves.

"Nagaro, why you do not come?"

Men stirred in the moonlit darkness, and there was the sound of indrawn breaths from several quarters. Inwardly Nagaro groaned. Why couldn't the young Mautep have just gone back to his own camp when he found no one at the meeting spot? Nagaro could have gone to the stream and told Roheed his decision. It wouldn't have been difficult, but he hadn't imagined the youth would be so persistent. Now he feared his fellow slaves would learn exactly what opportunity he had let slip.

When Nagaro did not immediately answer, Roheed spoke again. "You not understand?" he asked. Then he added, "You come. I take off chain." The youth's hand touched a small, telltale bulge in his sash.

Off to his right, Nagaro heard Moraga whisper something to Tego, and he thought he caught the word "key." Hastily he rose, gathering his feet under him with a clink of chain. "I will not leave my friends," he said in a firm voice, hoping to make himself clear to Roheed—but not too clear to the other slaves. His plan failed because the Hashti language lacked plurals, and so its native speakers tended not to hear them.

Roheed stepped forward to within an arm's reach of where Nagaro stood. "Which one your friend?" he asked, frowning. "This one? Or that one?" He pointed first at Pavo, then at Taru. "Maybe you take one with you, but you should not be shaku. You choose one now!"

Out of the corner of his eye, Nagaro saw Moraga gather himself into a crouch, and Tego was moving as well. To Roheed, they must be no more than shifting darker shadows in the moon-shadow of the cedar tree. Their chains wouldn't allow them to reach the young Mautep yet, but if Roheed came just a little closer... Silently Nagaro willed the youth to come no nearer, praying he wouldn't be forced to make an overt choice between helping his fellow slaves and fighting against them to protect Roheed.

"They are all my friends," he said, answering Roheed's question. "I told you before that none of them should be shaku. Will you free them all? —for I will not leave my friends."

"*Ai, Nagaro!*" The words, almost a moan, came from Taru.

Roheed stared at Nagaro, searching his face pleadingly. After a long moment, his shoulders sagged in defeat. "I not can do that," he said, shaking his head.

Nagaro spread his hands. "Then I think you had better go," he said quietly.

Roheed's gaze suddenly flicked to one side, looking past Nagaro to where Moraga and Tego crouched, ready to spring. He took two hasty steps back, his eyes now wary and frightened. "I go," he said quickly.

Turning, the Mautep youth beat a hasty retreat down the moonlit hill, leaving the galley slaves standing in a frozen tableau in the shadow under the cedar trees.

"By the Spirits, Nagaro!" Moraga burst out, when Roheed was out of earshot. "It sounded like he meant t' take off yer chain! He must ha' had the key!"

Nagaro swallowed hard. "I'm pretty sure he did."

"Ye could ha' knocked him down and taken it! We could ha' all been free! Why in Hakura's name didn't ye jump on him?"

Nagaro forced himself to meet Moraga's eyes and to keep his voice steady when he answered. "What would Urchak have done to him then, Moraga? He only came here with the key because he wanted to free me. How could I turn about and do him harm?"

Tredhold was the first to break the stunned silence that followed Nagaro's words. "Ye're an uncommon man altogether, Nagaro," he said.

Moraga spat on the ground.

"Uncommon ain't the word for it," he growled. "Nagaro, ye're a bloody fool!"

Chapter 21: A Tale To Pass The Time

Rain dripped steadily from the tarred-plank roof of the long, low stone building. Mostly it dripped outside, but here and there it dripped inside as well, and one of those places was about three feet from where Nagaro lay. Perhaps it was the splashing of tiny droplets onto his face that awakened him. Nagaro rolled over with a clink of chain and sat up in the damp, moldy straw. The shapes of the other slaves were visible around him in the gloom. They were chained to iron rings set in the floor about eighteen inches apart. The rings ran in two rows along the two longer walls of the long, narrow building. Most of the men were still sleeping. Nagaro glanced at the little rectangle of dreary gray sky that showed through the nearest of a row of small windows in the wall above where he sat. It was morning of another day that promised to be very much like the last one. A slave barn in the shipyards of Sar Tipaal was a dismal place in the month of Todrin in the rain. Still, he reflected grimly, at least there was enough to eat.

The Mautep crew of the *Fist of Death* had been in a great hurry to leave Chitaopa, as if they hoped to leave all memory of the plague behind them. Eight of their number they left behind as well in fresh graves near the mouth of the cave that had sheltered them all those weeks.

None of the Mautep who worked on the oar deck had been among the dead. Baruk, the slave master, and his lieutenant, Raak, had reappeared on that final morning, lean, haggard, and hollow-eyed. Seeing them, Nagaro had expected to be dealt eighteen lashes, three for each of the six slaves who had died under his care. It was not to be so however. He'd simply been marched back aboard the ship and chained with the rest. Whether Baruk had been impressed with his doctoring efforts or had simply forgotten, Nagaro never knew.

Two days out of Chitaopa, the first autumn storm struck the *Fist of Death* with terrible fury. The ship had been blown off course, and they had been forced to lie up a full day, anchored in the lee of a deserted bit of rock even smaller and less hospitable than the island they had left. Knowing the vessel was perilously low on provisions, Captain Urchak had ordered the crew to set sail again during the first lull, only to have the ship battered by a second storm that came hard on the tail of the first. The slaves had a miserable time of it, tossed about among the oars and benches by the heaving of the ship and given hardly anything to eat. At least they hadn't been expected to row. Most had been in no condition to do so.

Eventually, the *Fist of Death* had limped into Sar Tipaal's harbor, her sails in tatters, her decks and rigging sodden with rain. Her warrior crew had staggered ashore, half-starved, to be greeted with cheers and jubilation. The ship's homecoming had been so long delayed that the populace of Sar Tipaal had presumed her lost. Captain Urchak was hailed as a hero for having brought the ship and most of the men home. No one seemed to care that the plague had only been brought aboard the *Fist* as the result of her captain's ill-considered actions.

The *Fist*'s slave crew had been marched, dragged, or carried off of the oar deck the following day, with no fanfare whatsoever, and deposited in the slave barn where they now lay.

It was now nearly two weeks since these events, and in all of that intervening time, it seemed to Nagaro that it hadn't stopped raining. It wasn't, fortunately, a very cold rain in these southern climes, but everything was damp—the stone walls, the straw bedding, his clothing, his hair.

Taru yawned, stretched, and sat up beside Nagaro, giving voice to his most immediate concern. "Where's breakfast?"

"Not here yet," Nagaro informed him. "It's probably out there somewhere, getting rained on. Just once, I'd like to have something really dry."

Taru shrugged. "Maybe it'll be that cold porridge again. It's none the worse for a bit o' rain in it. I think I'll have a look."

The young Turo stood up and approached the window. His chain barely allowed him to reach the wall, and he had to carefully step across the gutter that ran parallel to it, one of two such channels running the length of the building and providing its only sanitation. By standing on tiptoe, Taru was just able to scan the yard outside for signs of activity. By the light from the window, Nagaro could see that Taru's cheeks were less hollow than they'd been a week ago, although the young man's ribs still showed more clearly than they'd ever done when the two friends had dwelt together on the shore of Wotana Bay.

On Nagaro's other side, Pavo stirred and sat up, brushing straw out of his hair. "Is food come yet?" the young Hashtep inquired, seeing Taru standing at the window. Neither Pavo nor Nagaro could reach the window to look for themselves. Nagaro smiled fleetingly to hear Pavo's words, an echo of Taru's earlier query. He supposed it was only natural that his two friends had their minds so fixed on the subject of food. They were both still very much in need of it. For his part, Nagaro had arrived in Sar Tipaal in better condition than most of his fellows, having had a mild case of plague and the advantage of full rations during his own recovery on Chitaopa.

"Well, there's something going on," Taru observed in answer to Pavo's question. "I hope it's breakfast... Say now," he added, with sudden interest. "It's that Roheed, come in by the side gate, riding on a horse. Looks like he's unloading some saddlebags. Hoy! Doesn't he look like a prince, though—all got up in black and gold! He's giving each o' the stable boys a little sack o' something. They're bowing and running about like a hill o' ants. D' ye have any idea what it's about, Pavo?"

Pavo frowned, then nodded. "It be Kaampo ko Set," he said. "Festival of—" he frowned harder "—time when fruit come. This time every Mautep give gift to Hashtep who serve him."

Taru was still watching the activity through the window. "Roheed keeps pointing this way. Now it looks like they're all coming down here, and they're bringing the saddle bags."

The "stable boys," as Taru called them, were a lot of ragged Hashtep lads who were employed—probably for very little pay—to distribute food and water to the slaves, muck out the straw bedding at intervals, and sluice down the floor gutters twice a day.

Most of the slaves were stirring by now. Those who could reach a window were on their feet, craning their necks, trying to see what was happening. Soon the murmur of their voices rose in the slave barn.

Only Simion showed no interest. Chained four rings down from Nagaro, the young Kelorin sat with his head down on his knees. Nagaro had heard the youth utter no more than a dozen words in as many days. Though he felt sorry for Simion, he was reluctant to speak to him for fear of encouraging the young man's unwanted interest. The other slaves near him shunned the young Kelorin outright. So it was that, amid the desperate comradery of the slave barn, only Simion was utterly alone.

Taru withdrew from the window just as the large double doors at the end of the barn were thrown open. Even the dull gray light of that gloomy morning seemed bright to the slaves. Those nearest the doors drew back, momentarily dazzled. Two of the stable boys entered the barn, clutching arm-loads of small bags sewn out of plain cotton cloth. They passed down the aisle between the two rows of slaves, tossing a bag to each in turn as they went.

Roheed didn't enter the barn, but stood just beyond the doorway, looking princely indeed in black silk pantaloons and vest, and a golden shirt with flowing sleeves. The fullness of his face and steady strength of his movements showed what proper rest and ample diet could accomplish against the after-effects of the plague. He appeared to be watching the two stable boys, making sure that they carried out his instructions.

The two Hashtep youths finished their task and scuttled out. Just before the doors were closed again, Roheed's gaze swept one last time over the ranks of chained men. Nagaro thought it lingered on him for an instant, but he couldn't be sure.

The bags turned out to each contain a handfull of sugared kuamka fruit and dried figs. These were a very welcome addition to the slaves' fare, which had so far consisted of unseasoned fish soup, dry bread, porridge, and onions. There was a distinct absence of talk as the men ate. Taru even devoured the kuamka without complaint.

Landros was sitting cross-legged in the straw across the aisle from Nagaro and studying him as he chewed on a dried fig. "I suppose," he observed, "that we must have ye to thank for this bit o' generosity from Lord Baalkir's nephew."

Nagaro shrugged. "Maybe."

The subject of his past dealings with Roheed wasn't a comfortable one. The initial responses from Tredhold and Moraga that last night on Chitaopa were representative of the range of reactions he had faced for having thrown away a chance for freedom and let Roheed get away with the key. Moraga had stopped just short of declaring him a traitor. Like all of the slaves, the former merchant seaman knew he would likely have died if Nagaro hadn't sought Roheed's help. Moraga had made it quite clear, however, that he thought Nagaro was far too high-minded for his own good—or anyone else's. At the other end of the scale, Pavo was of the opinion that Nagaro should give the Mautep lessons in kajadeem. What Taru thought, Nagaro wasn't sure. His friend hadn't said anything specific on the subject in all the days since, though Nagaro had noticed that Taru sometimes studied him with a worried look on his face.

Landros turned to Pavo. "What d' ye say lad?" he asked. "Were ye here last winter? Has Roheed done this sort o' thing before?"

Pavo raised his shaggy head. "Roheed not here last storm time," he declared flatly. "He only be sea-warrior two season."

This news startled Nagaro out of his thoughts. "How could he have learned so much of the Common Speech in so short a time?" he wondered aloud.

"Oh no." Pavo shook his head. "Roheed not learn that on oar deck. Roheed learn Droviri—what you call Common Speech—many year ago. You want I tell you story? Is very good story!"

Nagaro was immediately interested. "That's a fine idea, Pavo," he said. "A story is just the thing for a day like this."

"Aye," Taru put in. "I like a good tale."

There was a general murmur of agreement from the other slaves. As it happened, however, the stable boys arrived just at that moment with a bucket of water, a kettle of porridge, and a stack of wooden bowls and spoons. So the tale was delayed while the slaves drank their ration of water and ate their porridge.

As soon as the empty bowls were collected and the stable boys had departed, however, Nagaro reminded Pavo of his offer. So the young Hashtep nodded, stretched, and settled himself cross-legged in the dirty straw.

Three dozen faces turned towards him expectantly as Pavo began his tale, which he chose to tell it in the Common Speech for the benefit of the Edroviran slaves. The Hashtep slaves couldn't understand his words, but they seemed to already know this story well. Their avid looks and frequent nods showed that they could follow the course of Pavo's narrative from his pantomime alone. For the usually impassive Pavo turned out to be a surprisingly good story-teller. As he recounted the tale, he used the level of his voice, his facial expression, and movements of his hands and body to good effect.

"This story begin to happen many year ago," Pavo began. "When Hardeep, that was father of Baalkir, was lord of Sar Tipaal. But story begin with Notep—son of Lord Hardeep and brother of Baalkir. Notep is more young than Baalkir, but still very rich man. He make good marriage with daughter of very powerful lord. After one year, she tell him she is carry baby inside." Pavo patted his belly. "Notep think is good. He much happy to think maybe soon he have son.

"But before his baby come, Notep have to go to war. Lord Hardeep, he make war with other very powerful lord. Take many ship. Baalkir, he captain of one ship. Notep, he captain of another. They sail very far looking for ship of other lord." Pavo imitated with his hands the motion of ships riding over the waves, and the action of a sailor scanning the horizon. "When they find other lord and his many ship, they have big battle. All ship crash together. All man swing their sword." Pavo stood up to imitate parry and thrust. "Then, right in middle of battle, come very big storm.

So much rain come that one ship cannot see other ship. Wind blow very hard." Pavo made great sweeping movements with his arms. "Wind blow Notep ship very far. When rain stop and wind go away, Notep cannot see land. He cannot see his father ship. He cannot see other lord ship.

"Notep know he is far away west of land, so he sail east. He look for land." Here Pavo pantomimed with his hand, shading his eyes. "Notep sail until he see ship. But is not warship. It is Droviri ship that have broken mast. That mean it cannot sail fast. Notep think maybe ship have gold or other rich thing, so he tell all his man to catch that ship. Is very easy to do. They catch ship with many hook, and tie with rope. Then all Notep sea-warrior go to board Droviri ship. Droviri sea-man they fight like warrior. They fight hard with sword, but Notep have so many more warrior, and they kill them one by one—until only one man left.

This one man fight more hard than any. He very good with sword. He fight like tiger. Now Notep sure that ship must have very rich thing for man to fight like that. He tell his warrior all to fight this one man. Droviri man he fight like demon." Pavo was cutting the air, thrusting and parrying with an imaginary blade. "Is no man ever more brave, but Notep warrior too many. Droviri man he have wound in many place. He cannot fight any more. So Notep kill brave Droviri man."

Dramatically, Pavo illustrated the final, fatal thrust.

The young Hashtep paused, sweeping his audience with his eyes. All were staring up at him, enthralled. Pavo made a great show of sitting down, settling himself again in the straw. "What do you think they find when they go down inside ship?" he asked conspiratorially. "You think they find gold? You think they find any rich thing?" Pavo shook his head. "No," he said. "They find nothing. Until they look in last cabin. There they find... *woman*. She is woman with black hair, and white skin, and eye color like stormy sea—one of people like Nagaro, or like Mendorel. She have ring on finger. She is wife of brave man who fight like tiger, and she carry his baby inside." Again Pavo patted his belly. "Notep think maybe Droviri pay gold for woman, so he take her on board his ship. Again he sail east, and at end of day he see land.

"Now Notep sail south. Battle is long time finished, so he go home. He sail many day, and every day he go down to cabin where is woman. She is not look like Mautep woman, but every day he look at her he think more and more that she is very beautiful. At first she is crying, but then later she is just sit and look very sad. Notep ask her one day what is her name. She say is Emril. Notep go to his cabin to sleep every night, and he think of woman name Emril. He dream of woman name Emril. Soon he think Emril more beautiful than his wife. By time ship come to Sar Tipaal, Notep think Emril most beautiful woman he ever see.

"In Sar Tipaal, Notep take Emril to live in his big house. Notep wife is very angry that he bring in other woman. Everyone say Notep should send message to Edrovir to ask for gold for Droviri woman. His father say he should ask for gold. His brother Baalkir say he should ask for gold. They do not think it is good that Notep keep Droviri woman, because he have wife. But Notep think now he want Emril more than he want gold, and he not listen to any of them."

Pavo paused to moisten his lips with his tongue. "Now," he went on, "Emril is still carry baby of dead husband. That is reason Notep not take her to his bed. All through storm time he wait, and Emril belly grow big. Notep wife belly grow big too. It look like two baby come at same time. Finally storm is all gone. Flower time is come. Then is time for

Emril baby to come, and her time is easy. Her baby born quick. Is strong boy-child. She name him Sindar. One week more, and time of Notep wife is come, but her time is very hard. All day she lie in pain. She cry. She scream. She curse her husband for bring Droviri woman into her house. All night she lie in pain and grow more and more weak. And then, when morning come, she die with baby still inside. Then Notep take knife and cut his wife belly and take out baby. Baby is alive. Is boy-child too, but not so strong. Notep name his baby Roheed. So now he have son."

Pavo stopped and drew a long breath and let it out again.

"What happened then?" Nagaro asked eagerly. "If Notep married Emril, that would make her Roheed's stepmother, and Roheed could have learned the Common Speech from her."

But Pavo shook his head. "No," he said. "It is not that way. Story not finish. Still is best part."

"Well, get on with it then, laddie," growled Landros. "We're waiting."

Pavo cleared his throat. He settled himself more comfortably in the straw. "Notep take baby Roheed to Emril and tell her she have to feed his baby. Emril she try to feed two baby, but she is not have enough—" Pavo glanced hopefully at Nagaro and patted his chest.

"Milk." Nagaro suggested.

Pavo nodded his acceptance of the word. "Emril not have enough milk for feed two baby. Notep see Emril baby, Sindar, is more big and more strong. He think maybe Sindar live and Roheed die, and he start to be angry. Notep angry to see that Emril not look at him. He angry to see that she feed other man baby and that other baby grow strong. He angry to see she have other man ring still on her finger.

One day he get so angry he go and he take ring away. Then he take baby Sindar away. He tell his man to bring horse. Then Notep take ring, and he take baby Sindar, and he ride out from Sar Tipaal. He ride long way out into forest, to place where is stream. He get down from horse. He put baby down beside stream. He throw ring in water. Then he get back up on horse and ride back to Sar Tipaal. When he get to his house, is already night.

"Notep go to find Emril. He find she is sit holding baby Roheed and she is feed him. And Notep see she have tear come from her eye, but she not make any sound. Now Notep very sorry. He think he do bad thing. He turn around and get back on horse and ride back to forest. But it is night. Notep can not find stream and place where he leave baby Sindar. All night he ride, and he look. Just when sun come up, he find place, but is no baby there. Notep look on ground beside stream. He see mark made by foot of tiger. He look for ring in stream, but he can not find ring. Finally he give up and ride home. He feel very sad because he must tell Emril tiger take her baby, and water carry her ring away."

Pavo paused again to moisten his lips. "Now is best part," he said, leaning forward and sweeping the circle again with his eyes. "Many day go by. Emril she take care of baby Roheed. Notep he watch. He want to take Emril in his bed, but she always with his baby. And Notep begin to have very bad dream. Every night he dream of Emril, and every dream end with tiger. Sometime is even Emril turn into tiger in Notep dream. He begin to be much afraid. So he go to... god house..." Pavo gave Nagaro another questioning look.

"Temple," Nagaro said quickly, eager to hear more.

Pavo nodded again. "Notep go to temple. At temple is woman who tell what dream mean. She tell Notep he is have dream because he kill Emril husband and take her baby. Dream woman tell him he can not ever take Emril in his bed because he kill her husband when he cannot fight any more. She tell him he must always take care of Emril because she take care of his son. Notep go home. He sad and he angry. He tell everyone in his house not to speak ever again of what happen—how he kill Emril husband and how he take Emril baby away.

"So many year go by, and Roheed grow. Roheed is always small and much sick, but Emril love him, and he love her. He learn some of how she speak, but he not know her story. He know only she is slave belong his father, and she take care of him. Then one day, when Roheed have fourteen year, Emril is get very sick. She know is time for her to die. Roheed he not want to think it. He very sad, but she tell him to not be sad. She tell him she only stay to see him grow, but now he is big, and she can go. Then she tell Roheed story I just tell you—story Notep not want Roheed ever to hear. And then she die.

"Then Roheed feel very bad to know his father kill Emril husband. He feel very bad to know his father take Emril baby. Roheed begin to have bad dream. He dream of tiger. Sometime he see tiger come take baby from beside stream. Sometime he dream tiger come to kill him. Almost he can not sleep for dream. So he go to temple to tell dream woman. Is same dream woman his father see fourteen year ago. Dream woman tell him he always so much sick, and now he have bad dream, because other baby die for him. She tell him he have..."

Pavo paused, again at a loss for a word. He turned, as usual, to Nagaro. "What you say you have when you go to buy something, but you not have money, so you take it and say you go to pay another day?" he inquired.

Nagaro frowned. "You say you have a debt," he offered.

Pavo shifted his position in the straw. "This is special kind of debt," he said. "This we call *blood debt*. Blood debt follow man all his life, until he pay. Dream woman tell Roheed every time he find man who is like baby Sindar—man who lose father and mother when he baby—Roheed have to help that man. If he not do it, bad thing happen. She tell Roheed only way he ever be free from blood debt—only way he can pay—is he have to save life of man like that. So all this time Roheed have blood debt. And still he wait to pay."

Pavo looked around at his stunned listeners. There wasn't a sound in the slave barn except the dripping of the rain. Pavo cleared his throat. "Now you know story," he said, "of Roheed jir-Akaan."

Mendorel was the first to speak into the silence that followed the conclusion of Pavo's narrative. "Well," he observed, addressing Nagaro. "I'm thinking we know now why Roheed was so keen on helping ye."

Nagaro didn't answer. He was staring fixedly at the damp stones of the wall beyond Pavo's head.

Pavo frowned at Mendorel. "What you mean?" he asked. "Nagaro is man with no father and no mother?"

Mendorel nodded. "So he's said."

Pavo looked at Nagaro. "Is true, Nagaro?"

Nagaro started, and it was a moment before he answered. "Yes," he said simply. It seemed a safe admission. Leyel Virden had been introduced to the people of Edrovir as the Lady Maramine's son. The identity of his father had been left rather to the imagination.

All eyes were on Nagaro, and Pavo was looking at him curiously. "And Roheed know this?" the young Hashtep asked. "How?"

"He knows it because I told him." Nagaro answered quietly. And he explained, then, in a few words how he had come to tell Roheed. "I thought it odd that he wanted to know what happened to my family," he added. "And, to be fair, he was trying to find a way to help me even before I told him about my parents. After I told him, though, he became rather, well, excited."

Taru had been sitting silently. Now he addressed Pavo. "How old is Roheed," he asked. "Do ye know?"

"How many year?" Pavo looked thoughtful. "I think he have one more year than me. That mean he have nineteen year."

Taru's eyes widened and he looked hard at Nagaro. Nagaro was frowning. His right hand unconsciously fingered the tiny lump in the waist of his ragged pants that was his hidden ring. Feeling Taru's glance, he hastily moved his hand away and silenced his friend with a quick shake of the head.

"Well," Landros observed, "It seems Nagaro has set poor Roheed in the fork of a tree." He turned to Nagaro. "The boy thinks he has to help ye, and he tried to set ye free, but ye wouldn't let him—not unless he set the lot of us free! What a state o' mind he must be in right now! Do ye think he'll try again to turn ye loose?"

Nagaro frowned. He feared that Landros was right, and the thought made him very uncomfortable. "I don't know," he said. "Maybe he'll think he doesn't have to now, because I turned him down. After all, how could he be expected to help me if I said I didn't want him to?"

Pavo shook his head. "You do not know power of blood debt," he said portentiously. "I think Roheed is afraid something bad go to happen because he not help you." The young Hashtep was eyeing Nagaro with the look of someone who suspects that he has wandered into a fairy tale, and Nagaro wished he would stop.

"But Roheed *is* still helping ye," Mendorel put in, adressing Nagaro. "Didn't he put some o' that burn salve on your sore while we were still on the ship?"

Nagaro ran his fingers over the place on his right ankle where the chain had rubbed him raw. Putting salve on the wound had been the first thing Roheed had done after Nagaro had been returned to the oar deck. The sore had healed well, although it had left a scar. "Yes, he did," Nagaro acknowledged. "But that's no more than careful slave-tending. That wound could easily have festered in a filthy place like the oar deck. And as for the fruit," he added, glancing at Landros, "he gave the same to all of us."

The old sea-warrior shrugged. "So maybe he's helping ye by helping the lot of us," he suggested. "His curse doesn't say he can't do that."

There was some further discussion on the subject of the blood debt, although no more light was shed, and then the talk turned to other things. There was general agreement that telling more stories would be a good way to pass the time. They all promised that each would try to think of a tale, though most seemed to think they would be hard-put to equal Pavo's performance.

*

It was late that evening, when the slaves had all lain down to sleep, that Nagaro felt Taru's hand on his arm. He'd just been starting to doze, but he roused himself and asked in a whisper, "What is it, Taru?"

He heard Taru shift in the straw as his friend glanced around the room before answering. "I couldn't stop thinking all day about that tale o' Pavo's. How ye've got that ring, and no parents, and ye're just the right age and all."

Nagaro's brows came together sharply in the darkness. "What are you trying to say, Taru?" He kept his own voice so low it was scarcely audible.

"Well it seems like... I mean... Maybe we just heard the story o' what happened t' your parents. Maybe ye were that baby. Maybe ye're Sindar."

Nagaro could almost have laughed aloud. Instead he answered in an urgent whisper. "That's absurd, Taru! Pavo's story happened *here*. I grew up hundreds of miles away in Edrovir. How would a little baby have traveled all that way?"

"Well, someone could ha' found ye and carried ye there. Maybe someone even *saw* Notep leave the baby and throw the ring in the water. I don't know exactly how it happened, but there's just too many things that fit. Ye're nineteen. Ye were born in the spring. That baby's father was 'very good with a sword', and I'm thinking your father must surely ha' been so too. And the baby's mother was a very beautiful Kelorin woman..." Taru let the sentence trail, remembering perhaps how little Nagaro liked being reminded of his physical beauty. "And there's your ring," he finished hurriedly. "I saw ye feelin' for it. It's just too strange that ye have that ring. Weren't ye thinking the same thing?"

"No, I wasn't," Nagaro answered flatly. "It's very common among Kelorin folk for a man and a woman to give rings to each other as love tokens. The story made me think of my ring because that's probably what it was—a love token my father gave to my mother. Then when she died or... or had to give me up... it was bequeathed to me. I thought of all of that a long time ago. And as for me being nineteen, and born in the spring," he added after a moment. "I could say the same about you."

"Aye," Taru muttered. "But I'm not Kelorin. And I know who my parents were." Still he sounded a bit deflated.

"You're very clever, Taru," Nagaro told him seriously. "And I wouldn't want you to stop putting your mind to things. You just must be wrong this time, that's all."

There was silence, except for the rustling of men shifting in their sleep and the drip of rain.

After a long minute, it was Nagaro who reopened the whispered conversation. "Is there something bothering you, Taru? Since Chitaopa?" When Taru didn't immediately answer, he added, "If you're angry with me—the way Moraga is—I'd understand."

"Of course I'm not angry with ye, Nagaro! Not anymore, I mean. I guess I'm just, well... afraid..."

"*Afraid?* Of what?"

It took a moment for Taru to answer. "That we won't be able t' stay together," he said at last. "It almost happened on Chitaopa. Ye should ha' let Roheed set ye free, Nagaro. That's what I'd ha' done—at least I think I would. I'm glad ye didn't, o' course, and... well..." He paused again, then spoke all in a rush as if that made it easier. "We came into this together, Nagaro, and I guess I always thought we'd get out of it the same way."

"I've never wanted to go alone," Nagaro began. "It didn't feel right to leave all the—"

Taru didn't let him finish. "I mean just the two of us, Nagaro. Not the whole lot."

Nagaro shifted uncomfortably. He didn't want to admit that he'd been thinking more and more in terms of plans that involved setting the whole crew of slaves free. It was probably just guilt, he told himself, because he'd let Roheed leave with the key that night. "Listen, Taru," he said, with as much conviction as he could muster. "If you have a good plan that's just for two, you can count on me. But," he added, "if I see a chance to help the rest of these men, I'm going to take it. You'd do that too, wouldn't you?"

"Aye. 'Course I would." Taru sounded less than certain, but he also sounded a bit relieved.

"All right then. Let's get some sleep."

But Taru wasn't quite ready for sleep. "Did ye really think Roheed might ha' turned us all loose on Chitaopa?"

Nagaro sighed. "No. I was trying to make a point when I suggested it, but I think I failed. Roheed has a good heart in him. He sees clearly that slaves are men, not beasts. And he doesn't like to see men suffer needlessly. What he can't quite see is that men shouldn't be slaves at all. He thinks *I* shouldn't be one—and maybe he thought the same about Emril—but it's only because he thinks I'm *different* from all the rest. I was trying to make him understand that I'm not."

"Well, o' course *that* didn't work," Taru declared. "Because ye *are* different, Nagaro. Ye're completely daft! Trying to teach a Mautep that keeping slaves is wrong! What did ye expect?" He yawned audibly. "I thought ye wanted t' get some sleep..."

Nagaro sighed. It seemed that he had a better chance of convincing Roheed that slavery was wrong than of changing Taru's mind about the Mautep. Curling on his side, he tried to find a comfortable position—one where his chain didn't pull at his leg and his head was as far as possible from the place where the dripping rainwater fell into the straw.

Chapter 22: Vothra

The next morning the sun came out, which meant that those who had not previously wintered in Sar Tipaal were finally going to find out what life in the Shipyard was all about. And what it was about, was moving pieces of wood—everything from huge, rough, unshaped logs to planks, ribs, tillers and bowsprits.

Baruk and Raal appeared about an hour after the slaves had finished breakfast. The two Mautep from the *Fist of Death* came accompanied by a number of shipyard slave handlers. Fataan and Roheed—now in uniform—appeared a few minutes later, each carrying a handful of what looked like strips of dirty yellow cloth. Under Baruk's direction and Raak's whip, the slaves were assembled into work gangs, each one consisting of three or four men linked together in a line by their ankle chains. Baruk stumped up and down the slave barn, choosing men for each work gang according to their strength and physical condition to produce strings of men suited to more or less heavy work.

Nagaro found himself chained in a gang with Mendorel and Landros on that first day, while Taru was linked to Pavo and Tego. After they had been chained together, Roheed stepped up to Mendorel, the lead man in Nagaro's string, with one of the pieces of yellow cloth in his hand. This turned out to be a loop that the young Mautep hung, bandolier-fashion, over Mendorel's shoulder so that it hung diagonally across his chest and back. Fataan decorated Pavo, also a lead man, in a similar fashion. Roheed kept his eyes on his task and didn't look at Nagaro, who stood immediately behind Mendorel. The young Mautep came so close that Nagaro could see he was cultivating a mustache, but he didn't speak.

Each work gang was next assigned to a slave handler and promptly marched out into the watery sunlight. The slave handlers all carried pointed staffs, used as goads. Pavo later explained that the shipyard slave handlers were Hashtep who had begun as stable boys and distinguished themselves by loyalty to the Mautep warlords and aptness for the work. Aptness in this case seemed to include a distinct lack of sympathy for the slaves, even those who were Hashtep like themselves. The goads were put to painful use as the handlers lined up their work gangs in the area just outside the door of the slave barn.

As it turned out, there were a number of slave barns, all in a row, at one end of the shipyard. The work gangs issuing from each barn were marked by a different color of bandolier. Besides the yellow that marked the slaves from the *Fist's* barn, Nagaro soon noted blue, white, orange, red, and black. Pavo told him later that, although the slaves who served Lord Baalkir were all marked with the same brand, each of them also belonged, in a sense, to the captain of the ship he rowed. The captains engaged in a fierce if unofficial competition to demonstrate the superior performance of their ships and crews, both free and slave.

It was beneath Captain Urchak's dignity to personally oversee the performance of his slaves, however. This was Baruk's task, and the Slave Master took it very seriously. Like any good stableman who knows the strengths and weaknesses of every beast in his charge, Baruk made a point of knowing the men under his dominion. He'd teamed them carefully when forming the work gangs, and now he went down the line issuing work assignments. The slave handlers then proceeded to escort their strings of slaves across the shipyard to do whatever work they'd been assigned

Nagaro, Mendorel, and Landros spent that first day moving rough-hewn timbers from the area where they were cut to various locations where they were further worked into different pieces of a ship's skeleton. It was very hard work, made even harder by the fact that they had to learn how to move about without jerking each other's chains and tripping or falling. Mendorel, who had done it before, muttered instructions to Nagaro and Landros. Eventually, they mastered the art of always leading off with the right foot after a mental count of three whenever they were commanded to move, and of walking with a constant, shuffling rhythm. Baruk was everywhere, and Raak was with him, watching to see that the *Fist's* slaves were acquitting themselves creditably, and applying the whip as Baruk deemed necessary.

At noon, a gong was sounded and all of the free shipyard workers paused in their tasks to take their midday meal. The slaves got a chance to rest as well, though they were given only water. The water came from cisterns, and it was brought to the *Fist's* slaves in the familiar water skins by Fataan and Roheed. Nagaro had caught only occasional glimpses of these two during the morning's labor. Now Roheed moved impassively about his task, and Nagaro concluded that his best course was to ignore the young man as completely as possible. He would have liked to have asked Mendorel some questions, but talk among the slaves was quickly punished by whip or goad, so he turned his attention elsewhere.

It was his first opportunity to really look around the shipyard. The place was dominated by the shapes of six ships, like skeletal whales, in a row along the wharf. They were in various stages of construction. Nagaro studied the wooden skeletons with interest, noting how keel, ribs, decks, and planking all fitted together to make the whole. Two of the ships were clearly war galleys. In one case, he could see the row of gaps in the hull that would be the oar ports. The other was identifiable by an extension of the keel at its forward end that would form the core of the metal-clad ram. The four other ships were merchant craft.

The rest of the yard was a patchwork of different work areas, some covered by long roofs, others open to the sky. There were large stacks of timber, storage sheds, and the like. Sawdust and wood shavings were everywhere, although at the moment the carpenters had all paused in their work to fill their bellies.

Nagaro next considered the possibility of escape. He noted that the shipyard was surrounded by a high wall—too high for even a tall man to jump and catch the top of it. Besides the small gate near the slave barns at the farther end of the yard where Roheed had entered, there were two gates through which timbers and other supplies could be brought in. Both were heavily guarded by armed men. Nagaro sighed and looked about for any other possible means of exit. He'd just noticed that there were a number of rowboats tied up at several places along the wharf when the gong sounded again to mark the end of the lunch hour.

The afternoon passed in much the same way as the morning. Many of the *Fist*'s slaves were flagging well before the end of the day's work, not having fully recovered from the effects of the plague and their long period of short rations. By the time they were marched back to the slave barn, all the men were bone-weary and many were limping.

Chained once again to a ring in the floor of the slave barn, Nagaro sat and massaged his aching muscles. Baruk had kept the members of each work gang together in the barn, instead of returning them to their original places, and Nagaro was now chained between Mendorel and Landros. Taru was on the other side of Mendorel, with Tego and Pavo beyond him.

When the food was eventually brought—the usual flavorless fish stew—Nagaro ate ravenously. After the stable boys departed with the bowls, he was about to stretch out on the straw when Pavo's voice, raised above the rustle of straw and mutterings of the men, stopped him short.

"Who is go to tell story tonight? Someone Droviri, this time?" The young Hashtep spoke eagerly and loud enough to be heard by all of the occupants of the barn. His words were met with expectant murmurs from the Hashtep slaves and a general groan from most of the weary Edrovirans.

Pavo was not to be deterred. "Taru," he said. "You tell story?"

"Not me," Taru said quickly. "I can't think o' one. Maybe Tego's got a good yarn."

"I'm too tired to think, matey," Tego protested. "And I'm no yarn-spinner, neither."

"Mendorel? You tell story?"

"Ahh... well... I haven't thought of a good one..." Mendorel shifted uncomfortably. "Maybe tomorrow."

For a long moment there was gaping silence. The golden glow of the rapidly westering sun lit up the row of small, high windows along the western wall of the slave barn and shone in on the two rows of ragged, dirty men sprawling in the moldy straw.

Nagaro could see Pavo's face plainly and he read the disappointment there. "I guess I could try," he ventured.

All eyes turned towards him. He hadn't really wanted to be the first to go after Pavo, but it was obvious that no one else wanted to follow that performance, and he was afraid the whole idea of telling stories would collapse as a result. "I'm not a story-teller either," he added quickly. "But I've read about the history of my people, and you might find some of it interesting."

"Kelorin *history?*" Moraga was chained across from him, in the row along the farther wall. He sounded disgusted. "What make's ye think we're int'rested in Kelorin history?"

Pavo turned on Moraga. "Why not?" he demanded. He exchanged some rapid words with the other Hashtep in their own tongue. Then he turned back to Nagaro. "Is very good," he said, defiantly. "We like to hear story of Kelorin people. You talk some, and stop some, so I can tell my people what you say."

Nagaro nodded. "All right." He didn't look at Moraga. "But I'm not sure where I should begin. The whole history is rather long."

"Tell us about beginning—where your people come from," Pavo suggested immediately.

"All right." Nagaro cleared his throat to begin. "The Kelorin people come from the islands of Kelor, that lie far across the western sea. They came to those islands more than five hundred years ago, and they lived there peacefully for many lives of men. In the beginning, they were few in number and there was plenty of good land for all." He paused while Pavo translated in rapid Hashti.

Before he could continue, Moraga interrupted. "Ye're startin' in the middle," he objected, "if the Kelorin came t' those islands from someplace else! Where'd they come from before that?"

Nagaro frowned. "They weren't Kelorin before Kelor was founded, so that's why their history begins there. Before that, they called themselves the Lithenkelin—the Cloud Mountain People—and they came from the Cloud Mountains, of course."

"Well? Where's *that* then?" Moraga seemed to be in a particularly belligerent mood.

"The Cloud Mountains were on the mainland of the western continent of Ludea. It lies to the west of the Kelorin Isles." Nagaro was trying not to sound annoyed. "Some of the Cloud Mountain People were made slaves by another folk in Ludea. But there was a cataclysm—like the one the Turo call the Time of Fire and Water—and the slaves took advantage of the upheaval to gain their freedom. They acquired some ships and sailed to the isles that they named Kelor, where they became the Kelorin. And don't ask me where they came from before the Cloud Mountains because I don't know. There are no records, nor any spoken tradition that I've ever heard of, that tells of the Cloud Mountain People having ever lived anywhere else."

"Well that's easy then," said Taru. "That must be where they landed when they got off o' the boat."

Nagaro turned towards his friend. "What do you mean?" he asked. "What boat?"

"The Sky Boat, o' course. Ye must know the story—"

"Aye," Moraga interrupted. "Everybody knows the story." He proceeded to recite: "The first men came over the sea in a big boat from a place that's always night. They brought two of every kind o' animal, and they landed at Ulana Kura—ye call it 'Lankura.' And after that, the Spirits took the boat up into the sky an' set it on Naru's horn."

"Oh, *that* story." Nagaro sighed. It was a good thing he hadn't had his heart set on the other tale, since no one was letting him tell it.

"The Kelorin version of that story is a little different. We say men first came to this world from another world that was very like it. There were twelve races of men, and they came in a great ship that sailed the sea of night between the stars. They brought with them the seeds of all the kinds of plants and animals that they knew. They landed in many places—each race in a different place—and they planted their seeds wherever they landed. Our story says the moon we call Naru *is* the ship that sailed between the stars, and that it sails around and around up there in the sky waiting for the day when men will sail away again to another world—or maybe back to the one they came from. Only no one remembers how to sail it," he added, "or even how to get up into the sky where it is." He stopped speaking and frowned. "I always thought that story was a legend—not real history. Do your people have a story like that, Pavo?"

Pavo had been frantically translating into Hashti. He stopped to answer Nagaro's question. "Our story is part like Kelorin story. It say small moon is ship that bring Hashtep people from star. But it only say

Hashtep people come from star. Not all people. But after what you say," he added quickly, "I think maybe all people come from star."

"Well, let's test it then." Nagaro turned to Tredhold. "What about the Leithians? Where do your people say they came from in the beginning?"

Tredhold fingered his chin. "Well," he said, "our story says that our folk came to Leith from the sky in a great ship sent by the gods. Our story is a bit like Taru's, because it says Kroneg sailed the ship back up into the sky and tethered it to Naru's horn. We say Kroneg rides the small, dark moon, and the great, pale moon, Talebra, carries the goddess Lissafel. Kroneg chases Lissafel across the heavens, ye see, sometimes catching her up and passing her. Whenever Naru catches Talebra, it's said that we see which power is greater—Kroneg's sword, or Lissafel's kiss that turns the hearts o' men to love."

He stopped and laughed sheepishly. "But that's another tale. I'm afraid our story of the sky ship is a bit like the Hashtep one too, because it only speaks of our own folk. The idea that all the different men of the earth are like brothers is a Kelorin notion, I think. The men o' Leith never put much stock in it. But with all these sky ship stories being so similar, maybe there's something in it after all."

Shadows had by now begun to gather inside the slave barn as the sun slipped below the horizon. All the slaves could see through their little windows was the deep, luminous blue of the evening sky. Nagaro spoke into the silence that followed Tredhold's words. "It isn't a Kelorin notion," he said quietly. "It's part of Vothra's teaching. That means it's only as old as Vothra. Kelor was founded in the first year of our calendar, and Vothra didn't begin until the year 132. And not all the Kelorin chose to follow the Path in any case."

"I don't understand," Tego objected. "How could Vothra *begin?* Isn't Vothra one o' your gods?"

"No," Nagaro answered. "Vothra is not a god. Vothra is made up of human spirit—many human spirits, actually, gathered together into a single being with a single mind—a mind that holds the memories and knowledge of all the spirits that are part of it, gained from all the lives they ever lived. Vothra is very wise, but not all-knowing."

Mendorel cleared his throat. "The way ye talk, Nagaro, ye make it sound as if Vothra still exists. But everybody knows that Vothra's left us. He—I mean *it*—went away during the time o' the Rithral Lords. The Rithral Lords had a powerful magic. They could do things that Vothra couldn't do, and Vothra couldn't protect people from them. So nobody cared about following Vothra anymore, and the spirits that were part o' Vothra all blew away like the wind."

It was now almost completely dark in the slave barn. The only light was that of Talebra's half disk, shining weakly through the small, high windows. By that light, the men could see little more than each other's silhouettes and the gleam of each other's eyes. Nagaro spoke in the darkness. "Yes, I know all that. But the rithral magic ended generations ago, and there were always a few folk who kept to the Path—who kept Vothra's teachings alive. And now Vothra is gathering again—"

"Here now, lad." Landros spoke for the first time. "How do ye know that?"

Nagaro chewed his lip. "I suppose I shouldn't say I *know* it," he said. "But I *believe* it."

"Why?" This came from Mendorel.

Nagaro wasn't about to tell these men that Vothra had spoken to him in a dream, but he knew he had to say something. He chose the only thing he could think of that they might accept. "Because when my Lady Guardian died, Vothra sent me her Death Dream."

"A *Death Dream?* By the Eyes! Did it carry the Sign?"

The words had come from an unexpected place in the deep gloom of the barn, and it took Nagaro a moment to realize that it was Simion who had spoken. He answered without hesitation. "Yes, it did—first and last."

It was very quiet. In the dark, Nagaro couldn't see the expressions on any of the men's faces. He had no idea whether anyone besides Simion had been impressed by his words. He couldn't even tell how many of the men were still awake.

Pavo was obviously still awake because he'd been translating into Hashti in a rapid undertone and had just fallen silent. Now one of the other Hashtep said something in a hushed whisper, and there was some general murmuring among them. Pavo cleared his throat. "Nagaro," he said hesitantly, "we want to know... do Kelorin have god that made everything—that make thing happen? Good thing and bad thing?"

"They have Lokundas, what makes the bad things happen," Moraga growled, demonstrating that he also was still awake and listening. "I've heard 'em cursing him often enough."

Mendorel coughed. "It's Lokundas that sends men their fates," he said testily. "And it's the nature o' men to curse their fate when it goes against their wishes. But Lokundas didn't make the world. Have ye never heard a Kelorin speak o' the Maker?"

"Aye. I thought it was just another name for Lokundas."

"Well it isn't," Nagaro put in. "Lokundas is the 'Turner of Worlds.' The 'Maker of All Things' is Nomemduran. They're two of the Old Ones that were revered by the Cloud Mountain People—and the Kelorin, before the beginning of Vothra." He thought for a moment. "There's a passage from Oman's *Book of the Unseen* that explains the difference. It goes like this: 'Lokundas stirs the soup, but Nomemduran made the soup, and the pot, and the spoon—and Lokundas. And after Nomemduran made all of those things, he climbed out of the pot and walked away.' You don't hear us calling on the name of Nomemduran, because Nomemduran doesn't speak to us, and we don't really know if he's listening. And it's said that only a fool prays to Lokundas, because Lokundas simply doesn't care." He paused. "That leaves Vothra—who often is listening, and always does care—and who sometimes answers."

Pavo spoke again. "I think your Maker sound like our god, Sheptuum, and Lokundas is like Hiptatak, who is servant of Sheptuum. Hiptatak make thing happen that Sheptuum say. Many man make pray to Sheptuum, but Sheptuum not often give man what he want. Sheptuum do thing his own way. Is bad luck to pray to Sheptuum if you not ask for something very important."

Nagaro didn't think that Sheptuum and Nomemduran were so very much alike, but he decided not to say so. If the notion helped Pavo see some similarity between their two peoples, that was all to the good.

Again it was very quiet, and the silence lengthened. Here and there around him, Nagaro could hear soft, regular breathing, telling him that some of the men were now truly asleep. He heaved a sigh and stretched himself out in the straw, intending to join them.

"Nagaro?" It was Tredhold's voice. "I know that it's getting late, but I was hoping ye still might finish the story ye started. I'd like to hear how the Kelorin came to Arlinas."

"Is good," came Pavo's voice. "Also Hashtep want to hear story."

Nagaro didn't bother to sit up. He drew a long breath. "All right," he said. "But it *is* late, so I'll try to tell it quickly." He paused to collect his thoughts, then began.

"The Kelorin folk lived in peace for a long time after the founding of Kelor, but eventually their numbers increased and the Kelorin Isles became crowded. Then there was trouble between the heads of the different households—the Wared Lords as we call them. They'd made a council to choose the king who ruled the isles, and several kings had been chosen that way. But this time, the lords were so evenly divided between two rivals that they failed to name a king and there was war. One of the rival lords, Atheran, was a follower of Vothra. The other lord, Morengil, was not. Atheran wanted to use the wisdom of the Vothrin Path to guide the people, but Morengil thought Atheran and the other Vothrin were weak—that they wouldn't defend Kelor against enemies from outside."

Nagaro paused to allow Pavo's translation to catch up, then continued. "The war became very bitter, and Atheran was greatly troubled by the number of men who'd been killed, because Vothra doesn't like to see men kill one another. He decided to yield to Morengil to stop the killing. So he went to Morengil under a flag of truce and asked what terms they'd be given if they let Morengil be king. Well, Morengil either had a very hard heart, or he didn't trust Atheran and the other Vothrin lords, because he declared the price of peace would be that Atheran and the lords who had sided with him must all take ship and leave Kelor forever."

Again Nagaro paused to listen to the progress of Pavo's murmured translation. Through one of the little, high windows, he could see a single star sparkling coldly in the deepening blue of the evening sky. When the sound of Pavo's voice ceased, he picked up his narrative.

"Atheran wasn't happy about the terms, as you can imagine, and neither were his lords. But in the end, they all agreed it was best for the sake of peace. When they told their people, though, the people cried out that if their lords must go, then they would go with them. Well, Atheran's heart was gladdened by the courage and loyalty of his people, but he was worried because he didn't know where they could find a new home. He lay down to sleep that night with a troubled mind, and Vothra came to him in a dream. Vothra told him that if he sailed far into the east, he would come to a great body of land in the midst of which was a place where no people dwelt. There Atheran and his people could make themselves a new home."

Nagaro paused again. Pavo's voice droned in murmured Hashti and Nagaro stifled a yawn. "I'm sorry, Tredhold," he said. "I'm afraid I'm not being so quick in telling this, and now I can hardly keep my eyes open."

"I think I can guess what the ending is," observed the healer. "They all sailed away to find this land where no people dwelt, and they found it, and it was Arlinas."

Nagaro suppressed another yawn. "Yes, that's right," he said. "Of course it wasn't quite that simple. They started with a great many ships, but they had a hard time crossing the sea, and some turned back. Those who kept going ran out of provisions, but Vothra had left Kelor to go with the exiles, and the Spirit told Atheran to sail on because the land wasn't far. They finally made landfall on the northern coast, on the far side of the great mountain range—the Kor Vaskol. But there were people there, and the Kelorin had to fight a battle. They got separated into two groups. Atheran led the shore party over the mountains, and many died in the snow in the high passes. Those in the ships sailed on to the east, past the end of the Kor Vaskol, to the northern shore of a land where they found no people, just as Vothra had said. There they eventually met Atheran and what remained of his party. They called the empty land Arlinas, as you guessed, and they built their settlements there."

"So that's how it happened," Tredhold said when Nagaro stopped speaking. "It's similar to the story of how some Leithian lords came to leave the land of Leith and make their way to Arlinas. That's a tale of war betwixt rival lords and banishment as well. Those Leithians didn't have so perilous a journey because they didn't have to come by sea. And they came a few hundred years later. By then. the Kelorin had discovered rithral magic."

"You must tell us the story when it comes your turn," Nagaro told him.

"Aye, perhaps I will."

Pavo had finished translating. "Nagaro?" he asked. "Why do you say Vothra leave Kelor to go with ship? Is not Vothra be everywhere, and see everything, like Sheptuum?"

Nagaro stared up at the dark ceiling, his head cradled on his folded arms. "No," he said. "Vothra isn't everywhere and can't see everything. Vothra always has a center that is *someplace*. How far from that center Vothra can see is a matter of how strong the Spirit is—how many spirits have been gathered into it. Actually," he added, "Vothra can only see the world through the eyes of men. By looking into their minds. When we say 'By the Eyes', it's short for 'By the Eyes of Vothra's Mind'."

"Now where did ye learn all o' that, lad? I never heard the half of it." This came unexpectedly from Landros and his tone was more than a little curious.

"Nor I," put in Mendorel. "Is that something ye read in the *Book of Vothra?*"

Nagaro shifted uncomfortably. Here he was, explaining the nature of Vothra in the presence of two other Kelorin who both had more years than he. If what he'd just said wasn't even common knowledge among his own people, why should any of these men believe it?

"I don't think that's in the *First Book of Vothra*," he began cautiously, trying to remember exactly where it had come from. *He had known all of this for so long...* "It could have been in the *Second Book*, or one of the other Writings... Or perhaps my Lady Guardian told me. She had a copy of every book about Vothra that she could find, and I'm sure she'd read them all. I only read some of them."

"Well don't feel ye need to apologize to *us*," said Landros with fine irony.

"She must have been an unusual woman, this Lady Guardian of yours," Mendorel observed carefully.

"As long as I knew her," Nagaro said quietly, "she wanted one thing above all else—that her spirit should be gathered into Vothra when she died. I suppose maybe that's unusual. In these days at least..."

Mendorel coughed. "A bit."

"Aye, lad," Landros added. "Just a bit unusual, I'd say."

The slave barn was silent. Outside, the deep azure of the evening sky had faded into sable night. The small, high window was a rectangle of black on black, edged around by the faint silver light of the waning moon. Through that window, Nagaro could now make out two bright stars, like eyes gazing down at him. For a time he lay, unaccountably wakeful now, staring up at those twin points of light. Then at last he closed his eyes. For the first time in many a long day, what came into his mind as sleep descended was something other than images of the oar deck, the slave barn, or imagined escape.

A figure that was Maramine, and yet not Maramine, stood beside him in the dirty straw, untouched, and untouchable, by the filth and desperation of that place. Its skin shone like silver. Its hair was silver and ebony. The eyes were two midnight pools, and in the depths of each was reflected a single star. The figure spoke, and its voice was like leaves in the wind or the sound of raindrops falling.

Spirit that calls itself Nagaro, it said. *I have found you, though you have traveled far from the place where you were before. Know that we have become joined, you and I, by the gentle love of one noble spirit. Look for me ever in your times of greatest need. You have only to call my name, and I will hear you. For my name is... Vothra...* The last word came like a breath, sighing across his mind.

The figure faded, leaving a faint tracery of lines seemingly imprinted on his vision, as the after-image of some bright thing lingers in the eye. The Sign of Vothra, the circle-within-a-circle-joined, floated in the air between him and the window. Within the window's silver-edged rectangle was now only ordinary night—the star-eyes had moved on. Presently the Sign also faded from his vision. Nagaro closed his eyes though he couldn't remember having opened them. He didn't feel at all surprised by what had just happened, only comforted and strangely at peace.

When he awoke in the morning, both the dream figure and the subsequent apparent waking were etched with equal clarity in his memory so that he wasn't sure whether the figure had been a dream or a waking vision. That it was a true message from Vothra he didn't doubt. It had been too strange for an ordinary dream, even had it not been sealed with Vothra's sign.

Whether it had been dream or vision, it was clear that Maramine's spirit had achieved her dearest desire, and for that he was glad. He was less confident about the rest of it. To be "joined" to Vothra's mind, he knew, meant the Spirit should be more than commonly aware of him. The words of the dream seemed to say that the connection between him and Maramine during her life had somehow accomplished this, but it was such a rare honor that he scarcely dared believe it. After the previous evening's talk, he knew how strange such a thing would seem to his fellow slaves. He determined not to speak of it to anyone.

*

The days passed. Some had sun. More had rain—rain that drizzled, or lashed the walls, or drummed endlessly on the roof. Other days had only a leaden sky and chill, dank salt air—like a dying breath from the great, gray bosom of the sea. Whenever it didn't rain, the slaves were marched out to work in the shipyard. On the evenings of such days, they returned, bruised and cut, with aching backs and splinters in their hands. So the "storm time" of the Hashtep crept on towards midwinter with the gradual darkening of the days.

On most of these days, the slaves found someone who was willing to tell a tale. Nagaro had, as he hoped, broken their reluctance. Anyone, it seemed, could do as well as he—and many obviously thought that it couldn't be very hard to do better.

Tredhold did indeed tell the story of how the Leithians had come to Arlinas. It was a tale of treachery and violence, and it seemed to be all too typical an example of Leithian history—almost of the very soul of the Leithian people. Tredhold told the tale almost apologetically, seemingly uncomfortable with what it implied about his own folk. On the other hand, the other two Leithians among them—a seasoned merchant seaman named Farl and the young sea warrior, Gurd—told several such tales, filled with blood and betrayal, with gleeful enthusiasm.

From these tales, Nagaro was glad to learn that Leithians valued boldness, courage, and honor—at least when it came to being loyal to one's family or lord. What disturbed him, however, was that the men of Leith seemed equally impressed by ruthlessness and guile when these traits brought success against enemies. In the eyes of most Leithians, it seemed that victory was proof of worthiness, and revenge was the natural right of anyone who believed he had been harmed. Kelorin tales were more likely to be woven around themes of honor, compassion, and self-sacrifice. These virtues were extolled in the *Book of Vothra*, and they were so deeply ingrained in the psyche of Atheran's people that even Vothra's long absence hadn't entirely erased them. Though the heroes of Kelorin tales didn't always win the day, they strove to remain true to the principles that guided them.

In contrast, Turowan stories were mostly small in scope, dealing with ordinary men and everyday conflicts. The struggles of fishermen with the weather or with the scarcity of fish were common themes. Other stories told of troubles among close kin—the rivalry of brothers, a husband's jealousy, a father's disappointment in his son... The World Spirits figured in all of these tales. Sometimes they guided or protected. At other times they sent misfortune as punishment for offenses that were rather capriciously defined. The help of Hakura Kili was sought in such cases, and it was often delivered in the form of dreams—which usually required interpretation by a dream reader. The solutions put forward by these dream readers often seemed to Nagaro to be no more than common sense, but he refrained from saying so.

Pavo's original tale turned out to be typical of most of the stories of his folk. The other Hashtep tales tended also to feature dreams interpreted as portents, inescapable fates, and consequences dealt out by Sheptuum in the form of blessings or curses similar to the "blood debt" Pavo had described. Behind these marvelous manifestations, the Hashtep perceptions of right, honor, and justice could be discerned like images glimpsed through a transparent veil.

It naturally fell to Pavo to translate tales told by the other Hashtep. This the young fisherman did with obvious relish. Watching and listening, Nagaro soon began to suspect that Pavo was embellishing the stories as he retold them, and he began to wonder just how much of the story of Roheed had been fact and how much had been Pavo's invention. Eventually he summoned the courage to ask his new friend outright.

Pavo was not the least bit put out by the question. "Is mostly all true," he said, meeting Nagaro's gaze directly. "Notep have many Hashtep servant in his house. Hashtep see and hear. They talk to other Hashtep. Of course, I not know always what this one in story think, or what that one say. But is not hard to guess. Notep not want anyone to know his story, but everybody know it. Everybody in Sar Tipaal."

Nagaro found this last observation disquieting, considering how neatly his childhood history fitted into Roheed's tale.

Chapter 23: Blood Debt

The first month they spent in Sar Tipaal, the slaves were too grateful just to be alive to think much about winning their freedom. As the memory of the ordeals of the plague, near starvation, and the perilous voyage from Chitaopa faded, however, those who were inclined to think about the possibility of escape began to talk about it.

It was Landros, among the former Fleet men, who first brought up the subject, and it soon turned out that Tredhold and Gurd were of a similar mind. Moraga and the other more experienced slaves were quick with their derision, but the three sea warriors were undeterred. Simion just sat in miserable silence, his arms around his knees, following the conversation back and forth with nervous flicks of his eyes.

"We *have* to try to escape, mate. It's a warrior's duty!" Landros was explaining this to Moraga for the third time.

"I'll give ye *that* for your 'duty'!" Moraga spat into the straw and wiped his split lip with the back of his hand. "Ye don't think yer great Lord Kuran is comin' around here t' see ye doin' your duty, do ye? Ye'll end up with a bloody back, or worse!"

"Well, it's *my* back to risk," Landros retorted. "No one's asking ye to risk yours!"

"An' a good thing too, mate! *I'm* no fool!"

"Can ye tell us how ye're planing t' do it?" Mendorel interrupted the exchange, which sounded as if it might have come to blows if the two parties hadn't been chained at opposite sides of the slave barn.

"Aye." Taru spoke up. "Even if ye can get your chain loose, ye'll never get over the wall or past the guards at the gates. That leaves the small boats in the harbor, the way I see it."

Landros looked impressed. "Ye've been thinking the same way I've been thinking."

Taru shrugged. "I said *if* ye can get your chain loose," he observed pointedly.

"It's a greased knot, I'll give ye that," Landros admitted.

Moraga snorted. "That's what I've been trying t' tell ye!"

Landros ignored him.

"I say we should give that bloody bilge-rotter Baruk the jump and throttle 'im and take the key." This was Gurd's suggestion.

"But Baruk never comes in here alone!" Tego protested.

Tredhold finally spoke for the first time. "I say we should all keep our eyes peeled when we're out in the shipyard," he ventured. "There's so many tools about. Sooner or later, someone is bound to leave something with a sharp edge lying some place where one of us can pick it up when nobody's looking."

Landros gave his shipmate an appreciative glance. "Now there's an idea that's worth more'n a barrel o' salt fish!"

"That's all well and good," Moraga interrupted. "But what are ye goin' to do if ye ever get into one o' them little boats? Ye're hundreds o' miles from home—an' no provisions. How d' ye figure on getting back to Edrovir?"

"Ha! Salt-dogs like us? We'll row all the way if we have to! But with luck, we'll meet an Edroviran ship."

"Ye'll meet a dozen Mahuk craft first! If ye don't die o' thirst!"

"Well, dying is better'n rotting here like lobsters in a catch-pot!"

And so the discussion went. As the second mate of the *Fairwind*, Landros was the ranking officer and he clearly meant for the four Fleet warriors to go together, although Gurd would clearly have been glad to abandon Simion. "I tell ye, that boy jumps at his own shadow," the young Leithian muttered, glancing at Simion. "He'll give us all away—or let us down in the pinch!"

Simion gave Gurd a quick, wounded look, but he offered not a word in his own defense.

Nagaro listened to the sea warriors' plans and held his peace. He knew he had no answers.

Taru did more listening than talking as well, but he spoke quietly one evening to Nagaro while the others were engaged in a heated argument. "If I can find a way t' get to one o' those little boats, are ye with me?"

Nagaro frowned. "Of course. But Moraga has a point. What about provisions? Especially water?"

"Well, I was thinking... Didn't Pavo say he's got two brothers living just north o' the city?" Taru turned to the young Hashtep, whose face showed no emotion, though his sharp black eyes watched them keenly. "What d' ye say Pavo? Would your brothers help us? If ye were with us, I mean?"

Pavo considered Taru with his most inscrutable gaze. "Yes," he said at length. "I think my two brother help—if I tell them you both my friend." The answer was directed to Taru's question, but Pavo looked at Nagaro as he said it.

"Good!" Taru beamed. "That's settled then. We'll take Pavo with us, and make for his brothers' house."

Nagaro met Pavo's eyes. "Yes, it *is* good," he said. He was glad to have Pavo included in Taru's escape plans, although he couldn't see how they would manage to get out of their chains and into one of the boats without being caught.

Although Nagaro had agreed to Taru's partial plan, and he wished the sea warriors success as well, he couldn't help thinking of Mendorel, and Tego, and less affectionately of Moraga—not to mention all of the other men he'd nursed through the plague. Had he helped keep them alive only so they could continue to be slaves? Didn't he owe them all something for the chance he'd let slip on Chitaopa?

What was needed, of course, was an opportunity, but the weeks dragged by without any such opportunity presenting itself. Baruk never seemed to enter the slave barn with fewer than half a dozen Mautep or Hashtep stable boys, and the shipwrights guarded their tools all too well.

*

Nagaro found other things to occupy his mind during those weeks in the shipyard. First, he studied how the ships were made. He had no motive in this other than his interest. Pavo had once spoken with pride of the swiftness of the ships that came out of this shipyard. Pressed now for details, the young Hashtep explained that this was due to the great skill of Lord Baalkir's master shipbuilder. Several times they saw the man passing through the yard. He was well-dressed and surrounded by apprentices and underlings—a broad, squat man with a keen eye and gray beginning to streak his hair.

Nagaro also took advantage of some of the idle time in the barn to try to learn a little Hashti, and Pavo was more than willing to teach him. Though Nagaro didn't have the young Hashtep's gift for languages, he was fascinated by the many differences in structure between Hashti and his own tongue—what Pavo called Droviri. It was a revelation to him that there was more to learning another language than merely learning the foreign equivalent of each word he had learned in his own child-hood.

"They don't have any words that are like 'a' or 'the,'" he informed Taru on one occasion. "That's why Pavo always leaves those words out. He doesn't know when to use them and when not."

Taru looked contemptuous. "But that's *easy*. Ye just do what feels right."

"But none of it feels right to Pavo because he didn't grow up lis-tening to Droviri. I've been trying to think what rule I can give him, but for the life of me, I can't figure out the pattern."

Taru looked thoughtful. "Well, now that ye mention it," he said, "it's not quite the same in Turowan as in the Common Speech. But what do ye want t' learn Hashti for anyway?"

Nagaro shrugged. "I thought it might be useful to know what the Mautep are saying."

Despite his sincere efforts, he made slow progress. By the time midwinter arrived, he had several dozen words of vocabulary and had mastered a modest number of phrases. He could catch words here and there in the rapid speech of the Hashtep slaves and stable boys, but real fluency eluded him.

Little news of the outside world came to the men in the slave barns, and even less that was of any interest to the Edrovirans among them. There was really only one significant event that they heard about before midwinter. It caused a bit of a stir among the Hashtep, and Pavo's eyes went wide when he heard it.

"There is tiger hunting close outside city wall!" he said in a hushed voice. "Very big, strong tiger. It come hunting in farmer field every night for whole week. It kill two man already. All Hashtep very afraid. They want Lord Baalkir do something."

"Like what?" Tego asked.

"I do not know. Maybe he send warrior out to hunt tiger."

From his place next to Nagaro, Mendorel muttered quietly under his breath, "Roheed must be sweating tonight."

Nagaro tried to look as if he hadn't heard this. Several of the other slaves shifted and glanced at him, but no one else said anything.

*

It was on the morning of the third of Idrin, not long after they first heard about the tiger, that Nagaro was awakened early by Landros' hand on his shoulder. Turning his head, he made out the sea warrior's weathered face where he lay in the gloom. Landros put a finger to his lips, and gestured with a little jerk of his head towards the end of the barn where the doors lay.

The sun was not long risen and was veiled behind a thick bank of clouds, so the light was very dim inside the barn. Nagaro was just able to make out the moving form of a man working his way along the line of slaves, coming in their direction. Nagaro recognized him more by his size and manner of movement than by his face. It was Baruk, and the Slave Master was alone.

Nagaro lay very still, his mind racing. Was it possible that Baruk had come alone with the key? What could he be doing, and what did Landros mean to do?

Baruk was coming nearer. The Mautep could have kept out of reach by staying in the center of the aisle between the two rows of slaves, but instead he was walking along within a foot of the heads of the sleeping men. He seemed to be studying each in turn, treading quietly as if not wanting to wake them.

Tredhold and Landros must have already formed a plan, however. The healer lay just beyond Landros, nearer to the door of the slave barn. As Baruk stepped close to him, the wiry Leithian's hands shot out with the swiftness of a coiled spring. He caught Baruk's legs, tripping him. The Slave Master went down with a short, startled cry, and a heavy thud that seemed to knock the wind out of him.

Landros and Tredhold were on the fallen man in an instant, Tred holding the Slave Master's legs while Landros managed to get his hands around Baruk's neck, choking off any further cries. The grizzled Kelorin then brought the man's head down on the flagstone floor with a sharp crack. The thin layer of straw did little to cushion the blow. Baruk's body went limp.

The sounds of the brief struggle had awakened the other slaves. There were murmured voices in the gloom.

"What d' ye mean to do, Landros?" It was Tego's voice.

Landros had already started to run his hands over Baruk's tunic. "I'm looking for the key! If we can get everybody loose, they'll never catch us all." He turned to Nagaro. "Can ye hold his shoulders, lad? If he starts to come around, give a holler and I'll give him another crack!"

Nagaro didn't hesitate. Their chances here didn't seem to be even as good as on Chitaopa, but he'd promised himself he would help in any future escape attempt. He moved quickly to pin the Slave Master with a knee across the shoulders. Tredhold was kneeling on the man's legs. The short chains of the other slaves prevented them from being of any help.

All was not going well, however, with Landros' search. His movements were becoming increasingly frantic, and he was swearing under his breath in stronger terms than Nagaro had heard him use before. To make matters worse, there was a sound of voices coming from outside the barn.

"Ye don't think he'd have been fool enough t' come in here alone if he had it on 'im, do ye?" That was Moraga's voice.

Landros swore louder. Then he turned to the healer as the outside voices drew nearer. "He hasn't got it, Tred. We've gone and bodjered the ugly bastard for nothing!"

Tredhold had no chance to respond, for at that moment, the doors of the barn were flung open. Half a dozen Hashtep lads, come with the morning food and water, stood gaping at a scene that was suddenly suffused by the full gray light of day.

*

A row of posts stood near the end of the slave barn. They were seven feet tall, and thick enough that a man couldn't get both his hands around one of them. Nagaro had noticed them but had given no thought to their purpose. On that morning of the third of Idrin, he, Landros, and Tredhold found out exactly what those posts were for. Nagaro, for one, would have gladly remained in ignorance.

First he had been punched, kicked, and pinned on his back in the straw by a mob of angry Hashtep stable boys. Then, when the Mautep came, his wrists were bound together, and he was dragged out of the barn after Tredhold and Landros, and secured to one of the posts. This was accomplished by locking his ankle chain in a tight loop around the bottom of the post and lashing his forearms from wrist to elbow to the post just above head level. Landros had been similarly bound to the post immediately to his left, and Tredhold to the one beyond that. Thus the three men were arrayed in a row, immobilized and ready for the lash.

Baruk emerged from the barn at that point, moving under his own power. Nagaro caught a glimpse over his shoulder of the broken-nosed Mautep, rubbing the lump on his head and glaring at the three perpetrators with undisguised fury. The Slave Master ordered a dozen lashes apiece, and Raak delivered them with fiendish zeal. The ritual of punishment drew a cheering crowd of Hashtep, whose members gleefully counted out the number of the whip strokes. Nagaro noticed Roheed once, briefly, when he turned his head. The young Mautep was staring at him hard-eyed and silent, his face an expressionless mask.

The scar-faced Slave Driver worked his way from left to right so that Tredhold felt the lash first, and then Landros. Both men took their stripes in stony silence, unwilling to give their captors the satisfaction of hearing them cry out. Nagaro resolved to do the same. He squared his shoulders and clamped his teeth as he heard the grinding of Raak's boots on the muddy gravel behind him. The lash fell with a cruel sting. Again and again he felt the leather cut his flesh, and the blood trickle, but he let no sound escape his lips.

After the whipping, came a dousing with sea water. A bucket-full was sloshed onto each man's back in turn. The ice-cold water briefly numbed the burning sting of the whip cuts—until the salt in it began to bite. Then Nagaro had to clamp his teeth even tighter against the pain. Through it all, he was aware of some muttered talk among the Mautep. He caught a few words. At length he heard Baruk and Raak depart.

Seeing that the spectacle was over, the crowd melted away, leaving the three beaten men to stand, bleeding and dripping, bound to their posts.

The morning was still overcast, and the air off of the ocean was clammy and chill. As the fierce stinging of his back eased a little, Nagaro became aware that he was shivering with cold. He couldn't easily see what was passing at the slave barn's entrance, since it was behind him, but presently he heard the Hashtep stable boys departing. The morning's ration of food and water had been delivered to the slaves within. The three who stood at the posts outside received nothing.

"Seems we've missed breakfast," Tredhold observed in a light tone that sounded a little forced.

"No loss if it was more o' that infernal porridge," Landros growled. "Ye could caulk a ship w' that stuff!"

"Aye, that's true... Kronig's Blood, these cords are tight!" Tredhold was twisting his arms back and forth, trying to work a little slack into the lashings.

Landros tugged at his own bindings. "It puts me in mind o' when I was just a half-grown lad and my father signed me out as a scurry-boy on a merchantman. I was supposed to stay up on lookout every evening in the crow's seat, but I used to sneak down t' the galley when no one was looking and nab a bit o' biscuit. The mate caught me at it one time. Gave me a good lickin'. Then he hauled me back up to my post and tied me to the mast sprit!"

"So ye cut yourself loose with your whittling knife and nipped back down for another piece o' biscuit. I've heard that one before, ye old bootlace. I say ye made it up!"

"The part about being tied to the mast is the truth! I swear it on Lokundas' backside."

"Hoy, that'll make it true, all right!" Tredhold shook his head at his friend. "I'm wise to your ways, Landros, but ye shouldn't be misleading the innocent." He jerked his head in Nagaro's direction.

Landros shifted his footing, and turned his head to look at Nagaro. "I'm sorry to have pulled ye into this, lad," he said, suddenly serious.

Nagaro tried to shrug, but his back smarted too much. Instead, he flashed the older man a quick, hard smile and said, "Don't trouble yourself about it."

At this point, they heard the Mautep and Hashtep returning, and Landros muttered, "Stow the gab." Presently the other slaves were all brought out of the barn and lined up, amid a clinking of chains and barking of orders. Nagaro could hear a bit of low muttering that must be the other slaves, but he could catch no words in it. The slaves were not permitted to speak in any case. In due course, the work gangs were marched away to their toil in the shipyard. Again the three men were left alone.

After a little while, Landros muttered. "It's Idrin, isn't it? I should ha' known. No good ever comes o' things begun in Idrin."

"We should have known Baruk wouldn't have come in there like that with the key in his pocket," Tredhold countered. "Moraga's as bad as a bucket o' cold water in Genorel, but he was right about that."

"Humph! I'll take the bucket o' cold water." Landros wasn't going to concede Moraga anything. "What was Baruk doing sneaking around in there by himself anyway? That's what I'd like to know."

"Probably just taking stock of his stable-full o' horse-flesh. Looking to see which ones to pick t' pull the queen's carriage." The healer spoke with bitter irony. After a moment, he added, "I'd like to know where he keeps that key when he doesn't have it about him. That I would."

The two men went on in a similar vein for some time. Nagaro was grateful for the distraction, but he didn't bother to join in. After perhaps an hour, the morning clouds burned off and the sun came out. In that season it wasn't hot, but it was bad enough for men in their situation. All the cool mistiness of the morning soon evaporated and they were wracked by thirst as well as pain, and tormented by the smell of their own blood. Then there were the flies...

The necessity of simply *standing* became a torment as well. As their thirst waxed, the sea warriors' banter waned. Towards mid-morning Tredhold finally spoke the thought that must have been preying on his mind.

"D' ye think they mean to leave us here to die?"

"I shouldn't wonder." Landros growled through gritted teeth.

Nagaro realized for the first time that he knew more than the other two men. "I don't think so," he said. "I heard someone say 'night' and 'tomorrow.' I didn't hear anyone say 'die', or 'dead.'" By good luck, these Hashti words were in his limited vocabulary.

"Well that's good news if it's true. Maybe they'll cut us loose in the morning." Tredhold sounded relieved. "Did ye hear anything else, lad?"

"I could have told you how many lashes you'd get. That's all."

Landros leaned heavily against his post. "Well, I hope ye're right about the morning," he said wearily. "And I hope we make it through the night."

None of them spoke much after that. The afternoon wore itself out with excruciating slowness. Nagaro tried in vain to find a way to rest by leaning against the post. He could take a little weight off of his legs by holding himself up with his bound arms, but his arms quickly tired whenever he tried it. Once or twice he thought he heard Landros snoring. The older sea warrior seemed somehow able to sleep standing up. After what seemed an eternity, he heard the work gangs brought back to the barn. A little after that, the stable boys came and went with the evening's food and water for the men in the barn.

Finally, the sun sank into the distant gray mass of a gathering cloud bank and night descended, bringing first a blessed cooling of the air and then a chilling wind carrying the briny smell of the sea. Nagaro faded in and out of shivering awareness.

*

His mind struggled towards consciousness. He must have either dozed or fainted. His head had fallen forward, and his cheek was resting against the smooth wood of the post. It couldn't possibly be right, but it seemed that something like the rim of a cup was pressing against his lips, and there was water trickling through his beard... He couldn't move his hands to feel for the cup... *He couldn't even feel his hands...*

Water...

With an effort, he raised his head. He opened his mouth and felt the impossible water flow into it. He swallowed. The sensation of cool liquid flowing down his throat brought him back to himself. He managed to open his eyes and focus. There was a man standing right in front of him, bathed in moonlight, looking down at him and holding a water dipper. Nagaro was not entirely surprised to see that it was Roheed.

With a groan, Nagaro struggled to stand up. His knees must have buckled under him when his mind slipped into unconsciousness, and he'd been virtually hanging by his bound arms. Now his shoulders ached horribly. When he worked the fingers of his hands, he was relieved to feel a painful prickling as the blood began to flow back into them. His back stung and throbbed when he moved.

Roheed was still standing there in front of him, though they were eye to eye now that Nagaro was on his feet—or nearly eye to eye. Nagaro was slightly taller, barefoot, than Roheed was with boots on. Wordlessly, the young Mautep extended his hand, offering the dipper again. Nagaro accepted with a grateful nod. He had to swallow fast as Roheed poured the water into his mouth.

When Nagaro had drained the dipper, he felt much better. "Thank you," he said.

Roheed spoke then for the first time. "What I must do?"

It seemed to be a question, but Nagaro did not understand it. A movement from the vicinity of the next post suddenly reminded him that there were other sufferers, and he asked, "Will you give water to my friends?"

Roheed shifted uncomfortably. His face was hard to read in the moonlight. "Baruk say they attack him," he said reproachfully. "You not attack—only help a little."

It struck Nagaro that the young Mautep had something else on his mind. There was tension in his voice and his movements. Nagaro frowned. What Roheed had said was true, of course, but it also seemed to be another example of how the young Mautep tried to justify helping Nagaro by placing him in a category apart from the other slaves. "They didn't hurt him badly. They were only trying to get the key," he said defensively.

"They try escape?" Roheed's voice was disapproving.

Nagaro felt anger rise in him. "They are *warriors,*" he said tightly. "Like you, Roheed. What would you have them do? What would you do if you were taken and made a slave?"

"Tha's right," Landros suddenly spoke, his voice a hoarse croak. "A warrior has t' do his best t' 'scape."

"Or die tryin'." Tredhold didn't sound much better.

"Aye. Or die tryin'," Landros reiterated grimly.

Still Roheed hesitated. He addressed Nagaro. "On Chitaopa, you not try to escape," he ventured.

"That's because I told you that I wouldn't, if I were allowed to tend the men," Nagaro explained patiently.

"You not try to escape again," Roheed admonished. "Next time they maybe kill you."

Nagaro gave him a hard look. "Next time we might succeed," he said coldly. "If I see a good chance, I will take it." He paused, then added, as evenly as he could, "Will you give my friends some water?"

Roheed chewed his lip and glanced back and forth between Nagaro and Landros. Then abruptly, he turned and took a few steps to stand in front of the sea warrior. The young Mautep carried a large leather water flask slung from a strap on his shoulder. Now he filled the dipper from it and gave Landros a drink. Then he moved to Tredhold and did the same. He had no sooner finished, however, than he came back to stand in front of Nagaro. He thrust the dipper into his belt and crossed his arms. "Now you tell me," he demanded. "What I must do?"

Nagaro studied the young man. Roheed's stance suggested that he hoped to appear master of himself and of the situation, yet the youth couldn't hide his agitation. It seemed to Nagaro that he had only crossed his arms to keep them from shaking.

Nagaro shivered in a sudden breath of salt wind. He leaned against the post, still working his fingers, which had almost stopped prickling. "I do not understand," he said cautiously. "What do you want me to tell you?"

"You do not know what have happen?" Roheed sounded surprised. "You not know what happen this day just past?"

Nagaro was frankly indignant. "I've been here—tied to this post. No one has spoken to us all day. How could I know?"

Roheed took a step closer. He was staring fixedly into Nagaro's face. "My father hurt very bad," he said, and now his voice shook. "My father go hunt tiger. He go alone. Tiger attack him. Dakataar say maybe he go to die!" There was a hint of desperation in the young man's voice as he continued. "What I must do? Please... You tell me now!"

Nagaro heard Landros' sharp intake of breath. This news explained a great deal, but the way that Roheed was looking at him was alarming. "I am not a healer," he said, speaking carefully. "Maybe you should talk to Tred—the man on the other end. He's a ship's doctor."

"No!" Roheed was emphatic. "My father have very good dakataar already." The youth plunged on. "This morning just past, Raak beat you with whip, and I not stop him. When I go home, I find out tiger attack my father. Is happen just after Raak beat you! You tell me what I must do... to make it stop!"

Nagaro straightened. He shivered again, although this time there was no wind. He didn't like this at all. He had to make Roheed understand that this had nothing to do with him. "I am a follower of the Path of Vothra," he said. "We do not believe in curses or prophesies. Vothra says you should do what you believe is right because you feel it in your heart—not because you're afraid of punishment."

Even by the light of Talebra's half disk, Nagaro could see Roheed's eyes go wide. The young Mautep dropped his arms, and stepped back a pace. "*Keshaal!*" he whispered hoarsely. "That what *she* say! Now I know you are Sindar—come from dead!"

Nagaro was stunned. This was even worse! He couldn't let Roheed believe something like this. "What *who* said?" he asked desperately. "Not the dream reader surely... Do you mean Emril...?"

"See! *You know story!*" Roheed managed to sound excited, frightened, and accusing all at the same time. He was staring at Nagaro, his fists clenched at his sides.

"Everyone knows the story, Roheed! Everyone in the slave barn knows it because Pavo Maat told it to us. Everyone in the whole city has known it for years!" Nagaro wrenched at his bonds in his frustration. "Listen, Roheed," he continued. "The words I just said—about doing what you believe is right—are words from the *Book of Vothra*. If Emril said the same thing, it's because she was a follower of Vothra too, like me. That's all."

But Roheed either didn't understand or wasn't impressed. "Even you look like her," he said in an awed tone. "She have same eye, like you!"

Nagaro groaned. "That's because we're both Kelorin. We're *of the same people!* Most Kelorin people have gray eyes," he protested.

But it was no use. There was a light of revelation in Roheed's eyes. "I know what must I do," he said. "I take you to my father house—to live there. You be my brother. Then maybe my father not die, and tiger go away!"

Nagaro sagged against the post and closed his eyes. Invisible walls were closing in around him. There was no telling what other ridiculous notions the young Mautep's overwrought mind might produce if he didn't suggest a more reasonable alternative—and quickly.

"No, Roheed," he said. "I don't think that would do any good." He opened his eyes and fixed the young Mautep with his gaze. "Listen to me, Roheed," he said, speaking as slowly and calmly as he could. "And tell me. Why do you think your father went out alone to hunt the tiger? Was it because he believed he had to?"

He had Roheed's full attention now. The young Mautep's eyes were riveted on his face, and when the young man answered, the anguish in his voice was wrenching. "*He go for save me!* He think tiger come for *me!*"

Nagaro nodded grimly. "But he didn't have to go *alone*, did he? That was a dangerous and foolish thing to do. Is he still trying to pay for what he did all those years ago? Is he trying to die? To trade his life for yours?"

Roheed stood, rigid. "I not know," he said huskily. "I think... maybe is true."

Nagaro sighed heavily. "This is not good," he murmured.

"Why? *What I must do?*"

Roheed was still hoping for an answer. Nagaro was honestly trying to give him one, even if it wasn't the kind of answer the young Mautep wanted. "I'm not sure there is anything you can do," he said carefully. "Not if your father really believes he has to die. He will find a way—this time or another time. And if he's hurt so badly that his body cannot heal, of course, it's already too late..."

"But... must be *something*..." Roheed was pleading.

"There is just one chance that I can see," Nagaro told him earnestly. "You have to try to change his mind."

"Change his... *mind?*"

"Tell him that he has already paid enough. If he can believe that, he won't go looking for death anymore."

Even by moonlight, Roheed's stunned incredulity showed in his face. "You say my father *already pay enough?* How it can be true? How he can believe it?"

It was a fair question. How indeed? Nagaro considered. "I will tell you what Vothra says," he decided. "I think that Emril was Vothrin, so she would have told you the same thing if she had lived. Vothra says if a man makes a mistake—no matter how bad it is—and he cannot put it right, it is enough that he knows he did wrong, and that he is sorry."

Roheed's brow furrowed. "He know he do wrong, and he is sorry? Is *enough?*"

"Yes." Nagaro said it with all the conviction he could muster.

"How is it be enough?"

"It *has* to be. Otherwise there is no hope, and no life."

"And this what Emril say?"

"Yes. If she were here, she would say it." Nagaro was not entirely comfortable with expressing such certainty, but he had faith in Vothra's wisdom, and this was not the time for hedging. If only Roheed would stop looking at him as if he were some sort of oracle.

"Sheptuum send you for tell me this? You Sindar spirit come back from *Chofeer Naak?*"

Nagaro shook his head. There was a limit to what he could bring himself to say. "I don't think so, Roheed," he said wearily. "If the baby, Sindar, died before I was born, it's possible that his spirit walks in me, but I would never know it. That's what Vothra teaches us."

Apparently his words were enough because Roheed nodded. "I tell my father," he said, then added, "Thank you for tell me this." He took a step backward as if he meant to go, but then he suddenly stopped dead, and his brow constricted once again. "But still I must help *you,*" he said with renewed urgency. "I still not pay blood debt that dream reader tell me. Is because baby Sindar die so I can live. Tell me what must I do for *you!*"

"I have already told you, Roheed. You should do what you believe is right, because you feel it in your heart."

Roheed's frown deepened. "I want make you free man," he said seriously. "You should not be slave. But you not want to come live in my father house?"

"I will not leave all my friends."

"Then... is nothing?"

Nagaro heaved a sigh. "You could give me some more water."

Roheed made haste to do so. Without being asked, he gave more water to Landros and Tredhold as well. "In morning they cut you loose... all three," he told them. "Is already past middle of night."

The wind had been freshening, and a gathering mass of cloud rode suddenly across the pale moon, quenching Talebra's light. Roheed gave a little gasp and glanced at the sky. "My father...!" He turned and was gone, vanishing swiftly into the darkness, the sound of his running footsteps receding in the direction of the gate.

After a long moment of silence, Landros said, "Ye could have had anything ye asked for... and ye asked for *water!*" He didn't sound angry, just amazed.

Nagaro felt tired. "I couldn't use his belief for more than that."

"Ye don't think the gods might have sent ye here for some purpose then?" Tredhold asked. The healer sounded serious, although Nagaro couldn't see his face.

Nagaro laughed bitterly. "I'm afraid my life has been complicated enough without imagining that it was all arranged to bring me to this place just for Roheed's benefit."

"But ye've done him a service," Tredhold continued. "Ye may just have saved Notep's life—though I don't know why ye did it."

"That's easy, Tred," put in Landros. "Nagaro doesn't fancy being trotted off to Notep's palace and made into a Mautep prince!"

Nagaro frowned in the darkness. Landros was only half right, but he didn't feel like admitting that he had been moved by the picture of Roheed and his father, each desperately trying to save the other. "I've never had the slightest desire to be any kind of a prince," he muttered under his breath.

The storm hit an hour before dawn. Shortly after dawn, the Hashtep came slogging through the rain to cut the three men down and return them to the slave barn, wet, sore, hungry, and exhausted.

Chapter 24: Means Of Escape

Landros insisted on telling the tale of their encounter with Roheed to everyone in the slave barn. Nagaro waited only for the arrival of the morning food and then stretched himself on his belly in the straw with his face cradled in his arms to try to sleep. His back stung, and slumber did not come quickly enough to spare him from hearing the grizzled sea warrior launch into a detailed recounting of the night's events. Feigning sleep did spare him the need to say anything about it, however, and he resorted to the same tactic repeatedly in the days that followed, while the storm raged on raggedly, leaving the slaves nothing better to do than talk about the whole affair. Pretending to be unconscious allowed him to avoid the uncomfortable questions, as well as the looks.

Within a few days, it seemed that all the folk of Sar Tipaal—Mautep and Hashtep alike—had learned of Notep's fate and seemed to accept it as the judgement of Sheptuum. Lord Baalkir's brother would live, but his confrontation with the tiger had scarred his face and body, and he would probably never regain the full use of his right arm. The tiger on the other hand had been found dead from the wounds Notep had inflicted. This last was taken as a sign that Roheed's life was no longer in danger.

There was more, of course. For one thing, it was known among the stable boys that Roheed had been in the shipyard on the night following Notep's misadventure. It was even suspected that he had spoken with the three men tied to the posts. It seemed that the shipyard guards saw a great deal but knew better than to interfere with the doings of Lord Baalkir's nephew. Then there were some rather confused details: Notep (or perhaps it was Roheed) had been visited by the spirit of Emril (or perhaps it had been the spirit of Sindar), which had come to deliver the message that Notep had suffered enough.

All of this the slaves learned by listening to the conversation of the Hashte stable boys, who seemed to revel in a kind of vicarious involvement. Pavo was very nearly as bad. The story of Roheed was one of the greatest tales ever to come out of his native city, and here it was elaborating itself right before his eyes! He was indignant that the tales made no mention of Nagaro. Nagaro, for his part, was very glad they didn't.

Eventually, the storm did pass, and the slaves were returned to their labors. On the first such morning when the Mautep came to the barn, many eyes followed Roheed. The young Mautep went about his duties with a steady hand and a wooden countenance. Only once, when Roheed passed close to Nagaro while none of the other Mautep were looking, did the two young men's glances meet. It was only for an instant. Then Roheed inclined his head as if in acknowledgment. Glancing hastily away, Nagaro saw that Pavo was looking hard at him.

It was soon clear that Baruk had come to regard his three attackers as troublemakers. After the failed escape attempt, Nagaro, Landros and Tredhold were never chained close to one another. In fact, they weren't chained next to the same man two nights in a row. Nagaro had to wait several days to hear Taru's opinion of what had happened. When at last the two friends chanced to be chained next to each other, Taru wasted no time in getting around to the subject.

"So," he muttered, "why'd ye let Roheed believe that ye're Sindar when ye told me ye're not?"

Nagaro sighed. "He thought I was Sindar's ghost come back from the dead, not Sindar in the flesh. It's possible that his spirit walka in me, but not likely. And Roheed was going to believe it no matter what I said."

Taru sniffed. "Well, as long as ye're not playing favorites."

Nagaro managed a weak smile. "Do you think you could persuade someone to tell a story tonight?" he asked.

"Ye mean, to give them something else t' talk about?" Taru grinned. "Aye, I can do that."

There was immediate interest when Taru broached the subject to the men, and Tredhold volunteered to give them the tale of the fall of the Rithral Lords—how Naibarad the Destroyer had brought the other Rithral Lords down, one by one, and laid a curse on the land of Arlinas so that all the people of Arlinas had fled. It was a story unknown to the Hashtep, who listened to Pavo's translation with avid interest. Most of the Turowan slaves hadn't heard the story either, and even the Leithians and Kelorin who knew it in general terms couldn't offer an explanation of the exact nature of Naibarad's curse. Tredhold's description was as good as any:

"They say that all the old cities became places of fear, so that any man who tried to go into one of them was stricken with madness," the healer explained. "And many o' those who went in never came out alive."

"And this curse still there?" Pavo inquired after translating for his fellow Hashtep.

"As far as anyone knows," Tredhold replied. "We get stories from the town o' Kunai, that's to the north, on the other side o' the Goreitha Mountains. Folk say the land is still under a shadow."

There were more questions, although there were few answers.

Nagaro listened in silence, relieved that the men had finally found a new topic of conversation.

*

Shortly thereafter, the mystery of what Baruk had been doing alone that morning in the slave barn was finally solved. It turned out that the Slave Master had indeed been "taking stock of his stable-full of horse-flesh" as Tredhold had put it, and considering what sort of specimens would make the best additions to it. Long before the new men were brought in and chained in their places, the Hashtep slaves had learned exactly how many there would be.

The new galley slaves were drawn from the prisons of Sar Tipaal and arrived in the shipyard in big cage-like ox-carts. The various slave masters were allowed to pick from among the unfortunate wretches, with the number and order of the picks determined by both need and merit. Baruk was allowed a total of five because the ranks of slaves from the *Fist of Death* had been so badly depleted. He also had the first three picks because the *Fist's* slaves had worked so well in the shipyard. This still left the *Fist's* oar deck under-manned. The difference would have to be made up by slaves captured once they set sail—and by lone men.

No one was surprised to see that there was one very large man among Baruk's choices. The man's name was Chaheel, and the veteran Hashtep wasted no time in making him understand his special status. All of the new arrivals were quickly acquainted with the unusual com-radery that existed among the slaves of the *Fist of Death*. The Turowan lone man, Nanu, exchanged glances of commiseration with Chaheel. They might be of different races, but they were united by the knowledge that each of them would have no benchmate and would be expected to handle an oar alone.

With midwinter past, the Mahuk New Year came, and the occasion was marked by another gift from Roheed. This time the young Mautep brought small round cakes flavored with honey that were doled out one to each slave. Each cake was marked with a symbol pressed into the dough. Pavo explained that these were a traditional food eaten to celebrate the holiday. The symbols were letters from the Mautep writing system. Neither Pavo nor any of the other Hashtep slaves could read, but they all knew what the symbols meant. The letters represented various good wishes for the New Year—such things as health, wealth, and long life. The irony of this new revelation wasn't wasted on the galley slaves, though it didn't prevent them from devouring the cakes with relish.

Nagaro held up the cake that had been tossed to him by a disinterested stable boy. "What about this one?" he asked Pavo.

"That one say 'luck.'"

Nagaro looked down at the cake in his hands. *Luck.* A gift of chance was indeed what he needed. But the little cake was only honey-flavored bread.

*

Life in the slave barn settled back into its numbing routine, as one week ground its way into another. No opportunity for escape presented itself and even talk of escape became infrequent. So the winter dragged on, until the end of one drizzly gray day of labor in the shipyard when Nagaro felt someone jostle against him as the work gangs were returning and being lined up outside the slave barn. He glanced at the man who'd bumped him and found himself looking into the face of Simion.

For an instant, the youth's deep blue eyes locked with his. Then Simion glanced down at his right hand and Nagaro's eyes instinctively followed. Cupped in Simion's grimy fingers were two small pieces of blackened, rust-spotted metal. They were pieces of broken saw blade, the jagged saw-teeth running along one edge of each. Nagaro glimpsed them only for a second. Then Simion's fingers closed on them and he slipped the metal fragments into the pocket of his ragged uniform pants. The next moment, the two men were separated as Simion's work gang was marched away towards the open door of the slave barn.

Neither Simion nor Nagaro dared to say or do anything about what Simion had found while the stable boys were still about. As soon as the slaves had finished what passed for dinner and their Hashtep keepers had gone, however, Simion reached into his pocket and brought out the pieces of saw blade. Silently the youth reached out and offered the two objects to Tredhold, who was chained next to him.

Tredhold's face glowed with excitement as he turned the pieces of metal over in his hands and felt of the teeth with his thumb. "These are good, Simion!" he exclaimed. "*Very* good. Of course it'll be hard to use them without some sort o' handle. Just a bit o' wood would do—along the back of it here, so the edge wouldn't cut into your hand."

Without a word, Simion reached into his other pocket. He pulled out two small pieces of wood and proffered these to the healer.

Tredhold's jaw dropped. "By the Gods," he breathed. "Well done, lad! That's using your head, that is."

Simion's face lit up in response to this praise. The gratitude in the young man's eyes was almost painful to behold. The healer seemed not to notice, however. He'd already turned away and was passing the two objects across the barn to Landros. From there, the two fragments of metal soon made the rounds of the entire slave barn, amid a babble of excited voices. There followed a discussion of how the pieces of blade could best be used.

"How long do ye think it'd take to cut through your cuff with one o' these, Tred?" Landros asked. He was already busy using one of the metal fragments to cut a groove into one of the pieces of wood.

The healer made an experimental pass at the raw edge of his own leather cuff with the second piece of blade. "Several hours," he replied grimly. "The teeth are none too sharp, and the leather's awfully thick and tough. Ye might get through it by morning."

"So two men could get free in one night, with luck. But we need to get the four of us loose—all at once." Landros frowned thoughtfully. He'd succeeded in cutting a quarter inch groove in the wood and had slid the back edge of the blade into it, but the fit was too loose to be useful.

"Try wedging a bit o' straw in there next to the blade." Mendorel suggested.

"Good idea, mate." Landros gave the other Kelorin an appreciative glance.

"We'll have to pass them back and forth..." Tredhold was thinking aloud while he attempted to imitate what Landros had done with the other scrap of wood "If we cut all four of our cuffs the same way, and take two, maybe three, nights... we could all get free on the third night."

"The Mautep 'll see that your cuffs are half cut-through." Moraga had been listening and watching with interest. Though his comment was critical, it lacked his usual derisive tone, and there was a new light in his eyes.

Pavo spoke up then. "You not do like Tred show you," he said, illustrating with his finger held horizontally to imitate sawing at the edge of his own cuff. "They see cut that way. This is how you do." He turned his finger vertically and illustrated sawing up and down across the whole width of the leather. "That way, cut not show so much. And you rub dirt on it. Make cut place look dark like other part of leather."

Moraga nodded thoughtfully. "They *might* miss that for two days. Ye've maybe got a chance, mates. But if they do see it, they'll change yer leather and whip ye hard! An' if your lot gets away, they'll have every bit of straw out o' this place, an' strip us all t' the skin 'til they find what ye did it with. None o' the rest of us'll get a chance..." His voice trailed off.

Landros gave the Turo a questioning look. "So ye're feeling ready to risk the skin o' your own back now, are ye?"

Moraga shrugged. "I might be."

Landros nodded. "We'll try to find a place to hide the tools."

Moraga looked gratified, but his next remark was a challenge all the same. "Ye haven't said what ye'll do for provisions."

There followed a discussion of this problem. Provisions were difficult. Saving bread in their pockets was the best thing any of the men could think of as far as food was concerned. Water was harder. There were several cisterns scattered about the shipyard. All anyone could think of was searching around near one or more of these to see if the Mautep had left a bucket or dipper.

"If you can't find anything like that," Nagaro ventured, "you should at least drink your fill before you go."

From the corner of his eye, he caught Simion's anguished look. Nor was it the first time he'd seen Simion turn a pleading glance in his direction since Landros and Tredhold had begun to make their plan. It seemed that Simion either wanted to say something or wished Nagaro might say it. But Nagaro had no idea what it was.

Landros wasted no time in setting the plan in motion once it had been formed. The weather had been foggy the last several nights, which would aid their escape. While there was reason to think the trend would continue, no one knew for how long. No one was interested in a story that evening. Most of the men just lay down to sleep while the Fleet men plied their bits of saw blade. The four former sea warriors were still passing their improvised tools back and forth and sawing away in the dark when Nagaro drifted into slumber. They looked a bit haggard in the morning, having gotten only a few hours' sleep before being roused for breakfast.

Nagaro got a brief look at Tredhold's cuff as the men were eating their tasteless gray porridge. The healer had done a good job of darkening the cut place so it didn't stand out. Still, it seemed awfully obvious to Nagaro, who was looking for it. At least, he thought, Tredhold had made good progress during the night. He caught himself holding his breath when the Mautep came and began forming the slaves into the morning work gangs. This was the time when their captors usually inspected their cuffs and chains. The inspection must have grown a bit lax, however, for the slaves were linked into work gangs and marched out of the barn without incident. The day's work and the evening's return to the slave barn were also uneventful. Landros, who seemed able to sleep under almost any conditions, stretched out to take a nap before supper. Gurd, and eventually Simion, tried to follow his example. Tredhold sat tensely gnawing his lip.

As soon as the stable boys had departed after the evening meal, the two pieces of saw blade emerged from pockets, and the four men set to work again. For the second night in a row, no tale was told. The morning light revealed that there'd been less progress the second night than the first. All four men had blisters on their hands, and they'd decided sometime after midnight that less work and more sleep sounded like a good idea. Nagaro overheard Landros admitting to Mendorel that they weren't likely to be finished as early that night as he'd hoped.

Breakfast came and went, and the Mautep appeared as usual to form up the work gangs. It was while they were moving Landros into a line with two of the Hashtep that disaster struck. Fataan was stooping to secure Landros' chain to the second man's when he suddenly pointed at Landros' cuff and gave a shout. Watching from halfway down the slave barn, Nagaro felt his stomach twist as the Hashtep stable boys immediately converged on the sea warrior. Landros was flung to the ground and searched very thoroughly by half a dozen pairs of hands.

Apparently, no cutting implement was found on Landros' person, and there followed a kind of organized pandemonium. Nagaro had the opportunity to learn several new words in Hashti—words that meant "cut," "leather," "knife," and "escape." Baruk barked orders. Raak stalked up and down, making sure the orders were obeyed to the letter. Landros was quickly bound hand and foot. The slaves who'd already been linked together were hastily separated and returned to their places along the walls of the slave barn. Fataan and Roheed began an inspection of all of the slaves' cuffs, working their way from the end closest to the door, each taking one side of the barn. Behind them, and moving more slowly, came two teams of stable boys whose task was to carefully search every slave, regardless of the condition of his cuff.

Nagaro watched in a kind of agony as Fataan gave another shout when he came to Tredhold. From the corner of his eye, he caught a movement on the other side of the barn. Turning, he saw Simion standing at the small window that was closest to him. The young Kelorin withdrew his hand from the stone sill and stepped back. Then he sat down in his usual position with his arms hugging his knees and his head down as if awaiting the inevitable.

From where he sat, Nagaro could not see whether there was anything on the sill. He hastily dragged his eyes away from it, just as a shout went up from the stable boys who had been searching Tredhold. One of the Hashtep triumphantly held aloft a piece of broken saw blade with its improvised wooden handle.

Tredhold was immediately trussed as Landros had been. Despite the discovery of the tool, the search continued for the full length of the barn, although it became noticeably more cursory. The Mautep had no reason to expect that they would find any more cutting implements, and the damaged cuffs were easy to spot at a glance. They soon picked out Gurd and Simion and bound them as well. They did not, however, find the other piece of saw blade.

It was Roheed who was performing the inspection on Nagaro's side of the barn—perhaps not by coincidence. The young Mautep's face registered a flicker of relief when he found Nagaro's cuff intact, though he studiously did not meet Nagaro's eyes. He also gave Nagaro's pockets no more than a hasty pat.

It was only after Roheed had passed on along the line of slaves that it occurred to Nagaro to think of the ring he wore concealed about his waist. He was intensely grateful that he hadn't been searched more carefully.

*

This time the other slaves were all marched out and made to watch the whipping. The four former Fleet crewmen were each given eight lashes, and left hanging in their bonds as the work gangs were marched away to their day's labor.

Nagaro's mind was darkened all through that day by thoughts of the four men and the failed escape attempt. He remembered his own ordeal and found himself wondering whether the idea of escape for any of them was just an empty dream.

When the work gangs were returned to the barn that evening, they found Landros and the others already inside, lying stretched on their stomachs on a fresh layer of straw bedding.

After the Mautep had gone, Landros sat up gingerly. "Eight lashes, and half a day on the post," he observed, almost jauntily. "I guess trying to escape ain't so bad a crime as laying hands on our sweet friend Baruk!"

"Aye," observed Moraga. "That was bloody rotten luck, mate! All ye needed was one more day an' we could ha' seen how far ye got across the yard afore the guards nabbed ye." His tone was kinder than his words.

"Well, at least we've got us a fresh load o' straw," Tego pointed out. "The old stuff was stinkin' pretty bad."

"Huh! Don't talk to me about straw!" Gurd sat up abruptly, wincing. He pointed a finger at Simion. "That puddin'-livered crossy says he went and threw the other blade in the straw! And they've gone and swept it out! Probably thought he wouldn't get so many stripes if they didn't find it on him."

Simion stirred slightly at this, but he said nothing. Nagaro frowned. He was almost certain Simion had put the blade on the window sill. But if the youth had done that, why would he say he had thrown it into the straw?

Tredhold rolled onto his side. "Leave Simion alone, Gurd," he said quietly. "There wouldn't have been any blades in the first place if he hadn't found them."

"Well," said Landros, "if anyone finds another piece o' cutting tool, I think maybe we'd better keep it in our pockets 'til we're back aboard the ship and far to the north o' here. The more I think about it, the more I think Moraga is right. We'd never ha' made it out of this place in one o' those little boats. But if we were in Edroviran waters, we'd only have to swim ashore."

If the second piece of saw blade had indeed been swept out with the straw, the stable boys apparently failed to find it. The Hashtep slaves heard no mention of a second blade in the talk they overheard during the days that followed.

All the slaves were looking for tools now with redoubled interest, but they looked in vain. Perhaps the Mautep shipyard workers had all been warned to be more vigilant. Or perhaps Simion's find had just been uncommon luck.

*

Eventually the season turned, bringing fairer weather. On the first really bright, sunny day, Nagaro and the other fair-skinned slaves suffered a bad sunburn. Two days later, Roheed appeared with a bundle of squares of cloth, each with two crossed slits in the middle so a man might put his head through. These rude sun shades went to any of the men who wanted them. Many of the Turowan and Hashtep slaves, whose brown skins protected them from the sun, took one of the pieces of cloth to serve as padding when they had to carry lumber on their shoulders. More than one of them gave Nagaro a nod of thanks. He answered only with a shrug, refusing to acknowledge any connection between himself and the kindness of Lord Baalkir's nephew.

The approach of spring meant that soon Lord Baalkir's fleet would set sail, but before this happened, news came to Sar Tipaal of an event of great importance to all of the people of the Mahuk Baar. It arrived at the great house of Lord Baalkir in the dead of night, carried by a lone rider on a foam-streaked horse. By dawn, the news had spread to every manor house in the city, and the house servants had carried it to half the populace before the sun had reached its zenith. The other half knew by nightfall.

It was obvious even to the non-Hashtep slaves in the *Fist*'s barn that something was afoot from the tense, hushed conversation of the stable boys who brought them their breakfast. The Hashtep slaves exchanged significant glances as they ate their porridge. Nagaro could catch only one word consistently, but it seemed a significant one. As soon as the stable boys had closed the doors, he turned to Pavo.

"I'd guess that someone important has died," he said.

Pavo nodded. "Is old emperor," he said quietly. "Everyone expect this for long time, because he old and sick. But he live so long, sometime it seem it never go to happen. Now it have happen, and there will be very much war between warlord."

"What does that mean for Edrovir?" Nagaro asked. "If the warlords fight more among themselves, will they pay less attention to attacking Edroviran ships?"

Pavo looked doubtful. "Still they need have gold and slave," he said. "Maybe need more even than before."

Landros had been listening. "What does it mean for us, mate?"

Pavo turned his impassive face to the grizzled Kelorin. "It mean when we sail, we go to be in more sea battle," he said matter-of-factly.

"Can ye guess which one o' the bloody bastards is going to come out on the top o' the heap?" Gurd inquired. "Which one will be the new emperor?"

Pavo's brows knit together. "Everyone say is go to be Lord Baalkir or Lord Angkat," he said soberly. "Or maybe Lord Tuluptak. He also very strong. But Lord Baalkir and Lord Angkat, they hate each other long time. Some of warlord, they already start to join with one or other." He paused, considering. "Yes," he said after a moment. "I think most bad battle is go to be between Baalkir and Angkat. That mean we are go to be in middle of it."

Chapter 25: The Last Tale

It was mid afternoon of the last day in Sar Tipaal for the men of Lord Baalkir's fleet, free and slave. Tomorrow the ships would sail. It was a holiday for the Mautep crewmen—a final day to spend with their wives and families. The slaves were just left to sit idle in the barns in the stifling heat. For the slave crew of the *Fist of Death*, it was an opportunity for one last tale. They knew there would be no tales on the oar deck. It was simply too big, and a raised voice would bring down the wrath of the slave tenders.

The Hashtep slaves had pressed for a tale out of Turowan history, but the request presented some difficulty. History consisted mostly of exactly the kind of unpleasant happenings that the Turo preferred to avoid. Tego went so far as to claim that the Turo had no history.

Taru immediately objected. "How can ye say that?" he demanded. "The story o' Nevrath and Princess Minowei is history, isn't it?"

"Well, aye. That's so."

Nagaro had been lying on his back in the straw and he now sat up. "That tale is part of Kelorin history too," he pointed out. "Nevrath was a Kelorin lord."

"Aye, but Minowei was a Turowan princess," Taru countered. "So it's just as much a Turowan tale as a Kelorin one!" He tossed a handful of dirty straw at Nagaro, who easily dodged it.

"Then tell us story!" Pavo's eager voice rang from the other side of the barn.

"Aye! Tell it!"

"Tell it, Taru!"

Taru's expression said he would gladly have avoided the honor, but the men wouldn't hear of it. The Hashtep in particular insisted, once Pavo had explained the situation to them in Hashti.

Taru made a face. "Oh, all right! We all know that tale in Wotana where I come from, so I guess I can tell it as well as any." He sat frowning for a moment as he gathered his thoughts, then he cleared his throat and began.

"It happened just after the Time o' Fire and Water, when Takuma was chief o' the Turo clan that lived along the shore around the mouth o' the great river—in the place we call Ulana Kura. That's Lankura to ye lot," he added condescendingly to Nagaro and Mendorel, the Kelorin sitting closest to him.

"We all know where it was," Landros growled from where he lay stretched in the straw. "Just get on with the story."

"All right! I'm about to!" Taru shifted his position and continued. "Minowei was Takuma's daughter, and we call her a princess on account o' Takuma was a chief. She was the only child he had, because her mother died birthing her."

Tego cut in eagerly. "Minowei means 'dawn.' They say she was born just as the sun came peepin' over the hills, and afore the whole face of it even showed, her mother's spirit flew away to Hanuroa."

"Hoy now! Who's telling this story?" Taru scowled at Tego, and the older Turowan ducked his head. Taru resumed his narrative. "Takuma loved Minowei more than anything in the world. She was beautiful and kind... and brave too." Taru paused to swat at a fly. "Ye see, in the Time o' Fire and Water, when the flaming rocks fell out o' the sky, and the earth shook, and the sea came up over the land, Minowei didn't cry or scream or cover her head. She stood right beside Takuma. They told the people not to run away, and they led them up onto the top o' the mountain—Kel Lankura, ye call it—where the waves couldn't get t' them. And they stayed there 'til the fire stopped falling and the sea went back to its place. But when the people went down from the mountain, they found that all their houses and boats were smashed or washed away."

There was a murmuring and nodding of heads among the other slaves—Kelorin, Leithian, and Hashtep. They might have many different names for what the Turo called the Time of Fire and Water, but they all recognized the description. It was a catastrophe that had come to all the lands under the sun.

Taru went on. "So they had to make all o' those things again, and it was hard because there were so many storms after the fire-fall and the sky was dark for months o' time together. But Minowei and Takuma worked right along-side the rest, and they had their village built again by the time Nevrath came."

"Ye forgot t' tell about the *Place o' Shades*." Tego dropped his voice ominously when he said the name.

"Give me a minute!" Taru scowled. "I got distracted, telling about the fire and the storms and all. But I'll tell ye about the Place o' Shades right now, and no harm done. It's like this," he went on. "The Turo always lived along the shore, on account o' being fisher folk. They knew boats, and they knew water. And the great river—ye call it Edro, but we used t' call it Ulana—is nothing but a great lot o' fresh water running

downhill. So o' course the Turo tried long ago t' take boats *up* the river..."
Taru paused significantly. "And *that's* how they came t' find out about
the *Place o' Shades*..."

Taru let the words hang while waiting for Pavo to catch up. When
Pavo had finished his translation, he looked at Taru expectantly, as did
everyone else. The only sound in the barn was the buzzing of the flies.

Taru resumed in a hushed tone. "The Place o' Shades was some
ways up the river. It must ha' been there a long time, but no one knows
quite what it was. All we know is that it was something *dark*... and *frightening*... and *dangerous*. Men that came too close to it started t' see ghosts.
Men that went into it came back raving mad—*or they didn't come back
at all!*"

Taru looked around with satisfaction at the wide eyes of his listeners. Pavo's voice becoming hushed and dramatic as he translated the
last part did nothing to dispel the mood. Taru cleared his throat. "Well,"
he said, "as ye can imagine, nobody went very far up the river in Minowei's time... not on purpose at least. So when Princess Minowei came
back t' the village one day with a strange-looking man she said she'd
met a little ways up the river, ye can guess what folk thought."

"Aren't ye goin' t' say how she found him?" Moraga demanded.

Taru frowned at the merchant seaman. "She was gathering herbs
along the river bank, and she kept going a little farther... and a little
farther... and then she came around a tree, and... there was a man lying in
the ferns by the edge of the water! He sat up when Minowei came close,
and he spoke words she couldn't understand. He looked very strange
to her too, 'cause she'd never seen a Kelorin before, with pale skin and
pale eyes. Besides that, his clothes were all wet and torn, and he had a
bad-looking cut on the side of his head.

"Now a lot o' folk would have been scared—but not Minowei. She
couldn't tell what the man was saying, but it sounded like he was being
polite, and he never laid a hand on her. Minowei wasn't afraid o' much
anyway, I guess. She just sat down next to him and set about trying t'
work out how they could understand each other. So they pointed at
things and said words and made pictures with their hands—and she
figured out that his name was Nevrath and he'd come down the river—a
long way, floating on a log. It seemed he was lost and hungry, and pretty
much in need o' help. So being a kind girl, like I said, Minowei took him
back t' the new-made village of Ulana Kura."

Taru paused again for the translation to catch up before continuing.

"Minowei didn't see any harm in Nevrath, but she was afraid of
what some o' the people would do if they knew he'd come down the
river. Being clever, she didn't say anything about that part at first—not
even to her father. So Chief Takuma welcomed Nevrath according t' the

ways of our people. He gave him food and a house in the village to sleep in." Taru paused to scratch his nose, then went on. "Now Takuma was very curious to know more about foreign lands, and he wanted t' hear Nevrath's story. So he sent Minowei every day to talk to Nevrath and learn everything she could about him. She had t' learn some of his language, and she taught him some o' hers. It took a bit o' time for her t' get all of his story, but she did in the end, and it went like this:

"Nevrath was the second son of a lord, but his father had got killed in the Time o' Fire and Water, leading his folk from their own country— what ye call Arlinas—over the mountains to get t' what we call Edrovir. It was Nevrath and his brother that were leading their people when they came out o' the mountains and into a big valley a long way up the Ulana river. It seemed a good place, so they decided to settle there. Then one day, Nevrath fell into the river and hit his head on a rock—"

"He didn't fall! He was pushed!" This came from Mendorel, who knew the story from Nevrath's point of view.

"So who pushed him then?" Moraga demanded.

"Oh, I know that!" Tego volunteered. "It was his brother! On account of he wanted t' be lord!"

"But if Nevrath was the *second* son, like Taru said," Moraga objected, "then his brother would ha' been lord anyway!"

Nagaro had intended to let Taru tell the story, but at this point he had to say something. "By the old law, Kelorin people choose whoever they think will be the best leader to be their lord," he told them. "It doesn't have to be the oldest son, or even a son of the previous lord at all. Most of Nevrath's people favored Nevrath because he was very like his father. But there were some who didn't like him, and they worked on his brother, Hindrath, and got him to challenge Nevrath. Then, when it seemed that Nevrath would be chosen anyway, some of them plotted to kill him. He was trying to escape from them when he fell into the river and was carried over a great waterfall. He hit his head on a rock, and very nearly drowned..." Nagaro stopped, feeling their eyes on him.

Taru coughed. "Ye don't really need t' know all that," he said testily. "It's enough to know that Nevrath ended up in the river with a bump on his head—like I said. He pulled himself onto a log and got carried downstream—very fast, on account o' the river was a-flood from all o' those storms after the fire-fall. He fainted from the bump on his head and didn't know how long he was floating. But when he woke up, he was in a quiet pool t' one side o' the channel, and all around him on the banks there were big stone houses."

Taru stopped again to wipe the sweat from his forehead with the back of his hand. After Pavo had caught up, he went on. "Now, this is the strange part," he said, lowering his voice a notch. "All the houses looked very grand and well kept, but there weren't any people, as if everyone had left just a little while ago. And he saw a bit of open ground with a big statue in it that shone and sparkled like it was made o' gold and crystal. It was so beautiful that it had t' be magic—and Nevrath felt he had t' go closer, like it was pulling him. So he let go of his log and started t' walk towards it..."

Taru looked around the hushed barn at his listeners. Every eye was on him. "And now it gets *really* strange," he said. "Because when he got close t' that statue, he could *feel* it was evil, and he wanted to run away... *But he couldn't!* Somehow he knew he was going to have t' break it, so he picked up a big stone. But it felt like something was fighting with him! Something he couldn't see was trying t' keep him from throwing that stone. It took all his strength to throw it, but throw it he did. And when the stone hit the statue, it smashed into a thousand pieces, and the earth started t' shake, and all the stone houses began t' fall down! So Nevrath turned around and ran—back to the river! He got onto his log an' pushed it into the current and was swept away again, fainting like he did before. And he floated that way 'til he fetched up in the place where Minowei found him."

Taru paused. After a moment, one of the Hashtep said something, breaking the silence that hung in the stifling air of the dim slave barn. "He say, this is good story," Pavo explained. "He think this story as good as story of Roheed jir-Akaan."

"Yes, well, it's not nearly over either," said Taru. "There's something I haven't explained 'cause I wanted t' get Nevrath's story all told. Ye see, Minowei had to get this whole story from Nevrath, and it took a lot o' talking, which meant they were spending a lot o' time together. And pretty soon Minowei began to take a fancy to Nevrath. And he began t' take a fancy to her. And neither one o' them was in much of a hurry t' finish their task. They made it go on for days—'til finally Takuma lost patience and ordered Minowei to bring Nevrath before him.

"Now o' course Minowei was worried about this, but Nevrath said everything would be all right if he told the truth. Then he took her hand, and he asked her if she would marry him. And o' course she said yes, but that he had t' ask her father first, 'cause that was the way of our people."

There were murmurs of approval among the Hashtep at this turn of the tale.

"Minowei hoped that her father would be pleased to let her marry Nevrath," Taru continued. "On account of he was a chief's son, and he'd broken the evil heart of the Place o' Shades when he broke the statue." Taru took a deep breath. "But Minowei didn't know that her father had dreamed the night before that he'd seen her and Nevrath walking together beside the river—and they'd been *going upstream!*"

Taru drew breath. "The dream had worried Takuma so much that he'd got up early and gone t' the dream reader—an old woman named Funara. And it happened that Funara had a son she hoped would wed Minowei. She'd seen how glad Minowei was to spend hours with the pale-skinned stranger. So when Takuma told her his dream, Funara told Takuma that Hakura Kili had sent the dream t' warn him that Nevrath was an evil spirit from the Place o' Shades who'd come t' steal Minowei away."

At this point Pavo held up his hand for a pause. "This is not good dream woman," he said. "Takuma should not listen to her!"

Taru gave the young Hashtep a grim smile. "Well, Takuma did listen to her," he said, "but he didn't altogether *believe* Funara. The stranger didn't seem evil to him, and he guessed something o' what Funara might be about. But still ye can guess how Takuma's heart was troubled when Nevrath and Minowei stood before him t' tell Nevrath's tale."

Taru frowned a little. "The telling happened in the clan's big hall—a kind o' long wooden house. The clan elders were there, and Takuma's guards, and Funara was there too. And Nevrath told his story with help from Minowei. The tale was strange enough t' worry Takuma, but what worried him more was the way Minowei looked at Nevrath and Nevrath looked at Minowei. Before the tale was done, Takuma decided that Nevrath must ha' been courting Minowei without asking his leave, and that made Takuma very angry. So when Nevrath finished and boldly asked for Minowei's hand, Takuma spoke in anger, saying that Nevrath had taken advantage of his hospitality t' steal Minowei's heart, and now he meant t' steal the rest of her as well!"

Taru paused to draw breath and saw that his audience was listening with rapt attention. He plunged on. "Then Nevrath got angry. He said that among *his* people a woman could choose her own husband, and then Minowei said that she chose Nevrath! But o' course when she said *that*, Funara stood up and said that Nevrath was an evil spirit—with his pale eyes and pale skin—who'd come from the Place o' Shades. His story was a lie, she said, and he must ha' put a spell on Minowei to make her so disrespectful to her father. And all of the clan elders believed Funara, and so did the guards. Everyone called on Takuma t' kill Nevrath before he could do any more harm. Everyone except Minowei, o' course—"

Taru stopped speaking at a sign from Pavo, who was translating frantically. When Pavo finished, the barn was deathly quiet. Even those who knew this story were caught up in the telling of it.

Taru cleared his throat. "Well," he said, "Takuma ordered all his guards to seize Nevrath—to take his knife away and bind him. There were a lot of guards and only one o' Nevrath, so there wasn't much he could do about it Then Minowei pleaded with her father to send some men up the river to see whether the Place o' Shades was still there, and t' look for other signs that Nevrath's story was true. That seemed sensible to Takuma. Although he was angry, he was a fair man. So he sent three of his guards. If they came back with a good report, Nevrath would go free. But if they came back with a bad report—or if they didn't come back in a week—Nevrath would be slain. So Nevrath was bound hand and foot and thrown into the little house they used for a prison, with a strong bar on the door and a guard to watch day and night. And they wouldn't even let Minowei in t' see him.

"Well, a week went by, and the three guards didn't come back. The elders were sure the men had come t' harm and they called for Takuma to kill Nevrath as he had promised. But Minowei begged her father for more time. If Nevrath was slain, she said, and then the men came back with a good report, how terrible must her father feel? Takuma didn't like t' see his daughter so upset. He thought maybe this was evil magic, but then again maybe it wasn't. So he gave another day, and when that one passed, he gave another, and another. But the third time he said was the last time."

Taru stopped. For a long minute, Pavo translated, while the other listeners sat in silence. When at last Pavo fell silent too, Taru continued.

"By the end o' the last day, when still the three men didn't come, Minowei knew that she had t' do something. So she went and gathered some herbs she knew and mixed them in a cup o' ale to make a sleeping potion. And she crept into her father's room and took Nevrath's knife from where she knew her father kept it. And she took a bag o' dried fish from the village storehouse. She waited 'til after dark when the village was quiet. Then she went t' the guard who stood at the door o' Nevrath's prison and flattered him and offered him the cup o' ale. And he took it, and drank it, and soon fell asleep. So Minowei crept in and cut Nevrath's bindings, and told him they must both run away that night because her father would surely kill him in the morning.

"So they stole out o' the village and went to the forest, but Nevrath stopped at the edge o' the forest and told Minowei that she had t' stay. If she went with him, it would look like he'd stolen her, just as Funara had said. Then Minowei cried, and he put his arms around her and kissed her and told her that he would come back. He said he'd go to his people, far up the river, and some o' them would surely come back with him and help him make things right with Takuma so that he and Minowei could be wed. Then he gave her the ring off his finger, that was the only thing he had. It was gold, and had a stone in it like clear water. And Minowei gave him her necklace made o' abalone shell.

"But Minowei was afraid she'd be made t' wed before Nevrath could come back. The season was turning toward winter and he might not be able to come again until spring. So she asked him t' lie with her because then no one could wed her 'til it was sure she wasn't with child. So they lay together in the forest under the stars, on a bed o' pine needles. Then Nevrath took his knife and the bag o' dried fish and set off up the river, and Minowei went back to her father's house and crept into her own bed just before dawn."

Taru paused again. Pavo finished his translation and said, "This *very* good story!"

Taru beamed, basking in this praise. Then he cleared his throat again and went on.

"Minowei made no secret of what she'd done, and all o' the folk thought she was under a spell. Takuma sent men out t' hunt for Nevrath, but they didn't find him. So three days went by. And *then*, at last, the three guards came back! They'd traveled six days up the river, and seen no ghosts and felt no terrors. They'd come to a ruined city, all of tumbled stones. They'd even found the open place beside the river where pieces of the statue lay all over the ground. They brought back pieces of gold to show Takuma, but the crystal bits had melted like water when they'd tried t' touch them!

"So everyone could see that at least a part of Nevrath's tale was true. O' course Funara asked how they knew it was Nevrath that broke the statue. But Takuma saw that the magic of the Place o' Shades was broken, so Minowei's love for Nevrath was no evil spell. He was glad that he hadn't slain the pale-eyed stranger, but he was also glad that Nevrath was gone. He wanted Minowei to marry a Turo and stay close by him. He loved her too much t' bear being parted far from her."

This time, when Taru stopped, Pavo immediately said, "This cannot be end! Nevrath, he must come back!"

Taru grinned. "Will ye just do the translating," he said with mock annoyance, "and let me tell the story?" Then he made a great show of making himself comfortable again, just to keep Pavo waiting.

"Well," he went on at last, "Minowei waited all through the winter. The spring came, and still Nevrath didn't come. O' course, Takuma didn't think Nevrath ever meant t' come back, but Minowei wouldn't listen to that. She wouldn't give up hope, but she was beginning to worry that something had happened to Nevrath.

"By this time, everyone could see that Minowei wasn't with child. So, when the clan elders all began t' say that Minowei should be wed, Takuma hoped a good husband was all she needed to make her forget Nevrath. But there were so many o' the young men that wanted t' marry Minowei that Takuma didn't know how to choose—so he decided to have a contest. He put out the word, all up an' down the coast, that there would be a contest at the next full moon, and whichever man he judged t' be the best would marry Princess Minowei.

"Now, Minowei wasn't pleased at all! She told her father she didn't want to marry a man just because he was the strongest or fastest. What if he was cruel? What if he only wanted t' marry her because she was a chief's daughter? Takuma could see the sense o' this, so he promised her he wouldn't choose any man who wasn't kind and honorable and true-hearted. Minowei still wasn't pleased, but she saw that there was nothing more she could do."

Pavo signaled again for a pause at that point, and those who weren't Hashtep had to wait while the Hashti version of the story caught up. Then, at last, Taru continued.

"When the day o' the contest came, there were twenty men waiting in the gathering place at the edge o' the village to try to pass Takuma's tests. There were some from clans to the north, and some from clans t' the south, and some from the clan of Ulana Kura. And Takuma was just about to speak to them when—all of a sudden—Nevrath stepped out o' the forest!"

This turn of the story elicited gasps and expressions of satisfaction from the audience.

"Now Nevrath was standing tall and proud," Taru continued. "He looked like a chief's son. His clothes were not torn, and he had a sword at his side and Minowei's abalone shell necklace around his neck. When some o' the village men tried t' seize him, he drew his sword to show that he wouldn't be easily taken. That stopped the village men in their tracks! The Turo didn't use swords, ye see, so none o' them had ever seen one before. Then Nevrath put his sword away. He walked up to Takuma and bowed to him, and he unbuckled his sword belt and laid it at Takuma's feet. Then he spoke in Turowan, saying Takuma could keep his sword while he was in Ulana Kura because he'd come in peace and he wanted to compete in Takuma's contest!

"Well, Takuma couldn't help being impressed, and he couldn't say no because Nevrath was bein' so polite. Besides, Minowei was standing there with her face so full o' joy that Takuma hadn't the heart to say any-thing against the man. So he let Nevrath be part o' the contest.

"Takuma began by telling them all that winning was only part o' the contest because the man he chose to wed his daughter had t' be good-hearted, honest, and honorable. Then he told them the contest had three parts. The first was shooting with a bow at three different targets. They all lined up t' take their shots, and Nevrath was the best. A man from a southern clan was second best, and Funara's son was third.

"The second part o' the contest," Taru went on, "was a race t' the top o' Kel Lankura and down again. It was a steep, hard climb, but Nevrath was right among the leaders 'til they were almost at the top. Then a rock at the edge o' the trail gave way under the man from the southern clan, and he slid down to a place where he got stuck. The man cried for help. He was cut and bleeding and couldn't get up. Well, the others heard, but only Nevrath turned back to help the man. Most o' the other men ran past Nevrath while he was about it, but he passed half o' them again before they could reach the top o' the mountain and the other half on the way down. He came to the finish, leaping like a deer, and won the race! Funara's son was second, and the man from the southern clan was far behind on account o' being hurt.

"Well, ye can just imagine how Minowei's eyes were shining! But Takuma had a frown on his face because it looked as if he'd have no choice but t' give his daughter to this pale-skinned stranger. Still, there was one more part o' the contest, and this wasn't a good part for Nevrath. It was t' swim from the shore by the mouth o' the river to a rock called Gull Rock and back again. Nevrath hadn't lived all his life by the sea, and he hadn't had much practice swimming, but he plunged in with the rest. He kept pace with them for a little way, but before he'd got halfway to the rock, he'd spent his strength and he got a terrible pain in his side and couldn't hardly keep his head up. Then he called for help, or else he was going t' drown. But none o' the other men turned back to help him."

Taru took a breath, waited a little for Pavo to finish, and went on. "Now, Takuma and Minowei had gone out in a boat to watch the race. So when Minowei saw Nevrath in trouble, o' course she pleaded with her father t' save him. Takuma knew that Minowei would never forgive him if he let the man drown, so he told his rowers t' bring the boat in close. They pulled Nevrath out o' the water, looking half dead, and laid him in the bottom o' the boat. Then Minowei knelt by him and kissed his brow and wept over him. And Takuma could see how much Minowei loved this man. Finally, Nevrath opened his eyes and looked at Minowei, and he said in the Turowan tongue, 'I am sorry that I have failed you.'"

Taru paused. "When Takuma heard those words, he finally understood that Nevrath loved Minowei as much as she loved him, and he knew he couldn't keep them apart. So when the boat came back to the shore, Takuma helped Nevrath get out of it. Then he told the other men gathered on the shore that he had decided Nevrath was the best among them because he'd won two o' the contests, and because he'd turned aside to help a man in need. And he told Nevrath that he could marry Minowei, but only if he agreed to stay in Ulana Kura, because he couldn't bear t' have Minowei be parted from him.

"Then at last, Nevrath spoke, and he said he would take Minowei only as far as the other side o' Kel Lankura—because he'd brought some of his people with him, and they were waiting for him there in a place where they meant t' build their houses and make farms. Well, Takuma was very surprised and very pleased too, because the place wasn't far away. So he gave his consent.

"Funara objected, on account of her son had won the swimming contest, and been second and third in the other two parts, while Nevrath hadn't even finished the last one. But her son spoke up, saying he'd only tried the contest to please her, and he really wanted to marry someone else. Then Funara saw how foolish she'd been, and she told Takuma his dream really meant that the spirits wanted Minowei to wed Nevrath and live just a little way up the river. And so it was all decided, and Minowei and Nevrath were married."

Taru stopped and looked around at the faces of his listeners. "And that," he said, "is the tale of how Nevrath, who was the Lord o' the House of Loros, won the hand o' Princess Minowei, of the Clan of Ulana Kura, because he couldn't swim!"

The silence that followed was not allowed to lengthen. "Ye forgot t' say that their first-born child was Darion," Tego objected. "And how he brought all the folk of Edrovir together an' became the first king!"

Mendorel coughed. "Ye also forgot to say that it was the beginning of the House of Loros, because Nevrath and his brother split the old house between 'em. Do ye know how that came about, Nagaro?"

Nagaro sighed. He *did* know, and Mendorel *had* asked. "Nevrath and Hindrath were of the House of Tyronin," he said. "It was also the house of Atheran—the man who led the Kelorin people from Kelor to Arlinas. When Nevrath returned to the valley above the waterfall after meeting Minowei, he found that the people of Tyronin Wared had thought him dead and had chosen Hindrath to be their lord. Hindrath would have yielded the rule of the Wared to Nevrath, because he was sorry for how he'd behaved before and truly glad to see his brother alive. But Nevrath wanted to return to Ulana Kura.

Many of the people didn't want to leave the new homes they'd built, so Nevrath took only those who were willing to go, and he founded a new House. He named it 'Loros,' to honor Minowei, whose name means 'dawn.' Loros means 'a growing light' and it also means 'understanding.' So it all ended peacefully. But that valley above the waterfall, and the city that's in it, have been called Vered Mahir, the 'bitter place,' ever since, because of the trouble that came between the two brothers there, and the splitting of the House of Tyronin." Nagaro stopped, feeling that he'd said more than enough.

"It was the beginning o' the end for the Turo too," Moraga observed bitterly. "The Kelorin and Leithian lords moved in an' broke up the clans, an' now there ain't no Turowan chiefs anymore."

Nagaro spoke again. "You're right, Moraga," he said. "Though it wasn't quite that simple. After Takuma died, the folk of Minowei's clan became part of Loros Wared because they chose Nevrath to be their chief. There were other Kelorin houses that made alliances with the Turo by marriage in the early days too. It wasn't entirely a bad thing for the Turo. They were peaceful folk with no understanding of war. Being part of a wared gave them protection. And when Darion became king, he made three of the old Turowan chiefs lords in their own right to give them a say in the Council of Lords. But neither Nevrath nor Darion could stop some of the other lords from laying claim to Turowan lands and making the Turo their subjects whether they wished it or not." Nagaro stopped again, conscious of their eyes on him.

"I expect that's all in Sored's history book," Mendorel put in quickly.

But Nagaro shook his head. "No, that's not in Sored's *History of the Kelorin People*," he said. "Sored died before the end of the Age of the Rithral Lords. The story of Nevrath and Minowei, and the other things I just told you, are from the *Chronicle of Later Days*."

"And ye've read 'em both cover t' cover, have ye?" This came from Moraga, who managed to make it sound as if it were some sort of crime.

Nagaro shrugged. "Yes, I've read them," he admitted. Even Taru was looking at him oddly, so he said no more.

The talk turned to other things as the afternoon slipped inexorably towards night. Nagaro lay stretched on his back in the straw watching flies circle in the air above him. The truth was that he *liked* history. He'd read and re-read every book on the subject in Maramine's library. Why did so many things he had always taken for granted keep turning out to be so uncommon?

The next morning came too soon. The slaves were not eager to be back aboard the *Fist of Death*. The shipyard work might be hard, but at least it offered the chance to move about outside in the light and air, and there was no risk of being smashed by an oar or carried to the bottom of the sea with a sinking ship. And there had been the foul-weather days when they'd been left to themselves. The slave barn was undeniably damp and dirty during "storm time," but the straw was softer than deck planking, and they'd been able to tell tales.

The prospect of being carried north, possibly close to their homes, brought an ache of longing to the hearts of the Droviri slaves, but it was a longing made bitterly hopeless by the lack of any means of getting free of their chains. And of course, most of the Hashtep had originally lived in the part of the Mahuk Baar that lay close to Sar Tipaal, so they would only be going farther from their homes with nothing to hope for but the chance that they might return relatively unscathed to the slave barn at summer's end.

Chapter 26: A Desperate Gamble

By the time they were six weeks out of Sar Tipaal, Lord Baalkir's fleet had engaged in more than a dozen skirmishes with rival warlords. The warlords had all been minor ones. Most had been unaligned and had put up a flag of truce as soon as they found themselves getting the worst of the fight. Some of these had made pacts of non-aggression as a result; others had formally aligned themselves with Baalkir. Then there were the warlords who were already aligned with Angkat or Tuluptak. These had to be defeated outright.

It had been a harrowing time for the slaves. And it would have been even worse, Nagaro reflected, except that it was actually possible to be too exhausted to be properly terrified. Still, he wouldn't forget the horror-stricken looks on faces of the four Fleet men the first time the *Fist of Death* sent another ship to the bottom. The former sea warriors had surely heard men scream before when a ship was rammed, but their looks showed plainly that they now understood that the screams came from men like those all around them, chained to their places and unable to escape their fate.

Despite all the dangers, the *Fist* and her slaves had so far escaped unscathed. Some of the other ships in Baalkir's fleet had not been so lucky, however, and Lord Baalkir prudently put into a port for repairs. That evening found the *Fist* rocking gently at anchor beside her six sister ships as the slave tenders distributed the evening meal. Fataan was still working the oar deck, but Roheed had been promoted two weeks before and replaced by a new youth named Olam. Fataan had been out of sorts ever since. He clearly attributed Roheed's rapid advancement to birth rather than merit, and missed no chance to make disparaging remarks about his former co-worker. Olam, a gullible round-faced youth, hung on Fataan's every word.

The two slave tenders were both very excited about something that evening. Nagaro caught a word here and there, but rapidly spoken Hashti still ran too fast for him to follow. The Hashtep listened avidly, however, and as soon as Fataan and Olam had gone to eat their own dinner, Pavo told the non-Hashtep slaves what he had learned.

"Baalkir have decide to divide fleet in two part," Pavo told them. "*Fist* go north with two other ship that not so much hurt. They try to take gold and slave in water around those island called *Fa-ra-no*. Other four ship stay here for be mended. All seven ship meet at Sar Tipaal after eight week have passed."

The news caused an immediate stir among the Edroviran slaves. The mission would take them back to their home waters! Nagaro could see his own frustrated longing mirrored in the other men's eyes.

"All the way t' the Faranos!" Taru exclaimed. He took a bite of dried meat, chewed laboriously, and swallowed. "That's just off Wotana Bay—but it might as well be the dark side o' Talebra!"

Baruk had shifted some of the slaves' positions, and Nagaro was again chained next to Pavo, not far from the aft end of the oar deck on the starboard side. Taru was on the bench behind him, paired with Tego. Simion and one of the new Hashtep were chained at the bench in front of him.

"I'm thinking it must be Evrel by now," Taru went on. "That means it's been pretty near a year since they took Nagaro and me. A *year!*" He addressed Nagaro. "Can ye believe it? I never thought we'd be a year in these chains! I must ha' nearly turned twenty, if I haven't already!"

Nagaro swallowed a mouthful of biscuit. "I've almost surely passed my twentieth birthday, Taru," he said. "I try not to dwell on it."

"How can ye not—" Taru began. Then he stopped. "When *is* your birthday, Nagaro? Ye've never said."

Nagaro's brows came together in a frown. He supposed there was no harm in telling the truth. "I don't know exactly," he said. "I mark it on the third of Evrel because that's the day my Lady Guardian found me, but it's likely I was born in the last week of Madrel."

"But that'd make ye older than me by a whole month!"

Nagaro had to stifle a smile at the expression on his friend's face. Apparently Taru had imagined himself to be the elder. "Well of course I'm older than you, Taru," he said with mock severity. "And maybe you'll show me more respect now that you know it!"

Taru gaped at him for a second, then burst out laughing and leaned forward on his rowing bench to aim a quick punch at Nagaro's shoulder. Nagaro laughed as he dodged the blow.

Pavo laughed with them. "You not worry so much, Taru," he said. "You almost whole *year* more old than me."

Tego shook his head at them, grinning. Even Simion, who'd been listening shyly, managed a fleeting smile.

The friends' mirth soon died however. The impending anniversary of their capture hung like a shadow over Nagaro and Taru, and Pavo had been a slave even longer. Nor could they imagine that the year ahead was more likely to bring them freedom than the one just past.

*

"Look! A Hranji." A thread of hushed whispers ran along the oar deck. Nagaro twisted around to get a better look at the second man who was being marched in chains down the oar deck's center aisle. He'd never seen an inhabitant of Hran before.

The three Mahuk ships had been sailing north for several days and had overtaken a merchant craft somewhere off the coast of Jinara. The Mautep had seized the Jinari ship, taking her cargo as booty and some of her crew and passengers as slaves. The *Fist* had been allotted two men, the first of whom had already been chained next to the Turowan lone man, Nanu, on the aft-most port-side bench. This first man was a typical Jinari, lean and hawk-featured, with straight black hair and skin a shade darker than Nanu's. He'd moved to his place with a quick step, his black eyes darting to right and left.

The second man—the Hranji—was strikingly different. He was tall, broad-shouldered, and muscular, with skin that was nearly black. The features of his face were more in the Turowan mold—the cheekbones high and wide, the nose broader and more flat. But the thing that was most strange to Nagaro was the man's hair. It resembled dark wool and was cut short, sculpted into a form that was almost helmet-like. The Hranji held his head high and moved with detached dignity. He looked to neither right nor left as he passed Nagaro on his way to the seat next to Chaheel on the aft-most bench on the starboard side. This placed the Hranji just in front of Simion and directly across the aisle from the Jinari, his former shipmate.

Nagaro was frankly rather surprised that Urchak had taken another Jinari as a slave since the previous one had refused to eat and had been thrown overboard when he became too weak to row. He remembered Mendorel explaining that Jinari beliefs didn't allow them to eat the slave rations. Did Urchak merely expect to get a few weeks' work out of the man before he had to be discarded?

As it turned out, the Hranji was an even poorer choice than the Jinari. The trouble began as soon as Baruk gave the first command to row. The Jinari resignedly bent his back to the oar, following Nanu's lead. The Hranji, on the other hand, folded his arms across his chest and sat stubbornly still and silent while Chaheel plied the oar alone.

Raak applied the whip across the Hranji's naked back whenever his stalking prowl up and down the aisle brought him aft, but the big ebony-skinned man made no move to even put his hands to the oar. The slave driver grew angrier every time he returned to find the man not rowing. At first he dealt the Hranji a single stroke of the lash each time, before turning to stride back towards the ship's bow, swearing under his breath. Then he increased the number of lashes to two. The other slaves watched in dismay as the drama unfolded.

At first Pavo frowned in open disapproval at the Hranji's behavior. Between gasping indrawn breaths, the young Hashtep gave muttered voice to his thoughts as he rowed. "Why he not row...? Does he not... want help Chaheel?"

Nagaro only shook his head as he bent and pulled to the throbbing rhythm of the drum. He had no breath for speaking, even had he known the answer. Grimly he watched as stripe after scarlet stripe appeared on the Hranji's dusky skin. Sitting only two benches behind the man, he could hear the whistle and crack of the whip and see the Hranji's blood begin to trickle. The man's back was soon scarlet from neck to waist, yet the Hranji never made a sound. He began to sway on his bench, but somehow, incredibly, he held up his head. Nagaro could hear occasional gasps or muttered comments from the other slaves, expressing disbelief and admiration.

Meanwhile, Raak was working himself into a rage. Unaccustomed to such defiance, he was swearing in full voice now as he trod the oar deck, giving less and less of his attention to the other slaves. Twice Baruk called out directives to Raak. Nagaro caught the Hashti words for "stop" and "enough," but the Slave Driver seemed oblivious to his officer's commands. Finally Raak halted, spitting fury, and planted himself behind the Hranji, where he began to flail at the man with his whip, seemingly insane with rage.

Nagaro watched in horror, even as he strained to keep pace with the drum. The black man's back was already a bloody mess of lacerated flesh and Nagaro caught a metallic whiff of blood amid the general reek of the oar deck. *Surely this couldn't go on much longer...* Silently he began to pray that Raak would see the futility of what he was doing. But the blows continued to fall.

Then, just as Raak raised his arm for yet another stroke, the Hranji abruptly toppled forward without uttering a sound, and fell sprawling on the deck planks. Raak didn't even break his rhythm. He merely took two steps forward and continued his merciless rain of blows.

Nagaro and Pavo both sprang to their feet, holding their oar out of the water. They couldn't reach the Hranji, could do nothing to stop Raak... Half of the other slaves stood up as well, some letting go of their oars. The oar-shafts clashed together in confusion. Some of the men were shouting their outrage at the scar-faced Slave Driver. Others cried out as they were struck by wildly swinging oars.

Baruk's voice rose above the tumult, bellowing commands. The drum at last beat out the signals to cease rowing and to ship the oars.

Raggedly, the oars stopped moving, and some of the slaves had enough presence of mind to pull theirs in through the ports. Baruk came striding down the aisle—trailing Fataan and Olam—to where Raak still implacably plied his whip. The Slave Driver appeared furious beyond all reason, all but foaming at the mouth. His fellow crew members grappled with him, struggling hard. It took all three of them to wrest the whip from Raak's grasp. Working together, they eventually succeeded in dragging the man from the oar deck, still cursing. The little lame drummer, Ul, scrambled after them pulling the aft port door closed behind him.

The dim cavern of the oar deck was suddenly silent except for the creak of timbers and the sonorous wash of waves against the hull. The silence lasted several heartbeats and then there rose a hushed susurration of voices.

Nagaro sank down onto his bench. Numbly he stared at the Hranji's inert form. The man was lying in front of the last aft bench, his upper body extending into the aisle and plainly visible to all the slaves at the stern end of the oar deck. The lacerated flesh of the man's back was horrible to look at. Blood made a spreading stain on the deck planking. How was it possible, Nagaro wondered dully, that a mere strip of braided leather could do so much damage?

Simion had remained standing, frozen in place, just behind that last aft bench and only feet from the fallen Hranji. Now the young Kelorin seemed to come out of his trance. He stooped and leaned out over the bench. Placing his hand on the fallen man's leg, he shook him gently.

"Please, Zirda," he said in a shaken voice. "Are you all right? Are you alive?"

The Hranji's face was turned towards them and Nagaro was amazed to see the man's eyes flicker open. They were dark eyes in a dark face, but the whites showed clearly. The Hranji didn't speak.

"Please, Zirda," Simion persisted. "Tell us. Why didn't you row?"

It was the Jinari who spoke, then, from the bench across the aisle. He addressed the Hranji in a tongue that Nagaro didn't recognize.

The Hranji moved his head a little and rolled his eyes to fix their gaze upon the speaker. Then, for the first time since he'd been brought onto the oar deck, the Hranji spoke. His voice was deep and resonant. He spoke softly, words that were interrupted as if he drew each breath with pain. He addressed the Jinari in what sounded like the same language the other man had used.

The Jinari listened until the fallen man stopped speaking, then raised his eyes to Simion and spoke in accented, but very fluent, Common Speech. "I am Utabala," he said, his words falling in rapid cadence. "Dis man is called Zo-Hlan Tai. He is a Hranjili merchant from Pana, and I was sent by my merchant master to be his interpreter. To answer de question dat you ask, Zo-Hlan Tai says dat he will have no part of dis evil."

"What does he mean by 'this evil'," Nagaro asked. "Does he mean slavery?"

Utabala transferred his heavy-lidded gaze to Nagaro. "I believe so, yes," he said. "De Hranjili of Pana are a most es-strange people. Even de oder Hranjili do not understand dem. Dey do no evil, nor suffer it to be done. Dey do not even like to es-speak of it."

All the men chained nearby had overheard the exchange. Moraga spoke with cold finality. "If he don't row, the Mautep'll kill him."

"Raak may have killed him already." This came from Tredhold. The healer was staring at the fallen man, his face pale. "The poor fellow is in sore need o' doctoring and I can't reach him! Though there's little to be done for him here even if I could."

At that moment, the aft door was thrust open again and the slaves' conversation ceased. Baruk entered first, with the rest of the oar deck crew—all save Raak—close behind. Baruk seemed determined to act as if nothing unusual had happened. The *Fist* had fallen behind the other two ships and would have to row hard to catch up. Accordingly, the fallen Hranji was moved just enough to no longer block the aisle, and a quick bucket of sea water washed most of the blood away. Fataan assumed Raak's role. The young Mautep strutted up and down, inexpertly flicking the lash at slackers. The whip had evidently been cleaned by dipping it in the bucket of seawater. Nagaro noticed as Fataan passed that it was dripping red-tinged liquid onto the planking.

Twice they rowed before the evening fell, with only a short respite in between. Baruk didn't even pause to examine Zo-Hlan Tai until just before leaving the oar deck at the end of the day. Apparently he didn't like what he found then, for he went out scowling.

Water was brought around, then food, then more water. Nagaro noted that Utabala looked at the meat and biscuit with distaste, and handed them to his bench mate, Nanu. When the last round of water came, Chaheel tried to give the Hranji some, shifting the man onto his side and holding his head with surprising gentleness. The Hashtep was rewarded by a weak coughing sound, but that was all.

Later, when the slaves were left alone, Simion tried rousing the Hranji, and Utabala tried talking to his former shipmate. Once more the man opened his eyes, though his gaze was now unfocussed. He spoke again as well, in a voice barely audible. Utabala listened with his head bowed. When the man fell silent, the Jinari raised his head and turned to face the rest of the oar deck. He spoke to them all in a solemn voice. "Zo-Hlan wishes dat he be remembered wit good words to de Lord of de House of Tai, should any one of us ever come to Pana."

The Hranji did not speak again before the lamps were put out for the night. In the morning, Chaheel put a hand on the man's body and found it cold. The word passed from stern to bow in whispered Common Speech and muttered Hashti. A reverent silence followed.

It was Nagaro who at length broke that silence, speaking for all of them. "I don't expect that I shall ever go to Pana," he said soberly. "But I will not forget the name of Zo-Hlan Tai, nor the manner of his passing." A general murmur of agreement ran the length of the oar deck.

The two Mautep slave handlers entered a little later and found the corpse. They went out again, speaking in low voices. Shortly thereafter, the hatch cover was opened and the winch unceremoniously employed to remove the Hranji's mortal remains.

Raak was back on the oar deck later that morning, more surly than ever. The gossip among the other Mautep was that he'd spent the night roped to his bunk and had gotten a very stiff reprimand from Baruk. It seemed the Mautep considered losing one's temper so badly to be a serious disgrace and beating a slave to death something of a waste.

*

Two days later, Nagaro was wakened by a toe gently prodding his ribs. Opening his eyes, he found that it was early morning, judging by the light, and Roheed was standing over him. Baruk was there as well, standing behind the younger man, frowning.

Roheed made a gesture, indicating that he wished Nagaro to rise. Nagaro pulled himself up onto the bench and stood up, facing Roheed. As he did so, he noticed a small gold star on the right-hand side of the collar of Roheed's scarlet tunic. It was exactly like the one on Baruk's collar. The young man's mustache was well grown in by now and neatly trimmed. His expression was unreadable. Presently he spoke, gesturing as he did so towards Utabala's recumbent form across the aisle and two benches aft. "That man not eat. You talk to him, Nagaro. Tell him eat, so he not die." Roheed's tone suggested something more than a request, but less than a command.

Nagaro gave the other young man a hard look. He didn't care for the suggestion that he could, or should, have so much influence with his fellow slaves. "That man's name is Utabala," he said coldly. "And it is his choice, whether to eat or not."

Baruk clearly did not like the tone of this utterance, for the Slave Master sucked air sharply through his teeth and moved as if he meant to strike Nagaro. Roheed stopped him with a quick motion of his hand and a few words of rapid Hashti. He then turned back to Nagaro.

"Before, we have many slave die for not eat. But after you come, there is not one. Will you not talk to him?" It seemed a straightforward question.

Nagaro frowned. "Some men choose to die rather than be slaves— men like Taru's father, or the Hranji. Or Denoras, who chose to die while

I was tending him on Chitaopa," he added pointedly. "What right have I to tell a man that he should choose to live in this place?" Nagaro made a sweeping gesture at the surrounding oar deck. Roheed's glance flicked over the unwashed bodies, the iron chains, the filthy planking... When the young Mautep's gaze came back to rest upon him, Nagaro thought he saw understanding in the narrow, dark eyes. In contrast, Baruk was scowling. How much the Slave Master had understood of what had been said, Nagaro couldn't guess.

Roheed inclined his head once, briefly. Then he stepped back and turned as if to leave.

"Wait, Roheed..." A sudden thought had occurred to Nagaro, and he spoke on impulse. Baruk's scowl deepened at this shocking display of familiarity, but Roheed merely turned back with a questioning look.

Nagaro plunged ahead. "I have been told," he said, "that the Jinari do not eat anything that contains any part of an animal. If you offer this man some other food—some of his own food, perhaps—it may be he will choose to eat."

Roheed stared at him for a moment in apparent surprise. Then he gave another nod of acknowledgment. "Thank you," he said simply. It was Baruk's turn to stare. Roheed seemed not to notice. He merely beckoned for the Slave Master to follow him as he turned on his heel and strode from the oar deck.

There was a general stirring and murmuring among the slaves as soon as the aft door had closed behind the two Mautep. Many of the men had been awake, silently listening to the exchange.

Utabala apparently had heard at least the last part of it, for he sat up as soon as the two Mautep had disappeared and turned to speak to Nagaro. His black eyes were bright in a face that had begun to look a little pinched. "Why do you willingly serve dese men?" he inquired sharply.

"I serve them no more willingly than anyone here," Nagaro replied with some annoyance. "But I know that man, Roheed, a little. I've gotten some kindness from him in the past. I thought if I might possibly serve *you*, I should at least try to do so."

Utabala considered him narrowly. "Why do you wish to help me?" he asked suspiciously. "Do you not know dat your country and mine are at war?"

Nagaro met the Jinari's glance unflinchingly. "There is no war on this oar deck," he said flatly. "But perhaps you are seeking death when you choose not to eat, and my effort is unwelcome?"

Utabala licked thin lips. "If He Whose Name We Do Not Es-speak sends only food dat is unclean, His faithful servant must go hungry." The Jinari inclined his head, touching his forehead with the heel of his right hand. "But if de One We Do Not Name, in his mercy, relents and sends

His servant food dat it is permitted to eat, den surely it would be sin not to eat it and live to do His will." Utabala's teeth flashed in a fleeting smile. "Do you tink de Mahuk will bring oder food, only for me?"

Nagaro shrugged. "I believe Roheed will try. But perhaps Captain Urchak will not permit it, or perhaps there is none on board."

Again there came that fleeting smile. "Ah, dere were many barrels of yaba bread and bean cake among de cargo from our ship. I saw all of it brought onto dis one." The Jinari gave a little sigh. "But perhaps dese mis-believing servants of Eskarasi will have trown it all away when dey found out what it was."

Less than an hour later, the Mautep slave tenders appeared with the baskets of dried meat and biscuit. It was Olam who worked the port side where Utabala sat. The new recruit's basket contained two unfamiliar-looking lumps that he handed to the Jinari. Nagaro was momentarily distracted as Fataan moved past him, dropping his own breakfast into his hands. When next he looked at Utabala, he saw the man hungrily devouring a brownish lump that he supposed must be bean cake.

*

"That headland looks like the southern tip of Pakoa." Taru straightened from his crouch beside the oar port. "That's the most southern isle of the Lomoas!" It was during a rest period between stints of rowing, and the slaves were engaged in their frequent activity of trying to figure out the ship's position.

Tego looked around triumphantly. "Didn't I say we were comin' into Edroviran waters? It'll be good t' see those shores again." Then he shook his head. "But these are dangerous waters for this floating jailhouse. If Kuran catches us, he'll sink us for sure!"

Landros spoke from two benches behind Nagaro. He and the other former sea warriors had been scattered about the aft end of the oar deck where Baruk could keep an eye on them. "Now see here, Tego," he said. "The Mautep use their ships to attack our cities, steal our gold, and take our men for slaves. Every ship Lord Kuran sinks means less o' that."

At this, Moraga, who was across the aisle, muttered, "Right, mate. I'll remember that when we're all dead."

"Maybe we all be dead soon," said Pavo, "but I hope is not too soon." There was an odd light in his eyes. "I want to see Kel Lankura, at end of great river—where story happen that Taru have tell us."

"Ye had better hope we don't! That's Lord Kuran's home port." The words came from Mendorel, who was chained behind Moraga, and next to Tredhold. "Didn't ye hear what Tego just said about getting sunk?"

"Kuran can't sink us if he ain't there," Moraga observed acerbically. "Remember two years ago? Three Mahuk ships sacked Lankura 'cause Kuran was off protectin' somebody else!"

Tego turned worriedly to Pavo. "D' ye think Urchak and the rest o' this lot might try doin' that?"

Pavo shrugged. "Maybe. Mautep have many ship. Different warlord ship go to different place, and *Ku-ran* is only be in one place." He paused, considering. "But I tell you why I think maybe not. Two year ago it is Lord Angkat attack Lankura. We hear Angkat lose many man and not get so much gold as he hope. Angkat think it make him look brave, but Droviri ship very far away when he attack. Lord Baalkir say it not so brave. Maybe not so smart either."

At that point, the conversation was interrupted by the appearance of Fataan and Olam, coming to douse the lanterns.

*

Nagaro was nudged out of slumber by a hesitant touch on his arm.

"*What...?*" he mumbled, opening his eyes to the darkness and trying to shake off sleep. The touch came again, and he sat up, drawing his arm back. "Who's that?" he demanded, directing his voice in the direction from which he fancied the hand had come.

"I have something for you, Nagaro." The voice was Simion's.

"What is it?" Uncertainly, Nagaro put out his hand.

"Here. Take it."

As soon as his fingers closed on the object, Nagaro knew what it was. He could feel the saw-teeth along one edge and the rough wood of the handle along the other. "Simion," he murmured. "You've had it all this time! Did you hide it on the window ledge in the slave barn?"

Simion didn't answer the question. "I want you to use it to escape," he said eagerly.

"But *why*, Simion—?" Nagaro stopped, not sure he wanted to hear the answer.

The other youth hesitated. "For what you did for me on Chitaopa."

Nagaro shook his head in the dark. "I nursed all the men when they were sick," he protested. "And when I was sick, you gave me water. We all do what we can. No one owes me anything."

There was a pause, then, "Most of them don't even want to touch me."

Nagaro felt a welling of sympathy for the other youth. As hard as being a slave was for him and Taru, it must be worse for Simion. He felt for the top of the bench that lay between them and set the improvised tool down with a small, audible clunk. "You should keep it, Simion," he said decisively. "You're the one who needs to get out of here the most. You have no friends—no one you can talk to. Some of the others are cruel to you..."

"I can't go alone. I'm afraid," Simion said miserably. "But, if *you* were with me..." The young man's voice was pleading.

Nagaro felt his stomach twist. "I don't think that would be a good idea," he said desperately. He felt that what he said was true, but it made him feel terrible to say it. "You keep the tool, and do whatever you want to with it. If you don't want to escape alone, give it to Landros, or Tred. They're both decent fellows. I don't want to escape without all of my friends. I told Roheed that on Chitaopa," he added, trying to soften his rejection. "Now go to sleep, Simion."

He lay down again next to Pavo, turning his back to where he knew Simion must still be sitting in the darkness. He didn't see what else he could have done, but he still felt mean. After a moment, he heard the faint scrape of the tool being picked up from the bench top, and the sounds of Simion stretching himself out on the planking.

It was a long time before Nagaro was able to go back to sleep. In the morning, he said nothing to anyone about the night's conversation. All that day it seemed , even more than usual, that Simion wouldn't meet anyone's eyes.

It was after that evening's dried meat and biscuit was eaten, and after the dousing of the deck, when everyone was waiting wearily for the final return of Fataan and Olam to put out the lamps, that Simion quite suddenly turned around and gave Nagaro a quick glance. He stuck out his closed fist in Nagaro's direction. "Pass it back to Landros," he muttered urgently. Nagaro didn't have to ask what "it" was. He reached out and took the cutting tool from Simion. Turning, he held it out to Tego. "Pass it back to Landros," he said simply. Tego's glance flicked from the tool to Nagaro's face, to Simion's, and back to Nagaro, but he did as he'd been asked.

Landros held the familiar object in his hand, and stared at it for a long moment before addressing Simion. "So ye managed to save it then," he said carefully. "Well done, lad."

"*Well done?* Why'd he keep it to himself for so long?" The question came from Gurd who was chained next to Moraga.

Unexpectedly, Simion spoke. "It's not just for the four of us Fleet men this time," he said defiantly. "It's for everyone—anyone who wants to try."

This caused a stir. The more men there were sawing at their cuffs, the longer the whole process would take, and the greater the chance of discovery. Everyone knew this. But once the idea had been given voice, it wasn't easily set aside. The four former sea warriors were too scattered to be able to pass the tool among themselves without the cooperation of other slaves.

Despite the obvious drawbacks, it seemed to Nagaro that Landros was happier to have to allow the other men to try to escape as well. The grizzled sea warrior seemed actually relieved that Simion's unexpected announcement had forced his hand.

Taru was determined to be part of the escape attempt, so of course Nagaro had to join the effort as well. Pavo calmly declared, "I try too," despite the unhappy outcome of his earlier attempt at this approach, and the fact that they'd long since left his home waters behind. Mendorel asked to be included, and Tego threw his hand in as well, as did Nanu the lone man and also Utabala. In the end, more than twenty men joined the plot, including all of the Edroviran slaves.

Gurd rolled his eyes and declared that they hadn't "the chance of a damned soul in Hel"—even though he was part of the scheme. Moraga, the eternal skeptic, agreed loudly with Gurd, then threw his hand in anyway. "They can't beat the lot of us t' death," he observed with a fatalistic shrug. "There'd be no one left t' row the ship."

They began work that very night as soon as the lamps were extinguished, each man sawing away for a time in the dark, then passing the tool along, waking up the next man if need be. In this way, they were able to work all night without anyone missing much sleep. Lying awake after taking his turn, Nagaro did a mental calculation based on what the four sea warriors had been able to do the first time with two pieces of saw blade. He estimated that it would probably take them about two months to get free. By that time, of course, the *Fist* was supposed to be meeting the rest of Baalkir's fleet back in Sar Tipaal. He decided not to pursue this line of reasoning aloud.

Each day they rowed, and the *Fist of Death* made her way northward. By night, they scraped at the leather with blistered fingers. They were fortunate in that the Mautep were less vigilant now than they had been in the slave barn. For one thing, the slaves remained in their places on the oar deck. Their chains were not routinely unfastened and re-fastened as they had been in Sar Tipaal. Then too, the responsibility for inspecting the chains fell almost entirely upon the two young slave tenders. Fataan and Olam disliked their menial work and were often in haste to finish it.

External events helped them as well. Somewhere in the Faranos, the three Mahuk galleys encountered an Edroviran craft with several chests of gold and only a single warship for escort. The battle was brief. The escorting galley was caught by one of the Mahuk rams and sent to the bottom before anyone even had a chance to apply the grappling hooks. This windfall created a considerable distraction. The celebratory mood above decks lasted for several days.

After that, the three ships turned south, their mission already half complete. All that remained was to take on a few more slaves. Even half a dozen would probably do, the three captains reasoned, considering the quantity of gold they had acquired. The galleys skulked along the seaward side of the southern Faranos, looking for unwary fishing boats. After a week with limited success, a sighting of several ships flying the blue banners of the Royal Fleet sent the Mahuk craft speeding southward again. Landros spat, and muttered "cowards" under his breath, but most of the slaves were in no hurry to have the *Fist* tangle with Kuran's sea warriors. They were making good progress with the bit of saw blade—about half-way through. Even some of the more skeptical slaves had begun to hope. It was as if they could taste freedom on their tongues.

Then, somewhere among the Lomoas, the three Mahuk warships caught a small fishing fleet too far from land, and the *Fist of Death* was at last able to add two unfortunate Turowan fishermen to its oar deck compliment. Their capture was, of course, a bad enough piece of luck for the poor fishermen, but for the slaves who were part of the escape plan the event brought disaster. New slaves on the oar deck inevitably meant some rearrangement of those already there. And in the process of doing this, Baruk's sharp eye caught what Fataan's and Olam's had missed. The Slave Master spat an oath when he spotted the first damaged cuff. A short time later, when it was revealed that twenty-five slaves had partially sawed through their leather cuffs, Baruk could be heard cursing, not only the two slave-tenders, but also Captain Urchak for his folly in bringing sea warriors onto the oar deck.

One by one, the offending slaves were taken up onto the main deck. There, each was tied to a pair of stanchions and flogged, then untied and sat upon while his chain was re-riveted to a new leather ankle cuff. The entire process, for all twenty-five slaves, took the better part of a day, and the search for the cutting tool continued after the lamps were lit. Fataan and Olam weren't allowed to rest until the thing was found. The slaves' filthy rags were all carefully searched, and when that yielded nothing, every nook and cranny of the oar deck had to be searched as well. The men derived some thin satisfaction from watching the two young Mautep crawling about on the rank planking and poking among the benches while grumbling and cursing.

In fact, the slaves were able to significantly prolong their meager enjoyment by moving the offending object several times as the search progressed, before the two slave handlers grew suspicious and became very much more watchful. No one really dared to hope that the cutting tool would not be found, and of course it was—wedged in a crack under Landros' bench.

Nagaro's ring would have been discovered during the search if he hadn't done all he could to prevent it. As soon as he saw the pattern of the search, he surreptitiously untied the ring from around his waist and transferred the strip of cloth that bore it to his pocket. He managed to move it again, to a crack under his bench, just before his clothing was searched. When that danger had passed, he found a third opportunity to secretly retie the strip of cloth about his waist, preventing his treasure from being found when Fataan searched the benches.

The flogging was only seven lashes apiece. Apparently Moraga was right. There were too many slaves involved and they were needed to row. It wasn't the stinging of their backs that hurt the most however. It was the loss of that tiny sprig of hope that had sprouted amid the filth of the oar deck and been nurtured by their nights of toil.

Landros put the best face on it that he could. They only needed more cutting tools, he said, so they could free themselves faster. During the next winter in Sar Tipaal, they would all search for things they could use to cut leather. This time, they'd hide the tools and save them all until they were at sea again and close to their homes. It was a reasonable plan, but knowing there was nothing more that could be done through the rest of the summer and fall was very hard to bear. It might be a year before they could hope to make another bid for freedom.

Chapter 27: A Gift Of Chance

The day after the plot was discovered, Mendorel stopped eating. He said he'd held on long enough. Nagaro was disturbed by the older man's decision, but he didn't try to argue. As he'd told Roheed, he didn't feel it was his place to try to tell other men what they ought to endure.

The next day Moraga began to talk of "taking the Hranji's way." "It'd be quicker 'n starving yerself," he said. "And it'd make Raak madder 'n a hornet in a bottle!"

"It'd take a heap o' courage," Tego observed.

Nagaro frowned. It was evening, and they had just finished their dinner—those who chose to eat it. "Choosing death by any means takes courage," he said, glancing at Mendorel. "But it's true," he added, "that there'd be a certain satisfaction in refusing to row. It would be a last act of defiance before the end."

"Aye, Nagaro! Ye can't mean t' give up!" Taru sounded alarmed.

Nagaro shook his head. "No," he said. "Not yet." He'd already been brought to that extremity once in his young life. The slavery that he had sought to escape in the harness shed had been more horrible, more absolute, more final, than the chain that held him now. He'd believed, then, that death was the only way out. His attempt had failed. And then somehow... somehow... he had been delivered... Remembered words ran through his head. Scarcely aware that he was doing so, he spoke them aloud.

"Though burning gold or iron cold may weave my prison bars... My spirit wakes to wander still the shadows of the stars..."

"What is that?" Pavo asked.

Nagaro shook himself out of his reverie. "It's just part of a poem," he said, embarrassed. "I don't know the rest of it."

"What is it mean?"

"That iron bars or chains can only hold your body, I suppose. Your spirit is free. And as long as that's true, there is still hope." He stopped speaking, but his thoughts ran on. *Even if it's only a hope as frail as the shadow cast by starlight...*

Catching some movement, he turned his head and saw Mendorel

hastily look away. From the corner of his eye, he saw that Tredhold was studying him, frowning. The healer had been looking at him that way a lot since several new slaves had been added to the oar deck.

The two newest slaves, a father and son named Kojito and Kunoa, were chained near Nagaro, and inevitably the meaning of Nagaro's name had come up. Taru had handled it as he always did—with the same tale that he'd told on the day of their own arrival on the oar deck. The new Turowans had accepted the story without any comment as Turowans usually did. Neither Tredhold nor Landros had said anything, but he'd seen them exchange glances.

Nagaro looked down at his hands, so heavily calloused from rowing. His brows knit together. It was a long time since he'd thought about the words of that poem. He believed that Kale Fendred had first brought them to his attention in an effort to give him comfort. The Leithian lord had brought them up again later as well, to try to dissuade him from seeking death, for Kale was a devout follower of the Leithian gods. After the episode of the harness shed, the man had actually taken him to task. Nagaro could still picture Kale's worried face—see the troubled eyes that had searched his frozen countenance in vain for any sign of comprehension. He could still hear the man's words. *"What were you trying to do last night? Were you trying to die? Surely you know it's wrong to throw away Queen Solbrid's sacred gift. Thank the gods that Nevien came to us in time. Your soul would have gone to Hel carrying such a sin!"*

Nagaro, of course, believed no such thing. For him there was no Hel, and it was only the *other* thing that he'd been contemplating at the time that was a sin. Still, though Kale had watched him like a hawk and thwarted him repeatedly, Nagaro had never found it in his heart to hate the red-haired Leithian. Cruelty had never been the man's intention, and Nagaro suspected he owed his life as much to Kale as to the unknown piece of luck that had set him free.

For the second time, he spoke his thought aloud. "All I need is one piece of luck... one gift of Lokundas..."

Tego heard his words and the gnarled little Turowan asked, "What kind o' luck d' ye want, then?"

"Aye," Gurd put in ironically. "Just tell me, so as I can put in a word tonight when I pray t' Kroneg."

Nagaro shrugged. He was picturing some sharpened blade—*well-honed steel that would slice through a leather cuff in a single stroke...* What he said was, "I'll know it if I see it."

Utabala hadn't caught the irony in Gurd's statement. "Every day, tree times—morning, noon, and night—I make prayer to de One Whose Name We Do Not Es-speak," he said in his rapid Droviri. "Always I pray for our deliverance. Do you not all do de same?"

Pavo spoke up. "Always I ask Shepuum for help us." He turned to Nagaro. "Do you ask Vothra?"

Nagaro shook his head. "Vothra has no power to change the world, except through the hearts and minds of men."

Pavo considered this critically. "Then why you do not ask Vothra to tell Mautep it is wrong to keep us?" he inquired. "When they hear Vothra speak, they will let us go."

Nagaro sighed. "I might ask, and Vothra might even try to speak to them, but men may not hear. And they're free to do as they choose, no matter what Vothra says."

Gurd wasn't interested in the finer points of Vothrin belief. Perhaps he'd felt some reproach in Utabala's comment, for he now demanded, "What has your god sent ye then, Jinari, for all of your praying?"

Utabala's smile was brief and brittle. "He has sent me yaba bread and bean cake."

Gurd glanced at Nagaro. He started to say something, but Nagaro shook his head and the young Leithian closed his mouth. Before anything more could be said, the two slave handlers stepped onto the oar deck with buckets in their hands.

*

It was later, after the lanterns had been put out. Most of the slaves were already asleep, but Utabala stirred and spoke in a low voice that could just be heard above the creak and groan of the ship. "Pavo Maat, are you awake?"

There was a sound from Pavo's position as of someone sitting up and there came a single soft word: "Yes."

"Then tell me, Pavo, is Sheptuum de name of your god?"

Pavo's answer came immediately. "Sheptuum is mean 'most high lord.' Hashtep do not know any other name for Sheptuum."

There was a small pause while Utabala perhaps considered the possibility that the Hashtep and the Jinari might revere the same deity, each in their own way. At length he said, tentatively, "You have been an es-slave for many, many days, Pavo Maat. And you say you have prayed every day to your god, whose name you do not know. Has your god sent you anyting for all dose days dat you have prayed?"

Pavo hesitated. He kept his voice very low when he answered. "I think Sheptuum have send Nagaro. He is sleep now, or I would not say it, because he would not like to hear it. But this is what I know: Nagaro is one who save us on Chitaopa Island when plague come. Almost all man who are here, he save—because he talk to Roheed, and he make doctor with his own hand. He is in story of Roheed, too, and Roheed know it. Two time Roheed have tried to make Nagaro free, but Nagaro say no."

There was a moment's silence, then Pavo added, "And it is Nagaro ask

Roheed to give you other food."

"It is so, as you say," Utabala murmured. "But he is Droviri, an unbe-liever..."

Pavo answered quickly, defensively. "Nagaro say his people have god they call Maker of All Thing—that is like Sheptuum. Only, Nagaro say his people do not pray."

There was a pause while Utabala digested this. Presently he spoke. "De hand of de Un-named is everywhere, but is not seen," he intoned. "And de pattern of His foot-es-steps is not plain. So es-speaks de great Prophet Jembari. I, who am but His humble servant, shall not wonder at de wisdom of de One We Do Not Name if he choose to use an unbeliever to work His will."

There was a rustle in the darkness as Utabala moved to touch his hand to his forehead in the Jinari ritual gesture of devotion. After a moment, he added, "For what do you pray tonight, Pavo Maat?"

Pavo did not hesitate this time. "Nagaro have say he only need one piece of luck. So I pray for piece of luck—whatever thing he need."

There was a moment's pause, and then, "Dis I will pray for also."

For a time there was silence. Then, from another place in the dark-ness—where Mendorel lay—there was a quiet sigh and the sound of a man turning over in his place between the benches.

Nagaro slept soundly beside Pavo. In the days that followed he observed with great relief that Mendorel had begun to eat again. Since the former shopkeeper didn't seem inclined to talk about why he had changed his mind, Nagaro didn't ask.

*

The three Mahuk ships now flew southward, rapidly leaving Edro-viran waters. Their position was confirmed by Kojito and Kunoa, who hailed from Pakoa, the southernmost isle of the Lomoa chain. When the little fleet anchored briefly off of Chitaopa to take on water, Kojito told them that this isle was the farthest south of any land ever visited by the Turo.

They fought only a single skirmish on the journey between Chi-taopa and Sar Tipaal, one that was quickly resolved in favor of the House of jir-Akaan. Their arrival in the *Fist's* home port meant only a day's rest to take on fresh stores, since the remaineder of Lord Baalkir's fleet had reached the rendezvous before them. Then it was forth again to more battles.

Somewhere off the coast of the southern Baar, they met the ships of Lord Tuluptak. What followed was the fiercest battle of the summer. In the heat of it, one of Tuluptak's ships came too close, sliding along the *Fist's* port side with a horrible splintering of oars. Several men were struck by the flailing inboard shafts. Kojito was nearly disemboweled and died instantly, and a Hashtep named Umak who had survived the plague on Chitaopa had his arm and ribs so badly crushed that Baruk had the man put overboard. The injured Hashtep was conscious and moaning when his body was strapped into the leather harness and lifted from the oar deck. Those among the slaves who hadn't yet witnessed such horrors sat watching in dismay. Nagaro heard Taru behind him softly repeating, over and over again, "*Hamanei mata noa...*"

After the Mautep had finished removing the two men and had gone, Nagaro saw Kunoa staring stonily at the blood-stained bench where his father's life had ended. Silent tears had cut two tracks down his grimy cheeks. Potero, a Turowan who sat close to Kunoa, leaned forward to offer what comfort that he could. "At least it was quick, lad," he said gently. "He won't suffer any more o' this, and ye'll see him again in Hanuroa."

Nagaro didn't know which death cut more sharply across his soul. Only a few weeks before, Kojito and his son had been sailing free under the clear blue sky of Edrovir. Now the father was dead, leaving the son to face the brutal ordeal of slavery alone. And Umak would likely have died a year ago if Nagaro hadn't tended him through the plague. He'd kept that man alive, *for what*—so that he might be thrown into the sea with a bag of stones tied to his feet?

Lord Baalkir's war galleys sailed on under a Mahuk sun. Nagaro pulled on his oar. In his mind, he rehearsed and re-rehearsed a dozen unlikely scenarios. He spoke of them to no one since all of them required a piece of luck—that gift of Lokundas of which he'd spoken. He did not pray. Only a fool prayed to Lokundas, who was said to enjoy a good joke—especially at the expense of those who dare to hope too much.

*

The summer was waning fast, but the days grew hot, humid, and stifling. The *Fist of Death* skimmed with deceptive ease over the glassy swells, propelled by the straining slaves on her sweltering oar deck. Night came, bringing respite from the labor but not from the heat. Every night, the Mautep ordered the oar ports closed, sealing in the hot air—and the stench, which was always worst when it was hot. As they lay down to try to sleep, the slaves cursed the heat, the foul smell, and their masters.

"Why can't they give us just a little air?" young Kunoa's voice asked plaintively in the darkness after a few nights of this.

"In case o' storms," Potero told him wearily. "If one blew up in the night, she could be swamped an' go down afore we got the ports closed."

"Isn't it late for a summer storm?" the boy wondered.

"Aye," growled Moraga, "and early for a winter one. But they've got their rules an' the Spirits forbid they should change one of 'em for the sake of our comfort."

This brought a chorus of grumbled agreement.

A few nights later, however, the masters' precaution proved well taken. Two hours before dawn, while the slaves were all deep in slumber, the wind began to freshen and the ship began to rock on a growing swell. An hour later, the storm front struck, suddenly and with terrible force. Whether it was the last summer storm or the first storm of autumn, the slaves neither knew nor cared. What they did know was that they were being flung about among the benches like beans in a box—a black box with no lantern light. Crashes of thunder punctuated the groaning of timbers and the roar of the waves that washed over the ship.

Dawn came and went unheeded as the storm continued. With the ports still closed, the oar deck was as dark as the inside of a sack—a sack being tossed about by angry giants. Nagaro straddled his bench, clutching it with arms that ached, while Pavo was down on the planking, braced between the bench and the board they set their feet against for rowing. Between the rolls of thunder, Nagaro could hear the voices of his fellow slaves, raised in fervent prayer, all around him in the pitching darkness.

He heard a voice that he recognized as Tredhold's expressing an uncharacteristically heartfelt prayer for their safety. "Oh thou Great God Hrathgard, King of the Heavens and Lord o' the Wind, I pray ye let us live to see another day!"

No sooner had the Leithian finished speaking than a particularly large wave struck the ship. It swept across the deck above them with a deafening *whoosh* and carried away the aft hatch cover, pouring icy salt water down onto the heads of Tredhold and the other dozen slaves most immediately below.

Nagaro was one of them. Still clinging to his bench, he gasped for breath and twisted about to survey the damage. He found that he could now make out the shapes of his surroundings by dim daylight, which penetrated a dozen fathoms of black storm cloud to illuminate the pale rectangle of the open hatch.

"Hoy there, mate!" Landros shook the seawater out of his hair and raised his voice above the storm. "Bloody literal-minded, your Great God Hrathgard! We're all still alive, and he's showin' us the daylight!" He let go his hold on his bench with one hand long enouth to jerk a thumb at the uncovered hatch.

"We always say ye should be careful what ye ask for if ye pray to the gods of Leith!" Tredhold shouted back. The healer had barely uttered these words than the next wave came pouring through the hatch to give them all another dousing.

The Mautep crew understandably had more pressing matters to

attend to that morning than a missing hatch cover. By the time the storm had subsided enough for anyone to bother taking stock of the slaves, the oar deck was awash with enough sea water to have covered it to a depth of nearly two inches—had it been flat and remained level long enough for anyone to make the measurement.

The water was drained away through a number of scupper-holes, once these were unstopped, and the missing hatch cover was replaced with a makeshift construct of canvas and wooden splints. The slaves would have much rather seen the hatch left open now that the storm had passed. The heat had moderated considerably, but light and fresh air were still preferable to gloom and the stuffy, fetid atmosphere of the closed oar deck. Of course, no one among the Mautep asked for their opinion.

Lord Baalkir's storm-ravaged fleet was by now at the very northern edge of Mahuk waters, near the border of Jinara. As such, they were some distance from the nearest friendly port. The *Fist* had suffered only snapped lines and a broken spar, besides the missing hatch cover. Two of the other ships were leaking, however, and several had serious damage to their rigging. On top of this, it appeared that winter might be coming early, for the storm had been too cold to be the last storm of summer. All things considered, it seemed a good time to make for Sar Tipaal. Since speed was advisable, the slaves were set to the oars long and often during the day that followed.

*

Baalkir hadn't planned to meet Lord Angkat's fleet in the Strait of Jaamra. Plans, however have a way of requiring adjustments. Or, as the Kelorin would put it, Lokundas delights in playing games with the fates of men.

The Jaamra Strait was a narrow passage between two islands, and Angkat's ships were spread in a line across the width of it. Lord Baalkir could have avoided his rival by taking his ships around one or the other of the isles, but the lord of Sar Tipaal gave no order to take such a course, despite the damaged condition of his ships.

"I don't understand why he doesn't try going to leeward," Tredhold said as he crouched down, peering out of an oar port on the port side of the ship. He straightened. "It looks like the wind's in his favor and we'd make it easily."

Pavo had been listening to the mutterings of the other Hashtep. "No," he said flatly. "Lord Baalkir not run. All summer he look for Angkat. This be *very* big fight."

The oar deck was momentarily free of any Mautep, the crew having been called topside in preparation for the approaching battle. The *Fist* was rolling heavily on a westerly swell, her sails shortened and oars shipped. Her prow was pointing squarely at the mouth of the strait and the waiting enemy.

Taru had been squatting on his haunches, looking through his own oar port. Now he looked up. "There's another storm coming too," he said. "And it's going t' hit soon, sure as fishes drink! There's a great pile o' purple clouds out there to windward, and it's coming at us fast. I can see it move!"

Landros shook his head, frowning. "Here's a fine load o' flotsam," he growled. "A big battle is bad enough. But a big battle *and* a storm..."

There was a sudden shout from the deck above, like a barked order, and thudding of booted feet on the planking. The sounds reached them clearly through the improvised canvas hatch cover. The *Fist*'s little accident was making it much easier for the slaves to learn what was passing on the deck above. A moment after the commotion, Baruk and his crew burst through the aft door onto the oar deck. The Slave Master took his place by the speaking tube as Ul climbed to his seat at the drum. Raak strode down the aisle, whip in hand.

Orders were given, the drum sounded the signals, and the slaves all moved as one to un-ship the oars. "Row, shaku!" bellowed Raak, cracking his whip. "Row! Row for keep skin on your back!"

They rowed.

Baruk spoke some words to Ul, and the pace of the drumbeat quickened. The Mahuk crew had let out sail. The wind was raising whitecaps, now, and the *Fist of Death* surged ahead, slicing through the waves. To either side, other ships of Baalkir's fleet were keeping abreast of her. Over the drumbeats, the creaking, and the rushing hiss of waves against the hull, the shouts of the crew could be heard from the deck above. The Hashtep slaves could make out some of what was being said and exchanged words among themselves, gasped out between pulls on the great oars.

Pavo found breath to translate for Nagaro's benefit. "Angkat ship... they coming now! All ship... go to meet!"

Nagaro forced himself to stop counting the oar strokes. He knew that the *Fist* was moving at ramming speed. *Please*, he thought, *let the other ship turn aside. Let the ships miss each other!* It was a hope, not a prayer—not addressed to anyone. The lash fell across his back, a line of sharp fire. Raak was spreading his attentions around.

The slaves continued to strain at the oars. Nagaro felt as if his lungs were about to burst with the effort. He heard more shouts from the deck above. The voices were tense, excited. In his mind he could picture the two lines of ships about to crash into one another.

Baruk had his ear glued to the speaking tube. Now the Slave Master barked an order to Ul, and Nagaro understood it even before the drum beat out the signal. "*Ship oars!*" Nagaro and Pavo shouted in unison.

The slaves moved frantically to comply—barely in time, for there came a shuddering blow that threatened to throw them all backwards off of their benches. The shock was followed by a horrible grinding of wood against wood as two great hulls raked against each other. The oar ports along the port side were darkened by the hulking mass of another vessel.

Nagaro breathed a sigh of relief as he slumped, gasping. There had been no dreadful crunch of breaking timbers. Neither ship's ram had found its mark.

Then he heard it... from somewhere frighteningly close. The crash... the screams... Some other ship's ram had struck home. The members of some other slave crew were meeting swift, rending death—or a slightly less swift but no less horrible death in the icy depths below.

As always, under such circumstances, a wave of guilt overwhelmed Nagaro's gratitude at having been spared. He closed his eyes and murmured, "Vothra carry their spirits safely across the abyss..."

There was yelling from the deck above. Nagaro heard Pavo shout, "Is Angkat ship go down!" There was more shouting—more running feet above them and the clash of swords. Someone else cried in the Common Speech, "We're being boarded!"

Baruk shouted an order, and the Mautep oar deck crew members made for the aft door at a dead run, leaving the slaves to try to guess what was going on in the world beyond their prison.

It wasn't hard to tell that the *Fist* must be roped to another ship. The port-side oar ports were all still occluded. The grinding of wood on wood continued, though less forcefully. The slaves knew that nothing more could be demanded of them until the two ships were pushed apart again, and oars could be extended simultaneously on both sides of the hull. They should be comparatively safe for the time being. There would be no more attempts to ram, provided all the enemy ships had been sent into the fray. Only if Angkat had held one or more back, for a second wave, was there anything more to fear on that score.

It was much more difficult to tell how the battle on the deck was going. Shouts, curses, and the ringing of steel ebbed and flowed around the canvas-covered hatch, and it was impossible for the slaves below to tell who, if anyone, was gaining the upper hand.

Something else was happening as well. The slaves could feel it. Had they been on deck, they probably would have felt the rising wind. From their position, they were aware of the increased amplitude of the swell, felt in the rise and fall of the planks beneath their feet.

The sounds of sword play came closer again. A little bit of the battle for the deck seemed to have detached itself from the general melee. It sounded as if two fighters were going at it one-to-one just beside the hatch cover. Nagaro could hear grunting breaths and the impact of boots on the deck as the two opponents lunged at each other. He could visualize their movements from the crisp, cold ring of their sword blades coming together.

What happened next, Nagaro would remember for the rest of his days. Perhaps a sudden lurch of the deck—a harbinger of the coming storm—had something to do with it. Or perhaps the attacker stepped backward by mere chance. Whatever the case, the man came down with one boot on the improvised hatch cover, and the thing couldn't bear his weight. There was a brittle snap as the splints broke and a ripping sound.

The warrior made a desperate effort to maintain his balance, but failed, and he toppled backward. There was more ripping canvas as the man, clad in the brown and gold uniform of Lord Angkat's sea warriors, plunged head-first into the oar deck. He landed with a sickening crunch and sprawled across the aisle between the benches, his neck obviously broken. His outstretched right arm lay flung across the planking as if pointing at the bench where Nagaro sat. The dead hand still clutched the gold-inlayed hilt of his sword.

For an instant, the slaves all sat frozen in their places. Then Nagaro moved. *Here at last was the opportunity he had hoped for!*

Quick as a cat, he flung himself out into the aisle on his hands and knees, to the full length of his chain. Even then, he had to stretch—but his fingers managed to close on the sword hilt. Without hesitation, he jerked the thing free of the dead man's grasp. He scrambled up, then, and stood balancing to the ship's motion, feeling the heft of the sword in his hand. The leather hand-grip was still warm and slick with its owner's sweat. Turning, Nagaro placed his left foot on his bench seat. He carefully slid eighteen inches of steel between the leather cuff and the skin of his bare ankle, the sharp edge of the sword against the tough leather. Then, with a single motion, he drew the blade up and back, shearing through the leather cuff. It fell away with a rattle of chain and he stepped free.

"Ye'd best give that sword t' me, lad," Landros said, raising his voice above the mingled clamor of wind, sea, and battle. "It'll be of more use in the hands o' someone as knows how to use it."

But Nagaro wasn't going to let the sword go once he had it in his hand. He met the veteran sea warrior's gaze with a bold glance and shook his head. "This one came to me, Landros," he said. "And I *do* know how to use a sword."

"*Bishka!*"

The muttered word came from above their heads. Pavo glanced

up at the open hatch. "*Nagaro!*" He hissed, "It is Haotef! I think he come down. Right now!"

Captain Urchak's second in command did, in fact, come down—not the way his opponent had, but feet-first and very much in control. Nagaro barely had time to back up a few steps and come on his guard.

A murmur of Hashti ran among the benches. "They say he very good with sword, Nagaro!" Pavo's voice held an edge of fear. Nagaro only nodded his acknowledgment without turning his head. His eyes were on the Mautep.

"So is Nagaro!" That was Taru, sounding far too confident.

"Be quiet, Taru." Nagaro still hadn't taken his eyes off of the Mautep warrior.

Haotef had landed in a fighting crouch, his sword extended. From the deck above, the Mautep had seen a movement, and the flash of a sword blade below in the gloom. Now he found himself confronting the point of a sword in the hand of a half-naked slave. A slave caught out of irons was a slave in trouble in any case, and a slave who threatened harm to one of his masters might be slain at the master's discretion. Haotef knew the law, and besides, he recognized this slave. His quick appraisal had taken in the defiant gray eyes, the youthful beard, the hair tied with a bit of dirty rag, and the remains of what had once been fisherman's pants, now only knee-length because of the many pieces that had been torn off for one purpose or another.

Had Haotef's mind been open to the possibility, he might have read in Nagaro's stance the evidence that he was facing a trained swordsman. But to the Mautep, this was only the young son-of-a-dog who'd stuck a fish-gutting knife into his shoulder. So the fisher-boy who liked to play with knives was now playing with a sword. What of it?

"Hah!" Haotef gave a short, barking laugh. "Shaku raal!" He spat for emphasis, then lunged at Nagaro, expecting his revenge to be swift and sweet.

A gasp went up from the slaves on either side. Steel rang on steel as Nagaro parried. It was a bit awkward—not his best move, but it worked.

Haotef was momentarily startled by his opponent's success, but any fool could be lucky once. The Mautep warrior plunged forward, his sword expertly slicing the air where Nagaro had been an instant before.

Nagaro had sprung away, and he now continued adroitly to parry and dodge, giving ground as he did so to buy time, putting the body of the dead warrior between himself and his foe, his mind racing.

He had known, of course, that he would have to fight before this was over, but this was too much, too soon. Perhaps he should have let Landros take the sword after all. He was confident of his ability to fight a fair bout for "hits," but this Mautep meant to kill him. He could read it in the man's eyes. Nagaro had never fought for blood in his life, while Haotef had years of experience doing precisely that. Nagaro licked dry lips. There was nothing else for it. He was going to have to figure out how to kill a man, and he was going to have to get it right the first time.

And he had an audience. He was keenly aware of thirty-five pairs of terrified eyes fixed on him and his opponent.

Haotef, meanwhile, was getting over his surprise. So this slave dog had learned a few tricks somewhere, had he? Well, a little bit of a fight would make the inevitable end all the more sweet. Haotef feinted left as he leaped over the dead warrior, then whipped his blade around and drove the point at the errant slave's throat.

Steel rang on steel as Nagaro turned the thrust aside, then retreated up the aisle.

"*Keshaal!*" Haotef spat angrily. The son-of-a-dog was quick, but he kept running away! "Fight, shaku!"

Nagaro had now reached the place amidships where the aisle was widest. There he stopped retreating, shifting his grip on the sword hilt. He felt strangely calm. Defense, at least, was automatic. Even after three years, his muscles remembered what to do. The sword felt lighter in his hand than any blade he had handled before, and it was slightly curved after the Mautep fashion, but he could adjust to that.

The movement of the deck under his feet was another factor to contend with however. That movement was getting worse—but the Mautep had to deal with it as well. Nagaro mentally repeated Master Fendar's favorite adage: No matter how good you are, the other man can beat you. And, of course, the other side of the coin: No matter how good the other man is, you can beat him. The practical interpretation was simple. Always fight your best no matter who your opponent, beware of over-confidence, take advantage of the other man's mistakes, and don't give up before it's over.

It was time, Nagaro knew, to go on the offensive. If he was ever going to get a clear thrust at Haotef's chest, he had to know as much as possible about how the man moved. He had some idea already, but... Nagaro lunged.

Haotef parried and came at him. Nagaro stood his ground, neatly parrying the warrior's initial thrust. He then began a series of probing attacks, seeking to find his opponent's weaknesses while at the same time turning aside every fresh attack the Mautep aimed at him.

The approaching storm was making its presence more and more strongly felt. Both men had increasingly to work hard to maintain their balance on the heaving deck. The two swords whirled and clashed and rang together, as the combatants leaped and lunged and staggered back and forth. The slaves, still chained to their places, crouched between the benches, cowering away from the flashing blades.

Finally, Haotef came off of a feint with a particularly vicious thrust. Nagaro was caught off balance by an unusually strong lurch of the deck and failed to side-step quite far enough. The warrior's blade missed its intended mark but slid along Nagaro's ribs, drawing a four inch line of scarlet across his left side.

Nagaro felt the sting, and the warm trickle of blood. He heard an agonized groan from the watching slaves and saw Haotef's triumphant smile, a smile that said: *First blood!*

Being intent upon getting an opening for a killing thrust, Nagaro hadn't been thinking about hits. What good were hits when you needed to kill? Now, however, he understood. There was a psychological advantage to be gained. Nagaro looked the gloating Mautep in the eye—and smiled. It was a smile that said: *You think you have me, but you do not.* He gave Haotef little time to think about that smile, but moved with the quickness of thought, in low under Haotef's guard, to nick the man's thigh. Swiftly then, he parried the Mautep's furious counterattack and leaped away, leaning into the tilt of the moving deck.

Haotef sprang at him with a snarl, feinting left and coming in low to his right. Nagaro caught the thrust on the guard of his sword, deflecting it down and to the side as the ship rocked back the other way. Haotef staggered slightly, off balance, and Nagaro was in and back out again, raking the man's right side with his blade.

Now Haotef's face was a mask of fury. The Mautep gripped the hilt of his sword with both hands and brought it around in a terrible sweep at neck level and with decapitating force.

Nagaro ducked, feeling the swish of the air as the whirling blade missed his hair by a finger's breadth. Before his opponent could recover, he lunged forward and sprang away again, leaving a cut on Haotef's left side. He'd scored three hits in less than ten seconds. It would have won the bout, but he knew it wouldn't win this fight.

For a moment the two antagonists crouched, facing one another, breathing hard. There was no sound from the slaves cowering all around them in the gloom. Nagaro read something in the other man's eyes that hadn't been there before. Was it doubt? Perhaps even fear? He sighted along the blade of his sword, and smiled his most wicked, feral smile— white teeth in the midst of a beard as black as a raven's plumage. It was a smile that said: *You know I can take you.*

Haotef couldn't quite believe what had been happening. Where did a fisherman's son learn to handle a sword like this? What manner of man was he facing? Was it a man at all, or a demon? Well, he told himself, man or demon, it was going to die—*right now!*

Haotef's favorite move was a feint to the left followed by a cut to the right, but he'd used that move three times already without success. This time, the Mautep warrior feinted right.

It was a good gambit. The attack was so unexpected that Nagaro heard the other slaves gasp in alarm, but he was ready to respond. He'd been waiting for the left feint. Haotef's reversal of tactics surprised him for a fraction of a second, but in that fraction of a second he saw a way. He turned side-on to the oncoming sword—twisting right and arching his back to let the blade pass, feeling the guard graze his shoulder blade. At the same time, and before Haotef could stop his forward motion, Nagaro drove his own sword point straight at the man's chest, just left of center.

Nagaro wasn't sure how much force was needed to pierce a man's body. He and Master Fendar had talked about this, and he'd even tried putting a blade through a large bale of straw a few times. Still, when the moment came, all he could think of was that he didn't want his effort to be insufficient. He put all of his weight into his thrust. Combined with Haotef's unchecked momentum, the result was that the sword blade passed cleanly through the warrior's chest, right up to the hilt.

He found himself staring into Haotef's face, only two feet from his own. He saw the expression of startled disbelief, saw the spark of consciousness die in the man's eyes, and heard the gurgling rattle of the man's final breath. For a moment, time seemed frozen. Then Haotef's body toppled sideways, dragging Nagaro's sword with it. With a gasp, Nagaro staggered backwards, wrenching his blade free.

Chapter 28: Escape!

A ragged cheer went up from the slaves. Nagaro scarcely heard it. He stood with the bloody sword in his hand, chest heaving, balancing to the moving deck, and stared down at the man whose life he had just ended—whose spirit he'd just sent into the void. There seemed to be a roaring in his ears.

"*Vothra!*" he said, speaking aloud and scarcely aware that he did so. "Guide this spirit in its passing, as I would have you guide my spirit in the hour when my time shall come." Vothra help me, he thought, I've killed a man... *No! Don't think about it now. This isn't over yet.*

He shook himself. The roar in his ears was fading, replaced by the sounds of battle from the deck above and the groaning scrape of the two hulls grinding against each other as they rode the gathering swells— and the sound of the other slaves' voices.

"Hakura! Didn't I tell ye he was good?" That was Taru.

"Ye didn't say he was Kroneg's own godson!" Gurd turned towards Nagaro. "By the Mark, mate! I wouldn't want t' be crossing swords with ye!"

Nagaro didn't answer. Leaning down, he carefully wiped the blade of the sword on Haotef's tunic—scarlet on scarlet. He then went quickly back to the body of the first man, Angkat's warrior. He was surprised at how steady his hands were as he slid the blade of the sword back into its empty sheath, unbuckled the man's sword belt, and transferred it to his own waist. He found the dead man's dagger and drew it. Turning, he handed the knife to Taru.

"Here," he said in a flat voice. "Start cutting yourselves free."

Tego was looking at Landros. "D' ye still want t' be takin' that sword form him, mate?"

Landros laughed shortly. "I wouldn't dream of trying! But I *will* take the other one. If ye don't mind..." he added, addressing Nagaro.

Nagaro simply nodded. Re-crossing the moving deck to Haotef's fallen form, he retrieved the first mate's sword and its matching sword belt. Returning, he presented them to the grizzled Fleet warrior.

Landros took both objects in his hands. He was looking keenly at

Nagaro. "Where'd ye learn to fight like that, mate?" He spoke in a low voice as he put his foot on the bench in preparation for cutting his own leather cuff.

Nagaro looked away. "I trained with a master."

"Must ha' been a good one."

"I guess so."

Taru had cut himself free and had passed the knife to Tego. Now the young Turo strode out into the aisle. "So! Nagaro! What's your plan?"

Nagaro was glad to avoid any further questions from Landros. He drew a breath and said, "We're going to take this ship."

The murmur of voices around him stopped. Moraga made a choking sound. "Are ye *mad?* We're in th' middle of a battle!"

Nagaro bent to retrieve Haotef's knife. He handed it to Mendorel, who was closest. "I know," he said calmly. *Hadn't he thought about this a hundred times?* "It's the best time, really. Baalkir's other ships will all be too busy to give chase."

"But... the *storm!*" Gurd protested.

Nagaro frowned. "Yes... that may work to our advantage as well..."

Landros had freed himself and was busily cutting other men loose. He paused. "Nagaro has a good point," he said. "There's a lot o' confusion in a battle. And I can't see any of Baalkir's captains leaving a fight with Angkat to chase a ship full o' slaves."

"But we can't fight them! Mendorel exclaimed in dismay. "We're not sea warriors!"

"We have thirty-six able-bodied men," Nagaro pointed out. He had his own sword out again and had begun moving among the benches, cutting leather cuffs with it as fast as he could. "Five of them are trained with the sword, six if you count Taru. I trained him some before we were taken."

"But ye've only got two swords!" Moraga could be counted on to see the difficulties.

Nagaro's brows knit. "Yes," he said, "we will have to do something about that." He turned to Pavo, whom he'd just freed. "Can you get one or two Mautep to come down here? Pretend that you're Haotef, maybe? Calling for help?"

Pavo nodded. "I think I maybe can do that," he said. Then a slow smile spread across his face. "It pretty funny, I think, to hear Haotef ask for help!" With that, the young Hashtep rose and stepped easily across the moving deck to stand under the open hatch. He waited, listening.

Nagaro turned to face the other slaves. "Keep on working with those knives," he directed them. "And some of you come sit on these benches near the hatch as if you were still chained to them. We want everything to look normal. You can get out of the way again as soon as the swords start swinging." He turned to Landros. "Could you help me move these two bodies?"

A few minutes later, they were ready. Nagaro and Landros stood with drawn swords, each just outside of the patch of light from the open hatch, one fore and one aft. When Pavo heard someone passing on the deck above, he cupped his hands to his mouth and shouted something in Hashti. There followed a rapid exchange of words between the man above and Pavo below. Pavo's part sounded convincingly urgent. The young Hashtep's flare for drama was serving him well. Presently, Pavo stepped back hurriedly, signaling to Nagaro that the man was coming down.

The Mautep descended as Haotef had come, landing facing Nagaro. The man swore at the sight of a loose slave with a sword in his hand and promptly attacked.

This time, Nagaro didn't hesitate to go on the offensive. He launched himself at the Mautep, his sword flashing as he thrust and parried. The startled warrior gave ground before the force of Nagaro's onslaught, retreating backward—right into Landros' sword thrust.

Nagaro stared, stricken, as the Mautep went down with the tip of Landros' sword protruding from his chest. Landros calmly withdrew his blade and moved to wipe it clean. Straightening, he noticed Nagaro's look. "Ye'd ha' brought him down, I'm sure, mate," he said in a conciliatory tone. "This was just faster."

Nagaro was not mollified. "In the *back*, Landros?"

The grizzled sea warrior immediately stepped close and spoke into Nagaro's ear. "There's a time for honor, lad," he muttered, "and this ain't it. We *have* to win this, or we're all dead men. The whole lot of them are counting on us. Ye see that, don't ye?"

Nagaro swallowed and nodded. Though he didn't like it, Landros was right. He had no right to risk the lives of other men for the sake of his own personal sense of honor. But that didn't mean he wasn't going to try to do things the right way if he could.

When Pavo lured the next man down, Nagaro moved instantly to engage him, then gave ground so that the man came after him, moving away from Landros' sword. Before the Kelorin sea warrior could follow, Nagaro found his opening. He came in low under the Mautep's guard and ran the man through, this time saying his prayer silently instead of aloud. Having killed one man already, he now had a feel for how the thing was done. It wasn't as hard as he'd expected... *Surely it shouldn't be so easy to kill a man? Don't think about it...*

The third man's sword had been given to Tredhold. Now the fourth man's weapon went to Gurd. Pavo stepped forward again. This time, the young Hashtep enlisted the aid of the massive lone man, Chaheel, as a second voice, for added verisimilitude. Two warriors came down this time, together, and the resulting fight was a bit of a melee, hampered by the close quarters and the ever more pronounced heaving of the ship. Nagaro ultimately brought down one of the Mautep, stepping in when Gurd was too hard-pressed. Landros and Tredhold dealt with the other man. Nagaro was glad he hadn't seen exactly how the two sea warriors accomplished the deed.

After that, it was very quiet on the deck above. Pavo waited in vain for the sound of boots on the deck planks immediately above them, or any nearby shout or clash of steel. The sound of more distant shouts could be heard above the whistling of the wind across the hatch opening. Apparently the larger battle was still in progress. The one-time slaves exchanged glances. All of them were free of their chains now, and most were gathered in the aisle and among the benches closest to the open aft hatch.

"It's blowin' a bloody gale up there," Tego observed in a hushed voice.

Nagaro sheathed his sword and sat down on a bench. "What do you think has happened, Landros?" he asked. "You have more experience with sea battles than anyone else here." He was deliberately not thinking about the fact that he had now killed three men, and even more deliberately not thinking about the fact that it had gotten easier each time. *Think about here... now... How we're going to finish this.*

Landros considered. "Most likely the fight has moved to Angkat's ship. If it was over, they would ha' cut the grapples loose, and we'd be seeing daylight through our oar ports."

"Aye," put in Tred, "Ye don't want two ships tied together like this in a storm. The hulls knocking together will pound themselves to pieces."

Nagaro sighed. "We're going to have to go up there," he said decisively. "And I see no sense in waiting." He looked at Landros. The former second mate nodded agreement.

Nagaro turned to the circle of expectant faces. "I know most of you have never been fighters," he said earnestly. "Most of you don't have any weapon to fight with, either. We will welcome every man that decides to join us, but I won't think the less of any man who chooses to stay here below until it's over."

The response was prompt and emphatic. "We're with ye, Nagaro!" And from others, "Lead on, mate!"

Moraga growled, "Jus' show me a Mautep throat I can get me hands around!"

Utabala touched his hand to his forehead. "I am no warrior," he said in his rapid Common Speech. "But if it is de will of Him Whose Name We Do Not Es-speak dat I am to die today, I would have it be in de open air."

They made their preparations quickly. A number of the men went about, closing the oar ports against the coming storm. All of the knives that could be found on the bodies of the fallen Mautep were taken and distributed among those who were most willing to use them.

Nagaro picked up one of the two unclaimed swords and handed it to Taru. He gave his friend an encouraging smile. "Do you remember what I taught you?"

"'Course I do." The young Turo's words sounded bold, but Nagaro couldn't help noticing that his friend's hands shook as he was buckling the sword belt.

"Just remember, Taru," he said. "No matter how good the other man is, you can beat him."

"Ye mean like I always used t' beat *you?*" Taru asked bitterly. Then he brightened a little, and smiled crookedly. "But then *nobody's* as good as ye are, Nagaro. I'll bet most o' these Mautep aren't even half as good!"

Caught between modesty and his desire to be bolster his friend's nerve, Nagaro was momentarily at a loss. "You'll be fine, Taru," he said finally. "You're quick, and you've got good instincts. Just be careful, all right?" He gave Taru what he hoped was a reassuring smile and turned away. *If Taru gets hurt trying to do this... Don't think about it...*

Picking up the remaining sword, Nagaro looked around for Simion. He found the young Kelorin sitting, away from the others, on the same bench to which he'd been chained for so many months. Nagaro had cut Simion's cuff himself, but he realized that the young man hadn't moved since then. Approaching, he held out the sword and sword belt. "Here, Simion," he said. "These are for you."

Simion shrank away from the proffered sword. "I... don't want it..." he said brokenly, his eyes pleading. "I... I can't do this!"

Nagaro felt his heart sink. He'd been counting on all of the former Fleet warriors. They had so few trained swordsmen. What he said was, "You don't have to do it if you don't want to."

To his surprise, Simion responded with bitter anger that was apparently self-directed. "But I *should* do it! I'm *supposed* to be a warrior!" He paused, his face betraying his agony. "I'm not so bad, either—with a sword, I mean. It's... it's just that I haven't *killed* anyone yet," he went on miserably. "*And I don't want to!* I was going to sign myself out when the *Fairwind* got back to Lankura. I'm afraid of what I might have to do up there."

Nagaro felt something twist inside him. He sat down on the adjacent bench facing Simion, and laid the sword on the floor between them. "So am I," he said, with perfect honesty.

Simion gaped at him. "But you've already—"

"Killed three men? Yes. That's what I mean."

What could he possibly say to Simion? *I had to do it? They would have killed me?* He knew that it wasn't enough. It didn't stop *him* from feeling tainted. He looked at the floor while he groped amongst his feelings, trying to identify the thing at the center of his resolve. "I made myself a promise after Chitaopa," he said at last, "that I'd see all these men go free, if I could. I have to hope—whatever happens up there— that I'll have the strength to keep my promise." He raised his eyes and looked into Simion's. "We could use your help, Simion. But whatever you decide to do, I'll understand."

The young Kelorin sat strangely still, studying Nagaro with those eyes of midnight blue, so like the Lady Maramine's. Abruptly, the youth leaned down and picked up the sword. Then he stood up and silently began to fasten the belt around his waist with an air of determination.

Nagaro rose. "Thank you, Simion," he said quietly. "If I possibly can, I'll see that you don't have to do any killing."

*

In the end, no man chose to stay behind. The idea of waiting huddled among the benches, wondering what was happening on the deck above, held little appeal. Nagaro led the way, choosing to leave the oar deck by the forward door because he knew the layout of what lay beyond it. They went cautiously through the heaving ship, moving awkwardly up ladders and through trapdoors, with their blades ready in their hands. The forward part of the ship turned out to be quite deserted, however.

Presently they reached the crew's cabin and approached the door that gave egress onto the forward end of the main deck. There Nagaro stopped, listening. All he could hear was the hiss and wash of the waves and the howling of the wind.

There was nothing for it but to open the door to see what he could see. Nagaro turned the handle. Easing the door open took some strength because he was fighting against the powerful push of the wind. Eventually, however, he was able to put his head out far enough to get a view of the tilting, wind-scoured main deck. He squinted against the unaccustomed light, but it wasn't as bright as it could have been because the sun was already obscured behind the towering mass of purple storm clouds bearing down on the ship from out of the west.

At first glance, it seemed the main deck was empty except for the sprawled bodies of half a dozen dead sea-warriors, most of them in Lord Angkat's brown and gold. Then Nagaro spotted the men in the rigging. They were silhouetted against the sky, but he could just make out the scarlet color of their tunics. There were about a dozen of them, clinging to the spars of both the ship's masts, desperately trying to furl the sails without losing their grip and plunging to their deaths.

Nagaro forced the door a bit farther open, trying to determine the whereabouts of the rest of the *Fist*'s crew. Over the wind, he could hear the clash of weapons off to his right. He could see the port rail, where a half a dozen steel grapples and their associated ropes bound the *Fist* against the side of the enemy ship. Beyond the rail, on the deck of the other ship, he could make out the figures of men engaged in heated battle.

Nagaro pulled in his head, and let the door bang shut. Quickly he described what he had seen to the group of men nervously crowding the dim crew cabin.

"Well, that's a stroke o' luck," Landros said when Nagaro had finished. "Most of them being on the other ship. If we cut the ropes, quick and clean, and push her off with the fending pikes, we can strand 'em all there like fish on a beach."

Nagaro nodded. "If we can manage that, the only ones left to deal with are the ones in the rigging. They can't come down fast, either. Not in this gale. How many men do you need to manage those ropes, Landros?"

Landros squinted speculatively. "Give me three o' the swordsmen to do the cutting," he said, "and six strong lads for the pikes."

"Baalkir's men will try to come back as soon as they see what we're about," put in Tredhold. "It could get quite nasty."

"I'll be at Landros' back with the other swordsmen and those who are armed with knives," Nagaro explained. "We'll watch the men on the masts and be ready to move wherever we're needed."

Landros nodded appreciatively. "That's a good plan," he said. "But what about the rest o' the men? Those that don't even have knives?"

Nagaro had thought about this too. "They should stay in here until we're all in position," he said. "But there are several dead warriors out there that haven't been stripped of their weapons. Some of the men can run out, gather up the dead men's knives and swords, and fetch them back here. My group will give them cover. Then they can come to our aid if need be, or defend themselves if it comes to it." This idea was met with nervous nods and murmurs of approval.

It took only minutes to sort out the two parties who would make the foray. Landros took Taru and Gurd for his swordsmen. Pavo, Nanu, Chaheel, and three more of the biggest, strongest men were chosen to handle the long fending pikes. They would carry no other weapons. Tredhold and Simion were to stand with Nagaro, as were all of the men who had knives, except Moraga. The scar-lipped Turowan volunteered to take charge of the weapons scavengers and the men remaining in the crew cabin. Nagaro and Landros readily agreed to this. Tego and Potero were in Nagaro's party. Mendorel, Utabala, and young Kunoa were among the unarmed men under Moraga's charge.

As the foray parties lined up at the door, side by side, behind their respective leaders, Nagaro turned to Pavo. "How do you say 'put down your sword' in Hashti?" he asked.

"*Kia kaar hanuk-tak*," was Pavo's prompt response.

Nagaro carefully repeated the phrase. "Kia... kaar... hanuk-tak."

Landros gaped at him. "Ye don't think the Mahuk are going to surrender, do ye?"

"Why not?" demanded Taru. "*I'd* sooner surrender than have t' face Nagaro."

Nagaro gave his friend a hard look.

"The Mahuk never surrender," Tredhold protested. "And they never ask us to surrender either."

Pavo's brow furrowed. "Mautep say that Droviri have no kajadeem. They not surrender to man who have no honor."

Nagaro saw the indignant looks on the faces of Lord Kuran's former sea warriors. "It's likely that no one has ever tried asking for surrender," he put in quickly. "On either side. It's easy to assume things about other folk when you know nothing about them. And no," he added to Landros. "I don't expect Mautep warriors to surrender to men they think of as slaves. I just feel better knowing I can offer them the choice." He turned back to the door and put his hand on the handle. "Is everyone ready?" There was a chorus of affirmatives.

Nagaro and Landros both put their shoulders to the door, fighting against the wind to swing it wide. Then they were through it, and the next moment, they were running across the heaving deck, feeling the biting blast of the wind on their bare skin as they made for the port rail.

The two galleys were bound together, facing bow to stern. Eight huge grappling hooks were set fast into the *Fist's* rail, spaced out over a distance of several yards, their sharp tines gouging the wood, their ropes securely lashed to cleats along the other ship's rail.

The ship's fending pikes were normally secured by metal clasps along the inside of the rail, but they now lay scattered on the deck where the *Fist's* crew had dropped them after unsuccessfully attempting to ward off the attackers' grapples. It was the work of a moment for Pavo and the other pikemen to snatch up the long poles, each tipped with a metal hook and spike, and thrust them against the hull of the other galley along the stretch where the two ships' sides came closest together. The pikemen stood ready, their feet wide apart to steady themselves against the ship's motion, their hair whipping in the wind.

Landros, Gurd, and Taru started slashing at the thick grapple rope that was nearest to the *Fist's* bow. As Nagaro watched, that first rope parted under the fierce combined attack. The loosed grappling hook rolled across the tilting deck.

Nagaro turned back to face the center of the ship, knowing he dared not watch the progress of the men behind him, though he kept one ear tuned for signs of trouble. He stood poised, flanked by Simion and Tred and five knife-wielding former slaves. He balanced to the ship's motion, setting his teeth against the chilling effects of wind and salt spray as he watched first the Mautep crewmen in the rigging and then the four scavengers, Moraga, Kunoa, and two young Hashtep, who dashed out of the crew cabin to forage for weapons among the corpses on the deck.

On a calm day, the former slaves would surely have been noticed by the crewmen aloft, but the Mautep clinging to the spars in the rising gale had all they could do to make any progress with reefing the sails while avoiding being swept from their perches. They had no attention to spare for events on the deck below, and the wind drowned out or swept away all but the loudest and most piercing sounds. So it was that Moraga's men had finished their work and were scuttling back towards the crew cabin before the alarm was raised. Even then, the shout came, not from above. but from the deck of Angkat's ship. Nagaro couldn't understand the words, but there was no mistaking the tone. The shout was immediately answered by one of the men in the rigging.

Nagaro saw some of the men on the yardarms begin inching their way towards the masts, obviously bent on descending.

The next instant, Landros bellowed, "Here they come, lads! Don't let those bloody bastards get aboard!"

Nagaro spun around and took in the situation at a glance. The two ships were still roped together, but only just. The three slave swordsmen had ceased their assault on the ropes, leaving the aft-most pair of lines still intact, because they'd turned to face a half dozen sword-wielding Mautep in scarlet tunics who were bearing down on them across the deck of Lord Angkat's ship. Pavo and the other pikemen were standing firm, leaning on their pikes, but they all looked terrified.

Nagaro hastily looked behind him and found that Moraga's men were now standing at bay in front of the forward cabin door, awkwardly brandishing scavenged swords. A glance aloft showed him that at least one Mautep had reached the mainmast and started inching down it. "Simion!" he cried. "Protect Moraga and his men. Tego! Portero! Watch those men on the masts! Yell when they touch the deck. The rest of you, to the rail!"

There was no time for more. Nagaro turned back to the rail just as the scarlet-clad assailants reached it from the other side and swords came clashing together. Nagaro waded in, adding his blade to the rest.

The former slaves would have been easily overwhelmed if most of Captain Urchak's men hadn't still been fighting the crew of Angkat's ship. Only eight warriors had come to the rail. Four of these now tried to come over it. One succeeded, but fell to Landros' blade. The other three were pushed back by Nagaro, Gurd, and Tredhold. Gurd felled one of them with a savage cut. What the young Leithian lacked in finesse, he made up for in sheer ferocity.

With a chorus of angry shouts, the six remaining Mautep warriors threw themselves at the railing. Nagaro dodged back and forth along it, his blade a flashing blur that turned stroke after stroke. He parried a vicious cut that was aimed at Taru, striking his opponent's weapon up and away. Taru reached in under Nagaro's arm, thrusting upward to pierce the warrior's belly. The man went down with a cry. The eight Mautep swordsmen were thus reduced to five—even odds. One of the five shouted something and they all fell back, out of range.

The effects of having cut four of the grapple ropes were by now becoming evident. The two ships were pulling apart. The sails of Lord Angkat's ship had all been furled, but the *Fist of Death* still carried too much canvas for the weather, and only the two remaining grapple ropes now prevented her from heeling over in the wind. Those two ropes were stretched taut as bowstrings. Pavo and the other pikemen were pushing with their poles, and the *Fist*'s bow was swinging away from the other ship. The forward end of the gap was fast becoming too wide to fight across.

"Nagaro!" It was Tego's voice from behind them, tense with alarm. "The first man's on th' deck! He's got a sword. He's waitin'..."

Nagaro drew in a ragged breath. "Tred!" he yelled. "Go help Tego!" He saw the Leithian turn to comply. There was no time to turn around himself and take stock of the situation. The ropes were the key. Landros and Gurd were menacing the Mautep on the other ship, backed up by several knife-wielding former slaves. "Hold them, Landros," he gasped, then turned to Taru. "Go cut those two ropes! I'll keep them off you!"

Taru nodded and raced aft as Nagaro flung himself after his friend.

The Mautep plainly saw the danger. They shouted for reinforcements and converged on Taru, Nagaro, and the two ropes. Several more of Urchak's warriors responded. Landros saw the need. "We've got to flank Taru!" he shouted. "Those ropes need cutting and we can't let these devils over the rail!" As Gurd and the others pelted aft, Landros paused just long enough to call for Pavo and Chaheel to bring their pikes.

The clash of steel striking steel rose above the tumult of wind and waves. The Mautep were all furiously trying to stop Taru, slashing and thrusting at him, seeking to get past Nagaro's sword. They were hampered by the fact that they couldn't all reach Taru at once. Some sought to climb over the rail, but they met the blades of Landros and Gurd who were supporting Nagaro on either side. Pavo and Chaheel flanked them, in turn, ready to push the ships apart with their pikes when the ropes failed. The slaves who had only knives held back, crouching and ready in case the enemy presented any work that a knife could do.

Taru was doing his best with the first rope, but so many swords, moving so close to him, were keeping him getting in clean cuts, and the slaves' three trained swordsmen had their hands full. The Mautep were keeping them too busy to add a single stroke to Taru's task. Even with the aid of the two Fleet men, Nagaro felt as if he were trying to be everywhere at once. He knew the Mautep from the rigging would be on his back any minute, and if any more of those on Angkat's ship came to the aid of the ones he already faced, he feared all would be lost.

As it turned out, Lokundas chose this moment to play the Mautep an unkind trick. The rope that Taru was attacking was under a terrific strain, and before it was more than half cut through, it snapped. The *Fist* shuddered as the tension was suddenly released, nearly shaking loose the Mautep crewmen still clinging to her masts. Her bow swung even more sharply away from the other ship, bringing her stern closer to the wind. Her half-furled sails bellied as she strained forward, trying to drag the enemy vessel after her by the last remaining rope.

On the other ship, Captain Urchak felt the sudden jolt of the deck beneath him as the rope broke. He heard the frantic shouts from his crewmen near the rail, calling for aid lest the *Fist of Death* be lost. He swore violently. How in the name of Sheptuum could a band of mere slaves wreak so much havoc? And where was Haotef, his first mate? Here the fight with Angkat's warriors was nearly won, but now he must take men away from it to avert this other catastrophe.

Spouting oaths, the Mautep captain pulled three of his best men out of the fight, and made for the starboard rail at a dead run. He saw two men in the dark blue uniform pants of the Droviri Fleet, wielding swords. He saw the massive pikemen—and the young Turo who was trying desperately to hack at the single remaining rope. And there was a fourth swordsman, protecting the Turo. Urchak didn't recognize the man—pale-skinned, black-bearded, and clad in the rags of a pair of fisherman's pants. Whoever this slave was, he was fighting off two warriors at once, moving with the grace of a cat and the speed of a striking serpent.

Urchak had no time to worry about the man's identity. The young Turo might succeed at any moment. The Mautep captain barked orders as he made for a point opposite the *Fist*'s railing a few feet forward of where the slaves were making their stand. An instant later, he and his three crewmen had fending pikes in their hands and were extending them out across the gap between the two ships. The pikes' great steel hooks bit solidly into the *Fist*'s rail and the four warriors braced their feet and pulled, trying to bring the ships back together again.

At that moment, the last rope snapped.

Under other conditions, the four Mautep warriors might have held the *Fist*—but not with half of her canvas spread in that gale. When the rope parted, several things happened at once. Landros yelled *"Push!"* to his pikemen, and the *Fist* lunged to leeward as they leaned on their poles. At the same time, the ship heeled under the force of the wind, her port rail tilting sharply upward. The Mauteps' four pikes were swept upward as well, lifting Urchak and his crewmen into the air.

Two of the hanging Mautep let go. The first fell back onto the deck of the receding enemy ship. The second dropped into the widening gulf between the two hulls. The third man tried to work his way down the sloping shaft of his pike towards the *Fist*'s rail. He was met by the blade of Landros' sword. Urchak still clung to the fourth pike, dangling over the roiling water, the wind tearing at him.

Three swift strides brought Nagaro to the place where the hook of Urchak's pike gripped the rail. He caught the expression on the Mautep captain's face, the look in the warrior's single good eye. It was a look melded of rage, fear, and disbelief. Behind him Nagaro could hear Tego's voice, rising over the wind, edged with panic.

"Nagaro! They're all on th' deck! They're comin' for us!"

Nagaro hesitated. It would be easy to slay Urchak now. The Mautep captain was beyond the reach of a sword, but Nagaro could grab a pike from Pavo, not four feet away. The sharp point of a fending pike could easily impale a man. It would be justice too—payment for the needless slayings of Jomo and Olomi. But the man was defenseless, clinging to the pike shaft with both hands. It would be wrong, for the very reason that killing Taru's parents had been wrong. Nagaro's hesitation lasted only an instant. Dropping his sword, he seized the end of Urchak's pike with both hands, wrenched the hook free of the wooden rail, and thrust it away from him, out over the water. He watched as Urchak's body spun in the air and fell, flailing, into the foaming sea a dozen feet below.

Snatching up his sword again, Nagaro turned to discover that Tego and the other knife-wielding former slaves were backing towards him, away from the drawn swords of six of the crewmen of the *Fist of Death*, who had come down the main mast. One of the six was Roheed. Lord Baalkir's nephew stood front and center in the group as if he were the leader. The other Mautep flanked him, right and left, as they moved away from the base of the main mast with their swords at the ready. Nagaro caught a movement to his left near the fore mast. The other five Mautep who had been aloft were there, standing on the deck. They were none other than the members of the oar deck crew, led by Baruk.

Nagaro moved quickly, shouldering his way between Tego and Potero to take a stand at the front of the former slaves, directly opposite Roheed. Tredhold was already there to his right with Gurd. Landros and

Taru quickly followed, moving up on his left.

There was a shout from the five members of the Mautep oar deck crew as they dashed across to join their fellows, running with heads down against the wind, their swords in their hands. Baruk led them, and the lame drummer, Ul, limpingly brought up the rear. Another shout came, also from the left, as Moraga and Simion charged out across the slanting deck from the direction of the crew cabin. Kunoa, Mendorel, and two of the Hashtep pelted after them, inexpertly brandishing their pillaged swords. The six reenforcements to the slaves' cause came to a skidding halt beside Landros, even as the six pikemen moved into position behind them, pikes extended.

For several seconds, the two groups of men—slaves and masters—stood menacing one another, waiting to see which would be the first to move. The wild wind raked them as they balanced to the rise and fall of the heavy swell, their feet braced on the sloping deck of the heeling ship. The storm was fast bearing down upon the Strait of Jaamra. A mass of thunderous blue-black cloud now filled the western sky from horizon to zenith. In it, lightning flickered.

Nagaro mentally tallied up the balance sheet. There were eleven Mautep, all of them with swords, all trained—though Fataan, Olam and Ul probably wouldn't be challenging opponents. The former slaves outnumbered the Mautep by two to one—three to one counting those who were watching from the door of the crew cabin. But most of the slaves had only knives, or the unwieldy twelve-foot fending pikes which were impractical weapons in close quarters. Though the former slaves had eleven swords—including those that Moraga's men had taken—only six were in the hands of trained swordsmen, if he counted Taru.

Nagaro knew that both sides must consider their positions to be desperate. The slaves had to win the *Fist of Death* or die, while the sea warriors needed to fight their way through the massed group of slaves to reach the port rail and their only hope of escape. Angkat's ship was already separated from the *Fist* by a thirty-foot swath of storm-tossed water that was growing wider by the minute. If the slaves all attacked at once, picked up the weapons of the fallen, and kept coming, they could almost certainly win by the sheer force of thier numbers. But such an all-out battle would be terribly costly.

Baruk's face was set, his expression grim. He was not a man to willingly suffer a slave to go free.

Roheed was studying Nagaro, his narrow eyes unreadable. There was a chance there. Roheed might listen.

Nagaro lowered his sword point and took a step forward into the space that separated the two adversaries. Raising his voice to be heard above the whistling of the wind in the rigging, he boldly spoke the words that Pavo had just taught him: "Kia kaar hanuk-tak!"

Baruk looked startled for an instant, but then his face darkened, and he spat out some words and started to move as if to attack.

Roheed instantly flung out his arm to restrain the Slave Master and cried *"Wait!"* in Hashti. He lowered his own sword and stepped forward so that he and Nagaro stood face to face only six feet apart. He raised his voice above the storm. "What you want, Nagaro?" he asked in the Common Speech.

Nagaro answered in the same tongue. "We mean to take the ship."

"No!" Roheed's face registered dismay. "You not can do it!"

"I think that we can, Roheed," Nagaro answered levelly. "There is no other way for us. These men will not go back to their chains. You'd have to kill us all, and I don't think you can do that."

As if in answer to his words, the door of the crew cabin suddenly banged open and the rest of the former slaves came pouring forth onto the heaving deck, Utabala in the lead. They had no weapons, and they stayed well back from the other combatants, but the looks on their faces said clearly that they would fight if they had to. Nagaro saw with satisfaction that the Mautep had noted their arrival. Again he addressed Roheed. "If you go now—jump and swim—you can keep your swords."

Baruk interrupted in Hashti. Nagaro could understand enough to guess that the man was asking for a translation. Roheed said something in answer that contained the Hashti words for "ship," and "take," and also *hanuk*, which Nagaro supposed meant "sword."

Baruk's response was an explosion of curses, among which the word *shaku* figured prominently. Then the Slave Master shouted an order, even as Roheed again threw up his hand and cried "Wait!"

Five of the Mautep followed Baruk in his assault—the oar deck crew and a sneering bearded man from Roheed's group. Roheed brought his own sword up, but he appeared uncertain. The other four men with him continued to crouch beside him, confused but on their guard.

Nagaro had raised his sword at the first movement of the attackers, but then he stopped. Roheed was directly in front of him and therefore his natural opponent, but the young Mautep wasn't attacking. To his left, Nagaro saw Baruk close with Landros while Taru took on Olam. Simion moved to intercept Raak, stepping protectively in front of Moraga and Mendorel.

Suddenly Fataan sprang at Nagaro, apparently mistaking his hesitation for weakness. Nagaro immediately unfroze. He parried several of Fataan's thrusts with ease. The young slave tender's skill was so inferior to his own that slaying the youth would have been nothing short of butchery. Accordingly, Nagaro looked for an opportunity, saw one, and sent Fataan's blade arcing over Roheed's head to go clattering across the wind-swept planks of the deck.

Fataan stood weaponless, a look of sheerest terror on his face. Nagaro dealt him nothing worse than a hard stare. "Kia kaar hanuk-tak," he said, rather belatedly. Nevertheless, he'd made his point. With a yelp, Fataan turned and ran scrambling across the deck after his sword.

Then Nagaro heard Potero scream. He turned in time to see the bearded Mautep warrior in the act of pulling his blade from the Turowan's chest. Potero fell, lifeless, on the deck. One of Moraga's unskilled Hashtep swordsmen—a man named Hasaad—valiantly flung himself at the Mautep, but the bearded warrior struck the sword from the man's hand, and without hesitation, ran him through as well.

This dishonorable display ignited Nagaro's outrage. He had nursed Potero through the plague on Chitaopa. The man had been armed only with a knife! And Hasaad had been disarmed and then slain! He felt a wave of white hot anger rise in him. Three strides brought him to a spot between the Mautep and young Kunoa, the warrior's next intended victim. Simion had been moving in the same direction, trying to shield the young Turo, but Nagaro got there first.

"*Kia kaar hanuk-tak!*" Nagaro's voice grated between his teeth.

The warrior laughed at him and lunged.

The fight was intense. The Mautep was good, but Nagaro was better, and when he saw the chance to put his sword through the man's chest, he didn't hesitate. "*That was for Potero,*" he hissed, "*And for Hasaad!*" Stepping over the bloody corpse, he found Ul in front of him. The drummer was old and lame—not really a threat. With one quick motion, Nagaro sent old man's blade flying into the starboard rail, where it embedded itself. Ul emitted a squeak and scuttled after it.

A wild, hot song was singing along Nagaro's veins. It seemed to carry him forward, but it frightened him as well. This was what power felt like... *Too much power...* Suddenly Raak was in front of him. The scar-faced Slave Driver lunged at him, snarling, "*Die now, shaku raal! This be fast!*" Nagaro's anger surged afresh as he stepped forward to meet the challenge.

As it turned out, Raak was half right. The battle *was* over fast. After a few deft parries and thrusts, Nagaro found an opening and ran Raak through the throat, stepping aside to let the man fall. He looked down at the body. "That was for the Hranji," he said, in a voice of deadly calm that masked the maelstrom within. He looked up then, into the teeth of the wind, seeking another adversary on which to vent his fury—and stopped dead. He was staring into the face of Roheed.

In an instant, all the anger drained out of him. Roheed was staring back, shock etched on his features. Nagaro opened his mouth, thinking to call a halt to the fighting, only to realize that it had already stopped.

Everyone seemed to be looking at *him*. The adversaries had stepped apart. All of them were breathing hard, and most had been cut. Baruk and Landros were both still standing, bleeding in multiple places. Four men lay dead on the deck—two casualties from each side. The slain Mautep warriors had both fallen to Nagaro's hand and everyone knew it.

That makes five men I've killed today... No, don't think about it... He focused on Roheed and raised his voice over the gale. "Is this enough? Or must more men die?"

Roheed straightened out of his fighting crouch. The young Mautep had regained his composure. "It is enough," he said. Then he turned and said something to Baruk.

The slave master was looking pale. He shook his head, muttering "*keshaal!*" Eyeing Nagaro, he said something else as well.

Pavo must have moved up from behind Nagaro. Now he spoke low, almost in Nagaro's ear. "Baruk say he think you have demon inside."

Nagaro shivered. *Maybe I do...* But he didn't believe in demons.

There was a further exchange of Hashti between Baruk and Roheed. Nagaro caught the words *shaku* and *kajadeem*.

Once again Pavo spoke at Nagaro's ear. "Baruk say is no honor for surrender to slave, but Roheed say *you* have honor. He say you will let them go if they not fight any more."

Nagaro nodded. "No more shall die!" he cried. "Take your swords and go!"

Deliberately he wiped his own sword on the leg of his ragged pants and sheathed it. He turned to the group of former slaves who stood between the Mautep warriors and the port rail, and he raised his voice above the wind. "Let them pass," he shouted. "This fight is over!" Obediently and without a word, the ragged men moved aside to open a path to the rail.

Nagaro turned back to Roheed. "Take your swords and go. Now!"

Baruk glanced towards the rail. The distance to what had once been Angkat's ship had doubled since the fight began and was increasing by the second. The Slave Master made up his mind. Barking an order to his men, he sheathed his sword and made for the rail at a run. The rest of the oar deck crew sprang after him. Those who stood with Roheed hesitated, seeing that Lord Baalkir's nephew still didn't move, but Roheed spoke a word to them and they too dashed for the rail. Their departure was soon followed by a series of splashes.

Still Roheed stood with his feet braced against the deck's heaving motion, studying Nagaro, with his sword in his hand and the wind whipping his hair.

Nagaro looked to the west. The storm was now moving across the Strait of Jaamra. Already some of the more distant galleys were veiled in a curtain of rain. As he watched, a jagged fork of lightning crackled from cloud to cloud. Thunder rolled like the drums of titans. The deck swung and tilted under his feet. He turned back to the young Mautep "Roheed!" he cried. "You must go *now!* It will soon be too far to swim!"

Lord Baalkir's nephew followed Nagaro's glance with a quick flick of his eyes, but when his own glance returned to Nagaro's face, he only smiled. "I swim very good," he declared, and took a step forward. He raised his sword in a kind of salute, inclining his head to Nagaro. Then he sheathed the blade and asked, "Where is Haotef? I see he go down there." Roheed gestured towards the open aft hatch.

Nagaro swallowed. "He is dead." The gusting wind nearly whipped his words away. "I killed him." It was a confession, not a boast.

Something flickered in Roheed's eyes. It might have been admiration. "And other four man I see go down?"

"All dead."

"You kill them *all?*"

Nagaro shook his head. "Only two of them. The others were killed by Fleet warriors. They all died with their swords in their hands." That much at least was true.

The wind suddenly shifted, and a scattering of raindrops spattered the deck.

Roheed nodded, his narrow dark eyes considering Nagaro. Then he thrust his right hand into his pocket and stepped nearer, bracing against the ship's motion. Withdrawing his hand, he extended it with the palm cupped.

Without hesitation, Nagaro reached out and grasped the proffered hand. Their gazes met and Nagaro read respect in the other man's eyes. Then he realized that something small and hard was pressing against his palm. Looking down as Roheed released his grip, Nagaro stared at the object in his hand. It was a small gold ring, wrought in the shape of a salamander with its head resting on its tail and two tiny bright-green stones for eyes.

"It ring of Emril." Roheed spoke low and urgently. "My father find it..." He paused. "After she die..."

Roheed's pause had sounded uncomfortable, as if he were uncertain of the truth of what he'd just said. Nagaro found himself wondering whether the ring had ever really been lost. Another flurry of raindrops struck the deck, this time more numerous.

Roheed was speaking again. "He give it to me before we sail. I give to you. Maybe you find her family. Tell them... Roheed say... thank you..." The young man was obviously struggling to find words in the Common Speech. "I say thank you... for Emril... for she be so good to me. Tell them my father... he very sorry."

Nagaro couldn't think of anything to say. He nodded, and slid the ring onto the last finger of his left hand for safekeeping.

At that moment, a more steady rain started to fall—large drops, widely spaced, splashed Nagaro's bare skin. Roheed glanced towards Angkat's ship. The serious rain was out there, advancing like a moving curtain. Already most of the other ships were shrouded by it. Soon the ship that carried the rest of the *Fist*'s Mautep crew would be as well. The day had grown very dark.

Roheed started to turn away, then turned back one last time. "What you are, Nagaro? You are warrior?"

Nagaro shook his head. "I am only Nagaro," he said, then added, on an impulse, "Or maybe I am 'Shaku Raal' as long as there are slaves kept in the Mahuk Baar."

But now Roheed shook his head. "No, not *Shaku Raal*," he said seriously. "I give you other name—*Kiraam Shaku-Tal*." Then he spun away, raced across the deck, and leaped onto the port rail. For a moment the young Mautep stood there, balancing as the ship heaved. A flash of lightning outlined his form in sharp silhouette, his arms outstretched. Then Lord Baalkir's nephew executed a perfect arching dive into the sea and was gone.

Nagaro stood staring after him. "I hope he can indeed 'swim very good,'" he murmured to himself.

And then the rain came down in earnest. A dense wall of furiously pelting drops swept across the deck of the *Fist of Death*, obscuring everything that lay more than a few yards away. Within seconds they were all utterly drenched.

To men who had been unable to bathe their bodies for months or even years, that rain came like the blessed hand of heaven. All around him, Nagaro saw men stretching their arms wide and turning their faces up to the sky. He wanted to do the same. More than that, he wanted to shout or laugh or weep. The tide of emotion that swelled within him was almost too powerful to bear. *They had done it! They were free!*

But it wasn't over. They must sail away from this place—as far and as fast as they could—while the storm covered them, or else they might still be retaken. Nagaro cupped his hands to his mouth and shouted as loudly as he could into the storm. "*Who knows how to steer a ship?*"

"I can do that!" Simion emerged, dripping, out of the watery murk. "But it'll take two men in this gale!"

"Let me help ye!" shouted Mendorel, stepping around from behind Nagaro. "I've never done it before, but I can learn!"

"That's good!" Nagaro was glad to have Mendorel volunteer. He wasn't sure who he would have chosen to stand duty with Simion. "Put her stern to the wind and hold it there. Let the storm take us away from this place as fast as possible!"

"Aye, Zirda!" Simion saluted, and struck off across the deck with Mendorel right behind him.

Nagaro frowned at the younger man's response. He was no Fleet officer. Simion must be jesting...

He felt a hand grip his shoulder. "*We've got t' shorten sail!*" Landros bellowed the words into his ear. The grizzled sea warrior was holding onto him with one hand and wiping dripping hair from his eyes with the other.

Nagaro shook his head emphatically. "I want her to run before the wind! We need to keep sail on her!"

Landros tightened his grip on Nagaro's shoulder, shouting into his face to be heard over the wind. "I'm with ye, mate. But she's a galley, not a merchantman! She's got no ballast! If the wind shifts sudden, with this much sail on the yards, it'll lay her over! She'll founder!"

"All right then." Nagaro yielded to the veteran sea warrior. Landros had been second mate on the *Fairwind* after all. "You see to it. But leave every stitch you dare! How many men do you need?"

"About twenty."

"Right! You ask the Droviri. Where's Pavo...?"

"I am here!"

Nagaro turned about in the rain to find the young Hashtep standing right beside him, dripping.

"We need men for the sails, Pavo! Find Hashtep who are willing to go aloft and send them to the masts. Send the rest to me. We need to get these bodies off the deck!"

Pavo nodded and strode off through the rain. Landros had already gone. Somewhere to starboard, his voice could be heard admonishing the men to "look lively!"

"What can I do?" Taru appeared out of the swirling rain.

"Take your choice," Nagaro replied grimly. "The sails with Landros, or the corpses with me."

Chapter 29: After The Storm

The storm had largely spent its fury, and night had stolen over the world. The wind still blew stiffly out of the southwest, but the rain had stopped and the parting rags of cloud had revealed enough patches of sky to show them the blossoming stars. As soon as they could see enough of these to mark their course, they'd turned the bow northward. An hour later, when the thinning of the clouds to starboard had revealed the coast of the mainland rather close at hand, they'd altered course again to sail north by northwest.

Nagaro sat on the deck, leaning against the forward-facing wall of the structure that housed the aft cabins—the "stern castle," Landros called it. The last few hours had been exhausting, and his mind felt numb. Somehow Landros' group had managed to put several reefs in the sails without anyone being blown from a yardarm. The rest of the crew, under Nagaro's direction, had gotten the bodies of the slain Mautep flung overboard—minus their boots and their black uniform pants. Most of the former slaves' own clothing had long since been reduced to rags, and all of them were barefoot. The thought of being able to clothe themselves decently again was pleasing enough to overcome any squeamishness regarding the recent history of the clothing. The bodies of Potero and Hasaad had been wrapped in sailcloth and laid in one of the aft cabins, in the hope of burying them soon, decently, on dry land.

Handling all the bodies would have been unpleasant work in any case. The storm had made it difficult as well, for the heaving deck had been slick with rain and awash with waves that came over the railing. To make matters worse, Nagaro had felt the need to work fast, not wanting to leave a long trail of floating corpses behind them to show which way they'd gone. No one had wanted to go down into the oar deck to retrieve the six corpses there. In the end, Nagaro had gone down himself, and Taru had loyally gone with him.

After they'd cleared the decks above and below, Nagaro had stood a shift helping to hold the big tiller steady. Then, as the storm had lessened its fury, Landros had told him it was safe to let out a bit more sail, so he'd tried to find twenty men who weren't too exhausted to hold their place in the rigging. He'd gone up the foremast himself when the number had come up short. There he'd learned first-hand the perils of wrestling with soaked canvas while clinging to a yardarm twenty-five feet above the deck in battering wind and numbing rain.

He had only just come down from the mast when Utabala had asked if there shouldn't be some food handed around. Nagaro had put the merchant's agent in charge of the matter, with the massive lone men, Nanu and Chaheel, to assist him. The three had made sure that the distribution was fairly done, preventing what would otherwise have become a free-for-all. The food had come from the Mautep's store, and had been better than their usual slave fare, but Nagaro could scarcely remember what it had tasted like... *By the Eyes*, he was tired.

Nagaro wearily shifted his aching arms, clenching and unclenching his fingers where they rested in his lap. Emril's ring was still on his finger, tangible proof of the reality of the events of the last several hours. The elegant sword was there too, at his hip, as further proof. The hilt caught the light from the lantern hanging on a hook above the aft cabin door. There was a fine tracery of gold inlay on the hand-guard and a polished green stone set into the end of the pommel.

Such a beautiful thing to have done such bloody work... But of course, it wasn't the sword that had done the work. It was the hands... *his hands.* He stared at them. Thoughts that he'd been trying very hard to suppress for several hours had begun to work their way up through the numbness and the exhaustion. They were uncomfortable thoughts—disturbing, even frightening...

He wished he might seek comfort from Vothra, for he remembered the feeling of peace that had come to him that one night in Sar Tipaal. But he was afraid to try to call the Benevolent Spirit. *What if Vothra didn't answer?* He was terribly afraid that Vothra might never speak to him again.

At home, back in the Lady's house at Averwin, he'd read and reread everything that the Writings had to say about killing. It had all seemed so simple then, and so clear—all about fighting for just causes... defending those who could not defend themselves... ending suffering... the need, sometimes, to answer with violence those who brought violence into the world. But how great must one's suffering be to justify taking a life? It had been Nagaro's idea to lure those Mautep warriors down onto the oar deck, into what had amounted to a deadly trap. And on the upper deck, he had killed in anger, exacting payment for the deaths of others. Wasn't that vengeance? It seemed to him that he had done everything wrong.

The darkening downward spiral of Nagaro's thoughts was interrupted when the door of the stern castle opened and Taru and Landros emerged, their wounds freshly dressed. Tredhold was ministering to the wounded, having found the ship's infirmary, containing all the necessities of the healer's art.

Taru flung himself down beside Nagaro, and Landros sat next to the young Turo. "*Hamanei*, but I'm tired!" Taru exclaimed. "Doesn't it feel good to be free, though! I was beginning t' think it'd never happen, and now it has."

Landros addressed Nagaro. "Ye should go in and let Tred take care o' that cut on your side, mate."

Nagaro nodded, but he didn't move. Other thoughts were surfacing. It shouldn't be that easy to kill a man... It had gotten easier every time. And the last two, up on deck... The way it had made him feel...

"How many o' them d' ye think we killed, Landros?" Taru's question cut across Nagaro's thoughts like a knife blade.

Landros' tone was matter-of-fact when he answered. "Eleven, by my count. And we only lost two. We were dead lucky."

"Aye, lucky we had Nagaro!" Taru turned to his friend. "How many did ye kill, Nagaro?"

"Five." His voice came out flat, and he didn't look at his friend. It was almost half the total...

"The one I stuck in the belly... D' ye think I killed him?"

Nagaro could not meet Taru's eyes. "Very likely," he said, woodenly. *But that's not a quick way to die. I always went for the heart, or the throat... But I still killed them...*

Landros was looking at Nagaro. Now he said cautiously, "Ye never killed anyone before, did ye, lad?"

Nagaro kept his eyes fixed straight in front of him. "No."

"Sometimes it takes a bit o' getting used to."

Nagaro continued to stare across the deck. "Five men..." he said quietly. "Five men, whose spirits I sent into the void..." He paused to draw a shuddering breath. "I've crossed a line—from a place where I'd never killed anyone, to a place where I have. And even if I never kill another man as long as I live, *I can never get back across that line.*"

There was a short, stunned silence.

"Ye're not saying ye're *sorry*, surely?" The words burst from Taru. "They were *Mautep*, Nagaro! And ye were magnificent!"

"*No, I wasn't!*" Nagaro's voice shook. "I was *frightening*. Pavo said that Baruk thought I had a demon inside of me!" Nagaro shut his eyes and therefore didn't see how Landros silenced Taru with a gesture.

Landros stood up. "I'll go see if Tred is ready to have a look at that cut o' yours," he said, with careful casualness. Motioning for Taru to follow him, he made for the door under the gently swinging lantern. Once the two men were in the passage beyond, with the door closed behind them, Landros met Taru's questioning look. "This water's too deep for the likes o' you or me, lad," he said with a shake of his grizzled head. "This is work for Tred. The old barnacle's a fair hand at head-doctoring."

"*Head-doctoring?*" Taru was alarmed. "But Nagaro shouldn't need any kind o' head-doctoring! I don't understand what's wrong with him. He always wanted t' be a warrior!"

"Wishing and doing are two different things, lad." Landros led the way along the corridor.

"But *I* killed a man for the first time too! And... and it doesn't trouble *me!*"

"Doesn't it?" Landros paused to give the young Turo a searching look.

"O' course not! He was a Mautep. An enemy! I wish I could ha' killed more o' them!"

Landros shook his head and started forward again. "Well, Nagaro's not you, Taru. And he's Vothrin—takes it more seriously than most too. And Vothra doesn't much care for killing."

They'd reached the infirmary. One of the Hashtep was just coming out. As soon as the man had gone, Landros stepped into the doorway and addressed the healer.

"Tred, I want ye to have a look at Nagaro next. And I think ye'd better talk to him as well."

Tredhold looked up from his basin, towel, and bandages. "Nagaro? Ye don't think he's in trouble, do ye?"

"He could be."

Tredhold frowned. "I was worried about him for a moment, there at the beginning—when he said that prayer over Haotef—but I thought he looked solid as rock after that. I don't know that I've ever seen a new recruit handle himself so well. I was thinking that he'd make a fair Fleet officer when this is over."

Landros gave a short laugh. "I was thinking he could be captaining a ship inside of two years—and that's only because ye can't rise any faster." He shook his head. "It was amazing, Tred. I could tell he'd never fought for blood before—that he didn't know exactly how to go about killing a man. But he figured it out. Aye, did he! And once he'd figured it out, he just got better... and better... I don't know, Tred. Maybe he was just holding it inside. Or maybe he's just tired. Anyway, I hope ye can help him sort things out. That lad's got more born talent for the blade than anyone I ever saw. It'd be a bloody shame if he got himself so tied up inside that he couldn't use it."

Tredhold lifted his shoulders in a shrug. "Not everyone is cut out to be a warrior, old friend," he said. "I'll do whatever I can." He frowned to himself. It wasn't likely to be easy. Thinking men were always the hardest.

After Landros had gone out, Tredhold could hear Taru's worried voice receding up the corridor. "Nagaro's strong, I tell ye. He'll be all right! He *has* t' be!"

*

Nagaro sat silently on a stool while Tredhold cleaned his wound. The healer was seated on a bench beside him, dabbing gently at the cut with a wet cloth and talking about unimportant things. Nagaro wasn't listening. He was fairly sure that Landros had said something to Tred, and he did not resent it. He wanted to talk to someone, and if Landros thought Tred was the man to talk to, that was fine. He just didn't know where to begin.

The cut had been burning dully for hours—a pain so constant that it had ceased to register. Now, however, it was stinging viciously. At least it gave him something to focus on.

"It's a neat, clean cut," Tredhold was saying. "It should heal up well. Won't leave much of a scar."

The wet cloth stopped dabbing and there was a new sensation—or rather, a lessening of sensation. Nagaro twisted his neck to look at the wound. Tredhold was applying some salve out of a little pot. It was chutapak.

Tredhold grinned at him. "I wish I'd had a barrel of this back on the *Fairwind*," he said. "It seems to hasten healing." He gave Nagaro a careful look. "Ye look tired, lad," he observed. "Ye should try to get some sleep when I'm finished here."

Nagaro looked away. "I don't think I'll be able to sleep tonight," he said with complete honesty. "Not after what I've done..." *Will I ever be able to sleep again? What if I dream about sticking swords through men's chests all night...*

There was a pause. Then Tredhold said seriously: "This day asked a lot of ye, Nagaro. And everything it asked for, ye gave. I'd like to say thank you... for all of us."

Nagaro shifted uncomfortably. "Landros did as much as I did."

"Maybe. But it's work that Landros is used to doing. For you it was something new, if I'm not mistaken."

"Yes." Nagaro paused, then said, "I didn't like the way it made me feel."

"And how was that?" The healer's voice was gently probing.

Nagaro sought words to explain. It was more accurate to say that he didn't like the fact that a part of him *had* liked the way it felt. "Killing men is easier... and harder... than I expected," he said, at last. "Easier to do... Harder to live with..."

Tredhold nodded. "I've been in the Fleet for fifteen years," he said seriously. "I've seen a lot o' new recruits face their first battle—the first time they've had to kill a man." The healer pressed a dressing against the wound and began slowly to wrap a strip of bandage around Nagaro's chest. "I've seen all kinds of reactions—from the ones who can drop a man in his tracks and walk away and think nothing of it, all the way to the ones that just can't do it at all. Simion is one o' those. He's a good lad—even if he is crossed as a pair o' sheep shears. He can hold his own with a blade, but he can't quite make the killing stroke. He fights like a man who hopes that the other man'll give up and go home. Sometimes that's enough. When it isn't, someone else has to step in and finish the task. That hasn't made him very popular."

Tredhold paused, cocking his head to one side. "By the way," he said. "I've been wondering what ye said to Simion, down on the oar deck, that stiffened his spine. He came through for us better than I expected."

Nagaro was startled by the question. He gave the healer a puzzled look. "I told him I didn't like it either... and that I'd try to see that he didn't have to kill anyone..."

"Is that why ye stepped in between Simion and the warrior who killed Potero and Hasaad?"

Nagaro's expression changed in an instant. "No," he said wretchedly, turning away. "I got angry,,, because of the way the man killed them. I wasn't thinking of Simion. I just wanted to kill that man!"

"That's the way o' nature, Nagaro," Tredhold said quietly. "Ye see a man kill one o' your mates, and ye want to make him pay. I've felt it many times. Especially if it's a man I've doctored."

Nagaro frowned. "*Potero...*" he murmured. Then he looked down and noticed the stain of dark brown blood on his clothing where he'd wiped his sword clean after killing Raak. He felt suddenly sick. "But I shouldn't get so angry that I start killing everyone in front of me!"

"Do ye really think ye were doing that?" Tred sounded surprised. "Nagaro, that's *not* what I saw."

"What do you mean? I killed that bearded man who killed Potero, and I killed Raak..."

"Aye, and in between, ye *didn't* kill Ul. Ye disarmed him. Why?"

"Because he was just a lame old man. And he hadn't done anything that I knew of."

"And ye didn't kill Roheed either. Ye stopped fighting when ye came to Roheed."

"Because I didn't want to fight him! He'd told his men to wait—twice!" He felt Tredhold's eyes on him.

"Here's another thing," Tred offered. "Both o' the men that ye killed attacked ye first. Ye even asked the first one to put down his sword."

"But I didn't expect him to *do* it!" Nagaro protested. "I didn't even *want* him to!"

"Oh, aye," Tredhold said calmly. "But if he *had* put it down, would ye ha' killed him anyway?"

"*An unarmed man?*" Nagaro turned on the healer. "Of course not!"

"Ye said ye were angry—"

"Not *that* angry!" Nagaro's eyes blazed.

"All right then..." Tredhold was seeing the image of Nagaro's fevered face and hearing the cold fury with which the young Kelorin had said "*I'm going to kill you!*" He shook off the thought. "Nagaro," he said, "I've seen men so full of anger and blood lust that they couldn't see past the color o' the other man's uniform. But ye're not that kind of man. Ye were thinking the whole time—making choices."

"Maybe so..." Nagaro studied his hands. *Did that make it better... or worse?* After a moment, he looked up again. "Tell me one thing, Tred. Do you believe it was all *necessary?* I mean... Haotef would have killed me if I hadn't killed him. I'm pretty sure of that. And Landros would have killed the next two if I hadn't, and maybe not so honorably. But the two on the upper deck... did I really have to kill *them?*"

Tredhold met his gaze soberly. "Yes," he said. "I think ye did."

"Why?"

The healer frowned. "Because Baruk and his lot would never have given up and left so easily if they hadn't seen what ye could do," he said. "Men like that—men who live by the sword—need to see what ye can do with one, and that ye're willing to do it. If that's what's troubling ye, lad, ye can put it by. Ye did what had to be done, and ye did it uncommonly well."

Nagaro sat silent, staring at his hands and trying unsuccessfully to believe what the healer had said.

Tredhold stood up and fetched a cup from the table, and then a small bottle from one of the cupboards. The healer poured some water into the cup from a water skin and carefully added four drops of the liquid from the bottle. He swirled the cup and held it out to Nagaro. "Here, lad," he said, "I want ye to drink this."

"*Why? What is it?*" Nagaro's suspicion was reflexive. The words just slipped out before he could stop them.

"Only something to help ye sleep." Tredhold answered mildly, his searching gaze on Nagaro's face. When Nagaro still seemed to hesitate, he added, "That's *all* it is. I swear it! Ye need to sleep, Nagaro."

Nagaro stared at the cup. The last time that he'd been made to sleep to ease a troubled mind had been the day of the Lady Maramine's death. He hadn't had any choice about it then, but he had to admit, grudgingly, that it had probably helped. It was absurd for him not to trust Tredhold in this... "All right," he said. He took the cup and drank the contents quickly before he could change his mind. The liquid had an odd taste, but it was quite different from that of heskial. He felt himself relax a little. He stood up to leave.

Tredhold stopped him at the door when he started to turn in the direction that led to the deck. "Not that way, lad. Ye'd best sleep here in the officer's quarters tonight. I'll see that ye're not disturbed."

Nagaro offered no argument. He didn't want company.

The cabin Tred led him to contained four bunks, rather wider and more comfortable than those in the crew cabin. Nagaro stopped at the first one. Already his head was beginning to swim. He unfastened the sword belt and let the belt and blade fall to the floor. He left them where they fell. Dropping onto the bed, he stretched his aching body at full length and yielded to swirling, gray oblivion.

*

Spirit that calls itself Nagaro, wake!

Nagaro opened his eyes to the near darkness of the officer's cabin. The remnant of some disquieting dream fled, and he was glad not to pursue it. "Who is it? Where are you?"

I am here.

Nagaro rolled onto his side. Then he sat up and stared. The figure stood only a few feet away near the head of the bed. It was not so much illuminated by the moonlight streaming through the single porthole as it was shining by its own inner radiance. It wore a long-sleeved, robe-like garment that was black and silver. Black-and-silver hair fell softly about its shoulders, and starlit eyes gazed at him from a smooth, ageless face that was neither male nor female.

"Vothra?" He spoke the name uncertainly. "Am I... awake?"

Yes. I have been trying to wake you for some time.

The voice didn't seem to reach his ears in the normal way. It had a sweet gentleness that he couldn't describe, like love unspoken.

The healer meant well, but your mind has been clouded.

Indeed, Nagaro still felt half asleep. "But how am I able to see you if I'm awake?"

The face seemed to smile at him, and the dark eyes held his gaze. *Your mind feels my presence. It knows where I am. I have only to give it the image I wish you to see and the words I wish you to hear.*

Something nagged at him... something in what Vothra had just said. But there was a more immediate question in his mind. "Why don't you look the same as you did in the slave barn?"

Ah, you see, I have been growing stronger. The first time I came to you in a dream—more than two years ago—your mind chose to give me the shape of the one you call Maramine. The best I could do then was to

*send that image away before I spoke to you. The image you saw in the
slave barn was partly of my making, and partly of your own.*

"Oh." He knew, then, what it was that had bothered him about what
the spirit had said. Vothra had used the word "*presence*." He knew what
a "presence" was, or what one had used to be. He'd read about them, and
they were *not* commonplace. He remembered that Vothra had told him
before that their spirits were joined... that it was more *aware* of him...
And the next thing he remembered was the whole horrible cascade of
events of the day just past, and just exactly how unworthy he felt he was
of Vothra's "presence."

He was fully awake now, staring into the figure's eyes, as the pain
knotted inside of him. He groaned. "But I didn't *call* you! I didn't think
that I *should*."

Yes, I know. The gaze of those eyes held him transfixed. The voice,
however, was almost conversational. *In a sense, though, you did call—
three times—although that was many hours ago. I did not speak to you
then because you had a task to finish—and you have not been alone since,
until you came to this place. Indeed, you are not alone now. The healer is
here, but he sleeps.*

The figure pointed with a slender finger to a recumbent form on
the bed across from where Nagaro sat. He recognized Tredhold's sandy
hair, pale in the moonlight. He frowned, confused. "I called you? *When?*"
Then it came to him. "The prayer," he murmured. "I said it aloud for
Haotef, and I said it in my head for the next two. But when I got up on
deck, I forgot to say it for the others!"

*Once would have been sufficient. My mind is never very far from you.
I have been watching you, spirit that calls itself Nagaro.*

"Watching me? *Oh no!*" That ment Vothra had seen everything he'd
done—read every thought that was in his mind! He felt like weeping.
"Vothra!" He choked on the name. "I've killed five men! *I'm sorry...*"

The star-filled eyes did not waver, and once again the voice sighed
gently across his mind. *All of this I know. And you need not apologize to
me for any of it. Those five spirits are safe. They lie already, this night,
each wrapped in the warm velvet darkness of the womb, shrunk to the
tiniest form of being that can be called human... without awareness, or
remembrance, or understanding. In the fullness of time, they will grow
and blossom, and each will be born again into the world to learn anew
its ways, its beauty, and its wisdom. So flows the circle of our lives. So it
will be for you in that hour when your time shall come. Death is not so
terrible...*

Nagaro shook his head. "No, of course death isn't terrible... not for
the *dead*, I mean, once they're dead... But it's terrible for the *living*, for
those who are left behind to grieve, and to suffer from the loss! Death

ends dreams, destroys hopes—" He stopped. All of this was in the Writings. *And he was speaking to Vothra!* "Are you testing me?" he demanded, but he knew the answer before it was spoken.

That has never been my purpose, for life presents tests enough. The voice sounded almost sad, and the eyes were impossibly gentle, excruciatingly kind. *I am here to help you, if I can.*

If anything, Nagaro felt worse. "But you should be angry with me! Or at least disappointed." How could Vothra know everything he'd done and yet show no trace of disapproval?

The figure seemed to sigh. *How should I presume to judge you? I have the knowledge gained from a thousand lives, while you are finding your way through a single one, and recall no other. It is far easier to tell another man what he ought to do in his life than it is to do the right thing in one's own, while living it.*

"Then I *have* done wrong! How can I deserve your help?"

Another sigh. *How can you not? And I did not say that you had done wrong. Does it help to know that, in the course of all the lives that I have lived, I have held a sword in my own hand many times? That I, too, have killed—too many times to number? Here and there among those thousand lives, I have been the agent of every kind of violence and cruelty known to humankind—as well as every mercy and every kindness...*

"But that can't be! Unless..." Nagaro frowned. "Unless the violence was done long ago, before the Book of Vothra was written... before those spirits first became part of you..."

Some of it was, but by no means all.

Nagaro sat very still for a long moment without speaking, stunned by this revelation.

Will you let me try to help you, now, spirit that calls itself Nagaro?

A little part of the knot of pain and self-directed anger inside of him began to loosen. "Yes," he said huskily. "Please."

Then tell me about the things that trouble you.

So he began with the question of whether gaining freedom for the slaves justified taking lives. When he ceased speaking, Vothra answered as before, very gently.

You wish me to weigh the freedom of three dozen men against the lives of eleven. But these are not of the same coin. Slavery is without a doubt a great wrong. It is a lesser wrong, surely, than killing an innocent man—but perhaps a greater wrong than killing a guilty one. Does it help to know that all of those you killed were prepared to kill a slave simply for raising a hand against his master?

Nagaro frowned. "That helps some," he said. "But I didn't know it when I did it, which is when I had to choose. How can I make such a choice again if I can't know what's in a man's heart?"

The figure sadly shook its head. *Those who walk in flesh in the world must often choose without knowing. I cannot give you rules for choosing, nor can I counsel you not to choose if you are uncertain. But consider this: Those eleven men came prepared to kill, and to hazard their lives in battle. They lost their lives in a battle they did not anticipate, at the hands of an enemy they never imagined would raise a sword against them. I find that a fine irony. Never before in the history of the Mahuk Baar has a ship-full of slaves won freedom. No one can guess what may come of this deed when all its consequences have played out, down all the years. And no one can say now exactly what has been purchased with the price of eleven lives. But this is certain: Through your actions, something new has been wrought in the world. Is this new thing—this freeing of slaves—something good?*

Nagaro didn't hesitate. "Yes," he said with conviction. "I believe that it is."

Then be at ease. Trust the judgement of the healer, that what you did was necessary to achieve that good end, for he understands the ways of warriors. It is good, also, that you told the one called Roheed that those who died below decks died as warriors, for it means much to their people.

Nagaro felt a sense of relief, a surge of hope. "Did Roheed come safely, then, to the other ship?"

There was a little pause. *Ordinarily I would not answer such a question,* the spirit told him. *I prefer to deal in knowledge that leads to wisdom or to understanding, rather than in information about the doings of the world. If I begin to answer such questions, there is no end to men's curiosity. And such answers lead to actions, and actions to consequences—which are impossible to predict.* (A little sigh...) *Ah, but this is such a small thing, and one you might well come to know in time. And it will bring you peace. So, yes. Roheed is safe, and the others also. Nine lives were saved by your actions that otherwise would have been forfeit—ten including that of the one called Urchak, whom you could have slain, but spared.*

Nagaro closed his eyes and let out his breath in a long sigh. "That is good," he murmured. This knowledge meant as much to him as anything else the spirit had said. He felt a further easing of the knot of his feelings. A moment later, however, his eyes snapped open again as other thoughts intruded. "The Writings say one shouldn't be ruled by anger. Or kill out of anger, or for vengeance. I think I did all of those things!"

Ah... anger. The figure nodded in gentle understanding. *The healer was right about that also. Anger is a natural thing, and it is never more natural than when it comes in answer to cruelty or injustice—whether against oneself, or another. The simplest test of anger is also in the Writings. No matter how justified, anger should not lead you to commit an act that is itself cruel or unjust. By that test, you have not failed. You let your anger carry you some distance, but not too far, and that is important. You never gave yourself up to it.*

Nagaro was trying hard to accept the spirit's words, but he couldn't quite do it—and he knew why, though his thoughts shied away from the unasked question. "What about vengeance?" he asked quickly because he needed to say something.

The line between vengeance and just retribution is fine, the Spirit told him, *and not always agreed upon by all peoples. Most would say a sentence of death is just, for a willful murder. Had you and your friends been other Mautep, rather than former slaves, the Mautep you faced today would have had no difficulty seeing justice in your actions, and the injustice of their own.*

For the first time, Nagaro pulled his gaze away from the figure's shining face. He looked down, chewing his lip. This answer touched the edges of his pain without assuaging it, and the things that still weighed upon his mind were things he was afraid to put into words.

But I already know what they are.

The voice had breathed the words ever so gently. Nagaro looked up, startled, into those knowing eyes. He shivered. *It's true,* he thought. *You can see everything that's in my mind...*

The figure shrugged its ethereal shoulders. *More or less,* it said, with a quizzical smile. *But do not be disturbed. There is never likely to be anything there I have not seen before—and seen from the inside.*

Nagaro frowned. "If you know what my thoughts are, why must I speak them?"

There was a little soft rustle of laughter. *Well asked,* said the gentle voice. *But if you speak the thought that is at the heart of your fear—put it into simple words—it will cease to be so terrible. Try it.*

Nagaro swallowed and said one of the things, the one that seemed easier. "I'm afraid of what will happen if I get *too* angry... of what I might do." *There it was.*

The figure nodded. *So should everyone be, spirit called Nagaro, for anyone can be pushed too far. Yet your past has made you more than commonly distrustful of your anger. You are, in fact, less likely to stumble than one who is less wary.*

"Oh." *Was it as simple as that? And he'd been so worried?* He felt his spirit lift as pieces of the knot dropped away.

Vothra smiled at him disarmingly. *Now speak the rest of it.*

Nagaro was willing, but this was harder. It was both more painful and more difficult to explain. "When I was on the upper deck," he began, "after I killed the man who killed Potero... I... I felt as if I could do anything—with the sword, I mean—and no one could stop me. I felt *powerful.* And it felt *good.* And that frightens me."

Why?

He frowned, trying to find the answer. "Because I never thought I wanted power," he said after a moment. "It isn't good to want power."

The figure spread its hands. The starlit eyes were deep enough to drown in. *But everyone desires power, for power is nothing more than the ability to control the world around you—or bits of it. Who is there who does not wish to secure his own happiness and the happiness of those he cares for? It is impossible to do good in the world without exercising power of some kind, even if it is only the power of one heart to speak to another through love.*

Nagaro frowned harder. This sounded harmless, but it wasn't what he'd meant. What he was talking about was far from harmless. "I mean power *over other people.* I don't want *that* kind of power!"

And if you see someone doing something hurtful, do you not wish to stop him?

"Well, yes... of course..."

And if you see some great wrong? A thing like slavery?

"I would end slavery if I could, but..."

The figure lifted its hands in a gesture that seemed to say, "you see?"

Now Nagaro's spirit writhed, pinned between Vothra's inexorable logic and the rawness of his pain. "But I was *judging* them! Tred was right! I was choosing which ones should live and which should die!"

And still the deep, dark eyes regarded him sympathetically. *The world is made better when there is justice in it, spirit called Nagaro. And there can be no justice without judgement—just as there can be no good work without power. But judgement and justice are both too infrequently encountered on the field of battle.*

This was too much for Nagaro. "You don't understand!" he cried. "I hadn't any *right* to judge them! I shouldn't have been able to kill them so easily—"

Abruptly, the silver figure reached out and touched him lightly on the forehead. It felt like nothing more than the kiss of a cool breeze.

Peace...

The word moved across Nagaro's mind and through him like an echo of a sigh. Somehow it steadied him. He blinked, then drew a deep breath and let it out again. Vothra *did* understand. Of course... *He knew that.*

The figure smiled at him sadly. *You have a powerful gift, spirit that calls itself Nagaro,* the voice told him gravely. *It is a gift with great potential for making good things happen in the world, among those who call themselves warriors—those who are accustomed to deciding things by the sword.* There was a small sigh. *But it is not an easy gift for a thoughtful man—a man of your sensibilities. If you are to use it, you will not be able to entirely avoid violence and bloodshed—or choosing and judging. You would not be who you are if this did not trouble you, and precisely because it troubles you so much, I would rather see this gift in your hands than in those of any other living man of whom I have knowledge.*

Nagaro sat very still on the edge of the bed. The knot had all unraveled, but the strands that had formed it were not gone. Rather, each one lay in his mind, separate, clear, and comprehensible. And somehow it was all right—not easy, no, but all right. "Must I use this gift?" He was surprised at how calm his voice sounded.

The figure shook its head. *You need not, though you will find that others will want you to, once they have seen it.*

"*Should* I use it?"

That is for you alone to decide. If you do choose to use it, though, I offer these three pieces of advice: Be sure you always have good reason. Try not to strike the first blow. And slay no man unless you cannot see a better way.

Nagaro nodded. "I think I understand," he said quietly. "Thank you." And because he knew that all had been said that needed to be said, he added, "Will you go now?"

Yes. After I leave, you must speak to the one you call Tredhold. He has been awake some little time, pretending not to be. He neither sees nor hears me, except with the very edge of his mind. Therefore he is troubled. You must reassure him.

"All right, I'll try." Nagaro smiled faintly. He could imagine what sort of things Tredhold must be thinking. "Could I ask you one more question, before you go?" he asked, on an impulse.

Very well, but only one.

"I've read most of the Writings, and I... well... some of what you told me seemed different from what I've read. If it's going to be like that, how can I use the Writings? How can I know what is truly right?"

The silvery figure sighed, and a frown marred the high, smooth brow. *Ah, spirit called Nagaro, you are not an easy one to answer.*

"I'm sorry..." Nagaro faltered, chagrined. "I suppose I shouldn't ask such a thing..."

No, no. Do not think that. Let me answer you, although you may not like the answer. The figure seemed to stand for a moment in thought. Then it sighed again, more deeply. *Ah, young friend, when has it ever been possible to distill the wisdom of the world into a set of rules that could stand in all circumstances and for all time? Not a thousand words, nor a thousand pages of words, would ever be sufficient. Even if one could settle upon the number and form of the rules, the languages of men are too limited and too changeable to safely carry the meaning across ages of time, and generations of men. Already you are reading the Writings in translation, for they were first written in old Kelorin.* The figure smiled at him benignly. *The Writings are a beginning, no more. They are far from useless, but also far from finished. Read the Writings, by all means, and having read them, think about them and ask your questions. Then test everything against the consequences of what you do, and against what you feel in your own heart.*

Nagaro swallowed, and bowed his head in acknowledgment.

The silver figure stepped away from him and raised its right arm to trace a great circle in the air before it with a ghostly forefinger. The fingertip seemed to leave a glowing line, hanging shimmering in the air. *All spirit is one and the same in kind*, the voice intoned. *Born of the same spark, formed of the essential fire we call anim...* The figure placed its fingertip again at the top of the circle and drew a second glowing circle inside of it, half the diameter of the first. *Every spirit bound to onam— that is the flesh—is part of the whole, yet finds itself separate and alone.* The figure placed its forefinger on the shining line at the bottom of the smaller circle—a point that was also the center of the larger one—and drew one more glowing line in the air, straight and vertical, connecting the bottom of the smaller circle to the bottom of the larger one. *So does the will of the separate spirit, by its free choosing, join itself again to the whole, through me. Pledge for pledge is given. Follow the path as best you can, and I will not forsake you. Spirit that calls itself Nagaro, farewell.*

The silver figure raised its hand in one final gesture of parting, then turned, and vanished as if it had passed through some unseen doorway that let it pass out of the visible world. Nagaro felt almost physically the sudden absence of what had been there an instant before. The shining Sign of Vothra—the circle-within-a-circle, joined—lingered for several heartbeats in the air, fading gradually until it, too, was gone.

Nagaro let out his pent up breath. He was still sitting on the edge of the bed, and the cabin was awash with moonlight.

After a moment Tredhold stirred, and sat up. "Nagaro?" He spoke tentatively. "Are ye... awake?"

Nagaro answered calmly. "Yes, Tred, and so are you. And neither one of us is going mad, if that's what you're thinking."

"Oh, *well*, that's all right then," the healer responded dryly. Then he added, "I don't suppose ye'd mind telling me what just happened?"

"Vothra was here, talking with me," Nagaro answered matter-of-factly. "The Spirit just left."

"*Vothra?*" The healer was staring at him. Nagaro could make out the shine of the man's eyes. "But..." Tredhold was clearly uncomfortable. "Doesn't your guardian spirit come to ye in dreams?"

"Usually," Nagaro admitted. "This was what we call a 'presence.' Some part of Vothra was actually here, *present* in the world."

The healer continued to regard him closely. "Nagaro," he said carefully, "are ye saying that ye could *see* and *hear* Vothra?"

Nagaro actually laughed. "Yes, but only with my mind, Tred. There wasn't anything to be seen or heard in the usual way, and Vothra wasn't speaking to you. That's why you didn't see or hear anything. Maybe you... felt something?"

"*Maybe...*" Tredhold answered evasively. "Has Vothra... talked to ye before?"

Nagaro shrugged. "Twice, but never like this."

"Ah." Tredhold coughed. "So... what did Vothra say to ye then?"

"A great many things, Tred. Too many to tell. It seems things are both simpler, and more complicated, than I thought. It doesn't matter, though. The important thing is that I'm all right. You needn't worry about me—though I thank you for taking the care with me that you did." He rubbed his eyes. "I'm still tired," he added. "I'm going back to sleep now, and I suggest you do the same."

He didn't wait to see what the healer would do. Lying down, he stretched himself out upon the narrow bed and closed his eyes. Almost immediately, he drifted off into a deep and restful slumber.

Chapter 30: A Ship Needs A Captain

Nagaro awoke to sunlight streaming through the porthole. Assuming the ship was still on a northerly course, the angle of the light meant it was about midmorning. The *Fist* was moving with a surging roll, suggesting a favorable wind and moderate seas.

Tredhold had apparently already risen and gone. Nagaro was quite alone in the officers' cabin. There was evidence that others had been in and out, however. Someone had laid out some clothes at the foot of his bed. The sword and sword belt had been placed there as well. Breakfast had been left for him on a small table near the head of the bed. Finding himself both hungry and thirsty, Nagaro turned his attention first to the food.

There was a mug full of Jinari tokabi-leaf tea beside a plate bearing some smoked meat and generous portions of yaba bread and bean cake. He devoured it all, smiling at the latter items, which were surely Utabala's offerings. The meat was spicy. The yaba bread had a pleasingly delicate flavor. The bean cake was sweet and quite good, although he found it a bit sticky. The tea was still warm, though not steaming. It had a pungent aroma and a slightly musty flavor, quite different from sothiril. He drained the cup.

Once he had satisfied his hunger and thirst, Nagaro examined the clothing that had been left for him. The men must have gone through the Mautep crew's sea chests. Someone had found him clean underwear in addition to a pair of black uniform pants and a pair of black boots. There was no shirt, however, only a long, sleeveless vest of red-brown leather that laced at the front. The leather was well-tanned and the garment finely stitched—possibly an officer's piece of plunder.

Nagaro frowned. He would rather have had a plain white shirt, but he supposed that shirts without bloody holes in them might be in short supply. The vest would at least keep the sun from burning his back. Quickly he stripped off the ragged, dirty remains of his old clothes. The strip of rag that carried his ring was still around his waist, almost forgotten. He left it there and put on the underwear and pants. An ironic smile curled his lip as he pulled the boots onto his feet. They were the same color and of nearly as good quality as the ones that had been taken from him a year and a half ago. They actually fit quite well too. Finally he donned the vest, pulling it on over the bandage that wrapped his chest. It felt good to be wearing proper clothing again.

What he really needed was a bath. That, however, would have to wait.

Glancing down, his eyes fell upon the sword and lingered on the gold-filigreed hilt. He picked up the weapon. The black leather sheath that covered the blade was elegantly simple. The sword belt, also black leather, was graced by a gilt buckle. The sword itself was a truly superb weapon—light in weight, perfectly balanced, and razor sharp. Its owner must have been of high rank, or wealthy—but that hadn't prevented him from falling victim to Lokundas' whim.

Nagaro was glad he hadn't killed the weapon's owner. He couldn't have felt right about killing a man and taking his sword to keep. But this one had come to him by chance—a pure gift of Lokundas. The Writings had something to say about such windfall gifts, or "finder's gold." If chance brought gold or any valuable thing unearned, the finder might keep it and use it if he had need. If he had no such need, the finder was admonished to find someone else who did, and pass along the gift. Well yesterday, he'd certainly had needed this sword...

But he didn't have to keep it. He need not carry or use a sword, ever again, if he didn't wish to... He frowned at the object in his hands. He might need the sword again. The *Fist of Death* was still in Mahuk waters. Though it was late in the season, they might still meet danger before they came to an Edroviran port. And they had Hashtep aboard—and a Jinari—who would want to be put ashore close to their homes. Nagaro knew he couldn't stand by and see harm come to the men. If there was trouble, he would have to trust himself to deal with it... *appropriately*. It was more than a little daunting to realize that Vothra trusted him so much, but a tremendous relief to know that the Benevolent Spirit would understand and forgive him if he made a mistake.

With a sigh, Nagaro buckled the black sword belt around his waist. Though he hoped he wouldn't need it, the blade would be close to hand if he did. He squared his shoulders. It was time to venture out and see what the new day held for him.

He reached the door just as Taru opened it from the other side. The young Turo was still shirtless, though he had exchanged his rags for black pants and a pair of black boots, and he still had his sword. He gave Nagaro a long look up and down that lingered on the elegant sword at Nagaros hip before returning to search his friend's face. "Well," he said, with slightly forced jocularity, "Ye do look better this morning! Tred said he thought ye would, but he had such an odd look on his face when he said it that I didn't know what t' think."

"I expect he's not used to seeing someone talking to Vothra."

Taru's mouth dropped open. "*Talking to...?* Are ye jesting with me?"

Nagaro had to laugh at his friend's shocked expression, but he sobered quickly. "No, Taru, I'm not jesting. I thought I had done something very wrong, you see, and Vothra came and explained to me that I hadn't. I don't think you'd better spread that about though. Most of the other men aren't very sure what to make of me as it is."

Taru gave him an uncertain look. "Well, ah, no, I'd best not mention it," he agreed. "But ye haven't much to worry about just now... with the men, I mean. Ye're at the top of everyone's pole after yesterday." He eyed Nagaro warily as he finished, as if expecting him to flinch. When Nagaro only frowned slightly at the news, Taru went on. "Moraga and Gurd both had their eye on that vest ye're wearing. They were havin' a bit of a fight over it, but Pavo said ye should have it, and they handed it right over."

Nagaro's frown deepened. "They didn't have to do that. I don't need special treatment."

"Will ye let it go, Nagaro!" Taru chopped at the air with his hand. "Just forget I told ye. They couldn't ha' both had it, and the men 'll take it amiss now if ye don't keep it. Come on," he added, before Nagaro could make further protest. "I was coming to take ye to our barber shop. We found scissors, and things for shaving—and a *mirror!* Most o' the others have already had their turn, but I was waitin' so I could show ye how a proper Turo trims his beard."

Nagaro smiled to himself as he followed his friend. He knew that Taru had never trimmed a beard in his life. In point of fact, they had both watched Jomo having his beard trimmed on several occasions, so Nagaro knew every bit as much about the subject as Taru did.

The "barber shop" turned out to be the infirmary. A scissors and two combs lay on the little table, and a small rectangular mirror had been hung on the wall. The floor next to the mirror was littered with hair clippings. Most of them were black or dark brown, but there were a few locks of Leithian gold. Pavo was sitting in a high-backed chair having his chin shaved when the two friends arrived. Mendorel was carefully plying the razor. The older man had already been shaved, and he appeared to be nearly finished working on Pavo.

A beaming smile appeared on Pavo's broad face when he caught sight of Nagaro. "Good morning, *Kiraam Shaku-Tal*," he said, as soon as Mendorel stopped and stood back to take a look. "This is first time I be shave! Now I know I am truly man!"

Taru smirked a little. Pavo's beard had always been rather thin and scraggly, though this was apparently a racial trait rather than a sign of his youth. Without the beard, Pavo looked younger. One might have been tempted to say "boyish" had the young Hashtep not stood over six feet tall and been so impressively broad in the shoulders.

Nagaro gave Taru a stern glance, and Pavo an encouraging smile. "I always knew you were a man, Pavo," he said. "But what was that you just called me?"

Pavo's smile broadened. "Kiraam Shaku-Tal! That is what Roheed have call you."

"I thought it might be. What does it mean?"

Pavo frowned in concentration. "It mean 'man who take slave that not belong to him.'"

Nagaro's face instantly clouded. "You mean it's a man who *steals* slaves? He called me a *thief?*"

Pavo spread his hands. "Thief is bad thing?"

"Yes!" Nagaro was incensed. "Of course it's a bad thing! It's *wrong* to steal—to take things that don't belong to you! I didn't *steal* the slaves. I helped free them. Kelorin law says that one man can't own another, so the slaves never belonged to Lord Baalkir in the first place!"

Pavo sat stolidly throughout Nagaro's tirade. Then he shrugged his shoulders. "I do not think that Lord Baalkir know Kelorin law," he said calmly. "Mautep think one way to show you are better than other man is take away something that belong to him. If he cannot stop you, then you win!"

Taru and Nagaro exchanged glances. "But," protested Taru, "if the Mautep don't think stealing is wrong, why did Lord Baalkir make ye a slave for stealing two rabbits?"

Pavo shrugged. "Because I get caught. Also he is Mautep lord, and I am Hashtep fisherman. Besides," he added, "you both keep those sword you take."

Nagaro started to open his mouth to explain about finder's gold, but Taru jumped in first.

"That's different! That warrior fell right beside Nagaro! He had no more use for that sword, seeing as he was dead. And the man who had *this* sword is dead too!" He slapped the blade at his side.

Pavo stuck out his chin. "What about *clothes* you are wear?"

Taru bristled. "Do ye expect us t' give them *back?*"

Mendorel had been standing there looking slightly amused through all of this, but now he cleared his throat and said, "Landros called it spoils of war. That's an old custom—older than Kelorin law, I fancy. If ye win the battle, ye take what ye want. That doesn't sound so different from the Mautep custom Pavo was talking about."

Taru tossed his head. "Well, I don't care *what* ye call it," he said. "I call it fair enough! Didn't those Mautep take away everything we owned when they made us slaves? I figure that the very least they owe us is some new clothes!"

Mendorel laughed. "I'm not going to argue." The grizzled Kelorin was wearing black pants and a white shirt with a torn sleeve.

Pavo grinned. He was wearing black pants and boots, though he had no sword.

Taru finally dropped his frown and laughed too. "Come on," he said, turning to Nagaro. "Ye can cut my hair, and I'll cut yours. And then we can both trim our beards." He planted himself in front of the mirror.

Nagaro picked up a scissors from the table. He would have added something to the discussion of plunder and ownership, but the moment had passed, and at least his friends weren't fighting about it anymore.

"Ye don't want me to shave you then, Nagaro?" Mendorel enquired. "I'm getting good at it. The last three men I never nicked once, and that's on a moving ship!"

Nagaro shifted uncomfortably. "Ah... no, thank you, Mendorel. I just want my beard trimmed."

"Well, suit yourself," Mendorel said easily. "I guess ye were wearing your hair in the Turowan fashion when I first laid eyes on ye, at that. I'll just be going then. I never thought I'd see this day," he added, shaking his head. "I still can't quite believe it."

Pavo chose to stay. He sat on a stool and quietly watched while the two friends reinvented the art of Turowan-style barbering.

They first set about trying to cut one another's hair just long enough to tie at the nape of the neck. Taru had clearly never had the opportunity of seeing himself in a mirror before. He grinned and mugged shamelessly while Nagaro was working on him.

Then it was Nagaro's turn at the mirror. The black-bearded man who stared back at him out of the silvered glass was a shock. The last time he ha seen his reflection in a proper mirror he'd been a smooth-shaven youth just shy of his eighteenth birthday. The glimpses he'd gotten of his reflection in the little stream next to Taru's house while he was letting his beard grow hadn't prepared him for the change.

Nor was it only the beard that was new. The mirror also showed muscles bulging in his shoulders that the vest did nothing to conceal. "*Bishka!*" he murmured, borrowing a word he'd often heard the Hashtep use in moments of high emotion. He was wary, now, of uttering the name of the Benevolent Spirit in situations that didn't require Vothra's attention. For a brief moment he considered taking the razor and scraping his chin clean to see if he could find the person he'd once been—until he remembered that the person's name had been Leyel Virden. Resolutely, he took the scissors from Taru instead and began to trim his mustache.

They took turns experimenting. The object was to trim the beard as close to the face as possible, assuring the longest interval before the process had to be repeated. What they discovered was that they could do the parts in front themselves, but the sides were difficult to trim evenly without the aid of someone who could see what he was doing. Nagaro used one of the combs to work the tangles out of his matted hair and retied it with the bit of dirty rag he'd been using for want of anything better. Taru did the same. When they had finished, they took turns admiring their handiwork in the mirror.

"Do I look like my father?" Taru inquired as he stepped back and turned to face Nagaro.

"Yes, you do," Nagaro answered with perfect honesty. "Quite a lot, actually." Looking at himself in the mirror, he wondered for the first time in his life whether he looked like *his* father. He wondered whether he would ever know. He frowned at his reflection. The beard looked much better when trimmed—not so wild—but it made him look older by rather more than the two and a half years that had passed since he'd decided to let it grow. Well, that was all to the good. His eyes were still his eyes—dark gray with little flecks of blue and green. And there was the way his precisely-penciled black eyebrows came together in a strong, straight line when he frowned...

Pavo's face appeared over his shoulder in the mirror. "You look like proper man, Nagaro," the young Hashtep declared, then quickly added, "Taru also look like proper man."

Nagaro saw Taru's expression and laughed. "He just means that we both look like men, Taru. Don't look so worried. Come on, both of you," he added. "I want to find Landros."

*

They found the former second mate of the *Fairwind* outside the stern-castle door. He was sitting on the deck with his knees drawn up, leaning against the wooden planks of the stern castle, apparently enjoying the sun and the fresh sea air. Clean-shaven, he looked younger. There had been more gray in his beard than in his hair. He was also fully equipped with shirt, pants, boots, and sword.

The seasoned sea warrior gave Nagaro a long appraising look that took in the younger man's confident step, bold glance, and the sword at his side. If Landros was surprised by Nagaro's choice of the Turowan fashion of hair and beard, he didn't show it. Instead he smiled broadly.

"It's good to see ye back among us, mate," he said. "Take a seat if ye like."

Nagaro returned the smile. "Thank you, Landros," he said meaningfully, for he knew what the other man meant. "It's good to *be* back." He seated himself, and Taru and Pavo did likewise. Once settled on the planking, Nagaro wasted no time in coming to the point. "I've been thinking, Landros," he said. "This ship needs a captain."

Landros immediately nodded. "Right ye are—and ye're just the man for the task. Carry on, mate."

This caught Nagaro so completely off guard that for several seconds he could only stare at the older man. When he realized that his mouth was open, he shut it. Taru had said he was at the top of everyone's pole, but he'd expected Landros to have more sense. "I didn't mean *me*," he said. "I was thinking that *you* were the best man for the task. You were a second mate, after all, so you've had more experience commanding a ship than anyone else among us."

Landros didn't so much as blink. "Oh, I've had *experience*, all right," he drawled. "Enough to know that I'd rather be following orders than giving 'em. I was a second mate for close to twenty years, and I was a good one. But I never wanted to be first mate, much less captain. I suppose I could *do* it," he added. "But it ain't wise to change captains in mid-course."

Nagaro frowned. "What do you mean *change* captains?" he asked. "No one's *been* captain, so there's nothing to change."

Landros raised an eyebrow. "Ye looked like a captain to me yesterday. Sounded like one too."

"But I wasn't... I mean, I didn't... did I?" Nagaro looked desperately at Taru and Pavo, hoping for some support. He got support, but not the kind he wanted.

"Ye were doing first rate, Nagaro!" Taru offered staunchly.

"Oh, yes! You look like very good captain!" Pavo added, nodding vigorously.

Nagaro's frown deepened. This wasn't going at all well. "Now look," he said. "I know I'm good with a sword, but that's no reason to make me captain. You shouldn't just follow anyone who's good with a sword."

Pavo nodded some more. "Oh yes," he said brightly. "You very good with sword—*and* you very good captain. Hashtep all follow you anywhere!"

"But I don't *want* to be captain!"

"Ye should have thought o' that yesterday," Landros put in dryly, "before ye started hollering orders."

"I was just trying to do what was needed!" Nagaro protested. "I wasn't giving *orders!* I was just..." He cast about for a word. "...making suggestions."

"Suggestions? *Suggestions?*" Landros burst out laughing, and he laughed until the tears ran. Finally he managed to catch his breath. "Oh, laddie-buck!" he gasped, wiping his eyes. "Ye don't run a ship at sea on *suggestions!*"

Nagaro shook his head in exasperation. "I *know* that, Landros. *Why do you think I said this ship needs a captain?*"

Landros turned to Taru. "Has he always been like this?" he inquired helplessly.

Taru gave the sea warrior a look of pure commiseration. "As long as I've known him."

Nagaro gave Taru a severe glance before turning a rather cold eye on Landros.

The older man's weathered face suddenly became serious. "Now look ye here, mate," he said reasonably. "Captaining isn't about being good with a sword. It's about thinking about what to do next. It's about seeing what needs to be done, like ye said, and then seeing that it gets done. That's no different than what ye were doing. Now will ye just give it a try, lad?"

Nagaro sighed. When he actually thought about it, a good many of the ideas about what to do *had* come from him. And he *had* been telling men what to do—even if he hadn't assumed that they would necessarily do it. "Well, I suppose so..." he said grudgingly. "After all, it would only be until we get to Pakoa..."

"Pakoa Island?" Landros looked startled. "Why d' ye say Pakoa?"

Nagaro was suddenly embarrassed. He'd intended to discuss the matter of their destination with the sea warrior right after expressing his support for Landros acting as their captain. "Well," he said hastily, "Pakoa is the closest harbor that's in Droviri territory, isn't it?"

"Well, aye. But what's t' stop us from sailing all the way to Lankura?"

Lankura was, of course, the very last place Nagaro wanted to go. Fortunately there were good reasons why it didn't make sense. "Three things," he said, ticking them off on his fingers. "First, it's late in the season and we could get another storm at any time, especially as we go farther north. So it's best to make for the closest port, winter there, and seek our homes when spring comes. Second, we'll have to put the Hashtep ashore in Mahuk territory. It wouldn't be safe for them any-where near Lankura—or for Utabala either. That will take some time and make us even later. And third, we still look like a Mahuk war galley." He gestured at Lord Baalkir's flag, which still flew from the main mast. "We can pull that down once we're out of Mahuk waters, but we have no Edroviran flag to fly in its place. From what I've heard about Pakoa, it's just a fishing port, which means it won't be fortified. If we sail in there, we'll give them a fright, but at least we won't come under attack before we can sort things out with the local folk."

Landros stared at him. "Well I'll be blowed," he said. "I believe ye're right. But ye see?" he added. "That's what I mean. That's captain's thinking, that is. Seems ye're always one step ahead o' me when it comes to thinking."

"I'm sure you're exaggerating."

But Landros shook his head. "No. All I've been thinking about is whether we'd get more speed out of her if we brought her bow a couple points closer t' the wind. And, as for where we're headed, well, Lankura is my home, so that's where I thought o' going. I've seen it before," he added. "Some men are just naturally good captains. It comes as easy to 'em as falling off a yardarm does to a one-armed man. It's a gift, mate. And ye're one that's got it."

Nagaro's brow constricted. *Another gift? The Writings said one was supposed to use one's gifts...* But another thought struck him. "How can I be captain, Landros," he asked, "when I don't have any idea how to sail a ship like this one? You saw that yesterday when I wanted to leave all that sail on her."

Landros made a dismissive gesture. "The captain doesn't need to worry about that sort o' thing, lad. That's the second mate's job. Ye just tell me what ye want her to do, and I'll see she does it—or I'll tell ye why she can't. All I ask is that ye listen to me and take my counsel—just like ye did yesterday. Now what d' ye say, lad? Will ye do it?"

Nagaro sighed. He looked at his hands. "I suppose I'm willing to try, Landros. Call the men together and ask them if they want me."

"But we don't need t' ask," Taru blurted. "They'll follow ye, Nagaro. I know they will!"

Nagaro turned on him. "You don't speak for them, Taru! It has to be put to them. It has to be done right!"

"Well now," Landros put in quickly. "It don't always pay to give men too many choices. And it's not how we do things in the Fleet."

Nagaro's eyes flashed. "We're not in the Fleet here, Landros! Most of us aren't even sea warriors. I am not going to let you just declare me captain. We have to put it to the men!"

Landros raised an eyebrow. "All right then, mate," he said calmly. "We'll just do that." He stood up. "Come on then, the lot o' ye." Turning, he strode off across the deck bellowing, "All hands to the crew cabin! *Step lively!*"

Nagaro strode after him with Taru and Pavo tagging behind like a pair of eager puppies.

*

Landros could make himself heard over a howling gale when he wanted to, and making men jump was second nature to such a seasoned second mate. Minutes later, the crew cabin was packed.

Nagaro looked around the room. The men were all freshly shaven or clipped and dressed in a varried assortment of scavenged clothing. They were watching him and Landros with curious and expectant faces. Tredhold was standing off to one side with a healer's bag in his hand. The Leithian must have been doctoring some of the crew. His eyes met

Nagaro's for an instant, and Nagaro gave him a nod, but Tredhold hastily looked away.

Landros wasted no time. He surveyed the faces. "All here," he muttered. "Except Simion, who's at the tiller—but I'm sure I can speak for *him*." He raised his voice. "All right, ye load o' flotsam! Now listen to me. Nagaro, here, has generously agreed—after giving the matter *careful consideration*, to captain this shipload o' tar-hands and fisherman's sons as far as Pakoa Island—with stops as needed for the Hashtep and the Jinari. He says he'll do it only supposing there's no serious objections. Do I hear any objections?"

He paused for about two seconds. There were some murmurs from among the men, but no one spoke. "No objections? All right, then..."

Nagaro had stood slightly behind Landros, listening with a deepening frown. Now he abruptly stepped in front of the sea warrior and raised his own voice. "Is this what you all want? Do you want me to be your captain?"

This brought an immediate chorus of affirmatives from the Droviri and from the few Hashtep who could understand it.

Nagaro turned to Pavo. "Would you please ask the other Hashtep? Tell them what Landros said too, about stopping to put them ashore."

Pavo's rapid string of Hashti brought an enthusiastic cheer from his countrymen.

Utabala spoke up from his seat on one of the bunks. "I also tink dis would be most satisfactory."

Behind him, Landros coughed. "Are ye satisfied now, mate?"

Nagaro's throat felt tight with emotion. Mutely he nodded. He could feel all their eyes on him, eager and admiring.

Moraga stood up. He gestured for Nagaro to take the seat he'd just vacated on a small iron-bound sea chest. "Sit ye there, Capt'n. An' tell us where we're bound for first."

Nagaro moved to take the offered seat. He looked around at the expectant faces. "Well," he said, "the first thing we need to do is to bury Potero and Hasaad. I thought Chitaopa would do for that, unless there's a closer place the Hashtep know of that would be better. Does anyone have any idea where we are?"

There were blank looks from the Droviri.

Nagaro turned to Pavo. "Can you translate that? Ask them where they can be safely put ashore while you're about it. Just remember, we can't stop in too many places, and we have to stay clear of any place we're likely to find warships."

Pavo nodded, but before launching into Hashti, he said. "I already know I am go to Pakoa with you."

Nagaro was puzzled. "Why, Pavo? Your home is far to the south in the Mahuk Baar, near Sar Tipaal."

A look of sorrow crossed Pavo's broad brown face. "I can not go home ever, Nagaro. It is not safe for me. But Kunoa already tell me there are Hashtep on Pakoa. They live there long time. From before there is trouble between our two country."

Nagaro was surprised to hear this, but he smiled. "I'm glad, Pavo. What about the others? Will they want to go there too?"

"I go to ask them, but I think mostly no."

*

Landros quietly made his exit from the crew cabin. He wore a satisfied smile as he crossed the deck, making for his favored seat by the door of the stern castle. He had no doubt that Nagaro would work out a plan, and he would be ready to take the ship in whatever direction was needed. In the meantime, someone ought to keep a lookout on deck. His smile was replaced by a slight frown, and he glanced at the top of the mainmast. Someone really ought to be up in the crow's seat. He'd have to point that out to Nagaro. The lad couldn't be expected to think of everything.

Landros heard the crew cabin door open behind him, and a brief sound of excited voices before the door was closed again. Booted footsteps sounded on the deck. A backward glance revealed Tredhold with his bag. Landros paused to let the Leithian catch up. The healer had a troubled air. In fact, it seemed to Landros that his friend had worn the same worried look all morning. "What ails ye, Tred?" he inquired.

The healer didn't meet his eyes.

"Ye really must have worked your magic on Nagaro last night," Landros went on. "He came out o' the stern castle this morning looking like a sea warrior! A Turowan sea warrior, I'll grant ye, but a warrior none-the-less. And it only took me half an hour to talk him 'round to being captain... Now, what *is* it, Tred? I swear ye look like ye'd seen a ghost!"

Tredhold gave him a quick, startled glance, and looked away again. "Maybe I have," he muttered. "Except, of course, it wasn't *me* that saw it. It was *him!*"

Landros was genuinely worried, now. "What *are* ye on about? Get a grip on your tiller, mate, and lay the course out straight for me."

They had reached the door of the stern castle. Tredhold leaned heavily against the plank wall to one side of it and stared off across the deck. He nervously ran a hand through his freshly clipped hair. "It wasn't me, Landros," he said in a low voice. "Oh, I talked to him, all right. Maybe I helped a little. But if there was magic, it was the *other* one he talked to last night..."

"*What* other one? Who'd he talk to, Tred?"

The healer drew a quick breath, and finally met his friend's eyes. He lowered his voice to just above a whisper. "Vothra," he said. "He talked to Vothra."

Landros' eyebrows went up. "Do ye *believe* that, Tred?"

The healer looked away again. "*He* does, Landros. And ye've seen the result for yourself."

"But... I mean... did ye see anything yourself?"

Tredhold shook his head. "No, I didn't. But I *felt* something..." He shivered. "Come inside, Landros, and I'll tell ye what I can."

*

They sat in the officers' cabin—Landros on the bed where Nagaro had slept, and Tredhold on the one across from it. They each had a mug of pungent Jinari tea, raided from the pot Utabala had left on the brazier in the galley.

"I'd given him something to make him sleep," the healer explained. "He went down like a log o' wood too. I made it pretty strong. And he was real quiet for about two hours, so I lay down here to get some sleep myself. But then he got restless—started tossing about and muttering. It was plain he hadn't got past his trouble, and I wasn't looking forward to the morning." Tredhold paused to take a swallow of tea.

"It went on like that for a time," he continued. "I kept dozing and waking. But the last time I woke, he was sitting on the edge o' the bed... talking... and *listening*... like he was talking *to* someone. *Only there was nobody there!*" Tredhold took another gulp of tea.

Landros leaned forward. "Ye said that ye *felt* something, Tred," he prompted.

"Well... *ye-es*..." Tredhold sought for words. "He was looking, with his eyes open. And I had the... *feeling*... that whatever he was looking at was *right there*, by the head of his bed. I could *almost* see it—and I could feel it with my eyes shut! I tell ye, Landros, it gave me chills."

Landros studied the mug in his hands. "That sounds to me a bit like a *presence*..."

Tredhold started. "That's what *he* called it!"

Landros' eyes came up, and the two men stared at each other.

"*By the Eyes of Vo–*" Landros broke off and glanced nervously over his shoulder. "Bodjer me," he muttered. "It makes a body think twice about what he says. I can't say that I really understand what a presence is, Tred, but I've heard what they used t' be like—in the old days. Did ye question Nagaro about it?"

Tredhold nodded. "Aye. After *it* had gone. I *felt* it go, too. He said he was seeing, and hearing, Vothra, but only with his *mind*. And he called it a presence. He wasn't talking in his sleep either. He answered all my questions as plain as ye please. Then he told me to go back to sleep."

Tredhold sought refuge in his cup of tea. "But here's the strangest part," he said. "I was too wrought up to sleep. I kept tossing and turning. Maybe I started to doze, just a little. I'm not sure. But then I thought I heard a word—in my head, I mean. '*Sleep*', it was. And I just rolled over and went to sleep! I slept better than I've ever slept in my life too. I don't know what that was, Landros. Maybe I just dreamed it. But if I could put it in a bottle and pour a bit out whenever I wanted, I'd be a rich man."

"Do ye think it was Vothra that said that word?" Landros' eyes were steady on his friend's face.

Tredhold sighed. "Ye asked me out there if I believed he was talking to Vothra," he said, his eyes on his cup. "I'll be honest, Landros. I don't even half believe in the old gods o' my own people. I'm not above praying to 'em now and then, in a tight spot. And it makes me feel better, when I've just watched a warrior die, to say that he'll ride with Kroneg on the fields o' Seralind. But I don't really believe the gods *exist*. I haven't since I've been out o' my teens." He paused, looking up to meet Landros' eyes. "I couldn't quite say it out there in broad daylight, but if ye ask me here, right now, I'd say, 'Yes, I believe it.' Vothra is *real*."

Landros nodded solemnly. "Vothra isn't a god, Tred," he said. "And Vothra *was* real in the old days. I've always believed that. When Nagaro said Vothra was gathering again—back in the slave barn—I didn't think much of it. But I think I believe it now." He shook his head. "And Nagaro got a presence because he was upset about killing five men? A presence used to be a rare thing, Tred, a very rare thing." Landros paused, then asked. "What was he saying to Vothra, anyway?"

The healer frowned. "He talked about power. About not wanting it. And not wanting to judge people. And there was something about using his 'gift'. He did more listening than talking, though, really. He was very upset at the beginning, but he got very calm at the end."

"That sounds about right," Landros said, nodding. "Head doctoring is something Vothra is good at, or so they say."

There was a little silence. Then Tred asked, "What have we got our hands on, Landros? What manner o' man have ye got us for a captain?"

Landros shook his head. "He's all of twenty years old. He wields a sword like nobody since Darion. And he talks to Vothra."

"Didn't he say once that Vothra only had any power to change the world through the hearts and minds of men?"

"I don't remember if Nagaro said it, but it's true." Landros drained his cup. "And from the way he wears that sword, it looks like Vothra's told him it's all right for him to be a sea warrior. Ye don't suppose that's going to change the world, do ye?"

The healer met his gaze. "I don't know, Landros. Maybe it might."

Chapter 31: Passage To Pakoa

The voyage to Pakoa was somewhat circuitous. Whenever the *Fist's* crew sighted sails that might possibly belong to a warship, they quickly changed course, putting either distance or the shielding mass of some island between them and the other craft. Fortunately, none of these ships pursued them. Other encounters were less threatening. They saw many small fishing boats near the shores, and an occasional merchant vessel in more open water, but these naturally took the *Fist* for one of Lord Baalkir's prowling warships and either made way or fled before her. There were also several bouts of stormy weather that blew them off their intended course.

One of the first things Nagaro did was to have the oar deck sluiced down with sea water and scrubbed as thoroughly as possible. The men were at first loath to take up the oars again, but they saw the necessity the first time the wind wasn't in their favor. They found it wasn't nearly as bad without the whip. They were rowing for themselves now, which made all the difference in the world.

No one had been able to think of a better place than Chitaopa to bury their two dead comrades. It was the most westerly island along that part of the coast, lying well beyond the northern edge of Mahuk waters. It seemed neither the Mautep nor the Jinari made an effort to claim it. Though the Turo knew of Chitoapa from old tales, few if any had been there in recent years—not since the Mautep depredations had begun and Edrovir had made frequent war with Jinara.

They found their way to Chitaopa by using the knowledge of the Hashtep, and also the charts found in the captain's cabin. Landros discovered that he could easily interpret the Mautep charts by the shapes of the lands, even though he couldn't read what was written on them. When they at last reached Chitaopa, they found it deserted. Nagaro felt strange walking freely under the cedar trees, with their chain-scarred trunks, and looking out over the cove to where the *Fist of Death* rode peacefully at anchor, a prison once, but now their means to freedom.

For the grave site, they found a bit of level ground overlooking the sea, not far from the cedar grove. There they dug a single grave and laid the bodies of the two men in it—Turo and Hashtep, side by side. They smoothed the grave over and planted grasses and sprigs of herb in the fresh earth, so the place would look undisturbed when the new spring growth came. For a marker, they placed only a single large, flat stone that might easily be overlooked if one didn't know it for what it was.

Nagaro was bitterly sorry about Potero—a man who had left Chitaopa still in chains and now returned there only in death. But Tego said, "Don't ye grieve for 'im, Nagaro. His spirit's free in Hanuroa. And he was free on this earth too—on that ship down there. Maybe it was only for an hour, but he was free, and he had a hand in making it so."

Before leaving the island, they filled their water casks and gathered berries and wild onions to add to their food stores. They also made use of the island's streams to bathe. Nagaro stood naked under one of the slender waterfalls that cascaded down the sheer cliff face. The cold water splashed and tumbled over him, carrying away a little more of the grime from his skin, and some of the weight of memory from his soul.

From Chitaopa, they turned the ship eastwards and then south. They put a handful of Hashtep ashore on a sparsely inhabited island called Osfaraad in the territory of one of the minor Mautep lords. After rowing their way through a bit of calm weather, a half dozen more of the Hashtep were landed, under cover of night, on the mainland coast.

None of these men would ever be able to truly go home, for each of them bore Lord Baalkir's brand on his shoulder. They would have to make new lives for themselves, but at least they were among folk of their own kind who spoke their language. Though they would have to live warily, they might hope to send word of their survival to families and friends still living farther to the south. There wasn't a man among them that didn't take Nagaro's hand in parting and express thanks for his deliverance, in Hashti or in broken Common Speech. Besides Pavo, the only Hashtep who chose to continue to Pakoa was the lone man, Chaheel. The friendship he had forged with Nanu, the other lone man, seemed to explain his choice.

*

After putting the Hashtep safely ashore they turned north again, to thread their way among islands known to Utabala, before turning east to make for the mainland and the place the Jinari had chosen to be put ashore. The plan was to land him under cover of darkness on a sparsely inhabited stretch of coast at the very northern edge of Jinari territory. From there he would have to make his way overland on foot, about a dozen miles, to the port of Tambali.

While they were thus in transit, Nagaro decided to take inventory of the various stores and cargo, plundered and otherwise, aboard the *Fist of Death*. Utabala, being a merchant's agent, offered his expertise in identifying and valuing the items. Nagaro suggested that Utabala might take some things that were light enough to carry and return them to his merchant master, but Utabala waved the idea aside, saying that his master would have put down the loss to piracy—one of the normal hazards of the trade.

On the Jinari's last day with them, he, Nagaro, Taru, and Tredhold were going through the items looted from the merchant ship that had carried Utabala and the Hranji, Zo-Hlan Tai. The four men were working in a room under the stern castle, used for storage. Nagaro watched as Taru and the Jinari set down an iron-bound chest on the small table under the porthole where the light was better. "Is this the last of the things from your ship, Utabala?" he asked.

"I do tink so, yes, Captain."

Nagaro winced. Many of the men called him "captain" occasionally. Sometimes it was in jest, or when he said something that really sounded like an order. After nearly two weeks of this, he was beginning to become accustomed to it. Utabala, on the other hand, seemed determined to refer to him this way *all the time*. It made him uncomfortable, but he'd given up trying to persuade the man to stop, since his efforts clearly had no effect. He sighed, stepping forward to undo the latch on the lid of the chest. "What about that bundle you have, Tred? Is there anything in it we haven't seen before?"

"It seems to be more silk cloth," was Tredhold's response from the other end of the room. "But I mean to be sure there's nothing hidden inside it."

The latch on the chest yielded, and Nagaro raised the lid and surveyed the contents. They seemed to be an odd assortment. Three rolls of parchment with carved wooden rods protruding from the ends lay on top of a number of cloth bags and paper-wrapped packets, and there was a single plain wooden box.

Taru picked up one of the bags and pulled open the drawstring. "There's just dried leaves in here," he said in disgust. "Is this some o' your Jinari tea, Utabala?"

The Jinari glanced at it. "No," he said. "Dose are not tokabi leaves."

Nagaro had picked up one of the rolls of parchment. He pulled off the string that bound it and began to use the pair of rods to unroll the thing. It was, as he'd suspected, a scroll. The inner surface was covered with neatly penned writing in an unfamiliar script. A bit further down there was a meticulous drawing of a small plant, complete with flowers and roots. "I suppose this is Jinari writing," he said. "What does it say, Utabala?"

The Jinari took the scroll from Nagaro and began to scan it, deftly rolling the top end onto its rod with one hand while he unrolled the bottom end with the other. More drawings of plants, and parts of plants, appeared scattered among the text.

"Are those plants herbs?" Nagaro asked. "For cooking? Or maybe for medicines?"

"It is more like de second ting you say," replied Utabala. "Yes, more like medicines. But it tells mostly about de dangers of dese medicines—what will happen if dey are not used correctly. Dis one, for example, it says will cure palsy if a man rubs it onto de es-skin, but if a man makes de mistake of eating it, it will make him see tings dat are not dere."

Nagaro felt a chill creep along his spine. The Jinari had gotten to the end of the scroll. "What is that, there," Nagaro asked uneasily, pointing. "Is it the name of the man who wrote it?"

"Ah, yes," said Utabala brightly. "De name is Obiari. He was a very great lore master, and dis es-scroll seems to be from his own hand. I believe it is very valuable."

Master Obiari... Nagaro frowned. "What about the other two?"

Utabala picked up each of the other scrolls in turn and scanned them more quickly. "De second one is a description of how to make a liquor from de bark of a tree dat will render a man unconscious. It is not of great value, for it does not say who wrote it. Dis last one is all about poisons and de cures for poisons. It is a copy of anoder one of Master Obiari's works. It is worth more dan de second es-scroll, but not nearly so much as de first."

Tredhold had apparently finished with the bale of silk cloth and was examining the third scroll over Utabala's shoulder. "I wonder if we could get them translated," he said. "There's probably a great deal to be learned from them."

Again Nagaro seemed to feel a chill. *Yes, a great deal to be learned... But in the wrong hands... Poisons and dangerous medicines and Master Obiari!* A cold knot of apprehension twisted his stomach. "Utabala," he said slowly. "Do you know to whom these scrolls were to be delivered?"

"Indeed no, Captain Nagaro. I have seen de list of de entire cargo, and dese tings were not on de list."

"Could they have belonged to Zo-Hlan Tai?" Tredhold inquired.

Utabala looked uncomfortable. "I do not tink so. De Haranjili never es-spoke of anyting like dis. But sometimes de captain carried some... es-special cargo... for my master, and dose tings would not be put on de cargo list."

Nagaro's frown deepened. "Where was your ship bound?"

Utabala looked surprised, but he answered promptly. "She was going to Patamtala, in de islands."

Nagaro relaxed a little. It was only a Jinari port. He supposed there might be many decent folk like Tred who would be interested in the contents of those scrolls—just medicines, after all, and antidotes for poison. He shrugged to show a lack of concern and picked up the wooden box from amongst the other parcels in the chest. It was strongly made, but very plain, and fastened with a small hook. Nagaro undid the hook and raised the lid.

For an instant he stared in horror at the contents. Then he dropped the box as if it held a nest of scorpions. The box struck the floor with a sharp crack, but being well made, it bounced rather than broke. Half a dozen of the bladder-thorns inside were flung out and scattered across the planking. Nagaro felt the blood pounding in his ears. As if from a distance, he heard himself say, "Get rid of those things! Throw them overboard!"

Tredhold quickly knelt down on the floor and began picking up the scattered bladder-thorns and putting them back into the box. "There's no need for that," he said mildly. "I'll take charge of them." Having finished restoring its contents, he closed the box and stood up. "They can be very useful for the healer's art," he continued in a conversational tone. "Although I suppose they could be misused..." He glanced significantly at Nagaro.

Nagaro had succeeded in fighting down the wave of revulsion that had swept over him, though barely. He gave a rigid little nod. "Very well," he said tightly. "Take care of them, Tred. Perhaps you all can finish here," he added. "There's something I need to do." Turning, he made for the door and fled on up the ladder, along the passage, and finally out of the stern castle and onto the deck, seeking light and air.

Taru found him a little later atop the stern castle, leaning against the railing and gazing out over the main deck. The young Turo moved to a place at the railing by Nagaro's side. He cleared his throat. "After ye left, Tredhold told Utabala that he thinks ye must have had some bad experience involving bladder-thorns," he said, keeping his voice low. "He kept looking at me, too. I didn't say a word, but ye've got t' be more careful, Nagaro. Ye shouldn't have gone and dropped that box!"

Nagaro didn't turn his head. His jaw tightened. "I didn't *mean* to drop it," he said through his teeth. "I couldn't help it! I can't abide those things. And if you'd had somebody stick one into *your* arm every day to... to..."

"*I know!* But now Tredhold suspects something!"

Nagaro still kept his eyes fixed straight ahead. "Of course he does. He's a healer. He's already seen that I have scars all down my arms. And I... I said some things when I was in a fever with the plague. Tred asked me about the scars on Chitaopa, but I didn't tell him anything."

"Oh." Taru hesitated. "Nagaro? If he knows that much, why not just tell him the rest and—"

"No! I don't mean to tell anyone! *Ever!*"

Nagaro's response was so vehement that Taru instantly subsided into silence. After some time, he asked, "What were ye thinking about those scrolls?"

Nagaro turned to look at his friend for the first time. His gray eyes still smoldered. "I was thinking that the whole chest could have been on its way to Dreigen. It's just the kind of things he'd want—scrolls about poisons, and... and... bladder-thorns! And who *knows* what those herbs are for!"

"Dreigen!" Taru paled. "But Edrovir's at war with Jinara! How could those things be gotten all the way to Lankura?"

Nagaro frowned. "I don't know," he said darkly. "But it would have to be moved as secret cargo, wouldn't it? And it would be better if it passed through more than one port so it couldn't be easily traced..." He stopped and raised his hand to massage his temples. "No, you're right," he said. "It's a daft idea, and I'm probably imagining things." He shrugged his shoulders and glanced at the sun, which had already started down the sky. "Enough of this," he said. "It's time we changed course if we want to make Utabala's landing by nightfall."

*

They brought the ship safely in close to shore along the northern Jinari coast just as night descended. The remaining men all gathered on the deck to take leave of Utabala as the *Fist* rocked easily on the darkening sea. They hadn't dared to show a lantern, and so the only light came from Talebra's crescent and a myriad scattering of stars that were reflected in the glassy water.

Utabala stood by the starboard rail in his chosen costume—Mautep boots, and a Mautep uniform tunic over his own silk pantaloons, which, though dirty, were still serviceable. No one else had been willing to wear the scarlet of Lord Baalkir's livery, but Utabala had smiled and said it would be proof of the truth of the tale he would tell when he reached Tambali.

If the Jinari had been disturbed by Nagaro's behavior earlier that day, he didn't show it at their parting. He shook Nagaro's hand. "May He Whose Name We Do Not Es-speak look upon you with favor, Captain Nagaro," he said. "May He send you good fortune, and may your days be long upon de earth. And if it please de Unnamed One dat ever our two paths cross again under de sun, de heart of dis, His humble servant, will be glad."

Though Nagaro couldn't read Utabala's expression in the darkness, the Jinari's voice carried the warmth of sincerity. "That would please me also, Utabala," he replied. "And let us hope that the future will bring peace between our two peoples so that it may be possible."

Utabala bowed to him, then, and descended to the long boat, where a pair of oarsmen had been waiting. So the Jinari was rowed to the shore. Nagaro watched him spring from the boat and quickly cross the narrow beach. The Jinari raised his hand once in final parting, and disappeared among a stand of trees.

*

So they came to the last segment of their journey. Turning northward, they sailed into a storm that was the worst they had encountered since the one that had blown them clear of the Strait of Jaamra. It was no more than might have been expected at the end of the month of Sedrin at that latitude, but most unwelcome since they were all by that time very eager to make port. For two days they were tossed about and drenched, unable to keep much sail on the yards and uncertain of their position. On the third day, the wind and rain at last abated, and the clouds lifted far enough above the surface of the sea for them to make out the long, low shape of the mainland coast off their starboard beam. They adjusted their course a bit more westerly, and sailed on for another day through occasional wreaths of mist, under a leaden sky. Dawn of the fourth day at last brought the sun's face, and with it a jubilant shout from Kunoa in the crow's seat.

"An island! There! Off the port bow!"

An hour later, as they drew nearer to the island, there came the confirmation from Kunoa and the others who knew these waters well. It was Pakoa—the most southerly port in the Lomoas, and the southernmost habitable island within the territorial waters of Edrovir. South of Pakoa, the Lomoas became little more than a series of great rocks thrusting out of the sea. Nagaro directed Simion to put the tiller over. Landros sent men jumping to adjust the trim of the sails, and they set their course for their final destination.

The sea around Pakoa was dotted with small fishing boats since the weather was fair, but these boats scattered and made for shore as soon as their skippers caught sight of the *Fist of Death*, with her long, lean hull and ramming prow, and the red and black diamonds down her sides. Nagaro had ordered Lord Baalkir's banner taken down as soon as they were out of Mahuk waters, so the *Fist* flew no flag. Still, the folk of Pakoa were not inclined to take chances.

Pakoa's main harbor lay at the southern end of the island, on the mainland side. It was a deep and ample anchorage, well protected by a pair of steep headlands that flanked the narrow entrance. As the *Fist* made her approach to that entrance channel, there was not a fisherman's sail in sight.

Nagaro stood atop the forecastle, watching the headlands approach on either side, ready to call out orders to Landros to reduce speed or to the steersman to alter course. He was wondering how they would be received by the folk of Pakoa. The island had only a single town of any size, and it was here at the harbor they were about to enter. It was known as Pakoa Harbor, or as Pakoa Town to distinguish it from the associated anchorage.

There were other men crowding the forecastle deck. Taru and Pavo were there, and several others, mostly Turowans. Some of the latter might be known to the inhabitants of this port. Moraga, and a Turowan named Haruda, were merchant seamen who had formerly put in at Pakoa on occasion, though it was now some years since either had been seen there. And there was one named Obedo, a fisherman who came from the island—though his dwelling had been at the farther end of it.

Obedo had been taken only that same spring, just before Kunoa and his father, but Kunoa was by far their best hope to be recognized by the townspeople, for his family dwelt right here at Pakoa Harbor. Nagaro knew that the young Turo had a mother, a grandfather, and two sisters in Pakoa Town.

Kunoa was still up in the crow's seat, leaning out on a rope in his excitement, straining for the first glimpse of his home. The men were crowding the rail now, as the *Fist*'s prow came abreast of the headlands, and the ship slipped into the channel that ran between them.

Nagaro stood at the stern of the forecastle, watching, and he now called Pavo away from the rail. "Stand here with me, Pavo," he said. "There may indeed be Hashtep dwelling on this island, but the sight of your face on a ship like this one might still frighten some of the local folk."

Pavo nodded impassively. "Why you do not stand there at rail?" he asked.

Nagaro's face clouded. "I'll leave those places for the men who truly belong here... those who feel at home in Edrovir."

A sense of disquiet had been growing in him for days. Looking back at what he and these men had accomplished, he could feel satisfaction, even a modest pride. They had won free of their chains, seized their captors' ship, and now had brought it to this place of safety. But looking forward was a different matter. On the day following their escape, he had spoken to Landros of how the Edroviran men might seek their homes in the spring after wintering on Pakoa—but he, himself, had no such home to seek. What would he do? Stay here on Pakoa with Pavo? Or return to Wotana with Taru? Wotana held little enough for Taru and still less for him. There was only Gama, Taru's grandmother, and the little house on the bay where Taru's parents had been brutally murdered. Besides, at twenty miles distance, Wotana now seemed to him uncomfortably close to Lankura. And what would he do for his livelihood? Be a fisherman?

With an effort, Nagaro shook himself from his gloomy reflection.

The headlands were sliding by, and he could make out a number of folk concealed among the rocks or peering out at them from the shelter of twisted pines and junipers. Kunoa saw them too. Still clinging to his rope, the young Turo now waved frantically at them with his free hand. Raising his voice, the youth shouted at the observers. "Halloo! Halloo! It's me, Kunoa! I've come home!"

There came shouts then, suddenly, first from one side and then from another.

"Kunoa! Look! It's Kunoa!"

"That looks like Obeido! Didn't the Mahuk take him?"

"Where have ye been, Kunoa?"

"The Mahuk made us slaves!" Kunoa shouted back. "But we fought them, and we stole their ship! And here we are!"

There were more shouts then, and figures were leaping among the rocks—running in the direction of the harbor and the town. The *Fist* sailed serenely on. Presently she glided clear of the headlands and out into the calm, sheltered water that lay beyond. The town was directly before them. It appeared only a little larger than Wotana.

Little sails began to blossom on every side as the fishermen, who had so recently fled, cast off once more from the shore and came sailing out to meet this miraculous ship.

Nagaro gave orders, Landros shouted them to the men, and the *Fist* eased her way up to one of the long wharfs that lined the waterfront. By the time she came to rest there, she was surrounded by several dozen small craft. The wharf, too, was crowded with people. Men, women, and children were there. A burly, middle-aged Turowan man was standing at the front and center of the throng with his arms folded. Nagaro would later learn that he was the chief of the Town Council—which effectively governed the island. He was also the town blacksmith.

The children in the crowd were jumping up and down in their excitement as the gangplank was being lowered, and the older folk were waving and cheering wildly. Kunoa was the first one down the gangplank. He no sooner stepped onto the wharf than his mother rushed from the crowd to fling her arms about him and hold him tight, tears of joy streaming down her cheeks.

Nagaro had at last moved forward and stood watching from the forecastle rail. Yet the gladness he felt for Kunoa was still tempered by the emptiness he held inside. No such welcome awaited him anywhere in the land of Edrovir. If he was ever to have a place that would give him such a welcome he would have to find it for himself—or make it.

But a moment later, he shook off his frown, lifted his head, and squared his shoulders. Had he not just helped to lead a shipload of slaves to freedom when men had said it couldn't be done? If he could do that, was there anything that wasn't possible? He found himself smiling at last as he raised both his hands and his voice to join in the general jubilation.

The sun was bright on the water and the air was filled with the joyous clamor of the people's cheers. The wind off the island's hills was warm and tinged with the scent of juniper. He had his memory, and he had his freedom. It was a good day to be alive.

***

Glossary

Angkat (AHNG-kaht): A Mautep warlord, chief rival of Baalkir.

anim (AH-nihm): That of which spirit is composed, spirit energy.

Aramei (AR-ah-may): A Kelorin girl, daughter of Boronin the blacksmith of Wotana.

Arlinas (AR-lin-ahs): A country lying to the east of Edrovir, beyond the Goreitha mountains.

Atheran Tyronin (AH-ther-ahn teer-O-nihn): A Kelorin lord who lead his people from Kelornas to Arlinas long ago.

Averwin (AV-er-wihn): Nagaro's boyhood home.

Baalkir jir-Akaan (BAHL-keer jeer-ah-KAHN): A Mautep warlord, owner of the *Fist of Death*.

balandir (bahl-ahn-DEER): A Kelorin dance.

Baruk (bahr-OOK): Mautep slave-master on the *Fist of Death*

basirah (bah-SEER-ah): Hashti for "enough."

Berinar Sundorin (BEHR-ih-nar SUHN-dor-ihn): A Kelorin lord, one of the Signers of the Pact of Lankura and author of *The Rule of Loros*. Died under dubious circumstances.

bishka (BIHSH-kah): A relatively mild but expressive Hashti expletive.

Bodano (bo-DAH-no): A Turowan farmer.

bodjer (BAH-jer): Derived from a Leithian expression that was originally much cruder, 'bodjer' means roughly to 'do an injury to' as commonly used in the Common Speech.

Boka (BO-kah): An itinerant Turowan woman who wears a small gold earring.

Boronin (bor-O-nihn): Blacksmith in the town of Wotana, father of Aramei.

Brandle Furthing (BRAND-l FUR-dhing): A young Liethian man, Lord Madred Furthing's son. ("dh" denotes the voiced "th" sound in "this").

Bron Sobring (brahn SO-bring): A Leithian man, lord of Sobring Hold and one of Leyel Virden's "keepers."

Chaheel (chah-HEEL): A Hashtep galley slave, a "lone man" who could handle an oar alone.

Chitaopa (chih-TAOW-pah): An uninhabited island off the coast of Jinara.

Chofir Naak (CHO-feer nahk): Hasti name for "heaven", or the afterlife.

Chula (CHOO-lah): An old Turowan man, the gardener at Averwin.

chutapak (CHOO-tah-pahk): Hashti name for a salve used for burns and cuts to hasten healing.

dakataar (dah-kah-TAHR): Hashti word for "doctor", or "healer."

Darion Loros (Dehr-ee-ahn LOR-ose): Lord of Loros Wared and first king of Edrovir , called Darion the Great.

Denoras (DEHN-or-ahs): A Kelorin slave who chooses death rather than continued slavery.

dokan (do-KAHN): A gold coin. There are ten trokins to the dokan, and one hundred rins to the trokin.

Dreigen (DREHY-gehn): The king's Lore Master. ("g" is always hard, as in "get".)

Droviri (dro-VEER-ee): Among non-Edrovirans, the word used for the Edroviran language (also called the Common Speech) or for the Edroviran people. Also an adjective meaning pertaining to Edrovir.

Duleyin (doo-LAY-ihn): Seventh month of the Edroviran calendar, roughly equivalent to July.

Dunrel (DOON-rehl): Sixth month of the Edroviran calendar, roughly equivalent to June.

Edro (EHD-ro): Largest river in Edrovir, flowing roughly northeast to southwest and emptying into the sea at Lankura.

Edrovir (EHD-ro-veer): A country inhabited by the Kelorin, Leithian, and Turowan peoples, stretching from the Gorietha mountains to the western sea.

Elgurn Harlind (EHL-gurn HAR-lihnd): A Leithian man, third king of Edrovir, husband of Queen Semorel, and father of Princess Nevien.

Emril (EHM-rihl): A kelorin woman, mother of Sindar. She was enslaved by Notep jir-Akaan in the Mahuk Baar.

Eskarasi (ehs-kah-RAH-see): Equivalent to the Devil in Jinari belief.

Evrel (EHV-rehl): Fourth month of the Edroviran calendar, roughly equivalent to April.

Faranos (FAR-ah-noes): Two island chains off the northern coast of Edrovir. The Inner Faranos lie closer to shore. The Outer Faranos lie farther offshore and extend farther south.

Fargil (FAR-gihl): A young Kelorin man, son of the Lord of Galenor and suitor of Princess Nevien. ("g" is always hard even before "e" or "i" as in "get" and "give.")

farusia (fah-ROO-see-ah): A bushy plant bearing large white trumpet-shaped flowers, also the flower itself.

Fataan (fah-TAHN): Young Mautep slave-tender on the *Fist of Death*.

Fendar (FEHN-dar): A Kelorin swordmaster.

Funara (foo-NAR-ah): A Turowan woman who was dream reader for Chief Takuma.

Finorel (FIHN-or-ehl): The twelfth month of the Edroviran calendar, roughly equivalent to December.

Galenor (GAL-eh-nor): A coastal city to the north of Lankura.

Gama (GAH-mah): An old Turowan woman, Taru's grandmother. Also the Turowan word for "grandmother."

Genorel (GUEHN-or-ehl): First month of the Edrovirin calendar, roughly equivalent to January.

Gillard Marchent (GUIHL-ard MAR-chehnt): A Leithian lord, also called 'Gill". One of Leyel Virden's "keepers". Second husband of Princess Nevien.

Glenarl (glehn-ARL): An inland town in Harlind Hold, lying northeast of Lankura.

Goran (GOR-ahn): A Kelorin trader.

Goreitha (gor-EHY-tha): Mountain range forming the eastern border of Edrovir, separating it from Arlinas.

Gudo (GOO-doe): A young Turowan of Wotana, one-time friend of Taru.

Gundor (GUHN-dor): A Kelorin fisherman of Wotana.

Gurd (gurd): A young Leithian Fleet warrior on the *Fairwind*, captured and enslaved on the *Fist of Death*.

Hakura Kili (hah-KOOR-ah KEE-lee): Guiding Spirit of the Turo.

hamanei mata noa (hah-MAH-nay MAH-tah NO-wah): A Turowan exclamation to ward off evil or misfortune (literally meaning, "Spirits protect us").

Hamani (hah-MAH-nee): A Turowan girl of Wotana, friend of Aramei and childhood playmate of Taru.

Hanuroa (HAH-noo-RO-ah): The spirit world in Turowan belief, where the spirits of the dead are believed to dwell.

Haotef (HAH-o-tehf): A Mautep warrior, second in command on the *Fist of Death.*

Harl Sobring (harl SO-bring): A Leithian man, former lord of Sobring Hold, father of Bron.

Harmoth (HAR-mahth): Southern-most major port city in Edrovir.

Haruda (hah-ROO-dah): A Turowan man, formerly a merchant seaman, enslaved on the *Fist of Death.*

Hasaad (hah-SAHD): A Hashtep slave aboard the *Fist of Death.*

Hashtep (HAHSH-tehp): The common folk of the Mahuk Baar. (It is the Hashti word for their own race).

Hashti (HAHSH-tee): The language of the people of the Mahuk Baar (both the common people or Hashtep, and the warrior class or Mautep).

Hatakei Raal (hah-TAH-kay RAAL): Hashti name for Kuran Kel, the Lord of the Royal Fleet of Edrovir, (literally meaning, "running dog").

heeruk (HEER-uhk): Hashti word for "captain."

heskial (hehs-kee-AHL): A will-enslaving drug embodying spirit magic, distilled from the flowers of the heskia vine.

Hinda (HIHN-dah): A Kelorin woman, one-time cook and housekeeper at Averwin.

Hindrath (HIHND-rahth): A Kelorin man, older brother of Nevrath.

Hiptatak (hihp-TAH-tahk): Messenger of the god Sheptuum according to the belief of the people of the Mahuk Baar.

Hold (hold): A territory ruled by a Leithian lord.

Hran (HRAHN): Inland country south of Edrovir and east of Jinara.

Hranji (HRAHN-jee): The people of Hran. (Haranjili. to the Jinari.)

Hrathgard (HRAHTH-gard): Patriarchal god of the Leithians, known as

"King of the Heavens," and "Lord of the Wind." Also patron god of rulers.

Idrin (IHD-rihn): Seven-day month surrounding the winter solstice in the Edrovirin calendar. It follows Finorel and is followed by Genorel.

Jaamra (JAHM-rah): Place name referring to the Strait of Jaamra, a passage between two islands of the Mahuk Baar. Site of a sea battle between two rival Mautep warlords, Baalkir and Angkat.

Jembari (jehm-BAR-ee): One of the Jinari prophets.

Jinara (jih-NAR-ah): A coastal country between Edrovir and the Mahuk Baar.

Jinari (jih-NAR-ee): Word for the inhabitants or language of Jinara. Also an adjective meaning pertaining to Jinara or its people.

Jomo Nareyo (JO-mo nar-EHY-o): A Turowan fisherman, father of Taru.

kajadeem (kah-jah-DEEM): Hashti word for "honor."

Kale Fendred (kayl FEHN-drehd): A Leithian lord, one of Leyel Virden's "keepers."

Karidei (kah-REE-day): A Kelorin lady, the author of the poem *Song of Karidei*.

Katuk (ka-TOOK): A young Hashtep man, Pavo Maat's younger brother.

Kelor (KEHL-or): An island nation beyond the western sea that was the original ancestral home of the Kelorin people.

Kel Lankura (kel lahn-KOOR-ah): A small mountain near the mouth of the River Edro, on its northern bank.

Kelorin (KEL-or-in): A fair-skinned, dark-haired people originally from the isles of Kelor in the far western sea. Also their language or an adjective meaning pertaining to the Kelorin people.

Kelornas (KEHL-or-nahs): An island chain beyond the western sea comprising the nation of Kelor.

Kel Tierna (kel tee-EHR-nah): An Edrovirin port city to the south of Lankura.

keshaal (keh-SHAHL): A Hashti expletive, stronger than "bishka."

kia kaar hanuk-tak (KEE-ah kahr HAHN-ook-tahk): Hashti for "Put down your sword."

Kiraam Shaku-Tal (KEER-ahm SHAH-koo-TAHL): Hashti name given to Nagaro by Roheed, meaning "Thief of Slaves."

Kojito (ko-JEE-tow): A Turowan fisherman from Pakoa, father of Kunoa, briefly a slave on the *Fist of Death* before being killed by an oar.

Kor Vaskol (kor vahs-KOLE): A very high mountain range forming the northern border of Edrovir and also a portion of Arlinas.

Kroneg (KRO-nehg): The Leithian god of war, arbiter of the outcome of armed conflict and ruler of the dark moon, Naru.

kuamka (KWAHM-kah): A small, sour fruit used to ward off scurvy.

kuma (KOO-mah): An ointment that stains the skin brown to prevent sunburn, made from the nut of the kuma plant.

Kunai (KOO-nahy): A town on the east side of the Goreitha Mountains.

Kunoa (Koo-NO-wah): A young Turowan fisherman from Pakoa, son of Kojito, captured and enslaved on the *Fist of Death*.

Kuran Kel (KOOR-ahn kehl): A lord of mixed Kelorin and Turowan blood, Lord of the Royal Fleet of Edrovir.

Laash (LAHSH): A Hashtep slave on the *Fist of Death*.

Landros Torenin (LAN-drose tor-EHN-ihn): Older Kelorin sea warrior and second mate of the *Fairwind*, captured and enslaved on the *Fist of Death*.

Lanei (LAH-nay): A Turowan girl living in the town of Wotana.

Lankura (LAHN-koor-ah): The capital city of Edrovir.

Leithians (LAY-thee-ens): A fair-skinned, light-haired people originally from a land in the east called Leith.

Leyel Virden (LAY-ehl VER-dehn): The "idiot prince."

Lindra Loros (LIHN-drah LOR-ose): A Kelorin woman, wife of King Tevren and second queen of Edrovir.

Lissafel (LIHS-ah-fehl): (Also called "The Lady".) The maiden goddess of the Leithians, ruler of the hearts of men and women, and of the pale moon, Talebra.

Lithenkelin (LIHTH-ehn-KEHL-ihn): The Cloud Mountain People, who became the Kelorin.

Lithenkelir (LITH-ehn-KEHL-eer): The Cloud Mountains of Ludea.

Lokundas (lo-KOON-dahs): Also known as the "Turner of Worlds", he is the Kelorin personification of fate. One of the old gods of the Cloud Mountain People.

Lomoas (lo-MO-ahs): A group of islands off the coast of southern Edrovir. The Lomoa Islands lie south of the Inner and Outer Faranos and are separated from them by the straight known as "Farano's Mouth."

Lopo (LO-po): An aged, deranged Turowan slave on the *Fist of Death*.

Loros (LOR-ose): Name of the House founded by Nevrath, split from the House of Tyronin.

Loros Wared (LOR-ose WAH-rehd): A formerly existing Wared located on the northern bank of the River Edro, near it's mouth and extending to the sea.

Ludea (loo-DAY-ah): A continent that lies beyond the western sea.

Luka (LOO-kah): An old Turowan medicine woman.

Madred Furthing (MAH-drehd FUR-dhing): A Leithian lord, father of Brandle. Lord of Furthing Hold. ("dh" denotes voiced "th" as in "this.")

Madrel (MAH-drehl): Third month of the Edroviran calendar, roughly equivalent to March.

Mahuk (MAH-hook): An adjective meaning pertaining to the Mahuk Baar or its people. Used ignorantly to refer to the tawny-skinned, black-haired people from the Mahuk Baar, properly called Hashtep or Mautep.

Mahuk Baar (MAH-hook bar): The coastal country and islands to the south of Edrovir beyond Jinara.

Maramine Virden (mar-ah-MEEN VER-dehn): A noble Kelorin woman, Nagaro's "lady guardian."

Mautep (Mah-oo-tehp): Hashti word for the warrior class of the people of the Mahuk Baar.

Medrin (MEHD-rihn): Fifth month of the Edrovirin calendar, roughly equivalent to May.

Mendorel (MEHN-dor-ehl): A Kelorin shopkeeper and candle-maker, a slave on the *Fist of Death*.

Minowei (mih-NO-way): A Turowan woman considered a princess of her people, daughter of Chief Takuma.

Moraga (mor-AH-gah): A Turowan man, formerly a merchant seaman, enslaved on the *Fist of Death*.

Morengil (MOR-ehn-gihl): Kelorin lord, rival of Atheran, who remained behind in Kelornas.

Nagaro (nah-GAR-o): Name meaning "nameless man" in the Turowan tongue, given to him by his friend Taru.

Naibarad (NAHY-bar-ahd): A semi-legendary Kelorin rithral-wielder of Arlinas known in tales as Naibarad the Destroyer and associated with the fall of the rithral lords and onset of the shadow that fell over Arlinas during the cataclysm (Time of Fire and Water).

Nanu (NAH-noo): A Turowan galley slave on the *Fist of Death*, strong enough to handle an oar alone as a "lone man."

Naru (NAR-oo): The dark moon.

Nevien (NEHV-ee-ehn): Edrovir's princess, daughter of King Elgurn (a Leithian) and Queen Semorel (a Kelorin).

Nevrath (NEHV-rahth): A Kelorin man who founded the House of Loros, younger brother of Hindrath.

Nomemduran (no-MEHM-dur-ahn): Also known as the "Maker of All Things." One of the old gods of the Cloud Mountain People.

Nondorin (NOEN-dor-in): Eleventh month of the Edroviran calendar, roughly equivalent to November.

Notep (NO-tehp): A Mautep, younger brother of Lord Baalkir, father of Roheed.

Obai (o-BAHY): An island of the Inner Faranos, closest to Wotana Bay.

Obedo (o-BAY-do): A Turowan fisherman from Pakoa.

Obiari (o-bee-AR-ee): A Jinari lore master.

Olam (O-lahm): A young Mautep slave tender on the *Fist of Death*.

Olomi (o-LO-mee): A Turowan woman, wife of Jomo, mother of Taru.

onam (O-nahm): That material of which the physical world is composed (substance, flesh).

Osfaraad (ose-far-AHD): An island of the Mahuk Baar, near the northern border of Mahuk waters.

Otao (o-TAH-o): A simple-minded young Turowan slave on the *Fist of Death*.

Oteyin (o-TEHY-ihn): Eighth month of the Edroviran calendar, roughly equivalent to August.

Pakoa (pah-KO-ah): Island off the southern coast of Edrovir. Southernmost isle of the Lomoas.

Palu (PAH-loo): An old Turowan man, a fish-seller in Wotana.

Panila (pah-NEE-lah): A young Turowan woman of Wotana.

Patamtala (pah-tahm-TAH-lah): A Jinari port on the island of Judaba.

Pavo Maat (PAH-vo maht): A young Hashtep fisherman's son enslaved on the *Fist of Death*.

Potero (po-TEHR-o) A Turowan slave on the *Fist of Death*.

Raak (rahk): A Mautep warrior, slave driver on the *Fist of Death*.

Reith Hurn (rayth hurn): A Leithian lord, one of the Signers of the Pact of Lankura. Killed in the border war with Jinara.

Reivin (RAY-vihn): The woman who originated the reivinkor (Kelorin alphbet) and helped to found Kelor in the isles of Kelornas long ago.

reivinkor (RAY-vihn-kor): The Kelorin alphabet.

rin (rihn): A small copper coin. One hundred rins make one trokin.

rithral (RIHTH-rahl): A kind of crystal, an object of power wielded by the Rithral Lords.

Roheed jir-Akaan (ro-HEED jeer-ah-KAHN): A young Mautep slave tender on the *Fist of Death*. Nephew of Lord Baalkir jir-Akaan. Son of Notep.

Sar Tipaal (sahr tih-PAHL): A port city of the Mahuk Baar. Home to Lord Baalkir and site of his great shipyard.

scapala (skah-PAHL-ah): The scapala tree is the source of long, hollow thorns used to make bladder-thorns.

Sedrin (SEHD-rihn): Ninth month of the Edroviran, roughly equivalent to September.

Semorel (SEHM-or-ehl): A Kelorin woman, queen of Edrovir. Elgurn's wife and Nevien's mother.

Seralind (sehr-ah-LIHND): Name for the place of reward after death in Leithian belief, equivalent to paradise or heaven.

shaku (SHAH-koo): Hashti word for "slave."

shaku raal (SHAH-koo rahl): Hashti for "slave dog."

Sheptuum (SHEHP-toom): God of the Hashtep people of the Mahuk Baar.

shupat (SHOO-paht): Hashti for "rabbit."

Simion (SIH-mee-ahn): A young Kelorin Fleet warrior on the *Fairwind*, captured and enslaved on the *Fist of Death*.

Sindar (SIHN-dahr): Name given by Emril to her infant son.

Sobring Hold (SO-bring hold): The Edrovirin territory ruled by the Lord of Sobring

Solbrid (SOLE-brihd): The Leithian mother goddess. Ruler of earth, and giver and taker of life.

sothiril (SO-thur-ihl): Kelorin tea-like drink brewed from berries of the plant of the same name.

Taan (TAHN): A Turowan fisherman. Pavo Maat's older brother.

Takuma (tah-KOO-mah): Chief of the Turo dwelling around Kel Lankura during the Time of Fire and Water. Princess Minowei's father.

Talebra (tah-LEHY-brah): The bright moon.

Tambali (tahm-BAHL-ee): Northern-most port on the coast of Jinara. Utabala's home.

Taru Nareyo (TAR-roo nar-AY-o): A Turowan fisherman's son, Nagaro's first friend.

tavinskala (tah-vihn-SKAH-lah): A Kelorin dance.

Tego (TAY-go): A Turowan man, formerly a merchant seaman, enslaved on the *Fist of Death*.

Tevren Loros (TEHV-rehn LOR-ose): The second king of Edrovir, son of King Darion and Queen Selfira. Husband of Queen Lindra.

Thorlan (THOR-lahn): A Kelorin man, the stableman at Averwin.

Tira (TEER-rah): A respectful from of address used with a woman's name, roughly equivalent to "Ms." with no implied marital status.

tirka (TUR-kah): A short-sleeved upper garment, opening down the front, and cut long enough to cover the hips. Generally worn over a long-sleeved shirt and usually belted.

tirkyl (tur-KEEL): A closed-front, shirt-like garment with long, cuff-less sleeves, falling to the hips, usually worn belted.

Todrin (TOE-drihn): Tenth month of the Edroviran calendar, roughly equivalent to October.

tokabi (toe-KAH-bee): A Jinari tea-like drink, brewed from leaves of a plant of the same name.

Tor (tor): A respectful form of address used with a man's name, roughtly equivalent to "Mr."

Tredhold Ferth (TRED-hold FURTH): A Leithian Fleet warrior and the ship's doctor on the *Fairwind*, captured and enslaved on the *Fist of Death*.

trokin (TRO-kihn): A silver coin worth one hundred rins. There are ten trokins to the dokan.

Tuluptak (TOO-loop-tahk): A Mautep warlord.

Turo (TOOR-o): Turowan name for their own people, also a word for a Turowan man. Turowa is the female equivalent.

Turowan (toor-O-ahn): Member of a dark-skinned, dark-haired people native to the coastal region and islands of Edrovir. Also called the Turo. "Turowan" is also an adjective referring to anything relating to the Turo.

Tyronin (teer-O-nihn): Name of the house of the Kelorin leader Atheran from which the House of Loros was split.

Ul (ool): Lame Mautep drummer on the oar deck of the *Fist of Death*.

Ulana Kura (oo-LAH-nah KOO-rah): Turowan place name from which "Lankura" is derived. The place where the Turowans believe they landed when they got off of the Sky Boat.

Urchak tok-Faar (UR-chahk toke-FAHR): A Mautep warrior, captain of the Mahuk war galley *fist of Death*.

Utabala (OO-tah-BAH-lah): A Jinari merchant's agent and interpreter, captured and enslaved on the *Fist of Death*.

Vedorel (VEHD-or-ehl): The second month of the Edrovirin calendar, roughly equivalent to February.

Vered Mahir (VEHR-ed mah-HEER): A city on the upper reaches of the river Edro, in the valley just above the great waterfall. Also the "bitter place" where the brothers Hindrath and Nevrath quarreled and the House of Tyronin was split and the House of Loros formed.

Vothra (VO-thrah): The Benevolent Spirit of the Kelorin. A single being formed by the joining of multiple human spirits, each possessing the wisdom gained from having lived multiple lives.

Wared (WAH-rehd): Territory ruled by a Kelorin lord.

Worin (WOR-ihn): A Kelorin Fleet warrior from the *Fairwind* whose capture brings plague to the oar deck of the *Fist of Death*.

Wotana (wo-TAH-nah): A fishing village in Galenor Wared, twenty miles north of Lankura.

yaba (YAH-bah) root: A starchy, edible tuber growing wild or cultivated on the southern islands. Used to make Jinari yaba bread.

Zirda (ZUR-dah): A respectful form of address (masculine) used without a name, roughly equivalent to "Sir."

Zirdyn (zur-DEEN): A respectful form of address (feminine) used without a name, roughly equivalent to "madame."

Zo-Hlan Tai (ZO-hlahn TAHY): A Hranji merchant/trader captured and unsuccessfully enslaved on the *Fist of Death*.

Notes on Nagaro's World

Titles and Forms of Address in Edrovir

The titles **Lord** and **Lady** in Kelorin tradition were borne only by the chosen leader of a house and his/her immediate family, and only during the period of the person's service. In the Leithian tradition, the equivalent titles denoted hereditary status and were borne by all members of what were perceived as "noble" families. After these two cultures became enmeshed, Kelorin usage became a bit more relaxed, extending often as a kind of courtesy to previous living leaders and members of families that had included lords and ladies in the past so as to more closely resemble the Leithian usage. The Kelorin wished to remain on equal footing with the Leithians, and broadening their own definition was easier than persuading the Leithians to narrow theirs. These titles are always placed before the given name (or the given namd plus family name), not before the family name alone.

Addressing someone as "My Lord" only indicates the other person's perceived status, not that the person speaking is under the other person's jurisdiction. Proper formal forms of address for royalty are as follows: "My Lord King," "My Lady Queen," "My Lord Prince," and "My Lady Princess." A simple "My Lord," or "My Lady" can be substituted in less formal situations.

Zirda and **Zirdyn** are roughly equivalent to the modern American usage of "Sir" and "Madame," respectively. They are always substituted for a person's name, rather than preceding it. They are of Kelorin origin and their purpose was to show respect for the person being addressed. The Leithians had to adopt these terms to avoid insulting people, but some individuals can manage to make the words sound insulting by the way they are spoken. A subtle rebuke or insult may be implied by using "Zirda" to address someone entitled to use some other title, such as "Captain."

Tor and **Tira** are most similar to our "Mr." and "Ms." They always precede a given name, not a surname or family name. Family names are used primarily when a more precise identification is required, or possibly to boast if the family is a "noble" one. Tor and Tira are Kelorin in origin and used to show respect. They are used only for adults, not children, and their use shows a perception that the person addressed is an adult. They are not used between friends and family members, being for more formal situations.

Edroviran Calendar

Months of the year: The Edrovirin calendar has thirteen months. In order, they are: **Genorel, Vedorel, Madrel, Evrel, Medrin, Dunrel, Duleyin, Oteyin, Sedrin, Todrin, Nondorin, Finorel,** and **Idrin.** Each month has exactly four eight-day weeks (therefore thirty-two days), except Idrin, which has only seven days and therefore only one seven-day week. The winter solstice (referred to as the "turning of the year") falls on the fourth of Idrin.

Days of the week: There are eight days in a week, referred to by their numbers: **First Day, Second Day,** and so forth. If a person says, "on Third Day" or "on next Third Day," they mean the third day of the current week or of the following week, respectively. If a person says, "the third of Medrin," they mean the third day of the month of Medrin.

Edroviran Currency

The **rin,** a copper coin, is the base unit of the Edrovirin currency, rather like the dollar. There are half-rin and quarter-rin coins, as well as ten-rin pieces. The **trokin** is a silver coin worth 100 rins, and the **dokan** is a gold coin worth ten trokins, or 1000 rins. There are also half-trokin coins and half-dokan coins. People will often state larger amounts in rins, even though they could be stated in round numbers of trokins and/ or dokans. For example, people are more likely to say, "450 rins" than "four and a half trokins."

Edroviran Military Organization

Edrovir is a young nation with relatively rudimentary military institutions. The words I have chosen to represent their military ranks do not reflect the usage in any current branch of existing armed forces. For the **City Guard** or **Palace Guard**, I use "commander" for someone who is in command, and "lieutenant" for someone who is a step below that. I've used "sergeant" when I wanted something a bit lower still, and the rank and file are just "guardsman."

The **Royal Fleet** is more clearly defined. The Lord of the Fleet is in charge of the entire Fleet. He has some small number of "commanders," each of whom is in charge of a number of "captains." On board an individual ship, the captain is in charge and the other officers consist of "first mate," "second mate," and "third mate." The first mate in usually in charge of the oar deck crew while the second mate in charge of the main deck crew and therefore the sails. The third mate is there to add depth to the chain of command in the event that something happens to one of the other officers. There would also be a steersman manning the tiller, a drummer to beat time on the oar deck, a ship's doctor, and a cook – but none of these are officers. All crew members on a war galley are fighters, regardless of rank or other function served.

A Brief History of Edrovir

The **Turowan** people had lived for multiple generations as loosely organized clans along the coast and in the islands of the region that became the nation of Edrovir. The hinterland had previously been inhabited as indicated by some ruins, but was unpopulated at the time of the cataclysm known as the **Time of Fire and Water** which precipitated the arrival of the Kelorin and Leithian peoples from **Arlinas** to the east.

The **Kelorin** people, under the leadership of **Atheran** and the guidance of Vothra, had come by ship from the western islands of **Kelornas** several generations before and settled in the north of the land they named Arlinas, which they found unpeopled but marked by scattered ruins left by a vanished race. Those vanished people also left caches of strange crystals known as **rithrals** whose power-channeling properties seduced the Kelorin people away from the wisdom of Vothra's Path. **Leithian** people began arriving from Leith (lying still farther east) after the Kelorin were already well established throughout much of the northern, middle, and western parts of Arlinas and the rithral lords were rising to power. The Leithians settled in the southern and southeastern parts of Arlinas and coexisted with the Kelorin in a state of uneasy equality for perhaps a generation prior to the cataclysm. The cataclysm (caused by multiple meteorite strikes) coincided (not coincidentally) with the catastrophic ending of the **Age of the Rithral Lords** and descending of a "**shadow**" on the land of Arlinas. These latter events, associated with a mysterious figure known as **Naibarad the Destroyer**, possibly the most powerful of the rithral lords, were what truly drove the Kelorin and Leithian peoples to abandon Arlinas, crossing the Goreitha Mountains into the valley of the River Edro and its surrounding lands.

With the rithal lords dead and the rithrals either destroyed or left behind in a shadowed land, the Kelorin and Leithian people were forced to make a new beginning. In the power vacuum of the unpopulated region of Edrovir, they spread rapidly across the land as their rival lords staked out territories, some of which included areas inhabited by Turowan folk. The Turo, technologically less advanced and peaceable by nature, offered little resistance. Over the next twenty to thirty years, friction between Kelorin and Leithians grew and armed conflicts escalated, (as did border disputes with the neighboring nations of Jinara and Hran, to the south). Finally, a man named **Darion Loros**, the son of a Kelorin lord, **Nevrath**, and a Turowan chief's daughter, **Minowei**, emerged as a unifying figure. He pushed for the establishment of a **Council of Lords** made up of all the Kelorin and Leithian lords, and three Turowan chiefs, to provide common governance for a unified nation of **Edrovir**, with its capitol at **Lankura**. The Council of Lords, in turn, overwhelmingly chose Darion to be the new nation's king.

As Edrovir's first king, Darion wrote a **charter** that established the basic legal framework for the new kingdom. He had married a Kelorin woman, **Selfira**, and they had a son, **Tevren Loros**. After eighteen years of rule, Darion's unexpected and untimely death was widely blamed on his Lore Master, **Dreigen**, a man of mixed Kelorin/Jinari ancestry who had been presented to Darion by a Leithian lord, **Harl Sobring**. A badly divided Council of Lords narrowly chose the twenty-six-year-old Tevern to be Edrovir's second king. Tevren lacked his father's even temper and diplomatic skills. Pressed to marry a Leithian woman, he instead chose a Kelorin, **Lindra of Irvenen**, and his brief reign was marred by increasing tension between the more militant factions of Kelorin and Leithian lords. After Lindra bore Tevren a son at his ancestral home of Loros Hall, a group of Leithians, led by Lord **Reith Hurn,** waylaid the young couple as they sought to return to Lankura, leaving both Tevren and Lindra dead and their infant son missing.

Outrage over what was widely considered to have been a double murder led to serious internal strife, culminating in an incipient civil war that was prevented from coelescing when a truce was called by the six strongest lords, three Kelorin (**Anduar Tyronin, Berinar Sundorin,** and **Devral Sedras**) and three Leithians (**Reith Hurn, Pendrik Glenmark,** and **Odus Morbern**). They met at Lankura and signed a document known as the **Pact of Lankura** The pact stipulated that none of the six signers could serve as king but that they would choose the king, thus abrogating the authority of the Council of Lords. The **Pact Signers** chose a Leithian, **Elgurn Harlind**, to be the third king of Edrovir. Elgurn had been one of Darion's most loyal supporters and he had a Kelorin wife, **Semorel**, who in due course bore him a daughter, **Nevien**. The six Pact Signers continued to contribute to the rule of Edrovir, wielding substantial power by advising King Elgurn as the **King's Council**.

Religions of Edrovir and Lands Beyond

Kelorin beliefs: The Kelorin people originally had a pantheon of deities of whom two are mentioned: **Lokundas**, the "Turner of Worlds," who is basically a personification of fate, and **Nomemduran**, the "Maker of All Things." **Vothra**, the Benevolent Spirit of the Kelorin, and Vothrin teachings, (the Vothrin Path), were superimposed on these older beliefs. The older deities have been largely abandoned, but the habit of worrying about tempting Lokundas lingers.

 The Vothrin Writings: The *First Book of Vothra* is attributed to the spirit that first brought to the living world an awareness of the nature of the "void" and the existence of spirits in the state between lives. That spirit called itself Uona and came to dwell in the body of a man named Luzan. Luzan had found a way for his spirit to leave his body before that body was at the point of death, allowing Uona to enter it without having to pass through the womb. Luzan lived on one of the Kelorin isles and was blind from early childhood. Because the body Uona inhabited was blind, the *First Book of Vothra* was set down on paper by Luzan's sister. Ilira. Vothra came into being after the eventual death of Uona/Luzan. The spirit of Uona was able to maintain communication from the void with Ilira during her continued life. Uona became the founding spirit of Vothra and was gradually joined by other spirits, making Vothra stronger and more able to contact the spirits of the living. The *Second Book of Vothra* is a compilation of writings by living people who were in close communication with Vothra.

Turowan beliefs: The Turo have a guiding spirit named **Hakura Kili**, who is benign. There are also unnamed **World Spirits** that have power to affect men's lives and are generally described as "wayward" in the sense of being unpredictable. After death, Turowans believe that their spirits go to live in a place called **Hanuroa**.

Leithian beliefs: The Leithian pantheon consists of four deities. **Hrothgard** is the patriarch, called "King of the Heavens," who controls the weather and is also the patron of rulers. **Solbrid** is the mother goddess (sometimes called "Mother Solbrid" or "Queen Solbrid"). She is the giver and taker of life. **Kroneg** is the god of war and patron of all things male. He is associated with Naru, the dark moon. **Lissafel**, the maiden goddess, is sometimes called "The Lady" and is the patron of women and of lovers. She is associated with Talebra, the bright moon. **Seralind** is the Leithian equivalent of heaven, and **Hel** is a place of punishment after death.

Religiouse beliefs of the Mahuk Baar: The Hastep people, including the Mautep warrior class, revere a single god, **Sheptuum**. **Hiptatak** is Sheptuum's messenger. **Chofir Naak** is their heaven or afterlife.

Religious beliefs in Jinara: The Jinari have one god, whose name is not spoken but who is referred to by various circumlocutions such as, "The un-named one," or "He whose name we do not speak." **Jembari** is a Jinari prophet. **Eskarasi** is a form of devil or representative of evil.

About the Author

Carol Louise Wilde is the author of the Nagaro Chronicle, a seven-book fantasy-adventure series. She for long led a double life: biology research scientist by day, and by night, chief archivist for the nation of Edrovir and its neighboring states. The Nagaro Chronicle covers but one brief period in the long and eventful history of this world and its inhabitants. Ms. Wilde lives in Southern California with her husband of forty-odd years. They have two sons to carry on the tradition.